C000279390

Gavin Lambert is a novelist, director and author of several screenplays. His novels include *The Goodbye People, The Slide Area* and *Inside Daisy Clover* which was made into a successful film starring Natalie Wood. (These novels, along with *Running Time*, are published by Serpent's Tail.) He has been Academy Award nominated for his screenplay *Sons and Lovers* and film *I Never Promised You A Rose Garden*. He lives in Hollywood.

Also by Gavin Lambert and published by Serpent's Tail

Inside Daisy Clover
The Slide Area
The Goodbye People

Running Time

GAVIN LAMBERT

Library of Congress Catalog Card Number: 00–102190

A complete catalogue record for this book can
be obtained from the British Library on request

The right of Gavin Lambert to be identified as the
author of this work has been asserted by him in
accordance with the Copyright, Designs and Patents
Act 1988

Copyright © Gavin Lambert 1982

The characters and events in this book are fictitious. Any
similarity to real persons, living or dead, is coincidental and
not intended by the author.

First published by Weidenfeld & Nicolson in 1982

First published in 2001 by Serpent's Tail,
4 Blackstock Mews, London N4 2BT

website: www.serpentstail.com

Printed in Great Britain by Mackays of Chatham plc

10 9 8 7 6 5 4 3 2 1

To Lindsay Anderson

1919

Elva's Diary

February 4 • Baby so silent after the train pulled out of Chicago, I finally asked what was on her mind.

"How do you know I'm going to hit the jackpot out there?"

"Just be natural and you can't miss."

Our seats were upholstered in a rich brocade and had creamy lace antimacassars. Considering the state of my bank account it was reckless to travel first class, but I never doubted *our whole life* would be first class very soon, and thought we should get some practice. Besides, when you skate on thin ice, the faster you move the safer you are.

It began to rain, then it grew dark. We took our places in the diner as the train passed through Kansas City, and soon there was nothing outside the window except prairie that looked like the wrong side of the moon. Baby still silent, perched on her luxurious banquette and staring at her face reflected very white, like her own ghost, in the glass.

On the way back to our roomette de luxe it was so dark that I couldn't see the numbers on the doors properly, opened the wrong one and walked straight into the Ritz on wheels. A gorgeous suite with a velvet sofa and matching chairs, lamps with beaded shades, and a vase of huge, almost sinfully deep red roses on a mahogany table — but no sign of human habitation. I sniffed a heavy perfume in the air, not from the roses; it was more oriental and suggestive, like the aroma of Ahmed Ben Hassan's tent in *The Sheik,* so racily described by Mrs. E.M. Hull. Baby sniffed it too, and pointed (she can be incredibly quick on the mental draw!) to the far corner of the suite. At first I saw nothing but shadow. Then a single, darker shadow. And realized someone was standing there, rigid

as a store dummy, sending out waves of silent musk. It remained so still, I
began to think it *was* a store dummy, unlikely though this seemed. Or
maybe not so unlikely if you thought of doors in legends and dreams,
opening to another world!

Then the figure gave a sudden twitch. I glimpsed a plump white hand
and a pointed finger. An overhead light came on, and we were gazing at a
woman in a long black gown, her hair and face completely hidden by a
hat with a thick veil. Draped around her shoulders was a silver fox fur
with a stuffed head.

Baby looked frightened, but I was so excited I never thought to apologize for being in the wrong compartment, or even to wish its occupant
good evening. "I've seen that woman before and I'd know her anywhere," I said. "She can't show her face in public and they only let her
out at night."

Baby looked confused, then the woman stepped forward and spoke in
some kind of foreign accent. "I can tell you worse than that." She gave a
long discouraged sigh. "They forbid me to enter a Turkish bath."

"Is it a very difficult life?" I asked. "Have you ever regretted it?"

She pressed her hands together. They looked pale and soft and curved
as doves. "I wept at first. But then I laughed. They may tell me not to do
this, not to do that, and yet I am nobody's slave." I felt sure she was
baring her teeth in triumph behind the veil, as I'd often seen her do. "I
am *feministe*, you see, and always prove it in the end. Because I get to
knock the pants off every man in the world!"

"And do we admire you for it," I said warmly.

She seemed genuinely touched and invited us to sit down.

Baby Looks Back

Until I found Mother's diaries I had forgotten how seriously she took
our little soirée with the Wickedest Face in the World, AKA Theda Bara.
Now it comes back, she thought of it as Fate. When you're high on the
occult nothing just *happens*, everything's part of the kismet plan. "In the
very first hours of our new life, we meet one of the all-time greats,"
Mother said next morning. "Always trust your vibrations, Baby, and always travel first class." Then she gave me the inside story on Theda, born
Theodosia Goodman, just another hefty Jewish blonde from Cincinnati.
A director at the Fox studios noticed her dark burning eyes as she stood in
the extra line, and decided to fix her up as a black-haired Arab princess.
She was given foreign accent lessons and unveiled at a press conference

by Mr. William Fox himself, who announced that his Corporation's new star was born on the banks of the Nile. ("The Left Bank," Theda told a reporter who wanted details.) Then he filled in the rest of her legend — weaned on cobra's blood instead of mother's milk, mystic bride of the Sphinx, kept serpents and bats as household pets — and launched the deadly vampire who sucked men dry.

Although it got me nowhere at the time, there was something about Theda that *I* took seriously as well. If she came from Cincinnati and never knew one bank of the Nile from the other, if she was nobody's mystic bride but the daughter of a neighborhood tailor, she couldn't be *real*.

"Of course she's real," Mother said. "To thousands and thousands of people."

"But you told me she was all fixed up. From nowhere and nothing."

"It's a *game*, Baby. Like Let's Pretend."

"You know she's not real but you believe in her anyway?"

"I'm one of the thousands and thousands. That's what the movies are all about. I suppose you'll be wondering next if Cinderella's not *real*, just because she never existed!"

Food for thought, as they say. On her way from New York to California, Theda had stopped off for a vacation in Chicago, veiled to the gills and driving around in a limousine with curtained windows. Then she boarded the Super Chief, all set for a mysterious personal appearance at the Los Angeles premiere of her latest, *The Lure of Ambition*. One considerable turkey, as it turned out, not her first but almost her last. Although Mother never realized it, Theda was heading for the skids by the time they met, so frankly I would take her whole act here with a barrel of salt. Miss Evil-Kiss-Me-My-Fool had no need to slink around heavily veiled in the dead of night, and could probably have entered a Turkish bath in broad daylight with no one giving a hoot.

Incidentally, Mother writes that I was confused by Theda, which is understandable, but I don't believe she frightened me. Not seriously. Not for more than a moment. You have to grow up before you can be seriously frightened. For more than a moment.

Elva's Diary

February 5 • Only a few more minutes of Kansas left outside the window, and it's snowing hard. Baby suddenly wonders what a mummified Negro infant looks like. At first I'm startled by the dark recesses of her mind, then notice she's reading Sherlock Holmes again. She often says she wants to be a detective when she grows up, and certainly asks enough questions.

Last night I was too tired (and pie-eyed) to finish writing about TB, so I'm getting the rest of her down after breakfast. A strong inner glow warms me as I write. No doubt in my mind our meeting was an omen: Baby and I are *definitely* on our way!

After opening a bottle of bootleg bubbly (I let Baby sip from my glass), TB talked some more about knocking the pants off every man in the world. Claimed she was the first to do it. The Gish sisters are still playing victims, sacrificial lambs, crushed violets, frightened birds. Pickford refuses to grow up. Mae Marsh and Blanche Sweet are just divinity fudge. I said the most thrilling moment in any TB movie was the scene in *When a Woman Sins*, after she discarded her lover like a used glove and he shot himself. "You looked at his dead body, and you *laughed*. Then you dropped rose petals all over him."

TB lifted her veil and I saw her face was painted frost-white, her lips almost purple, her eyes ringed with the blackest kohl. "The rose petals were *my idea*," she told me. "I felt the need for more than vulgar triumph. I wanted poetry."

I said she had a truly original mind and once again she seemed genuinely touched.

"There comes a moment in the life of even the greatest sinner, my friend, when the heart cries out." She pressed her pale hands together. "Never forget the heart."

TB talks exactly like the dialogue titles in her movies, although sometimes she forgets her foreign accent. Cynics might pick on this and call her phony, but I disagree. To err is human, and we must forgive TB an occasional lapse as she strives ceaselessly to keep up the illusion created for her and for us. She clearly believes, night and day, in her great Role. Isn't that the secret of true Art?

Noticing the current issue of *Woman's Home Companion* on the table, I asked TB if she'd read the article on Madame Blavatsky. It contained an account of the noted psychic materializing a cup and saucer in midair during a picnic on the tropical shores of the Bay of Bengal. TB nodded. "Most vivid. Madame is one of the great women of the age. Like her, I am *spiritualiste* as well as *feministe*." My heart leapt to my throat, for two of my consuming passions are the Movies and the Unknown, and here I sat opposite a woman who embodied both. On a mundane level I opened the wrong door last night, but on another deeper level I opened the right one. Would TB understand if I tried to explain?

She understood. "If you submit to the vibrations, it happens all the time. And we are both en route to a city, my friend, where the vibrations are unusually strong." Madame, she told me, tagged Los Angeles as a Power Spot. Its vibrations came from the earth itself, which was *magnetically charged.* "Never forget the Indians lived there first. They were the true founding fathers, making magic and drugs."

We finished the bottle and I felt drunk on more than champagne. TB glanced at Baby, who had fallen asleep. "Tell me. You are going to Los Angeles because of the little one? To make her a star?"

Once again she astonished me. "How did you guess?"

"Just a vibration," TB said modestly.

"There's no doubt in my mind Baby can take that place by storm. You'll see what I mean if I wake her up and get her to dance a tango."

TB shook her head. "You mustn't wake her, she looks so peaceful. And so *small,*" she added, giving Baby another glance. "Can she be more than three years old?"

Many people ask this about Baby, who is sublimely healthy but in no hurry to grow. Part of my plan is to keep her age a closely guarded secret, so I withheld the news that she recently turned seven. "A fourteen-carat pocket genius," I said. "Reads and writes as well as dances, sings "Shine On Harvest Moon" and imitates Charlie Chaplin."

"And so small."

I explained that Baby's all-time greatness was *willed* from the start, for I believed in prenatal preparation. While I was carrying her, I kept her fetus away from negative influences like the stockyards, the dirty lakeside beaches and her father. Determined to expose it as much as possible to the soul-stirring experiences Chicago had to offer, I carried it around the Art Institute, on a Votes for Women float where I paraded in costume as a Liberty Belle, took it to a concert by Caruso, a matinee of the classic motion picture *Quo Vadis?*, and an exhibition of magic by Houdini during which he escaped from a sealed chest under water.

When TB asked how Baby's father fitted in with all this, I said he never did. "The most negative influence of all. Any time I brought up the subject of Baby making good on the silver screen, Mr. Kay swore he'd never let me use her as a one-way ticket to California."

"But now he's changed his mind?"

"Not to my knowledge. He died in the influenza epidemic last month."

One of the roses on the table was full-blown and had shed a few crimson petals. TB scooped them up in her hands and dropped them one by one to the floor. Then she looked across at sleeping Baby and spoke another dialogue title. "Little one, it will be hard. You must be very brave."

Typical of her great role and most effective, but I felt glad Baby was asleep and unable to hear. She might have been frightened.

Baby Looks Back

Theda was a pacesetter in her way, one of the first old-timers to make her whole life into a movie. But it didn't end there. Other people, Mother included, started making *their* lives into *her* movies. A confusing situation and more food for thought.

About Father. I never got close to him, partly because Mother saw to it, partly because he spent so much time on the road drumming up business for Coca-Cola. I remember he used to complain about the expense of my dancing lessons, accused Mother of going haywire in stores and buying me unsuitable fancy clothes. "Why do you want to turn our kid into a performing monkey? Why can't you be satisfied with a normal life?" Mother had some standard comebacks, I remember them like phrases of old songs that lodge in your head forever. To prove Father had no imagination: "And to think — when we talked about a name for Baby — you wanted to call her *Myrtle*." To taunt him: "My husband's a failure, but why can't my child be a success?" And to warn him she'd always keep trying: "My kind never runs out of rainbows."

Another thing she never ran out of: black eyes. There was still a trace of the last one Father gave her when she scattered earth on his grave. In those days she had a favorite saying about Death. "It's a cause for celebration," she told any friend who lost a loved one. Death was not an end but a beginning, you moved to another sphere and became part of the Eternal Wheel. But when she talked about a cause for celebration after Father died, it sounded different. More personal.

Elva's Diary

February 7 • Why has TB locked her door? I knocked loudly several times at all hours, calling out, "It's your new friend and greatest admirer, Elva Kay!" But she never answered. Is she, after all, as her movies claim, The Woman Who Does Not Care? More likely she has a drinking problem!

February 15 • After a week in the city of Los Angeles, I'm still not sure *where* I am. We got off the train at a place called Arcadia, they told us it was the end of the line and it was certainly the beginning of nowhere.

More than twenty miles from Hollywood. Mr. Van Tassel, who offered to share a taxicab with us, explained that everywhere is twenty miles from everywhere else out here. Baby said, "It's not winter anymore," and after a trip that began in rain and continued in snow we found ourselves breathing lemon-blossom air warm as spring, saw a row of palm trees across the street from the station, and a wall covered with ruby bougainvillea. In the clear hard sunlight they looked unnaturally still, as if they were painted. But then a line of gray houses with front porches and pitched roofs and cupolas took me right back to Des Moines and my childhood. When I remarked on this to Mr. Van Tassel, he said most of the people in Los Angeles actually *came* from Des Moines or places nearby, and built the kind of houses they lived in back home. All the same, he added, it's the New Italy out here.

TB had a white curtained limousine waiting at the station. She walked past us as if we never existed. Unsteady on her feet, though, and don't tell me it was because she couldn't see through that veil. Our taxicab trailed her limousine for a while, then outside the town it speeded ahead of us, across a long stretch of scrub desert. This was a real shock. People lived in tents and frame shacks in this desert, which looked like a frontier settlement, tin lizzies parked outside the tents, chairs, old clothes and junk sticking out from their rumble seats. Signs announced Goldfish and Canaries for Sale. Mr. Van Tassel explained that some people make their way out here and can't find work, so they set up in makeshift villages and start a small business. Baby wanted to know where they got the fish and the birds for a small business, she could see no water or trees around. Mr. Van Tassel looked surprised and said, "I never thought about that. But you can find anything to buy and sell out here. Frogs, rat poison, bicycles, notions, anything." Then he turned to me. "That's a really cute little kid. She ought to be in pictures." I smiled — like the Mona Lisa, I hope.

The taxicab ride seemed to take almost as long as the trip from Chicago. We passed through an orchard of avocados, then a flat open stretch of nowhere that turned out to be an abandoned real estate development. Builders' trash lying around, a faded sign advertising Lots for Sale. "Some speculators are plumb crazy," Mr. Van Tassel said, "and *deserve* to go out of business. Just because it's a boom town they think people will live *anywhere*. I knew a man who bought up acres of *pure swamp* near the coast and called it Jerusalem. People took one look, got bitten by mosquitos or sank knee deep in mud, and thought he had to be kidding. But he wasn't. When he couldn't get Jerusalem moving, he blew his brains out."

Mr. Van Tassel came out here from Nebraska and made a bundle, so he claimed, selling supplies to the infirm. Kneebraces, crutches, air cushions, trusses and so on. "It was a cinch. Thousands of ailing old folk from Iowa heard the climate out here would fix anything from pinkeye to, pardon me, piles. It was too late for some of them, they dropped dead on arrival, but the others bought up anything to help them move around or stand up or sit down or stop itching." These days, so he claimed, Mr. Van Tassel has a genuine cure for most diseases, for he's invented several gadgets to improve health and preserve youth. His latest is called Magnetro, a little band you strap on your arm. It has a battery which sends out electric waves and gets rid of cancer, insomnia and arthritis, as well as restoring color to hair that's gone gray or white. Mr. Van Tassel is certainly very spry and dapper. As well as a diamond stickpin he wears his own Magnetro, and says it turned his own hair black again. But it looked dyed to me.

A citrus grove, a bean field, and still no Hollywood. "Where is it?" Baby kept on asking. "Where *is* it?" Finally Mr. Van Tassel gave her a solemn look and spoke like a minister in church. "Whoever asks where Los Angeles is," he intoned, "to him I shall say: Across a desert without wearying, beyond a mountain without climbing." We stared at the little man. "I read that in a Chamber of Commerce brochure," he said. "It impressed itself on my mind."

Baby sighed, then hummed a snatch of "Let Me Call You Sweetheart." I asked Mr. Van Tassel if he could recommend an elegant but modest apartment house near the Hollywood Hotel, which I'd read about and knew was frequented by the all-time greats. He suggested the Yucca Riviera Plaza, only two blocks away and not expensive. "I'm not worried about expense," I said. "I just don't happen to care for luxury or ostentation." He blinked and wanted to know what brought me out to California. I saw no point in confiding my plans for Baby to a man who sold peculiar and probably useless appliances, so I told him I was recently widowed and suffering from asthma, which I hoped the climate here would improve. "I'd never have taken you for a widow, you're so cheerful and you're not wearing black," he said. And then tried to sell me a Magnetro band at a special discount, $40 instead of $55! What a nerve, I thought, he never claimed it cured asthma, but when I reminded him of this, he said he'd forgotten to mention how many other ailments Magnetro banished practically overnight — goiter, flatulence and earache, too. He offered me a bottom line price of $28. At the same time, accidentally-on-purpose, his hand brushed my knee, he remarked I was unusually attractive as well as unusually cheerful, and invited me out to dinner. I turned him down flat on every count and the rest of our journey passed in a frosty silence. No matter. By this time the brute had served his purpose.

It was almost dusk as we passed the Hollywood Hotel, which looked like a cross between a Swiss chalet and the Tower of London, with the American flag flying high above it. (I'm gradually getting used to the fact that most places out here look like somewhere else.) Our taxicab turned into a side street, and since Mr. Van Tassel had been looking sleazier by the minute to me, in spite of his diamond stickpin and glossy black hair, I feared the Yucca Riviera Plaza might turn out to be a rat's nest. But we stopped in front of a charming romantic place with white walls and a red-tiled roof. Separate single-story residences built around a patio with geranium beds, gnome statues and an old-world fountain with water trickling out of a stone frog's mouth. It struck me as positively Mediterranean, although the locals refer to it in rather mundane terms as a bungalow court.

I gave Mr. Van Tassel 50¢ for the taxi fare, and a quick brush-off. The manager of the court, knee-high to a mosquito, wearing a fez, affable if not completely sober, showed us a residence at the back. It was not spacious, but the bed had an elegant brass frame and could accommodate the two of us. There was also a red leather armchair, a beaded satin-glass light fixture hung from a chain, a knotty pine dresser and a stained glass window in the bathroom. $29 a month.

"It's only temporary, of course," I explained to Baby, who nodded and said I certainly knocked the pants off Mr. Van Tassel. She doesn't miss much. We freshened up and asked the manager where we could find a bite to eat. "You'll be lucky," he said. "After eight o'clock at night you can fire a cannon down Hollywood Boulevard. There's no one around to hit." And when we stepped out, he seemed to be right. An almost empty streetcar clanged by, probably the last of the evening, and the store windows were dark. I thought of my childhood again. We passed a Masonic Hall, a paint store, the Sun Drug Co., a ticket office for the electric railroad, and then a little barred door in the wall that turned out to be the overnight jail. After a few blocks we reached a street called Vine, and beyond it lay nothing but dark empty countryside.

"Are you sure we've come to the right place?" Baby asked. "You said this was your street of dreams."

We turned back, and two old ladies on bicycles drew up outside a house. They wore long black dresses, shawls and mobcaps. I began to feel depressed, then cheered up when I noticed a palm tree beside the entrance. It took my mind off Des Moines.

In a side street opposite the little police station we found a Tea Room Buffet with the lights still on, but a man wearing a check suit, bow tie and fedora hat was just about to close the shutters. "You're out late tonight," he said. I explained we were new arrivals from Chicago, hungry after a long ride from the Arcadia railroad station, and he agreed to make us a couple of tuna sandwiches. Baby wanted a root beer special, but he said the fountain was closed. "Planning to get your little girl in pictures?" he asked. Smiling, I informed him my only plan was to escape the Chicago winter. "If you stick to it, you'll also escape a broken heart," he said, adding that many started at the bottom of the screen's ladder of fame, but few reached the top.

Instead of going straight back to the Yucca Riviera Plaza, we stood outside the Hollywood Hotel for a while. I knew all about it from *Photoplay*. A few years ago Mira Hershey, the chocolate bar heiress, took it over and made it a favorite rendezvous of the stars. In one of its sumptuous apartments, Carrie Jacobs Bond wrote her immortal ballad, "The End of a Perfect Day." And on Thursday nights they held a dance in the grand ballroom, which had gold stars on the ceiling, each one engraved with a glittering name, Doug Fairbanks, Francis X. Bushman, Norma and Constance Talmadge. Unfortunately it was Wednesday night, and although I noticed a few smart roadsters parked outside, no one famous came in or out. In fact, at 9:20 p.m. in the motion picture capital of the world, there was no one around except Baby and me.

"Are you sure this is the right place?" Baby asked again. "You said this was your Starlight City." For a moment it seemed crazy to have taken a train for more than two thousand miles, only to stand in the main street of a town that looked deader than Des Moines even on a Saturday night, with no friends or connections and a meager $575 in the bank. And only to be reminded of a place and time I prefer to forget.

Then the moon came out from behind a cloud and turned both of us a dazzling silver. It was a glorious effect, Baby and myself like human sequins on the empty sidewalk, and it gave me a strong vibration. Yes, I told her, this is our street of dreams, our Starlight City and more, and we are *definitely* on our way!

Baby Looks Back

I remember that moon. It *was* uncannily bright and seemed to shine right through us, but I had a different reaction. Apart from Sherlock Holmes my favorite reading then was stories about mad scientists and the fantastic rays they invented. Once their ray struck, you found yourself in their power and changed without knowing it.

Elva's Diary

February 15 (continued) • Next day I bought a map of the city to find
out where the studios were located. Once again everywhere was twenty
miles from everywhere else. "This place has studios all over," I said to
Baby, "from the San Fernando Valley to the sea. We can walk to Mr.
Chaplin and Famous Players Lasky, but Mr. Griffith and Mr. Fox are almost downtown, Inceville is way out near the Pacific, and Mr. Laemmle's
fabled Universal, the home of your favorite actor Lon Chaney, is way over
the other side of the mountains." Mr. Hendrix, the manager of the Yucca
Riviera Plaza, was sitting on his porch, so I went over and asked how
people out here managed to get around. He told me there's some public
transportation if you're not in a hurry, an electric railroad runs Big Red
Cars here and there, but an automobile's the thing. "My brother's in the
business," he added, "and can give you the best deal on wheels." I
thought how everyone in Los Angeles wants to make some kind of deal
right away, and promised to let him know.

As Baby and I moved off, a pudgy freckled boy in a Buster Brown suit
came out of a nearby apartment, followed by a woman with fluffy blonde
hair and startled eyes, like Constance Talmadge in *Happiness à la Mode.*
She was dressed in a long white gown with puffed sleeves and a cascade
of starched frills down the front, wore a strand of pearls and carried a hat
with a wide brim and butterfly bow.

"That's Mary Louise Cloud." Mr. Hendrix glanced at Baby. "She's
pushing her kid into the movies too, so you girls should get together."

Since I never mentioned my plans for Baby to Mr. Hendrix, this took me
by surprise. I was equally surprised and none too pleased to discover a
rival under the same roof. Impossible to avoid the creature, for she hurried up, peered at Baby and gave an affected laugh. "Oh my, what pretty
lace drawers." Her accent sounded deeper than a Delta shrimp bed, and
her costume might have got by if she was serving iced tea on the plantation. "And what lovely curls," she went on. "They look so natural."

My smile was cool. "They're as natural as they look, you know."

"How old is she? I can't believe she's a minute over three."

I sidestepped this by guessing her boy was around six, and asked what
she called him.

"His real name's Baxter. Professionally he's known as Baby Peaches."

Mr. Hendrix guffawed from his porch. "They should get up an act together. Peaches and Cream."

I pretended not to hear, but Mary Louise appeared to find it amusing and gave her affected laugh. Then she asked my Baby's name.

"Jewel. Baby Jewel."

"How charming. What's her real name?"

"I told you. *We* saw no reason to change anything she was born with."

I smiled at Baby, who began to hum "Jealousy" and invited Peaches to tango. The oaf only gaped at her, so she tangoed happily around the patio by herself, holding an imaginary partner.

"That's charming," Mary Louise Cloud said again, watching with eyes more like gimlets than saucers now. "You could probably get her a part as a midget, if she wasn't almost too small."

"I didn't bring Baby out here to play midgets," I said. "Besides, if they *want* midgets, who don't they get real ones?"

"There just aren't enough to go around right now. Oh my, this sun." Mary Louise put on her enormous hat. "So many circus pictures. Peaches did two midgets last month."

"Has he ever done anything else?"

"Not yet. How about your Jewel?"

"We only just got here, Mrs. Cloud. I came to California for my health, with no idea of a career for Baby in mind. But the moment we set foot in this town, everyone began saying how cute she is, so now I'm prepared to consider it. If the right part comes along."

Peaches, still gaping at Baby, broke wind so loudly it had to be on purpose. Once again I pretended not to hear. Mary Louise looked at her watch. "Oh my, come along, Peaches, or we'll be late for our appointment at Century."

I had no idea what Century was, but they had an appointment there, which was more than Baby and I had anywhere, so I decided to drop my superior attitude. Why should there be any competition between us after all? Peaches was a boy and obviously no threat to Baby in terms of talent, personality, beauty or charm. And although any mother who boasted of her doltish child playing midgets had a low-class mind, she at least knew some of the ropes. Swallow your pride, I told myself, and go to work on the backhanded bitch later.

Shortly before dark a Model T drew up with a man at the wheel, Mary Louise in the passenger seat and Peaches on her lap. She said goodnight to the boorish child, who clambered out. As the car drove off I felt certain Mary Louise had no intention of returning until morning, and Peaches seemed used to this kind of behavior. He slouched across the patio, whistling foolishly. But was the man Mary Louise's steady date, or had she picked him up at Century that afternoon? She looked ready to pick up a man anytime, and in any case I thought it cruel to leave a child, however unappealing, alone all night in an apartment house room. Did he have anything to eat? Should Baby and I bring him a tuna sandwich, keep him company and see if we could draw him out? Better not, I decided, Peaches would be sure to tell his mother and she *might* suspect my motives.

Next morning I kept watch on the patio again, and saw the Model T return around ten o'clock. Mary Louise sauntered brazenly back to her apartment in her frilly white gown and pearls, twirling her picture hat. Half an hour later I knocked at her door. Peaches opened it, his face so blank it was hard to tell what he felt, but I detected some ill humor there. The room smelt of cheap talcum powder. Mary Louise appeared from the bathroom, wearing a soiled polka-dotted wrapper, and apologized for receiving me in her *robe de chambre*. "Good morning to you, Mrs. Kay, I only just got up." I told her how much I'd enjoyed our meeting yesterday and asked how it had gone at Century for Peaches. She said her boy auditioned for a part in an animal comedy. The producer liked the look of him (I supposed he must have *wanted* an overweight ugly child), walked him to the back lot and introduced him to a donkey. "Well now, the donkey seemed charming enough to me, Mrs. Kay, but it scared Peaches to the bone. He let out a howl and tried to run away. So we missed *that* boat for sure." Her eyes opened very wide and she laughed. "Imagine, a big little fellow like Peaches scared of a donkey."

Peaches ran to a corner and began gobbling candy out of a paper bag. I invited Mary Louise to take a cup of coffee with me on the Boulevard. She looked surprised, then accepted ungraciously. "Well, I've got nothing else to do right now." While she opened her clothes closet and wondered what to wear, Peaches broke wind in his dreadful rude way, swallowed more candy, went out and slammed the door. She seemed too busy to notice, slipping off her wrapper, diving into another plantation gown and checking herself in the mirror. I told her how pretty she looked, found flattery an easy way to her shallow heart, and as we walked to the Tea Room Buffet I sang the praises of Peaches, called him handsome and cute and bright as a button. "But do you think he's got *talent*?" she asked. I assured her it oozed from every pore and he must have inherited it from his mother. "He certainly didn't inherit it from his father," she said, and over coffee confided *that* story.

Two years ago, she informed me as she stroked her pearls, Baxter Cloud Senior had fallen for a crazy goldmining scheme in Mexico. He uprooted Mary Louise and Baxter Junior from North Carolina, where he farmed tobacco, and took them south of the border. First there was no gold, then a revolution broke out. "You should see those revolutions down there."

Her eyes grew round as saucers. "They come once a month, more regular than the trains!" After Baxter Senior got killed by a stray bullet from one of Pancho Villa's soldiers, she decided to head for Los Angeles and put her boy in the movies. "I just couldn't think of anything else to do," she said.

"But I guess you had some connections here?" She shook her head, and I kept my voice very casual. "So how did you set about it? Where was the first place you took little Peaches?"

"Mr. Evansmith. I'm sure you've taken your Jewel there too."

"Not yet, we're only just settled in, but I was planning to take her to Mr. Evansmith this afternoon," I said, wondering who he was and making a mental note of the name. And then, at a venture: "They do say he's the best."

She nodded. "And so convenient, just across from First Methodist."

"You may not have struck gold, Mary Louise, but you're wearing the finest string of pearls I ever saw. I could rip them off you."

"Baxter went out and bought them after the first night of our honeymoon. And believe me, dear, I earned every precious bead."

"I believe you, dear. Where did you take little Peaches next?"

"Hauled him off to the Standard Casting Directory and had him listed, like everyone else."

"That's so convenient too," I said at another venture.

She nodded again. "Just across from Masonic Hall."

Two out of two, Elva Kay, I told myself. And out loud: "I just can't get over the way you dress!"

Mary Louise looked like a cat with cream on its whiskers. "You've got to have a *style* out here." She ran her eyes over my tasteful beige suit, but didn't compliment me on it. "I guess you know the studios are always sending out calls for toddlers. Especially for Mary Pickford movies. She orders by the crate. But remember one thing." Glancing around the Tea Room as if she feared someone might be listening, Mary Louise lowered her voice. "If a call goes out for a toddler to play Lillian Gish's baby, *don't answer it.* Not even if the money's good. Which it won't be. You'll know what I'm talking about if you saw *Hearts of the World.*"

"When she got carried off by a pirate?"

"No, Elva, when she dragged some screaming tot all around the battlefields of France, with cannons and the whole German army firing away. The worst things always happen to Lillian's babies."

"And to Lillian, come to think of it," I said, remembering TB called her a sacrificial lamb. But I thought to myself, the woman's a star, and Baby — who's no coward like Peaches and could handle herself on a battlefield, let alone a donkey — might get her career off to a tremendous start on Lillian's lap.

To cement my friendship with Mary Louise, I touched her hand and told her we had something very personal in common.

"Kids who are going to make it big in pictures," she said.

"More than that, dear. I too am a widow."

It seemed to please her. "Bless your heart. When did you lose Mr. Kay?"

"Just a month ago."

"And you're not wearing black." She laughed. "Neither did I, it's just too depressing."

This led naturally to the subject of husbands, and men in general. Mary Louise claimed to be through with them, unaware that I knew she'd just spent the night with a lover. "Well now, we've got even more in common than I thought," I said. "I'm only thirty — a little younger than you, I guess — and I feel exactly the same." She wanted to know Mr. Kay's line of business, and when I told her Coca-Cola salesman, she laughed again and then wrinkled her nose. "You look as if you could have done better than that. But if Baby Jewel's got any talent, I'm sure it comes from *you*." I longed to kick her, but kissed her instead and said I had some shopping to do. Mary Louise decided to treat herself to a 10¢ matinee of Erich von Stroheim in *Blind Husbands,* and we parted on the best of terms.

I hurried home to pick up Baby, put a little rouge on her lips and take her straight to Mr. Evansmith. His shop had a window display of Picture Kiddie Portraits, all of them Guaranteed Natural. He offered me a special deal, ten portraits for $6, explaining we could check the proofs next day and choose the best for the Standard Casting Directory. Mr. Evansmith was extremely impressed with Baby, not a bad angle to her face, he said, obvious star material and a born winner. And although it was the first time she ever posed for a professional, Baby acted as if she really *lived* in front of the camera. You don't always know what's going on in her mind because she doesn't talk much; when she comes out with something, however, it's always to the point! But I could see that the closer Mr. Evansmith moved with his camera, the happier she looked. Then halfway through the session she stopped smiling. "Smile, please, keep smiling," Mr. Evansmith said. She shook her head and told him, "Nobody smiles all the time." Mr. Evansmith seemed quite startled. "But they should look as if they do," he said. Baby gazed straight into his eyes and did something extraordinary. Actually smiled without smiling! "I've never seen any Baby take direction like that," Mr. Evansmith said.

Every portrait turned out so well it was hard to choose the best, so I

brought them all to the office of the Standard Casting Directory and asked
the girl for her opinion. A brisk young lady in a shirt and tie, she told me
in a superior tone that she was much too busy, but when I held up the
portraits one by one in front of her face, she began to look interested.
"Humdingers all," she said finally. "So what do you suggest?" I asked,
and she voted for Baby smiling but not smiling and holding the American
flag, which was a last-minute inspiration of Mr. Evansmith's. Then the
secretary explained I had to write a line of copy to be included with the
portrait, and I asked her to show me the latest issue of the Directory.
Children come almost at the back of it, after Leading and Feature and
Character Adults, but before Animals. Beside a hopeless addled portrait
of Baby Peaches his mother had placed the words, Incredibly Versatile. I
thought for a moment, then wrote on the form, Baby Jewel — A Real
Sparkler! The secretary found this smart as a whip, was sure it would pay
off, and offered me a special rate of $40 for three issues.

Baby Looks Back

According to Mother I wasn't much of a talker in those days, which is
hard to believe now. Maybe I kept quiet because, although I adored her
unconditionally, I suspected she was God. Open any page of her diaries
and you meet one of the powerhouses of the world. From the Eternal
Wheel to my fourteen-carat genius, everything Mother believed in was
totally real to her, and she left me no choice but to go along with it. As a
result, all her beliefs about me came true. When she arranged for me to
start singing and dancing lessons at the age of four, she told the teacher
he'd be amazed how quickly I learned every step and how perfectly I
carried a tune. It happened. On my sixth birthday she decided to enroll
me in school — not the local Elementary, which wasn't good enough —
and over Father's objections went to see the principal of a fashionable
academy in Villa Park. It was way beyond our means, so she struck a
bargain with him, offering to wash dishes and do light housework five
days a week if the school accepted me at reduced fees. Then she struck a
bargain with *me*. "I am sacrificing myself to the hilt, Baby, so you can get
the best education around, and I want your solemn promise to work twice
as hard as all the other girls and come out Top of the Heap." I did, just
before she yanked me off to California.

Mother had to be right because she could only be wrong if I disappointed her, and letting down God was naturally out of the question. My
first moppet photographs were nothing less than the knockouts she expected, and not long afterwards, when she worked out a wild plan to

show me off in front of Mr. Griffith and Lillian Gish, I followed it to the
letter. She got away with the pushiest behavior because she was a non-
stop dynamo and yet a real lady. *Almost* a classic beauty as well, only her
jaw was a shade prominent and usually working overtime. (Years later,
when I first saw Irene Dunne in *Back Street*, it occurred to me: If they ever
make a movie of Mother's life, there's the actress to play her. And *Roberta*
clinched it. I watched Irene, who was incidentally one of Mother's top
favorites, give herself all those grand opera airs and then heard her hit all
those flat notes. It gave me what they call the shock of recognition.) I
suppose her dreams and ambitions created a lot of pressure, yet I took it
for granted. She made every demand seem so natural and right, just as
she dismissed anything not up to snuff — our poky Chicago apartment, a
black eye, a blister on her hands from too much dishwashing — as *only
temporary*. The bad passed away, the good lasted forever. Once you understood that, nothing could hold you back.

Elva's Diary

February 20 • Mary Louise Cloud supposes that until the Casting Directory with Baby's portrait comes out, we can do nothing except wait
around. That kind of attitude shows why, in almost eighteen months,
she's managed to land her Peaches no more than a couple of midget
parts. After only two weeks in this town the big break may still be just
around the next corner for Baby, but at least the Queen Bee, success, has
winged by and almost kissed her!

Taking our usual Boulevard stroll to the Hollywood Hotel, we found a
movie company shooting a scene for a Norma Talmadge picture right outside the entrance. Norma was not in the scene, but I noted the assistant
director picking people off the Boulevard to act as extras on the hotel
veranda. They had to sit or stand and watch Norma enter the lobby offscreen. (I'm boning up on movie technique and lingo pretty fast, and
passing it on to Baby.) Although I drew the assistant's attention to Baby
several times, he affected to ignore me. Finally he said, "No kids! Abso-
lutely no kids!" and affected to ignore me again when I demanded to
know why. A man stood near the camera, wearing breeches, a check cap
and tinted glasses. He looked important, and after making inquiries and
learning he was the director, I took Baby over. "Look at her," I said.
"Have you ever seen anything like her? She's ready and able to add a
special touch to your scene." He told me to consult his assistant and
moved away.

The assistant was now lining up his extras (a very mundane bunch, no one worth looking at in my opinion), and telling them what to do. All eyes were focused on a section of the veranda near the camera, so I snuck Baby to the other end, which was empty, and lifted her over the railing. Soon the director called "Action!" which she knew was her signal. She crept along the veranda to the back of the crowd, burrowed her way to the front, stood up and waved! The director didn't care or didn't notice, and I dare say nobody will notice Baby when Norma's movie comes out. But I felt crowned with success, having maneuvered her in front of the camera and watched her seize the moment like a perfect trouper.

In any case something important came out of this. Overhearing two extras discuss a movie Mr. G was shooting with Miss G, I got a powerful vibration. Play your cards right, Elva, I thought, and we walk off with the game. Next morning I rouged Baby's lips, made her put on her white tutu and carry her ballet slippers, and ordered a taxicab to take us to the end of the Boulevard, where Hollywood met Sunset. We could have boarded a streetcar, but I wished to appear above the crowd. Mr. G's studio looked like nothing much, just a fenced compound with a few barnlike buildings inside, but right above it stood a huge open air set, the city of Babylon. It was deserted and silent, with a long flight of steps leading up to a temple, statues of elephants lining the ascent. They perched on their hindlegs and their trunks curled like question marks into the air. A peculiar group of people hung around the studio gate, I supposed they were extras waiting for work. Two men in cowboy outfits, an Indian wearing feathers, a trio of little Chinamen, and a genuine Fat Lady from the circus, dressed like a child, her legs just rolls of white fat and roses peeping out from her ankle socks. I informed the guard that Mr. G was expecting Baby, and would he please direct us where to go. He suggested I think up a better one or go home, which made the Fat Lady squeak and wobble with laughter. Then I nodded to Baby. She began to cry, emitting the most fearsome sobs, and suddenly bolted past the guard, straight through the gate, running hell for leather in her white tutu. I accused the guard of giving her a terrible scare and ran inside after Baby, who'd disappeared by now. "It's all right, I won't let the brute hurt you, come to Mother!" I called, while the guard hollered after both of us. Looking back, I saw him preparing to give chase, but fortunately a car pulled up at the gate and distracted him. The Fat Lady continued to pitch like a boat.

Baby waited for me on the other side of the first barn. She changed calmly into her ballet shoes. We heard the guard shout again, then his voice was drowned out by *bloodcurdling screams* from inside the barn! It sounded as if someone was in ghastly pain or danger, and I said to Baby,

"Whatever's going on in there, we can't turn back now." I opened a door
and we entered a movie stage. As we tiptoed forward I noticed a camera
crew and a couple of lights trained on a set representing an old-fashioned
living room. Desperate shrieks came somewhere from this set, but I could
only see a burly middle-aged actor trying to break open the door of a
locked closet. Finally a voice called "Cut!", the actor turned away and the
screams stopped. Then the closet door opened and a girl walked out. She
had a frail white face, huge eyes, disheveled fair hair. A tall thin man
wearing a panama hat and brightly checked suit moved slowly toward
her. She smiled faintly and murmured a question that ended in "... *real
enough*?" The man nodded and they went off to the sidelines.

As I pondered our next move, an assistant spotted us and asked what
we were doing. "Baby and I would like to see Mr. G," I said. He asked if I
thought people could simply walk on a set uninvited and get an appointment. "Well, now I'm here," I said, "why don't you invite me?" He
stared at me in amazement. "And before you fix an appointment for me,"
I went on, "I'd like you to explain something. Why does Miss G act away
inside that closet when no one can possibly see her? And what's the good
of screaming when she'll never be heard?"

"I don't believe this," the assistant said, but before he could make up
his mind what to do, Mr. G himself came up! I saw him full face and
close, looking like a handsome bird with a slightly beaked nose and
hooded eyes. Baby gave him a little smile and raised herself on her points.
Mr. G seemed interested but puzzled. Then he turned to me and said in a
slow, deep, patient voice, "I'm going to shoot *inside* the closet next. Miss
G has been working herself up for that scene."

"I hope you're taking this in," I told Baby. "I hope you'll always remember to work yourself up to a scene." I made a sign, her smile faded,
and my fourteen-carat genius began to dance the Dying Swan. There was
no music, of course, but she fluttered her arms in perfect rhythm, making
them like wings. She glided around in a circle, then sank gradually to the
ground. She arched her neck, fluttered her arms more pitifully, as if her
strength was fading, and let her head droop forward. She grew very still,
very sad, until in complete silence she expired. It was so beautiful I felt
tears come to my eyes. Some of the camera crew had gathered around,
openly admiring, to watch her little death. Miss G stole up beside Mr. G.
She still looked ghostly and distant, but I knew Mr. G was stirred to the
depths. In his deliberate thoughtful way he walked over to my crumpled
Baby and lifted her to her feet.

"What else can you do?" he asked.

She held on to his hand, catching her breath as she looked up at him. "I can imitate Charlie Chaplin but I didn't bring the costume."

"Would you like to see her tango?" I said. "She can do it without music, just like the Swan."

Mr. G frowned. "A child should not tango. A child should study nature. Flowers, animals, the world of being." He gazed intently at Baby. "Did you ever play with a squirrel?"

"No," said Baby, not in the least surprised, "I never did."

"Imagine you're playing with one now."

Without hesitation Baby knelt on the floor and held out her hand to a small invisible animal. "Don't be frightened," she whispered. "I only want to play with you." She looked up at Mr. G. "He's very wild, you know. He's not sure. . . ." She held out her hand again, crooking a finger. "Come along, you're so pretty, I really love you." To Mr. G: "He's coming. But don't move or you'll frighten him." After a moment she smiled, pretended to tickle the squirrel's neck, then gave a bleat of pain. "He bit me! And ran away!"

Once again Mr. G lifted Baby to her feet. "The kid's got it," he said, looking almost stern. She stared at him as if hypnotized. "A natural," he said, then turned to Miss G. "See how quickly she breathes. She's nervous."

"She'll get over being nervous," I assured Mr. G, "now she knows she's got it."

Mr. G frowned again. "I hope not. Nerves are a sign of imagination."

There was a long, strange silence. He gazed into space, alone with his secret thoughts. I smiled at Miss G, who still looked remote and said nothing. Finally Mr. G turned to her. "I should like to see this child at fourteen. Won't she be lovely, in the rosebud garden of youth?"

Miss G looked rather cryptic but still said nothing.

"In the meantime," I suggested, "couldn't she be lovely as Miss G's baby daughter?" But Mr. G said she had no baby in this picture, only a doll. He patted Baby's curls, promised not to forget her, and ordered his assistant to take my phone number. Then he asked Miss G if she'd like an ice-cream soda before going back to work. She decided to wait until the scene was finished. He started toward the set, turned back and beckoned to us. "The kid's got it," he repeated. Baby never took her eyes off him. "But she'll lose it," he went on, "if you make her do artificial things. Artifice is the death of art. Nature is feeling and life." He nodded, left us to rehearse Miss G in the closet, and as we went out the door she began screaming again, loud enough to wake the dead.

"Sit down," I said to Mary Louise, "I don't want you to faint when you hear this. I arranged for Mr. G to give Baby an audition today, and he was deeply impressed. He told me *she's got it*."

"Oh my, how clever you are. Has he signed her up?"

"Not yet. But he asked for my phone number."

"Sit down, Elva, I don't want you to faint when you hear this. But they ask for your phone number just to get rid of you."

"In *your* experience, maybe, dear."

She shrugged. "Did you know the man's half Jewish, by the way? Like Douglas Fairbanks?"

Baby Looks Back

Mr. Griffith said he wouldn't forget me, and I certainly didn't forget *him*, even though it was years until we met again. He made a big impression that day, so quiet and gentlemanly and sad, yet full of authority. The Ideal Father, or so I thought.

Elva's Diary

February 22 • Yesterday I found Baby lying on her stomach on the patio, watching a lizard. She said she was following Mr. G's instructions and studying nature.

Baby always had this desire to *learn*, she inherits it from me, and it reminded me not to neglect her education out here. So much on my mind since we arrived, I never thought about sending her to school again. But when I asked Mary Louise where she sent Peaches, she laughed.

"Nowhere. Right now it's more important for that boy to lose weight. He doesn't want to, so I may start giving him enemas."

Underneath the magnolia and satin manner, there's a heart of stone. "Isn't that against the law?" I asked.

Her eyes opened very wide. "Giving enemas?"

"Not sending your child to school."

"Maybe. But hundreds of people come out here every week, Elva. It'll take years to check up on all the kids who don't go to school."

"Suppose I reported you to the authorities?"

She laughed again. "You have the best sense of humor."

I kissed her and went to consult Mr. Hendrix. He told me Lakewood Elementary was only a few blocks away, so I immediately took Baby to see the principal. A most unattractive person with jowls and a prairie twang, he dared to say after giving Baby only the briefest glance, "We only take normal children, not picture kids."

It was enough to make me realize I'd never allow him to take Baby anyway, but I saw no reason to let the man off lightly. "And what is normal? A voice like a hick? A face that would stop a clock?"

He got up from his desk, showed me the door and said, "Try Mrs. Root."

I asked who Mrs. Root might be and he said, "Your only hope. My secretary will give you her address." I wanted to go around there at once, but Baby said, "Let's wait until tomorrow. Take me to a movie by Mr. G." But none of Mr. G's movies was playing, so we settled for Mary Pickford in *Poor Little Rich Girl*, and it's certainly true she refuses to grow up. Playing a child of ten! Still, I had to admire the way she surrounded herself with *real* youngsters and managed to look (almost) no older than they did.

"You know what they call her?" I said to Baby as we came out. "The first woman in America to earn a million dollars!"

She stared at me. "Is Little Mary a woman?"

"A woman who'll never see twenty-five again. Married, too." *And* enjoying a torrid romance with dashing Mr. F, I thought to myself, even though she claims to be a Catholic.

"Then why doesn't she act grown-up?"

"People don't want her to, they just love to see cute kids."

"Doesn't *she* want to?"

"Not a bit. Little Mary says she was so unhappy as a real youngster, she makes up for it on the silver screen by *acting* a happy one. I told you before, it's all a game up there."

Baby fell into one of her long silences, getting ready to ask one of her deep questions. "Why can't people be happy in both places? Up there and down here?"

"Look at it this way. It's more than a question of being happy or unhappy. No matter how good a person has it, a person always imagines having it better."

"Why?"

"Human nature."

Next morning we walked to Mrs. Root's place, just around the corner from the little studio on Santa Monica Boulevard where they make *Tarzan* pictures. Baby gazed wistfully at the entrance and I asked if she hoped to catch a glimpse of Elmo Lincoln in his loincloth. She shook her head. "Boy?" I said. She shook her head again. "I want to see Edgar Rice Burroughs." She doesn't care for Tarzan but she's an avid reader of Mr.

Burroughs' romances about the planet Mars. Although we waited a few minutes, the only arrival was a truckload of jungle foliage.

The schoolhouse looked from the outside like an English Tudor cottage. I rang the bell and a tall woman of maybe forty-five opened the door. She had a round face, bulging eyes and a brightly painted bunched-up mouth. A winding turban covered her head and she wore dimestore bracelets on each snaky wrist. "My horoscope told me to expect an important stranger today," she said, glancing at Baby. "But I must also use care in motion. Welcome aboard." We followed her through a hallway to the livingroom. There seemed to be a considerable racket going on upstairs, several kinds of music playing at once, people jumping around, maybe a chair knocked over. Mrs. Root gave no sign that it bothered her. "Yesterday I was supposed to put more effort in the right direction," she murmured. "But what *is* the right direction?"

The livingroom had a rustic atmosphere, curtains and upholstery with a cherry blossom pattern, china animals, bowls of potpourri, and a big reproduction in an antique frame of my favorite George Frederic Watts painting, *Hope*. (It shows a blindfolded lady on her knees, which might seem gloomy, yet Mr. Watts makes you feel she'll get up and come through, so it's really inspiring.) Cordial and gracious from the start, Mrs. Root struck a very different note from the brute at Lakewood Elementary. "How about a pick-me-up before we get down to business?" she suggested, opening a wooden box packed with dried fruit. "The dates are out of this world, the figs are more than delectable, but leave the prunes alone unless you enjoy chewing leather." She watched approvingly as Baby selected two dates and a fig, then laid a hand on my arm. "My dear, I specialize in educating picture kids and I know a winner when I see one. You laid a Golden Egg."

I gave my Mona Lisa smile. "People keep saying that, ever since we set foot in this town. Now what kind of education can you offer?"

"The basics. Reading, writing and counting."

"Baby knows those basics already, Mrs. Root."

"God bless her. Too many toddlers earn three hundred dollars a week and can't even write their own names. Shall I give her history, then? Or geography? You name it."

"I'll name it," Baby said. "I want to study nature."

"She's superb, Mrs. Kay. I'll give her all the botany she can take."

"You teach every subject yourself?"

"Certainly. I had a very fine education in Oklahoma City."

I asked Mrs. Root how long she'd been at the teaching game, and she told me the school opened five months ago. "I came out here to stay with my elder sister, right after poor Root cashed in his chips. ..."

"Excuse me," I said. "You lost your husband too?"

"Yes, my dear. Root's pushing up daisies now. So you're a widow yourself?"

I nodded. "And it's amazing how many widows I get to meet out here."

"That's because it's a woman's town whichever way you look at it. Now let me get back to the school. My sister teaches at Riverdale and happened to mention how many schools refuse to take picture kids, who might as well belong to the tribes of Israel for all the welcome they get. But say what you like, picture kids are the kids of the future out here, and I had an inspiration. *Start a school that takes no other kind.* Maybe you noticed I put a public telephone in the hallway? That's so the studios and my little stars in the bud can touch base whenever they want. You were asking about Root. He was shot through the head."

Baby looked up with sudden interest. "Who did it?"

"She's more than superb," Mrs. Root said. "She's iridescent. Root was a night clerk, my dear, at the Redbud Hotel in Oklahoma City. He went off for a tinkle in the small hours, came back to the lobby and found a man wearing a stocking mask with his hand in the till. The bandit shot him on sight and made off with Root's pocketbook as well." She sighed. "And as poor Root pointed out in the hospital, just before croaking, he never carried more than five dollars and the till was almost as empty as the hotel."

"You couldn't expect the bandit to know that," Baby said.

Mrs. Root handed her a dried fig. "You are one of a kind. You see through to the heart of things." She turned to me. "As I was saying, it's a woman's town whichever way you look at it. All doors open for the female of the species out here. She can become a star, or the Mother behind a star, she can write photoplays, she can even direct pictures and run her own studio like my friend Lois Weber."

"I never heard of her," I said.

"Never heard of Lois?" Mrs. Root looked shocked. "But she's monumental. A mind as deep as a well. Her pictures deal with basic issues of the day, divorce, abortion, Christian Science, and always give both sides the benefit of the doubt. On Christian Science her picture told us, there's certainly something to it but consult your doctor first."

"I'll take Baby to see her this afternoon. Where's her studio?"

"On the rocks, my dear, I'm afraid. Lois is going out of business." Mrs. Root moved to the door. "Now come and see my schoolroom."

As we followed her upstairs, the racket sounded louder than ever. "Talent Hour," she explained. "My kids get their basics from eight to eleven, then one hour to work on their acts."

In the main room upstairs, the school desks had been stacked at one end so that Mrs. Root's picture kids could go through their paces. A boy with bangs played the piano and sang "Put Your Arms Around Me Honey," while a girl wearing a white top hat and tails tapdanced on the lid. A toddler juggled with colored balls, a little fellow in a sailor's suit practiced somersaults and handstands, a pocket señorita with a rose in her hair clicked a pair of castanets, and in a corner four youngsters played "Alexander's Ragtime Band" together on drums, xylophone, harmonica and ukulele. "That's a very musical family," Mrs. Root said. "They're going to audition for Winnie's Date Room next week. In blackface."

A sprightly old woman sat in a high-backed chair, watching the acts and giving an approving nod from time to time, or clicking her teeth when the juggler dropped a ball. She was dressed like a Dutch doll, silver curls peeping out of her bonnet. "One of the biggest little troupers up north sixty years ago," Mrs. Root said. "They called her the Barbary Coast Kidlet, she played Little Eva in *Uncle Tom's Cabin* and Little Nell in *The Old Curiosity Shop.* Later she brought vaudeville to Alaska during the Gold Rush. Imagine the thrill when she answered my ad for Talent Supervisor."

No doubt in my mind, we had found the ideal place for Baby to continue her education. And for only $18 a month.

Baby Looks Back

Haphazard is the word for Mrs. Root's teaching methods, even though she gave me special attention. Way ahead of the others in basics, I was pretty much on my own from the start, and after setting the rest of the picture kids multiplication and spelling tests, Mrs. Root came over to my class of one at the back. "I'll begin by opening your eyes to the true story of mankind, my dear, which regular education in our country ignores. It stuffs you with so-called essential facts and leaves the imagination to fend for itself." Her voice suddenly dropped to a whisper. "The footprint of an unknown beast in the Himalayas tells us more than the Lincoln Memorial, because it makes us ask, *Why?*"

"*Why?*" I asked.

"You're sublime. And if I knew, I'd tell you. Just bear in mind the world is largely unexplored. You've learned your Julius Caesar and your

Napoleon, but what about El Dorado, William Tell and Prester John? You can show me India or Germany on the map, but can you find Atlantis or the Seven Cities of Gold?"

I took Mrs. Root's word on everything and for a long time believed these people, places and footprints really existed. At least her rundown on presidents of the United States, from Madison to Wilson, was offbeat but correct. Ulysses Grant ate cucumber dunked in vinegar for breakfast, because it kept him sharp. Thomas Jefferson invented the revolving chair. John Quincy Adams liked to swim nude in the Potomac. Grover Cleveland had an artificial jaw. And my new education involved spending one hour a day with a fine illustrated album called *State Flowers, Birds and Trees of the Union*. I learned to identify the Common Loon of Minnesota, the Dogwood of Virginia, the Bluebird of Missouri, the Single Leaf Pinon of Nevada and a whole heap more, although it was probably not what Mr. Griffith had in mind when he told me to study nature.

In Talent Hour I showed the ex-Barbary Coast Kidlet my Dying Swan, my Charlie Chaplin and my tango. She taught me to sing "Hot Time in the Old Town Tonight" and to dance a very fancy twostep. After we whirled around the floor together, knocking the other kids dead, she pronounced me champion of the month and earned me dirty looks. Incidentally, she got more calls on the public telephone than anyone else, for she was listed in the Casting Directory as an Old Character Woman. Once, I remember, she hurried off to play a corpse in an open coffin. Not as easy as it looked, she said.

Elva's Diary

May 15 • Downtown today I noticed a sign with an arrow pointing to the Highest Point in the City. We seemed to have reached the lowest point in our lives since we got here, so I said to Baby, "Let's go up, we could certainly use a lift!" Which is how we came to take a 5¢ round trip on the Court Flight cable car, with a visit to the observation tower at the top included.

It felt like our lowest point because no one has telephoned for Baby since her crackerjack photo appeared in the Casting Directory two weeks ago, and we've had no word from Mr. G either. I hate to admit Mary Louise could have been right, especially after the wretched Peaches got another midget call. And this morning, during Talent Hour at Mrs. Root's, *two* of Baby's front teeth fell out! Mrs. Root advised there were good cheap dentists around Broadway and Fifth, just walk right in and they fix you up, so we took a streetcar downtown and rang the bell of Dr.

Zola, Painless. He led us into a room that smelt of lye and had choppers in glass cases on the wall. He sat Baby in a chair with a drill looming over it like an instrument of torture, stepped on the foot pedal by mistake and started the motor. The sound was even more bloodcurdling than Miss G's screams in that closet. "I bet you're glad we don't have to use it on you," Dr. Zola said to Baby with a cheerful smile, made her bite into pink wax and told us to come back in a week, when he'd have a plate ready that she could clip over the gap for interviews. $9.

As we came out of the building, Baby noticed a soda fountain across the street and wanted a root beer special. Then we took a walk and I saw the sign. On the tower at the top of the hill was another sign, One Big Look, and we stood on the platform with a view all the way from the mountains to the Pacific. There was no one else around, and the day was perfectly clear except for patches of mist along the coast. For the first time since we arrived in Los Angeles I could see it whole, and see it *wasn't* whole at all. It reminded me of a jigsaw puzzle I once started and gave up, scattering a lot of pieces on the floor. In the long spaces between all those pieces there seemed to be no connections, nothing to help you guess how the pattern might turn out. So much desert. One Big Look showed that all the way from the mountains to the ocean was just basically desert. You had to cross the biggest stretch to get from Hollywood to Santa Monica and the beaches, along dirt tracks or a railroad that passed nothing except a few tall spindly palm trees and a few derricks where oil had been struck. To-day all the tracks looked very lonely, occasional automobiles and a Big Red Car moving as slow as camel caravans. Between Hollywood and downtown the roads were at least paved, but they passed through acres of wilderness, broken up from time to time by clusters of houses with whitewashed walls and red tiled roofs like the Yucca Riviera. But on some of the front lawns, oil pumps nodded up and down. Only the foothills looked cultivated, bright green oases with planted estates and houses as grand as castles on the Rhine. Two things struck me as especially strange through the telescope. First, on a hillside above the Hollywood Hotel, was an ugly bare patch of land hollowed out in the shape of a huge bowl, an old ranch house stuck in the middle. Then at the edge of downtown, stood a gleaming artificial lake with dark Des Moines houses dotted along the shore. People were out in sailboats, but the air was so still that the boats hardly moved. They looked stranded forever, like everything else in the desert.

The stillness and the long empty spaces felt ghostly, especially with Baby and me alone on the platform. She wanted to look through the telescope, so I lifted her up and she pointed it toward the coast more than twenty miles away. There was another space out there, like bluegrass, and it joined the sky. "Is that the ocean?" she asked, "where there's no more land?"

"The Pacific. Biggest and deepest ocean in the world."

"What's the other side?"

"For a very long time, nothing. Two thousand miles away you come to a bunch of islands. Another three thousand and you come to Japan."

"Did you ever go on an ocean?"

"Never in my life. And right now is the closest I ever got to one."

After a while she said, "I'd like to get closer. And put my feet in it."

"First things first, Baby. Wait till you hit the jackpot."

She fell silent again. Then she asked, "Which way is Atlantis from here?"

"Nobody knows. It might have been near Iceland, or Jamaica, or Long Beach. But nobody's even sure it existed."

"Mrs. Root is sure." Baby swiveled the telescope and gave an excited cry. "They're shooting a movie! Have you ever seen a movie set like that in your life?"

Through the telescope I saw the Far East — but it wasn't on the other side of the ocean, it was almost directly behind us. Streets of tumbledown wooden pagodas, balconies and arches tilted every which way, a rooftop sign that said Chew Tun, and two men in long yellow robes on the roof beside it. "You're looking at Chinatown," I explained. "Sometimes it's difficult to tell a movie set from a real place out here."

Baby sighed. "Sometimes I have dreams like that."

On the point of asking Baby about her dreams, I felt a sudden *vibration*, the most powerful since I got here. It came from the earth itself, a hidden faraway shiver. The desert in front of us, the high palms and low houses, the lines of dusty tracks, the dead lake and a great pink stucco turreted mansion in the foothills, everything we could see from the platform went blurred and shaky. Shuddering brightness made the whole desert like a mirage. "What is happening in this place?" I asked. "Am I seeing what I imagine, or imagining what I see? In any case this vibration is going on much too long!" Baby said, "Too long for what?" and then it stopped. The city looked as clear and still as usual. I took Baby's hand and we walked back to the cable car in silence. At the bottom of the hill, the man who sold tickets gave us a wide grin. "I ought to charge you extra for the earthquake!" he said. "But it's only a ten cent one," he added, "the kind of minor shock you get out here several times a year."

"It's a major shock as far as I'm concerned," I told Baby on the streetcar back to Hollywood. "And it's given me a very troubling idea. Do you suppose, every time I feel a personal vibration in Los Angeles, it's not in my mind but in the earth?"

June 2 • This morning my spirits were almost as low as my bank account, and it felt as if the Queen Bee had flown away for good. The greatness of Baby shines out from that portrait for all the world to see, why doesn't the world see it? I walked her to Mrs. Root's as usual and said, "You know where we are? We're almost at *rock bottom*, and I may have to sacrifice myself to the hilt again." Perhaps I spoke more bitterly than I intended, for a look of alarm crossed Baby's face. "It's only temporary, isn't it?" she asked.

"Of course. But sometimes temporary can seem very long." I kissed her. "Just keep studying nature and developing your imagination as Mrs. Root says and working on your acts. Mother will think of something, somehow."

It was the second day of a heatwave, with a sticky wind blowing in from the desert. On the walk home I noticed a new billboard outside the Church of the Golden Dream, Do You Really Know What Happens When You Die? The Reverend Cora stood outside wearing sandals, cloak, braided hair, lipstick and eyelid paint the same color as her church's dream. She carried sprigs of a dried golden plant and shook them at me. "Grown in earth charged with minerals from the gold mines of the San Gabriel mountains," she said. "This plant sends out chemical rays to enrich body and spirit." I got a whiff of something nauseous and hurried on. "It lasts a lifetime and costs only one dollar!" she called out, and I thought, people like the Reverend Cora give the Unknown a bad name.

So exhausted when I got back to the Yucca Riviera that I took off my clothes and lay down on the bed. Elva Kay, I told myself, if you can wash dishes in Chicago, you can wash them in Starlight City. The Tea Room Buffet has an ad in the window for Kitchen Help. A tear splashed down my cheek, then I dozed off. I started to dream I was on my knees with my back to a wall. As someone covered my eyes with a blindfold I said, "This will get you nowhere, I am Hope, I spring eternal!" As I jumped to my feet, groping the air, a knock on the door woke me up.

"Are you there?" Mary Louise's voice, then her laugh. "And are you decent?"

"No, I'm in the 'altogether.' "

The laugh again. "Alone, I trust?"

"No, with a roomful of thoughts."

"You have the best sense of humor. Now pile into some clothes and let us in."

"Is that dear clever Peaches with you?"

"Peaches took the Pacific Electric to Long Beach. He loves to ride the railway. I want you to meet my friend Harvey Pancoast."

She meant her lover, I supposed. "Just a minute," I called, and thought as I dressed, all these weeks I've never met the man, only seen him from a distance in his Model T, picking the bitch up or dropping her off. And she's never even mentioned him before, so she must have wanted it that way, and has a reason for bringing him out in the open now.

I opened the door and saw Mary Louise frilled up in a peach-colored gown, cheeks a bit flushed and looking tickled silly. Obviously they'd been fooling around at high noon in spite of the heat. Pancoast was almost as snappy a dresser in his way. He wore white knickerbockers, stockings and moccasins, a black shirt open nearly to his belly button, and carried a cowboy hat. His granite face and narrow frontier eyes reminded me of William S. Hart, although one of the eyes looked around the room while the other didn't, and I realized the still one was glass. He told me he owned a studio on Poverty Row, where they produce the cheapest stuff in town, cliffhanger serials, knockabout comedies, circus stories. I glanced at Mary Louise and thought, can a woman sink any lower than spreading her legs to get her boy a midget part?

The creature lolled on my bed. "Oh my, it's so hot, I'm quite tuckered out." She plumped a pillow. "Where's your Jewel?"

"At school. Naturally."

She plumped the pillow some more and lay back with a contented sigh. "I guess you're wondering why we're here?"

"No, dear. I never look a gift horse in the mouth."

"We've come to do you a favor."

"Bless you, but your presence here is a favor in itself."

Harvey laughed. "You girls really kill me. Are you always so polite to each other?"

I decided I could never like him. "Life is short, Mr. Pancoast, but not too short to observe the amenities."

He stared, then joined his sweetheart on the bed. "Mary Lou, I can't tell if your friend is kidding me or not."

"That's one of the fascinating things about Elva. She keeps you guessing." Mary Louise did her old trick of studying my outfit (a suit of pearl-gray cotton) and making no comment. Then she asked, "How would you like to go out on the town tonight with Harvey and me?"

"Thank you so much. But two's company, three's a crowd."

"We'll be a crowd anyway. It's a party!"

"You're full of surprises this morning. But I never leave Baby by herself at night."

"I leave Peaches by himself all the time. Just slip Mr. Hendrix a quarter and ask him to look in once."

I shook my head. "You know he starts hitting the bottle at sundown."

"Where does he get his stuff?" Harvey asked.

Mary Louise sat up. "Now come on, Elva, it's time you started getting around." She sounded impatient. "You're still a very attractive woman and good things shouldn't go to waste!"

"Hear, hear," Harvey said unexpectedly and winked with his good eye. For a moment Mary Louise looked frightened, almost grim. Had she wanted to keep Harvey and me apart because she feared I might snatch him away? God forbid, I thought, she's more than welcome to the brute. "They want extra girls," Harvey went on. "I promised to try and help them out."

I gave him a long cool look. "This is beginning to sound like the fishiest offer I've had in this town. And I've had one or two."

It stunned him. "Mary Lou, I don't know if she's kidding again or not."

"Neither do I, but she's certainly in a strange mood."

"I'm not in the mood to be *procured* for a night of unbridled lust," I said. "You may call that strange if you like."

"Holy cats," Harvey said, "this friend of mine is giving a party, and it turns out there'll be more guys than girls, so he asks people to bring extra girls. What's so fishy about that?"

"I thought of *you*," Mary Louise said, going rather shrill, "because you're never asked out and it's a shame. But if you want to stay home and brood about your Jewel getting nowhere, I'm sure you're welcome."

"Just don't act high and mighty, and give me unbridled lust." Harvey laid a hand on Mary Louise's knee. "You never told me she was such a nervous person."

Mary Louise shrugged. "I've never seen Elva like this before." Her eyes went very round as she gazed at me. "Do you have a fever, dear? What a pity that would be. This friend of Harvey's is a big-time director, and he's giving this party for the opening of a swank new supper club. You'd make *connections*, which is another reason I thought of asking you."

Then Harvey mentioned the director's name. I'd never heard of it, and couldn't decide whether they were telling the truth or bluffing. The prospect of making connections was certainly enticing, but at the same time a wild thought entered my mind. No doubt I *was* on edge — about Baby's future, my shrinking bank account, the idea of having to sacrifice myself

again — but as I looked at Harvey Pancoast and Mary Louise Cloud side
by side on my bed, she with a playful smile and he with a glass eye, they
seemed positively sinister. It was impossible not to imagine them as
agents for the white slave racket! I could go to that party in all innocence,
hoping to meet some all-time greats, be slipped something sweet and
drugged in a crystal goblet, and *wake up in a locked room in Rio.* Only a
week ago I'd seen a movie in which it happened.

"Are you all right, Elva?"

I felt unable to answer Mary Louise at once, remembering with a chill of
fear how often she slunk home at dawn after Harvey dropped her off, and
wondering if their nights were full of crime as well as passion. Then I
pulled myself together. "I'm fine, dear. Maybe just a little giddy from the
heat. If I offended you and Mr. Pancoast, please forgive me."

"We'll only forgive you if you come to the party." She laughed. "Otherwise we'll be dreadfully offended."

"When Baby gets home from school," I said, "I'll see how she feels
about being left alone."

Baby Looks Back

As it happened, I didn't feel like being left alone that night, but never
told her. When we sat down in class that morning, Mrs. Root seemed
upset and said she had an announcement to make. The ex-Barbary Coast
Kidlet had answered another call for a corpse in an open coffin the previous day, an unusually grand corpse, Mrs. Root told us, the Queen of
somewhere or other in Europe. She had to lie in state in a cathedral while
mourners filed past to pay their last respects. When the final shot was in
the can the director called "Cut!", but the Kidlet continued to lie very
still, her eyes closed, her face powdered dead white, a tiara of fake diamonds on her head. Someone came up to tell her she could go home
now, but the Kidlet had already gone home. "A pro to the end," Mrs.
Root said. "She succumbed on the job."

The news stunned me. I realized how fond I'd grown of the old pro,
and was appalled when Grace Baggett, who specialized in dancing on top
of pianos in white tie and tails, called out at once, "So who's going to take
over Talent Hour?" Mrs. Root felt the same way. " 'The Show Must Go
On' is a fine idea, Grace, but don't push it too far." Until a replacement
was found, she added, she would supervise Talent Hour herself. Later,
when we stacked the desks and began working on our acts, I noticed the
ex-Kidlet's chair standing empty against a window. Tears came to my
eyes. I remembered the day she fell into it, gasping for breath after our

spectacular twostep, and patted a silver ringlet that had gone awry. At
least the Conway clan, so popular with the customers of Winnie's Date
Room that they'd been booked for an extra two months, showed the right
feeling. They got out their instruments and played "After You've Gone"
with a lot of drum taps.

When I broke the news to Mother, she had her usual reaction to death
and promised me the ex-Kidlet was now happily aboard the Eternal
Wheel. Looking out the window, she drew my attention to a large yellow
butterfly fluttering around the patio. "Maybe she's on her way there this
very moment, Baby. Butterflies are bearers of souls." Maybe so and
maybe not, I thought as the butterfly took off and disappeared, but I'd
rather have the ex-Kidlet alive and singing and dancing and reminiscing
about her nursery days on the Barbary Coast — how she wore blackface
and strummed the banjo on one night, and on another danced Irish reels
in a green suit and leprechaun hat.

When Mother asked if I'd mind being left alone that night, it struck me
she wasn't in the best shape either. She seemed distracted and impatient,
complaining about the heat and the wind from the desert. "It's only temporary," I said. She agreed, yet still looked uneasy and ready to talk about
rock bottom again. I didn't want that. It made the world crack and gape,
which was against the rules. *Rock bottom*, if we ever hit it, would be my
fault. So I told her not to worry, it was time she cut loose and went off on
a spree.

She gave me a strange look. "What makes you think it's going to be a
spree, Baby?" Now that I've read her diaries, especially the crazy part
when she's afraid of being drugged and carried off to white slavery, I
think I understand her problem. Mother was feeling another kind of heat,
and since she always saw herself as a real lady, she must have hated to
admit she was desperate to get laid.

"Whatever it's going to be, go ahead and let off some steam," I said.
She gave me another strange look, stroking her throat with one finger,
and walked to the mirror. You might call this whole scene ironic in view of
what happened when Mother went to her first party out here, but I never
knew about any of that until much later.

Elva's Diary

June 3 • Wind still blowing as we packed into Harvey Pancoast's Model
T last night, and a tinge of smoke in the air. Harvey said a fire had broken
out in the hills, it often does when the thermometer climbs and the wind
gets up. Mary Louise in white chiffon, fluffy as a meringue pie, pearls

coming out of her everywhere. Yours truly in the Grecian style, having nipped out to the Boulevard to buy a little outfit for the occasion. Gauzy and flowing, like TB in *The Forbidden Path*. ($22.50.) Mary Louise looked it up and down but said her usual nothing.

On the long, feebly lit road downtown, I wondered about Harvey driving so fast with only one eye. He told us President Wilson was coming out to Los Angeles soon to drum up support for America joining the League of Nations. Mary Louise wanted to know where Harvey stood on this. "What's it going to cost us?" he said. "I can't tell till I see the figures." Through the Broadway tunnel to a narrow street, where we stopped outside a building with no sign. On a vulgar billboard opposite, a mouth with great luminous teeth parted to crunch what looked like a piece of chocolate. For Better Results *Chew* Your Laxative! "If it *tastes* like chocolate," Mary Louise said, "I'll buy some for Peaches and pretend it's candy." An attendant hurried over to park the car, and a young man wearing Turkish trousers and an embroidered vest opened the door. Felt immediately on my guard. He led us down a long dim passage to a room with flickering candlelight, oriental masks on the walls, low divans, pillows and carpets on the floor. More like the Arabian Nights than a supper club.

People lay around and talked in whispers, but it was too dark to see who they were. Smartly dressed on the whole, glimmer of jewelry, some of the women wore painted feathers. More young men in exotic costumes wheeled around carts with silver ice-buckets holding champagne and what I mistook for silver teapots and sugar bowls. At a white grand in an alcove, a Negro pianist played "Melancholy Baby."

Like a movie, I thought. Everywhere you go is like a movie. Another Negro, very tall, dressed in a kimono, came up to Harvey and introduced himself as Big Fella. I noticed a scar on his cheek. He led us over to a divan, whispering to Harvey on the way, and Harvey told us his important friend would arrive in a few minutes. "If he's giving the party, shouldn't he arrive before his guests?" I asked. "Not if he's important," Mary Louise said. She arranged pillows on the floor and struck what she imagined to be a seductive pose. "Is Big Fella the headwaiter?" I asked. Harvey shook his head as he sprawled on a divan. "He owns the joint." Felt more on my guard than ever, unwilling even to sit down. "Who are all these people and do you know any of them?" I asked Harvey, who looked around and informed me he knew Jack Pickford over there! I couldn't believe he meant Mary's brother, but he insisted he did, nodding toward a mixed group way across the room. I still found it too dark to see anyone clearly, and wondered whether Harvey could. "Well, which one is Jack?'' I said, and Mary Louise laughed. ''What a lot of questions, dear, do sit down.'' And a young man came up with a cart. Harvey lifted the lid of a silver teapot, then of a sugar bowl. ''Holy cats, what tidings of joy.'' He shook some white powder from the bowl on to his thumb, then held it out to Mary Louise. She plunged with her nose and took a sniff.

For a moment I was confused. What could Mary Louise's nose be doing in Harvey's thumb and why did he allow it? Then I caught the drift, and what happened next was like a scene from a movie. Very quick, one shot flashing after the next.

Harvey shook out more powder, sniffed it from his own thumb.

I said I was leaving at once.

Mary Louise told me to cool down and have some champagne.

The young man with the cart picked up a bottle.

I shook my head and started to walk away.

Harvey tugged at my sleeve and said something about a wet blanket.

I jabbed my elbow straight in his face.

A mask grinned from the wall as I hurried out of the room.

In the long dim passage I paused to steady myself, feeling quite faint.

At the other end, the doorman let in someone from the street.

(A round of applause for the pianist in the candlelit room!)

He wore a seersucker suit with a red carnation in his buttonhole.

Suddenly so weak with fear I couldn't move.

He came up and asked in a British accent, ''Are you unwell?''

The face reassured me instantly. Such kindness in the eyes. And the rest of him had a comforting aura of success, silk handkerchief in front pocket, platinum watch, diamond ring, manicured fingernails. Like a leading man in a society picture. Mature but not old.

''I can't stay in this place. Please call me a cab.''

He looked amused and asked who brought me.

''Do you know Harvey Pancoast?''

''An old friend. I invited him.''

This took a moment to sink in, like Mary Louise sniffing. Then I thought, if he's a big-time director, he can't be a drug fiend. ''I'm Harvey's extra girl,'' I said, trying to sound as ironic as possible.

Instead of answering he took my arm and led me straight back to the room! It never occurred to me to resist. The scarred Negro clapped him on the shoulder, people looked up and called hello. No doubt in my mind he commanded great respect, and I had a sudden thrill entering on his arm. ''I know you're famous,'' I whispered, ''but I have to admit the only picture directors I've ever heard of are Mr. Griffith, Mr. Ince and Mr. de

Mille." He smiled, said he was not quite in their class yet, and snapped his fingers. A young man came up with a cart. He helped himself to white powder and sniffed like all the others.

"Please call me a cab," I said, rigid with fear.

He lowered his hand from his face. "If I do, you'll be disappointed for the rest of your life." I turned away, but he took my arm again. "Or perhaps not quite as long as that," he said.

"How long?" I asked, wondering at myself, helpless now in his strong grip.

"A year. A night. An hour." He let me go, as if he knew I would stay after all, filled a glass with champagne and held it close to my lips. "All the way home, at least, sitting in a cab and asking yourself why, if you did the right thing, you're not feeling better about it."

What a connoisseur of the human heart, I thought. And WDT's charm was like the finest honey, he had spoonfuls of it. I took the glass and sank willingly to a divan at his side. "What are you so afraid of?" he asked, leaning very close, and I felt his breath on my cheek. "We seem to be in a den of vice," I said. "Suppose the police raid it?" He smiled again. "Where have you been? That's never a problem out here." A heavy, broad-shouldered man wearing dark glasses and a dark suit walked past, giving us a friendly wave. "Vice squad," WDT said. "He runs a gambling syndicate on the side." The man stopped by a cart, lifted a silver bowl and helped himself. "I can't believe what I'm seeing," I said. WDT leaned close again and remarked I seemed hardly dry behind the ears.

When he confirmed Jack Pickford was sitting three divans away, I said, "Does Mary *know*?" He assured me Mary knew a lot of things, and one of them was never to cast the first stone. More bubbly flowed and I found myself gulping it. I inquired how long WDT had been in Hollywood. "Two years," he told me, and I supposed he'd made pictures back in his native England. But he shook his head. "Prospecting in Alaska was my previous career. Then I decided I'd find more of what I was looking for out here." I stared at him. "Gold!" he said. I refused to believe such an elegant man of the world had roughed it in the frozen north. "Most of us come from nowhere and we get somewhere very fast," he explained. That sounds good for Baby, I thought. "Mack Sennett was a plumber," he went on. "Little Adolph Zukor, who runs the studio I work for, used to peddle furs, and his partner Jesse Lasky played cornet in a vaudeville band."

The sound of these names, so casually dropped, gave me the best kind of goose bumps. Then a very young girl with short dark hair walked past in a most provocative costume, a silver satin tunic, white fishnet tights, bangles on both arms above the elbows. As she blew a kiss to WDT, I knew I'd seen her before. It was Barbara Lamarr! A sensation at sixteen in *Souls for Sale*, and a sensation at seventeen in juvenile court, when they accused her of indecent behavior in public and the judge called her "too beautiful for her own good." Gazing after her, WDT remarked in a strangely cool impersonal way, "Not long for this world." I felt the worst kind of goose bumps and wondered how he knew. "Some have it written all over them, Elva."

The pianist was playing "By the Beautiful Sea." Barbara went up to Big Fella, stroked his scar, kissed him full on the mouth, put her lovely pale arms around his black neck. They started to dance. "I see why she landed in juvenile court," I said, then gasped as Big Fella pushed her roughly against the wall and opened his kimono. This happened just a few feet from where we sat. Barbara unbuttoned her satin tunic and an exhibition followed, the kind I imagined only went on at certain nightspots in Paris, France.

I covered my face with my hands, but WDT pulled them away. "Never turn down a free show," he said and refilled my glass. I saw him smiling again, his eyes still looked unbelievably kind. What happened next was like another quick scene from a movie, although you could never show it.

Barbara sank to her knees and Big Fella stripped naked.

I gulped more champagne and stared helplessly into WDT's eyes.

Dialogue title (WDT): "Don't look at me, look at them."

I looked. Barbara kissed Big Fella's. I looked away.

Dialogue title (WDT): "Don't be shy."

I looked back. Barbara began to perform an act in which Mr. Kay had often tried, with no success, to interest *me*.

Mary Louise plumped her pillow.

Dialogue title: "Oh, my!"

I finished my champagne and glanced around the room.

Some of the guests mildly amused, others indifferent, Jack Pickford concentrating, an oriental mask grinning from the wall.

It was over, they disappeared together and the pianist changed his tune to "Give My Regards to Broadway."

As if nothing had happened, WDT said in his opinion that Barbara had less talent than Mary Miles Minter, whom he'd recently directed in a picture. He saw unplumbed depths in MMM. More bubbly flowed and he watched me drink it with that mature, intent, protective look in his eyes. Although fairly rattled by what I'd just seen, I was aware he never left my side, and felt flattered. "I'm hardly the most fascinating woman in this joint," I said. "I'm just a mother from Chicago who believes her little daughter was born to make it big in movies. Her name's Baby Jewel, by the way, and that's exactly what she is." WDT leaned very close. "It's true, Elva, you're dreadfully ordinary. That's why you fascinate me."

Did he mean this or was he making fun of me? Either way I felt hurt, and disappointed that he asked nothing about Baby. But there was no time to tell him so. Two people came over to our divan and I gasped to find myself shaking hands with Jack Pickford and his bride Olive Thomas. Newspapers call them the Ideal American Couple and they certainly looked it. In the excitement of meeting them, I forgot to wonder how an Ideal Couple happened to be frequenting a den of every kind of vice! When WDT introduced me, they said, "A great pleasure to meet you," in the most charming and natural manner, then Jack turned to WDT and asked about some deal. I hardly listened to their conversation, too busy star-tasting as my mind seemed to be licking their skin and their clothes. Olive started as a Ziegfeld Girl at sixteen, and you'd have thought sixteen was yesterday. She had the face of an angel. Her hair fell in long ringlets to her shoulders, and she wore a simple white dress with a rose pinned to the front. I'd admired her in *Limousine Life* and adored Jack, of course, in *Seventeen*. In his case I had to admit seventeen seemed a bit longer ago than yesterday. He was shorter than he looked on the screen, tired and almost old around the eyes. But when he smiled, he looked as boyish and carefree as when he played Tom Sawyer.

I asked myself whether Jack and Olive (and WDT) were really hopeless addicts caught in a gilded trap, or just indulged occasionally at parties. They didn't twitch or sweat. WDT seemed to read my thoughts, for when the Ideal Couple left, his eyes sparkled and he said, "What's your idea of dopers, Elva? People in dirty rooms, rolling their eyes and letting their tongues hang out?" I admitted that was pretty much my idea. "Better throw it away," he advised. "If you read Freud, you'd know the great Sigmund took coke to cure a fit of depression."

"I know very little about Mr. Freud, but I'm not surprised to hear he got fits of depression. Do you get them too?" He denied it smilingly. "Then why take the stuff?"

"To get hard," WDT said, looking down at his groin.

I pretended not to have heard and drank more champagne.

"Baudelaire put me on to that," he went on. "He said, the more you cultivate the arts, the less often you get hard."

The pianist was playing "Shine On Harvest Moon." I listened for a moment, thinking of Baby. Then I told WDT I'd never heard of Baudelaire. If he recognized the coldness in my voice, he gave no sign. He told me Baudelaire was a French poet who believed there was no beauty without corruption, snapped his fingers as a cart was wheeled by, and took a long deliberate sniff. When he finished he said, "I think you're ready for it now, Elva," and before I could protest, "let's have no more crap about calling a cab." I must have looked terrified, for he added, "Sweetheart, it's not rape. Give my your hand."

How can you resist a man like that? WDT could charm you into letting him murder you. He made me feel foolish and ignorant for not going along with anything he suggested. I'd already watched a display of unbridled lust and now I held out my hand. He stroked the palm lightly, then shook powder on my thumb. I took a deep breath and a sniff. For a while I insisted I felt nothing at all, then said, "Well, maybe a little. It's very strange. I feel *more* normal instead of *less*. I'm not in the least anxious or scared, which is quite a change."

WDT looked pleased. "Exactly what Sigmund found. Go on."

"That's all. Except ..." I leaned toward him and couldn't believe what I heard myself saying, "I feel like clay in your hands. And it's delicious."

"Stop it or I'll get hard."

Couldn't believe it, either, when I heard myself laughing at this. And then Mary Louise was standing in front of me, rather wild-eyed, obviously vexed to see me so intimate with WDT and making the connection she'd missed out on herself. "You've certainly changed your tune," she said. "Elva didn't even want to come here," she told WDT. "I had to talk her into it."

"You did good work." WDT sounded brusque and I could tell he had no time for Mary Louise. It made me feel more normal than ever. When she went away I said, "I had a strong vibration someone was going to drug me at this party, and ship me off to white slavery in the tropics. At least half my vibration was right." To my surprise I laid my hand on his knee. "What about the other half?"

"I promise you it'll be different," he said. "And even more exciting."

Later we sat close together in the back of his chauffeured limousine. It was after midnight and the streets were empty. The darkness felt soft and deep, like black mohair pile.

"How many men have made love to you?" he asked suddenly.

I'd taken a couple more sniffs, so the question failed to shock or alarm. "Only my late husband, and I never enjoyed it."

"You must have had dreams of a lover who'd show you how to enjoy it."

"For a while. But I never really believed they'd come true, so I put them out of my mind and concentrated on Baby instead."

He laughed.

"Everything amuses you. Why?"

"If it's not funny, what is it?" he said.

We drew up outside a bungalow court in Westlake. It was much grander than the Yucca Riviera, built in a kind of Alpine style, the apartments like separate chalets. WDT's livingroom had an open fireplace, a high beamed ceiling and a signed photograph of Mary Pickford on the bureau. There was a wall of bookcases and a landscape painting he told he me was an original Pissarro. Then he mocked me, supposing I'd never heard of Pissarro.

"I know beans when the bag is open. The Art Institute of Chicago was a constant refuge during my marriage."

The night was still warm, WDT took off his jacket and stood behind me while I looked at the painting. "It's a mistake to take you for granted, isn't it, Elva?"

"It's a mistake I'd never make with you." He began to stroke my arm with what I imagined to be *an expert touch,* although I'd never felt one before. "You can take your pick, yet you don't. You ask people to invite extra girls to your parties and then bring one of them home. I'm dazzled, of course, but bewildered."

His other hand began to stroke me even more expertly. "I like to get off the beaten track. Away from the old faces and the old situations." I felt a squeeze. "So you admire my Pissarro?" I nodded. "It's a beauty," he said. "Did you know Sigmund believes that any kind of beauty — not just the human form — arouses lustful thoughts?"

WDT had a puzzling attitude toward beauty, quoting an obscure French poet who says it's always corrupt, claiming it's just a matter of sex. But perhaps, I thought, everything's a matter of sex for him. They say it's a trend.

"Look at the lake in my painting, Elva. Think of it as a symbol and tell me what it does for your libido." As he explained what libido was, his hands moved underneath my Grecian draperies. "Use your imagination," he said.

"I'd rather use yours, it's obviously stronger."

How right I was. In a low voice WDT said a lake always reminded him of a vagina. (It's not easy to write that word down. Maybe I need another sniff!) I told him a lake was far more beautiful, in my opinion, than the human part just mentioned, but he merely swung me around and planted his mouth on mine. What happened next is not easy to write down, either. As first I thought, it's going to be like Mr. Kay taking his brute pleasure. In fact it *was* like Mr. Kay taking his brute pleasure, except that I enjoyed it. And I denied him nothing, which was certainly not the case with Mr. Kay. And the more I allowed WDT to feast on me like a tiger, the more excited I became. What would Mr. Freud have to say about that?

Or about something that occurred later? While I lay dazed but happy under a sheet on his bed, WDT came naked out of the shower, looking as if he wanted to start all over again, stroked me fiercely and *asked for my stockings*. As a keepsake, he said. To remind him of our night. I wondered if this meant he wouldn't be seeing me again, but he denied it, stroking me even more fiercely and explaining he needed the feel of my presence when I wan't there. When I suggested a photograph instead, he said, "No, Elva. A memento's more personal."

It was the night of anything goes. Playful, almost wanton, I stood naked on the bed and flung all my lingerie at him like TB scattering rose petals. Then WDT put a ragtime record on the phonograph, swung me to the floor and danced me wildly all over the apartment. Later he threw me on the bed for a tigerish encore. I couldn't believe my lack of shame. "Am I really so dreadfully ordinary?" I asked after I got dressed, and he was walking me to the door. He shook his head and told me I had unplumbed depths. "I think they've just been plumbed," I said, and he laughed, then promised we'd see each other again very soon.

In the small hours his chauffeur drove me home. Not far from the bungalow court we turned into a street running alongside a lake. It still didn't look like any kind of symbol to me, in fact I recognized it, from the domed and turreted mansions outlined on the opposite shore, as the lake in the desert I saw from One Big Look. Dawn was breaking as the limousine glided to a stop outside the Yucca Riviera. The wind had dropped and there was a faint scent of jasmine in the air. I took off my shoes and stole across the patio like Mary Louise after a night with Pancoast.

Can a woman's life, I wondered, be changed in a few unbelievable hours? Baby slept peacefully in our bed. I lay down beside her, careful not to make a sound, but afraid she might be wakened by the beating of my heart.

Baby Looks Back

Never heard a thing. Next morning was Sunday and Mother slept late. When I saw her wriggle and stir, I made coffee on the hotplate, and when I brought it to her, I noticed a red mark on her throat. She said she had no idea how it got there, and in any case it was only temporary. She told me to fetch her beige chiffon scarf, which she wound around her neck and kept there for several days. Nothing special happened to her at the party, she said, apart from meeting Jack Pickford and Olive Thomas, and because I'm no talebearer I said nothing special happened to *me* during her night on the town.

"You didn't mind being left on your own, Baby?"

"It was fine. I ate some liverwurst and an apple, and read *Thuvia, Maid of Mars*."

True as far as it went, as far as Mother's account of her party. I read a couple of chapters, decided to look up Peaches across the patio, knocked on the door and got no answer except for a horrendous fart. The door was unlocked, so I went inside. Hendrix lay on the bed, his fez askew, a bottle of liquor cradled in his arms, Peaches sprawled on a chair wearing one of his mother's wide-brimmed hats with the ribbon tied under his chin. They were both zonked. "Hello there, little woman," Peaches said. His voice sounded strange, hollow as well as slurred. "I'm a secret drinker. How about you?" Not yet, I told him. "Well, maybe you don't hate your mother," he said.

"No. Why do you hate yours?"

"She's a filthy slut. The biggest stinking whore in town."

Surprising language for an untalented boy of six, but more surprises followed. Mary Louise was pussy for sale. Mary Louise spread for any lousy parlor-snake, even if he only had one eye and (probably) one ball. Mary Louise caught the clap in Mexico from some scummy greaser trick, and again in Hollywood from some dago bastard bit-player. Peaches was going to kill her. Or run away. Or watch her take it up the ass. Or maybe all three.

Technically, I suppose, some of this was beyond my scope, but I caught the drift. Hendrix guzzled and cackled. When Peaches finally ran out of threats against Mary Louise, he turned on *me*. "Now that you know my secret," he said, looking really mean and wall-eyed, "what am I going to do with you?" He turned to Hendrix and asked if he desired my body, but the old man was clearly in no state to do anything about it, even if he felt in the mood. "Well, little woman, you better have a few drinks," Peaches said, and reached for another bottle on the floor. When I refused, he looked meaner than ever, so I took a sip of scotch, found I disliked the taste but enjoyed the sensation. Peaches became more friendly. "It's the only thing for a broken heart," he said.

So while Mother sniffed her first coke, her Jewel knocked back her first bootleg scotch. Peaches and I passed the bottle back and forth in silence, then he got up and stumbled to the toilet. He spent a long time there. I heard another fart, an oath, sounds of violent pounding and flushing. Wondering what he was up to, I went in and saw him tossing Mary Louise's cosmetics into the toilet bowl, lipsticks, shampoos, pots of rouge and cream, false eyelashes, a powder puff. Then he slapped and cuffed the tank when it wouldn't flush. "It's no good," I told him. "You've just stopped the whole thing up." He slumped on the seat and began to cry, still wearing Mary Louise's hat.

By now I was feeling queasy and wobbly, so wished him goodnight and lurched home across the patio. Lying on the bed a while later, I heard Hendrix stumble into the fountain on the way back to his own apartment. Then I fell not into peaceful sleep as Mother imagined, but an alcoholic stupor.

In a way it was the beginning of a change in our life together. Of changes at the Yucca Riviera, everywhere. A few months later Peaches had run away, Mother and I had moved away. We joined the crowd outside the theatre at the premiere of Olive Thomas in *The Follies Girl,* Mother broke through the cordon to greet her as she stepped from her limousine, but Olive looked pale and blank and an escort hustled her away. I remember she wore a gorgeous fur cape. It must have been the same one that she wrapped herself in not long afterwards, before drinking half a pint of liquid mercury and lying down on the floor to die. People in the know, who included everyone I met, called it the tip of a glittering iceberg. A lot of dopers and degenerates, they said, were passing themselves off as all-American boys and girls on the silver screen. So poor Olive opened the Purple Age out here, and two or three years later Barbara Lamarr closed it, still too beautiful for her own good but found cold and stiff in her own bed. Her studio blamed a crash diet, but people in the know talked of suicide at the end of a long trail of sin. If you boast of ordering roses and lovers by the dozen, you can't expect to go out quietly. Between the first and last of the purple exits, Starlight City turned into Sodom and Gomorrah West, where America's reckless idols paid out half their salaries to pushers, held orgies, carried on secret affairs, seduced minors and were hauled off screaming to padded cells. If you want to escape the rumor mill, Mother used to say, for God's sake go to church. She certainly sampled quite a few places that called themselves churches, from the Temple of the Sacred Monad, where they kissed an ancient symbol of balance, to the Fellowship of the Lost Ages, where new light on the past was shed by a man who believed himself a reincarnation of the Queen of Sheba.

Most important of all the changes, although Mother found her heart's desire when Baby Jewel began to shine, she lost something, and so did I. She found it increasingly hard to understand my life except on a mundane level, to use one of her favorite expressions, and I found it a growing problem to understand hers on any level at all. I often thought of our first night on the Boulevard, when we got caught in sudden moonlight, and often wondered if a mysterious ray hadn't struck us after all, and was working on our lives without our knowing it.

All said and done, though, we stayed very close.

1922

Elva's Diary

January 5 • This morning I telephoned Charlotte Pickford and Lillian Coogan and invited them to tea at the Hollywood Hotel. Although we'd never met, both Mothers accepted graciously. Such is the power of the Queen Bee, success, even if my own glory is a mere reflection of Baby's. Feeling the need for a pick-me-up before leaving the house, and finding supplies had almost given out, I called WDT. The butler said he was not at home. The butler says that all too often these days. Am I just an old face and an old sensation? I dismissed the hateful thought and got behind the wheel of Baby's Packard.

On my way into the hotel I glanced at the veranda and was overcome as usual by memories. Baby and I on our first night in Hollywood, alone on the empty sidewalk with no friends or connections, and the moon that drenched us with silver. The day I snuck Baby into that Norma Talmadge picture and she waved at the camera. Did I ever mention we went to a matinee when it opened, and the scene was cut out?

Lillian arrived first. Quite a shock to reflect that such a stout bulky woman, wearing a chinchilla coat and a potty-shaped hat trimmed with the same fur, was a vaudeville Baby not so very long ago. I could have seen her hoofing on some dingy stage in downtown Chicago. She peeled off a glove, made me admire a ruby ring she claimed little Jackie gave her last week, and suggested we order tea right away because Charlotte was always late. Then she asked if I didn't find our new president thrilling.

Politics never interest me. All I could remember about Mr. Harding was a secret Mary Louise told me the last time we met. She had it on the best authority that his family was octoroon. Naturally I didn't pass

[49]

this on. "Anyone who believes in *normalcy* gets my vote," Lillian said. "Harding's kept us out of the League of Nations, he reckons that making money is a God-given creative impulse, and he's promised to lower taxes." She leaned forward confidentially. "You wouldn't know this, Baby Jewel's not a real big earner yet, but the tax situation right now is highway robbery. Jackie stands to make a hundred and fifty thousand this year, and the poor little kid's got to hand over five percent to Uncle Sam."

Lillian told me she also looked to our president to do something about the crime rate. It was rising everywhere, she just read in the newspaper that Los Angeles had overtaken New York in murder, robbery, fraud and even suicide. "Too many of the wrong kind coming out here, Mrs. Kay. They don't have jobs or anything, just *hope*. And when hope gives out, they start robbing and killing!"

Dreadful, I agreed, but confessed that murder cases fascinated me all the same. "Well, of course, nothing thrills me more either," Lillian said eagerly, and wondered if I was following the case of two old men in Santa Monica who fell in love with the same sixty-year-old woman. "One man sent the other a box of poisoned rejuvenation pills. You must admit that's original."

"Right now I'm reading everything I can about Madalynne Obenchain," I said. "They call her the most amazing woman ever clapped in the county jail. Do you believe she shot her faithless ex-lover through the head, or were there really two rough-looking types lurking in the brush?"

"Obenchain's no saint in my opinion." Lillian stroked her ring. "And there's more to that case than meets the eye."

"She's a woman without fear," I said. "She's convinced nothing is really decided down *here*. She puts her final trust in the Beyond."

"If they send her there, I hope it doesn't let her down." Lillian smiled grimly. "I heard on the grapevine, by the way, that Obenchain's faithless lover rented women's clothes to wear at parties."

This certainly bowled me over. "What can it mean?"

"What I told you. There's more to that case than meets the eye."

I decided not to reveal I'd sent Madalynne an anonymous gift of cologne, along with best wishes for acquittal, for her Christmas in the jug. But according to the *Times* last week she received a total of 107 packages, plus a hamper of turkey and a $1000 greenback, so I was not alone in my attitude. Thanks to the male animal, the woman must have suffered greatly. *"Is it possible you could hold me, kiss me, caress me,"* I murmured, quoting from one of Madalynne's letters to her two-timing lover quoted in court, *"and be laughing at a bleeding heart?"*

"It seems very possible, considering what I heard on the grapevine."
Then Lillian stared at me. "Is something the matter?"

For a moment I saw WDT's smile, and his eyes that no longer seemed
so kind, and it must have shown in my face. Luckily Charlotte Pickford
arrived at that moment, carrying the evening *Express*, said she was delighted to meet me but turned at once to Lillian. "Get an eyeful of this.
Fatty's in some hole."

Lillian snatched the newspaper and read aloud the opening paragraph
of its front page story. At Mr. Arbuckle's trial for rape and Murder 1, the
District Attorney in San Francisco had just testified that Famous Players
tried to bribe him to call off the case against their star. "Heavy nail in
Fatty's coffin," Lillian opined. "He's no saint in my opinion, but he's an
old friend of my husband, so let's keep it to ourselves."

Charlotte smiled. "I don't see how we can unless you lower your
voice."

"It's not Fatty's first orgy. We all know about those sultry roadhouse
revels back East last year. I hate to cast the first stone, but can we be sure
he's not trying to ruin the character of an innocent girl this time? After
making her submit to unnatural acts?"

"Did you hear what I said?" Charlotte asked. "The whole room can
hear what *you* said."

WDT had told me the girl was just a tramp who worked in a couple of
Mack Sennett comedies and was always catching "the crabs." After she
infected so many ac'ɔrs that he had to close the studio and call in an
exterminator, Mr. Sennett fired her. I wanted to pass this on to Lillian,
and cap her story about Madalynne's ex-lover renting female clothes, but
feared it might harm my image.

Besides, it would never have gone down with Charlotte. Although she
worked in the Toronto fish market before Little Mary hit the jackpot, she
seemed naturally high-flown, and has a reputation as perfect Mother and
devout Catholic. No taller than her Mary, just 5 feet, she's notably
broader around the beam, with a bosom like a retired soprano's. I glanced
at my own svelte reflection in a mirror on the wall. It assured me I was the
most glamorous Mother in show business, as *Photoplay* commented last
month, and I resolved to stay that way. Too many Mothers, including my
tea guests, let themselves go.

"A doctor for the defense testified the girl died of a ruptured appen-
dix," I pointed out.

"Let's hope Fatty didn't rupture it," Lillian said, and I marked her
down as a difficult woman.

Now Charlotte changed the subject by congratulating me on Baby's success. Lillian echoed her, but more grudgingly, and both started giving me
advice. Charlotte reminded me her Mary was trained by Mr. Griffith, and
it took Mr. Chaplin to launch Jackie in *The Kid*. Baby needed an artist to
guide *her*, and seemed unlikely to find one as long as she went on making
two-reel comedies. "Make her *develop*, Mrs. Kay. If you stand still for
more than a minute in the picture business, you're left behind." Moving
on to Baby's salary, which she knew all about, Charlotte told me it wasn't
good enough. In the future I must stand my ground and always demand
50 percent more than the studio offered. She'd always done that for
Mary, and it accounted for her millions. "After I made a deal with
Zukor," she added proudly, "he told me he was planning to go on a
diet, but I saved him the trouble. He lost ten pounds agreeing to my
demands."

Lillian hoped I wouldn't let Baby *grow up too fast*. "A kid should stay a
kid as long as possible. That's the American Way and I'm strong on it. I'm
raising Jackie 100 percent normal and protecting him from wrong ideas.
He never gets to see any of those movies about life or sex. No *Foolish
Wives* or *Forbidden Fruit* for Jackie." Charlotte revealed she had a chair
placed at her disposal, right next to the director's, on the set of every
picture Mary made. Lillian dismissed the rumor that Mr. Coogan had
taken over Jackie's career kit and caboodle. "He makes the deals but *I*
make the character. Only a Mother can do that."

I thanked them for taking such an interest, then saw from their faces it
was time to get to the point. In this town you don't invite people to tea
just to be social. You're after something, and after some light gossip and
shop talk, you aim to get it. Usually I'm an exception to the rules of life,
but this time I admit I conformed. Pouring more tea, I explained that on
Baby's birthday, February 1, the Los Angeles *Herald* planned to host a
party and present her with its Baby of the Year award. A truly important
affair with national press coverage, and a tribute not only to Baby but to
the whole community of picture kids. "They occupy a special place in the
American heart," I said, "so naturally I want you both to come, and bring
Mary and Jackie as well."

They looked at each other. Finally Lillian said, "I had no idea *your* Baby
was getting this award." Charlotte announced she would be happy to
come, but couldn't answer for Mary. Her daughter was no longer a child,
she reminded me, in spite of still playing children in the movies, but a
young married lady who led an independent social life and entertained
all-time greats with Doug at Pickfair. For dinner last week they had Elinor
Glyn, novelist of passion and adviser extraordinary to the stars on the

finer points of making love. "Oh, that woman dazzles me," I said. "Is it true she's writing a jungle romance for Gloria Swanson?" Lillian brushed cake from her lap, agreed she'd be happy to attend Baby's party, but was unable to vouch for her Jackie, who had a very tight schedule this month. Apart from appearing in almost every scene of his current picture, *Oliver Twist,* he had appointments to be photographed with Valentino, John Philip Sousa and Babe Ruth, and the Chamber of Commerce was planning to give him a banquet. Also, when his picture finished shooting at the end of the month, the studio wanted him to go to Europe and be received by the Pope.

"Mary's going to receive George Bernard Shaw," Charlotte said. "He'll be staying at Pickfair at the end of the month."

"Bring him to Baby's party!" I exclaimed, and they laughed, so I pretended it was a joke.

After a cordial round of goodbyes I headed for the lobby, certain my plans to make Baby's birthday tribute a glittering event were well under way, and deciding to get the *Herald* to invite Mr. Shaw. Then I passed the desk and my heart almost stopped. Standing there was a man who looked from the back exactly like WDT, with a girl wearing the latest in taffeta dinner suits. He must have sensed I was watching him, for he turned his head briefly as they moved off to the elevator together. A stranger after all. But even the *thought* of WDT these days produces a low heavy cloud that hangs right above my head, and I sank into a chair with my mood of elation utterly destroyed. I drove home with tears pricking at my eyelids, hurried into the house and called WDT again. The butler said he was not at home. I remembered a letter Madalynne wrote to her deceitful lover, she had a cold feeling in her heart and felt it must be her love struggling in death. The black cloud still hung above my head, and my own heart started to grow cold.

Baby Looks Back

One more example of the change in our life together was that Mother never understood why I dreaded my birthday party. She always made plans for me without thinking about what was really happening to *me*. In a way, of course, it wasn't her fault, for I didn't often tell her. After she described her tea with the Mothers at the Hollywood Hotel, for instance, I kept quiet about my own afternoon, which was spent clinging to the back of a truck. Once, after a tire exploded, it almost turned over. "Okay, Baby?" they asked, dusted me off, changed the tire and got ready for Take 2.

Now I'll go back a little in time, for Mother's diaries have many years missing. I found them after she died, stashed away with other personal belongings, scrapbooks, photographs, letters, cocaine and cassettes. A lot of the stuff had been nibbled beyond recall by kangaroo mice, still leaping around hillside canyons in those days. They probably fed on Mother's life in the winter, when there was little other food around.

Mary Louise, who must have got it from Harvey Pancoast, told her about the Poverty Row producer who was searching for a new child wonder. Kiddie parodies of adult movies were exceedingly popular at the time, one little trouper had a big success as a sharp-shooting, pint-sized Tom Mix in the Wild West, and another wowed audiences as Gloria Swanson, Norma Talmadge and smoldering Nita Naldi. So when Sam Goldwyn announced his plan to star John Barrymore as Sherlock Holmes, a genius from Poverty Row dreamed up a Kid Sherlock series and sent out audition calls to discover a pocket sleuth. Mary Louise got an appointment for Peaches and saw no risk in boasting about it to Mother, because the producer was only seeing wonder boys. A week or so later she realized what a mistake she'd made.

"Now, Baby. This is the chance we've been waiting for. You're always reading Sherlock Holmes, you love him, you're the natural choice to play him!" For a moment I thought Mother had finally cracked under the strain, then looked at her face and knew she had to be right. The only crazy person around was myself, who actually doubted her word for ten seconds. She called the studio, learned the producer was holding two days of auditions in two days' time, and went to work. "When *rock bottom's* around the corner, Baby, you play for the highest stakes. I'm not only disguising you as a boy, I'm fixing you up as Holmes himself!" Unable to find a satisfactory costume in the clothing stores, she proceeded to run one up herself, borrowing a sewing machine from Mrs. Root and pedaling away all night. In less than twenty-four hours she made a Victorian frock coat and trousers, and a few hours later fitted me with a peaked cap and an opera cloak.

"And *now,* Baby, you've got be very brave." She held a pair of scissors in her hand. "It's a sad moment when we crop these glorious curls, but remember they'll grow back as soon as we need them again." Removing my cap, she snipped and sheared, then decided the remains of my hair should be darker and rubbed in black shoe polish. After sticking a little cherrywood pipe in my mouth, she led me to a mirror. "You may need a minute to adjust, but I know you'll agree it's a triumph." The mirror image, a solemn and frightened midget in fancy dress, showed me nobody I knew. It wasn't myself or Sherlock Holmes either. But Mother said, "Take it from me, you're the famous sleuth to the life!"

I remembered the ex-Barbary Coast Kidlet on the art of acting: "If you feel it, you *are*." Banishing the Yucca Riviera, Mother and my doubts, I walked mentally into the mirror like Alice through the looking-glass and began to feel evening in London, a gaslit street, a hansom cab passing by, a muffin-man who rang his bell. Then Mother jolted me out of it by saying, "There's some shoe-polish over your left eye, Baby, let me clean it off." That night I had another dream in which I walked down Hollywood Boulevard and it turned out to be a movie set. Opening the door of Mr. Evansmith's studio with its window display of kiddie portraits, I found nothing on the other side.

Because Mother knew Peaches was auditioning next morning, she took me to the producer's office late that afternoon. "Any encounter would be distinctly unfortunate and I'd have a hard time explaining you away. Besides, the end of the day is best. The poor man will be tired and desperate for an answer to his prayers." It was a cool day toward the end of fall, an overcast sky made the street they called Poverty Row look as dreary as its name. Not long ago this part of Hollywood had been farmland, and the old barns were still there, fixed up as shooting stages, brown paint peeling off the walls. A grim frame bungalow fronted each lot, with rows of small dusty windows and the studio's name above the entrance. We walked under S. Gordon and found ourselves in a yard that was empty except for a black monkey in a cage. I supposed it had been used in an animal comedy earlier that day, and was waiting to go home. It chattered angrily at us. A fierce acid smell hung in the air. I imagined it was monkey pee, but the guard who took us in explained it came from raw film stock. Part of the front bungalow served as a processing laboratory, and the rest had been split into offices no larger than cells in the county jail.

They were no more comfortable than cells, either. Nowhere even to sit down in the bare gray room overlooking the yard, where the last Boy Wonders of the day waited with their Mothers. They stared at me with surprise and a kind of fear, for no one else had thought of dressing up for the part. I leaned nonchalantly against a wall, following Mother's orders to look as butch as possible and keep my mouth shut. For a while nobody spoke, then one Mother broke the ice. Yet another widow, she'd sold her late husband's beanery in Wichita and driven out here with Sonny in a beat-up truck. "Los Angeles was easy to find, I just followed the sunset," she said. Summoned in turn to another office, each Mother and Boy Wonder disappeared for a few minutes, and nobody came back smiling. A sudden thundershower broke, infuriating the monkey and making the smell of raw film stock even more bitter.

We were the last to be called. If an office containing only a desk and chair stood a man drinking black coffee from a tin mug. He wore a cheap twill suit, shiny with age, and a straw hat. Short, homely and impatient, he was maybe no more than twenty-five but looked as if he'd never been young. My costume seemed to displease him at once. "Now what the hell is this?" he said. "This is little Toby Kay," Mother answered promptly, while I continued trying to play butch. "Toby's got show business in his blood, Mr. Gordon. His late father was a touring actor and actually appeared as Sherlock Holmes all over the country!" Sid Gordon walked around me, muttering "Toby, eh?" I stuck the cherrywood pipe in my mouth. "He's pretty damn small," Sid Gordon said, but Mother told him it was part of my appeal.

Sid Gordon walked around me again. In the yard, the monkey gave his loudest cry. "Why don't they pick it up?" he asked. "It's getting on my nerves. Toby, eh? What can Toby do?"

Mother ticked off my accomplishments on her fingers. "He sings and dances, tap and classical, imitates Charlie Chaplin. . . ."

"We don't need any more runts who imitate Charlie Chaplin," Sid Gordon said. "Give me a song, Toby. I'll tell you when I've heard enough."

Mother had worked this part out. She particularly admired my rendition of "Shine On Harvest Moon" and felt sure it would score a bull's eye. I had my doubts. I felt ridiculous performing it dressed as Sherlock Holmes, but I put the pipe back in my pocket, went into a smooth old-time shuffle and got through the first verse before Sid stopped me.

"Well, he can carry a tune."

"Of course," Mother said rather grandly. "We haven't come here to waste your time. When Mr. Griffith saw Toby dance, he told me The Kid's Got It. If you don't believe me, ask him."

"If he's got it, why didn't he get it?"

"There was nothing to get at the time," Mother said. "No moppet role in the picture Mr. Griffith was making. Miss Gish only had a doll."

"What? You're confusing me," Sid complained, then tapped me on the shoulder. "So you think you've got Sherlock Holmes in your blood, eh, Toby? Let's see what you know about him."

This was not in the scenario, as they say, and just as well. I had to go out on my own, as I did when Mr. Griffith asked me to play with a squirrel, and this time I was secretly waiting for the moment. With experience behind me, I knew that if I felt it, I *was*. So I told Sid Gordon about Sherlock Holmes without saying a word.

Sitting down in the office chair, I began playing an imaginary violin. Instinct told me to take my time, even if Sid Gordon burst out impatiently, "Now what the hell is this?" But he said nothing. I jumped up and stalked around the place with an imaginary magnifying glass, checking the door, the windows and the drawers of his desk. In one drawer I found a girlie calendar, a photograph of a nude with her back turned and the tear-off calendar leaves glued to her ass. I held it up and gave Sid Gordon a knowing smile. He walked up and down irritably, sipping coffee. I stood in front of him and checked Sid himself, starting with his shoes and going as high as I could reach, which was his stomach. I poked it. I marched around him in a circle, exactly the way he'd done with me, delved into his trouser pocket and came up with some small change and an old rabbit's foot lucky charm. Holding up the charm, I looked very grave and suspicious, stuffed it away and produced a pair of imaginary handcuffs. I snapped them on Sid's wrists, sat down in the chair, stuck the pipe in my mouth and pretended to smoke, having solved "The Case of the Rabbit's Foot."

A silence followed. Sid Gordon gave me a long unfriendly stare. Finally he said, "Give me back my lucky charm. And my money."

I did so, and there was another silence.

"See how quickly Toby breathes," Mother said. "Mr. Griffith told us it's a sign of nerves, and nerves are a sign of imagination."

Sid Gordon ignored her. "How old are you, Toby?" he asked, but Mother got in first. "Little Toby Kay is just four years old. Isn't that amazing?"

He stared at me again. I thought he had a kind of Sherlock Holmes look on his own face now, so I spoke for the first time, in a voice as deep as I could muster. "Four and a half," I said.

He nodded, then almost exploded with rage as the monkey gave another shriek from the yard. He opened the door and called out: "Someone get a blanket and throw it over that goddam cage."

"It won't work," Mother informed him calmly. "A monkey is not a parrot."

He glared at her, then sighed. "You never know. Leave your phone number at the desk on your way out."

That was it. A last quick look at me, a "Toby, eh?" but no goodbye. As we left the monkey shrieked again, he shrieked back at it in a furious imitation, then slammed the dirty window shut.

The guard showed us out and it started to rain again. We ran up toward Sunset and into the first cafe we saw. Everyone stared at me. "It's warm in here, take off your cloak and have a glass of milk," Mother said. Then she patted my hand. "There's only one little bridge left to cross now. We'll have to let Sid Gordon know you're a girl before he signs you up."

"What makes you think he'll sign me up?"

"He knows fourteen-carat genius when he sees it. Finish your milk, Baby, and I'll take you to a movie to celebrate."

For three days her confidence never wavered. She bought me a long velvet bathing suit with silk ruffles — "very much in fashion right now among kiddie stars, they wear them to premieres as well as to the beach" — and took me to see *The Last of the Mohicans* and Chaplin in *Sunnyside*. Early on the fourth morning Mr. Hendrix told us Sid Gordon was on the office line. She picked up the phone and said calmly, "Elva Kay speaking, I've been expecting your call." An hour later we entered his office, where Sid stood exactly as before, wearing a straw hat and drinking black coffee. But there was no monkey in the yard outside.

"Now what the hell is this?" he said.

The shoe polish had been washed out of my hair and I wore the velvet bathing suit with silk ruffles.

Mother smiled. "Baby Jewel is a master of disguise. Just like Sherlock Holmes."

Sid Gordon walked around me several times. "Jewel, eh?" he said. "Baby Jewel?" His expression was not friendly. "Now tell me this, Mrs. Kay. When Griffith saw the kid, *who was she?* Toby or Jewel? Or Charlie Chaplin? Or Lon Chaney?"

When he got over the shock, he became very excited. "Let me handle this. It'll make an incredible story. There's no adult actor in the business who could get away with a stunt like that." He called for more coffee and started to plan an ad campaign on the spot. Part of it concerned my late father who toured from coast to coast playing Sherlock Holmes. It made me nervous. I looked at Mother, who still smiled calmly, and realized she had no intention of coming clean about this one. Well, I thought, it's certainly Let's Pretend up there. Father had never been real to me, and in a strange way he became *more* real by turning into Mother's fantasy. Although, remembering how many of her fantasies Mother made me believe in, it was perhaps not so strange after all.

"Okay, Baby Jewel, your mother and I are going to have a private talk. Any questions before you wait out in the yard?"

"Just one," I said. "Who gets to play Doctor Watson?"

"No Watson. You're on your own."

I felt outraged. "You can't have Sherlock Holmes without Watson."

"I can have Romeo without Juliet if I want." He suddenly beat the desk with his fist. "Forget about Watson. And while you're at it, forget about Holmes. We're not even using his last name, because we don't own the goddam rights. We're calling you Kid Sherlock, putting you in costume, making you solve mysteries and go after criminals. For laughs! Like you

Everything was getting worse by the minute. "You thought I wanted to make you *laugh?*" Sid Gordon nodded. "But you never laughed once," I said.

"I never do." He glared at me. "And just for the record, here's a couple of other things you should know about me. I make animal and kiddie comedies, and I *hate* animals and kiddies. Now go and wait in the yard."

While I did so, an open truck drove up with a cage on the back. This one contained a bear. They wheeled the cage inside a barn. The air smelt of acid and the truckdriver stared at my velvet bathing suit.

Until Sid Gordon broke the story of how he came to discover Baby Jewel for Kid Sherlock, Mother said nothing to Mary Louise. Then one morning she handed her a copy of the *Herald*. "I wanted you to be the first to know."

Mary Louise saw my photograph in the movie section and scanned a report of the trick I'd pulled, which Sid Gordon found more sensational than Mary Pickford playing two parts in the same picture. All of her face, including her lips, went completely white. Then she managed to laugh. "Oh my, Elva, how clever you are." She gave me a cheerful look. "There's really nothing your Mother won't do to claw her way to the top." Her color started to come back. "But what's all this about your late lamented father going on the road as an actor? I thought he went on the road for the Coca-Cola company."

Mother never blinked. "Whoever gave you that idea, Mary Louise?"

"*You* did, Elva Kay, the first time we had coffee together in the Tea Room Buffet."

"How can you say such an extraordinary thing?" Mother's display of astonishment was in the Lillian Gish class. "You must have imagined it."

"I *heard* it, Elva Kay."

"Not from my lips, dear."

All this time Peaches sat in the clothes closet with the door open, watching me intently. He jerked his thumb toward Mary Louise and silently mouthed the word "whore," just as Mother glanced in his direction. She looked puzzled, then turned to Mary Louise. "Is your Peaches all right in there? And does he have another midget part coming up?"

Peaches slammed the door closed. Later Mother told me, "Don't worry about what Mary Louise said. Whoever's going to believe a story like that? From a woman like her? But I'm worried about that dreadful Peaches.''

So was I. Since the night he confessed he was a secret drinker, his behavior had grown increasingly peculiar. Sitting in Mary Louise's clothes closet was the least of it. Often he waited to catch me alone and utter hideous threats about what he'd do to me if I ever breathed a word. Yet *he* went on mouthing ''whore'' and worse behind Mary Louise's back. None of my promises reassured him. He stuffed warning notes in my lace drawers and my shoes. He pinched my neck and my ears. And he must have been living on bootleg scotch and candy, for he put on a lot of weight. Mother said he was beginning to *look* like a real circus midget, but Mary Louise gave no sign she noticed anything.

Two weeks later we moved out of the Yucca Riviera, into a small rented house. It was full of Early American maple furniture and patchwork quilts, and Mother described its style as Hollywood Rustic. ''We're not quite in the Pickfair bracket yet, Baby. Mr. Gordon drives a hard bargain and I had to settle for a starting salary of two hundred dollars a week. But it's still a good contract. I got a movie director friend of mine to vet it.''

In the middle of our first night in the new house, the doorbell rang. After I heard Mother go to answer it, I got out of bed and opened my door. Mary Louise stood in the hallway, wearing a long white gown with a scarf wrapped around her head. ''Is Peaches here?'' she asked, and Mother said, ''Certainly not!'' Mary Louise opened a closet door and peered inside. ''He might be hiding, you know, he loves to hide.'' Then she sank into a wing chair. ''I got back late tonight, which is very unusual, and found he'd run away.''

''What a dreadful shock for you, Mary Louise, and what an extraordinary thing for Peaches to do. But why should he come here?''

''He's in love with your Jewel.''

Mother stared at her. ''I don't believe it!''

''It's true. I've seen the way he looks at her.''

''But he's only seven, dear.''

''Puppy love. It can hit them hard.'' Mary Louise dabbed at her eyes with her scarf. ''I've tried everything to help that boy. But I just couldn't get him to lose weight and stop sulking at auditions or in my closet.''

''It's a difficult age. But I'm sure he'll come back. They often run away for one night just to make you feel worried.''

Mary Louise shook her head. ''He left a note calling me horrible names and saying I'd never see him again.''

''Then you should go to the police.''

"And show them that insulting note? I'd rather die!"

Mother told her to burn it first.

"I never thought of that. How clever you are."

The next thing puzzled me. Mother asked Mary Louise if black coffee or some crackerjack bootleg gin would improve her situation. Mary Louise whispered in her ear, and Mother said, "It so happens you're in luck. My ship came in again last week." And they went up to her bedroom. Before I fell asleep again, I heard Mary Louise laughing.

There was still no news of Peaches a month later, when Mother brought me to the studio for my first day's work as Kid Sherlock. We went into the same barn as the bear. I was nervous, not from imagination but because I still wondered what Sid Gordon meant about playing for laughs, and had no idea how to do that, especially as he never laughed. Mother told me again not to worry, just do exactly what everyone said, and it was sounder advice than she realized, for I had no time to do anything else. Sid waited inside the barn with a particularly anxious and irritable look on his face. "Come on, come on, come *on!*" he said, as if I'd arrived late instead of ten minutes early. He hurried me over to a dressingroom the studio carpenter had fixed up in a corner. It looked almost as large as a double bed. I changed into a costume similar to the one Mother made, but oversized. Sid nodded approvingly and said a toddler in grown-up clothes was always good for a laugh, not to worry if I tripped, slipped or took a pratfall. "No matter what happens, Baby Jewel, *keep going! Make time!*"

I did what he said. For two years I did what everyone said, and everyone said Baby Jewel not only made time but had a fantastic comedy talent. As one of the more fancy critics wrote, I was a born farceuse. This was certainly true of the director, a breezy unruffled fellow who specialized in gags and slapstick, and fortunately laughed most of the time. His name was Jim Horne and he later directed comedy shorts for Laurel and Hardy, for my money the funniest pair in movies if you except Helen Hayes and Ramon Novarro as an oriental couple in *The Son Daughter*, which was only a one-shot and unintentional. A Kid Sherlock movie usually opened on the little detective at his solemn breakfast, seated in a high chair at a long table. A whale-sized housekeeper brought me coffee and bacon and eggs on a tray, and while I ate my breakfast I read the newspaper and occasionally paused to play the violin. Then someone rang the doorbell and the housekeeper showed in a person needing help. A girl in distress, a mysterious widow in black, a bandaged stranger, a fat man trembling with fear, a frantic thin one in dark glasses, another I immediately tagged as a gold king because he carried a stetson and had a speck of gold dust on his vest.

It took only a minute to set up the plot, a murder, a disappearance, a kidnaping, a robbery, and we were out the door and into the action. For the exterior of my rooming house we moved a few blocks away, to an old clapboard bungalow with my flivver parked beside a palm tree. No London, no gaslight, no hansom cab, no muffin-man. "No time," Sid Gordon said. But I did have an arch-enemy like Holmes's Moriarty, a mustache-twirling type with a cane, and his gang was always behind the dirty work. When I wasn't spotting a vital clue with my magnifying glass, or rescuing someone tied up in an attic, or chasing a villain, I was in danger. They trapped me in a cellar with a mechanical ceiling that moved lower and lower until it threatened to flatten me out, they set a poisonous snake on me at breakfast, sneaking it through an air vent, they almost pushed me off a barn roof, a mountain top, a belfry and a ferris wheel. I chased my arch-enemy by flivver, boat, train, pick-up truck and motorcycle. They faked close shots of me gripping a steering wheel or astride a bike, and used my stand-in, a genuine circus midget, for the rest. Sometimes I disguised myself as a bishop, an old vagrant with a limp, a jockey, a maharajah, a blind clairvoyant, a retired admiral and a foreign princess (the only time I "played" a girl).

For the first week Mother was always on the sidelines, then Sid told her not to stick around unless she felt like it. "I don't feel like it," she said. "Surely you realize by now I'm not the Stage Mother type." In fact, it made her uneasy sitting there while I did all the work. Her Baby was the breadwinner and she preferred not to watch me slave for every crumb. And Sid had his own motive for wanting her out of the way, as I discovered after my first accident. When they stuck me up a tree to spy on a house, a branch gave way and I plummeted to the ground on my head. "Who are you? Who am I? What day is it?" Sid asked while the director mopped a speck of blood off my forehead. "Baby Jewel. Sid Gordon. Thursday. So what?" I said. He looked impatient. "So you haven't lost your memory. No point in telling your Mother about this, by the way. It'll never happen again." A week later they stuck me on the roof of a disused hotel. I had to peer through the skylight into a room below, and halfway through Take 1 the roof caved in. Luckily I missed the skylight by inches and a bed broke my fall. It had a mattress, so I merely bounced around for a while like someone on a trampoline. Sid Gordon looked grim. "If we'd had a goddam second camera in the room, we could have used that fall," he said. Instinct, not Sid, persuaded me to spare Mother the information that her Baby was risking her life to get in the Pickfair bracket. So you see our situation was changing all the time.

When I finally got to see the Pacific Ocean, it was not because Mother took me there as a reward for hitting the jackpot. We had to shoot a scene with the mustache-twirler planning to push me off a launch. As he crept up behind me, an unexpectedly high wave broke over the side and my head. Screaming like Gish I back-flipped into the icy deep. They fished me out, I vomited a quart of ocean, said "Baby Jewel, Sid Gordon, Tuesday," and got ready for Take 2. "But don't ever ask me to go near the ocean again," I added, "or I'll tell Mother."

When my first *Kid Sherlock* opened at a Hollywood theatre, the main attraction was Mr. Griffith's latest, *Way Down East*, with Lillian in major trouble again. This time she had a baby instead of the doll she carried around in *Broken Blossoms*, but it died of exposure to the cold. "A heart-stopping moment," Mother whispered, "but I'm glad Mr. Griffith never called back and offered you the part. As Mary Louise said, Lillian's little ones have the worst luck in the world. And you'd have been dead less than halfway through the picture." When Lillian herself got trapped in the raging ice floes, Mother wept, and so did I, but for a different reason. In fact I'd been weeping for some time, because Mr. Griffith was not at the theatre for the opening. I'd imagined him coming up to lift me in his arms, staring deep into my eyes and telling everyone, "The first time I saw this kid, I knew she had it." Afterwards Mother said not to take it so hard because the audience obviously knew I had it; they laughed at *Kid Sherlock* as hard as they cried at *Way Down East*. When they discovered I was in the theatre, I had my first experience of signing autographs and all kinds of people wanting to kiss me. But it was Mrs. Root who really lifted my spirits. "Don't tell me you just did what Mr. Gordon and the others said. Everything up there is because of *you*, my dear. I bow to your talent." Until then I was unsure what I really felt when I saw myself on the screen. But I thought over what Mrs. Root told me, and decided she had a point.

Theatres all over the country started to book my *Kid Sherlock* two-reelers, and Sid Gordon said they were screaming for more. Soon I had less spare time and less education, because I had to give interviews and pose for photo sessions. I also modeled children's fashions for a department store, cut the ribbon at the opening of a new toy shop, went into the ring when the circus came to town, and took an IQ test at the University of Southern California, which was a favorite publicity gimmick for kiddie stars in those days. I scored 172, which put me in the genius class and gave a completely false impression of me. The questions were so elementary, it would have taken a Peaches not to reach that level. And I was three years older, anyway, than my official age of five. ("What a blessing you're still so small," Mother said, "and likely to stay that way.") Although Mrs. Root was unaware of my real age, she agreed the IQ test was a racket. "Your report stressed that all picture kids are special cases because they're subjected to the influence of creative adult minds. Humbug and poppycock, my dear. *You're* the creative mind and you influence the adults." Interviewers fired off the usual questions at me: "Who is your favorite star?" "What are your hobbies?" "How does it feel seeing yourself on the screen?" "Do you long for a dramatic role?" I usually answered the first thing that occurred to me, although Mother sometimes got in first. I certainly never said my hobby was cooking and I made us blueberry pancakes for Sunday breakfast. I *did* say my favorite stars were Lon Chaney, with John Barrymore in *Dr. Jekyll and Mr. Hyde* as runner-up, and I was glad people liked me when I saw my films with an audience, and I would play a dramatic role if Sid Gordon told me to, and I hoped one day to work for Mr. Griffith. Interviewers often described me as older than my years.

After I hit the jackpot Mother became increasingly elegant, but not in an obvious way. She kept to her color range of pearl-gray, olive green and beige with a hint of mauve, which the fan magazines found tastefully understated, but she added a subtle femme fatale touch. A white rose in her belt. The fashionable aigrette, a thin ostrich plume that stuck up like an antenna from her head. Sometimes a fan to match her evening gown. She copied Mae Murray's Apache ties and Gloria Swanson's tortoise shell bracelets. "Mae put me on to Apaches," she used to say, or "Gloria put me on to tortoise shell," implying she knew them personally when in fact she'd just been to see *Jazzmania* or *Her Gilded Cage*. At the time I admired all these touches for themselves, and found them wonderfully grand. Now I see them as badges of her own secret affair, and realize she was acting as hard from the start as I ever did.

But in spite of being consumed by her passion for the movies and the Unknown, as she liked to say, she kept her feet on the ground. The only additional items in our household budget were Hattie, the live-in maid, and "my" Packard, which of course she learned to drive herself. Her director friend sent her to a lawyer who formed the Baby Jewel Company Inc., and she explained I was now a corporation as well as a star, with a trust fund approved by the court. Although she often mentioned her director friend, I only met him once. They were very discreet and were never seen in public together. He came by the house on my birthday and gave me a diamond and platinum watch, a tiny replica of his own. "Diamonds are lucky," he said. "I bought my watch after my first picture,

Diamonds in the Sky, was a hit. I've been lucky ever since, and now you will be too."

The day after we went to see *Four Horsemen of the Apocalypse*, Mother told me Mary Louise had disappeared. Although Mother couldn't really stand her, she couldn't resist the opportunity of feeling sorry for her, and they continued to meet for more than a year after we left the Yucca Riviera and Peaches ran away. "I'm never high hat, Baby, and I'm not going to drop the wretched creature just because you're a success. Mind you, she's more than pathetic these days, she's on the edge of *rock bottom*, ditched by Harvey Pancoast and Peaches still officially a Missing Person." But when I suggested the Baby Jewel Company Inc. could loan her fifty dollars, Mother said the situation was not that hopeless yet. Mary Louise got work as an extra and had at least one new man in her life, the electrician at a downtown burlesque house. "She may be a fallen woman, but she's not a completely rejected one." The mystery of Mary Louise's disappearance began when Mother went to the Yucca Riviera and found her apartment closed. Mr. Hendrix only knew that she checked out and left town, saying she was going to hunt down Peaches herself, come hell or high water. He had no idea whether a clue had finally come her way, nor did the electrician, whom Mother interviewed backstage at the burlesque house while he trained his spotlight on a stripper. Mary Louise never even told him she was leaving, he said, but he didn't appear too sorry or surprised. Then postcards began to arrive. Mary Louise was in El Paso. She wrote nothing about Peaches, only that the Mexican border brought back memories of Mr. Cloud in that terrible revolution. Mary Louise was in Galveston. Again nothing about Peaches, only that she got caught in a hurricane. Finally Mary Louise hit North Carolina, which brought back more memories. "Somehow she's worked her way back to the plantation," Mother said. "I wonder if a Cloud still runs it, and what kind of welcome she'll get." But no more postcards arrived. "I fear the worst," Mother said. "She must be rejected as well as fallen."

Soon after the last postcard, another mystery occurred. I used to get home and find Mother staring unhappily at the telephone. Now I realize this must have been when her secret affair started to go wrong, but at the time I only wondered why she was always expecting the phone to ring. Once she answered it, listened for a moment, hung up and almost burst into tears. "There's nothing I hate more than wrong numbers!" When I asked if anything was the matter, she looked startled. "What strange questions you sometimes ask!"

It was probably a mistake to let her know I felt worried. It made me too adult, like *her* parent, when of course things were supposed to be the other way around. Any sign I was growing up made her nervous, for the kid could only stay a breadwinner by staying a kid. A columnist in the *Times* begged me to do the world a favor by remaining Baby Jewel forever, and she cut it out for her scrapbook. "Lillian Coogan told me not to let you grow up too fast. Mature emotion can put years on a child." The longer I obliged the *Times* and the world, the longer Mother felt young and saw the money rolling in. She often explained to interviewers that I loved my work because she'd taught me the movies were a game of Let's Pretend, and now I roamed at will in the innocent fantasy world of childhood. This said more about Mother's fantasy world than mine, of course.

"Drink your milk, Baby, finish your tuna sandwich and go to bed. You've got a big day in the sewers tomorrow, chasing after that Russian spy, and you need your beauty sleep."

Elva's Diary

February 1 • That low black cloud hanging over my head this morning when I woke up. Why should it settle there on the day of Baby's birthday celebration? With a pang I remembered yesterday's conversation with Miss Sophie, hairdresser extraordinary to the stars and a few other privileged customers like myself. She told me Elinor Glyn had been under the dryer, confiding a piece of advice she gave Rudolph Valentino for a scene of passion in *The Sheik*. "*A man is only cruel to a woman he loves or has loved.*" This bitter truth made it impossible to get WDT off my mind, and I realized I woke from a dream about him this morning. He stood alone, with a mocking expression and a red carnation in his buttonhole, in a field of glittering snow. When Hattie brought me breakfast and the *Times*, I turned to the latest account of Madalynne Obenchain and confronted another bitter truth, spoken from a barred cell. "*A woman will go through hell to be near the man she loves.*" Reading how she continues to hold up nobly and reaffirms her trust in the Beyond, once again I felt strangely close to Madalynne. Victims of the faithless male, our natures combine the psychic and the carnal. (Elva Kay, you would never have written those words two years ago. Do I know you anymore?)

Baby had the day off and was sleeping late. I drank my coffee and decided to go through hell once more myself. There must have been vibrations around, for instead of that lying coon butler, my slippery lover answered the phone. I wished him good morning and he said, "Who is this?" It takes him a mere seven weeks, I thought, to forget the sound of my voice. "You may not be happy when I tell you who it is," I said quietly. "It's a person you've been avoiding, getting your butler to call up and cancel our dates."

"Elva. The Lady of the Great Lakes. How are you?"

"Not at my best, considering the last time I saw you was nearly two months ago, and you had to go out almost as soon as I arrived. What have I done? Why have you cooled?"

"You want the truth?"

"The whole and nothing but, please."

"You won't like it."

"I'll have to risk that."

WDT, who considers his sense of humor to be on the dark side, once described himself as a man who always winked at the blind. So I laughed when he compared me to a vampire. It annoyed him. "No joke," he said. "You use me up and wolf me down." And before I had time to protest, he turned psychologist and explained *why* I was such a predator, constantly in a state of heat. Of course he brought Sigmund into it, quoting one of the brute's most misguided remarks, something about the sexual principle being a female invention. Then he compared me to Pandora's box, blaming himself for opening it, but excusing himself because he couldn't have known what lay inside. A praying mantis, apparently, shut up and ignored far too long, biting and frothing with desire.

At first I was stunned. Finally I said, "How dare you accuse me of always being in a state of heat when you hardly ever see me?"

"You're always in it when I *do* see you. Which is why I hardly ever see you."

WDT was clearly in a mood to wound. I kept very calm. "If you feel used up and wolfed down, it must be on account of the *other* women in your life."

"Let's not go into that again, Elva."

"Let's not have the pot calling the kettle black. I only brought up your other women to make my point. I'm not jealous, in spite of all your boasting about them. I always said I'm willing to share you rather than lose you completely."

"But you want the lion's share."

Another unbelievably wounding accusation. How could anyone call four rendezvous and eleven cancellations in six months the lion's share? And how could I reconcile the WDT I used to know, his charm and good humor *and* sexual principle, his acts of kindness like giving Baby a watch, with the voice I heard comparing me to a vampire and a praying mantis? I began to feel I'd never understood him.

"As long as I never understood you," WDT said, "I found you rather attractive. Like a cat. Always fun to guess which way you'd jump, until I discovered it would always be on me."

"Well, I never did feel like jumping on anyone else." I tried to sound ironic. "Shouldn't you be flattered?"

But he told me we were living in a New Age. And shedding illusions like old clothes. We used to believe mutual attraction lasted forever, now we know it's only a seasonal thing, like dahlias or lettuce. Then he asked if I read the volume by Havelock Ellis he lent me a while ago. I said I never wanted to hear another word about the great Havelock or the great Sigmund, that in my opinion these so-called experts on human behavior were only experts on taking the romance out of life.

WDT sighed. "You're too old to be trapped at an infantile stage of sexual evolution. Romance is for creatures of habit, like the animals. But the human species is blessed with a sense of erotic adventure, and it's time you discovered the joys of *constant stimulation*, Elva. The highest desire lasts only as long as lovers remain strangers. When they really get acquainted, routine sets in and it's time to move on."

"I call that the most cynical thing I ever heard."

"If you insist on turning back the clock and being in love for keeps, stick to masturbation." He sighed again. "That way you'll never risk getting to know anyone too well."

"Except myself, I suppose," I said lightly.

WDT laughed. "But what could be more boring?"

The next part is painful to write down, not that it's been easy up to here. I don't understand it, but the more ruthless, indifferent and depraved WDT claims to be, the more I long for him. I'm ready to *grovel*, not to his face, of course, but secretly my heart beats faster.

"Thank you for all your kind words. Can I see you just once more if I promise not to jump on you?"

"Does that leave you with any reason to see me?"

"My stock's running low and I'd like something to remember you by."

After some hesitation WDT told me to come at 5:00 and be punctual, because he had to go out at 5:15. When I explained that Baby's party would not be over by then, he told me to come at 8:00 and be punctual, because he had to go out again at 8:15.

"Very well. Hasta la vista, you busy man."

Baby ambled into the room as I hung up. I felt a terrible joy at the sight of her, swept her up in my arms, told her she would always be the greatest blessing of my life, wished her many happy returns and gave her a diamond bracelet.

Baby Looks Back

I came into Mother's bedroom to beg her to call off my party, then changed my mind and never did, because I knew she never would. I had no doubts about my ability to handle the scene, and was even ready to say, "This is a great American honor and I'll remember it for the rest of my life," when they presented me with the Baby of the Year award. I had no qualms about passing for seven, in fact I'd begun to believe it was my real age, just as I automatically thought of Father as a touring actor by now. But the whole stunt felt like *work*, which seemed unfair on a day off and doubly unfair on my birthday. Like any other pro, my idea of fun was to relax, not to get dressed up and fussed over by strangers. There was nothing sentimental on my mind, either, no yearning for simple childhood pleasures, a picnic, a potato race or games with the neighborhood kids, or even a tour of the place they call Venice-by-the-Sea, where you played the pin-tables, took a gondola trip and listened to an imported mandolin band. For my birthday I wanted a feast of barbecued chicken, waffles and an ice-cream soda, the latest Edgar Rice Burroughs romance of Mars and the latest Fu Manchu, a *Lone Wolf* movie and a trip to a real estate jamboree.

The jamboree, where real estate salesmen opened new homesites and put new tracts of land on the market, was almost top of the list. Mother often drove me in my Packard to these openings. We looked at developments in California, dreamed of living with glamorous names like Montebello and Mar Vista, and of the house we would build. They had brass bands, lotteries, sometimes free lunches. We toured the foundations and the parceled out lots; then someone cut a tape in the middle of nowhere. Once we went down the coast to Palos Verdes, where Spanish dancers stamped their feet and clicked castanets on a cliff above the Pacific, while a stunt pilot dived his plane at our heads. At another site cowboys staged a rodeo, and at another the famous soprano Madame Johnstone Bishop sang hymns with organ accompaniment. We inspected Mack Sennett's development up in the hills, but Mother saw a coyote sitting on the jumbo sign that said Hollywoodland, and told me we could never live in the wilds. She felt too close to the jungle again at a site way out on the edge of the chaparral, when a rattlesnake slithered down an Indian trail and the salesman ran for cover just as he was offering lots for $450.

We loved to imagine what style of house we would live in, Spanish or Old Plantation, California Ranch or English Tudor, and where we would build it, in the canyon above Beverly Hills they called Little Switzerland, because it stayed cool in summer, or in Westlake where her director friend lived, and a new development offered fantastic lakeside panoramas. Once she noticed a billboard, Buy Land in Los Angeles and Wear Diamonds, and decided not to build but to invest. They nearly took her to the cleaners. A group of real estate sharks dumped building materials around a new site in the San Fernando Valley, and marked most of the lots Sold to make it look as if business was really booming there. After a free hot dog, Mother agreed to buy four half-acres of dust at $700 apiece, and they had their first sucker. Fortunately the lawyer from the Baby Jewel Company Inc. checked it out and stopped her from losing some of my hard-earned money.

Although there was no time for a jamboree that day, at least Hattie cooked up a storm for lunch. But Mother seemed distracted and ate hardly a mouthful of the feast. In fact, right after Hattie dished it up, she left the table and the house, returning half an hour later without a word of explanation. She drank a shot of gin and wondered if she was getting old. I said she never looked better, but it didn't help. She was even more jangled than on the day she feared we were on our way to *rock bottom,* yet now we were on our way to the top. It puzzled me, but I knew she would only say, "What strange questions you sometimes ask!" if I wanted to know what was wrong. So I ate a pile of waffles and told myself it had to be temporary.

The *Herald* sent a limousine to pick us up, big enough for twelve and so low-slung I had to stand up to see out the window. I wore a filmy evening gown and a load of diamonds, the only gems Mother approved of for either of us. The watch given me by her director friend, my new bracelet, a pair of ear clips from last year's birthday, a pinkie ring and a brooch from Christmas. On the drive Mother seemed to recover from that mysterious attack of nerves. "Nothing like a limousine to make you feel safe and taken care of. And it goes so much faster than everyone else." As we reached the Hollywood Hotel, she clutched my arm. "Baby, they're giving you a standing ovation!" She exaggerated, of course. Although there was a crowd outside, it must have been waiting for other stars besides myself, and had no choice but to stand anyway. We got out, I signed autographs, showed off my diamonds and thanked a woman who said she'd kill to have a daughter like me. A couple of shabbily dressed boys who looked like trouble hustled their way close to me and blew raspberries. When I asked Mother what they had against me, she said they were jealous, waved and blew kisses to the crowd, then swept me into the lobby, acting like a true and very great star.

The party was already under way in a banquet room the size of a barn, and a smell even more noxious than raw film stock hung in the air. It was sulfur from photographers' flashbulbs, which in those days sent up clouds of yellow smoke, like the latest in poison gas. They popped at Mother and me, but I knew all about smiling in public no matter what happened, and tried to look as if I smelt roses.

Almost at once Mother spotted Charlotte Pickford and Lillian Coogan. "I knew I'd get them!" she exclaimed as she dragged me over and they took pictures of all four of us, smiling under another cloud of yellow smoke. It turned out that Mary and Jackie had sent heartfelt regrets, and George Bernard Shaw never even acknowledged his invitation, but Mother took it in her stride. "They're just missing the party of the year, that's all!" And she hurried me on to the president of the Baby Jewel fan club, a motherly type who couldn't get over how small I was, and hoped I would like the Dutch doll my fans had sent me. More picture sessions followed, with the editorial staff of the *Herald* and Sid Gordon who never cracked a smile.

All this time I was looking anxiously around for Mr. Griffith, the only person apart from Mrs. Root that I cared to see. But it was another case of heartfelt regrets. "He had to go out of town," the publicity man for the *Herald* told me. I asked if he sent any personal message, about liking my movies or looking forward to seeing me again, but the publicity man shook his head. I told Mother I felt seriously let down, and she said she hoped I wasn't developing a *complex* about Mr. G. As usual Mrs. Root lifted me up. "You don't know what you've done for my business. I sent out a brochure with a photo of you as my star pupil, and the kids have been swarming in like maggots." And she bowed to my influence as well as my talent. I told her I was sorry the last two months left me no time for school, and she promised her door would always be open for me, any time of the night or day.

Mother was on the lookout for several all-time greats (she'd asked the *Herald* to invite almost every star in Hollywood) but I only remember two that showed. Theda Bara created a sensation, although not the kind she used to create. You saw how quickly time moved on, a few years turned her into someone from a century ago, ready to be framed and hung in a museum. Heavier and no longer veiled, she still wore funeral black and that fox fur with a stuffed head draped around her neck. She found an old Spanish chair like a throne and occupied it while people stared in amazement and disbelief. Beside her stood a man whom she introduced as her husband. He was a director and made *The Lure of Ambition*, the turkey

Theda was coming out to launch in Los Angeles when we met her on the train. I suppose Mother asked her out of revenge, just as she continued seeing Mary Louise for the same reason. She certainly high-hatted Theda in her grandest manner. "I can't believe no one's offered you a picture in more than a year. Of course, they do say if you stand still for more than a minute in this business, you're left behind." Theda gave it back with a smile. She warned Mother that success was often only a flash in the pan, and apologized for not having seen any of my little comedies yet.

Another yellow cloud went up as Ruth Roland, the western serial queen, made an entrance in her famous gun-toting outfit: cowboy hat, check shirt, gloves, leather holster, white pants with RR embroidered down the sides. She was a special guest of the *Herald,* and when they took me over to meet her, she pumped my hand. "Remember this, Buster. If you start a Kid Ruth series and make a goat out of *me,* it's shoot-out time at the O.K. Corral." A hearty wink, and she went off to be interviewed by a reporter from *Motion Picture Classic.* Then the publicity man brought over another special guest, Adolph Zukor, commander-in-chief of Famous Players, almost as wide as he was tall, but not much taller than me. Charlotte Pickford joined us, looked him up and down with a majestic twinkle in her eye, and notes that he must have put back the ten pounds she made him lose after negotiating a new contract for Mary. Mr. Zukor told Mother he'd like to have a talk with her, but Sid Gordon suddenly appeared between them from nowhere. "No Baby-snatching!" he warned. "I've got her tied up for another year." Mr. Zukor asked Mother why she ever agreed to it, then found Theda kissing his cheek. Spotting a big wheel, she'd risen from her throne.

She was still clinging to Mr. Zukor's arm when the ceremonies began and he made a speech, thanking the *Herald* for inviting him and wishing Baby Jewel many lucrative returns. Then it was Mother's turn to talk about the movies as a game of Let's Pretend, and to promise I would never leave the world of eternal childhood. Finally, in another cloud of smoke, Ruth Roland pronounced me Baby of the Year. I thanked my fellow Americans for the honor and went to cut my cake. Three tiers high, it stood on a long table, and they had to lift me over the top in order to reach it. The publicity man whispered not to cut the lowest tier, which was fake, cardboard sprayed with icing.

Except for opening a stack of presents in public, the worst was over. Package after package contained a doll or teddy bear or game or hoop, none of which interested me. The department store I modeled for sent a selection of kiddie sports and evening wear, and I was obliged to pose in a smoking jacket and a Red Riding Hood cape. Not one package contained

what I really wanted, something to eat or read. When I told Mother I had
no intention of carting home a load of junk, she looked shocked and
called me ungrateful. "I'm not ungrateful, I just don't want any of it," I
said, "although there must be other kids ready to kill for it." This
changed her attitude. She looked mysterious, called me a genius and
went to confer with the publicity man. Minutes later he made an announcement. Baby Jewel thanked everyone for her sensational gifts, but
didn't feel it was right to have so much when less fortunate children had
so little. So she planned to make a personal tour of hospitals and orphan-
ages, distributing her dolls and teddy bears and fashions. Applause and a
few bravos. Ruth Roland sang, "For she's a jolly good fellow!" I managed
to smile. The following week I had to go through with it. The orphans sat
around politely, clutching or wearing my gifts, staring at me in a silence I
thought would never break. The hospital kids lay pale and still on their
beds. One had a halter around his neck, another had lost a leg, another
looked on the point of death and closed his eyes. This time I barely managed to smile. Nothing unpleasant occurred, no one cried out in pain or
blew raspberries, but without knowing why, I felt afraid of them all. But
the flashbulbs popped and smoked, the *Herald's* publicity man beamed,
and Mother said it was all beautiful, that I created birthdays wherever
I went.

In the meantime, riding home in the limousine after the party, she told
me I had the magic touch. "Everyone adored you. Mr. Zukor was chewing his nails as he wondered how to get you away from Sid. And what
about Theda? She must have married that man to get back in pictures. He
seems mundane but they say he's going to direct *Ben Hur*." I asked if
she'd knock the pants off him if she failed to get a part in it, but Mother
said rather grimly, "Theda will never knock the pants off any man in this
world again." Then she fell silent and gazed out the window. By the time
we got home she was mysteriously jangled again. It seemed an effort for
her to ask what I wanted to do now, and I felt she didn't want me around.
So I explained that standing and smiling and answering questions really
tired me out, and I had to take a nap. Mother stared at herself in the
mirror. "Have *I* got the magic touch, Baby?" "No doubt about it," I said.
"There's a doubt about it in certain quarters," she answered, went to her
bedroom and closed the door.

When I woke up, she'd gone out. Hattie didn't know where, and gave
me a glass of milk. I drank it and felt suddenly overcome by a mixture of
confusion and anxiety and disappointment. A few tears plopped down
my cheeks. Hattie put her arms around me, wondering why the birthday
girl was unhappy. "What strange questions you sometimes ask!" I said.

Elva's Diary

February 3 • Impossible to write down anything for a while after that exhausting night. Then I thought, maybe some things should never be written down. But I started this diary because the moment Baby and I set out for Starlight City, I felt *historic*. My life was going to be one of a kind and future generations will want to know! Baby up there on screens all over the world now, for everyone to see and love and remember, but what about Elva's story? I once told WDT I was keeping this diary and baring my soul without fear or shame, but refused to let him see it. "Why do you want to confess everything?" he asked. "Do you have secret guilts after all?" Shades of Mr. Freud again. Better for WDT if he'd never heard of the man.

On Baby's birthday, triumph though it was, I actually considered ending my life. Thrilling moments like Mr. Zukor wanting to meet me, and my inspired notion that Baby should get additional press coverage as a moppet Florence Nightingale, giving away her toys to poor and sick children, went for almost nothing. All I could think of was Baby dressed in black, with a veil, laying a wreath on my marble tomb at Hollywood Memorial Park Cemetery. Although I managed to laugh off WDT's lacerating remarks on the phone, by lunchtime I was feeling even more bruised and crushed than Norma Talmadge at the end of *The Passion Flower*. I realized I still had much to live for, yet it no longer seemed enough. One voice said, "Elva, you had almost two years of him, be grateful and let it go," but another voice said, "You can't let it go, it's like a taste of blood." For WDT gave me an experience that most women only get in their dreams, or the movies. I was not just Baby's Mother but desired and desirable, my secret romance with its hint of danger as perfect as anything Elinor Glyn could devise. After such a glamorous double life, how could I go back to a mundane single one? Better a praying mantis, I thought, than a desperate moth without a flame. Not that WDT really meant it when he called me a praying mantis, or a vampire, he was only trying to wound, but the fact remained he was eager to show me the door. Thirty-three is a vulnerable age for a woman to find herself alone and rejected, no matter how svelte and inviting she appears in the mirror. She imagines the end of youth approaching, and grows very sensitive to any sign that the end may be nearer than she thought.

As I drove out to Westlake, elegantly attired and subtly perfumed, I hoped against hope that WDT would realize his mistake the moment he saw me. I imagined him moved and excited by the pleading bewildered look in my eyes, sweeping me up in his arms and bringing back those

nights outside time. If not, at least he would get a shock he never bargained for. It was dark when I reached his quiet street, and instinct told
me to park a discreet distance away, around the corner from his bungalow
court. How right it was. I walked stealthily to an alley, catty-cornered
from the entrance, and saw a limousine waiting outside. A moment later
WDT came out with a lady wrapped in furs. Probably MN, but I couldn't
be sure on account of the darkness and the way she kept her back to me. I
pressed myself against the wall and watched while they talked quietly in
front of the limousine. Like a movie, I thought, and the idea occurred to
me to slip into the court behind them! They were too preoccupied with
each other to notice a figure darting through the night. WDT's front door
was open and I hurried inside the apartment. Somehow I felt furiously
calm. I looked at his desk and saw he'd been at work on his income tax.
Next to the forms lay a book sealed in cellophane, *The Crimes of Love* by the
Marquis de Sade. I was unfamiliar with the author but guessed he was
obscene, for WDT once read to me from *Miss Coote's Confession*, a volume
wrapped in the same way.

Strange how the mind wanders unexpectedly. I remembered that Miss
Coote found her satisfaction in the rod, giving or taking it, and was always suggesting a "game of slaps." Then I heard the front door close. I
looked across at WDT with a smile and said, "I see you've been doing
your income tax." He seemed annoyed, and asked why I sneaked into his
apartment that way. I smiled again. "The door was open. And I didn't
care to interrupt your tender goodbye to the lucky lady in furs." He made
no reply, only shrugged. From the way he looked at me, then turned
away, I knew I could never move or excite him again and felt in the grip of
an icy rage. "A man takes what he wants when he wants it," I remarked,
"but a woman gives her all."

WDT showed no trace of emotion. "God knows," he said, "I never
asked you to give your all." He glanced at me with the faint glint of amuse-
ment in his eyes that I once found reassuring. "How amazing you are,
Elva." He came very close and for a moment I was foolish enough to feel
reassured all over again. "Every time you open your mouth I realize
you've learned nothing at all from me." The moment was gone. "Never
confess you love a man who doesn't love you, Elva. It only makes him
despise you. And never bow down and let him take over. It makes him
lose interest. It's a dull fellow who enjoys a willing slave." All this was
spoken in a voice of honey, dripping more sweetly as worse followed. "I
wonder what mistake you're going to make next. Will you accuse me of
turning you into a coke head?"

"Didn't you?" I knew as I said this I made my next mistake, but for the moment had no strength. He stood too close. I forced myself to back away, but he followed.

"I gave you a sniff, Elva, and you asked for more. You always ask for more. More of everything. You're the most anal-expulsive creature in the world."

I told WDT I was unfamiliar with the expression but could guess where it came from, so no need to explain it.

"There you go again, Elva, closing your mind and refusing to learn. Don't you want to hear about yourself as a little girl on the potty? What the little girl did on her potty, Elva, is a clue to the voracious woman standing in front of me now."

"You're disgusting," I said.

WDT sighed. "Anal-retentives hold it back, you see, they're hoarders who grow up thrifty and careful. But expulsives love getting rid of it, they're spenders who grow up full of greed and desire." His eyes seemed almost caressing. "Expulsives are all gobble and shit, Elva. Gobble and shit."

I backed further away and sank to a chair. WDT remained in the center of the room, hands in pocket, idly tracing the pattern in the carpet with one foot.

"Well," I said, trying to keep it ironic, "you've certainly called me every insulting name in the book. Some people might say you've been vile and cruel, but of course *I* know you've been honest if not kind. And I suppose you talk this way to all the girls?"

He nodded. "They love it. Even the little taxi dancer last week."

"And even the lucky lady in furs I saw you escort to her limousine?"

"I know you're dying to know who that was."

"I know you won't tell me. One of your stars, anyway. She had the aura."

"She loves it specially," WDT said. "Of course, she's younger than you. They're all younger than you and they don't cramp me with illusions. They know there's a whore inside every one of them, and they want me to bring it out."

He smiled, and it made me realize everything had gone too far. The smile was so lofty and scornful and deliberately humiliating. It amused WDT to trample me in the mire, and yet if he suddenly decided to romance me again, I'd fall for it. I felt so angry with both of us.

He went on smiling until I opened my purse, as if reaching for a handkerchief, and brought out a small revolver. "Where did you get that?" he asked.

"I went out and bought it at lunchtime today."

His eyes flickered. "To kill me?"

"To kill myself. In front of your very eyes." He stared at my little weapon. "It's real, you know," I said. "It's not an illusion. You can't laugh it away." And I pointed it between my breasts.

"Killing yourself is better than killing me," WDT said. "But it's still a very immature idea, even from you." I gripped the revolver with both hands. "Be a good girl, Elva," he went on, "and give it to me."

After a moment I said, "Yes, I will," and without getting up fired straight at his heart. I think I missed it, he clutched his left side near the rib, staggered back and fell into the chair opposite his desk. We sat looking at each other, quite close, WDT in a kind of slump, trying to speak, myself completely lightheaded, like a person able to walk on air. "Gobble and shit indeed," I said, still pointing the gun. "There's more in my Pandora's box than you ever guessed." He tried to speak again, stumbled to his feet, knocked over the chair and collapsed on the floor. As he lay on his back under a chandelier, the light caught his face and his lucky diamond ring. The position of his arms and legs disturbed me, they looked unnatural and contorted. I packed my gun away, knelt down and straightened them a little. Touching his hand gave me an odd tender thrill. I pressed it to my cheek, felt its warmth and kissed it before letting it drop gently on the floor. I noticed his watch had stopped an hour ago, he must have forgotten to wind it. His eyes looked different, rather glassy with shock, but WDT still seemed the most attractive man I ever met!

A car passed outside, making me jump to my feet. It didn't stop, but I knew I had to be going now. Forcing myself to think practically, I glanced at my pearl-gray cotton gloves and knew I'd left no fingerprints. No letters from me in the apartment, either, for I never wrote him any, and if he still had the silk stockings I gave him after our first night together, there was no way of tracing the owner. In fact, there was no trace of Elva Kay left in WDT's life, although more than a trace of WDT in mine. Giving his body a last look, I wondered how long it would take me to forget him, then opened the front door a crack, saw the patio was empty and hurried into the night.

As I started to drive home I wondered what to do with my little revolver, considered dropping it into a mailbox, then stopped by the lake. I threw it in and watched it sink. The lights of WDT's bungalow court glittered across the water, and a dreadful thought struck. I forgot to ask WDT for my snow before I shot him, and my cupboard was almost bare. Getting back into Baby's Packard, I turned over possible alternative sources in my mind. At first, I could only think of Harvey Pancoast, who was unthinkable. Then I remembered the club where WDT and I first met, wondered if Big Fella was still around and decided to make discreet enquiries. It was only 9:30 when I got home, but Hattie said Baby had felt very tired, cried a little and gone to bed early.

The news filled me with remorse. "It was still her birthday, I shouldn't have gone to the movies without her," I said, and tiptoed to her bedroom. Baby's face looked so happy and peaceful, it was hard to resist the temptation to gather her into my arms. She was all I needed to love. A gleam of diamonds and platinum came from the bedside table. I wanted no reminders of WDT in our house, picked up the watch and resolved to take a hammer to it in the morning, smash it to pieces and throw it out with the garbage. I blew a goodnight kiss to Baby, feeling suddenly very tired after my long busy day, and went to bed early.

Baby Looks Back

Mother carried her secret with her to the grave, as they say, and I only discovered it through her diary. Then I burst out laughing. It seemed too long ago to be shocked. By this time the unsolved murder of William Desmond Taylor was distant Hollywood folklore, and I could only feel amused that Mother got away with her crime. Unconsciously she must have known she would, for didn't everything she want always come true? Maybe that explains why she never expressed a twinge of guilt, or even seemed aware she had committed a capital offense.

I also had to admire her terrific strength, some of which she used on me and some of which she passed on. Strength in our family, which was not really a family, came through the female line, for Mother herself had a powerhouse Mother, whom she must have written about in a diary that got nibbled away. Among her belongings I found an old hand-tinted photograph of Little Elva with braided hair, smiling up at Carrie Watts with a rose pinned to her blouse just above the heart. They had the same classic nose and obstinate jaw. The same cat's eyes, intent yet blank, and I'm sure Carrie's changed color according to the light, like Mother's. Back of the photograph was written *Des Moines, Xmas Day, 1896*. Seven years earlier Carrie Watts was just out of college and working at her parents' clothing store in Omaha, Nebraska. A touring actor copped her cherry and left town without saying goodbye. When Carrie found she was pregnant, her parents could only talk of eternal shame. "Hard-shell Baptists," Mother explained when she told me the story. "They put her through total immersion at the age of twelve and couldn't forgive her for turning out a sinner." Emptying the store till, lifting a sheepskin coat from the rack, making and keeping a vow never to see her family again, Carrie took

off for Des Moines and her best friend's house. With the friend's help she
passed herself off as a widow and gave birth to Mother in the back parlor.
(So we had thespian blood in the family after all.) A month later, Carrie
found a job in a garment shop. Three years later she was running her own
business, and enjoyed a successful career in the rag trade until she died at
the age of thirty-seven after eating canned shrimp. "Then Mr. Kay came
through Des Moines on Coca-Cola business," Mother said, "and was
smitten. I married him because business was slack, I despised small
towns and at least he lived in Chicago."

Although the William Desmond Taylor case made a big splash in Los
Angeles, it seemed almost to pass me by. I suppose I was too busy. But I
remember waking up in the morning after my birthday to find my watch
gone. Mother said I must have lost it at the party, and although I felt sure I
put it on my bedside table before going to sleep, she repeated "You must
have lost it at the party, Baby," with such conviction that I decided she
was right. Then she asked if I ever told anyone who gave me the watch.
Only Mrs. Root, I said, because she admired it one day. "Do me a favor
and don't tell anyone else. Someone murdered Mr. Taylor last night —
isn't that terrible? — and of course if the police need my help I'll be happy
to give it, but I'd prefer to be spared embarrassing personal questions."

My Sherlock Holmes instincts were aroused. "What kind of embarrassing questions?" I asked, and Mother confided that Mr. Taylor had a crush
on her and even proposed marriage. She turned him down because she
liked him well enough as a friend but he inspired no romantic interest. It
sounded very convincing, but of course I still wanted to know who killed
Mr. Taylor. Mother said there was no definite suspect so far, but he had a
secret life and we should get ready for surprising developments.

I also wanted to know where Mother went that night. "Forgive me,
Baby, I did something very selfish and abandoned you, but I had a great
urge to go see Gloria's latest society romance, *Don't Tell Everything*. You
were sleeping so soundly I hadn't the heart to wake you. Besides, you
don't care for society romances." Once again she convinced me. I knew
she had this violent craving for movies, sometimes needing one the way
other people rush out for chocolate bars. And she was always excited by
Swanson's clothes.

A few days later she bought me a diamond watch from Tiffany's with
gold instead of platinum casing, and revealed that she always felt platinum was *not for us*. "Some things are rare and yet curiously vulgar,
Baby." That same week I noticed she stopped wearing white roses in her
belt and aigrettes on her head. The fan was put away in a drawer. I suppose she thought it wise to cancel any suggestion of the femme fatale.

One other event connected with the case I remember very well. Sid Gordon, always on the lookout for a gimmick, dreamed up a Kid Sherlock episode based on Mr. Taylor's murder and rushed it through. The little sleuth was consulted by two movie actresses, a Mabel Normand type who turned back flips, and an ingenue with blond ringlets like Mary Miles Minter. They had both received blackmail letters after the mysterious death of a famous director. By this time both Normand and Minter had been questioned by the police, so Sid knew he had a winner. I forget who was the real killer, although my arch-enemy must have been back of the whole business, but I know I got trapped in an empty movie stage at night with an escaped cobra.

Elva's Diary

February 5 • Life has its contradictions. I killed a man and now I miss him occasionally. Or miss the *possibility* of him, which never failed to stir my blood. But I order myself to think of the times he really *did* stir it, and find memory more satisfying than possibility. Anyway, this feeling will soon dissolve in the mists of time.

The story only broke in the afternoon editions next day, for Desmond's body lay undiscovered all night. (Now that the case is making banner headlines from coast to coast, I see no reason to conceal identities with initials, WDT, MN and the rest. Besides, more and more people are involved and I'll get confused.) Arriving for work at 7:30 the next morning, the wretched butler found his master's corpse and ran screaming into the street. I read conflicting accounts of what happened next, then the phone rang and Lillian Coogan came on the line. Knowing I shared her fascination with murder and had even met Mr. Taylor casually a few times, she was eager to talk things over. "Of course, he was no saint in my opinion," she said. "I wasn't aware you ever met him," I replied. Never did, Lillian told me, but she'd heard plenty on the grapevine and knew I'd like to hear it as well.

"One hears so much gossip," I remarked airily, although I'd heard none at all, but Lillian insisted she had the goods. Although I realized she was going to be very useful, I took care not to seem breathless with anticipation. So I told her how great she looked at Baby's party and wondered whether the big new emerald ring was another present from Jackie. Then I let her dish out.

According to Lillian's grapevine, the wretched butler calmed down in the street, returned to the apartment and phoned the news to Mr. Zukor, for whom Mr. Taylor was due to start a new picture shortly. In the meanwhile his screams had woken everyone in the bungalow court, including its other famous tenant, Edna Purviance, Mr. Chaplin's leading lady and former lady love. Edna at once phoned the news to Mabel Normand, then put in a call to Mary Miles Minter but got her mother instead, Mary having left the house to report for her last day's work on *Drums of Fate.* (Desmond always told me Edna was just a nodding acquaintance, but as it turns out she was wise to the whole set-up, the nods they exchanged were clearly not of the usual kind.) The police were the last to get the news. So much telephoning went on behind the scenes that no one thought to call them in for an hour or two. When they arrived, Mabel was snooping around the apartment in search of her love letters to Desmond, Mr. Zukor and his studio manager were burning a stack of private papers in the fireplace, and a couple of their employees had just whisked crates of bootleg liquor out the back. All this time Desmond lay in his final sleep on the floor. And in the meanwhile, the Minter mother had rushed to Famous Players to break the news to Mary, and much speculation arose because they got into a slinging match and slapped each other in front of everybody!

February 6 • Desmond's funeral. I longed to go, even tried on a costume, but finally stayed home. A triumph of discretion over curiosity. I was naturally eager for a glimpse of Mabel and the Minters paying their last respects. Also, if either star of the silver screen happened to be wearing a fur coat, I might possibly have recognized it, and discovered who was the lucky lady I saw that night.

February 7 • All over the papers today that Mabel was probably the last person to see Desmond alive. She told the police she visited him at 6:45 p.m. and stayed more than an hour, which means of course she was the lady in furs who loved it when he talked dirty. Asked why she ransacked the bungalow for her letters, she said she wanted "to prevent terms of affection being misconstrued." (Go tell that to the marines, Mabel!) Then she came up with her own theory about the case. "The jealousy of another woman enters the mystery," she said. This gave me a momentary turn until I realized it was a dig at Minter. When are they going to put the heat on Minter? I wondered, and the phone rang. "When are they going to put the heat on Minter's mother?" Lillian asked. "I just heard on the grapevine she was part of the harem too!"

My first reaction was disbelief. "They're all younger than you," Desmond taunted me on that fatal night. Then I decided it was a lying taunt, one more attempt to hit below the belt. Another moment from the past came back. Desmond once annoyed me by suggesting I take a lesson in genuine maturity from the Minter mother, and I annoyed *him* by agreeing to do so when I reached her age. The lady in question reminds me of Lillie Langtry when she faced the cameras twenty years too late and fifty pounds too heavy in *His Neighbor's Wife,* but no doubt it amused Desmond to have mother and daughter at his beck and call. "Such curious things go on in our city," I said. "Imagine three women allowing themselves to be used as slaves to one man's desire."

Lillian had the explanation for that. He got them all on dope. Then she added, "There used to be four. But the *Photoplay* writer killed herself."

Rumor or fact, this was a shock. I had no idea who Lillian was talking about. "You've certainly got the goods on Mr. Taylor," I said lightly.

"I thought everyone knew about Zelda Crosby."

"Poor Zelda," I said, wondering why Desmond never mentioned her name.

"They hushed it up, of course, and the verdict was natural causes, but everyone *heard.*"

Everyone, I thought grimly, except yours truly. Lillian had never even met Desmond, yet in some ways she knew more about him than I did.

"And everyone heard about the waitresses and shopgirls he picked up for the night," Lillian went on. "Never telling them who he was and taking them to a low hotel."

This at least was no news to me, for Desmond loved to boast of his casual adventures. "I can hardly believe that," I said. "The man had to stop somewhere."

"Not until somebody stopped *him,* Elva. I know he was only an acquaintance, but did you never sense his unusual power?"

"No, isn't it strange, I sensed nothing at all."

It was a relief when Lillian hung up and I could stop playing a role that would have taxed even a professional actress. Besides, my mind was aflame. If one girl killed herself on Desmond's account, and *I* seriously considered it, who knows what further tragedies were averted when I decided to kill Desmond instead? It began to seem as if I performed a service, almost a mission for womankind. If that sounds on the grand side, just call it a damn good thing I plugged the brute.

February 8 • This morning, looking in the mirror, I saw the face of a liberated woman. I no longer miss Desmond. That feeling has dissolved in the mists of time.

Then a limousine from the *Herald* arrived to take Baby and me downtown on her goodwill tour of a children's hospital and an orphanage. Although suddenly carefree, I went for the sniff that always gives me an extra sparkle at public functions, and found myself literally scraping the bottom of the barrel. This problem must be solved, and quick. Yet every time I resolve to go in search of Big Fella, a strong vibration holds me back. The man is surely deep in the underworld, and I'd be dealing with a criminal nature.

The tour was no less a triumph than expected. Baby had a fine time handing out gifts and signing autographs, she smiled with simple unaffected pleasure and was touched by the gratitude on so many dear brave faces. According to the *Herald*'s publicity man there's strong nationwide interest, from *Photoplay* to the Hearst press, in this unique event. He congratulated me again on my inspired idea, mentioned he was looking for a new assistant and said I could have the job if I wanted it! A joke, I think. Anyway, I responded in kind and arranged to have pictures taken while I gave an orphan a teddy bear.

February 10 • Woke up this morning in terrible discomfort. An enormous lump in my throat made it almost impossible for me to swallow. Only temporary, I told myself, I'm never ill, and picked up the *Times* to read that our district attorney, Mr. Woolwine, has ordered his assistants to wind up the prosecution of Madalynne Obenchain on their own, so he can devote all his time to the Taylor case. One more link in the psychic chain between me and Madalynne, I thought. Mr. Woolwine should really be prosecuting Elva Kay, but he doesn't know it and never will! According to the *Times*, he complained that certain people in the motion picture colony were trying to block his investigations, just as they tried to block Mr. Arbuckle's trial. And he promised not to let them get away with it, although I would say Mr. Zukor got away with at least half of it when he burned Desmond's private papers. Now I'll never know what was in them, of course, but hope Mr. Woolwine will at least see fit to release Mabel's love letters to the press.

My throat *looked* all right, but the lump in it felt bigger by the minute. During the first months of our affair, when I was finding it hard to calm down and get a good night's rest, Desmond sent me to a doctor who fixed me up with a prescription. I phoned him now, and luckily he was able to give me an appointment almost at once. By the time I arrived in his office my lump felt the size of a golf ball, but after a thorough examination, "Dr. Gregory" (as I shall call him here) said my throat was in perfectly normal shape. Impossible, I protested, and he gave me a glass of water to drink.

There was no way I could swallow a drop. Dr. Gregory showed no surprise, even looked quite pleased, and asked if I was under any kind of nervous strain.

"What a strange question. Everything's coming up roses."

He gave me a thoughtful look. "One of us has got to speak frankly," he said. "Don't be alarmed. Nothing I say will go beyond these walls." He reminded me he was bound by the Hippocratic oath, and quoted part of it, something about keeping his mouth shut if he saw or heard anything in the lives of men not fitting to be spoken.

The lump in my throat felt bigger.

"In the course of my examination, Mrs. Kay, I looked up your nose. Its membranes show the kind of damage with which I'm very familiar, for several of my patients have the same vexing problem. I always tell them cocaine is highly stimulating and gives you a lot of energy, but can have harmful effects in the long run. Eating away the nasal membranes is one of them."

And Dr. Gregory smiled pleasantly. For a moment I bowed my head, then looked him directly in the face. "Doctor, you have guessed my secret. I'm maybe a little nervous because my supply's run out, and I don't know where to get any more."

He nodded. "That explains your *Globus hystericus.* Or in plain language, your Hysterical Globe. An imaginary lump in the throat is a not uncommon anxiety symptom, especially in women."

He handed me the glass of water. Without thinking, I took a sip and then realized I'd been able to swallow it.

"There you go, Mrs. Kay. We bring it out in the open and it's a little better already."

I tried to swallow more water, unsuccessfully this time. Dr. Gregory smiled pleasantly again and told me not to expect complete results until I made a decision. Either give up cocaine or go back on it. And something in his voice confirmed my suspicion I'd come to the right doctor.

"You'd prefer it if I went to a sanitarium and withdrew, of course," I said lightly. "But I'm so busy right now. It would save a lot of time if I went back on the stuff." I looked him directly in the face again. "If only I knew where to get it."

Dr. Gregory picked up a fountain pen, wiggled it between his fingers and set it down on his desk again. Then he told me how much his complete guaranteed cure for *Globus hystericus* would cost. The lump in my throat felt bigger again, but I managed to stay calm and get the price down a couple of notches. At least Baby starts her third year with Sid Gordon very soon, I thought, and her salary goes up.

"What about my nose?" I asked.

"We'll keep an eye on it." He sounded almost casual about the subject now. "If you don't overdo it, you'll be living with a kind of sinus problem. And if there's real trouble, we can always switch to the needle."

I thanked my lucky stars for the vibration that kept me away from Big Fella. This way everything felt so straight. The good doctor watched me take my first treatment, said he was a great fan of Baby's and wished us both all the luck in the world.

Outside his office building, a limousine was parked right behind Baby's Packard. I noticed a young woman with dark bobbed curly hair sitting in the back. She wore a mink coat and ate peanuts out of a brown paper bag, throwing the shells on the floor. Then a chauffeur opened the door. Mabel Normand got out, looking prettier than she does in the movies. She handed her chauffeur the paper bag and went into Dr. Gregory's building. She left a trail of delicate perfume behind, and as it wafted away I realized the lump in my throat had disappeared. Meanwhile the chauffeur gathered up Mabel's peanut shells from the limousine floor and dropped them in the paper bag.

February 11 • A day of thunderbolts in the press. After completing their search of Desmond's bungalow, the police found two items Mr. Zukor must have overlooked. First, a gold locket engraved *To My Dearest*, with a photograph of Mabel inside. (Go tell the marines how to misconstrue *that*, Mabel!) Then, as they fine-combed his library, a letter fell out of a volume wrapped in cellophane, no doubt *Miss Coote's Confession* or worse. It bore the large butterfly crest of Mary Miles Minter and read, "Dearest, I love you, I love you, I love you!" So the heat is now on Minter as well. Mr. Hearst's *Examiner* ran a stern editorial on the finds, complaining about putrid vice among picture people and warning that America won't stand for it much longer.

And in the late afternoon Lillian Coogan launched another thunderbolt over the phone. The Minter mother skipped town early today, and the grapevine says she's fleeing to Europe. "Now we know why she and Mary were spitting at each other like cats after they heard about Mr. Taylor. Each thought the other killed him!" I felt indignant with the police for letting the Minter mother make a getaway, but Lillian assured me the Feds would be on her tail.

February 13 • After my visit to Dr. Gregory I calculated that in spite of Baby's hike in salary we would need a bit more of the green stuff coming in. Some months ago I thought of investing in real estate, but knew no one to ask for guidance and found that respect for the law is curiously lacking in this town. Today I recalled Charlotte Pickford once telling me that she made a bundle out of land, and phoned her for advice. She put me on to her real-estate operator, who drove me out to a huge flat empty tract of land beyond Fairfax. "I know it looks about as exciting as Nebraska right now," he said as we stood on the edge of a poppy field, "but things change very fast in this town. If you snap up a couple of acres here, you'll make a killing when someone wants to build." This time my lawyer not only approved the scheme and promised to arrange a bank loan, he was interested in grabbing some territory for himself.

February 15 • Baby had the day off and I drove her to our parcel of land. She complained there was nothing on it. "Don't be deceived by appearances," I said. "There's plenty *in* it."

We stood all alone out there, way beyond where Hollywood ended. Bare stony mountains loomed in the distance. Spotting a single red poppy in the field, Baby picked it. It looked unusually bright in her hand. For a moment I thought of blood, then took a breath of pure air, which acted like champagne, Valentino on horseback and Rachmaninoff's piano concerto all at once. "You'll look back on us standing here," I said, "as the moment the Baby Jewel Company Inc. really got under way," and felt more secure and hopeful and free than ever before in my life.

February 20 • The first time I met Desmond, he told me he'd recently directed Mary Miles Minter in a picture and felt she had unplumbed depths. In *Moonlight and Honeysuckle* I found her professionally mundane, but as regards her personality off the screen, I imagine no one would disagree with Desmond now. For some time Mr. Zukor has been molding her into another Mary Pickford, complete with morning dew on her curls. To protect her maiden image he even put a clause in her contract forbidding her to marry, and encouraged the fan magazines to run articles on her simple home life with her Mother. Now, not yet turned twenty, she behaves like a blend of Lola Montez and Salome. Today she told the press that she felt no shame about her letter to Desmond, but was proud to admit she loved him deeply and passionately. Many young girls, she added, would have fallen for a man with such poise and position. Cool and defiant as the flashbulbs popped, she even claimed they were secretly engaged. An interesting contrast to Mabel, quicksilver bright on the screen but a little slow off it. To questions about that incriminating locket, she could only reply, "I have nothing to conceal." Nothing *left* to conceal would be nearer the truth. The *Examiner* has warned us again that America won't stand for this much longer, and printed a letter from a women's club, ordering Hollywood to clean house. Asked for comment, Mr. Zukor said he sympathizes and will be glad to help.

February 21 • Lillian regaled me with another item she heard on the grapevine. "The police found stacks of women's lingerie in Mr. Taylor's bungalow. Nightgowns, chemises, brassieres, step-ins, silk stockings, you name it, Elva." I wondered casually if any of the owners had been traced. "One nightgown was embroidered with the letter M," she told me, "but I doubt whether Mabel *or* Mary will be eager to claim it." When I observed that Mr. Taylor seemed to have a little quirk in common with Madalynne Obenchain's lover, who rented female clothes, she laughed. "How innocent you sometimes are. Mr. Taylor never dressed up, he just gloated over mementos of his unusual power."

"Which I never sensed," I reminded Lillian. "Isn't it strange?"

February 25 • Thunderbolt. Opening the *Times* this morning, I read that the police have checked into Desmond's past and found he was really *someone else*. Real name Tanner, not Taylor, and a few years before the war he was living in New York, making good money as a broker. And married, to boot! One day he suddenly vanished, no one knows why or where, may have gone to Canada, but in any case turned up here five years ago as William Desmond Taylor, bachelor. It seems he came to Hollywood by way of Alaska, so he told the truth about that part of his life, although he lied about his age. Fifty, not forty-four. No explanation of why his wife never tried to catch up with him, but Lillian's grapevine has the answer to that. She did. Saw a newsreel of a Hollywood premiere and recognized her husband in a group of famous people. It cost Desmond a bundle to keep her quiet. Then, just as mysteriously, *she* vanished.

Like a movie, I thought. A mystery plot to keep you on the edge of your seat. So many ways it could go. *Suppose Desmond killed his wife?* That means I fell in love with a murderer, and it makes the denouement of our romance more than ironic. In any case I loved and hated a man who was not himself.

February 27 • The police have revealed more information about Desmond to the press. He got his foot in the door of the picture business as a dope dealer, and had several important clients, among them two star actresses who cannot be mentioned by name. But you don't need to call in Sherlock Holmes this time. Mr. Hearst warns that the drug angle, coming so fast on the heels of passion and murder, may be too much for our unsuspecting public to take lying down. Protests have already poured in from the federation of women's clubs, groups representing our major churches, the American Legion and the Boy Scouts.

Naturally I felt worried about Baby's reaction to the turn of events, but when she got home from work this evening, she said she'd had no time to read the papers recently. Then she scanned the *Examiner* over supper and yawned. "A lot of people who come out here are really someone else," she said. "They change their names or make up stories about themselves. Look at *us*."

March 1 • Letters about the cesspool of Hollywood continue to flood the newspapers. I was beginning to find them monotonous when my eye caught these words, from an English teacher in Whittier: *"Whoever fired the fatal shot that ended the life of William Desmond Taylor made a bang to echo in all our lives for years to come."* This was never my intention, of course, yet the words gave me an odd, secret flush of pride!

March 3 • Lillian's grapevine says Mr. Woolwine might just as well hang up his hat, the Taylor case will *never* be solved. It's too much for the motion picture industry, let alone our unsuspecting public to take. After the press got hold of Mabel's locket, Minter's letter and Desmond's past, Mr. Zukor and his cohorts decided to call a halt. Any moment now the case will be officially closed. "A wise decision in a way," I said. "The whole thing is obviously bad for business. But how can Mr. Zukor and his cohorts stop the police going on with their inquiries?" Lillian remarked again on the innocent side of my nature. "How can you live out here all this time, Elva, and not realize money can do anything?"

I thought it over and decided she was right. After all, when I'd been here less than a week, I noted that everyone in Los Angeles seemed eager to make some kind of deal. At the end of the day, a special bulletin on the radio confirmed Lillian's prediction and increased my respect for her sources. But although the news took a certain load off my shoulders, I felt disappointed in a way. The last few weeks have been like a movie that's so exciting you hate for it to end. Also, the police gave Mabel back her letters and I'll never get to read them now.

March 6 • According to the newspapers, over 300 people have written to the police and confessed they shot William Desmond Taylor. I asked Lillian if she understood the motive behind such behavior. "I told you before, Elva, too many of the wrong kind come out here. They don't have jobs or anything, and they'll grab any chance to get ahead." To risk the electric chair for a place in the sun, I pointed out, was like cutting off your nose to spite your face. "But if you're famous, you're famous," Lillian said. "You get your picture in the papers, and nobody can call you just a rube any more."

I asked if the grapevine knew whether the police actually solved the case before they closed it. "No, they were stumped because they couldn't pin down the motive," Lillian said. "If it was passion and jealousy, they ruled out Mabel as not the type, and bet fifty-fifty on Minter and her mother. But if it was a drug war, it could have been almost anybody. By the way, Elva, you never let on who *you* think did it."

After a moment I told her I inclined toward drug war as a motive, so it could have been almost anybody.

March 15 • My fatal shot, it seems, continues to echo. Yesterday Mr. Zukor and other studio chiefs called a press conference to explain that recent events have made it necessary to appoint a moral leader for the motion picture industry. Our former Postmaster General, they felt, was the natural choice, and they had great pleasure in welcoming Mr. Will H. Hays to Hollywood. Mr. Hays spoke not only as the president of a new association that would improve our way of life, but as a Presbyterian, Freemason, Rotarian and Grand Elk. The day of indecency on the screen, he announced, was over. Couples must never be seen making love in bed again, and women taken in adultery must always be punished. Off the screen, if any star gets involved in a public scandal, the studio is entitled to cancel his contract. Decency, Mr. Hays said, was the new watchword out here, and decency meant respect for the family and the institution of marriage.

Then Mr. Zukor spoke. The wheel of fortune has not been kind to Mr. Zukor recently, for Mabel Normand, Mary Miles Minter and Fatty Arbuckle are all on his contract list, but he was still ready to make a great sacrifice for the new cause. In response to public protest, he has withdrawn Mabel's latest picture from the theatres, and to avoid any future protest he has put *Drums of Fate* with Mary Miles Minter on the shelf. It will rest there alongside Fatty Arbuckle's latest comedy, completed just before his trial began. Whether the jury reaches a final verdict of innocent or guilty, Mr. Zukor explained, Arbuckle has dragged our industry through the mud and must pay the price.

In hard cash, according to Lillian's grapevine, Mr. Zukor's studio will lose a price of at least $2,000,000. The sacrifice may not leave him in the best of humor, but I intend all the same to phone him soon. If he really wants Baby, he must promise to wait for her. And I'll promise to deliver. Surely she's worth waiting for. Mr. Zukor needs a bit of tone on his contract list. And Baby needs the big league as soon as she's free of Sid Gordon.

March 21 • Mr. Hays, who takes his new job very seriously, has just advised the motion picture colony to respect "that clean and virgin thing, the mind of a child." I had an inspired notion and told Sid Gordon he must invite Mr. Hays to visit Baby on the set, with a full press corps in attendance. He sniffed some useful ballyhoo and called Mr. Hays' office. A secretary there promised to pass on the invitation, but warned that a great many stars, from Mae Murray to would-you-believe-it Theda Bara, were anxious to be photographed with our new moral leader. Imagine my satisfaction when she called back with the news that Mr. Hays was a great fan of Baby Jewel and we had a date.

March 24 • Mr. Hays was due at the studio midmorning, but the secretary phoned to say he'd been delayed. I heard later, on the usual bush telegraph, of yet another moral crisis in our colony. Handsome and popular Wallace Reid, whom I first admired romancing Gloria in *The Affairs of Anatol,* had just collapsed from morphine poisoning. Mr. Zukor, to whom the wheel of fortune continues curiously unkind, for Wally is also on his contract list, summoned Mr. Hays to an emergency meeting. He claimed he simply couldn't afford another great sacrifice, but offered to make a small sacrifice to Mr. Hays instead. After some haggling, they both came out smiling. Mr. Zukor had permission to release *The Ghost Breaker* as planned, as long as he got the press to inform our unsuspecting public that its star was in a sanitarium recovering from overwork. And our good shepherd had quickly learned what money can do out here, especially for his own pocket. "I think," Lillian said, "we can all start to relax now."

In passing. Lillian seems to have changed her tune since the first time we met, when she talked about the American way and 100 percent normality. But sooner or later, I suppose, we all change our tunes out here.

When he heard Mr. Hays was going to be late, Sid Gordon fell into a terrible rage. Baby's scene, specially chosen for its innocent heartwarming appeal, was all ready to be filmed, and he felt obliged to delay it. It was also necessary to pacify the press corps with coffee and cookies, which made Sid complain about extra expense. After thirty minutes went by he barked: "No time, I've got no more goddam time to waste, let's shoot."

Then word came that Mr. Hays was on his way. As soon as he arrived, the camera whirred and Baby went into action, using a jimmy and drill to crack a safe three times larger than herself. The door swung open at last and she crawled inside for a look at the secret papers. But while she examined them, a creeping hand appeared and stealthily swung the door back closed. Kid Sherlock was trapped again. Mr. Hays fairly slapped his thighs with laughter, especially when Baby hammered on the door with her fists and the safe rocked from side to side.

Knowing Mr. Hays came from the Middle West, I confided that Baby and I shared his grassroots. He reacted most positively. "Our kind settled this town, Mrs. Kay. It got away from us, but don't worry, we're starting to get it back."

"With Baby and me standing right behind you," I said.

Our new mentor is not a particularly attractive man, with crooked yellow teeth, a mole on his chin, ears like a jack rabbit and an unusually strong aroma of deodorant. When he kissed Baby, I thought she winced, but she never complained when one of the photographers demanded a repeat performance.

March 27 • Only her famous smile came through, and the photographs of Baby and Mr. Hays are the sensation of the hour. It seemed a good moment to call Mr. Zukor and lay my cards on the table, but Mr. Zukor said it was a bad one. He had too much on his plate right now and needed to think.

"Think about the crackerjack project I have in mind," I said.

"Call me back about it next week, Mrs. Kay."

"You can't beat *Alice in Wonderland*."

"What? You can beat it to death," Mr. Zukor said. "They did it just two years ago."

"But it fizzled."

"So that's a good reason to do it again?" Turning a deaf ear to my argument that a homely deficient moppet actress was to blame, he said rather disagreeably, "Call me back next year if you get a better idea."

I concluded Mr. Zukor was still not in the best of humor.

April 3 • Today Sid Gordon informed me it's a good idea to pull out while they still want more. Kid Sherlock could certainly keep audiences happy for another year, but he feels the time has come to launch Baby as herself. In other words, as a girl. He's been mulling several ideas and finally come up with the cat's eyebrows, a new series of two-reel comedies with Baby as Cleopatra, Joan of Arc, Salome, Queen Elizabeth, Madame Butterfly, Mata Hari, the Queen of Sheba, Carmen and other great women of history.

"Madame Butterfly and Carmen are not great women of history," I said. "They're from opera."

He looked impatient. "No need to split hairs. They'll go down in history when Baby gets through with them."

"But why must she keep on making two-reelers? She's more than ready for a feature."

"I don't make features," Sid Gordon said.

"You can't beat *Heidi*."

"A guy named Chaplin did pretty good out of two-reelers."

I tried another line of attack. "You told me you want Baby to be herself, but you're putting her in disguise again. At this rate, no one will ever know what she really looks like."

"Baby Jewel in disguise *is* herself, Mrs. Kay. Audiences go crazy about it. Not just her Sherlock Holmes but her bits as a blind man and a maharajah and a jockey. She's the most versatile kid in the business and I plan to keep it that way."

"A talent like Baby's must be allowed to *develop*."

He pounded the desk in one of his sudden rages. "Name me *one adult actress* getting a chance to run the gamut from Sherlock Holmes to Joan of Arc to Madame Butterfly!"

The man doesn't know a winner when he sees one, I thought, as he showed me to the door.

Baby Looks Back

My great women of history left the theatres, as Sid Gordon liked to say, screaming for more. In a way they even allowed me to develop, for it was a challenge to act people I knew practically nothing about. This time the Kidlet's advice, "if you feel it, you *are*," was no help. This time, this kidlet had to fall back on technique. More than he knew, Sid was right about Baby Jewel being herself only in disguise, for she still had no idea who she was when the disguise came off, and no time to think about it. Somehow I took the situation for granted. In spite of days when I felt definitely tired or vaguely depressed, I assumed my life was wonderful. After all, a woman once stepped out of a crowd to say she'd kill to have a daughter like me.

In those days, interviewers never asked really smart-assed questions like: "What is the real you? Where does it belong?" If they had, I'd have said it belonged to Mother. Around this time she read a new uplifting bestseller called *The Prophet* and used to quote, more or less, from one of its poems about parents and children. "I am the bow, Baby, and you are the living arrow I've sent forth!" I agreed it summed us up pretty well. But I suppose Sid Gordon was partly responsible for sending me forth, so a part of the real Baby Jewel also belonged to him. He was never the type to show or demand affection. Most of the time he seemed impatient or furious, yet I knew he was pleased with me, and we became like two hardened professionals, each giving the other his due without having to say a word.

And one other part of me, the most secret, belonged to Mr. Griffith. In my dream as opposed to my waking life, my Father figure remained the Father of Motion Pictures, as they called him then. They called him other cosmic names as well, the First, the Inventor, the Master. He had watched me dance and the clouds parted when he bestowed his solemn unbelievable accolade. I never forget the towers of Babylon on the hillside above his studio, and they always seemed like a monument to the Father-Master. Once I suspected Mother was God, then I met Mr. Griffith and really found Him. Three years after I first saw Babylon, it was still standing, a few more statues overturned, a plaster elephant slumped on its side, one pillar of the temple dangerously on the lurch, yet even more grand and mysterious in decay. From time to time I asked Mother to drive me over for a look, and compared Mr. Griffith's kingdom in my mind to Sid Gordon's unmagical dump, my familiar yard and barn and gimcrack sets. And I always hoped for something that never happened, for Mr. Griffith himself to appear in the splendor of an archway as he wandered around his domain in a panama hat. All I ever saw was a black cat streaking down the temple steps.

My act of worship was truly religious, for it had a quota of fear. I was afraid the Master disapproved of me. Otherwise, why did he never get in touch? Around this time his pictures were having less success, his stars went to work for other studios, even Gish left him, but instead of coming to *me*, Mr. Griffith chose sweet little puppets who never made it. "I don't understand your complex about Mr. Griffith," Mother said. "It's clear you're not his type." Maybe that was my complex. Even past his prime, he conferred something called prestige. If you'd worked for him, you'd gone as high as you could get. No matter what happened later, you were among the blessed.

Way down below, in the workaday world, my new comedies actually spanned more centuries and places than *Intolerance*, but that was no reason for Sid Gordon to spend extra money or take extra care. Discounting a few of the tackiest sets on Poverty Row, he shot them on location, and after a few weeks I realized Los Angeles itself was a series of incredible open air movie sets, the biggest back lot in the world. For Spain we went to Olvera Street and the plaza in the Mexican quarter, for my Butterfly we moved on a few blocks to Little Tokyo, with its kimono market and Pagoda Inn. Venice-by-the-Sea, some of which looked more like Old Bagdad on a budget, came in handy for Salome's palace in Galilee, Cleopatra's in Alexandria, even Madame du Barry's private apartments at Versailles. (Mother protested to Sid Gordon about this, complaining he had no taste, and Sid Gordon said he had no time.) Joan of Arc raised the siege of Orleans on an empty stretch of land in the Hollywood foothills, a French-type chateau complete with drawbridge in the background. It belonged to a plate-glass tycoon who came over to watch and wanted to make his movie debut, so they fitted him out as a soldier. Catherine the Great drove her buggy through a street in the downtown section known as Russian Village, founded by a religious group from Siberia. They made perfect extras because they walked around in Cossack boots and embroidered blouses, although they weren't too pleased at being sprayed with artificial snow. I even got to see the desert for the first time when they filmed Cleopatra delivering herself to Julius Caesar in a rolled-up carpet. Set in motion by concealed wheels, I was trundled along and unrolled at the foot of a cardboard pyramid just off the road to Palm Springs.

Some of my great women of history had been previously played by stars, and Sid Gordon found an extra joke in fixing me up like Theda as a wild-eyed Cleopatra, or Nazimova as a haughty Salome with a scarecrow's thatch of pale blond hair. My Queen of Sheba was modeled on Betty Blythe. They smothered me in pearls and a gown with a peacock sewn across the front. When Pola Negri made a big splash over here as Madame du Barry in a German movie called *Passion*, Sid rushed me into production wearing a silver court wig like a beehive, and smoldering with desire in a low-cut blouse and hoop skirt. "Each of these broads chews up scenery in a different way," he said and ordered me to flare my nostrils, narrow my eyes to slits, drape my body around a pillar. As usual I acted everything straight, and the critics described some of my scenes as comedy classics: Carmen strutting down Olvera Street with an outsize sombrero on her head and a rose between her teeth, Butterfly's eye-rolling hara-kiri with a saber on the Pagoda Inn roof, a poster for California oranges in the background, Salome stripping off her veils and tossing them at John the Baptist's head on a platter, in fact a store dummy's head with a fright wig and a splash of tomato catsup.

Today I wonder which would look funnier, the originals or my imitations. The originals, I suspect, but at the time Sid Gordon told me my
performance not only wowed the public but intrigued the stars, eager
to see themselves and each other. Betty Blythe claimed she never
saw my Queen of Sheba but found me perfect as Theda, and Theda
claimed she never saw my Cleopatra but found my Betty Blythe
devastating. Nazimova walked out of my Salome after three minutes, bitterly offended, and Sid Gordon said, "Well, show me a Lesbo with a
sense of humor." I asked him to explain this, but he told me to discuss it
with Mother in a few years' time. I discussed it with her that evening. She
looked startled, then said she had no idea what Sid Gordon meant. The
next time I went to school, I asked Mrs. Root to clear up the Lesbo mystery, and she shook with laughter. "My dear, Mr. Gordon's so right, you
should meet my sister." She offered me a dried fig. "And if you promise
not to breathe a word, I'll give you a course on the birds and the bees and
a couple of rarer species. An actress who's just played Cleopatra and
Carmen ought to be ready for the facts of life." Ready or not, that's how I
learned them, and Mrs. Root appended a vivid tribute to Margaret
Sanger and her movement for birth control.

Having written off Sid Gordon as a vulgar exploiter who kept me in
two-reelers for quick money, Mother was delighted with the quick money
but riled that vulgarity made him (and me) more successful than ever.
"It's time you were recognized as a great artist, Baby, but the brute won't
let you play Heidi." She also blamed Sid for cramping our social pros-
pects. My fame was solid but too mundane, Mother explained, to open
the gates of Pickfair or San Simeon. She longed to be invited to a dinner
party with Mary and Doug, or a weekend with Hearst and Marion
Davies, but most of all she longed to join the glamorous occult set headed
by Valentino and his wife Natacha Rambova. She knew the sultry Latin
lover took down spirit messages and consulted Black Feather, his Apache
guide from the Beyond, before agreeing to start a new picture, and she
knew that Natacha double-checked his horoscope and conferred with the
astral body of one of Madame Blavatsky's hidden Tibetan masters. But
their friend Nazimova also sat in, and my Salome killed any chance of
Mother being persona grata at Falcon's Lair.

Mother's nature, she believed, combined the psychic and the carnal.
With William Desmond Taylor gone, she apparently decided to accentuate
the psychic, and I believe she actually eliminated the carnal until her next
great romance some fifteen years later. In any case she began spending
most weekends at a mystic center down the coast near Point Loma, run

by a widow who called herself the Veiled Mahatma. The name conjured up Theda in her glorious prime, but Mother showed me a photograph in which the Veiled Mahatma, although she wore a long robe and braided hair, was unveiled and looked more like Lillian Gish playing a nun. It was a look that Mother cultivated as well. The resident followers at the center worked the land, practiced yoga, meditated in an Egyptian-style temple and believed in reincarnation. The Veiled Mahatma even declared that her late husband had been born again in the shape of a terrier dog called Spot. "Of course, she doesn't force you to go along with that," Mother said. "It's a curiously bad-tempered little animal, by the way." She described the atmosphere of the place as wonderfully pure, and told me about a ceremony at which they all gathered on a sacred beach at night, under a full moon, turning their backs on the world to face the Sea of Life and feel the magnetic, energizing pull of the Pacific. Then they spread rugs on the sand and enjoyed a piquant picnic. But a year after Mother joined the center, a female follower sued the Veiled Mahatma for alienating her husband's affections on the sand, under a full moon, after feeling the pull of the Pacific. It was pretty much the end of the place.

Then Mother switched to the Angelus Temple, not because she believed in Aimee Semple MacPherson, but because she loved the show and thought her a true star. "I only wish she'd chosen a less mundane vehicle than Christianity to appear in." One time we went to the temple together, and it was a memorable experience, although I had a misunderstanding with one of Aimee's usherettes. Mother bought me a pair of smoked glasses so I wouldn't be bothered by autograph fiends, but the usherette took me for one of the blind hoping to be healed. Seizing my arm, she hustled me into the Children's Miracle Room, with Mother elbowing her way through the crowd in pursuit, yelling I was just resting my eyes. Before the situation was cleared up, I had a weird glimpse of a roomful of moppets, some with leg braces and crutches, some with skin eruptions and spasms, some wearing smoked glasses like me.

The temple had batteries of Kleig lights, like a movie set, and held around five thousand extras. Dressed like a traffic cop in white leather, her blonde hair in tight marcel waves, Aimee tore up the aisle on a motorcycle and warned we were all speeding to hell. "Apply the brakes of repentance," she advised. "Turn around and start riding to heaven." She really made her audience want to do this, and got them high on the general idea that good was happy. All those anxious-looking people from Iowa and Kansas (you could hear on all sides what Mother called the prairie twang) began to smile. They cheered, applauded, embraced each other. Then Mother stared at me in astonishment. "Baby, are you clapping your hands for Jesus?" she asked. "No, I'm just clapping my hands," I said, "because Sister's got it." But Aimee, like the Veiled Mahatma, eventually found it impossible to balance the psychic and the carnal. After disappearing for six weeks, she came back and told the press she'd escaped from kidnappers, but it turned out she spent the time with her secret lover, the radio operator at the temple. Mother, who saw the man once, told me he limped and had a shriveled left leg. "Maybe Sister was just trying to heal it," I said.

In her own life Mother was moving toward a new combination, the psychic and the financial. Less than a year after she bought that poppy field, the real estate operator had an offer for it, almost half as much again. An insurance company wanted to build offices there, but he advised Mother to wait for an even bigger offer, and in the meantime to snap up another half-acre on Santa Monica Boulevard beyond Beverly Hills. "Am I making enough money to buy up Los Angeles like this?", I asked when she drove me to see the lot. "We only have to come up with a down payment," she explained. "With Baby Jewel as collateral, the bank loans me as much as I want." When she told me just how much she wanted, I reckoned we needed a contract for three features a year pretty soon. For openers. "Be careful," I begged, "I may not want to work in pictures forever." Mother looked as if an electric shock had passed through her body. Then she pulled me down to the ground and we sat on my damp new investment. "A star must never abandon her public, Baby." I stared at an orange orchard and some redwood bungalows beyond the empty lot. "Furthermore, Mary Pickford has been in pictures fourteen years already, and only just played *Little Lord Fauntleroy*. Everyone agrees the end's nowhere in sight, and you started much younger, so you can have a much longer run!"

Once again I found no holes in her argument and bowed to it.

Elva's Diary

August 1 • This morning I measured Baby to check her height. She hasn't grown a hairsbreadth since I started the log five months ago. Naturally I count my blessings, but still wish I'd taken another year off her age when she auditioned for Sid Gordon.

August 6 • Madalynne Obenchain, after suffering more than both Gish sisters combined in *Orphans of the Storm* — a hung jury and a second trial

— stepped out into the world a free woman today. I sat in the back of the courtroom to hear the verdict, and when the reporters crowded around, moved forward for a closer look. Maybe I was studying her more intently than I realized, searching her face for some clue to the actual events of that fatal night in Beverly Glen, when somebody shot her faithless lover on the steps outside his country cabin. For she turned and looked directly at me. I gazed into Madalynne's eyes, and they seemed to answer my question. They were very soft and appealing, but with a glitter in their depths, like mine.

September 19 • Over tea at the Hollywood Hotel, Lillian passed along the latest cuttings from her grapevine. Fatty Arbuckle, unable to get a job since he was acquitted, has become a slave of the bottle. Wally Reid went mad after they withdrew him from morphine, and is confined to a padded sanitarium cell. Mr. Hays and Mr. Zukor have become excellent friends, and Mr. Hays is not only delighted with the cooperation he's getting, but notes a sincere desire in the motion picture colony to improve itself. The American Legion has a move afoot to make little Jackie an honorary colonel.

October 2 • Just finishing breakfast in bed when Hattie came up with the news that a plainclothes detective and a sergeant in uniform were waiting to speak to me. I guessed at once that the Taylor case must have been reopened so secretly that not even Lillian's grapevine got the word. It didn't faze me. Months ago I reckoned with the possibility that Desmond's hateful butler might mention my name, among countless others, as a visitor to the bungalow. And I prepared myself then for an interrogation that never happened. After telling Hattie to bring the men coffee, I slipped into a housecoat, applied discreet make-up and went to greet them with a friendly smile.

On the way downstairs I made up my mind to fire the first shot and inform the police, with disarming sincerity, that Mr. Taylor was a casual but kindly acquaintance and I was most grateful for his interest in Baby. Luckily the detective cut in just as I opened my mouth, and saved me from a possibly awkward blooper. For he launched into an odd story about a family of four that went camping high in the hills a week ago. In a clearing behind some bushes they found a tattered jacket with a hound's-tooth check, an empty bottle and some human remains, mostly bones. The bones were analyzed as those of a seven- or eight-year-old boy, and the bottle contained a trace of bootleg scotch. My mind was ticking over by the time the detective explained how a tag on the jacket led to a dry cleaner in Hollywood, then to the Yucca Riviera Plaza and a talk with Mr. Hendrix, who recognized the garment in question.

"Dear God," I said. "That family must have stumbled on the bones of Baxter Cloud Junior, known as Baby Peaches!"

The detective confirmed this, and asked if I knew anything about Mary Louise's subsequent disappearance. "Only what she told Mr. Hendrix," I said. "She went off to find her runaway son come hell or high water. And later she sent me three postcards, but with never a word about poor Peaches. Maybe," I added, "Mr. Harvey Pancoast who produced animal comedies on Poverty Row, and the electrician at the burlesque house on Spring Street, knew more than I did."

While the sergeant noted this information, the detective wondered if I agreed with Mr. Hendrix that the late Peaches had a drinking problem. I did indeed, for my daughter, the famous Baby Jewel, made a casual allusion to it some time after he disappeared. Upon close questioning, she gave me quite a vivid account of Peaches left alone all night by his mother and knocking the stuff back. "And now," I said, "please explain how that poor boy ended up just a heap of bones in the hills."

"Peaches must have passed out drunk," the detective told me, "on the first night he ran away, gone to sleep near the top of Laurel Canyon and been eaten by a pack of coyotes. No doubt the lad was too fuddled to resist. Parts of the sad remains bore crunch marks." Then the sergeant grew philosophical. "Two kids in the same apartment house, both trying to make it in the movies, but they end up so different," he mused. "In a way it's the same old story," I said. "Some make it and some don't." Then he asked if Baby would send him a signed photograph and I promised to see to it. Both officers thanked me for being so helpful, and I told them it was a duty and a pleasure to cooperate with the law.

October 14 • When the phone rang, a voice said, "Señora Obligado calling from the Green Hotel in Pasadena." A moment later, Mary Louise came on the line. "I just got into town, Elva. The police traced me to Pinar del Rio in Cuba and passed on the sad news. Can you come to Peaches' funeral tomorrow?"

Naturally I felt bowled over. Mary Louise had not only turned into Señora Obligado, but was putting up at one of the grandest places in town, past its prime maybe, but still famous because John D. Rockefeller always stayed there. "My poor long-lost friend, what a terrible moment for you," I said. "Of course I'll come, and bring Baby too. She finishes playing the Queen of Sheba tonight and gets a day of rest before her next starring role."

"Oh my, the Queen of Sheba. What a thrill. We're out of touch with show business in Cuba, of course, but I did hear Baby was doing quite well."

Mary Louise heard more than that, I felt sure, but was too jealous to admit it. "Well, Señora," I remarked, "you've come a long way since your last postcard, I can tell."

"I married another tobacco farmer." She laughed. "And moved up from cigarettes to cigars!"

"You were born under a lucky star, dear, in spite of poor Peaches. I never heard of such a turnabout. Last time we met you were really singing the blues. And then that long wild goose chase after your boy."

There was a pause, then Mary Louise said, "I could have shipped the remains to Cuba, but I felt Peaches deserved a Hollywood funeral, and Felix agreed."

I made another reference to her mysterious trip across country and again got nowhere.

"When things turn really bad, Elva, I just blot them out from my memory later. I honestly couldn't tell you what I did between the time poor Peaches disappeared and the time I met Felix."

"Yes," I said. "And you were always vague about what you did between the time they shot Mr. Cloud in Mexico and the time you arrived in Hollywood."

"You're right. I can't remember that either." After inviting Baby and me to come and take tea at the Green Hotel after the burial, Mary Louise apologized for having so much to do and hung up.

The creature hit pay dirt and is not telling how, I thought, but I can make a few guesses. That excuse about leaving town to go after Peaches was a blind. She ditched her electrician for a more promising beau, a traveling salesman most likely, which would explain her safari all the way through Texas to North Carolina. One of them ditched the other out there, and she landed Felix Obligado, who was in the neighborhood on tobacco business. No doubt it took a backwoods Cuban with a taste for white flesh to consider Mary Louise a prize worth carrying off.

October 15 • At the Chapel of the Psalms, just Baby and me, Mr. Hendrix barely sober, and La Obligada with her new husband. Plus a reporter and photographer from the *Tribune*, alerted by La Obligada herself, who told them Baby would be a mourner at the funeral. After men, publicity is clearly top of the creature's list.

The Cuban is fiftyish, on the stout side, with a sleek black mustache, a fair amount of jewelry, and skin the color of his cigars. He also wears

Cuban heels. We had a brief conversation in the Garden of Memories before the service, and I learned at least one of my guesses was correct. He met Mary Louise "out walking" in Fayetteville, where he'd come to inspect a new American method of bug control. During the service he stood with his arm around her, occasionally stroking her back in a manner that suggested more than the desire to console. And once she wriggled in a manner that suggested she was ready for it anywhere.

We followed an unnecessarily large mahogany coffin past the Wishing Well and along an avenue of pines. The reporter whispered in my ear that the Hollywood Park Memorial Cemetery is the most expensive in town, so it must have cost the Cuban a sack of pesos to get Peaches in. Wearing a mantilla straight out of *Blood and Sand*, more suitable for the bullring than the graveyard, Mary Louise laid her boy to rest not far from the marble tomb of General Harrison Gray Otis, founder of the *Times* and our Chamber of Commerce. She pulled a rose from her corsage and threw it at the coffin. When the earth finally covered it, she turned and kissed Baby. "Oh my," she said. "You were poor Peaches' best girl." I couldn't believe she could top this for bad taste until she told the reporter, "If he'd lived, he'd have been a star too!"

Longing to hit her, I knew I could never bear Mary Louise lording it over a gracious tea at the Green Hotel. So I took her aside and pleaded a sudden headache. She professed to have forgotten about the tea, but hoped Baby and I would stay at her *finca* if we ever found ourselves in Cuba. I promised to do so in that unlikely event. We embraced, then she smiled at the photographer and nudged the Cuban to give Baby a farewell kiss. A flashbulb popped and they walked to their rented limousine.

"My headache's completely gone," I whispered to Baby. "But I can't take any more of this pretentious vulgar display over a boy who had no future, except as an extra playing circus midgets. Let's go and see Norma Talmadge in *Smilin' Through*."

Baby Looks Back

Mary Louise had reversed all Mother's predictions and come back with a winning streak. Inviting us to stay at the Obligado plantation was the final blow, and she turned quite pale. To get over the shock of knowing she could never act superior to Mary Louise again, she needed a movie at once, and lost no time driving to the theatre, where she sank into a mezzanine seat and wept through *Smilin' Through*. But the picture left me cold. Somehow life was more real than the movies that day.

During the service I compared Peaches' funeral with Father's, a routine affair that began in a musty suburban church and ended in a cemetery with rows of packed anonymous headstones. The sky was heavy and gray that day, the air had a tinge of smoke, a train rattled past in the distance. But Peaches' funeral seemed to take place on a movie set, and it was the kind of day that made people long for the beach. I saw a few bright, prosperous, kingsized tombs scattered around a country estate, and then Peaches himself, or rather his remaining bones, sealed in a handsome box under the earth. Above him gleamed a huge bank of flowers, then a blue sky and a warm sun. I looked at the flowers, felt the sun, and thought of Peaches glaring at Mary Louise as she told how he lost a part because donkeys frightened him, and he ran screaming off the back lot. I thought of him gotten up as a circus midget, riding the Pacific Electric alone, trying drunkenly to flush Mary Louise's cosmetics down the toilet, squatting in her clothes closet and mouthing "Pussy for sale!" when she turned her back, leaving weird threats in my shoes, stealing up behind me and giving my neck a mean, painful nip. I tried to fit all this in with Mary Louise showing up at our house in the dead of night, saying Peaches had run away because he was in love with me. With Mary Louise herself running away, getting caught in a hurricane at Galveston and coming back as Señora Obligado in a black mantilla. With hearing her tell a reporter that Peaches could have been a great star as she tossed a rose into his grave. With watching her hold on to her husband's dark, ringed, powerful hand as they entered an Isotta-Fraschini and drove out of our lives, to a famous hotel in Pasadena, to catch the train next day for New Orleans, and then the boat for Havana, which a poster in a travel agent's window called the city of voodoo and marimba nights.

But the next morning they fitted me out as Calamity Jane, drove me to the San Fernando Valley and taught me how to act quick on the draw. Dressed like a frontier scout, with a coonskin hat, I rescued the pony express from a gang of outlaws, shot them off their horses one by one and let the mail go through again. By the end of the day I was too tired and pleased to worry about the answers I needed to various questions, and by the time I reached home, I had forgotten the questions. Grabbing a turkey and mayonnaise sandwich, drinking my milk and hitting the sack, I was back in my usual situation, no time to live anywhere except the present.

1930

Elva's Diary

February 1 • "You and I know you're eighteen today, but the world believes you're only fifteen, and in a pinafore you can still pass for twelve," I said. "This calls for a very special celebration." Taking Baby by the hand, I led her out the front door to our driveway. Beside my beige Dusenberg stood a new Stutz convertible, silver-gray and upholstered in matching leather. Baby pronounced it the snake's hips but feared I'd been wildly extravagant. "A Stutz doesn't come cheap," I admitted, "and yet I didn't feel a thing. Last week I sold our little citrus grove on Pico to Colonial Drive-Ins, at a profit I can only describe as soul-stirring."

I handed her the custom silver-plated keys. Baby got in her convertible and sat at the wheel with its jeweled monogram on the horn. After a while she said, "It's a pity I won't be officially old enough to drive it for another three years." I pointed out the fine impression she would make just riding around in a machine like that. A Kissel might be sportier, but Clara Bow had one. A Lancia might be more sophisticated, but who dares compete with Gloria? One Dusenberg in the family is enough. The Coogans offered me a discount on a white Rolls-Royce (they own the concession out here) but a white Rolls no longer sets you above the crowd. It's about as rare as sunshine.

"I shudder at the thought of a white Rolls," Baby said, and tooted her horn. After we went back into the house I weighed and measured her for the last time, knowing a girl seldom grows taller when she's turned eighteen. The results could not have been more desirable. On the *Youth and Health* scale, Baby registered as an ideal twelve-year-old, eighty-nine pounds and a mere jot over five feet without her shoes. And I noted her

[105]

skin was more glowing than ever, no telltale hint of muddiness or acne
thanks to her pint of yogurt at breakfast, and her midmorning tomato
juice taken ice cold with a squeeze of fresh lemon and a spoonful of active
dry yeast.

The doorbell rang, Hattie answered it and brought in a lavishly gift-
wrapped package. "I knew Mr. Mayer wouldn't forget you," I said, spotting the MGM trademark on the birthday card. Baby opened the package
and tossed me the most luxurious orchid corsage I ever saw. "You wear
it. I shudder at the thought of orchid corsages." Was she making a joke or
becoming spoilt? "And how about dinner at the Coconut Grove tonight,
with all the stars crowding around to congratulate you?" I asked. "Do
you still shudder at the thought of that as well?" She begged me not to
make her throw up. "Then I suggest we go see Jeanette MacDonald in
The Love Parade instead," I said. "I heard her sing *Dream Lover* on the radio
and it's sensational. Or would you prefer a sneak preview of *The Divorcee*,
Norma Shearer in her first shameless role?"

Baby fell into one of her long silences. "I'd prefer both," she said finally. "But first I want to take One Big Look."

I stared at her, having no idea what she meant.

"Don't you remember? Two of my front teeth fell out, we went to a
dentist downtown, then took a cable car to the highest point in the city.
And there was an earthquake as well. I always loved that day."

Sometimes I don't understand what goes on in Baby's mind, but suspect she has the same problem. Maybe she's like the Divine Garbo who
recently told us, "I can only express myself through my roles." I was
certainly struck by the way Baby expressed herself in her triumphant version of *The Bluebird*, when she entered the Kingdom of the Future and
watched all those galleons sail across the sky with cargoes of unborn children, soon to begin their little lives on earth. Such a strange wistful expression on her face, almost as if she felt sorry for them! At a moment like
this she reminds me of Mr. Chaplin, another great artist who brings happiness to thousands and yet suffers from a secret melancholy.

Toward noon I took the silver-gray wheel of Baby's birthday Stutz and
we headed downtown on its maiden voyage. We passed two white Rolls
on Beverly Drive and five more after we swung onto Wilshire Boulevard
and purred along the ritzy new shopping and business center they call
Miracle Mile. "I told you, a white Rolls is a drug on the market," I said,
then slowed down as we approached the first piece of land I ever bought,
and the only poppy field for miles around that never yielded a drop of oil.
Mrs. Cudahy, the packing corporation widow who used to dress as
Nefertiti at her parties for the smart set, grabbed the adjoining fields a

year or so later and found herself awash in black gold. Still and all, the
Royal View Towers, an apartment house in Regency style, now stands on
my lot with an unending view of derricks and pumps, and I made a bundle on the deal.

Nobody goes downtown these days, and I saw why as soon as we
reached it. The less fortunate oriental, black and Latino types have taken
over almost everything except the business district. Store signs in various
languages, even billboards advertising a lotion to straighten the kink in
Negro hair. Sidewalks teeming with aimless wanderers, they swarm in
and out of 5 and 10¢ stores, mill around hot dog stands, gape at the
photographs outside rundown burlesque houses. A permanent traffic jam
created by rattling streetcars and all kinds of jalopies. We drove bumper to
bumper. Once a drunken old vagrant lurched right in front of us, and
once a Mexican woman stepped off the sidewalk as her shopping bag
burst, and rows of oranges bounced before the Stutz's gleaming hood.
The only encouraging sight was a new movie palace, built in the Mayan
style, with a fine colored poster of the Divine One herself above the entrance, and a sign that promised Garbo Talks in Anna Christie Next
Month. At least, I remarked to Baby, these drifting thousands can escape
to the movies and find solace for their souls. "Just like you and me," she
answered, then spotted another theatre. It was playing *Abraham Lincoln*
and she wondered whether we should go see it instead of *The Divorcee*,
but I told her everyone said that Mr. Griffith had completely lost his
touch.

I found a parking space by the Hotel Broadway, Baby put on her
smoked glasses and we walked around the corner to Court Flight. Just
before we reached it, a sleazy-looking man in shirtsleeves beckoned urgently to us from a doorway. I ignored him, but Baby went up and asked
what he wanted. He offered to sell us a cask of Dago Red. "Thank you,
but I have my own bootlegger," I said. He spat on the ground and I felt
more than ever in a different world. The cable car rested at the bottom of
the hill, looking positively abandoned, the ticket man dozed in a chair as
if he'd given up hope of clients. It was no surprise this time to find ourselves alone on the observation platform with its rusted railings and
grimy telescope. The surprise lay in the view itself. We suddenly saw
what the newspapers told us had been happening for years, but it took
One Big Look to bring it home.

The city had grown and spread so much that empty spaces became an
event, and the desert had almost vanished beneath houses, office blocks,
buildings of all kinds. Most extraordinary of all, fantastic towers were
springing up everywhere. No one lived in them, it was forbidden on ac-

count of the earthquake risk, but they rose in all shapes, dimensions and colors. The highest was the great Richfield pylon, a network of bright steel that soared above an edifice in gleaming black and gold. Then came the white pyramid of the new City Hall, and the pale gray one of Bullocks Wilshire department store, and the lofty spire of St. Vincent's, copied from a Mexican cathedral and more decorated than a wedding cake. Not so tall but equally surprising were the scarlet pagodas of Sid Grauman's Chinese Theatre, the rich brown imitation hat atop the Brown Derby restaurant, and more than a dozen striped minarets signaling a chain of new drive-ins. Hardly a bank without its confident steeple or an insurance office without its solid belfry, it seemed all of Los Angeles was reaching to the sky. "No yellow brick road needed here," Baby said. "Could it be anywhere else but Oz?"

The boulevards to the ocean were all paved now, and a steady line of automobiles moved along them. More sedans and tourers were parked on lots behind markets and drugstores of clean white stucco, and on endless streets of houses with green lawns and pink geranium hedges. The view was so onward and upward that you could hardly believe our country was in the grip of a Depression. The *Times* was right as usual last week, I decided. The only Depression we have to watch for out here is psychological, because the rest of the nation wants to convince us we share its problems.

Looking through the telescope, I was suddenly dazzled by bright water. It was the artificial lake in the desert that I noticed on our first trip, but standing now in the center of Westlake Park, where palms and pepper trees had been planted to create another oasis, and the old houses pulled down to make way for a booming residential area. Even the bungalow court where Desmond leased an apartment had vanished into the past. I wondered if the lake's watery depths still held a trace of my deadly weapon, then felt this trip down memory lane had lasted long enough, and told Baby it was time to go home. "Just one last One Big Look," she said, training the telescope on Babylon. Like Mr. Griffith it had almost fallen, nothing remained except scaffolding and a flight of steps tilting up to nowhere. Baby sighed, then suggested a visit to the soda fountain where she enjoyed the best root beer special of her life. "I'm giving up sodas, finally," she said, "but I'd like to down a last one there." It was welcome news, *Youth and Health* strongly disapproves of them, but then she added, "From now on it's gin fizzes all the way."

We rode the cable car down to the street, walked to Fifth and Broadway, and found ourselves caught up in a seething crowd. I gave a wide berth to a bearded tattered man complaining loudly to the air about the sins of the

rich. The *Times* frequently warns that downtown is a breeding ground for
Bolshies, and approves President Hoover's policy of denying government
aid to the unemployed, who must help themselves instead of attacking
the system. Having no taste for politics I usually take no stand on these
matters, but now I suspected the Depression was more than psychological in this neck of the woods. There was hostility in the air, much stronger
than the irate spittle of a bootlegger when he failed to interest me in cheap
wine, and I felt myself becoming the target of angry or mocking glances. It
may have been due to my costume. Had I known that Baby planned to
drag me through a ghetto, I would never have worn my Persian brocade
coat and a cloche hat modeled on the Divine One's in her recent *A Woman
of Affairs*.

An obviously destitute mother with a ragged child blocked my way,
staring at me with tired yet ravenous eyes. I had the impulse to hand her a
quarter, and she smiled vaguely. Other unfortunates at once pressed
around me, and it seemed only right to dole out the rest of my loose
change to a crippled Negro, a decrepit old lady, a rather menacing young
derelict. "I never saw you do anything like that before," Baby said as we
moved on again. "I never found myself in a situation like that before," I
told her. "And it brought a wonderful sense of relief. The unfortunates of
this world actually smiled at me. Now why don't we go home?"

But my way was blocked once more. Another derelict, older and much
filthier, with blackened teeth. Finding a solitary nickel left in my purse, I
dropped it in his outstretched hand. He face went ugly and mean. "Don't
crap me, what do you think I can get for this?" Baby reached in the pocket
of her jeans, added a dime to the nickel, and he smiled. "Remember the
price of everything's going up," she said as we moved on again. "You
can't buy a smile for a nickel any more."

Like so much else, the soda fountain had vanished into the past. In its
place stood a discount store with hard soap, cans of paint and garden
hoses in the window. We started to turn back, then Baby noticed a large
crowd across the street in front of a movie theatre. People gazed up at the
sky, waving and applauding. Seizing my arm, she hustled me expertly
through the traffic. We reached the edge of the crowd, looked up and saw
a man climbing a flagpole erected on the roof of the theatre. He had almost reached the top.

"What gives?" Baby asked a cop, who told us the man was hired to sit
on top of the flagpole until *High Society Blues* with Janet Gaynor opened in
three days' time. "Publicity," he explained. "The studio thinks it'll help
the picture." Baby hoped the studio paid the flagpole-sitter well for going
to so much trouble, and the cop said, "You can be sure of it, kid, the

movie studios always pay well." He spoke in an amused fatherly way, making it clear he took her for a smart brat of twelve or less. "That fellow up there," he went on, "is the famous stunt artist Shipwreck Kelly. The new Miramar Hotel in San Diego paid him $2000 last month for doing the same thing."

The cop seemed to regard Shipwreck Kelly as quite a hero, and so did the crowd. The little Negro on crutches and the two tough derelicts had joined it, but like everyone else they looked in a good humor now. And I no longer felt unwisely conspicuous, because every pair of eyes concentrated on the entertainment in the sky. A huge wave of applause broke as Shipwreck Kelly reached the top of the pole, strapped himself into a platform seat and waved. "Won't he get hungry?" Baby asked the cop, who promised that hamburgers, doughnuts and coffee would be sent up by rope at mealtimes. Also shaving equipment in the morning, because Shipwreck liked to keep himself neat on the job.

Then, not for the first time, the cop gave me an admiring look. "Haven't I seen you in the movies?" he asked. I smiled and shook my head. "You look like you could be a star," he said. I thanked him, amused that he never suspected he was holding Baby Jewel's hand. But Baby has the knack of blending into her surroundings, no matter what they are. I guess her personality is somehow more *democratic* than mine. And I've never been able to get her interested in clothes.

A woman in a ratty fur-trimmed jacket joined us, looking up very disapprovingly at Shipwreck. Soon she began shaking her head and clicking her teeth loudly. "Something bothering you?" Baby asked, and the woman complained that Shipwreck was setting a bad example to youth. Last month her best friend's fourteen-year-old daughter sat on top of a pole in her own backyard for two days, while her parents and neighbors and even the local minister begged her to come down. Worst of all, the woman said, the police refused to help when they learned she was doing it for a bet, and stood or rather sat to win $80. She thought it pretty disgraceful that an officer even shouted up at the girl through a megaphone, saying he believed in free enterprise.

Not liking this slur on his department, the cop holding Baby's hand said he believed in free enterprise as well. Outbursts of juvenile flagpole-sitting, he added with a wink in my direction, had been reported from Culver City to Long Beach, and in his opinion they showed the pioneer spirit. "You're doggone right," Baby agreed, which convinced the cop of *her* pioneer spirit. He hoisted her up on his shoulders for a better look. She gazed for a long time through her smoked glasses at Shipwreck Kelly reaching for the sky, not saying a word but occasionally waving her hand. Once again I had no idea what was going on in her mind.

Baby Looks Back

I'd found an idea for my next picture. But first, thanks to the kangaroo mice, there's another time-gap to fill.

After my contract with Sid Gordon expired, he offered to double my salary if I would agree to star in a new Baby Jewel series, *The Invisible Woman.* "It's a cinch," he told Mother. "Baby gets hold of the H. G. Wells formula and ends up, a hundred reels later, running the world." She turned him down flat, even when he offered another $100 a week. "Can you imagine? First the brute keeps you in disguise, then he doesn't even want you to be *seen.*" A few weeks later she almost engaged in hand-to-hand combat with Adolph Zukor, although when he first called to summon us to his office, her vibrations were encouraging. "He wants you for *Little Orphan Annie.* That sounds more like it." After some friendly conversation about my great future at Famous Players, Mr. Zukor asked me to leave the room. I knew he wanted to talk about money, for on my way out I heard him tell Mother, "I am so generous with artists, even you will be amazed." But she overdid the Charlotte Pickford approach. The sound of angry voices soon carried way out to the corridor, and then Mother emerged looking grim and slightly disheveled. "I only asked for a three-picture contract starting at half a mil. When I wouldn't come down, Mr. Zukor showed no signs of losing ten pounds. But he lost his temper, called me a harpy and began shaking me by the shoulders. Naturally I took a swipe at him with my purse, and you're not playing Annie after all. He'll be sorry."

Undaunted when she heard through Lillian Coogan's grapevine that both Mr. Goldwyn and Mr. Zukor considered her a menace to the business and likely to wreck my career, Mother sold her half-acre lot on Santa Monica Boulevard to a moving and storage company for a soul-stirring profit, then made a down payment on a house in Beverly Hills. "I know it sounds reckless, Baby, considering you're unemployed and don't have a single offer on the horizon. But although I'm no poker player, I know how to bluff. What counts in this business is the *aura of success.* It so happens I stumbled on a heartwarming bargain, the former residence of slinky Louise Glaum, star of *Sweetheart of the Doomed* but now on the skids. Wait till you see the impression it makes when we move in next month." In the meantime, through her friend in the publicity department of the *Herald,*

she planted a couple of outrageous lies. Broadway was paging me to play
Peter Pan and Ziegfeld had offered me a special spot in his latest show. I
went back to study with Mrs. Root, where a large tinted photograph of
Baby Jewel now hung above the public telephone.

The heartwarming bargain and former residence of Louise Glaum was a
Southern Colonial mansion with twelve rooms, none of which Mother
could afford to furnish properly. On our first evening there we sat facing
each other on two French Provincial chairs, with an imitation Chinese
chest between us. The rest of the enormous livingroom was bare except
for a pole lamp in Victorian-gaslight style and a built-in bar with Mexican
tiles. "Rome wasn't built in a day," Mother said as she mixed herself a
hefty orange blossom. Then she looked suddenly enigmatic. "Tell me,
Baby, do you know the facts of life?"

I acted puzzled and shook my head.

Mother seemed disappointed. "I thought maybe you picked them up at
work. But you'll be going back to work any moment now, of course, and
you could use the info. Why don't you ask Mrs. Root tomorrow?"

At first Mrs. Root was amused. "So you no longer have to pretend you
believe in the stork. What a relief, my dear." Then she looked grave. "But
what an enigma, your mother's mind. Why does she suddenly bring the
subject up, and why won't she give you the lowdown herself?"

"She works in mysterious ways," I said. "Like God."

Part of the mystery was solved that night when Mother inquired how I
felt about the facts of life, now that I knew them. "I'm sure they'll come in
handy," I said. She was pleased but not surprised at my attitude. "You
were always quick on the mental draw. Did Mrs. Root fill you in on the
Lesbo situation?" I nodded. "You *might* run into one when you go back to
work. But you're more likely to meet the kind of man who chases underage girls. Did Mrs. Root fill you in on that situation as well?"

I shook my head, and I wasn't acting. Mrs. Root had originally briefed
me on the biological situation, the contraceptive situation, the marriage-
and-adultery situation and the third sex situation, but the child-lover situation was news.

"Then let me put in my two cents' worth," Mother said. Sipping her
orange blossom, she explained that Mr. Chaplin, who was a genius but
had his special kink as so many of them do, met his first wife at a beach
blanket party when she was only fourteen, and fell instantly in love.
"Now I hear he's about to take another child bride, although I don't remember how *they* met. I bring this up in no spirit of gossip or criticism,
Baby, I just want you to know it's *the kind of thing that goes on*. So if

an actor invites you to his dressing room for cookies and milk, better say no."

I promised Mother I certainly would, thinking to myself I probably wouldn't. Although I had no intention of going any further than cookies and milk, it gave the idea of getting back to work an extra something.

In the meantime Mother continued to play her own brand of poker, rejecting offers for me to tour the country on one-night vaudeville stands, to play opposite a comedy dog in a new series of two-reelers, and to take a supporting role in the latest Jackie Coogan picture. "Lillian may think she's doing us a favor, but seems to forget that Jackie needs you more than you need him. His last two movies took in maybe a nickel apiece." But we still dined by candlelight, as Mother liked to say, sitting on basket chairs around a rickety card table while Hattie served us open-face tuna or bacon sandwiches.

Finally a call came from Mr. Louis B. Mayer, top man at the new MGM studio since Sam Goldwyn left it to make pictures on his own. He invited Mother to go over for a talk, and she returned in a state of high-voltage excitement. "Imagine a studio that's been operating hardly a year and has already signed up Mae Murray, Ramon Novarro, Marion Davies, John Gilbert, Lillian Gish, your favorite Lon Chaney, and a pair of young lovelies on the way up, Norma Shearer and Joan Crawford! Now they want to ink *you* as well."

"But will they pay half a mil for a three-picture deal?" I asked.

Mother shrugged. "From a man like Mr. Mayer we'll take less. He explained I tried to push Mr. Zukor a jot too far." Obviously they'd hit it off together in a very special way. "So what is Mr. Mayer like?" I asked.

"Like all the others in a way. One of the wretched homeless Jewish millions washed up on our shores, short and plain and not overly educated, but strangely alert to our dreams. *All these men seem to know what America wants.*" Mother's eyes grew very bright. "They're witch doctors, Baby, with some dark primitive magic in their souls. And Mr. Mayer even makes an agreeable personal impression. Better manners than Mr. Goldwyn, better clothes than Mr. Lasky, you can understand his accent better than Mr. Zukor's, and he's got *genuine human warmth.*" She told me they got on so well that after settling the general terms of my contract, Mr. Mayer ordered coffee brought in and discussed the world in general. He believed the two greatest men alive today were William Randolph Hearst and Mussolini. He handed it to President Coolidge for opposing the right of workers to strike and reminding the nation "the business of America is business." And he signed off by confiding a personal secret that he felt

Mother was the kind of person to appreciate. Morning, noon or night, his favorite dish was his own mother's homemade hot chicken soup. "His voice broke when he said this, Baby, and I realized how deeply human he was."

"Who's Mussolini?" I asked.

"He just took over Italy. But he loves the movies. Mr. Mayer says he's most helpful to the MGM company shooting *Ben Hur* in Rome, and actually visited the set." Mr. Mayer, she went on, was not receptive to the idea of my playing Alice or Heidi because he felt my MGM debut should be in a role no other moppet had played, so he called in his vice-president, Mr. Irving Thalberg, who suggested a wonderful children's classic, *The Secret Garden*. "When Mr. Thalberg told us the story, Mr. Mayer was so moved that tears came to his eyes and he decided to buy it at once." Mr. Thalberg was only in the office for ten minutes, not long enough for Mother to get to know him. He was surprisingly young, better looking than Mr. Mayer, but she suspected not as warm. "But I'm sure it's true what they say. He's a boy genius and reminds you of Napoleon, Peter Pan and J. P. Morgan all at once."

"Who's J. P. Morgan?" I asked.

"You never heard of J. P. Morgan *or* Mussolini? Sometimes I wonder if Mrs. Root's doing her job. Mr. Morgan is a *mastermind*, Baby. He owns the best banks, shipping lines and steel companies, and he even raised the money for our country to get in and win the Great War."

Add J. P. Morgan to hot chicken soup, I thought, stir in Mussolini and genuine human warmth, and you cooked up an impressive but confusing personality. In any case we were obviously making a long jump from Poverty Row. Mother seemed to read my mind. "This is where we walk off with the game," she said, wound up her phonograph and played a record of Valentino singing "Pale Hands I Loved Beside the Shalimar." It always sounded like amateur night in an Italian tenor contest to me, but in Mother's opinion Valentino could do no wrong. As usual she sat in one French provincial chair and listened to it, as usual I sat in the other, watching her grow very calm and soft and still, thinking she was really a classic beauty.

From the outside, Mr. Mayer's studio gave nothing away and stood nowhere in particular. Parceled out and developed only a few years previously, the stretch of flatlands called Culver City was still wild mustard and alfalfa fields on the outskirts, then you reached a grid of neat suburban streets and turned into a wider boulevard with stores, real estate offices and a church. The studio was the largest building in the neighborhood, a solid blank front that still gave nothing away when you passed inside. The guard led us through several crisscrossing alleyways lined with concrete buildings and silence, then into the lobby of an office block. A man was leaving it as we entered. Fortyish, huskily built, he had a creased, rough yet melancholy face. "Why are you staring, Baby? It's nobody." I went on staring in silence until Lon Chaney disappeared around the corner of an alley. Then I said, "It's the Man of a Thousand Faces, but today he's wearing the Thousand and First, which is his own, which is why you don't recognize him."

While we waited in Mr. Mayer's office, Mother said she never quite understood my fascination with Lon Chaney. "You can tell he loves his monsters," I explained, "and he makes *me* love them too. Not that I consider myself beautiful, but I wish we could make *Beauty and the Beast* together." Mother looked horrified, felt sure the idea would not appeal to Mr. Mayer, and begged me to get my mind off Lon Chaney at once. But it took me awhile. At first, when we went in to meet Mr. Mayer, it was difficult to focus on the stocky figure standing behind a large polished desk, wearing a somber business suit and eyeglasses that gave him an owlish look. In my mind the Hunchback of Notre Dame was carrying me to his bell tower. Then I realized Mr. Mayer was gazing very intently at me, so I pulled myself together and took stock. He was only forty then, but seemed older. Not physically, but to borrow Mother's phrase, he had a very strong aura of success and I felt he must have been around a long time to acquire it. Maybe it was the eyeglasses, but he had an aura of dourness as well and I wanted to cheer him up.

Apparently Mother had the secret. Mr. Mayer looked glum at the sight of me, then brightened at the sight of *her.* He held her hand almost tenderly and said how wonderful she looked. Then he knelt down in front of me, so that we met face to face. He held my arms, found me smaller than he expected, and asked whether I thought it more important to make people laugh or cry. "I don't know," I told him. "So far I've only made them laugh." He nodded briefly, stood up and returned to his desk. After a pause he said, "We've all seen a monkey laugh. But only human eyes can weep, and that's the difference between humans and animals." Mother gave him an eager smile. "This may surprise you," Mr. Mayer continued, "but I have only to imagine Baby Jewel in *The Secret Garden* and tears come to my eyes." The desire for happiness, according to Mr. Mayer, was a basic universal emotion, and no one in the world could fail to respond to the plight of a lonely orphan child, unloved by her guardian uncle but still searching for a Promised Land beyond the wilderness.

Unmistakable tears filled Mr. Mayer's eyes. Mother dabbed at hers with a handkerchief. Later I understood one reason they got on so well. Their fantasies about childhood coincided, and I also came to see how alike they were in another way: you never knew when their hearts would turn soft, at garbage or the real thing. (You never knew, either, when they'd turn hard.) But at the time, although I felt unmoved by the orphan child set-up, the MGM set-up impressed me. It was the other end of the earth from Sid Gordon waiting impatiently for me to get back in front of the camera after I fell through a roof or into the ocean.

Wiping his eyeglasses with a silk handkerchief, Mr. Mayer said the policy of his studio was Talent. Personality and the human factor made the world go around, which was why he'd recently coined a slogan for MGM, *More Stars Than There Are in Heaven*. Baby Jewel, he went on, would soon be a star in this heaven, but he saw our association as more than professional. Although I had a wonderful unique Mother, a girl my age needed a Father as well, and he looked forward to assuming this role. Privately I drew a line here, and disqualified Mr. Mayer because he had none of Mr. Griffith's romantic quality. On the other hand he was a candidate for Millionaire Uncle, swank and touchy but liable to hand out extraordinary presents if you played up.

Mr. Thalberg came in briefly. He had an elegant, almost offhand manner but dark, urgent, preoccupied eyes. "We may be in the business of mass production," he told Mother, "but individuals are our product." Mr. Mayer nodded approvingly, then looked grave after his vice-president left the room. "That's a very original brilliant boy, but he worries me. Only gets four or five hours sleep a night." Then he stood up and informed Mother we'd be hearing from him as soon as the contract was ready. She became discreetly flirtatious as she said goodbye, and Mr. Mayer lost his dourness as he pressed her hand again, looking her up and down and repeating that I had the most unique Mother in the world. And he knelt down in front of me again. "She could easily have been a movie star in her own right. But she chose to put her daughter first. Never forget how much she's sacrificed for you." To my amazement his eyes filled with tears again.

When we got outside I asked Mother if Mr. Mayer had ever been an actor. "Whatever gave you that idea, Baby? He started in the junk business. But did no one tell you Russians are very emotional people?" When she was specially delighted with Mr. Mayer, Mother referred to him as a Russian, not a Jew. Today he was Russian because he believed she could have been a movie star in her own right. "You ought to be able to recognize sincerity when you see it," she said.

Next day I asked Mrs. Root for her opinion of Mr. Mayer's character, and she came up with a different reading. "I never met him but I know the type. Always remember, my dear, men like Mr. Mayer are *a breed apart*. They saw the light of day in some murky ghetto, escaped to the Promised Land and found the Old Testament prophecies coming true. When I gave you my rundown on great religions of the world, I explained that the descendants of Jacob always believed Jehovah would come to their rescue after centuries of persecution."

If there was a connection here, I missed it. But Mrs. Root found it quite simple. The God that delivered Mr. Mayer and his colleagues from persecution was the Movies! "The Red Sea parted for them right here in Hollywood, my dear, so naturally they feel most special and Chosen. In fact they look on their studios as temples that produce the Commandments and the Word."

"Is that why Mr. Mayer means to have *More Stars Than There Are in Heaven?*"

"Once again you see through to the heart of things. These men speak the language of high priests."

"Mother says Mr. Mayer speaks the language of money like a native. When they got down to the details of my contract, she found less human warmth than she expected."

"Tell your dear Mother, all that humbug and poppycock about not serving God *and* Mammon comes from the New Testament, not the Old."

Mrs. Root rang the bell for end of class and we stacked our desks for Talent Hour. It was supervised now by an ancient ham in a black cloak, who used to tour the West with a traveling show in the frontier days. He told us he occasionally went to the races with an old friend from Arizona who recently settled out here, retired gunfighter Wyatt Earp.

Reporting for work on *The Secret Garden*, I was nervous not from imagination but lack of it. In the world of childhood fantasy I never had time for Cinderella or Mother Goose, and never saw myself as an angelic orphan who invented playmates or wrote to Santa Claus and got an answer. My fantasies began with crazy inventors and rabid foreign spies from the pulps, and continued with a wild movie serial called *Patria*, in which the Japanese and the Mexicans got together to invade the U.S.A. They were foiled by Irene Castle, who gave up ballroom dancing for the secret agent business. (Later I discovered this serial had been produced by one of Mr. Mayer's favorite Americans, William Randolph Hearst.) Sherlock Holmes, Fu Manchu, Lon Chaney and life on planet Mars completed the picture. So encouraging talk of Let's Pretend at rehearsal time only set me on the track of the yellow peril, poisoned darts, garotted corpses, master-criminals disguised as old ladies, hunchbacks and purple airships. I had to fall back on the old rule of doing what everyone said, and this time everyone said I had an amazing instinct for characterization, which allowed me to develop from born farceuse to born actress in my first feature film. I was no longer the adorably funny kid who mimicked adults but the adorably serious kid who made fairy tales come true. In *The Bluebird* everyone said I reached new depths of feeling, although the scene that Mother mentions, when I watched all those unborn souls sailing into life, felt far from deep at the time. I was only wondering to myself if there was a new child star in the bunch.

A version of *Treasure Island* was my greatest pre-talkies popular sensation, in spite of the New York critics who condemned Hollywood for destroying yet another classic. I played a girl called Jill Hawkins who wanted to be a boy and longed for daredevil adventures. Dreaming herself into the land of Long John Silver, she got more than she bargained for and finally woke up in terror from her escapades as Jim. A man's world was too rough and dangerous, she decided, reconciling herself to girlhood after all. Recently one of those dumb feminist movie buffs wrote a book about sexual chauvinism in Hollywood movies, and singled this one out as maybe the period's most disgusting artifact. But she missed the basic point. The studio was just trying to solve a problem: how to combine two of its favorite properties, *Treasure Island* and Baby Jewel.

And looking back now as a human artifact of more than one period, I see those years as among my best. The studio wrapped me in security as warm and soft as a comforter. It was not only in the business of producing individuals, as Mr. Thalberg said, but of making its products *feel* individual. It worried over every detail, the best camera angles for my face, what flowers should grow in my secret garden, whether my Bluebird of Happiness should look like a peacock or a bird of paradise, the cut of my Jim Hawkins wig. Every day I arrived for work, the gateman gave me a personal welcome. I had a dressing room twice the size of our old apartment at the Yucca Riviera, a secretary to answer my fan mail, a special doctor on permanent call, a special limousine with an armed guard to drive Mother and me to my premieres. My official eleventh birthday occurred just as we were finishing *The Bluebird*, and hundreds of gifts were sent from all over the world, crates of flowers, candy, bicycles, perfume, even a baby zebra which I gave to the Los Angeles zoo.

When talkies came I had no problem adjusting to them, unlike quite a few stars who made voice tests and found themselves lost in the shuffle. Everyone said I recorded as naturally as I cried, and the studio put me straight into another hit, *Freckles*, about a poor country kid who wanted to be a naturalist and paid her way through school by hunting rare moths and butterflies in the swamps of Indiana. The last reel left her on the verge of growing up into the famous Gene Stratton Porter. I remember Miss Porter died two or three years before we made the picture, and the Hollywood Park Memorial Cemetery named a foyer after her. The studio arranged to take publicity shots there, and I was photographed holding a butterfly net not far from the tomb of Peaches Cloud. Mother quickly made friends with the head of publicity at MGM, and they mapped out a Baby Jewel Campaign, Ramon Novarro teaching me to Charleston on the set of *The Bluebird*, Rin Tin Tin joining me to lead the Santa Claus parade, a visiting Costa Rican admiral pronouncing me the official mascot of his country's navy, a kidnap threat that made good headlines. But its high point was my own idea: a visit to a neighboring stage when Lon Chaney was playing the armless wonder in a circus picture. Although busy working out how to throw knives at Joan Crawford with his feet, he took time off to order a vase of roses. When it arrived, he picked out a rose with his toes, ignoring the thorns, and offered it to me. While the flashbulbs popped, I kissed it. Afterwards, I realized he never spoke a word to me, even though he was very friendly, smiling and bowing as well as doing the number with the rose. "Lon likes mystery," the publicist explained. "He's afraid people will get to know him too well if he talks to them."

The studio always invited me to the premiere party for a new MGM picture, even when Mr. Mayer considered the picture itself too adult for me to see. One evening a limousine drove me to meet Mother at the Coconut Grove after the opening of *Flesh and the Devil*. Mother was a Garbo-maniac. She could imagine no greater glory than the two of us being introduced in front of a battery of cameras, and once more she hoped the Divine One would overcome her dislike of official functions. Once more it failed to happen, so she cruised the Grove for alternatives and came back to our table with a small procession in tow. The publicity chief, several photographers, screen siren Billie Dove, known as the Voluptuous, and a tall rangy young man who seemed very uncomfortable in his tuxedo. Billie clung to him with one hand and held an enormous plumed fan in the other. As I wondered who he was, whether he hated tuxedos in general or his own in particular, which was too short in the sleeves, he left Billie and picked me up in his arms. While the photographers got to work, I sat on his shoulder and smiled brightly as usual at everyone, still wondering who the hell he was. The stranger asked if I liked flying. "You mean airplanes?" I said. He turned his face close to mine, and for a moment it had an anxious dazed expression. (Later it came out he was slightly deaf.) "That's right, airplanes," he said in a quiet Texas drawl. I told him I'd never traveled in one, and he promised to see about that and take me up in the air very soon. Then he set me back on the ground and went off with voluptuous Billie. "You've just been paid a rare compliment," Mother announced. "Howard Hughes is very shy and usually doesn't cooperate with publicity, but he brightened at the mere mention of your name." I was flattered but had to admit I never heard of Mr. Hughes. The publicity chief told me he recently inherited a fortune and was now producing pictures. Then he added solemnly, "By all accounts, that young man is a favorite of the gods."

It was twenty years before Howard kept his promise to take me flying, but in the meantime he provided Mother with her next inspiration. Aviation pictures were coming into fashion at the time, and the famous stunt pilot B.J. Langdon was working on a big one called *Sky High*. Mother described him as a daredevil in private life as well. "Going out with Clara Bow is even more dangerous than a crash landing, Baby." She got the publicity department to contact BJ and ask him to take me up in his plane. He agreed enthusiastically, and after some hesitation Mr. Mayer okayed the idea. "He was afraid you might get killed or disfigured in an accident, Baby, but I *swore* you had a charmed life." A costume designer at the studio created a silver leather flying outfit for me, and we drove in a limousine to a private airfield near Santa Monica. Mother fortified me with a shot of brandy as we drove across the field and pulled up beside a rickety-looking monoplane.

I stepped out to meet the great BJ, newsmen and photographers crowding around. A stocky sunburnt blond with blue eyes and a broad smile, he lifted me off the ground and kissed me on the cheek. "Are you scared?" he whispered. I shook my head. "But please do me a favor," I said. "Do not go higher than five thousand feet." He wanted to know why and I thought of explaining, then decided it was too complicated. I remembered a horror story by the great Sir Arthur Conan Doyle in which a pilot took his plane too high in the sky, and strange flying beasts came out from the clouds. A huge squid with wings and a kind of jellyfish with a terrible purple beak circled the plane, then moved in for the kill. They not only smashed his machine but ate the pilot up. According to Sir Arthur, too high in the sky meant over five thousand feet, so I said, "BJ, just keep us below five thousand if you don't mind," and BJ assured me he had no intention of taking us higher than a few hundred. He strapped me in my seat, I fastened my silver leather helmet, the plane shuddered as the propeller whirred, then we lurched into the air.

I looked down and saw Mother waving. I waved back, and soon we were out over the Pacific. So far, so good. In spite of the vibration and the fierce rumble of the engine, being airborne was an interesting experience. As BJ changed course and turned back inland, I gave the city below One

Bigger Look, and was astonished to catch a glimpse of an enormous sailing ship, with tall masts and billowing canvases, in the middle of a wide
empty field. I had time to realize it was the back lot where Douglas
Fairbanks was making *The Black Pirate* before the plane turned a kind of
somersault. Too shocked to make any sound, which BJ would not have
heard anyway, I could only close my eyes as the world turned over.

After a while the plane righted itself. This time there was just a moment
to see BJ grin at me, then he spun us into another somersault, and I
realized he was not only a daredevil but a prankster. Flat on my back in
space, I closed my eyes again, quaking with fear and rage, refusing to
look at a ghastly confusion of earth and ocean and sky. By the time we
landed, I managed to smile for the cameras, but as BJ unstrapped me I
whispered that I hated him. "I hope you fly higher than five thousand
feet, and soon," I said. Then we posed for more pictures, Mother getting
herself into quite a few of them, and I answered the usual sappy questions. Great, I said, thrilling, bang-up, a sensation I'll never forget. BJ
hissed in my ear, "Why do you hate me?" The lunk honestly had no idea.
"I hate you too much to explain *why*," I hissed back. "Now flub off!"

BABY JEWEL TAKES TO THE AIR! was the *Tribune* headline next day. "She'll
take to the bottle," I said, "if she's ever thrown around like that again."
But Mother refused to believe that BJ's stunt really frightened me. "It's so
unlike you, Baby. Besides, *I* wasn't frightened. I knew he was just having
fun." Once again her conviction was so total that it gave me the old feeling of never wanting to disappoint her. "It was only temporary," I said. A
few days later BJ went into a power dive for a scene in *Sky High* and lost
control of his plane. It caught fire when he crash landed, and he was
badly burnt. Mother went very pale when she heard the news, but made
no comment. I sent flowers to the hospital, and a note telling BJ I really
loved him.

In the visiting celebrity stakes, Mother felt I moved ahead of Jackie at
last when the press recorded my curtsy to Rama VII, King of Siam, and
my burlesque high-kicking contest with the comedienne Fanny Brice,
which brought about the headline BABY SNOOKS MEETS BABY JEWEL.
"Should have been the other way around, all the same, Baby." A special
thrill was when Edgar Rice Burroughs paid a visit to the studio and auto-
graphed my copy of *Thuvia, Maid of Mars.* It still stands on my bookshelf
today. A deep shame was the Kiddie Soap bearing my name that I en-
dorsed on billboards all over the city. "But it pays a bundle in royalties to
our company," Mother said. Fortunately Mr. Mayer came to my rescue
when she asked his permission to mastermind a similar deal for my seal of
approval on a new brand of peanut brittle. "Enough is enough, Elva,"

he said gently, pressing her hand. "We don't like our stars going too commercial."

The one prize that continued to elude her was Garbo. She found this particularly frustrating because Mr. Mayer had personally discovered the Divine One and brought her to the studio. Sometimes we worked only a stage away from each other, but no visitors were allowed on a Garbo set, and not even Mother could beg or bluff her way in. The prey she stalked had a sixth sense for escape routes, leaving the stage by a side door, ducking out of the wardrobe department through the back, apparently never eating in the commissary, where Mother sometimes joined me for lunch while her eyes monitored the entrance.

One day, as we were lunching late and about to leave, the Divine One appeared in the commissary doorway. She wore a tweed suit and slouch hat, walked calmly to a corner table, rested her chin on her hand and stared into space. She seemed to create an invisible circle of barbed wire around that table, and the few people still at lunch respected it. Nobody spoke to her or even reacted to her presence. Her solitude was mysterious and forbidding until Mother rushed over to invade it. Stiff with embarrassment, I stayed behind and hardly dared to watch. She sat down at Garbo's table and began talking fast. Surprisingly, although the Divine One made no answer, she made no attempt to bolt either. Then to my astonishment she gave the faintest of smiles, and a nod, and Mother signaled frantically for me to join them.

As I reached the table, her Garbo-mania was at floodtide. The Divine One, I heard her explain, was the first screen actress to make love to men instead of being made love to, more dashing than Ronald Colman, more subtly brutal than immortal Valentino. She described the electric shock of a scene in *The Temptress* when Garbo kissed Antonio Moreno all over his face and finally reached his mouth, where she lingered before walking away into the moonlight. The Divine One nodded and seemed aloofly pleased. Mother recalled the scene in *Flesh and the Devil* when Garbo flicked a cigarette from John Gilbert's mouth and seized him by the shoulders. This got another remotely approving nod. Since neither of them took any notice of me, I was able to study Garbo's lustrously pale skin, and her eyes that seemed fixed on a point in the far distance. And without knowing why, I began to feel uneasy and disappointed. Now you see her, I told myself, now you don't. As Mother began praising the amorous punch of a scene in *The Single Standard*, I realized I was due back on the set and made my excuses. The Divine One merely nodded, looking a thousand miles beyond my face.

During a set break that afternoon I asked Mother, "Did that lady actually *say* she was Garbo?"

Mother smiled. "Garbo doesn't have to *say* she's Garbo."

"But did she?"

"I don't remember." A dreamy, reminiscent look came over her face. "But I believe not. In fact, I believe she never said a word. I hope I didn't talk too much, but she seemed to like it." Her eyes grew very bright. "I really feel we made contact."

Unfortunately, as the publicity chief revealed, Mother made contact with an imposter, a former extra chosen as Garbo's stand-in because of her uncanny resemblance to the star. And he told us the story of a girl from the Middle West who went by the name of Geraldine de Vorak, often found herself mistaken for Garbo, and began to enjoy it. Gradually she started to believe she *was* Garbo, and got trapped in what psychology buffs today would call an identity crisis. She copied the Divine One's clothes, maintained an enigmatic silence, lunched alone in the commissary, ventured to walk along Hollywood Boulevard in dark glasses and even signed a few autographs. Recently a columnist in a fan magazine wrote that the star seemed less reclusive than before, appearing boldly in Bullocks Wilshire one day to buy a pair of gloves, dining at a restaurant with friends and looking quite animated in a gown exactly like one she wore in *The Kiss*. (Geraldine had bought it at a discount from the wardrobe department.) The studio, of course, knew all about Geraldine's game, but saw no reason to discourage it. She did no one any harm and made good copy, you even had to admire her for playing it so well.

At first Mother looked more crushed, to borrow one of her own descriptions, than Norma Talmadge at the end of *The Passion Flower*. Then she made a commanding recovery. "I *felt* there was something fishy about that woman, isn't it strange, even though Baby wouldn't believe me." A few weeks later, as my driver took me home in a limousine after work, I saw Geraldine walk slowly past the studio gate. It was raining but she didn't seem to notice or care. She wore no raincoat or hat, just a tweed suit and flat heels. I called out to offer her a ride. She stared at me with a confused, desolate look on her face, and walked on a little faster. It was weirdly like the fadeout of *The Single Standard* when Garbo disappeared along a street in the rain, ignoring a man who tried to approach her, and the final title came up, "I am walking alone because I want to be alone." Next day I learned that Geraldine, in a fit of over-confidence, had shown up three hours late for work and refused to give an explanation. No stand-in could get away with that, and she was fired. "I wonder what she'll do now," I said to Mother. "Can she go back to being an extra after believing she's Garbo?"

Mother shook her head. "She's more likely to go mad, Baby. It happens when you live too much in the world of dreams."

I was just finishing up *Freckles* at the time. The last scene was a school graduation ceremony with the mayor of Wabash handing me a special prize and predicting a great future for little Miss Gene Stratton Porter. The actor cast as the mayor looked familiar, I puzzled over his face and then remembered he had a small part in the Master's most recent movie, *Lady of the Pavements*. (Mother didn't care to see it, but let Hattie take me. "In the age of *Sadie Thompson*, Baby, I'm afraid you'll find Mr. Griffith sadly old-fashioned on the subject of Love for Sale.") Although the graduation scene went smoothly as I ran it through with the actor, he kept looking at me in a stealthy uncertain way. "Something bothering you?" I asked finally, but Ralph Haines only smiled and shook his head. I went back to my dressingroom while they set up the first shot.

Someone knocked on my door. I opened it and found Ralph Haines outside. When he asked if he could come in, I got the message at once, even though in Mother's book a man of that kind should have invited *me* to *his* dressingroom. "What can I do for you?" I said, but instead of answering he walked in, sat on the couch and gave me another stealthy look. "Close the door," he said, and then, patting the couch, "Come and sit down." I was fascinated, but perched carefully at a distance. He cleared his throat. "Do you know where your Mother happened to be born?" he asked.

"Des Moines."

Ralph Haines nodded, then asked where *Mother's mother* was born. I began to think the scenario had gone wrong. "I'm not sure, but I know she died in Des Moines. From food poisoning."

He nodded again and edged toward me. The scenario was obviously back on the track, so I got up and moved away. When he followed, I said loudly, "I know all about your kind!" Ralph Haines made no attempt to come any closer, but looked confused and asked what kind I knew about. I repeated Mother's warning about actors who chased underage girls. This time he laughed. "I promise you I'm too old for that." And then, because he thought I didn't believe him, "Don't I look old enough to be your grandfather?"

"Hard to say."

A casting director would have called Ralph Haines a timeless homespun type, also a natural for costume pictures. *Freckles* took place in the 1900s and he looked as if he belonged there. A slight paunch, wavy gray hair, and a rumpled, weathered face. When we ran through the scene, he struck me as a ripe old-time professional, but now he seemed suddenly unsure of himself, marooned in the center of my dressingroom. I wondered if he might be suffering from a secret illness.

"Well, I *am* your grandfather," he said at last.

It was my turn to feel confused. I seemed to have slid into a dream sequence without knowing it, just like *Treasure Island*. Then I heard Ralph Haines telling me about a thespian friend who went on tour in *Peg o' My Heart* years ago. Knowing the company was booked to play a week in Omaha, Nebraska, Haines asked his friend to find out what he could about a girl named Carrie Watts. The friend wrote that Carrie had moved to Des Moines, where she gave birth to a daughter called Elva. "An unusual name," my grandfather said. "You don't forget it." Many more years passed, he went on, and then he saw a photograph of Mother and me in a fan magazine that carried a story about the discovery of Baby Jewel. He had never met Mrs. Elva Kay in his life, and yet he *recognized* her, even though he couldn't explain why her face seemed so familiar. A while later he saw another photograph, read that Mother was born in Des Moines, and suddenly she looked right at him with the gray, longing, trusting eyes of Carrie Watts.

"Her eyes were gray?" I said.

"Definitely. Well, sort of." He shot me an uncertain glance. "Maybe they had a touch of green. And of hazel, like yours. Yes. In between was the color of Carrie's eyes, and in between colors we all see different."

"How long since you saw the photograph that looked right at you?"

"I'm not sure." He sounded vague. "Maybe five years. Maybe six."

"You've taken a long time to do anything about it."

"This is not the kind of situation you want to rush into. You have to weigh the pros and cons." Haines lit a cheroot. "But when they cast me in your picture, and we ran through our little scene today, it felt as if I'd thought things over long enough, and I had a hunch it was time to take the plunge." He flashed me a smile that struck me as almost cunning. "So I wrestled with my soul for another three minutes outside your door, and then knocked."

Haines dropped ash on the floor and I handed him an ashtray, wondering whether he was very calculating or very undecided. He flashed the smile again. "Between ourselves, think Elva would like to see me?" I wasn't sure, so declined to commit myself beyond remarking that Ralph Haines was her father and she hadn't seen him yet. Mother had warned me about stars who came from broken homes and people who suddenly turned up, claiming to be long-lost members of the family and expecting handouts. She described a very dramatic scene in *The Lady*, Norma Talmadge confronted by a young man insisting he was her son. Well, here was Haines waiting to confront Mother and insist he was her father. It might be genuine or he might be after a handout, for he was clearly not a successful actor, ending up in bit parts after years on the road.

"If you've got blackmail on your mind," I said, "Mother knows the time of day." Haines denied it indignantly, and I almost believed him, then remembered he was an actor. "How can you talk that way?" he asked. "You seem like a nice kid." And the tip of his cheroot seemed to burn with anger. "If you think I seem like a *nice kid*," I said, "why do you come in here and spill dirt on my Mother? That's no way to treat a *nice kid*. I'm really shocked. And in Mother's opinion, if a man gets a girl in trouble and abandons her, he's a selfish coward. If you're anything better than that, why didn't you go straight to *her* instead of getting at me?"

Looking at me in a distinctly unfriendly way, Haines blew out a cloud of smoke. "It won't work. You can't stop me from seeing her." His voice sounded hard and obstinate, and I began to suspect him of playing a very subtle game all along. When he turned away to leave, an extraordinary thing happened inside me. It scared and excited me at the same time. I suppose it was a sensation of power. Baby Jewel's a valuable property, I thought, and no stranger, even if he claims to be her grandfather, threatens her like that. Or if he does, he reckons without her friend and protector.

"If I told Mr. Mayer you came in my dressingroom because you chase underage girls," I said, "he'd fire you. And you'd be ruined."

His hand on the door, Haines turned around and stared at me. "Are you really such a coldblooded little horror?"

This was unexpected. In my dressingtable mirror I saw the two of us reflected, an old actor wearing a floppy cravat and carrying a stovepipe hat, Baby Jewel in a white graduation outfit looking not a day over twelve. Haines had no idea she was really almost seventeen, so maybe he felt a natural chill in his bones when he heard me talk that way. But what kind of person talked that way? Nobody ever called me a coldblooded little horror before. Once, as I arrived at the premiere of *The Bluebird*, a crazy young lout put his fist through the limousine window and called me Baby Pig Meat. He even made hideous obscene gestures and began unbuttoning his fly before a cop kicked him in the stomach. But you couldn't blame me for that. Baby Jewel was always deeply adorable. She was on *Photoplay*'s list of the Top Ten Most Beloved. She was the Costa Rican navy's official mascot, with a gold engraved plaque reading *Pequena Diosa* to prove it. In Tucson, for the opening of *Treasure Island*, they proclaimed

Baby Jewel Day. In Detroit they made her honorary sponsor of National Doughnut Week. She tugged at the heartstrings of the world. When she caught the flu, cables and flowers poured in, the press called to check her temperature night and day. Her fan club, increasing by the thousands every year, stretched from Germany to Japan. And a woman once said she would kill to have a daughter like Baby Jewel.

This had to be the person I saw in my dressingtable mirror. And Haines had to know it. I wrote down our phone number on a slip of paper. "Give me time to get home and warn her first," I said, pressing it into his hand. He thanked me and apologized for insulting me. "You're really a nice kid. And we're both in the grip of conflicting emotions." Then he left. Five minutes later we faced each other on the set and shot the first part of the scene. The mayor made his speech about kids with real initiative, little Miss Porter looked demure but excited, and it was time to break for the day.

Mother took the news more calmly than I expected. "You handled it very well, Baby. No good shutting the door right away, he might turn vicious. I'll have to see the brute." When the phone rang, she assumed a carefully polite voice. "Good evening, Elva Kay speaking, be so good as to come around in an hour, when Baby and I have finished our supper." She hung up, went upstairs, and returned a few minutes later looking suddenly radiant. I tried to find out what she was really feeling, but she wouldn't have it, and swept me up in movie chatter over fried chicken, succotash and pecan pie. "It seems Doug and Mary are not getting along so well these days!" An atmosphere of rift, she'd heard, hung over the set of *Taming of the Shrew*. The previous year, Mary had finally broken with her image of childhood on the screen and cut off all her curls. Photographs of the result were wired all over the world. "I said at the time and say it again, Mary aged twenty years in less than five minutes. Nothing's gone right for her since, and it's a lesson for *us*."

In everyday clothes, Haines had a touch of the seedy old bachelor. He wore a wrinkled blazer, a shirt with a wide frayed collar, and scuffed shoes. And he'd overdone the cologne. The moment he entered, he tried to clasp Mother's hands with a warm dramatic gesture, but she turned nimbly away and invited him to follow her to the livingroom. Haines complimented her on the house, but I couldn't tell whether he thought it looked expensive or genuinely admired Beverly Hills Colonial. When the good times began, Mother opted for what she called the antique look, overstuffed velvet sofas, high-backed chairs with embroidered footrests, coffee tables with engravings under glass, junk statuary, ornamental china elephants. "We bought this little place from Louise Glaum, last of the Vamps," she said grandly, and offered Haines an orange blossom. Most welcome, Haines assured her, to a man who'd been wrestling with his soul. Then he sighed heavily. "I was right about those eyes."

Mother wore the official smile she reserved for interviews. "Do you mind answering a few questions, Mr. Haines?"

"I mind you calling me Mr. Haines. I'm your father."

Her eyebrows shot up. "That's what we've got to find out." And she grilled him so thoroughly, I knew she must have worked out everything in advance. For she hardly overlooked a single detail, the name of the touring company that took Haines to Omaha in 1889, which play, what part, the location of the Watts house and clothing store, how Haines first met Carrie, the name of the hotel in which they managed to make love.

"You're pretty hard, Elva."

"Please don't call me that, Mr. Haines."

"Call you hard or Elva?" I asked.

"Elva," Mother said, and when Haines inquired what she would like to be called, "I won't know until I've finished with you." She finished with him and gave a long enigmatic pause. "Well. It seems you're not exactly an imposter." I supposed she had impostors on her mind since meeting the false Garbo. Flashing his crafty smile, Haines asked if he could call her Elva now. She saw no reason why not, although I never heard her call him Father.

"Doesn't this call for another drink?" Haines said.

Mother sighed and told me to get it. When he lit a triumphant cheroot, I thought she was going to jump on him for not asking permission first. She almost did, then settled for a refined wince.

"Now tell me about your life these past years." Mother's voice suggested duty more than caring. "Have you been in our city for long?" Haines told her he came to Los Angeles ten years ago and never stopped working. She nodded. "I've surely seen you in the movies then, but I've got a bad memory for small-part actors." Then she found it strange that we all lived in the same city, but our paths never crossed until now. "No, Elva, it's not strange," Haines said. "People keep to themselves out here, they don't reach out. You ask them why they've come, and they always tell you, to escape their backgrounds and start over. They want to get away from the past, they're not looking for it to catch up with them."

"It's their privilege," Mother said, her eyes steely.

Haines suddenly looked like a man with nowhere to go, no one to call up, all his lines of connection down. I felt a twinge of sympathy, imagined him sitting home night after night, alone with his past. Then he smiled again. "Well now, Elva. How does it feel to meet your old Dad at last? Are you glad or embarrassed?"

Mother's eyes grew even more steely. "I'm never embarrassed. Not even when somebody's got no right to ask a question, but asks it all the same." And she reminded Haines of his heartless and cowardly past. She found it difficult to understand a man who abandoned his unborn daughter, then decided to look her up years later and expected a warm welcome. But she supposed human curiosity was stronger than anything, even the sense of shame. "I don't mind satisfying your curiosity, Mr. Haines, but forgiveness is out of the question."

She was playing Norma Talmadge, noble and wronged, with a seasoning of Lillian Gish the porcelain prude. Untouchable Garbo hovered around the edges, and maybe at the very back of her mind, she heard an echo of Theda knocking the pants off every man in the world. "So that's how I feel about your past. It doesn't look good for your future." I dare say she made Haines wish he'd left his human curiosity unsatisfied, it must have sounded pitiless to someone with no previous experience of Mother as a performer. And reading between the lines, which Haines could not have been expected to do, I understand now why Mother put forgiveness out of the question. She saw no contradiction in literally getting away with murder and continuing to feel respectable at heart. Things always had to *look* right, but Haines made them look wrong, in fact illegitimate. If she accepted him, concocting a story to explain to the world why they'd been separated so long, he would always be there to remind her she was secretly misbegotten in a back room. As I heard her annihilate Haines, I felt there ought to be a drop of affection somewhere. Then I noticed how tightly she clasped her hands together, and knew she simply didn't want him to intrude on our lives at all. Her sense of family began and ended in exclusive concentration on Baby Jewel. Too late, and unnecessary, to change focus. She was convinced she had everything she needed.

I suppose Haines never knew exactly what he needed. No blackmailer, just a drifting aging man with what they used to call a guilty secret, perhaps he nursed a fantasy of being taken back into the fold with open arms, all is forgiven, we love you, we always hoped it would turn out this way. When he saw there was no chance, he simply finished his drink and got up to leave. By the front door he looked at Mother as if expecting a last-minute change of heart. It never happened. He cleared his throat, then kissed her clumsily on the cheek. She withdrew as if stung by a bee, and went to pour herself another orange blossom.

"We'll change our phone number tomorrow, so he can't call again. And I'll have guards put on the house for a month, just in case he tries to pay another visit and make me change my mind."

I took a shot of gin. "Unless you're playing very hard to get, it looks like you never want to see him again."

"Why do I need a father at my age?" Almost automatically, Mother glanced at herself in a mirror. "Not that I feel old, or *look* it. Do I?" I shook my head. She turned her profile to the mirror, firming her chin. "It would be different, Baby, if I was still a child like you." For a moment she must have forgotten my real age and the drink in my hand. "Besides, I never felt for half a shake that Mr. Haines and I had anything in common."

Next day, in the final scene of *Freckles*, I thought my grandfather used some effectively restrained emotion when he wished me goodbye and good luck. But our director, Lionel Barrymore, found him too low-key. Like other actors from the theatre, Mr. Barrymore was brought in to direct talkies because he understood the human voice. He certainly liked it to carry to the back of the gallery, and I used to think his idea of a really subtle weapon would be a sledgehammer. And since he couldn't call out instructions during a scene, as they used to in silent movies, he wired his actors with electrical receivers hidden under their costumes. One buzz from Mr. Barrymore meant you're giving too little, two buzzes meant you're giving too much. He buzzed you three times for too slow, and four for too quick. Also, you never knew when you'd get a signal in the middle of a scene, and you had to remember instantly what each signal meant.

Haines started to wish me goodbye and got a single buzz. He started the scene over and almost turned it into *The Singing Fool*. I'd have given him two sharp buzzes, but it was none of my business. At the end our director looked very pleased. "Thank you, Mr. Haines. That was top notch and you're through." I told my grandfather it was a pleasure working with him. After returning the compliment he walked off the set, out of my life, but looked back to wave briefly.

When I worked on the same stage in later movies, I imagined I saw Ralph Haines occasionally, on his way out, turning back to wave. My other studio ghost was Geraldine de Vorak, who used to walk sadly past the gate in the rain. She haunted me the day I went to see Mr. Mayer about my idea for a flagpole-sitting movie, except she looked different this time. She wore a red slicker, and her hair was bobbed and dyed blond. She smiled in a nervous awkward way, and I realized she was not a ghost at all. "Geraldine de Vorak as I live and breathe!" She told me she'd changed her name recently to Virginia Page, because American names were more popular now, and changed her style as well, so she could answer an extra call at MGM without getting thrown out on her ear. "I just finished two days on a Marion Davies picture and no one recognized me. In fact a couple of people think I'm a dead ringer for Marion now." I advised her not to push this, but noticed a gleam in her eye. It faded when she went on to explain times were not so good. Last month she moved to a shantytown that just sprang up in the Valley, near Universal, joining a group of extra girls who lived for free in huts made out of scrap iron and junk lumber. They pooled their money to buy Sterno heat so they could make coffee and warm up a can of frankfurters for supper. "But now I need a pair of eyeglasses and I don't have four dollars," she said, looking embarrassed but hopeful. "Your sight's failing?" I said, "that's terrible," but she shook her head. "No, there's jobs I'm missing out on because they want a girl with eyeglasses and I don't have any." I handed her a $10 bill and wished her luck.

Mr. Mayer was on the phone backing a racehorse when I came into his office. He hung up and told me he'd placed $300 on an outsider to win, because it was called Elva. "And now, does my one smart girl with one beautiful mother have a problem? Is that why she wants to see me?" Because I knew he liked it, I sat on his lap. There was a mirror on the wall and I watched Baby Jewel's reflection as she gave Mr. Mayer's hand an affectionate squeeze. "No problem," she said, "just an idea," then described the sight of Shipwreck Kelly on his flagpole and her talk with the cop.

"Isn't there something for a movie in that situation?" I asked. But Mr. Mayer saw no situation beyond someone sitting on top of a flagpole for three days, and it felt static. "Then listen to this," I suggested. "There's a neighborhood kid who seems kind of shy and left out of things, but she's really longing to prove she's got the pioneer spirit. Everyone laughs when she enters a flagpole-sitting contest, then by golly she wins and bails her family out of hard times."

Patting my knee in an affectionate Millionaire Uncle way, Mr. Mayer wondered what I meant by hard times. I brought up the Depression, and he frowned as if I'd uttered a dirty word. Of course you never feel it at MGM, I went on quickly, plenty of good black ink around here thanks to your policy of More Stars Than There Are in Heaven, and am I proud to be one of them. But in less fortunate parts of the country, I explained, times are not quite as easy as they used to be, and although Mother believes it's only temporary and she may well be right, it seems a good moment to give people a family story that plugs free enterprise.

Mr. Mayer assumed his poker face, admitted I might have something there, and promised to think it over. I knew this meant he was rising to the bait, he loved to play games and keep you in suspense. Then, almost smiling, he told me he'd just heard from Marie Dressler. "She thinks it's a lulu," he said. The lulu in question was a script everyone at the studio saw as a perfect vehicle for the two of us. I thought it was crud, kept hoping old Marie would thumb it down, but now the green light was on for the most lovable mother-daughter team in the world. We were cast as a pair of freelance domestics, hired to help in the kitchen when the rich gave grand parties, but secretly the most amateur thieves you ever saw, always trying to make off with jewelry and silver. Finally caught in the act, we explained my brother was going blind, and needed an expensive operation to save his sight. Stunned by a moment of *real life* intruding on their frolics, the rich proved they had hearts by dropping charges and reaching for their pocketbooks.

Mr. Mayer *loved* this story, and now that old Marie loved it too, I had no choice but to act thrilled. We ran through the final scene together yet again, Mr. Mayer playing Mother and crying. When he reproached me for not crying along with him, I said I felt the scene was somehow beyond tears. But when they previewed the movie in Long Beach, I admit I wept up a storm like everyone else in the theatre. And I had to hand it to Uncle Louie, he could put his finger on the pulse of the nation.

Being a good girl usually paid off anyway, for by the time of that preview in Long Beach, Mr. Mayer had a posse of writers developing my tribute to free enterprise and the pioneer spirit. It was called *Top of the World*, racked up some of my highest grosses, and gave me a special credit: "Based on an Idea by Baby Jewel." Although friendly critics saw no end to my talent, a few unfriendly ones feared they saw no end to my Babyhood. In an attempt to head this kind of thing off, the studio had started to bill me as "Baby" Jewel, but cruel voices were heard in the land all the same. They insisted a child star had a moral obligation to reach the awkward age and lose her appeal, they reproached me for not living up to it. "Some people are very superficial," Mother said. "They can't trust appearances."

Elva's Diary

April 21 • When did I first realize how vital it was for Baby and me to grow young together? Miss Sophie, hairdresser extraordinary, asked that question today as she gave me an oat and cucumber rinse. Unable to remember exactly when the vibration struck, I told her I was profoundly impressed by Anna Q. Nilsson in *Vanity's Price*, the outspoken drama of a

woman's daring quest for eternal youth through plastic surgery. (Not that
I intended to follow Anna's route, one heard too many stories about slips
of the knife. Lillian Coogan knew a woman who came off the surgeon's
table looking much younger but unable to close her left eye.) And I was
naturally shaken when Pickford stepped into the barber's chair, had herself plucked like a chicken and caused the greatest public outcry since the
execution of Sacco and Vanzetti. We might have withstood the shock of
seeing those ringlets mown to a flapper's bob if poor Mary, after years of
passing for a juvenile, had been able to pass for a flapper. Shorn of her
image as well as her locks, she brought the Temple of Time down on her
own head, exposing every minute of her thirty-seven years in no longer
than it took for a flashbulb to pop. I wondered if she realized, too late,
that an imaginary child could be happier than a flesh-and-blood adult,
and vowed never to throw Baby out with the bath water.

"Baby's the Jewel," I once told Miss Sophie, "but I'm the setting." If I
started to age by even a few years, surely Baby herself would start to look
less miraculously young? It was no problem, of course, to keep the years
at bay with yogurt, plenty of positive thoughts and sleep, plus a fountain
of advice from Miss Sophie on the fountains of youth. She put me on to
the Velvetskin Patter, a nightly stimulator that toned up facial muscles
and smoothed the skin all over my body, and to HG2, an elixir that guaranteed a rejuvenating flow of two pounds of liquid bile from the liver to
the intestines, thereby banishing gray hair, mental sluggishness and lackluster eyes.

But after a while, not looking any older failed to satisfy me. I wanted to
look positively, glowingly younger. The results of my first attempt were
so humiliating that I felt unequal to baring them in my diary at the time.
Youth and Health ran a most persuasive ad for goat-gland suppositories, a
breakthrough in rejuvenation techniques by the famed Dr. Clayton E.
Wheeler. I filled out the mail-order form, enclosing a $250 check, and the
suppositories arrived with a brochure promising visible results after a
month. There was even a photograph of Dr. Wheeler's goats, a herd from
Catalina bred specially for their serum, on the way to his laboratory. After
inserting for three weeks, and confiding my hopes to no one except Miss
Sophie, I read in the *Times* that the U.S. government intended to prose-
cute Dr. Wheeler for fraud. His suppositories contained nothing but desiccated hamburger, and far from prime quality at that.

I resolved not to make another move without consulting Miss Sophie
first, and soon learned that fraud was not the only danger in this field.
Intrigued by an article in *Woman's Home Companion* on Dr. Voronoff of
Paris, France, I asked what she thought of his monkey-gland serum injec-

tions. "Elva," she said, "let me freeze your blood with this." One of her clients, a famous star whose name she declined to reveal in spite of my best efforts, went to Paris for a course of the doctor's injections and came back to Hollywood looking triumphantly younger. Then she developed a sore on her lips, and another on her private parts. It appears Dr. Voronoff is not what Miss Sophie calls a detail man. His client caught about the worse case of clap in the world from those French monkey-glands.

I often suspected Europe was no place for me, and Miss Sophie's story confirmed it. Health hazards apart, I never heard anything that truly convinced me it was worth the trip. When the great Mr. Lubitsch arrived to make pictures in Hollywood, they took him on a tour of Paramount Studios, where he paused to admire a typically magnificent set. "I have seen Paris, France, and Paris Paramount," he commented. "I prefer Paris Paramount." If you asked him, I believe Mr. Lubitsch would not limit the comparison to Paris. For the movies take us everywhere, from Venice to Rio, from Buckingham Palace to Shanghai, and improve on the originals every time. To travel the world, I feel sure, is to risk severe disappointment as well as illness.

Our first day in Los Angeles, Baby and I shared a cab with a man who called it the New Italy. Since then I've heard it called the New Greece, the New Palestine, the New Dawn and the Last Frontier, and found one name as apt as the other. Why leave a city that allows us to live wherever we care to imagine we're living? And to meet any foreigner worth meeting, since they all come out here to work in the movies, or even simply to live? When I put these questions to Miss Sophie, she confessed she'd put them to herself years ago. Miss Sophie arrived from Sioux City in 1901 on a very slow train with a special $5 fare, and apart from a one-day excursion to Catalina, which she doesn't recommend, has never left the city limits. A client once offered her $2000 to go to San Francisco and dress her hair for the opening of the opera season, and although Miss Sophie was tempted at first, she felt her personal security threatened. The idea of even a brief separation from our fair shore caused her to lose an entire night's sleep.

And now, after my rinse, Miss Sophie suddenly drew the curtain across the cubicle entrance. She asked if I could keep a secret, and I assured her I'd kept a few in my time. "Then I may have the answer for you, Elva, right here in the City of the Angels. Did you ever hear of the Phenol Peel?" News to me, I said, and Miss Sophie described it as a new caustic solution applied to the face. "It *burns* the years away. And I've heard the results look incredibly natural."

Miss Sophie could not confirm but inclined to believe a rumor that Agnes Ayres had been peeled before her comeback in *Son of the Sheik.* I found this unlikely since Agnes was only twenty-nine at the time. Miss Sophie winked. "So she *claimed*, Elva. But in any case, the early bird catches the worm." She placed me under the dryer, then wrote down a phone number on a piece of cleansing tissue. "The Peeler used to operate on a boat outside the seven-mile limit. Now he runs a clinic in the hills, but he still can't get a license to practice, so it's extremely hush-hush."

"You said his stuff burns. Suppose I get scarred for life?"

"Sue him." Miss Sophie laughed, then patted my shoulder. "But seriously, Elizabeth Arden wanted to buy her way in, and offered a bundle. And although it's a step into the Unknown, you're not the girl to turn anything down on *that* account."

April 25 • Last night I told Baby I was suffering from overwork and she asked how that could possibly be. I reminded her that my real estate dealings subjected me to constant pressure. "Dr. Gregory says I'm near the breaking point and advises two weeks of complete rest. So I'm going into seclusion at a private clinic." Baby thought it sounded a terrific idea and she wouldn't mind joining me. "But I start shooting this heart-warmer with old Marie next week." She seems oddly discontented at the prospect, although the story strikes me as a winner. "I check in tomorrow," I said. "No phone calls are part of the treatment, but don't worry. When I get back, you'll be surprised what a good rest can do. You'll probably notice it at once in my face."

Although Baby and I have never been separated for more than a day before, she seemed to think she can handle it. "Have a good time and keep your mind off property. God knows we can both retire on what we've got already."

April 26 • Soon after Baby left for a conference at the studio, the phone rang. Dr. Gregory's ever-thoughtful receptionist informed me that her employer had been murdered some time before dawn.

A gangland affair, apparently, the result of an argument over territory between Dr. Gregory and the top *capo* out here. The police had seized my doctor's files, but there was no cause for alarm. Officially he treated Mrs. Elva Kay for a sinus problem. After thanking the girl for her kindness and expressing sincere regrets, I hung up and felt relieved that at least the man chose a convenient time to go. My stock on hand is high, and I know of two possibilities for future business. The clever little comedienne

Thelma Todd runs a restaurant in Malibu, a convenient police-protected front for bootleg liquor and prime dope. The only problem is her involvement with Dr. Dragna, the top *capo* who presumably wiped out Gregory. I prefer not to deal even indirectly with a killer, so it seems a better idea to get in touch with Norma Talmadge's doctor, an open secret like Norma herself, and ask him to take on my sinus problem!

April 27 • Dr. Spivak likes his patients to check in on the night before their peel for a brief examination. I followed the road to Lookout Mountain, then turned into a private driveway marked Chateau El Sereno, and arrived at an impressive mansion in the Victorian style. It reminded me sharply of the haunted house in *The Cat and the Canary*. A parking attendant took my Duisenberg, a nurse showed me to my room and took my blood pressure. After listening to my heart as well, she handed me a red and green capsule. I wanted to know what was in it, and she said, "Just a sleeping pill." It knocked me out for ten hours and I still felt groggy after breakfast, when she helped me into a smock and led me to Dr. Spivak's office in the basement.

We had only spoken on the phone, so I knew no more than to expect a foreigner. I found a tall, brisk, charming man with fair hair and dark penetrating eyes. He looked thirty-five but admitted to forty-eight. When I asked if he peeled himself, he only smiled. A native of Belgrade, he said, with royal blood in his veins, second cousin to the King of Yugoslavia. He studied biochemistry in Paris, developed his formula there and found himself trapped in a jungle of intrigue. One doctor employed a private detective to try and steal it, another claimed Spivak stole it from *him*. Hoping to escape this kind of thing, he came to California and submitted his formula to the American Medical Association. It refused him a license. When I asked why, Dr. Spivak explained it's dangerous to move ahead of the times, wherever you are. You find yourself trapped in a jungle of intrigue, wherever you are. Only last year, after he refused the House of Arden's partnership offer, they sent a spy. A woman booked herself in for a peel, pretended to swallow the sleeping pill, and tried to force the locked door of the Theatre with a hairpin during the night. Still in all, business was booming. He could mention many famous faces he'd peeled, but etiquette forbids. I asked about Agnes Ayres and he repeated, "Etiquette forbids."

In his spotlit Theatre, an enormous converted cellar without windows or mirrors, Dr. Spivak motioned me to a streamlined chair. It tipped back automatically when I sat down. He handed me a blue and yellow capsule, and I wanted to know what was in it. "Just a pain-killer," he said. Not that I would necessarily feel any pain at all, maybe a little discomfort, but he never took risks. One by one he switched out most of the lights, until the room beyond my chair almost vanished in darkness. The nurse came up and stood nearby, holding a batch of cotton swabs.

"At this point," Dr. Spivak said, "most patients like to say a mental goodbye to their faces, which they won't be seeing again for two weeks. And those with a religious turn of mind like to say a prayer as well." I said both, crossing my fingers. Then panic seized me, I had a vision of being confronted in the mirror by a creature more ravaged than Ruth Chatterton at the end of *Madame X*. But it was only temporary. A pleasant floating sensation took over, no doubt due to the speedy blue and yellow capsule. For a while it intensified, and I seemed to plunge through a trap door and into a tunnel of floating lights. In a strange way this felt perfectly agreeable.

Then Dr. Spivak opened a bottle of pale liquid that filled the room with a violent acid smell. I guessed it was the Phenol and wanted to know what was in it, but he revealed only that it derived from benzene, a versatile property found also in weed killer and dynamite. Training a spotlight on my face, he warned that even a drop of Phenol in the eye could cause near-blindness, so I must lie very still and relax. Luckily, wherever that capsule floated me, through more trap doors and down more glittering shafts, it always seemed to be in the direction of confidence. And Dr. Spivak provided another boost when he said that relaxation comes more easily if you hold the right thought. He suggested the right thought was Youth. The secret of it, and keeping the secret of it. I held the thought as he started to brush the liquid over my face with a cotton swab. Although my skin tingled and smarted, there was no real burning sensation. Just a mild impression of being bitten by a horde of mosquitos.

When he finished, the doctor told me not to speak for an hour, lit a cigarette and remarked that my face had turned white as a sheet. But this was normal. Shortly it would turn red as a live coal, also normal. The nurse came up with a spool of black ribbon and a white cotton scarf. "Mrs. Kay looks good and red to me," she said. The doctor put out his cigarette and they got to work. The ribbon turned out to be waterproof tape that held in the Phenol, and the scarf, when tied securely around my face, held up the tape. The remarkable capsule had now put me in a mellow mood. I no longer plunged or floated underground, but lay back on bright sumptuous pillows, listening contentedly as the doctor told me the tapes had to stay on for two days, until the Phenol completed its peel of the outer layer. The next thing I remember, I woke up in my room feeling most refreshed.

Getting out of bed to look in the mirror, I saw only a face in a white
cotton mask, with slits for eyes and mouth, that might have belonged to a
member of the Ku Klux Klan. A nurse entered carrying a tray with two tall
glasses and a pack of straws. Lunch. No chewing of solids for a week, she
said. The movement could cause deep rents in my skin, like cracks in a
wall after an earthquake. But consommé and milk would take care of the
protein level. Adding that patients may order cocktails at any time, she
handed me the bar list. It offered a wide selection of bootleg liquor at
prices to make even the Mafia blush, and I was glad to have packed my
own. There was a nice little pile of snow stashed away in a cold cream jar
as well. No way of sniffing it until the mask came off, but I wasn't fazed.
They'd doped me to the gills from the moment I entered the place, and at
such an early stage of the game it seemed imprudent to risk a sneeze.

Sipping my lunch, I leafed through Dr. Spivak's booklet of special instructions. He recommended patients to spend Day One in seclusion, or
at least not in conversation. Various aids to passing time alone, radios,
jigsaw puzzles, cards and dice, were available on request. The library also
provided newspapers and magazines. Although eager to find out what
had happened in the world since last night, I didn't feel up to appearing
in public yet, so ordered the *Examiner* sent up to my room. A victim of real
estate fraud, who jumped to his death from Suicide Bridge in Pasadena,
made the front page headlines. In an editorial, Mr. Hearst noted that two
stockholders in bankrupted corporations, and a writer of silent movie titles unable to find work since the talkies, have already thrown themselves
into the Arroyo Seco this year. He echoed the Chamber of Commerce's
complaint, four suicides in as many months represents a serious threat to
nearby property values. A high barbed wire fence must be built around
the area at once.

Turning to an interview with Clara Bow, who looks plump and frazzled
unless the *Examiner*'s camera lies, I read that she's suing her secretary for
libel. The creature sold the New York *Graphic* an inside account of Clara's
gambling mania and rambunctious love life. No details given of the latter,
but I received an advance tidbit on the usual grapevine last week. It seems
the It Girl invited each and every member of the University of Southern
California's football team to her Beverly Hills hacienda for a "tackle."
Gather ye rosebuds while ye may, Clara, but don't rock the boat! Things
have stayed quiet for so long that Mr. Hays nods peacefully over his
Code. At the climax of our Purple Age, it was predicted that Hollywood
would never recover from a certain "fatal shot," but fortunately Mr.
Zukor and his cohorts knew how to play their cards. Realizing it was
more important to save face than save money, they threw Fatty and Co. to

the winds, and found a little repentance goes a long way. The wings of screen romance were scarcely clipped, as immortal Valentino in *Son of the Sheik* soon proved to Vilma Banky in his tent. And these days the Divine One's affairs grow ever more tempestuous, while *Photoplay* predicts that Marlene Dietrich, a newcomer from sinful Berlin, will offer hot competition in *Morocco*. So in the end my "fatal shot" was just a personal bull's eye, hitting only the target in mind at the time, and I have nothing to reproach myself for.

My face began to itch violently, interrupting my reverie and obliging me to call a nurse. "Just the Phenol at work," she said, gave me another blue and yellow capsule, and I soon floated off on flashing lights. As dusk fell, I was aroused by a ghastly distant howl. Not human, but a coyote making my most unfavorite sound in the world. When the nurse arrived with my liquid supper, I complained that my face had turned ice-cold. "Just the Phenol at work," she said, and gave me a brace of sleeping pills.

April 28 • The next thing I remember clearly, two women in cotton masks sat rolling dice in the solarium. According to the custom here, we made ourselves known to each other only as Mrs. K, Mrs. B and Mrs. W, anonymous though we were already behind our masks. Eager for the next stage of treatment, Mrs. B and Mrs. W told of a trip to the Caribbean they planned to take soon. They expected their new faces to attract a crowd of Latin lovers, but struck me as too talkative for their own and the Phenol's good. The instruction booklet warns us not to speak much and refrain from smiling on Day Two.

Unsure whether my face itched or froze, I sometimes wished I knew how it looked.

April 29 • Although Dr. Spivak unmasked me today, I never saw my face, owing to the absence of mirrors in his Theatre. This was intentional, he explained. All patients look flushed, blotched and swollen after the peel and a glimpse of themselves might induce anxiety. The nurse handed him a large powder puff and he dusted me with particles that looked like bread crumbs. As my face was still moist, they clung. They also stung quite a bit, but when I wanted to know what was in them, the doctor reminded me of his watchword. Secrecy. I felt the powder building up and setting into a kind of layer crust, and surreptitiously licked the corners of my mouth. The first taste was metallic and distinctly poisonous, the second reminded me of eggnog pie.

Patients are encouraged to spend time in the open air on Day Three, so I took a walk in the sunlit grounds after leaving the Theatre. My face no longer itched or froze. Instead, I had the odd sensation it was no longer there. As the voice of Al Jolson drifted across from a portable radio, I saw two women playing croquet on the lawn. Another rode past on horseback. All faces were hidden by the same dark brownish crust.

May 6 • Miss H has livened up our dreary afternoons, when time seems hardest to kill between liquid lunch and the cocktail hour. Soon after her crust formed, she came into the game room and began playing the piano. Mrs. B and Mrs. W foxtrotted together, then one of them suggested we hold a regular tea dance until we were sprung. The tinkle of the ivories brought Dr. Spivak into the room. Mrs. B and Mrs. W jostled each other to get him for a partner, making it all too clear they have only one thing on their minds.

May 12 • At the end of an hour, after repeated applications of warm oil, my crust came loose and the nurses lifted it off. Dr. Spivak trained a spotlight on my face and handed me a mirror. I gazed into it for several minutes. No word passed my lips. Finally I heard the doctor ask if something was wrong, and explained I felt too moved to speak.

Apart from a suggestion of bloat around the eyes, which he promised would disappear in another day, I looked better than at thirty. Only the most tactful of furrows on the forehead and lines around the mouth, as if a magic glaze had passed gently and naturally over all. The steal of a lifetime for $3500!

May 13 • When Baby came home from work, she found me sitting on a sofa, listening to Bing Crosby's record of "Lazy Bones." I kept my face in a soft shadowy light. Throwing her arms around me, Baby hoped I felt rested. "I feel like a new woman," I said, then reached out nonchalantly to switch on another lamp.

When Baby gasped, I gave her a puzzled look.

"What is this?" she asked. "Why do I look at you now and suddenly feel six years old?" When I told her not to exaggerate, she ran her forefinger up and down my face. "I'm not exaggerating. I just can't believe what I see." I smiled faintly, and she accused me of holding something back. "When have I ever done that?" I said. She parted my hair gently above the ears, then moved it back from my temples. "No scars. And yet I could swear you've been under the knife."

I denied it. She searched again, and of course found nothing.

"I told you a rest would work wonders," I said.

"It's turned you into my big sister." Baby still looked suspicious. "For God's sake don't go for another rest, or you'll turn into my *little* sister."

I told her again not to exaggerate, and asked if she missed me. Everyone missed me, Baby said, Mr. Mayer most of all, and made her little joke that he was secretly in love with me. As usual I found the idea preposterous, and as usual she insisted I was Mr. Mayer's ideal type, a mother and a lady, sexy yet refined. She thought it a shame he was too respectable to get a divorce, although he might change his mind when he saw me now.

Baby Looks Back

Maybe I was joking about the divorce, but not about Mr. Mayer's hot pants. No old goat like some of your moguls, very buttoned up on the surface, shaking his head at cheap stuff and dirty talk, he had a terrific yen for real ladies. Or ladies he decided were real. If they didn't fit the bill, they never got that peculiar, subdued, ardent look. Joan Crawford *wanted* to be the most real lady of them all, but Mr. Mayer never saw it that way and came on strictly paternal, treating her like his favorite shopgirl. It drove her up the wall, especially after she married Douglas Fairbanks Jr. and felt like one of Hollywood's aristocrats. But when Mother walked into Mr. Mayer's office, she made a bigger effect than fire on Frankenstein's monster.

Sometimes he gave a dreamy contented sigh, sometimes a discreet woof. And sometimes he popped like a bottle of soda that had just been opened. A great actor, of course, with a cunning line in flattery, he probably put on a show with Mother at first, to disarm her before getting down to business. But later, when he had no ulterior motive, I watched the eyes of this glum powerful man blink and cloud with longing at the sight of her, I saw him turn awkwardly gallant, even felt he was shy. Then I used to imagine what a rewrite job the history of this town would meet if they ever got married, Mother playing Josephine to his Napoleon or maybe Mr. Mayer playing transformed Beast to her Beauty.

About the clinic. I knew there was more in Mother's face than met the eye. When I saw it, I truly felt like a genuine child again, for she had somehow lost fifteen years and looked younger than the day we got off the train from Chicago. After checking her for signs of a lift, I supposed one of those miracle creams or stimulators in her bathroom might have lived up to its billing, then doubted it and gave up. Her story about only needing a rest to turn the trick was ridiculous, but I pretended to believe it because our situation had changed again. In fact, it had reversed itself.

With an important secret of my own to keep, I was happy to let Mother keep hers.

At first I worried that my secret might start showing, but any two people who settle down together develop habits to cover a lot of tracks. So when Mother found me discontented for no reason or hard to figure out, she fell back on a useful ingrained attitude: it was my deep mind, one of my moods, the secret melancholy of the artist. And we covered even more tracks because we were both natural performers, with only a simple difference between us. They paid me to act. It paid Mother to act. I used to think of our life together as a show we took on the road, picking up the rest of the company as we went along: Theda, Sid Gordon, Mary Louise, Mr. Mayer, Geraldine de Vorak, Mother's long-lost father, all kinds of fantastic hams, straight men, character bits, standbys and role-players, onstage and behind the scenes.

My juvenile lead made a late entrance, although I met him a few times before I realized he was going to play the lead. Walking past the prop department at MGM one day, on my way to a costume fitting for *Treasure Island,* I heard someone playing jazz piano. When I looked through the open door I saw a boy in blackface at an old mahogany upright, surrounded by furniture from different periods, old beaded lampshades, statues, mirrors. Without looking up from the keys, he said, "I know you but you don't know me," introduced himself as Jimmy Gabriel, rounded off the piece he was playing and asked my opinion of it. "Pretty good," I said, and he told me, "Thanks, I'm the composer." Privately I doubted this, but was wrong, for I later discovered Jimmy Gabriel made a lot of improbable claims that turned out to be true. At that time, playing a bit part as a speakeasy entertainer in a flapper movie starring Joan Crawford, he was a genuine fifteen to my official twelve. The son of a vaudeville couple, born while a twister hit Kansas City and almost blew off the hospital roof, he grew up on the boards and made his debut turning somersaults at the age of three. His early triumphs included an act in which he escaped from a locked straitjacket, and a straw-hat and cane rendition of "I Wonder Who's Kissing Her Now," but the audience booed when he fouled up a mind-reading display. He learned to tap dance, roller skate, juggle, ride trick bicycle, play poker like a pro, imitate W.C. Fields, George M. Cohan and Sophie Tucker. All this he told me at our first meeting, which lasted barely five minutes, including an impersonation he threw in of Cohan singing "Hello Broadway." It was so good, I forgot he was in blackface.

Overdue at a costume fitting, I had to say a reluctant goodbye, and left Jimmy starting up a rag at the piano. While they adjusted my breeches and vest, I decided he was an extraordinary bundle of talent and energy, and would go far. But by the next time we met, on our way to different stages along a studio alley, he had gone nowhere much. In costume for a bit as an African native in a Lon Chaney movie set in the Congo, he wore dark tan makeup and a grass skirt. So I didn't even recognize him. "I guess I failed to make much of a first impression, which is unusual," he said. I explained the impression had been fairly deep but in blackface, so I never knew what he really looked like. "I still don't," I added. Jimmy was sorry that I missed him in a reform school picture, where he had a nice little part, epileptic but not racially disguised. Then he warned me that versatility could prove more of a problem than an asset. Casting directors liked Jimmy because there was no age, type or race he seemed unable to play, but this made it hard to establish a strong personal image. "I can see that," I said. "You certainly look as if you came straight from the jungle now." He launched into a hula dance, making deep drumbeat sounds and alarming contorted movements. Duty called once more, I wished him luck and continued down the alley. Caught up in his act and his tom-tom effects, he never even noticed my departure. But when I looked back to see an audience forming, I decided again that Jimmy Gabriel would go far.

I made two more pictures before meeting him again, in the meantime looking hopefully at any Indian rajah, Mexican colonel, Roman centurion or tonsured monk I happened to pass, but finding only strangers and extras. A while after my official fifteenth birthday I was walking back to the set from the MGM schoolroom. Secretly old enough to have finished school, I was trapped in my age racket and obliged to keep going until I reached an official sixteen. By the time Mr. Mayer signed me up, education laws were seriously enforced, and although I wanted to stay with Mrs. Root, he wouldn't have it. So I put in four annoying hours a day on the studio premises. It so happened, when Jimmy and I met again, that we were in the same movie without knowing it. Just a few days before my heartwarmer with Dressler was due to start shooting, the studio decided to include me in an all-star MGM revue, one of those movie variety shows for which Mr. Mayer rounded up his top contract players. Marion Davies did a wonderful Black Bottom, Buster Keaton did a plumber act, John Gilbert and Norma Shearer did Shakespeare, Joan Crawford led the Broadway Melody Girls parading fashions on skates. I had two sketches, one with Wallace Beery, one with Jack Benny, and in both was eighteen passing for twelve. Jimmy was engaged for a bit in the circus number with Grace Moore, glamorous soprano from the Metropolitan Opera, cast as a bareback rider who sang Puccini. At eighteen passing for fifty, he played a broken-down clown with white makeup and a false red nose. Not being on the lookout that day, I failed to recognize him yet again.

"You ought to know me anyway," he said. "Doesn't my personality shine through by now?"

"It does when I know who you are." For the first time I realized how short Jimmy Gabriel was, maybe the baggy pants accentuated it, or maybe after three years I expected him to have grown. "Don't be offended, but will you always be knee-high to Gary Cooper?" I asked. "Always," he said firmly. "It's part of my personality." The smallest bodies, he added, often harbored the greatest souls. I told him I saw no reason why not, then duty called both of us and we parted once more.

At the end of the day, two notes arrived in my dressingroom. The first, in an envelope with the MGM trademark, was a revised shooting schedule for the rest of the week. It placed me On Call. The second, in handwriting as large and careful as a child's, asked for a date on Saturday night. It ended, "I want you to see me as I really am." Although uncertain what Jimmy Gabriel had in mind, I determined to accept. All my previous dates had been publicity stuff arranged by the studio, this month's promising contract juvenile escorting me to a party or inviting me for doughnuts at Kitty's Come-On-Inn, favorite teashop rendezvous of the stars. Promising juveniles were always tight-assed with jealousy, wanting to know how much I earned. A date with Jimmy Gabriel promised something different, and was a matter of free choice, not of being placed On Call. When I read my publicity, it seemed that On Call was becoming the story of my life. *"Baby Jewel is one child star who doesn't long for an 'average' childhood. 'How can I miss what I never had?' she asks, and tells you the only thing she ever misses is the studio when she's between pictures."* Or: *"Baby Jewel has been in pictures so long, she can't imagine any other life. All she wants is to go on working hard, and become a truly great actress. If you tell her many people consider she's truly great already, she looks at you in astonishment."* Or: *"Baby's Mother, the vivacious Elva Kay, puts her finger on Baby's secret. The kid believes in everything she does, and that's why the public believes in it too."* I only protested once, when the MGM schoolteacher set us an English composition on the theme, If I Had One Wish. My composition was brief but pithy. *"Known to thousands but a stranger to myself, too busy living up to other people's wishes, I've never had time to find out what I personally wanted."* But after getting that note, I found I personally wanted a date with Jimmy Gabriel.

It had to be secret, because Mother always expected me to act fifteen, in public at least, and Mr. Mayer thought I *was* fifteen, so neither would approve Baby Jewel going out on the town with a bit player from vaudeville. But I felt sure that Mrs. Root, still my friend although no longer my teacher, would help an actress who needed to unwind on Saturday night. I called her up, explained the situation and asked her to invite me to a cozy supper, letting me know later what I had to eat.

She loved it. "Frankly I've been expecting a romantic development in your life, you always struck me as advanced for your age. I'll be thrilled to alibi for you, my dear."

I warned her not to get carried away. "There's no romantic development. I just need someone to relax with."

When I told Mother about Mrs. Root's invitation for Saturday night, she looked up from *Modern Screen* and wanted to know the guest list. "No other stars, just a few of Mrs. Root's favorite ex-pupils," I adlibbed. "You can forget about calling the reporters on this one." She studied the cover picture of Lupe Velez on her magazine. "It sounds like a good idea, Baby, you need to spend a little time with youngsters. But I wish you'd find an interesting hobby as well."

This was familiar advice, for Mother connived with the studio publicity department to invent hobbies for me: miniature golf, making hooked rugs, giving fudge parties. "I'm really disappointed that nothing seems to appeal. Other stars can't wait to relax and find ways to take their minds off the camera."

"Tell me how other stars do it. Maybe you'll come up with something that finally tempts me."

Mother looked hopeful and said, "Lupe Velez plays the ukulele. Joan Crawford drives up the coast on moonlit nights and watches the ocean lash the rocks. The Divine One goes shopping on Olvera Street for rare painted pigs." She glanced at my face and sighed. "You're hard to please, Baby." And then, after a pause: "Gloria Swanson retires to her perfumed elevator."

"None of this tempts me, even if any of it's true."

"You don't believe it?" She shook her head sadly. "Sometimes I just don't understand what goes on in your mind."

And sometimes Mother was like a boat that slipped its moorings and left reality behind. She invented my fudge parties and yet she believed in Swanson's perfumed elevator. According to Mrs. Root it was typical behavior, everyone out here tends to drift toward some imaginary sea. "We live in the City of Dreams, which has its risks, my dear, but it's only through dreams that we learn about our inmost selves."

"Great, as long as you know dreams from lies."

"Once again you see through to the heart of things."

Mrs. Root must have been waiting eagerly for the cab that brought me to her house on Saturday night. She opened the front door before I rang the bell, and confessed she felt like the nurse who set up Juliet's assignation with Romeo, although she naturally hoped my assignation with Jimmy Gabriel would turn out better. "We are not Romeo and Juliet," I insisted, warning her again not to get carried away. She only smiled, and complimented me on the stars in my eyes, which she couldn't have seen, for I was hiding most of my face under a hat with a downward brim. Then a horn tooted outside. I kissed her and thanked her for providing my alibi. "We had spaghetti with meat balls, cherry pie a la mode for dessert," she called out after me. "And later we played charades!"

I only recognized Jimmy Gabriel because I was expecting him. The first time I saw him as he really was, he stood on the sidewalk under a street lamp that hit him like a spotlight. Almost glaringly blue eyes looked out from a face that contradicted itself, endearing turned-up nose and aggressive turned-down mouth, reddish hair slickly parted in the center and an obstinate cowlick. He wore a pinstriped suit, a jaunty spotted necktie, and carried a cap. With a bow, he opened the door of his beat-up Dodge roadster. "Madam's faithful chauffeur awaits." The seats in those old automobiles were high off the ground, and when I looked down at Jimmy on the sidewalk, he seemed shorter than ever. He put on his cap at a rakish tilt and gazed into my eyes. "Am I or am I not dreambait?"

I told him I never judged by appearances, dreambaits being a dime a dozen out here, and asked where we going to eat. He knew a place that served the best enchiladas in town. I loathed Mexican food but was trained to smile when I felt like throwing up, and smiled again as we entered a dim cantina in some nowhere section of town built around a cut-rate drugstore, a small oilfield and a cemetery. The long dark room had a stuffed parrot beside the cash register, vases of bright paper flowers on the tables, and a loud strolling guitarist with a grin and a sombrero. We sat in a secluded booth at the back, near the kitchen with its fierce peppery smells. Jimmy offered to order for me, and I knew he wanted to, so I nodded and kept smiling while he asked for hot tamales, beans with special hot sauce, in fact the whole enchilada.

"Show people never come to this place," he said. "So if you take off that hat, we can both see each other as we really are at the same time." When I removed it, he thought he saw a faraway look in my eyes. "Just wondering if we can get something to drink," I explained. Jimmy snapped his fingers at a waiter and ordered two colas. Not at all what I had in mind, and it seemed the evening was starting so badly it could only improve. But not yet. The guitarist came up to our table flashing gold teeth, leaned over me and sang one of those mournful serenades called

Adios Chiquita or Que Noche Triste. I reached for my hat, but Jimmy said, "Relax, nobody here has any idea who you are. They don't even know Garbo from Beery, all they know is Lupe Velez, Dolores Del Rio and Spanish movies downtown."

The waiter arrived with two cola bottles and a wink. I took a polite sip and tasted rum in the cola, in fact more rum than cola, in fact a mighty Cuba Libre. The evening began to improve, and I even hoped that with enough liquor under my belt I could eat the whole enchilada without knowing it. Jimmy leaned across the table and asked, "What shall I call you? Do people really call you Jewel?"

I shook my head. "Almost everyone calls me Baby. But recently they had a meeting at the studio to decide what to call me in future. I'm the oldest Baby in the business and they realize it can't go on much longer."

"I've seen and heard a few cracks on that subject," Jimmy said.

"That's why they had the meeting. They want to stop the cracks but keep cashing in on Baby Jewel. Finally Mr. Mayer came up with an inspiration. In future I'll be known as 'Baby' Jewel." Jimmy looked puzzled. "Baby in Quotes," I explained. "If we do that, Mr. Mayer thinks we'll have it both ways. We admit I'm not really Baby Jewel anymore, passing for twelve makes you a juvenile, not a toddler, but we don't lose the name."

Anything to do with show business fascinated Jimmy. He listened very solemnly, drumming his fingers on the table, thinking it over. "They're sharp as tacks at Metro," was his verdict. "From now on I'm going to call you Baby in Quotes." We drank to that, then the hot stuff arrived and Jimmy served me professional advice along with it. He went into his wise old trouper act, eyes growing veiled with experience as if he'd seen it all, and I actually sniffed stale cigar smoke and greasepaint instead of tabasco in the air.

Too many toddler stars remained mental and emotional babies, he said. They grew up but never became real adults. Remember Baby Parsons, a has-been at ten, unable to make a comeback because she lost her kiddie appeal and never acquired any other kind? I remembered Baby Parsons, drained my Cuba Libre and asked for another. Then I got the lowdown on Baby Helen, who used to yodel in Alpine costume but had not been heard from in years, on Baby Peggy, who co-starred with a dog and lost her savings in the stock market crash just as she reached the awkward age, and on Baby Doris, who tried to stay infantile by wearing rompers and an Alice in Wonderland switch, but ended up in the chorus line of a burlesque show.

Then Jimmy pointed a reassuring finger and told me not to worry about *my* future in spite of everything. He promised I would never drift into the ranks of extras, stand-ins, second-row chorines, find myself slinging hash or pumping gas, even though I still peddled innocence at the dangerous age of fifteen. Well liquored up by now, I had to stop myself confessing my age was even more dangerous than he knew. I smiled and heard him explain how he never doubted *I* would become a real adult when he first saw me offscreen, in the doorway of the MGM prop department. There goes one Baby, he thought, who knows the score. "What score is that?" I asked, and he made a sweeping gesture. "The whole mysterious kit and caboodle called Life," he said.

According to Jimmy, it was all in my face. He watched my face and it was always running the gamut, from sunshine to sorrow, hope to despair, trust to suspicion, love to hate. I felt pleased but doubtful, nobody else had ever seen anything like that before. "Haven't *you* seen it in the mirror?" he asked, and I shook my head, then told him about the English composition in which I described myself as only a mirror for other people. He found this not a good attitude and ordered me to imagine I was driving a car, my hands on the wheel, the motor running, the brake released. I imagined it. "Now why doesn't that machine move, why doesn't it *go*, Baby in Quotes?" I suggested it could have been paralyzed by a secret invisible enemy ray. "No, what a crazy idea, it's in perfect shape. You've just got to make the right connection." But I made the wrong one, something about a hidden force locking the brake even though I released it. "What is all this secret hidden stuff in your mind? The right connection is between your foot and the gas pedal. Step on the gas and you can go anywhere you want, as fast as you like." He made another sweeping gesture and a sound like vroom.

I found his confidence truly amazing and supposed he was born with it. Jimmy agreed. Making his debut at the age of three, turning somersaults to a packed and rowdy audience, he felt no twinge of anxiety or nerves. He always knew he was good, and the sweet sound of applause confirmed it. After that first test you could lock him in a straitjacket, fling him around, teach him pratfalls, set him on a trick bicycle, and he felt supremely confident. The world might box him in or turn him upside down, but he was still free and right side up. Furthermore, although a screen part worthy of his talents had not yet come his way, he never doubted the big break lay just around the corner. "It's going to happen for me soon, like it happened for Gary Cooper. One good close-up is all it takes. And my kind lasts longer, by the way, than tall, dark and handsome." I remembered Mr. Griffith saying nerves were a sign of imagination, and asked Jimmy if he thought he lacked it. "No, *you* lack confidence," he said.

Like Mother, who was certainly loaded with imagination, Jimmy believed that if he wanted it, he would get it. This was one reason he impressed me. People with a will and a plan always did. Although I had a will and a plan, they were not my own but belonged to Mother, and although Jimmy insisted I had only to make the right connection and step on the gas, I doubted I would get far. The warning honk of a horn, and the rearview mirror would show me Mother at the wheel of her beige Duisenberg, catching up fast.

The musician came back to our table, his guitar throbbing, but Jimmy sprang to his feet and seized it. He seized the man's sombrero as well, and launched into his own version of Adios Chiquita-Que Noche Triste. As usual, when he put on an act, he vanished into it like magic. In spite of his reddish hair, freckles, blue eyes and natty suit, he convinced me he had crocodile tears, a drooping mustache and a gold tooth in his soul. The most greasily plaintive voice I ever heard serenaded me with the only Spanish words he knew, mainly the dishes on the menu, and the most energetic body I ever saw performed passionate flamenco stamps, a cakewalk, and finally a bolero in which he did the splits. Halfway through I began playing the coy señorita with an imaginary fan, at the end I tossed him a paper flower. Customers and staff crowded around to watch, and gave a long round of applause.

"The sweetest sound in the world," Jimmy said quietly. "Doesn't it lift you to the moon?"

It was my first experience with a live audience, I told him, so I wasn't sure. But I knew I never heard the same sound. The applause only set me down firmly on earth, where I saw everyone smiling at us, felt afraid of being recognized and reached for my hat. Then I remembered they wouldn't know Garbo from Beery and asked for another Cuba Libre.

"Baby in Quotes, you seem to be a heavy drinker."

"But always sober on the job."

It was hard to bring Jimmy down from the moon, but he had to take me home. Mother wanted me back by 10:30, and although she'd gone to the preview of *A Lady Surrenders*, she told Hattie to wait up and clock me in. Half a block from home, under one of the fanlike maple trees that graced our quiet exclusive street, as Mother liked to say, Jimmy stopped the roadster. He switched off the engine and the lights, and there was no one about, no sound except for the buzz of cicadas on exclusive front lawns. We listened to it for a while, then Jimmy said, "I always wanted a kid sister." It was not the role I saw myself playing, but I smiled and thanked him for a terrific evening. He suggested a repeat next Saturday night, and I thought it could be arranged. We said goodnight, shaking hands, and I walked up the street to my house, looking back once before I let myself in. Watching me from the sidewalk, under a street lamp again, Jimmy took off his cap and bowed.

Mrs. Root's spaghetti and charades turned out such a sensation, I told Mother next day, that she decided to make them a regular fixture, and I wanted to be part of the fixture. "Charades are my hobby now. Nothing else really takes my mind off the camera. I'm crazy about them." Mother hoped Mrs. Root's spaghetti would not be part of the fixture, it was much too fattening.

"Tell your dear Mother we ate extra lean Swiss steak," Mrs. Root said when Jimmy's horn tooted the following Saturday night. We drove toward the ocean and Jimmy told me he planned a surprise. "But you're not wearing that Mata Hari hat. Do you have any shades?" I shook my head, explaining I thought he only went to places where no one knew Garbo from Beery. "Not tonight," he said, pulled up outside a drugstore, ran inside and came back with a hideous green eye-shield, the kind gamblers wear. "All the shades had rhinestone frames. Not your style." I wondered if he imagined a green eye-shield was my style. "You can make it cute, Baby in Quotes. And I'll keep you company." He produced another from his pocket.

At Venice-by-the-Sea we had to park a couple of blocks from the ocean, beside a putrid canal with the remains of a half-sunken gondola. We walked toward the beach and I saw how much the place had changed since I played several great women of history there. The oil strike brought rows of derricks and a reek of sewage, many canals were dry or filled in; the private villas shuttered and derelict. Things looked better along the boardwalk at first, the strings of ornamental lights and the ferris wheel glittered as usual. Then I noticed almost every attraction was closed, no Temple of Birth, no Magic Lagoon, no Palace of Darkness and Light. A waffle parlor and a Mother's Root Beer stall, but nothing for the inner man. Still, at least my favorite pavilion survived. Although it looked straight out of the Arabian Nights, with blue onion-shaped domes, pink minarets, a long yellow arcade, it was really the MGM of bathhouses, with a salt-water pool known as the Cavernous Plunge. I told Jimmy I played Salome and Cleopatra with the bathhouse as background, then we approached the Venetian Gardens dance hall with its winged lion over the entrance, and I remembered we ran up flags and used it for Madame du Barry's private apartment at Versailles.

"It's changed since her day," Jimmy said, "as you'll see." At first I thought the surprise was to take me out dancing, then noticed a poster announcing a marathon contest. "A friend of mine entered it," Jimmy explained, "and I want to see how she's doing tonight." He told me to wear my eye-shield, and put on his own.

It was the 239th hour, or almost the end of the 10th day, and the orchestra played "Singing in the Rain." The grandstand was not very crowded, so we took seats a couple of rows away from the other spectators, close to the last remaining couples on the floor. Some wore smiles that looked painful, others seemed on their way to the grave. Jimmy pointed to a tall girl with a great figure, hair rippling down her shoulders, strange fierce eyes, bandaged ankles. "That's Marie," he said. Although not exactly dancing, Marie was at least on the move — "That's all they expect after a week," Jimmy said — but her partner's eyes were closed and his head slumped on her shoulder. She suddenly lifted her arm, clenched her fist and brought it down on his neck with a whack. He opened his eyes, raised his head groggily. She slapped him twice on the jaw and he managed to stay awake until the orchestra finished its number. A paunchy master of ceremonies, wearing a straw hat and holding a cigar, announced a fifteen-minute break. "Let's have a big round of applause for these kids," he said, and the spectators obliged as the couples staggered off to eat, get a massage, snatch some sleep or sniff ammonia to wake up.

"Who's Marie?" I asked. Jimmy told me he was one of the judges when they voted her Miss Half Moon Brand Orange of 1929. "Now she wants to get in pictures," he said, and I thought she'd certainly chosen the hard way.

When a few spectators began drifting off, the master of ceremonies ordered them sharply to stick around. "Two visiting celebrities will be visiting this contest very shortly," he announced. "You don't want to miss two ladies of the silver screen." Then canned music blared out through loudspeakers.

"Do you mind that I brought you here?" Jimmy asked. "I wanted to check on Marie, you see." I told him marathons were obviously part of the whole mysterious kit and caboodle, on which I felt glad to get a fresh angle. "You're right. It's crazy but it's Life, and you can't learn too much about Life." I wondered how much the surviving couple stood to win, and Jimmy thought $1000. "Not enough," I said, thinking of the agonized smiles, the bandages, the clouts on the head. I looked around at the spectators, mainly middle-aged women and kids. They ate popcorn, drank cola, hardly talked, and the blank concentration on their faces reminded me of a street crowd waiting for stars at a premiere.

Halfway through the next dance, a man wearing a red jersey began to hallucinate. Trying to break away from his partner, who held on desperately and knocked him around, he shouted something above the music. A nurse hurried up. He stared at her, then laughed and returned to normal, as they say. Marie's partner went to sleep on her shoulder, which she allowed for a while before giving him a couple of whacks. And another couple collapsed at the same moment, their knees gave way together as they tumbled to the floor in each other's arms. The nurse tried to revive them with handkerchiefs soaked in ammonia, but they only moaned, clawed weakly at each other's faces, then lay still. A doctor came up, listened to their heartbeats and signaled to a pair of male orderlies, who carried them away piled on the same stretcher. Everyone watched this with the same blank concentration. When the dance ended, the master of ceremonies assured us the couple was not dead, just dead tired.

Watching Marie drag her partner off the floor, Jimmy raised his eyeshield for a moment. "That girl's a real hard worker," I said, "I hope she wins." Jimmy remarked that it would solve a lot of problems, and I wanted him to explain this, but the emcee came back, waved his cigar and ordered a big hand for Thelma Todd and her friend Zasu Pitts. Waving and smiling, they took their places in special box seats, and the crowd seemed more enthusiastic about Zasu, probably because it had seen her play all those dumb maids and knew who she was. But the emcee seemed more enthusiastic about Thelma, probably because she was the pretty one. "I hear you and Zasu are going to make a comedy series together!" he called across, and Thelma called back, "Laurel and Hardy, watch out!" A Paramount starlet and a smart cookie, Thelma had just opened her Roadside Rest along the coast highway, figuring she needed something to fall back in on case she never made it, or never made Laurel and Hardy watch out. This was the only time I saw her in person. A year later I saw her in one of the first Marx Brothers movies, then in a two-reeler with Zasu, and not long after that on the front page of every newspaper. Another unsolved Hollywood murder, she slumped across the wheel of her car, wearing a nightgown and a mink coat. At the marathon she wore a keen little beret and a dress with a high-flounced collar, and laughed a lot with Zasu, who munched on a sandwich.

During the next dance, Marie began to wilt like her partner. For a while one of them came to and slugged the other, then she dropped to the floor on her knees in a praying position. Her partner stood over her, looking dazed, while she swayed back and forth. He tried to pull her up, but she broke away and began beating her head on the ground. As the orderlies carried her off on a stretcher, Jimmy leapt to his feet, told me to wait and hurried toward the dressingrooms. The emcee gave us all a breezy smile.

Only three couples were left on the floor now, at the 240th hour, at the end of the 10th day. One girl sagged badly, her head drooping almost level with her partner's crotch. He dragged her up by the armpits and slapped a bag of ice against the back of her neck. It seemed to do the trick. Thelma and Zasu were busy signing autographs.

"Marie's conscious but doesn't seem to know who she is anymore," Jimmy said when he came back. "The doctor's worried about brain damage and they're sending her to the hospital." I had never seen Jimmy anxious or frightened before, his face showed a childlike bewilderment, as if Life was not supposed to turn out that crazy. We left the ballroom and strolled along the boardwalk, not talking. Before we got in the car, I looked at the half-sunken gondola in the stagnant canal and guessed how Marie must be feeling.

"Let's get some chow," Jimmy said, and we stopped at a completely empty Chinese restaurant. I preferred Chinese to Mexican chow, but only just. He ordered shark-fin soup for both of us and apologized for giving me a rotten evening. I told him I found it educational, but he insisted it was rotten and felt sure I'd never want to go out with him again. "Stop it," I said. "The only rotten thing is Marie passing out when she got so close to the jackpot. I hope there's no brain damage and she gets in the movies anyway." Jimmy decided I was the most understanding person he ever met, but he looked curiously unhappy about it. Finally, speaking through a mouthful of chop suey so I wasn't sure I heard right at first, he said, "I've got another surprise for you this evening. Marie's my wife."

I asked him to repeat that. "She's my wife. We met at the Miss Half Moon Brand Orange contest, and I fell hard. She seemed to feel the same, so we tied the knot four months ago. But we soon realized we'd been too hasty. Neither of us was ready to settle down." I agreed that a trip to the altar at eighteen was asking for trouble, and wondered why Jimmy ever believed it could work out. "I believed I'd found the right girl," he said. "I'm impulsive and I do things in a hurry."

"So what are you planning to do now?"

"We were planning a divorce as soon as I could afford it." He looked bewildered again. "When I knelt down by the stretcher and asked Marie how she felt, she didn't know who *I* was either. Even though we're still married."

We drank some pale weak tea and asked for fortune cookies, but the place had run out of them. When Jimmy looked at his watch and thought it was time to drive me home, I detected a note of regret in his voice. Maybe he wished I was more than fifteen and more than a kid sister. Or maybe I just hoped he wished it. On the way back he told me some more about Marie. "She was always ambitious. She couldn't wait, like me. She had to be a star by her nineteenth birthday, or she'd do the Dutch act." I said I never heard of the Dutch act. "In Japan it's hara-kiri," Jimmy explained. "Marie had the act all worked out. She'd jump off Suicide Bridge in Pasadena, on New Year's Eve."

He stopped the car under the same maple tree, we listened to the cicadas and I thought how much of Jimmy's life was unknown to me. It made him romantic, once I was over the shock of discovering I'd gone out on two dates with a married man. He had fallen wildly in love and suffered, had seen his wife carried out from a dance marathon on a stretcher with her memory gone. I wanted to say I was as happy to share all this as to hear him talk about his built-in confidence, or to watch him impersonate a lousy Mexican singer. Most of all I wanted to ask how much Marie still meant to him, but instead I answered the question myself. If he cared how she was doing in that marathon, he cared.

So in the end I said nothing at all, except when he supposed I would never go out with him again, and I told him to pick me up as usual next Saturday night. He got out of the car, opened the door for me, wished me goodnight and shook hands. I walked up the street and looked back just before opening the front door. This time he was sitting in the roadster with his cap on, and as soon as he saw me turn the key in the lock, he drove quickly away.

Mother was enjoying one of her quiet evenings at home, getting her scrapbooks up to date, nostalgically skimming old interviews. She asked how the charades went. "They're really beginning to stretch my imagination," I assured her, took to my room and sat for a long while on my bed in the dark.

Next Saturday night I drank two gin fizzes before meeting Jimmy, which was just as well, for he chose a Greek restaurant in Hollywood where the food tasted greasy spoon with vine leaves, and they had no liquor in the cola. He told me he'd visited Marie in the hospital, she now knew who both of them were. She threatened to kill her partner if she ever saw him again, but the doctor put this down to exhaustion and frustration, and called it normal. One problem of marathon dancing, it turned out, was that you often decided you hated your partner after a few days, but had to stick with him. "It's one problem of the movies as well," I said. "I loathed the sneaky scene-stealing kid who played my brother in *The Bluebird*, but day after day I led that little bastard lovingly by the hand through the Land of Memory and the Kingdom of the Future." As Jimmy looked at me in surprise, and I realized I must have sounded like a tough Baby by any standards, some Greek in boots began folk-dancing on a long table. I waited for Jimmy to respond, take over and do a stomping peasant act, but nothing happened. "Marie's lost twelve pounds," he said, and I privately cursed her as an offscreen wet blanket. She had taken away the Jimmy I knew, and I wanted him back. On second thought, I just wanted him back any old how, but free of *her*.

"If you're not in a public mood," I said casually, "why don't we go somewhere private? Like your place?" Jimmy agreed he felt no urge to cut up or stay on the town, but warned me his place was not exactly Beverly Hills. "Who cares as long as it's private? I'm not in a public mood either, by the way," I said. We drove to an apartment house in the foothills. It reminded me of the Yucca Riviera, except it had three stories and no elevator, and Jimmy lived on the top floor. His livingroom overlooked the city and was directly in line with a silvery beacon light that flashed all night from the pylon above the Richfield tower. I remember its almost hypnotic effect, RICHFIELD, then darkness, then RICHFIELD again. The room had almost no furniture and only one table lamp, fairly dim, so it grew suddenly bright each time the neon winked, and the faces of show folk glinted from posters tacked on the walls, W.C. Fields, Buster Keaton, Chaplin, Fanny Brice, Al Jolson, and to my surprise Clara Bow in *Dangerous Curves*. "You like Clara?" I asked, and Jimmy said he liked her dangerous curves. Then I noticed a phonograph on the floor and suggested music. He put on a Paul Whiteman record of "I Wonder Who's Kissing Her Now." I remembered the song was one of Jimmy's big hits as a vaudeville kid and asked him to show me how he did it. At first he seemed reluctant, then opened a closet from which a pair of orange velvet short pants fell out. After rummaging around, he came up with a battered straw hat and a cane. He disappeared to the bedroom and returned wearing nothing but the velvet pants, which had suspenders attached. When he put on the hat, it was too small, and when he leaned on the cane, it was so short he almost fell over. But he managed a neat shuffle, then an intimate tap, and sang a verse.

At first, something was missing. It lacked the verve of his Cohan and his hula, his sobbing Mexican. When I gave him the sweet sound of applause, he shook his head. I thought Marie must be holding him back still, and cursed her privately again, but suddenly he threw away the hat and cane, said in a perfect Al Jolson voice, "Hey, Ma, listen to this, you ain't seen nothin' yet!", puffed out his bare chest, did a slow bump and grind and turned into Sophie Tucker. As the neon sign flashed on and off across the room, he seemed to grow a foot taller and a hundred pounds heavier in spite of the skimpy ridiculous short pants, and he vanished completely into his red hot momma act, belting loud enough to hurt my ears. Finally, he sank exhausted to the floor. I gave him more of the sweet sound, but he lay there without moving and apparently fell asleep.

Some situations you fall into like an old glove. I walked into the bedroom, which was in darkness but had the neon sign flashing across it, took off all my clothes and lay on the bed. After a while I called, "Jimmy?" I heard him groan, then saw him come to the doorway. At first he only stared at me. I asked if he could keep a secret. He continued to stare, frozen in the doorway. "Mother and I have kept this secret for years," I went on, "and now I'd like to unveil it to you. But only to *you*. Let's keep it strictly within these walls."

After a long silence and a longer stare, Jimmy offered to promise anything if I put on my clothes. No deal, I informed him, adding not to change out of those velvet pants either, which I found unusually provocative. He complained I was acting as crazy as Marie. "To hell with Marie," I said, which made him angry, which made me explain I didn't really mean it. "All I meant was, Marie's got nothing to do with it."

He laughed rather nervously. "You can say that again."

"Marie's got nothing to do with it."

Another silence, then a sigh, and he promised to keep my secret.

"Here it comes, Jimmy." The room flashed with neon. "I'm older than the world has been led to believe."

"It's not true!" he said, and then, "How much older?"

"I'm eighteen. Same as you." I gave him a quick history of the situation: Mother deciding to lie about my age when we first came to Hollywood, getting away with it because I looked so small and Babylike, sealing my fate when she convinced Sid Gordon I was only four, and he gave it out to the newspapers.

Jimmy asked in a low voice, "Why did you take off your clothes before telling me this?"

When I answered, I had the odd sensation of hearing someone else speak and wondering who wrote my dialogue, it really flowed. "I wanted to lay myself bare to you, Jimmy. And let you in."

He thought this over, walked slowly to the bed and sat on the edge of it. He started to take my hand, then changed his mind. "Baby in Quotes, I'm a married man."

"But you're planning to get divorced."

"When I can afford it."

"I'll give you the money tomorrow."

He laughed nervously again. "First you take off your clothes, then you offer to give me money. Since when does a girl behave like this?"

"Since Garbo, Jimmy."

"You've had all the answers so far." He took my hand very gently. "But I'm not in love with you. What do you say to that?"

"Give it time. It might happen. I wasn't in love with *you* until last week." I wondered again who threw me the lines and felt myself performing Jimmy's trick, vanishing into my own act. And when the neon flashed, I saw he was smiling.

"Why did it take you so long?"

"Maybe because, until last week, I only saw you so happy and cocksure I couldn't really get near you."

"You're growing on me," Jimmy said, "every time I look at you." But he got up suddenly and turned away. "Same old story, same old trap," he muttered to the air. "They always wait until I'm not feeling so good." I feared I was losing after almost winning, like Marie, then noticed him slip neatly out of those short pants. Turning back, he leaned over me, so sturdy and sinewy that he no longer seemed short. "Am I or am I not dreambait?"

"You are not tall, dark and handsome."

"What the hell has that got to do with it?"

"Nothing. It's personality that counts, and lasts longer."

"Never forget it." He leapt on the bed like a ballet dancer and stood looking down at me. "I'm working on my legs. Some critic wrote that Cohan had *sardonic* legs, and I'd kill to have some critic write the same about me." Then he lay beside me. "This is crazy."

"Maybe so, but it's Life."

"Maybe so." He laughed. "And maybe I'm not feeling so happy, but I sure am cocksure." He took my hand. "Feel it."

"Yes," I said, "I feel it," and then I felt the whole mysterious kit and caboodle as well, running the gamut from nerves to utopia. From the infallible way he handled the situation, I guessed Jimmy was not unused to virgins, and we vanished together into the same act, in a final flash of neon.

A few minutes after 10:30 he stopped the roadster under the maple tree. I wanted to relax and listen to the cicadas, but didn't want to stay out any later, because Mother was home. Jimmy looked around to make sure no one was on the street, then hugged me and kissed me a long goodnight. "We'll give it time," he said. "It may happen." I told him to pick me up as usual the following Saturday, walked to the house and looked back from the front door. Jimmy sat in the car, almost invisible under the tree, then winked his headlights before driving away.

Mother smiled as I came into the livingroom, and I had a moment of imaginary terror. "Baby, I'm getting a vibration. Whatever you played tonight, it wasn't charades!" Instead, she announced she was suffering from overwork and had booked herself into a clinic for two weeks of rest. Preoccupied with getting away from it all, she only noticed I seemed a bit distracted, put it down to the movie with old Dressler and correctly predicted I would cheer up when I found I had a hit on my hands. Going up to bed, I realized she was giving Jimmy and me the perfect opportunity to see each other more often and make it happen more quickly, and sat again for a long thoughtful while in the dark.

But things hardly turned out as I hoped. A few days later I started the Dressler picture and had to work overtime on the all-star revue, while Jimmy landed two bit parts, as an Indian scout and a Filipino butler in love with a blonde taxi dancer. He even canceled a date because Marie, who simply could not get over losing that marathon, and was depressed over her chances of stardom, called him up after she swallowed a bottle of sleeping pills. Privately I cursed her again, then said I was so relieved he got her to the stomach pump on time.

At least we talked a good deal on the phone, and one Saturday night, when neither of us wanted to leave that bed with the silvery neon flashing across it, I got home very late, and on the Sunday, because Hattie took the afternoon off, he came over to the house. Our Beverly Hills style made him stiff and uneasy, so I returned to the subject of paying for his divorce, feeling sure I could fix it with the Baby Jewel Company Inc., but he grew even stiffer and wouldn't hear of it. "Jimmy Gabriel doesn't play things that way." He loosened up after I made him a drink, then went into one of his most inspired acts after I put Mother's favorite record on the phonograph, Valentino singing "Pale Hands I Loved."

Stripping to the waist, he wound his shirt around his head like a turban, cracked an imaginary whip and ordered me to get down on my knees. "I'm not sure Baby Jewel plays things that way," I said, but he gave me such an excitingly brutal look that I groveled at his feet. When I begged him to spare me, his eyes smoldered and his chest heaved magnificently. "By Allah," he cried, "I'll make you remember this night!" He jabbed me with his foot, turned me over on my back and straddled me. While I cringed, begging him again to spare me, he sneered with triumph. Another crack of the imaginary whip knocked an end table over. He ordered me to undress, took off his pants, picked me up, flung me roughly down on an overstuffed sofa and stood over me, bulging with passion.

Then he looked across the room and gave a slow incredulous smile. Sitting up, I realized he'd caught sight of himself in a mirror. "This is getting out of hand, this is getting *too* crazy," he said. "What's happening to us?" He unwound the shirt from his head and let it drop to the floor. I stood beside him and saw our naked reflections, our clothes strewn all over the room, Jimmy's pants slung across one of those ornamental china elephants. "The movies are happening to us," he said. "We're living there. We're always trying out new parts and watching ourselves." He moved closer to the mirror, gazed into it, and I saw Jimmy try out another new part, world-famous star, idol of the crowd, slightly weary of success and adoration. "Our lives don't really belong to us. They belong to the public. It's the price we have to pay." He put an arm around my shoulder. "And yet, maybe we only find ourselves when we're playing a part. And maybe we play so many parts, we find too many selves. What a mystery. But we have to live with it."

The front doorbell rang and continued ringing while I dived into my clothes, and Jimmy disappeared with his shirt and pants behind a high-backed chair. Opening the door, I found a man with a pale, strict, businesslike face waiting outside. He wore a light raincoat, although the day was fine, and a derby hat. Maybe a private detective, I thought, or a child molester, or a bank teller, or a spy. "I am a Russellite," he announced. "What is that?" I asked, and he handed me a publication to explain it. I thanked him and closed the door, ignoring the bell when he rang it again. Jimmy sat back in a chair, his feet stretched out on a rest, his hair combed, generally spruced up, back to playing himself as far as I could tell. When I showed him the publication, he riffled through it and gave a whistle of disbelief. "These people are crazy, but it's not Life." The battle of Armageddon, he read, was drawing near. All over the world, governments in league with Satan had lined up the forces of evil. Our only chance of salvation was to refuse to fight or salute the flag, and prepare ourselves for the Second Coming when the battle ended.

The Russellites sobered up the rest of our afternoon. Jimmy became suddenly anxious and asked if I always answered the doorbell when I was alone in the house. I told him I did, although few people rang it. I could only remember a Boy Scout on a recruiting drive and some movie-struck tourists who thought Tom Mix lived here. "Promise me never to answer it again," Jimmy said. "You might open the door to a hold-up or a kidnaper next time. And if it's a kidnaper, it might be the Organization." A spasm of alarm crossed his face. "Now I think about it, I won't sleep tonight unless you promise." Touched and pleased by his protective attitude, I gave my promise and asked if he really believed there was so much danger around. If you avoided downtown, Los Angeles always struck me as peaceful as a summer's day.

"The air's the only thing in Los Angeles that's still clean," Jimmy said after an impressive pause. "You lead such a sheltered life, Baby in Quotes. There's a lot you don't know." Gangsters had moved in on almost everything out here, he told me, rum-running, dope-dealing, horse-racing, prostitution, the restaurant and kidnap business, even the movies. Theatre owners hired gangs to plant bombs in rival theatres that refused to increase prices. "I could go on, but I don't want to alarm you." He went on. "This town makes it so easy, because the protection's fantastic. Would you believe a gangster from New York or Chicago can move in here with his way paved?"

I shook my head and asked who paved the way. "A crooked attorney, a crooked bailbondsman, a crooked physician in case he gets stabbed or shot," Jimmy ticked them off on his fingers, "and two crooked officials, in the police department and city hall, he can bribe to get charges withdrawn." This sounded almost as fantastic as Armageddon and the Second Coming, but Jimmy assured me it came from the horse's mouth. When he played a bit in the reform school picture, he met a cop who was acting as special adviser on the story. They became friends and kept in touch. "We have dinner once in a while, and he really opens my eyes." Then he had to be going, gave me a long hug and told me to be very careful. "I never want to lose you," he said, and it seemed we were finding enough time and really making it happen after all.

The next Saturday, with Mother back from the clinic, I was back at Mrs. Root's when alibi hour struck. She opened the door with an expression on her face that reminded me of the time she announced the death of the ex-Barbary Coast Kidlet, and handed me a letter that someone had dropped through the mail slot ten minutes ago. Remembering Jimmy's warning about the danger all around me in this town, I expected a blackmail or kidnap threat, then recognized the large careful handwriting and felt a worse kind of fear. Mrs. Root watched me sit down in a chair, light a cigarette, open the envelope and read that Jimmy Gabriel had decided, when the chips were down, that he still loved his wife. And he felt responsible for Marie because she was going through such a bad time. He still loved his Baby in Quotes, of course, but in a different way. It sounded crazy but it was Life. At first he planned to keep our date and tell me in person, but at the last moment he felt a clean and definite break would be better. He asked me to forgive him, promised never to forget me, and thought I deserved someone who could give himself heart and soul. XXX Always.

"Read this, but don't say a word," I told Mrs. Root. I went out to the hallway, called a cab on the public phone, and came back to see tears in her round doleful eyes. She opened her mouth to speak, remembered my instructions and opened a box of dried fruit instead. I took a date. "The only date I'll get tonight, ha-ha," I said. She took a fig, we chewed in silence, and when the cab arrived I pocketed Jimmy's letter and kissed my old friend. "The charades are over now," I said. Then, as every girl in this situation is supposed to do, I went home to Mother.

On the drive back, for no reason I could fathom, an image of Jimmy turned up in my mind. He raised his eye-shield rather furtively as Marie dragged her partner off the dance floor at the Venetian Gardens. And I understood he was really hiding out that evening, unable to stay away from Marie but unwilling to admit it, and making sure she wouldn't recognize him. She didn't, of course, but not under the circumstances he expected. Then I began to wonder what role Jimmy was playing this night, the man who renounced his love in the cause of duty, and felt good, or the man who betrayed it under pressure, and felt bad. The cab stopped outside my house, and I wondered what role *I* was going to play with Mother.

As I paid the driver, he gave me a startled look. In the hallway I caught sight of myself in a mirror, like Jimmy at the climax of our Valentino scene, when he was smiling and naked except for a shirt wound like a turban around his head. This person in the mirror was crying, and at first I preferred not to know her. In the movies I looked particularly appealing when I cried, but now I looked ugly. Blotched and wretched, almost tacky. Then Mother appeared in the mirror behind me. I turned around, held out Jimmy's letter and told her to read it. While she did so, I tried to improve my face, watching Mother in the mirror as she turned the page. Her eyes had grown moist and bright, her face remained superbly calm. A classic beauty, I thought, how does she manage it, but forgot about my appearance, or playing any kind of part, as she came over and put her arms around me. She led me into the livingroom and sat me down beside her on a sofa. "Now tell me the rest, Baby," she said. "And don't leave anything out."

I gave her the works. Sympathetic and tender beyond belief, she reproached me for nothing, not even for deceiving her, not even for losing my virginity. "What a misleading phrase, by the way. When the circumstances are right, as they obviously were at first in your case, a girl gains far more than she loses." She patted my hand and headed for the bar. "As for the rest, I've been through the passion mill myself and sung those brushed-off blues. Let me make you a gin fizz." She rattled the cocktail shaker. "Just when we need it most, our famous woman's intuition leaves us in the lurch. We give our all, and let *them* take what they want when they want it." I asked if there was no way around this, and she shook her head. "It's a law of nature. We can't change it, we can only accept it. In the long run, keep hoping as we may, the male animal *never* makes us happy."

There was no bitterness, only a quiet yet rather thrilling conviction in her voice. I felt unable to imagine any man daring to try and prove Mother wrong. She went on to explain another law of human nature, that childhood was the only safe place. "It protects us from carnal heartbreak. As long as we stay there, we're touchingly untouched. A pity you didn't stay there longer, Baby, but at least you can still *act* touchingly untouched on the screen. You may have lost it down here, but they can't take it away from you up there."

Suggesting we concentrated on the brighter side of things, she handed me the *Express* and went to fetch a pill that would knock me out for ten hours. "You need all the rest you can get, and I'll give you another pill to make sure the sandman comes tomorrow night as well. The camera never lies, especially on Monday morning." I stared at a photograph of Baby Jewel wearing her best smile and an American Airways button in the lapel of her jacket. To publicize my election as Honorary Hostess of the Air for their new eleven-hour flight from Fort Worth to Cleveland, I read, American planned to hang my picture in every terminal along the way. "This is a first, Baby," Mother said as she came back, handed me a capsule and another gin fizz. "No airline in history has conferred such an honor before." I felt a tear roll down my cheek. She wiped it away with a perfumed handkerchief. "Everything dissolves in the mists of time." I hoped she was right. "Take it from me. And here's another sensational piece of news to chase the clouds away. Next Saturday night, you've got something much better than a date with Jimmy Gabriel. Marion and Mr. Hearst have invited us to a shindig at the beach!"

Elva's Diary

May 20 • After her dramatic confession of a secret affair, Baby retired to bed obviously braced by my good sense and compassion, a couple of gin fizzes and a knock-out pill just starting to work. For a few minutes I sat alone, torn between sadness at my daughter deceiving her Mother and astonishment at how neatly she covered her tracks. Couldn't have put up a better smoke screen myself! I was also torn between anger at Jimmy Gabriel for taking Baby over body and soul, and relief that he brushed her off before the scandal broke and Baby was headlined as the Clara Bow of child stars, launching a new Purple Age with a love nest in the Hollywood hills.

A glance into her bedroom revealed that my poor child had fallen asleep without switching off the light. There was no sign in her face that a secret affair had aged her by even a day. I had to resist the temptation to gather her up in my arms with a terrible joy, but left her to darkness instead, took off my clothes and lay down with the Velvetskin Patter. As it purred over my body, I thankèd our lucky stars that Baby could still pass for a stainless twelve.

All the same, as in the case of my wretched father, I felt obliged to double-lock the door on Mr. Jimmy Gabriel.

May 21 • As I arrived for my appointment with Mr. Mayer, the door of his office opened and Ramon Novarro came out, seemingly burdened with more than overweight. I reminded him of the day he taught Baby to Charleston, but he only kissed my hand and hurried away. The secretary asked me to wait while Mr. Mayer took a call, so I had time to leaf through *Film Daily* and learn that movie attendances showed no signs of falling off in spite of a deepening Depression. When the door opened again, Louis came out to welcome me. Clasping my hands, gazing deep into my eyes, he couldn't believe how young I looked. "It must be the way you live," he said, putting an arm lightly around my waist as he drew me inside. "But I wish Ramon knew how to live. Such a problem, such a problem with that boy." He sat behind his desk and frowned for a while. "I'd like to discuss it with you, Elva, but I'm afraid it's not fit for your ears."

I told Louis not to worry about my ears. "They've heard a bundle in their time. I won't faint if you tell me Ramon's as queer as a three peso bill."

He gave a blink of surprise. Then he said, "But his fans will, if they ever find out. Oh, Elva. Of course you're right and there's nothing I should be afraid to discuss with you. Ramon confides in me like a son. I understand why. The boy needs a father. He was never close to his real father, try to imagine such a thing. Maybe that's how the whole problem started. But what can I do?"

The extraordinary man got to his feet and re-enacted his scene with Ramon, imitating a Mexican accent in his unique fashion. It went like this. Louis spelled out the risks, moral and practical, of living outside the laws of God and man. Ramon saw the point but still wanted to live there. Louis reminded Ramon of his obligation to the studio that made him a great star. Ramon thought he fulfilled it by making great pictures. Louis informed him that his latest, *In Gay Madrid*, laid one big egg. Flashing with Latin pride and anger, Ramon told Louis to read all the reviews panning the script but praising *him*. Louis saw the point, but begged Ramon to stay out of trouble if he insisted on living dangerously.

"A difficult assignment, Louis, but I'm sure the boy does his best."

Humor is not the extraordinary man's strong point. His mouthed puckered, I foresaw tears, but he smacked the desk instead. "If it costs me thousands to bury a scandal, what's the good of his best?" He dropped to his knees in the middle of the office. "Ramon, I told him, you keep getting into trouble and costing me thousands. Right now I have no new picture for you. Retire to a monastery and find spiritual strength." He got up and straightened his eyeglasses. "Ramon promised to think it over. You must admit it's a nifty idea."

I ventured that Ramon in a monastery would make colorful publicity, but he shouldn't retire for too long. Also, he could kill two birds with one stone and lose some weight.

"You're right, Elva. Almost my very words." Mr. Mayer returned to his desk. "Now what did you want to see me about?"

Although Baby implored me on no account to tell her boss about Jimmy Gabriel, I found the strongest of reasons to break my promise. Knowing my man, I gave him a skillfully laundered version of the unhappy romance, aiming to touch his heart without overly disturbing his mind. "Louis," I began, "a young man who may or may not be talented, but has made no name for himself as yet, only played a few bit parts, began paying unwelcome attention to Baby a few weeks ago." A thunderous frown appeared on Mr. Mayer's brow and I went on quickly. "Nothing really happened, of course. Just hand-holding, and some light petting at the boy's insistence. Yet it was enough for Baby to develop a crush. Fifteen's a wholesome but impressionable age." Louis nodded, but the frown remained. "Then the poor child discovered her crush was married."

Louis sprang to his feet, but I hardly paused for breath. "Poor, innocent, romantic, bewildered Baby," I said. "She made a brave but painful decision, and gave him the brush-off. But how she cried, Louis. I never saw her cry like that before." The frown began to clear and I knew his heart was touched. "Now, of course, she needs your help."

"Anything. You know I'll do anything for that little girl."

"I know, Louis. And bless you for it. But let's keep it between our-selves. She must never suspect I came to you." He crossed his heart. "Here is what you and only you can do. She'll forget the brute more quickly if there's no chance of running into him at the studio again."

As Louis sat down slowly, he looked pokerfaced. It was a sign I knew well, it meant his deepest feelings were involved. "As you spoke, Elva, I heard my own thoughts." He asked for Jimmy Gabriel's name, wrote it down on a slip of paper which he placed under his blotter. "Such scum will never work at my studio again. And I'll make him one unlucky boy. He'll find himself a leper, an Ishmael, in other places too."

I felt sorry about this, for I meant no long-lasting harm, only planned to keep Gabriel out of Baby's way for a while. "No need to ruin the boy," I said, but Louis shook his head. "He almost ruined your child." He clasped my hands again. "I'll fix him for life. You'll see. Every girl should be so lucky to have a Mother like you," he went on, as he led me admir-ingly toward the door. "And a studio like mine, of course. We take good care of our family here. Family," he repeated. "Never forget we're a fam-ily that looks after its own."

"Louis," I said, "I like to feel I'm a part of it. In my modest way."

Baby Looks Back

This cloak-and-dagger episode was another secret Mother carried to the grave. Mr. Mayer as well, I suppose. It doesn't make me laugh, like Mother committing murder, but doesn't make me angry, because of the way things turned out.

The first week of no Jimmy was the worst, especially Saturday night with Hearst and Marion. Far from having the effect Mother predicted, it gave me a terrible longing for other Saturday nights. But then I never shared her feeling that the gates of Pickfair and San Simeon opened on somewhere close to paradise. Pickfair was too much iced tea and high society talk, although Mary seemed gracious as they come and Doug put on a flashy acrobatic show, leaping over a grand piano and running up a tree. San Simeon was a sleepless night in a canopied bed because of the ruckus outside from WR's private zoo. No problem with the camels, bears, ostriches or giraffes, but the apes howled and the lions roared from midnight to dawn. And Hearst, although friendly, never got it through his head that I was more than six years old. I told him my earliest movie memories were of *Patria*, his serial about Mexicans and Japs trying to take over the good old USA, which should have dated me and provided a happy topic. But it only led WR into a long diatribe against Woodrow Wilson, who denounced the serial as racist which hurt it at the box office.

Sweetly devoted to her solemn tycoon, much prettier and funnier than in her movies, Marion won me over for life on that visit with her opening remark to Mother. "When B-baby g-grows up, d-don't ever let her b-be kept, like me. It's tough enough b-being an actress without b-being a f-fallen woman as well!" The industry's moral bodyguard, Will H. Hays, came up as she said this, but gave no sign that he heard. He kissed Marion and me, shook hands heartily with WR, and stood under a pair of old church bells mounted on a wall bracket, watching us all with his crocodile grin so fixed you felt sure he woke up with it in the morning. "If WR made Marion a fallen woman," I asked Mother later, "how come Mr. Hays keeps smiling at them? I thought he wanted to clean all that up." Mother explained you could never clean up a man as rich as Mr. Hearst, who paid his dues anyway with editorials approving every speech Mr. Hays made and calling him a boon to the industry.

Some people described the beach palace as more informal than San Simeon, which only proved that some people found it cozier to eat dinner in a gold-leafed room under a raft of imported chandeliers than in a duplicate of part of Westminster Abbey. At San Simeon you could play a pinball machine with a medieval tapestry hanging on the wall behind it, but at the beach palace you could walk through a Regency ballroom to a veranda that overlooked a marble swimming pool with a Venetian bridge, and the Pacific Ocean as backdrop. On Saturday night Mother and I stood there among all kinds of famous and beautiful strangers, while the band played a Charleston and moonlight glittered on the surf. She whispered that we were living in the Mecca of the world, then noticed a small, graceful, white haired man who drew an admiring crowd as he pantomimed a juggling act with imaginary rubber balls. "Baby, look at Charlie Chaplin!" That's not Charlie, I said, he always had dark hair, but Mother told me it turned white after his second child bride divorced him and won a $600,000 settlement. Now he had to dye it for pictures. She joined in the applause and bravos, then took me by the hand and boldly introduced me. "I'm sure you're a fan," she said.

Mr. Chaplin looked me over, told me he saw *The Bluebird* and liked me very much, but expected to like me even more in my comedy with Dressler. "Very smart of Mayer to let you do that. I was afraid he'd make you weep for ever." Mother said she could kiss him, because she'd told me exactly the same thing herself. "But I weep in the end," I warned Mr. Chaplin. "So does old Dressler. You wait." Mr. Chaplin laughed, and I believe might have asked me to dance. But his date for the evening, also jailbait, took him off to the floor. Mother looked ecstatic. "You made a real hit. I bet you ten dollars he comes after you later." I stared at her. "But *suppose . . .?*" I said quietly. She put her arms around me and whispered, "An all-time great, unlike Jimmy Gabriel, would get you somewhere. Let's have no more digs at old Dressler, by the way."

As the moon grew very silver in the sky, a titled houseguest at Pickfair, the Duke of Jamaica or some such, partnered Mother on the dance floor. WR and Marion, who wore a gold satin gown with Ziegfeld feathers as silver as the moon, found me wallflowering the scene. Pegging me at eleven or twelve this time, WR asked if I wanted lemonade, but Marion handed me her glass of champagne. "M-maybe you're a b-bubbly B-Baby!" she said. When WR looked disapproving, she did a tremendous high kick and ordered him to shake a l-leg. They joined the dancers and started to Charleston, WR like the oldest beginner in the class, Marion giving it her all as if she were on stage at the Follies, and both of them happy enough to make me sad. How lucky to be a case of Until Death Do Us Part, I thought, instead of a case of Until Life Do Us Part, like Jimmy and me. I walked by myself across the Venetian bridge and back again, sipping Marion's champagne. Then I wandered to the library, found a picture postcard of Mussolini and wrote a note to Mother on the back. *I'm going home with a headache but stay and get somewhere.* Dodging Louella Parsons with a gleam in her eye, I escaped to the hallway and asked a footman to give Mother the note and call me a cab.

In the movies, faced with playing a scene that made no sense, I never worried about motivation, as they call it these days, but learned my lines and took direction, and very often that scene got singled out for praise. So when the cabdriver asked, "Where to?", I picked up the cue with a real horseshit line, knowing only that somebody had written it and I was supposed to say it. I gave Jimmy's address. The cab drew up outside his apartment house, and although I still had no idea what the scene was about, I paid the driver off and walked up two flights of stairs. Marie opened the door and told me Jimmy was out. Jimmy opened the door and told me Marie was out. Nobody answered. If Jimmy was out, I had a losing situation on my hands. If Marie was out, I had a winner, locking eyes with Jimmy as he realized we were made for each other after all. If nobody answered, nobody was home, or possibly I heard tremendous love-sounds beyond the door, but in either case I ran blindly downstairs, tripped and fell on my head, then woke up in a hospital to find Jimmy in tears at my bedside, begging me to live.

I rang the bell and nobody answered. I rang it again, and was about to give up when a middle-aged man in woolen pajamas opened the door, his eyes blinking sleepily behind steel-rimmed glasses. It seemed the studio ordered a rewrite, but no one handed me the new pages. "I'm looking for Jimmy Gabriel," I said, coming up with a line to cover the situation. The man told me Gabriel moved out a week ago and left no forwarding address. His news dried me up completely. "It's the way the world goes," the man said, then gave it as his opinion that people out here constantly moved away and left no trace, maybe they wanted to disappear, maybe they were in a hurry, or maybe just forgetful. In any case they were certainly moving away most of the time.

It was the start of a long monologue about people moving away, all the different places they came from, everything changing from one week to the next. I couldn't stop it or walk out on it, the man's eyes were no longer sleepy behind their glasses and took on a fierce crazed loneliness. While he blathered on, I looked over his shoulder into the livingroom. It had changed so much, there was nothing to miss. It had moved away and left no trace. This room was full of furniture in Mission style, but empty of posters, and window blinds shut out the flashing neon sign.

When the man finally paused for breath, I wished him goodnight and hurried downstairs. He called out after me that he'd forgotten an important reason why people kept moving away out here. "They're always changing jobs, along with everything else," I heard, then his voice faded. By the time I reached the lobby, I was so confused by all this change in the air that I lost my sense of direction, mistaking the door to the janitor's closet for the exit. I even seemed to lose my sense of Jimmy, who began merging with the thousands moving away and leaving no forwarding address.

Walking down the narrow foothill street, I looked out for a cab but passed only a couple of deer who fled at the sight of me. At Franklin Avenue I passed only a line of trucks with labels for Half Moon Brand oranges on their doors, another of life's charming ironies. I walked on toward the Hollywood Hotel, finding it a change to walk in this town, and noticing more changes. I made a point of passing the Yucca Riviera, and at first it was no longer there, then I saw it had been repainted adobe pink and renamed The Apache Arms. The Boulevard looked like Mother's street of dreams at last, movie theatres, glittering signs for stores, banks, more hotels, and an all-night café in the shape of a huge owl blinking light from its yellow glass eyes. As I headed for the hotel to call a cab, a few passers-by stared at me, not because they recognized Baby Jewel; they wondered why I was so dressed up. The hotel had changed as well, it was no longer fashionable and only a hick would stand outside waiting to catch a star.

No Dusenberg in the garage when I arrived home, and the house was silent. My bedroom faced west, toward the ocean, and I leaned out the window, imagining the party still in progress at the beach palace. With a glass of champagne in her hand, Mother apologized to Charlie Chaplin for my headache and promised I'd be dreaming of him tonight. She informed Louella of my latest hobby and pumped her for the latest dirt, she talked to anyone who would listen about the grosses of my latest picture, about her latest real estate deal, and her latest mystic. Then I heard cicadas buzzing on exclusive front lawns and found my sense of Jimmy again. But he had moved away a little, and I thanked God that someone rewrote the scene where I rode back to the apartment house on a cloud of romantic fable. At least it turned out less MGM than anything in *my* script.

But a few weeks later, when we came to the last scene of my heart-warmer, and I had to explain about my brother going blind, old Dressler mugged and hammed so much that I was obliged to get even, pulling out every stop to make a super-MGM climax. I wept so sincerely the crew applauded, and afterwards I realized Jimmy had moved further away. He was another studio ghost, he joined my grandfather walking out of the stage and my life, and Geraldine de Vorak lost in the rain. One day I passed the prop department and saw Jimmy in blackface playing jazz piano, even though the piano wasn't there. And then I saw his photograph at the head of Louella's column, and read her tip-off that the top brass at Fox, mightily impressed by a test he made, had signed him to a contract and were grooming him for stardom. Mr. Fox himself described the young Jimmy Gabriel as a wholesome versatile gee-whiz kid, an all-American adolescent, a new kind of hero for our time, and predicted the public would go wild. So Mother and Mr. Mayer, like mice and men, found even their best-laid plans subject to change.

Right before Jimmy's first big hit opened, Marie claimed he deserted her and filed suit for divorce. By then he was dating a flock of starlets, but the day after his divorce became final he married a model he met at a party. "I'm impulsive, I always do things in a hurry," he told Louella. "Gabriel is definitely on his way," Mother told me, "but I don't think he's going to handle success as well as you."

Six months or so after our first date, we were officially introduced in front of news cameras at a premiere. "I'm so glad to meet you at last," I said. "I've heard so much about you." And Jimmy felt so excited to meet me at last, he simply had to kiss me. "Baby Jewel!" he exclaimed. "When I think of all the beautiful moments you've given me, what can I say?" He kissed me again. "I only hope I never disappoint you."

1940-1941

Elva's Diary

November 5 • Arriving a few minutes early at the Brown Derby, I asked for the Countess di Frasso's table, followed the maître d' to a secluded booth and scanned the lunchtime crowd. It was less all-star than usual, only Gable and Lombard still the most romantic lovers in town after more than a year of matrimony, and Jimmy Gabriel, a long way from anyone's idea of the all-American adolescent these days, with his fourth wife.

Half an hour late, looking as if she'd just got out of bed, which was likely, for Dorothy's dawn never breaks before noon, the Countess sauntered in. She's dynamic even put together as casually as a garage sale. Wearing a sailor hat, satin blouse, old tweed skirt and beaded moccasins, her eyebrows plucked beyond the call of duty, she waved to the Gables, winked at a handsome waiter, kissed me, ordered a double martini and launched into an account of her recent visit to the di Frasso estate outside Rome. Guards with machine guns surrounded her taxi at the gates, the Italian government having commandeered the place in her absence — for Hermann Goering, who was paying a call on Il Duce. While the Nazi bigwig gave banquets followed by rumors of orgies at her fabled villa, Dorothy had to sleep in the stables, but luckily she'd converted a loft into servants' quarters the previous year, so was not obliged to bunk down in a manger.

"Was there nothing Count Carlo could do?" I asked, and Dorothy said there was never anything the Count could do, except pick up his monthly allowance and avoid her. As she reminded me yet again, their marriage of convenience was now inconvenience all the way. Dorothy wed the Count for his title, and the Count wed Dorothy for her millions, but as a certified

Countess since 1923, she felt she'd paid her dues. "I'll divorce the old fox if I ever catch up with him again. A title's not like an insurance policy, Elva, it doesn't run out, so I've got nothing to lose." She also reminded me yet again that she's not as rich as people imagine, the $12,000,000 she inherited from her father shrank in the Depression like denim at the laundry. "You're probably worth ten times more than me, Elva. You certainly look it. No one I know wears so many diamonds for lunch."

I presumed Il Duce never called the stables to give Dorothy a hello, let alone apologize, and she shook her head. Seems that relations between the Countess and Mussolini cooled last year, after she brought him a crackpot inventor who claimed he could revolutionize the art of war with a new high explosive. Il Duce ordered a demonstration near the slopes of Mount Vesuvius, but it turned out hardly more impressive than a show of damp firecrackers, and he made Dorothy foot the bill. "Benito's always been tight as Kelsey's nuts." It's not the Depression that shrinks her millions, I thought, but her crazy schemes, the soya bean plantation, the company she floated to bring dog-racing to Italy. "How are conditions in Europe?" I asked, and she passed on a hot tip from a blackshirt guard at the villa whom she lured into the hay. "The Luftwaffe's bombing Britain to its knees, Elva, and Churchill's under pressure to sue for peace." Although miffed with Il Duce and Herr Goering, she seemed eager to believe it, and I didn't tell her that Mr. Hearst, who blames the British for starting the war and feels they deserve to lose, planted the same chestnut in the *Examiner* a month ago.

Politics still strike me as mundane, but they grow increasingly difficult to ignore these days. My own view of the unfortunate temporary situation in Europe is conservative enough, even if Dorothy and WR find it too radical for their tastes. Of course I agree that we Americans must stay out of the conflict, for with the Depression lingering on, our transatlantic cousins can hardly expect us to come to their rescue yet again. But while my two dear pro-German friends dismiss stories about concentration camps as parlor pink propaganda, and see Russia as the real enemy, I believe Britain deserves to win the match *on points*. Like most thinking moviegoers, I compare the different ways of life depicted in *Confessions of a Nazi Spy* and *Goodbye Mr. Chips*, or *The Mortal Storm* and *Lloyds of London*, and cannot doubt the British way is better.

Luckily the war clouds threatening to hover above our conversation were swept away by a fascinating stranger. As the maître d' escorted two men to a nearby booth, my head was literally turned by the younger of the pair. He had a touch of diamond-in-the-rough newcomer John

Garfield, half beautiful, half ugly, and all stallion. Dressed in a fine cashmere suit and gripping a Panama hat with both hands, he walked like a
sneak thief on the prowl. Although his face seemed familiar, I was unable
to place it at first. Then the older man reached under the Panama hat just
before they both sat down, and I caught a gleam of metal as a pair of
handcuffs slipped off. The younger one snapped his fingers at a waiter,
and in a flash as quick as the pocketed bracelets, I knew him for
Hollywood's star gangster, the *capo* nicknamed Bugsy.

Columnists label Mr. Siegel the glamor boy of Murder Inc., or in a less
friendly mood the man from Kosher Nostra, but Dorothy has always
called him the most exciting love of her life, high praise from the lady who
snatched Gary Cooper on the rebound from fiery Lupe Velez. As soon as
their romance hit the headlines, I longed to meet Mr. Siegel, but he
ditched her before I even met Dorothy. An invitation to San Simeon always raised hopes that Baby and I would run into Dorothy and her lover
there, but we only ran into Dorothy, for although Mr. Hearst encouraged
his news hounds to give plenty of space to Gentleman Ben (it boosted
circulation), he and Marion never played weekend host to famous unmarried couples. On principle.

According to the newspapers our star gangster was locked up in jail
right now, awaiting trial for the murder of a rival hood known as Big
Greenie, so it stumped me to see him drop in for lunch at the Brown
Derby. Sitting with her back to the action, Dorothy missed it all and was
reminiscing anyway about another colorful ex-lover, the prizefighter for
whom she threw a grand Hollywood party. She installed a boxing ring in
her home so he could entertain guests by sparring with a fellow pugilist,
but the night ended in a drunken free-for-all and left her with only a sharp
left hook to remember him by. When she finished this typical saga, I
advised Dorothy to take a gander over her shoulder. "Benjy!" she cried,
and rushed to give him a hug. They whispered together, Mr. Siegel
glanced in my direction, and she beckoned me over.

After introducing his lunch companion as Deputy Sheriff Pascoe of the
police department, the glamor boy of Murder Inc. fixed me with the most
welcoming of smiles and blue eyes. In a ruggedly appealing Brooklyn
accent he admired my diamonds. "Heavy sugar, I bet you got that one
from Flatow's," he said, laying a finger on the spray above my heart. He
was right. Then he admired my person, insisting I looked more like Baby
Jewel's sister than her mother, a compliment I never doubted was sincere.
In all modesty and truth it turns up at least once a month, and Mr. Siegel
impressed me as a man who spoke his mind, not cheap flattery. When

Dorothy called me the undisputed queen of real estate in this town, as legendary in my way as Baby, his eyes flashed and he smiled even more hospitably. "I bet they take one look at you and pay the asking price," he said. I feared all this attention might put Dorothy's nose out of joint, but my eternally adventurous friend was giving all *her* attention to Pascoe, a solidly willing Randolph Scott type.

"She's my dream, the kid I always wished I grew up with," Mr. Siegel said, getting back to the subject of Baby. "The only other movie star ever made me wish the same thing was Jean Harlow. In a different way, naturally. But why hasn't Baby made a picture this year?" I explained we were taking a breather and mulling various offers since deciding not to renew our contract with MGM. Surprising me with his inside knowledge of the business, Mr. Siegel wanted to know if our problem was scripts or salary or loan-outs or options. It was Mr. Mayer, I told him, the brute no longer seemed to understand or even care about Baby's best interests. Mr. Siegel heard the same thing happened, in a different way, to Jean Harlow. He knew for a fact Mr. Mayer could change overnight from Santa Claus to Simon Legree, and believed power had twisted his mind. Then he said we had to call each other Elva and Ben, and drank to Baby's next hit plus a load of mud in old Louie's eye.

Gangsters love the movies as much as the movies love gangsters, I thought, remembering the time Mr. Al Capone was so delighted with *Scarface* that he threw a party for the director and gave him a beautifully inscribed submachine gun. It seemed almost telepathic when Ben confided that his best friend in the New York speakeasy days was another kid from Brooklyn called Georgie Ranft. "He hit Hollywood, dropped his N as in Neat, now he's the smoothest tough guy on the screen. And when *I* moved out here, Georgie had the red carpet waiting. That's how I met my favorite Countess." Dorothy took time off from Pascoe to blow a grateful kiss, and then Gentleman Ben got back on the subject of Baby again. His favorite among her pictures was *Girl on the Wing*. She really touched him on the raw playing the teenager who died in a plane crash but came back to earth as an angel and straightened out so many tangled lives. "Believe me, I don't usually go for that kind of crapola," he added, hoping I would forgive the frank expression. I told him I'd forgiven franker, and he switched to his other dream, regretting he never met Jean Harlow before she died. "But I met her mother a few weeks *after* Jean died, and wait till you hear this." Seems that Mrs. Bello was sitting alone in the house when Jean strolled past out of nowhere, wearing her favorite white sweater, slacks and sneakers. "Hi, Mom," she said, then vanished into the garden. "So maybe," Ben said, his blue eyes fastened on my face, "the whole business ain't exactly crapola after all."

I agreed we must never rule out the Unknown, and met his gaze directly, remembering how Dorothy told me on the phone only yesterday that nobody as sensitive as Ben could be a trigger man. "The press keeps calling him a hoodlum, but it's a wicked smear. The only criminal charges Benjy ever faced in his life, until Big Greenie, were peddling heroin and carrying a concealed weapon. Why don't they write about his *other side*?" Ben longed to improve himself, she went on, he valued refinement and even asked her to fix up his mansion out here in the same style as her Roman villa. "I hope you see his place one day, Elva, then you'll appreciate his love of the spiritual. Sixteen rooms full of the best that money can buy."

And maybe that ain't exactly crapola, I thought, Benjamin Siegel knows heavy sugar from Flatow's when he sees it, wears the best cashmere, admires Baby, respects the supernatural, and now his eyes gleamed with boyish pride as Dorothy began to rake over old times, telling Pascoe how the boy uncovered a mural in one of her Roman cowbarns. On a tour of the di Frasso estate, Ben complained of a noxious smell in the air, ordered her to clean the barn out and convert it to a game room with pinball and jackpot machines. After carting away a few tons of vintage manure, the workmen exposed a fresco in almost perfect condition on one wall. Dorothy called in an expert who identified it as *Virgin Ascending to Heaven* by Raphael. "Never heard of the guy before," Ben said. "But it was some painting, and the Countess insured it for three hundred grand. How's that for beginner's luck?"

Over asparagus, broiled lobster and several bottles of Dorothy's favorite vino, they started down memory lane and she grew misty-eyed. Ben told how the Countess met a sailor in a waterfront dive who convinced her that pirate gold, to the tune of $1,000,000, lay buried on an uninhabited island in the Caribbean. She chartered a yacht, stocked it with champagne, caviar and a crew, invited a few friends aboard, and set off with Ben for a treasure hunt. Although they dug up the isle for three weeks, they found not a single doubloon. On the voyage home the steward pulled a gun on Dorothy and tried to hold her for ransom on the high seas, but Ben dealt with him, then some of the crew stole Dorothy's champagne and tried to mutiny, but Ben dealt with them as well. "I adored every moment," Dorothy said. "It was okay but we had nothing to show for it," Ben said. Next time around, he steered the Countess to a more likely proposition, and she invested a few thousand smackers in a gambling ship outside the international limit. When an elegant crowd arrived in water taxis on opening night, Ben saw the good times coming, but a freak storm broke, waves poured over the side of the ship, drenched and seasick guests were trapped under falling roulette machines, and he began to wonder if Dorothy brought him bad luck. "I adored every moment," she said. "It was okay but we had nothing to show for it," he said. Their lives sounded daffier than a screwball comedy. Maybe, I reflected, *My Man Godfrey* and *Bringing Up Baby* were no less typical than *Dark Victory* of the world we live in today.

Over coffee and cognac, and a cigar for Ben, his favorite Countess grew even more misty-eyed. "You always gave a girl the time of her life," she said, and Pascoe offered his handkerchief. I felt Ben's hand rest lightly on mine, looked up and received an emphatic but mysterious wink. As I wondered if he meant to convey that life with Dorothy was fun but too crazy to last, his knee pressed not at all lightly against mine under the table, and I realized he meant to convey something quite different.

Struggling to conceal inner turmoil, I heard Pascoe announce it was time to leave. Ben took a wad of dollar bills from his pocket and sent his companion off to settle the check. And while Dorothy smiled at him through a haze of vino and memories, he leaned back with a kind of lazy insolence, rubbing his foot up and down my legs. I avoided his eyes but not his furtive caresses, which he even kept up as Pascoe returned to slip the bracelets discreetly over his wrists. Then, holding his hat as before, he said, "It's been real, Elva," got up and kissed Dorothy on the cheek. "I adored every moment," she said, and waved them both goodbye with the Deputy Sheriff's handkerchief.

All that remained of Ben was his cigar, less than half smoked, lying in an ashtray between us. As I gazed at it, Dorothy picked it up with a sigh and relit it. "I always loved to do this," she said, and ordered another cognac. I retired to the ladies' room, locked the door and gave myself a quick fix, hoping it would bring me back to reality. After the first dizzy rush to the brain, I suppose it did, if reality was the fact that a young street Apollo had sent out tango signals. I told myself a woman of fifty had no right to think and feel that way, then looked in the mirror and told myself a woman of fifty had no right to cover the tracks of age so well. And thanked Fate for introducing me to Ben only a week after my annual "booster" peel!

But the upward rush subsided, producing my usual attack of cold shivers, and my face turned ghastly pale. Closing my eyes, I seemed to plunge down a chute of despair, all the way to rock bottom, where I hit the dismals and collapsed on a stool. Then came a fierce struggle against panic, which as usual I won, summoning the presence of the Mighty I Am. As I willed the Master to my rescue I heard a strong reassuring crackle and felt the warmth of his Violet Flame. Leaping all over me, it cleansed and burned. The Master's voice spoke to me above the roar. "When it's all in the mind, put it *out* of the mind," he ordered, prompting me to remember that our dismals are always the work of an Inner Secret Service abroad in the world, a conspiracy to sap our natural energy and power. "Blast!" I heard. "Blast and fight with everything you've got!"

Someone knocked impatiently at the door. "Just a minute," I called, and stood up to look in the mirror again. Calm and confident, if slightly breathless, my familiar self looked back. Another close call, I thought, wondering why the Inner Secret Service kept after me this way, then remembered the Master despised negative thinking, and rubbed a little rouge on my cheeks.

"Admit you found Benjy a knockout," Dorothy said, still puffing on his cigar as I returned to the booth.

There was a welcome drop of cognac left in my snifter, and I drained it. "Jimmy Cagney plays gangsters in the movies," I remarked with a smile, "and many people find he makes them more fascinating than in real life. But Ben Siegel in real life is even more fascinating than Cagney in the movies!"

Although this was intended as a compliment, Dorothy seemed to take it as an insult. "I don't see why you have to bring gangsters into it, Elva."

"I don't see how I can keep them out of it. The boy's no killer, of course, you can tell that at once, but you must admit he carries private enterprise beyond the usual limits."

Dorothy sighed. "I suppose he's a bit naughty sometimes. He shouldn't be running a labor union racket. Or a call girl ring."

"I didn't mean to criticize. I've always secretly admired gangsters because they're so honest. They make no bones about breaking the law when it's not on their side."

"Now that's very true, Elva. I wish the world wasn't so prejudiced, and saw Benjy through your eyes."

Feeling my way cautiously, for I realized Dorothy was sensitive about any attempt to impose a criminal image on her favorite ex-lover, I confessed my pleasure and surprise at meeting Ben in the Brown Derby when he was supposed to be in jail. "And in such good spirits, too, for a man with a murder rap pinned on him. I longed to ask how he managed."

"You were right not to," Dorothy said. "It's bad taste to talk shop when a man has to go back to the pokey after lunch. A man in that situation needs to take his mind off his problems."

"But we can talk a little shop now he's locked up again. Ben must have very good friends in the police department."

"You bet your ass, Elva. He's got very good friends everywhere. And Pascoe's a real sweetheart, by the way. He's going to let me send Benjy a case of champagne." Her eyes grew misty again. "Imagine what the poor boy's going through, knowing he never harmed a hair of Big Greenie's head."

Not for the first time I was struck by her forgiving heart. Dorothy lives for her men, they exploit her and then ditch her, yet she bears no grudge and goes on living for them all the same. The only time I heard her make an unforgiving remark was when she called Gary Cooper a son of a bitch because he never invited her to his wedding. But she still sent a gift.

November 7 • Stirred to my depths at a matinee of *A Free Soul*, on citywide reissue this week. Had to hold on to my seat when Norma Shearer, refined yet passionate in a filmy evening gown sans underwear, goes to visit devil-may-care racketeer Clark Gable. "A new kind of man, a new kind of world!" she murmurs as she yields to him on a white couch. In a vortex of emotion I recalled the impact of Desmond Taylor on my innocent youth, then yesterday's impact of Gentleman Ben on my full bloom, and wondered if the secret pattern of my life, romantically speaking, spelled D-A-N-G-E-R.

November 12 • Or maybe D-I-S-A-S-T-E-R.

A photo of Ben on the *Examiner's* front page today, and a scoop story of his life of ease behind bars, the work of one of WR's eternally burrowing news hounds. Seems that our star gangster paid out $30,000 for a month of special privileges. Lobster and pheasant dinners and champagne delivered to his cell, permission to employ a fellow inmate as valet, and to have a barber shave him every day. Permission to visit his Beverly Hills dentist almost every other day, then drop in after "bridgework" at the Brown Derby or his other favorite lunchtime haunt, Lindy's Boulevard Café. But according to the dental assistant at the County Jail, who's clearly not one of Ben's good friends, the prisoner boasts a perfect set of teeth. WR's news hound predicts a major shake-up at the jail, hints of corruption at the highest level. Meanwhile Ben is confined to basic rations in his cell, and Dorothy's latest heartthrob, Deputy Sheriff Pascoe, has been transferred for duty to some Siberian suburb.

And now, for yours truly, comes the sidewinder. The *Examiner* landed its scoop as follows: *Only two days after Ben played passionate footsie with me at the Brown Derby, the news hound spied him lunching at Lindy's,* SNUGGLED IN A BACKROOM BOOTH WITH ACTRESS-PLAYGIRL WENDY BARRIE. This former Paramount Protégée of 1935, dropped by the studio and now grinding out quickies wherever she can, keeps her name in the gossip columns by getting the likes of Ty Power and Rudy Vallee to escort her to parties, and almost getting the likes of dimestore heir Woolworth Dona-hue to escort her to the hitching post. She obviously grabs any man and headline that comes her way, but Gentleman Ben has proved no slouch at coming her way and letting her grab him. An old kind of man and an old kind of world, I thought grimly, threw the paper with Ben's photo in the wastebasket and wrote him off as a two-timer who sent out tango signals just for the heck of it.

Then I summoned the Violet Flame for a good cleansing and burning, heard the Master's voice warn me that animal habits sap our finer ener-gies, and advise me to concentrate on business in future. I gave him my solemn promise and thought of Baby about to return from Hawaii. She faces important decisions about her career, which makes it no time for her Mother to get caught in the passion mill again.

November 13 • Too excited, or ashamed, or both, to continue this wild saga until today. The Flame had hardly finished crackling when the phone rang, and Dorothy invited me to lunch at Lindy's because she felt sure Ben would be there! One of her temporary lapses of memory after a bender, I decided, but she went on: "I know there's been a spot of trouble at the jail, but don't underestimate that boy. Benjy never takes a spot of trouble lying down."

Another vortex of emotion. I refused to go, then agreed, ran upstairs, opened my clothes closet, remembered Norma in *A Free Soul*, picked out a twin set in silver-gray rayon and dispensed with underwear. As I entered Lindy's, a pair of small, intense, bloodshot eyes fastened on my outfit. They belonged to W.C. Fields, who was lunching with Jimmy Gabriel, whose fourth wife has just left him. He muttered and raised his glass in my direction while we waited for Ben. "I checked with the Brown Derby and he's not expected," Dorothy said. "So he's bound to come in here today."

An hour passed with no sign of him. Dorothy ordered another bottle of vino, then a phone, and called the county jail. They confirmed Ben was inside, but refused to put her through. "Everyone's turning against the boy," she complained. "Except you and me." She reached for my hand.

"You're a good person, Elva. I bet you never did anything low or mean in your life. I felt it the moment Mary introduced us at Pickfair."

This time I had to blame the bottle for Dorothy's lapse of memory. "Marion introduced us at San Simeon," I said.

"I really don't believe so. But it doesn't matter." She was still holding my hand. "I'm trying to explain why Benjy needs a woman like you."

I was stunned, and at first could find nothing to say. Then I decided to adopt the light approach. "But he's well and truly locked in the hoosegow, Dorothy, and goes on trial next month for rubbing out Big Greenie. I just don't see what I can do for him."

"You're made for each other. And don't worry about that silly trial. He'll leave the courtroom a free man."

I was stunned again, then disbelieving. "I certainly hope so, but how can you tell?"

"Benjy's lawyer slipped me the word. He's a real sweetheart and he's got plenty of friends in this town. They'll dismiss the case for lack of evidence."

"But what about Ben's bodyguard? Haven't they persuaded him to sing?"

"They've persuaded him to fall out of a hotel window, Elva. Just last week. So you see, that lawyer wasn't fooling." Then she sighed. "But it won't be easy for Benjy when he gets out. He's been badly hurt by the press and he'll find a lot of cold shoulders in this town. It makes him reckless and angry when he's not appreciated, so I want *you* to appreciate him and help him make good." She sighed again. "Or watch his step, anyway."

"I don't know what to tell you."

"Tell me you'll do it. You're still looking damn good, you've got the money and the figure to go out and get yourself a man. What's stopping you? Don't you want one? And hasn't Benjy got something to offer *you* as well?"

"Honestly, the idea never occurred to me," I said, heard a strange echo of Mary Louise urging me to go to that fatal party, and wondered again about the secret pattern of my life. When Desmond took me over body and soul, he certainly freed me from the mundane here and now, showing me nights outside time and tuning me into some magical station of the air. Although the Queen Bee success arrived by the time he departed, I never felt the same freedom and magic again. In all these years the nearest I've come to it is an occasional embrace from the Unknown, the perfumed twilight of the Mighty I Am tabernacle and the Master releasing his ecstatic power. But when Benjamin Siegel played footsie under the table, I tuned in loud and clear to that old station, and felt something even more crackling than the Violet Flame.

"Anyway," I went on, "Wendy Barrie seems to be more his type."

Dorothy shook her head. "Quickie time, whether it's the movies or the sack. Benjy likes to boff class, he thinks something rubs off even if it's only for one night." As usual, her language acquired a dash of color when she was really on the sauce. "So along comes a Mayfair accent telling him her godfather wrote *Peter Pan,* and it works like a dose of Spanish fly."

"I've got no Mayfair accent and no famous godfather."

"But you sound closer to Boston than Boston. You could send a dozen Wendy Barries packing, Elva. Wherever it comes from, you just naturally drip with tone."

"Well, thank you. You make me feel right up there with Barbara Hutton, who won't hire a maid unless she speaks French." To cover my deep emotion, I was still playing it light. Dorothy knows what she's talking about, I thought, she mingles with bluebloods from Park Avenue to Capri.

"I married tone but I don't naturally drip with it," Dorothy said. "That's my problem. And I don't have quite your figure, either." She reached for my hand again. "Now promise me you'll take Benjy on. You're the only woman I know who fits the bill and can foot it too."

I stared at her. "But he's got fingers in quite a few underworld pies. Don't tell me they're not full of plums."

"Underworld's an exaggeration, Elva, almost as bad as gangster. Benjy just crosses to the shady side of the street now and then."

"Well, don't tell me there's no money on the shady side of the street."

"There's plenty, but Benjy's a big spender. And a high roller as well. It stops him getting ahead the way he should." She lowered her voice. "Having to support a wife and two kids back East doesn't help the poor boy any, either."

I was stunned again. Even the light approach failed me. "I never knew Gentleman Ben was a married man," I said.

"It's his one guilty secret. He feels deeply ashamed. But you mustn't blame him. Blame his wailing wall momma, always pushing marriage and matzo balls to make him settle down."

"Obviously Mrs. Siegel didn't know her boy," I said, and ordered a cognac.

Dorothy ordered the waiter to bring her a cognac as well, then begged me again to take Benjy on and bring out his *other side.* I tried but failed to interest her in black coffee. "Promise me you'll do it," she said.

"I promise you this, Dorothy. In my book you'll always be a living saint. The way you go on living for a man, after he's stopped living for you, it's just nothing less than saintly."

"A few boffs from Benjy and you'll start feeling saintly yourself. Now come on, Elva. *Those hot pants are waiting for you.*"

The waiter served our cognacs and another lapse of memory loomed over the horizon. "Never ordered this, handsome, but I'll order *you* any time." I tried but failed again to interest her in black coffee, saw the tip of her tongue begin to hang out Pekingese-style, and feared I would soon be losing her completely. "Loved you the first moment I set eyes on you in Grauman's Chinese," she said. "At the preem of that horrible picture."

"We met at San Simeon. What horrible picture are you talking about?"

"*The Women.* Two hours with a pack of silly rich bitches, nothing but sex on their minds, don't tell me you ever saw creatures like that in your life. And don't tell me you forget what happened when we came out of the theatre. Newsboys shouting war, war, war in Europe, up and down the Boulevard!" As the waiter passed our table, she gave him a wink. "But we went dancing at the Grove all the same," she said.

"Yes. And now it's time to go home."

Dorothy shook her head, ordered the phone and wanted me to call Ben at the county jail. "Tell him you'll be waiting when he gets out." Luckily another lapse of memory occurred when the waiter brought the phone. "Never asked for this, handsome. Try me with something else." I had a cunning idea, and whispered to the young man to help the Countess to her feet. It worked. She clamped an arm around his waist and gazed into his eyes. While everyone watched, I followed them across the restaurant at a discreet distance. Then Dorothy slid to the floor and lay with a contented moan across the waiter's feet.

Somehow it was less embarrassing than I feared. Strange, at difficult moments, how the mind wanders unexpectedly. Mine wandered to Norma in *A Free Soul*.

Baby Looks Back

Sitting on the beach in front of the Royal Hawaiian Hotel to watch the sunset, I heard a bellboy page me to take a long distance call. Across the Pacific a man's voice said, "Let me tell you about your Mother and the Countess di Frasso today," then described the scene. "Just a minute, do I know you?" I asked, but he only laughed. "Your Mother's fantastic, a knockout figure and the greatest deadpan technique since Buster Keaton. She might have been pouring tea for Eleanor Roosevelt instead of watching di Frasso on the floor of Lindy's Boulevard Café, batting her false eyelashes at a waiter.''

"Ah. Now I know you.''

Jimmy Gabriel laughed again. "Your Mother could walk off the Hindenburg as if it never crash-landed. Now when do you get back?''

"I'm sailing on the *Lurline* tomorrow. Unless I change my plans.''

"Get on that boat. I've got something very important to talk to you about. By the way, are you all right?''

"I'll be interested to hear your impression,'' I said, and hung up in case Jimmy Gabriel started to tell me what he wanted to talk about. I wasn't ready for anything more important than a banana daiquiri. Although I wrote on a postcard to Mother that I planned to stay on the islands until I died, I was sure of catching the boat home in the morning. Ten years after my first date with Jimmy, I still needed to learn his lesson properly. Making the connection between my foot and the gas pedal, I knew how to drive off on my own by now, but not how to stop myself getting carried back in reverse after a while. It seemed inevitable, given what Mother called the secret pattern in our lives.

This pattern was clear and symmetrical, like a mirror-image. Either she needed me or I needed her, search the world for two people more dependent on each other at all the crucial moments. We were the moon and the earth, two traveling companions on a circuit of the sun. And no way to go back on the deal. Mother drew up the papers while I lay in her womb, and I signed them on board the train from Chicago to Hollywood, letting her play the fondest of devils to my moppet Faust. She swore the biggest jackpot in the world was waiting for us, and we hit it.

"How long do you think you'll be gone?'' she asked when I told her I planned to leave for Honolulu as soon as my final MGM option expired. "It depends,'' I said. "If I really like it, I'll stay on and retire.'' She shook her head. "Unheard of, Baby, for a daughter to retire before her Mother.'' This was a switch from the usual applesauce about a star never abandoning her public, but not even Mother could try that on when the public was abandoning *me*. I suggested instant retirement for both of us, God knows we could afford it, and she gripped my arms fiercely. "Must you always think about money? Think about Life, which is Energy, which is a Flame we're *obligated* to keep burning, which is a law of nature!''

"There's nothing to think about,'' I said after thinking for a while. "If it's a law of nature, we can't fight it.''

"You were always quick on the mental draw. Now answer this. If *I've* got twenty years of top Energy left to burn, how many more does that leave *you*?"

After thinking again for a while, I found something to think about, and accused Mother of loading the dice by growing younger while I grew older. She denied it. "If anyone's loading the dice, Baby, it's you. The way you *look* now is only the way you *feel* now. You could start growing younger tomorrow if you put your mind to it." Then she prophesied I would soon snap out of my negative mood, and come back from Hawaii with a change of heart.

But I felt my heart had already changed. One night in the small hours it woke me up, beating too fast, and I listened to it. My heart's desire was for the day when no one who looked at me could possibly mistake me for "Baby" Jewel. And I found an amazingly simple solution, which was to gain more than fifteen pounds and wear glasses with heavy tortoise shell frames. The weight I could have taken off, but not the glasses, not for most of the time, because I grew seriously farsighted. Quite suddenly, as I remember it, while reading a script Mr. Mayer sent me, the pages blurred and I was unable to make out a line. "It's no good, I can't see the damn thing, so what can I tell you?" I asked, and at first he thought I was playing games. "No, I can't even see *you* clearly anymore," I insisted, "unless you keep your distance. When you come near, you go out of focus, like the script." Mr. Mayer looked alarmed and sent me to an optometrist that same afternoon. My tests confirmed the problem, anything in the distance clear as daylight, anything under my nose a puzzle.

At the Royal Hawaiian, nobody mistook me for anybody except the kind of person who stayed there. Like all really exclusive hotels, it sheltered its guests from the outside world, and in the outside world we even had our own private enclosed beach, roped off like a block of the best seats at a premiere. I still never cared to go near the ocean since falling into it during my Kid Sherlock days, but outside the Royal Hawaiian I sat with my back to it and usually forgot it was there. Most days the surf was light and I seldom heard a wave break. But I did hear plenty of roped-off conversation among the upper crust guests, talking endlessly of golf and polo and safaris in Kenya, never of movies, which seemed to play no part in their lives. They even ordered afternoon tea on the terrace, a scene I accused myself of imagining until I took off my glasses and saw it clearly. And when I drove up to an extinct crater full of banyan trees and looked across a misty silent rain forest, walked through a pineapple grove that drugged me with perfume, saw the moon like an outsized pearl in the sky or peered into Crystal Falls Cave and thought of Martian palaces, the islands turned into a dream of perpetual escape. The air drew no breath of change and I saw hardly a sign of real time in a real world, even though Pearl Harbor was only a year and a few miles away.

So here you see the deeply adorable "Baby" Jewel gone heavy and weird in a muumuu and eyeglasses, idling around her tropical fool's paradise, and if you want to know the reason, so do I. Even a memory as sharp as mine has its blurred edges. Forty years later I'm looking back on an impression of myself, not the exact person I was. And memory plays tricks with time, unhappiness seems longer and happiness shorter, or vice versa, depending on your state of mind when you retrace the past. For what it's worth, memory suggests I was trying out a new role at that time, playing unlovely and unloved as if hoping to erase an eternity of beloved loveliness on the screen. This eternity in fact lasted around fifteen years, from my first Kid Sherlock hit to my final MGM turkey, which made Mr. Mayer realize that with or without quotes I was "Nobody's Baby" anymore. For half of that time, getting paid and loved for singing the same old song up there, I lived mainly in the present. Then, thanks to Jimmy Gabriel, I began to wonder when the future would arrive, and if there wasn't some way of hurrying it up. It would help, I used to think, to find out who I was going to be before the movies gave up on me as a has-been.

By the mid thirties I was in my early twenties, but around sixteen on camera, a public teenager who was no kind of child and yet no kind of adult either. Eternally bright-eyed on the threshold of life, I peddled my little piece of blue sky. Mrs. Root once laid a book on my desk and said, "Far less truly spiritual than Marie Corelli, my dear, but required reading in schools, so better look it over." When I came to the part about the pure in heart being blessed because they saw God, I knew the Bible was not for me. "Show me someone not so pure, who's been around but still sees God, and we'll talk," I said, and Mrs. Root congratulated me on seeing through to the heart of things again. But Mr. Mayer believed firmly in the pure in heart, on the screen at least, and put me in movies that grew increasingly purer. I reached the same Mr. and Mrs. America who smiled a deepening Depression away when Judge Hardy advised his son Andy never to make a promise he wasn't prepared to keep, and never to run away, because things would always catch up with him. I made them believe in happy endings as surely as Shirley Temple when she marched into the White House, sat on Lincoln's desk dangling her cute little pantalets, and persuaded Uncle Abe to release her Confederate father from a

Yankee jail. But while millions sat in the dark feeling closer to each other, and less frustrated, as they watched our cheerful bloated images, I just sat in the dark feeling nothing at all, except a twinge of frustration at feeling nothing at all.

To give you an idea: *Footlights,* one of my blockbusters, set me up as a small-town girl determined to make it as a Broadway star. Her family disapproves, so she runs away to New York, raising money for the trip by holding out a tin mug and pretending to be blind. A few adventures and hard times later, she auditions for the ingenue lead in a Broadway play. A total hush falls over the theatre, she thinks it's disaster, but it's really because people sniff genius in the air. If you know anything about old movies, you know this is where her real troubles begin. Her father turns up, tries to drag her back to Gloversville, and when she refuses, tells her never to come home again ever. The Barrymore-type leading man puts the make on her. The jealous leading lady, in love with the Barrymore type, almost succeeds in getting her fired. If you're still with me, you know that sincerity and cuteness see her through.

To give you another idea: we're still in *Footlights* but nearing the end, thank God. At the party after my opening night triumph, the Barrymore type proposes a toast to my talent, and says he'd be honored to play Hamlet to my Ophelia. Applause and tears, especially (how did you guess?) from my proud parents, up from Gloversville after a last-minute change of heart. The famous actor and reformed human being takes me aside and apologizes for putting the make on me. On camera his lips brush my cheek with chaste professional admiration. Offscreen we've been lovers for a month.

The Barrymore type was played by Warren William, who got the part because studios thought of him then as a new Barrymore, which they needed on account of the old one taking to drink. The first time I saw Warren, his tall lean figure and strong bony face with its proud nose reminded me more of Mr. Griffith. He had the same air of keeping his distance, although in a different way, not solemn but suave, not judging but skeptical and secretly amused. He wore double-breasted suits and black snapbrim hats with terrific style. He even looked elegant and relaxed in a toga, lusting discreetly after Claudette Colbert in *Cleopatra.* But he could never play hero. When they cast him as Sam Spade in an early version of *The Maltese Falcon* no one believed it, least of all Warren, who didn't believe in heroes. He went back to playing polished con artists and classy lechers so perfectly that he failed to become a star. It was impossible to trust him up there, and you've got to trust a star.

I began not trusting Warren personally when we shot the scene in which he invited me up to his apartment for a champagne supper. At the end of each take he kept his arm around my waist, casually enough to suggest he'd forgotten to remove it, but long enough to let me know he hadn't. By not coming on strong, he came on much stronger. One afternoon they finished with him around 4:00, and he went off. They finished with me around 7:00. I told my dresser not to wait because I always hated anyone hanging around at the end of work, and walked to my dressing-room. Warren lay asleep on the couch, his long legs stretched out, his long arms folded across his chest, his black hat perched on his crotch. I switched on my portable radio but he never stirred. I removed my make-up and went into the bathroom to change my clothes. The door opened and Warren moved in close, yet still seemed to keep his distance.

He yawned and said, "They work you pretty late."

"Yes," I said.

"You shouldn't let them. Not if you want to live a long life."

"I never thought about that. Maybe I do."

"I don't." He put on his dashing hat. "But taking you out to dinner could change my mind."

"I hate to think of you deciding to live longer on my account," I said. "It's a terrible responsibility. But you can take me out to dinner anyway."

We went to Musso and Frank's, which Warren considered one of the few civilized places to eat in Hollywood, it reminded him of a New York chop house with its paneled walls and leather booths and old-fashioned gloom and waiters almost as peevishly efficient as they were back East. He dropped the subject of long lives, but warned me nothing out here was going to last very long anyway, because geologists were predicting that a fatal earthquake would destroy the place sooner or later. Sooner being too late in his opinion. He viewed the Long Beach quake of two years ago as just a rehearsal and looked forward to next time, when a huge convulsion would rip the city from the mainland and hurl it into the Pacific. He had an affectionate mental image of the scene, and described a fantastic ruined island of French chateaux, Colonial mansions, Chinese pagodas, movie billboards, gilt chandeliers, gas stations, palm trees, fake Titians, orchid farms, oil derricks, white Rolls Royces, store dummies wearing Fredericks of Hollywood evening gowns, thousands of oranges rolling out of burst crates, bits of modern Paris and ancient Rome from back lot sets, part of Aimee MacPherson's temple, Santa Claus Lane floats with dead starlets slumped across the reindeer, and semi-nude Busby Berkeley girls trapped in the keys of a musical typewriter as big as the Ritz.

"Don't you feel it? Can't you tell the bubble's on the point of bursting?"

I told Warren I felt the opposite, each morning I drove to the studio it looked like the rock of Gibraltar, built to last as long as Mr. Mayer's dreams and his new circular white desk.

"My friend over there knows better," Warren said, and pointed to a man alone on a stool at the long bar.

The man wore an old tweed suit, held a pipe in his mouth and a glass in his hand. "Our greatest American novelist," Warren said. "And they appreciate him so much out here, they put him to work on a three-hand-kerchief story about Barbara Stanwyck falling in love with a Mississippi bargeman." I watched the man climb off the stool and head much too carefully for the door. Still holding his glass, he disappeared into the street. "Our greatest American novelist is fairly loaded tonight," I said. "Show me a great or near-great American novelist who isn't fairly loaded almost every night," Warren said. "But William Faulkner knows what to do if that earthquake fails to deliver." And he explained how Mr. Faulkner thought of Los Angeles as a city built on millions of celluloid spools worth millions of dollars, which a single careless match could destroy in a single moment of time.

We got into an argument. I could appreciate that Mr. Faulkner was ready if not eager to strike the match, but I couldn't see it destroying all the celluloid in town, however carelessly he struck it, even with a mighty Santa Ana wind blowing. Warren told me not to be so literal. He defended the idea as a figure of speech, and I attacked it as a dumb exaggeration. "Tell your friend, when he sobers up, to concentrate on Barbara Stanwyck, who's worth concentrating on, instead of sweating over some useless scheme to set us all on fire."

Leaning toward me across the table, Warren was still distant as ever. "Do you never go out of character? I guess not. Everyone out here follows their script. You're stuck with playing Little Miss Pipe Dreamer and I'm the sum of all my parts." Then he was suddenly close. "The movie never ends. It goes on and on, all the way to the most popular whorehouse in town, where the girls are made to look like different movie stars, and the customer gets to screw Barbara Stanwyck, or Joan Crawford, or Claudette, and gets to feel he's Clark Gable. The madam, by the way, has been lost for years in the role of Mae West."

This whorehouse was news to me, and I wondered if Geraldine de Vorak fell on her feet or her back there at last, playing Garbo every night.

"You've been to this place?" I asked. Warren nodded. "So who did you choose to screw?"

"That's my business. But I know who I'd choose tonight."

"I'm really shocked. I can't believe there's a whorehouse in town with someone pretending to be me."

He nodded again. "You'd be surprised at the business she does."

"Better than Shirley Temple?"

"She's not on the menu. You can't screw Shirley Temple."

Warren put on his dashing hat, we walked to the parking lot and made a big show of saying goodnight. Then he drove off. His car waited around the corner, moved on again as I reached it, and I followed him to the Sunset Strip. Only three years ago it was still mainly farmland, with a bridle path in the center, but when Prohibition ended signs of night life sprang up almost overnight, and it turned into one of those smart uptown streets from the movies. The bright streamlined Trocadero was RKO, you expected Fred Astaire to come out through the swing doors in white tie and tails, then improvise a tap number on the sidewalk. The Café Lamaze a few blocks further on was Warner Brothers, the couples waiting outside for their cars were always George Raft and Ann Dvorak types, a bit gangsterish and flashy, like the place itself. Half a block up a side street you reached the plush Clover Club, which was MGM, too exclusive to stand right facing the Strip. It had floor shows, after hours gambling, police protection and, as a final unmistakable sign of class, chandeliers. Then the glitter ended and you were suddenly deep in the country.

Warren's car vanished into darkness, broken up only by a few dim street lamps that shone on high wrought-iron gates and shadowy driveways leading to houses I couldn't see. As he turned up a winding canyon road, a sprinkle of rain began. The street lamps became dimmer, a coyote streaked in front of my car, and the city felt hours away. He turned up another narrower canyon road, which came to a dead end below a wall draped with vines, a garage entrance hidden there and a smell of damp leaves in the air.

I followed Warren up a flight of steps to a ranch-type house under a hillside thick with trees. A heated pool steamed in the light rain. He opened the front door, which was unlocked, switched on a couple of lights, led me through a livingroom with fur rugs and low couches, to a small bedroom with fur rugs and a low bed. He disappeared without a word through another doorway, and I supposed he was visiting the bathroom. I lit a cigarette, walked to the window, listened to the stealthy rain, then felt a pair of hands pressing hard on my waist and found Warren right behind me, having sneaked up naked except for that hat. He asked what I was waiting for, so I took off my clothes while he lay on the bed the way he lay on my dressingroom couch, closing his eyes and stretching out

his legs. But he had some kind of sixth sense. The moment I finished
undressing he threw the hat at me and snapped his fingers. I walked to
the bed, he pressed hard on my waist again, turned me around until I
stood with my back to him. "Here we are," he said quietly. "In the same
old place, a room with a bed. And we're going to play the same old
game." He didn't sound too enthusiastic. "As the wise man said, it's just
an exchange of two momentary desires and a contact of two skins. But I
like to be told I'm loved."

All this must be in his script, I supposed, and picked up my cue. With
my back still turned, and his mouth tickling it, I said I loved him, even
wishing it was in *my* script to mean it. Not that I wanted to fall in love
with Warren, but I longed to hear a violin play. No violin had played for
me since Jimmy Gabriel. Then Warren pulled me around and made me
feel that although the game might be old, it was the only one in town, and
well worth playing. He obviously felt the same way, yet afterwards he
became distant again. Smooth and satisfied in a black silk robe, he kissed
me on the forehead with an insulting God's-gift-to-women charm, and
suggested I drive home. As I left, he was mixing himself a drink. He's not
allowed to play it any other way, I thought, and walked past the steaming
pool, down the steps to my car. I looked up at the house and saw the
lights turned off one by one.

On the set next day Warren's attitude was so offhand, almost callous,
that I feared he must be a type Mother warned me about, the man who
lost interest in a girl after making out with her. But later Warren flashed
me a wry apologetic signal, and I understood he was following an old
Hollywood rule: the only sin is the sin of getting found out. In those days
we had to be officially virtuous, a tough order with columnists and studio
spies close on our heels, labeling a couple "constant companions" if they
were seen out together more than twice, and advising them to order a
bagful of rice if it happened again. We learned very quickly never to dine
with a lover at Romanoff's or any smart place where Louella and company went on regular night patrol, and some of us moved out to beach or
hillside hideaways, where distance and darkness protected. No one could
avoid the grapevine for ever, it had eyes and ears that could see in the
dark and hear through soundproofed walls, but the grapevine was strictly
home entertainment and respected its own unwritten law: this is just between you and me. It knew everyone's screwing habits, which marriage
was a front because the groom liked boys and the bride liked girls, who
was the real father or mother of so-and-so's child, but never cast the first
stone by talking to the press.

At the end of shooting that day, Warren flashed me another signal and I followed his car up the winding canyon road. There was another car parked below the dead end wall. "Flynn's here," he said. "He always moves into my poolhouse when he's had a row with Damita." Flynn was not yet a star, but on the verge of becoming one, for he'd just finished playing *Captain Blood* and the studio publicity department predicted that women all over the world were going to swoon at his feet. In the meantime, he seemed to be groveling at Damita's feet. Columnists wrote that passion had this couple in a death-grip, and compared them to tigers in the jungle. But Warren, who once made a picture with Damita, compared her to a jackal, and when Flynn joined us for a drink he struck me as a very sad bewildered tiger, with a black eye. "Why do I let this happen to me?" he asked, described life with Lili as the greatest heaven and the greatest hell, but couldn't find words for the heaven. "Anyway, this time it's really over, it's finished," he said. "And there's nothing to be sorry about. When the party's over, we all have to pay the price."

Warren shook his head. "Not me, Flynn. I leave before the party's over."

The almost unnaturally handsome specimen laughed, knocked out his pipe and went back to the greatest heaven the next day. On the weekend he came back from the greatest hell, and the three of us sat around Warren's pool on a gorgeous Sunday afternoon, drinking French wine and eating South Seas buffet sent over from The Beachcombers. "It's so damned uncivilized out here," Flynn said, lying in the sun, his mouth full of lobster and pineapple. "It's positively greasy," Warren agreed, lying in the shade, his mouth full of squab salad. "The only mistake we make," Flynn said, "is expecting to be happy in a place like this." Warren said it was a mistake he never made, because he never expected to be happy here. "All I can do now is make my pile and quit," Flynn said. "You'll die before you quit," Warren said. Then he added, "You should have followed my example."

"What is that?" I asked Warren.

He smiled. "I died before I stayed."

The moon rose, the stars came out, the night was warm, the air was scented with jasmine, and I felt more content than in a long time.

Warren gave me a suspicious look. "What's the matter? Why are you so happy?"

"It just occurred to me we're not really in *Footlights* at all. We're making a different movie and I like the script much better."

"I'm not sure I do," Warren said. "I'm a lazy actor and *Footlights* is easier to play."

Flynn laughed and lit his pipe.

"Warren, are you serious? You'd rather be in *Footlights* than our own movie?"

"I like to please the audience, and I don't see the audience going for our own movie. We're only making it to please ourselves." Warren turned away from me and gazed up at the moon. "That never works out so well."

"You're too smart for me."

"I'm glad you realize it."

Flynn yawned and said he was going to take his glorious body off to bed.

"Do you honestly believe it's so greasy out here?" I asked Warren. "And do you never expect to be happy? And are you really dead?"

"Stop worrying and remember what the wise man said. Happiness is a negative state."

I decided to go home, but Warren wanted to exchange momentary desires and hear again how much I loved him. In the morning we had to play the scene where he apologized for putting the make on me, and halfway through I kept breaking up. It was embarrassing and finally Warren got annoyed.

"What's the matter with you?"

"This whole situation just kills me. It's so unreal."

"Which situation? Ours, or *Footlights?*"

I broke up again. "Take your pick," I said.

It made him even more annoyed. "Get back and do the scene right, or you and I don't *have* a situation."

I stared at him. Warren's eyes looked even more cold and crafty than when he played con artists. I went back and did the scene straight through, with an edge of panic that came out like excitement. (One critic found it uncommonly truthful. He thought I seemed in a real daze after my first night triumph.) We broke for lunch and Warren walked abruptly away. That afternoon he was distant as the horizon, but when he spoke his lines about being honored to play Hamlet to my Ophelia, he looked at me with a close, intense admiration. We broke for the day and he flashed a signal. I followed his car up the canyon road, then called out as he walked ahead up the flight of steps, "Did you mean all that? Would you really have walked out on our other movie if I balled up again, or are you just one hell of an actor?"

Warren turned around, looking very thoughtful, and then he smiled. It was the only answer I got.

Sometimes, for the contact of two skins, we went to my apartment, which I moved into a few weeks before *Footlights* began shooting. Al-

though it had been on my mind for some while to take a place of my own,
I put it off because I dreaded Mother's reaction. But when I finally broke
the news, she surprised me once again. "I've been waiting for you to
suggest it, Baby. What took you so long? Afraid I wouldn't like the idea?"
Switching to her role of real estate queen, she immediately tried to sell me
a house. "I've got the best buy in town, cozy little Tudor mansion right
behind the Beverly Hills Hotel, nine rooms, two patios, landscaped garden, heated pool." I told her I only wanted to rent, and she had an inspiration. "Move into the old Valentino estate, just think of the publicity if
you rented Falcon's Lair! It's a dream hideaway, classic Moorish-Mediter-
ranean, tiled roof, beamed ceilings, servants' wing, four-car garage, stables and kennels, total privacy guaranteed in ten acres of land. They don't
build them that way anymore, you know." I told her it sounded great but
a little too elaborate for a girl just starting to live on her own. Mother
sighed. "I could offer you a special deal. I hate to see you let an opportunity like that slip through your fingers." After I let a few more opportuni-
ties slip through my fingers, including the former mansion of razor blade
tycoon King Gillette, modeled on an old Hawaiian palace, and a Jacobean
castle where John Gilbert lived for a month, I settled on a second-floor
apartment in West Hollywood. "Simple yet luxurious, Baby, split-level
studio-type livingroom, open fireplace, private terrace with french windows and sunrise view. Plus A-1 maintenance like all my buildings, full
janitor service, daily maid, valet parking, manager on premises twenty-
four hours a day. And if you find you don't like living alone after all, I
won't hold you to the lease."

The day after the picture finished shooting, Mr. Mayer summoned me
to his office. He told me to sit down on the white davenport, gave me a
long pokerfaced look from behind his circular white desk, and asked if I
was happy.

"I get by," I said. "How about you?"

He shook his head. "I am sick to my heart, sitting on thorns." He took a
sheet of paper from under his blotter, stared at it, sighed heavily, and
counted the times Warren had visited my apartment at night, then the
Saturday nights I never came home at all.

Naturally my first reaction was to wonder how he got the information
on that sheet of paper. Warren and I had always been smart, never leaving or entering the apartment together, parking his car around the corner,
but someone on the premises must have been smarter. I could only
suppose Mr. Mayer made a deal with the manager on duty twenty-four
hours a day.

"We had dinner a few times," I said, "and he's seen me home. Sometimes I guess we talked late. You know how it is.''

Mr. Mayer gave a weird moan. ''Yes, I know how it is, and I never thought you'd lie to me. Is it really you sitting there and pretending you never had secret dates with an old wolf, a known vulture, a schlub Blue-beard?''

''What is schlub?'' I asked.

''Not so good. In fact, lousy. The first time you came to this office, with your beautiful Mother, I welcomed you to our family. A good family al-ways looks after its own, even the black sheep.'' He moaned again. ''So young and so black,'' he said. ''Don't you know every scandal breaks sooner or later, every dirty secret starts at the bottom and rises to the top? When it comes out this little girl is dating an old wolf, you're in such trouble.'' He stood up and pointed accusingly at me. ''Your public won't stand for it, all the millions who love you and believe in you feel betrayed, we get millions of protests, letters, telegrams, phone calls, suicides, and they all say 'Down With Her, we never wish to see her or hear about her again!' '' His pointing finger almost hypnotized me. ''If you were differ-ent, if you were not a sweet child, maybe we could ride the situation. But the way you are, the way everyone sees you, we're helpless. We bow to pressure.'' Mr. Mayer dropped his hand to his side and sat down again, his shoulders actually bowed, as if he felt a terrible weight on them.

He acted out this scene so vividly, my disgrace, my public turning against me, the studio dropping me like a hot potato, that for a moment I believed it was really happening. Then Mr. Mayer reassured me it was only something that *could* happen if I failed to obey orders.

''Stop seeing the old wolf.'' He gave me a dour puzzled look. ''You know it's not love. It's a lower kind of thing.''

''How do you know what it is?'' I asked. ''How can you tell what I feel?''

Mr. Mayer gave a thin smile. ''It's my business.'' He paused. ''Besides, I already talked to the old wolf. He painted the picture.''

''Please stop calling Warren an old wolf. He's only forty.''

He ignored this. ''I explained it meant trouble for him as well as you.'' Another thin smile. ''He doesn't want trouble. He's one sharp fellow. He won't see you again.''

''I don't believe it,'' I said, feeling queasy, on the verge of believing it.

Mr. Mayer buzzed his secretary and told her to get Mr. Warren William on the phone. When the call came through he said in a genial voice, ''Warren, my good friend, I just told her you're one sharp fellow and she wants to let you know she's not dying.''

He summoned me to the phone. I picked it up and heard Warren's voice, casual but guarded. "I warned you it was greasy out here," he said.

"Then let's not make it any greasier. I'm not dying." And I hung up, aware that Mr. Mayer was wiping his eyeglasses with a silk handkerchief. Having checkmated me, he put the glasses back on and gave me a tender gaze. He led me to the couch, sat down beside me and patted my knee. "Now your Mother need never know you almost turned her dreams to ashes. Think of it, think of the tragedy of a Mother who gives her only child all the love and hope and sacrifice in the world, only to die of shame." He patted my knee again. "No, don't think of it. I've saved you from letting it happen."

Mr. Mayer had fixed Warren, made me imagine millions of people shaking their fists and yelling "Down With Her," and now he stirred up my old fear of betraying Mother. Yet he seemed to believe he was doing me nothing but favors. It was even more confusing when I detected a glint of tears in his eyes, and tears came to mine, not for Warren, but for myself, whoever that was. For my life that didn't belong to me on the screen or off it.

"It's natural to seek attention from an older man when you never had a Father," Mr. Mayer said. "But it's not natural to spend the night with him. You need one decent fellow, older or younger but not a wolf. You need a normal, romantic, beautiful love, the kind your public expects." He went back to his desk. "The picture's a lulu, by the way. You and the old wolf make a wonderful team."

He handed me a script called *Girl on the Wing* and told me I could go home. But this time I didn't go home to Mother. I walked to the parking lot, saw the ghost of Warren driving off and expecting me to follow him, got in my car and drove to my apartment. I changed into a swimsuit, took sun on my private terrace, read through *Girl on the Wing* and marked a few lines I would refuse to say. Then I drank a glass of tomato juice with a squeeze of lemon and a spoonful of activated dry yeast, ate a pint of yogurt and took a long nap. I had a dream about Warren in the whorehouse, and the madam saying, "But you can still have her, Baby Jewel will be free in a few minutes." After I woke up, I took a long shower, got dressed and drove over to Mother's house. We had a date to see *The Magnificent Obsession*, and settled in our mezzanine seats just in time to catch the previews of a new Mae West comedy, with Warren up there playing one of the men in her life. I never said a word. Mother wept a little when Robert Taylor cured Irene Dunne of blindness. Afterwards she discussed the boom in Motor Inn Hotels and told me she aimed to get in on it.

Years later, reading her diaries and realizing she tried a little cloak-and-dagger stuff with Mr. Mayer over Jimmy Gabriel, it occurred to me Mother might have tried it again when she leased me that apartment. Maybe she put Mr. Mayer in touch with the manager on duty twenty-four hours a day. And maybe, when Mr. Mayer accused me of almost turning her dreams to ashes, he was only bluffing to cover up their operation. Then I doubted it. Mother never employed anyone to do anything she could do herself, and if she really wanted to find out how I spent my evenings, she would have turned private eye and trailed me from studio to passion mill in her new olive-green Chrysler Coupe de Ville.

On a happier note. It was amusing to learn from the diaries that *Girl on the Wing* touched Bugsy Siegel on the raw, because it gave him something in common with Eleanor Roosevelt. When she came out on a visit to Hollywood and the studios invited her to view their latest product, Eleanor found my picture almost as inspiring in its way as *Lost Horizon* and *The Life of Emile Zola*. Mr. Mayer was a dyed-in-the-wool Republican, but he threw a lunch for her, and the newspapers carried photographs of Eleanor smiling at Mr. Mayer and me, telling Mr. Thalberg and Norma Shearer how much she also admired *Romeo and Juliet*, shaking hands with the studio's latest juvenile discovery, Mickey Rooney, being introduced to Clark Gable, watching Eleanor Powell rehearse a tap routine for *Born to Dance* and China take shape on the back lot for *The Good Earth*. Mother elbowed her way into a few shots and vowed to vote Democratic if Mr. Roosevelt ran for a third time. But she reneged when the time came, because she feared he was leading our nation into war.

Unfortunately Eleanor and the Bug failed to start a trend and *Girl on the Wing* failed to show a profit. Mother told Mr. Mayer the public stayed away because it refused to sit there and *watch me die*, even though I came back to life as an angel. "You never killed Baby before," she said, "and I hope you've learned never to kill her again." Irving Thalberg, looking frail but urgent, told Mr. Mayer and company he had his finger on the pulse of America and knew better than anyone in Hollywood what the public would and would not buy. "It won't buy Pollyanna over the age of ten," he said. "Keep Baby wholesome, but let her cut up. Andy Hardy's wholesome, but he's always cutting up. Jane Withers is not so wholesome, but everyone bought her when she turned an imaginary machine-gun on Shirley Temple in *Bright Eyes*." When he left the room, Mr. Mayer sighed. "That's a very brilliant man, but he worries me. He only gets four or five hours sleep a night."

A few weeks later Mr. Thalberg caught pneumonia, then fell into the longest sleep. At his funeral Mother whispered, "My heart breaks for Norma, of course, but I still think Irving was wrong about the public *and* your picture." I said nothing. I hardly knew Mr. Thalberg, but after his remark about Jane Withers and Shirley Temple, it felt as if I'd lost a friend.

After they studied reports on *Girl on the Wing* from theatre managers all over the country, Mr. Mayer and company decided Irving Thalberg had a point. "Leave this kind of stuff to Shirley Temple, or better still, just leave it," one manager commented, and he was relatively kind. Mother hit the roof when she heard I was being compared unfavorably to Shirley, whom she hated from the moment she saw *Stand Up and Cheer*, and members of the audience actually stood up and cheered the moppet's rendition of *Baby, Take a Bow*. I suppose she felt time stealing by and maybe running out when the press called Shirley the greatest little package dropped down creation's chimney since Baby Jewel, and when she saw her accept the awards I used to accept, elected Honorary G-Woman, kissed by J. Edgar Hoover, listed as a bigger annual wage-earner than the president of General Motors, and of course begging never to grow up.

Several weeks went by with no mention of my next project, although I reported to the studio to have new portraits taken, and Mr. Mayer always gave me a friendly smile. "We'll have news for you soon, tomorrow maybe," he said. But when he finally summoned me to his office, he gave me his best pokerfaced look and held up a paper doll. "Do you see that?" I nodded. "Does it remind you of anyone?" I shook my head. "You're not so bright today. It ought to remind you of the person you used to be." He let it dangle for a moment, then said, "Goodbye, nice knowing you," and dropped it in the wastebasket. "Time's up. You are no longer one paper doll."

"What am I now?" I asked.

"Who knows? I only know *where* you are." Mr. Mayer sighed heavily. "You are Nowhere," he said in a voice as hollow as an empty grave. "That's where you are today." He explained I could pass for a poised and quite pretty seventeen, but who needed it? Almost every star of the time was thirty and up or fifteen and down. In between was Nowhere, too young for serious romance, too old to write letters to Santa Claus. "Nobody buys a person in a situation like that. They buy Greta, Norma, Myrna, Joan, if you're talking real women, they buy Shirley, Mickey, Freddie Bartholomew, if you're talking real kids." Another heavy sigh. "But you know what the cash register rings up for a person like you? No Sale," he said in a voice as dead as dust.

This time Mr. Mayer never wiped his glasses, I saw no glint of tears and wondered where the conversation was leading. The point of no return seemed the most likely destination. He rescued me from angry millions shouting "Down With Her," but he couldn't rescue me from Nowhere. He could only call it quits and settle my contract. I glanced at the mirror on the wall, which used to show Baby Jewel sitting on Mr. Mayer's lap, squeezing his hand, giving her most adorable smile, knowing it was always Baby Jewel Week somewhere, and feeling loved from Sweden to Australia. Now it showed me someone who could usually pass for a poised seventeen, but revealed every year of her secret twenty-five as she stared at the crumpled paper doll in Mr. Mayer's wastebasket.

"You look worried. Why are you worried? You're not going to turn your Mother's dreams to ashes. Not yet." Mr. Mayer almost smiled. "In spite of everything, we haven't lost faith in you. We're making plans." He told me to stand up, looked me over with no apparent enthusiasm, gave me permission to sit down again. "Yes, I can see it," he remarked, then clammed up, not divulging what he could see. Part of the act, of course, he was waiting for me to ask, and held one of his best pauses before replying. "We're creating a new image for you. We're throwing out angels, secret gardens, flagpoles, winning prizes for catching butterflies. No more fantasy in your life." He frowned briefly. "No low-class realism, either." His face cleared. "This is who you're going to be. *One young American girl, special yet typical.* She sets out in the world with a dream, like they all do, her head maybe touching the clouds but her feet on the ground."

In a way I despised Mr. Mayer and in another way admired him, in a way I was afraid and in another way fond of him, so when I glanced at the mirror again it actually showed me one young American girl, special yet typical, setting out with a dream. She forgot about the crumpled paper doll in the wastebasket, she held her head high instead of low. Then a doubt occurred and I asked Mr. Mayer, "What kind of dream?"

"The pursuit of happiness," he said grimly. "What else?" He went on to explain that the studio intended to play down my small-town folksy side and groom me for high style, which he believed I could handle because Mother was obviously born with it. I longed to ask what Mr. Mayer meant by high style, but longed even more to wind up the interview, escape from his office and take a few deep private breaths. So I nodded knowingly and waited to put the question to Mother.

"White-walled sets and gowns by Adrian," she said. "And maybe a director to match, Mr. Lubitsch or Mr. Cukor. This calls for champagne." She toasted my new image, then confessed, "You and I and the bedpost know I was born with no style at all. But people do say I positively glitter with it, so there's no reason you can't glitter too. Take Norma Shearer. The queen of Hollywood chic started out as Miss Lotta Miles, modeling ads for automobile tires in Canada." Her eyes gleamed. "That's the magic of the movies, Baby!"

That night I dreamed I was walking past Bullocks Wilshire, saw a display of winter fashions in the window and decided to go inside for a look. A glass door slid open to the usual false front of my dreams. Stepping into sudden darkness, I took a pratfall down a flight of stairs to the sound of applause. A few days later I received the script of my next picture and found most of the action took place in a department store. It was described as a store with high style, so at least I'd get a white-walled set, but otherwise my new image looked like a false front. Maybe the pages blurred as I read on because I failed to find anything special yet typical in my character, a rich sorority girl who took a bet she could hold down a job during summer vacation, and had a chaste romance with the millionaire storeowner's son, who promoted her from notions to lingerie. "Mr. Mayer is cooking with less gas than I expected. But at least he's upgraded your social background and you go to a lawn party at the end," Mother said when I came back from the optometrist. "Try and see it as a step in the right direction." My vision wasn't up to that. "Where's my dream?" I asked. "And what kind of happiness am I pursuing? The bet is stupid, any dumbbell can hold down a job in a store for a couple of months, and the rich boy's a jerk."

No Adrian, I wore a salesgirl uniform for most of the picture, and no Mr. Lubitsch or Mr. Cukor, two smart fellows who were otherwise engaged. I was back with the low style director of *Girl on the Wing*, who used to make serials and had been turning out five MGM movies a year for several years, including the Hardy Family stuff. Mr. Seitz was a reliable handyman with a crack commercial record, not too fond of me because I'd already spoiled the record once. In my new farsighted condition it was no surprise that I spoiled it again. The picture opened to lukewarm reviews, box-office reaction ranged from cool to Siberian, and the theatre manager who trashed *Girl on the Wing* seemed intent on bringing my career to a speedy close. "One more picture like this, and Baby better stick to selling lingerie."

More than two months went by with no mention of my next project, and Mr. Mayer's smile grew less friendly, until it vanished and came back as a remote frown. "We'll have news for you soon. Next week maybe." Finally a script was brought out from someone's bottom drawer and given a quick polish by a contract writer. Scott Fitzgerald received no credit on *Rich Girl, Poor Girl*, which made him luckier than me, and the director said quietly at our first meeting, "When all this is over, I hope we're still friends." But Dorothy Arzner looked as if she doubted it. She tightened the belt of her trench coat rather grimly, like an experienced sailor buttoning up for the storm ahead, and I guessed the negative mood of Hollywood's only woman director had something to do with *her* last picture. Dorothy's feminine touch was supposed to launch a new Joan Crawford, mysterious and unpredictable, in *The Bride Wore Red*, but the new Joan sank and they failed to remain friends. Now the same touch was supposed to bring out a new "Baby" Jewel, and Dorothy looked at me as if wondering whether there was anything new to bring out. "I'll do whatever you want and never hold it against you," I promised. She gave me another long thoughtful look and finally said, "I'd love to put you in lamé, with a high collar and a tight short skirt. But I can't find the scene to justify it." When I reported on this to Mother, she smiled. "I wonder why Lesbos are so keen on lamé. In *Christopher Strong* she put Hepburn in almost nothing else." Then she shook her head. "I could name quite a few male directors with a more feminine touch than Miss Arzner, but at least she won't make a pass at you. You're not her type, Baby. They say she still carries a torch for Clara Bow."

It would have taken more than lamé to save *Rich Girl, Poor Girl*. I played the daughter of divorced parents, spending part of the year in the luxury mansion of my father, a big-time defense attorney, and part in the modest apartment of my mother, a small-time nightclub singer. My parents hadn't spoken for years, but when my mother was unjustly accused of murder, I persuaded my father to defend her. "Now let 'Baby' find someone to defend this picture," my friendly theatre manager commented. "Three times in a row nobody buys you, you are still Nowhere," Mr. Mayer said, and contrasted me with his latest find, one lovely girl who was definitely Somewhere. "Judy Garland is quite appealing in *The Wizard of Oz*," Mother said, "but I doubt she's more than a flash in the pan." All the same, she wept when the *Times* included me in an article on fading juvenile stars, comparing me to Pickford, who failed to adjust to adult parts because she took too long to grow up. "Some people have short memories. Has the *Times* forgotten it once begged you to stay five years old for ever?"

I'd forgotten it myself, but then I was only eight at the time. Now I was yesterday's news and the studio gave me what Mother called the John Gilbert treatment. When he decided Gilbert had lost his popular appeal, Mr. Mayer made him sit out his contract and report weekly for no work. He issued similar orders to me through his secretary, and in Mother's mind reverted once and for all to the Jewish type, after years of being

Russian and emotional. "The brute was brought up on Jehovah, he believes in smiting and punishing." But I never knew what Mr. Mayer believed in, for I never got to see him when I reported. "No news today," his secretary always said. No portrait sessions, either, and only a nod instead of a "Good morning!" from the gateman when he waved me through.

Since *Girl on the Wing* I had seen Nowhere coming, in the shape of smaller dressingrooms, quicker schedules, costumes off the wardrobe rack. Now I saw it in the billboards that surrounded the parking lot. There was always a row of them to advertise current productions, the Divine One in *Ninotchka*, Norma Shearer and Joan Crawford in *The Women*, Norma Shearer and Clark Gable in *Idiot's Delight*, William Powell and Myrna Loy in *Another Thin Man*, Judy Garland and Mickey Rooney in *Babes in Arms*, but my name no longer appeared on any billboard, even though the posters changed after a few months to Clark Gable and Spencer Tracy in *Boom Town*, Katharine Hepburn and Cary Grant in *The Philadelphia Story*, Jeanette MacDonald and Nelson Eddy in *I Married an Angel*, Judy Garland and Mickey Rooney in *Strike Up the Band*. Baby better stick to selling lingerie, I thought, and remembered Jimmy Gabriel telling me not to worry about my future.

"*I'm* not worried," Mother said. "The other major studios are going to be knocking at your door." She called Mr. Mayer to ask if he would agree to loan me out, and he had no objection provided he took 75 percent of my salary. "He's of the greedy persuasion, but I beat him down 10 percent. Now you're officially ready and willing and available, so just sit back and let the offers pour in." I sat back and eventually had an offer to test for a bit as an ex-child star in a Jane Withers comedy. "Baby never tests," Mother said, and said it again when a minor studio wanted to see how I looked in native costume for a South Seas cheapie. Then she told me she was going to call Scott Fitzgerald and ask him over for a drink. "Although he didn't do you justice last time around, he only had a week to do it in. And I hear he's turned one of his own stories into a screenplay now, which should make a perfect vehicle for you. Especially with Cary Grant as your father." I stared at her. "Cary's hardly ten years older than me," I said. "I'm sure he can play older," Mother said. "We'll test him and see."

Early one evening Mr. Fitzgerald came to see us at Mother's mansion, redecorated now in white moderne and streamlined like a ship. Down the open staircase, remodeled in pure MGM art deco, Mother made her entrance in a cocktail dress copied from Adrian and asked him breezily to name his poison. He refused, because he was on the wagon at the time. At first he looked a little sad for no particular reason, then bewildered for a very definite reason. Mother announced his little Honoria for *Babylon Revisited* was sitting in front of the built-in mirror across the room. I lit a cigarette and avoided Mr. Fitzgerald's eyes. "I know your little Honoria is *supposed* to be nine," she went on, "but Baby can easily pass for fifteen, and your story will be even more moving if we play the girl older. Besides, you need a star name for the part, and who else is there?" Mr. Fitzgerald agreed about the star name but felt it would wreck the story if he made Honoria older. Then he told Mother he planned to send the script to Shirley Temple.

She shook her head calmly. "I don't see Shirley in the part," she said. "And you must have heard her box-office is starting to slip."

Mr. Fitzgerald was kind enough, or stunned enough, not to point out that *my* box-office had slipped much further. Instead, he announced he had a deal for the picture if Shirley accepted the role. "Think it over," Mother advised him. "You'll be dealing with Mrs. Temple, who's not easy, and has ideas of her own." Mr. Fitzgerald didn't answer this, but got up, stood in front of me and gave me a long enigmatic look. "I always wanted to meet you," he said. "I wanted to ask if you ever got tired of smiling."

It was a remark you could take either way, ironic or sympathetic, and I took it in silence, hoping it was sympathetic. I was also careful not to smile.

After he left, Mother shrugged and made us another round of martinis. "Some people just can't adjust to the realities of show business." A few weeks later we heard that Shirley, or Mrs. Temple, turned the part down. "Didn't I warn him? He'll be coming back to us, Baby. Wait and see." But Mr. Fitzgerald never came back, and I decided his question about smiling was ironic, his look a disguise for pity.

"Will you please give up now?" I said. "You told Scott Fitzgerald I could play fifteen, and before that you told David Selznick I could play twenty-five, which made me ideal for Melanie in *Gone With the Wind*. Maybe you even told Darryl Zanuck, without telling *me*, I could play sixty-eight and be perfect as the old Indian dowager in *The Rains Came*. But there's a problem you refuse to face. I'm dead."

"Don't exaggerate. There's reincarnation in life as well as after death. Everything goes in cycle and you're between cycles."

"Then let me stay there."

"You can't. It's a law of nature."

John Gilbert sat out his contract drinking. I decided to sit out the rest of mine eating. I gave up yogurt and tomato juice for chocolate bars, french fries, ice cream, peanut butter, pasta and pork chops. "It's my new cycle and it's a law of nature," I told Mother when she begged me to stop, and went out to buy the ugliest cheaters I could find.

"What are you trying to prove, Baby?"

"I just want to make sure you don't call Fred Astaire, and suggest I'm the perfect dancing partner now that Ginger's gone straight."

Reporting for no work a few weeks before my contract expired, I met Mr. Mayer outside the new executive building dedicated to Irving Thalberg. At first he failed to recognize me, then said I ought to feel ashamed.

"I'm sorry. It took me a long time to reach the awkward age, and I hoped you'd admit it was worth waiting for."

He looked as if he'd stepped on horse manure. "How can you do this to me, after all I've done for you?"

"You haven't done much for me lately," I said, and Mr. Mayer hit the roof, which was the sky, as we happened to be outside. He flew into a public rage, and yelled at anyone who passed by, a couple of secretaries, a messenger boy, a studio cop, to look at this child, this hideous child who was once charming and pretty and loved. He wondered if anyone could believe a great star had fallen so low. "She made *Top of the World* and that's where she was! Is it my fault they don't buy her now? Would *you* buy a schlep like that?" They shook their heads. Mr. Mayer turned back to me. "Get a traveling circus to book you, *if* you're lucky," he said. More people stopped to watch the scene, some of them pulling up in cars on their way to the parking lot. He must have yelled at me for about five minutes, and then he wept. At first I was alarmed, but by the end I was enjoying it because he obviously enjoyed it too, and later I heard the experts voted it Mr. Mayer's best public performance since he went up to Mr. Chaplin in a restaurant and slapped him in the face.

Before signing off, he accused me of turning Mother's dreams to ashes, but he was wide of the mark. Not only a star in her own right, Mother had become more of a star than her Baby by now. She might wince at the sight of me, but the sight of me encouraged her to grow younger and peachier and richer and if possible more energetic. I fell, she rose, and her glory absolved me. She continued to acquire block after block in Beverly Hills and Hollywood, and blocks of shares in General Motors, Standard Oil, Burger Master, Sears Roebuck and a South African diamond mine. And now the automobile age was here to stay, she produced endless lots from up her sleeve to satisfy the demand for new drive-ins, service stations, supermarket sites with parking areas, even a stretch of land the city needed for its first freeway. Her circle of friends extended beyond the real estate elite to top executives of Carnation Milk, Purex and the *Times*. They escorted her to premieres, Hollywood Bowl openings and Chamber of Commerce luncheons. She was a guest of honor at the National Orange Fair, where lifesize dummies of local luminaries were propped against citrus trees, and I walked through a grove containing Clark Gable, Marlene Dietrich, Howard Hughes, Mother, and clusters of oranges that turned out to be dummies as well.

Once she took me to the Shrine Auditorium for an anti-Franco rally, even though she supported Franco in the Spanish civil war. But she knew Joan Crawford would be there, because Joan was married to Franchot Tone at the time, and Franchot, as Mother said, was a smooth enough actor but a rabid lefty. We sat in the celebrity block right behind Ernest Hemingway and Dorothy Parker, and applauded Joan, wonderfully glamorous in a huge sweeping hat and a fur muff, as she pledged one thousand dollars for a Loyalist ambulance. Equally glamorous in a silver turban and minaret tunic, Mother stood up, smiled at Joan, changed sides on the spot and pledged two thousand dollars. Next day the *Times* published her picture in a group with the Tones and Mr. Hemingway, a blurred uncredited Baby in the background.

Sitting out my contract in Mother's long shadow, I found the world just a suburb of the movies. I saw Mother edge in front of photographers at the Museum of Natural History as Dorothy Lamour presented the board of directors with a sarong from *Her Jungle Love*. I watched her cut the opening day ribbon in the showrooms of a new furniture company that specialized in reproducing designs from studio sets. She was a major investor and made a killing when the livingroom from Bette Davis's house in *Dark Victory* sold by the thousand. I followed her on a private tour of Forest Lawn, where she planned for us to lie side by side throughout eternity and picked out a couple of plots. We strolled through a Shangri-La of tropical flowers, bright pavilions and marble statuary, sniffed mimosa air in the Mystery of Life garden, stood in a chapel where artificial sunlight streamed through the windows while Wurlitzer music played, lingered on a hillside terrace with white doves circling above our heads. "I know we're living in the movies," I whispered, "but do we have to die in *Lost Horizon?*" Speaking personally, Mother felt there was no movie in which she would rather die. After checking out the graves of Jean Harlow, Lon Chaney and old Dressler, she advised me to think of my cemetery lot as real estate. "Naturally I want us to stay together for ever, among the stars and under the stars, but imagine the resale value if you change your mind. Property's got nowhere to go but up, even for the dead!"

And once I followed Mother into the temple of the Mighty I Am, where an attendant handed out American flags at the door. We stood among maybe five hundred people, all holding flags, and watched the Master, also known as Blessed Daddy, make his entrance in a violet robe and a lot of gold jewelry. For the benefit of newcomers he gave a short lecture on the Violet Flame, describing it as the only foolproof human security system. Nothing else could drive away the hostile entities surrounding us. The air was full of these entities and the Master could spot them far and wide. Recently he spotted unidentified enemy submarines planning to torpedo the Panama Canal, and turned them back through sheer violet force of will. But the most hostile, hostile entities, he warned, were silent and invisible. Communists, free-lovers and suchlike sent out little mental devils of the mind to poison the atmosphere of our country, and we must constantly be on our guard against them. "Turn them back like those enemy submarines," he advised. "Fight them with everything you've got."

Then the Master's wife, known as Little Dynamite, joined him at the altar. Also wearing a violet robe and a lot of gold, she handed her husband a gold incense pan that hissed with a violet flame. It sent out currents of sickly heavy perfume that nauseated me even at a distance, but the Master inhaled until violet flame seemed to be coming out of his nostrils. His followers, including Mother, closed their eyes and breathed deeply while Little Dynamite encouraged them by beating a gong. When it stopped, they opened their eyes to reeking smoke, waved their flags and chanted "Blast! Blast! Blast!" They did this until the violet flame in the incense pan gave out and the Master made a sign. "We turned back a record number of hostile entities today," he said. "I love you all."

Mother chanted more quietly than the others, blasting away in a ferocious whisper like the hissing of the flame. After we handed in our flags and got outside, I asked how she could believe in such junk, and she told me the answer was simple. "*It gets results*, Baby." Since she joined the Mighty I Am, all her business ventures had made tremendous strides, and with the secret of energy and power in her pocket, she never put a foot wrong. "What about those hostile entities?" I asked. "You really believe they're all around us?" She nodded, and astonished me by confiding she had moments of anxiety and depression that only the Master's technique could banish. "Don't forget the *Times* calls me a one-woman empire. Running an empire, especially when it runs the gamut from real estate to your career, creates terrific strain. Sometimes I get tired and nervous, and even hit the dismals."

"I had no idea," I said. "I've seen you on edge from time to time, but never truly in the dumps."

"I should hope not, Baby. No one, not even you, will ever see me that way. But please don't worry. I've got the Flame on my side."

The she told me the reason she brought me to the temple. "The hostile entities are getting at *you*, Baby. They've made you gain weight."

"No, I made myself do that," I said, and wondered about those enemy submarines turned back from the Panama Canal. "If anything like that really happened, we'd have heard about it. One of WR's reporters would have scooped the story."

Mother suddenly swung the Chrysler toward the curb and braked beside a large vacant lot, sprouting weeds and a few white poppies. "Look at that piece of land. I bought it for peanuts years ago, and Rexall Drugs just made me a heartwarming offer. But I've decided to hold out for more." Gliding into traffic again, she returned to spiritual matters. "Has it never occurred to you that things happen in this world way beyond the reach of the Hearst press? Stop being so literal. Sit back and ask yourself the cardinal question." Horns tooted as she nipped through a red light. *"Who knows?"* she said.

Hindsight makes it easy to see Mother as not far from going crazy, but craziness can be much less obvious than people imagine. In those balmy Los Angeles days many borderline things went on, and no one called them insane. Gary Cooper joined a secret society, the Hollywood Hussars, set up by a retired colonel who believed America was in danger of invasion by a foreign power. Like the other Hussars, Gary promised to ride out on horseback if the enemy struck. Mr. Mayer and Mr. Hearst connived to put out a fake newsreel to discredit Upton Sinclair when he ran for Governor of California. It showed migrant workers, the unemployed and the down-and-outers all eager to vote for him, and asked how we dare support a pinko politician who aimed to raise taxes to help a bunch of losers. But the shots were clips from MGM movies, with Mexican peasants from *Viva Villa!* working overtime, and Mr. Mayer and WR enjoyed a good crazy chuckle when Sinclair went down. I also remember Corinne Griffith, such a hit during the twenties in *Syncopating Sue*, then a casualty of sound. She made herself a new career heading a movement to abolish income tax, canvassing showfolk year after year, and I happened to drop by Mother's house on the afternoon she sat showing off her famous legs and explaining why taxation was an un-American idea. Mother listened carefully, wondered which way to jump, then quoted Carole Lombard. "I enjoy living in this country and I don't mind paying the freight," she said. Then Hattie served tea from a silver service on a silver tray, a custom Mother borrowed from Gloria Swanson. Handing around a plate of raisin cookies, she told us she'd just heard the guns of Armageddon coming nearer.

When she picked up that Russellite leaflet left at the house years ago, Hattie's life changed. She heard the guns and prepared herself for the Second Coming. The Russellites turned into Jehovah's Witnesses and Hattie moonlighted for them, traveling from door to door at every spare moment, warning of the guns. For old times' sake, and because she remained a good worker, Mother kept her on and occasionally begged her to shut up. News of Armageddon came as no surprise to either of us that day, but I was certainly surprised at the way Corinne took it. She never blinked, crossed her famous legs, sipped her tea and nibbled a cookie while Hattie told her not to worry, the Second Coming would surely save her.

"Thank you and can it, Hattie," Mother said. "But she's a dear, so interesting and such a positive outlook," Corinne said when Hattie left the room. "Not long ago I fired a maid for pessimism. She kept on and on about California falling into the ocean, and told me 'None Shall Escape.' " Then she asked Mother about some investments. As life returned to normal, to coin a phrase, it struck me how people as different as Mother, Corinne, WR, Mr. Mayer, Gary Cooper and Hattie shared the same kind of fear and the same positive outlook. Someone was always threatening to attack them, take their money or their lives away, and something always had to be done about it, practical or mystical or both. In those days hardly a day passed without our city being described as an oasis in the desert, and the desert meant the Depression, strikes, communists, war, any kind of bad news. The desert stopped at the city limits, arrested like the Okies no one wanted to know about, but the oasis was blessed with a magical ongoing boom. Every week it had an exploit to celebrate, a new building to house the *Times,* a new neon-bright theatre to house the showgirls of Earl Carroll's Vanities, a new post office for Beverly Hills, a new automobile or aircraft plant opening up, and of course the movies spinning more money than ever before.

The oasis was smothered in fog the day I came back from Hawaii. Sitting on the boatdeck, I took off my glasses and saw a gray gap in the world. Edging its way toward the gap, the *Lurline* hardly moved. The air was clammy and still; I felt suspended in no place and no time. Across the Pacific I heard Jimmy Gabriel's voice, hollow with long distance. "By the way, are you all right?" This time I had no smart answer ready.

Then the fog started to clear, and so did my mind. As we drew near the quayside, an opening in the fog showed a patch of land beyond the harbor, empty except for a strip of highway and a huge billboard on stilts, with the outline of a huge face. It cleared my mind further. If I had my name on one of Mr. Mayer's billboards, I thought, imagining Baby in *Boom Town*, Baby in *Strange Cargo*, a herd of reporters would be waiting on the quayside for a person who was someone even if she didn't know who. And maybe Mother was right about reincarnation for the living. My present cycle had taken me as far as I could go, all the way to Hawaii.

Wishing herself better luck next time, a reincarnated Baby walked off that boat. I saw Mother waiting near the gangway in her silver Cadillac Executive Sedan De Luxe. Her smile glazed when she looked me over, I knew she was hoping for a sign of change, a few missing pounds at least. "Well," she said finally, "I see you got a nice tan." On the drive home we passed the huge billboard, and a girl smiled down at me, her face framed with oranges. She was advertising California Half Moon Brand. I told Mother about Jimmy Gabriel's phone call. "Incidentally," I said, "he thinks you're a great deadpan artist with a knockout figure."

"If you're going to see him, Baby, better practice *your* deadpan. Jimmy Gabriel is looking quite terrible. What do you suppose he wants?"

"I didn't ask."

"Fox just let him go. They dropped his contract."

We pulled up outside my little Mediterranean hideaway above the Strip, where I moved to avoid managers on duty twenty-four hours a day. A few minutes later the phone rang and Jimmy invited me to dinner at Lindy's that night. I accepted and hung up, aware of Mother watching me.

"Mr. Gabriel doesn't let the grass grow under his feet. What does he want?"

"I didn't ask."

"His fourth wife just left him. And she's pregnant."

"That's funny. I can't imagine Jimmy a father."

"You don't have to. The father's her dentist. Or so I heard on the grapevine."

As I neared the table, Jimmy got up and bowed. He still wore a striped suit and jaunty spotted necktie, was still full of grin and bounce, but his face looked ravaged. As if a great shock made it fall apart for a moment and it never quite fitted together again. In spite of a few deep lines and the reddish cowlick tinged with gray, he seemed no older. Or maybe beyond age, an incredibly vital ruin. Since he never was handsome, it didn't matter. But he obviously still knew he was the greatest, which did.

We gazed at each other in a mutual electric silence. Finally Jimmy put on a pair of eyeglasses. We both laughed at the same time, then fell silent at the same time.

"What happens if we try the naked eye?" he asked. "Do we still see each other as we really are?"

I removed my glasses. "The fine print's blurred, Jimmy, but I'd know you anywhere."

"Sure you would. Didn't I tell you my kind lasts longer than tall, dark and handsome?" He removed his glasses and made a curious rumbling sound, in perfect imitation of W.C. Fields about to deliver a backhanded compliment. "I heard you were in great shape, but the shape's even greater than I heard."

We flung our arms around each other.

Elva's Diary

November 22 • Oddly excited, with an almost feverish gleam in her eye, Baby dropped by and announced she was going on a diet. Said she'd given her word to lose at least twenty pounds.

"That's certainly good news. You gave your word to Jimmy Gabriel?"

She nodded. "We're going to make a picture together."

"That's certainly news and I hope it's good."

Baby glanced at herself in the mirror. "I don't believe anyone could go around looking so disgusting. Unless, as Jimmy said, she was really disgusted with herself."

"Has he just discovered the great Sigmund? Anyway, he looks much worse than you, so I presume his self-disgust is even more profound."

"No, he doesn't mind the way he looks. Neither do I. And he thinks the movies overrate the whole idea of beauty. It's getting monotonous. Looking like Wallace Beery and still coming across sexy is much more original."

"I should hate to see it start a trend. Now tell me about the picture, Baby. Is it comedy or romance?"

For some reason she laughed. "I haven't read the script," she said. "But don't expect a happy ending."

I wondered exactly what went on during or after dinner that night if Baby agreed to team with Jimmy Gabriel without even reading a script. "Which studio are you signing with?" I asked. "Paramount? Warners?"

She laughed again. "Republic."

"But that's almost Poverty Row." I felt stunned. "It makes nothing but reach-me-down westerns with singing cowboy Roy Rogers, who I understand is so desperate for publicity he takes his horse to church."

"That's not for publicity. He honestly believes animals have souls."

"Well," I said. "Maybe so. And maybe Jimmy Gabriel can't get a job anywhere else, but why let him drag you down?"

"Goddammit!" There was a note of hurtful impatience in Baby's voice. "I'm as down as Jimmy. No major studio wants us. If de Mille remakes *The Ten Commandments* and needs a crowd of thousands when he parts the Red Sea, we might get walk-ons. In the meantime we're going out on our own, producing a picture we can bring in for four hundred thousand dollars if we invest half our salaries."

It confirmed my worst suspicions. Obviously Jimmy Gabriel was exploiting Baby to revive his own career. "Does he have a cent to invest?" I asked. "I heard he was flat broke, owed a lot of alimony and couldn't keep up the payments on his house."

"I promised to take care of all that."

For the first time in my life, I wanted to slap Baby's face. Instead, I changed the subject and asked whether it came to light during dinner that the fourth Mrs. Gabriel was pregnant by her dentist. It did. The guilty couple plan to marry as soon as their divorces become final. Then my errant child informed me she had an appointment with the trust fund lawyer, and sailed off to arrange a loan of God knows how many thousands from the Baby Jewel Company Inc. to Jimmy Gabriel. Wishing I knew how to break his strange hold over her, I went upstairs for a quick fix.

The phone rang as I left the bathroom, and brought further comfort. Rexall Drugs finally agreed to pay my asking price for the La Brea lot! I was still in a trance of satisfaction when Miss Sophie arrived for a champagne brunch. We had it poolside, taking advantage of the Indian summer, and discussed the Baby situation. She deplored the news about Gabriel, and added that Baby's comeback vehicle ought to be nostalgic and stirring, like *Little Women*. I confessed my own secret hopes for a return to greatness in the romantic style, and wondered whether Miss Sophie had seen *Till We Meet Again* with Merle Oberon and George Brent. She loved it, and we exchanged memories of the earlier version, *One Way Passage*, with Kay Francis as the lonely young heiress stricken by an incurable disease, and William Powell as the man she met on board ship, unaware he was sailing home to face a murder charge.

"There's always room for a picture that tugs at the emotions," I said.

Miss Sophie agreed. "And when Merle went off to die alone, the audience reaction was almost reverent. I believe she created an even greater hush than Kay."

"Baby could have created a greater hush than either," I said.

The phone rang again and I hoped it might be the Countess, still wisely in retreat at Palm Springs since her performance at Lindy's. Gentleman Ben's trial comes up very soon, and I wanted to know if the lawyer still had everything fixed. But the hello was from Earl Gibson of Ace Foods, inviting me to open house on Christmas Eve. No doubt Dorothy was having such a good time in the desert with her good friend Elsa Maxwell that she couldn't spare a moment to return my calls. I wondered what those two girls could possibly be doing down there, and felt certain they were not playing golf, unless Dorothy had her eye on a caddy.

After Miss Sophie left I made a quick trip to look over Ramon Novarro's mansion, which he's putting on the market, promised to get him a tidy price and hurried home to dress for the preem of *The Letter*. Sessue Hayakawa and his charming oriental housemate were my escorts. We agreed that Bette Davis scaled new heights, and I had a secret thrill of identification when she confessed, "With all my heart I still love the man I killed!" I don't, of course, not anymore, but for a few days I did, and understood her temporary confusion. Home again after a long day of ups and downs, I found my mind wandering restlessly from Baby to Ben to Bette to Rexall Drugs and back to Ben. Then I set the Velvetskin Patter to work, and it purred my body to sleep.

November 26 • Soon after 9:00 this morning Baby arrived with a gleam in her eyes and a script in her hand, saying she'd lie around the pool while I read it. By the time I turned the last page I was in shock. If someone asked me to imagine the most obnoxious fade-out in the world for Baby, asked me to see in my mind what I least of all hoped to see on the screen before the curtains closed, I might perhaps have conceived her hauled off to a women's penitentiary in a police van — but never lying disheveled and riddled with bullets beside a dusty highway! Closing my eyes, I tried to shut the image out, for it threatened to destroy all the fine tender visions of Baby that I lived with for so long, from the time I took her to hear Caruso before she was even born.

Walking out to the pool, feeling as helpless as Norma on the tumbrel in *Marie Antoinette*, I saw Baby in her swimsuit and closed my eyes again. She looked like a pocket whale. Then I pulled myself together, threw the script on a table and said I would prefer she never faced a camera again, and remained a living legend, rather than shatter her image this way.

She laughed. "It's not *my* image. It belongs to you and Mr. Mayer and strangers sitting in the dark. I long to shoot it dead."

The sky was the same, and my landscaped garden with its orange trees in imported Mexican urns, its Japanese teahouse and rose arbor with a replica of the Venus de Milo, but a strange Baby lounged beside my pool. She was going to play a ruthless killer in a B movie, with the remains of Jimmy Gabriel as her partner in crime, and seemed to think it the best thing that ever happened to her. And as she stretched out a plump arm and reached into her purse, I prayed I was dreaming, for she came up with a six-shooter.

Sinking to a chaise lounge, I begged her to put it away.

"Jimmy gave it to me, he wants me to get the feel of always carrying a gun. You've gone pale. Do guns make you nervous?"

Before I could answer, a voice called my name. I turned around to see Dorothy making her way from the house to the pool. "Baby, don't let the Countess see you playing with firearms," I said, but she only shrugged and assured me the weapon wasn't loaded. Clicking the safety catch free, she took aim at Dorothy, who ducked nimbly behind an urn. "It's all right," I called, "Baby's just getting into character for her next movie!"

Dorothy broke cover, came up and stared at Baby. "So that's who it is. I didn't recognize you." She turned to me. "Just got back and am I beat. Elsa threw a party last night which ended with a conga line in the desert at dawn. So naughty of me not to return your calls, but life at the Springs was one damn caper after another."

"It was nothing urgent," I said, keeping it light, not wishing to pursue the subject in front of Baby.

"You had Benjy on your mind, Elva. Don't deny it. And don't worry either, I'm here to tell you that lawyer wasn't fooling."

Baby wanted to know who we were talking about, and although I shook my head at Dorothy, she ignored it. "Benjy Siegel and that wicked plot to frame him for murder," she said.

Baby was suddenly on the alert. "Didn't you go around with the Bug for a while? I'd like to ask you a question."

"Never call him the Bug. Or Bugsy." Dorothy's voice crackled like ice cubes pouring from a tray. "It's a vicious label the press stuck on him when he went on trial for carrying a concealed weapon. Benjy blew his topper because the judge was so unfriendly, and the judge told him to stop carrying on like a candidate for the bughouse."

"I'm very interested in how it feels when you press the trigger," Baby said. "Did he ever tell you about that?"

"Of course not." The Countess glared. "He never killed anyone."

"What about Big Greenie?"

"I told you, it's a wicked frame-up. The police are out to crucify Benjy, just like the cops. Sometimes I wonder if we're living in a free country."

Dorothy's patience was clearly fraying, but my errant child seemed unaware of it. "Are you sure there's no smoke without fire?" she asked.

"The boy's no more a killer than Hitler's a threat to the world. If you don't believe it, ask your Mother to back me up."

Baby gave me a look of surprise. "You never told me you met the Bug."

"Once, very briefly, when Dorothy and I were lunching at the Brown Derby," I said. "You were in Hawaii. If I never told you, I suppose I never thought it important."

"Now, Elva. It wasn't so brief, we all had lunch together and Benjy never took his eyes off you." I could have hit the Countess. "They should have hung signs," she went on. "Danger, Love at Work. Road to Romance Ahead."

With Baby's hateful script and that image of her body riddled with bullets still on my mind, and Baby herself bursting with curiosity and overweight, I felt close to the breaking point. "Dorothy, stop telling the world!"

"I only told Elsa. And Marion and WR, on the phone."

Without a word I ran into the house, flung myself sobbing on my bed. A few minutes later Baby said, "Di Frasso's gone," and put her arms around me, so wonderfully affectionate that I wept all the more. She wiped my eyes with a handkerchief. "It's okay. I'm wise to the whole situation now and it sounds great."

I pushed her away, protesting I had no idea what situation she was talking about. Baby smiled. "If you can't come clean with yourself, at least come clean with me." I wept a little more, and protested a great deal more, and finally admitted that Benjamin Siegel's tango signals had plunged me into a vortex of emotion. "But I'm not even sure he's serious, Baby. It's only Dorothy who keeps insisting we're made for each other and I'm his kind of woman."

"Why shouldn't she be right?"

"Why is everyone trying to push me into the arms of this man?"

"From where I stand, you don't need much pushing."

"But I'm too old. Fifty-two next year."

"You don't look it. What have you been keeping yourself so young for? Don't tell me it's just the mirror. You've been getting ready for someone for years, whether you know it or not."

"Shades of the great Sigmund, Baby."

"Well, you'd make a sensational case history. Carrying on like the Legion of Decency because I'm going to kill people in a movie, but secretly hoping to become a gangster's moll yourself."

"Wait a minute. Ben Siegel's not really a gangster. He just crosses to the shady side of the street now and then, as Dorothy said."

"I don't care if he plugged Big Greenie."

"Baby!"

"And neither do you. Admit it. You *hope* he didn't, but you want him anyway. It's a great situation," she said again. "A challenge. Something to lift you out of the same old routine of making zillions. You're getting too like Rosalind Russell for your own good."

"I certainly admire Roz, but never felt any resemblance."

"I feel it every time I see one of those movies where she puts her career first. Then Melvyn Douglas or Robert Montgomery takes her by the shoulders and says he knows there's a real woman inside her, waiting to be freed."

I hugged Baby and said it was a long time since we acted so close with each other, it filled me with happiness and I hoped she felt the same.

"Right hand to God I'm tickled to death. And just to set the record straight, I'm not in love with Jimmy Gabriel. I'll never even go to bed with him again. I'm just seeing my way clear for a change."

Wishing she could see her way clear to ankling that movie, I kept silent for fear of letting a shadow come between us. We parted most lovingly, convinced we were both setting out on new cycles, and reminding ourselves how far we'd traveled together since boarding the train from Chicago. I lay back and let the past unreel in soft, tender focus. Baby solemn in lace drawers as we walked along Hollywood, quiet as a village that first night. Her Dying Swan at Mr. Griffith's feet. My inspiration to disguise her as a boy for Sid Gordon. Those long golden years as the Beloved, sharing her dreams with a grateful world, acclaimed by Howard Hughes, Ramon Novarro, Eleanor Roosevelt, Charlie Chaplin. Boarding a plane in her silver leather uniform and helmet, and rising to the sky. I waved to her up there and thought, that's where Baby belongs.

The phone rang, I picked it up and heard my broker advise me to invest $200,000 in gold right away. He explained why, but I was in no mood for facts or figures, hardly listening, and then told him to go ahead and buy $250,000 worth. A quarter million was always my lucky number. "That's my girl," he chuckled, and promised I would be very glad of it in the future.

Baby Looks Back

"At this rate we'll never get to the clinch," di Frasso said when Mother fled into the house. "Yet all she really wants is Benjy, and all Benjy wants is to be a perfect gentleman. There's no woman alive who can help him more, and no man alive who knows more about making a woman feel appreciated." Nobody, except the police, knew very much about the Bug in those days. Gangsters were supposed to behave like Humphrey Bogart in *The Petrified Forest*, a scowl on his face and a machine gun on his lap. But Ben Siegel was a smiling fixture on the nightclub and racetrack scene, and what we saw seemed to contradict what we heard — that he used to go around with Meyer Lansky of Murder Inc. in New York, and that he ran a neat extortion racket out here, muscling in on the movie extras' labor union and shaking down the major studios by threatening to call a strike the day before a crowd scene was due to be shot. According to Jimmy Gabriel, the studio chiefs paid up and bore no grudge. "It takes one to know one, Baby. Remember *Mr. Deeds Goes to Town?* The hick who knocked a bunch of crooks and shysters on their big city asses by being so honest and sincere and cute? That was a Columbia picture, so you might take Harry Cohn for some kind of corny idealist. Forget it. Ben Siegel came to town the same year as Mr. Deeds, and Cohn not only pays him off, he admires his nerve and buys him a drink whenever they happen to meet at the Clover Club." So I saw no real danger in Mother getting bitten by the Bug, and felt sure she could handle the situation. After all, Norma Shearer was dating his friend George Raft.

At that time I was seeing my way very clear, thanks to Jimmy. I might have been ready for reincarnation when we met again at Lindy's, but he decided the form it would take. As we got mildly high on martinis, I heard him tell how success turned his head and almost wrung his neck. And as I hear it now, he covered ten years of his life in one long amazing breathless truthful sentence. "This is the story of a very smart guy who did everything dumb in the book," he began. "I married one tall gorgeous conniving whore after another, they called themselves models or starlets or secretaries but whores is what they were and are, I treated money like water until I was living on credit, I believed everything I did was great, and mind you some of it was, but not all, especially later, so every goddam pitfall I warned you about the first night we had dinner, remember? I fell into every goddam one, chewing up too much scenery, peddling every trick in my bag, losing touch, losing my youthful appeal but never acquiring any other kind, never becoming an adult, becoming a totally unreal person instead, not bad or cruel, I don't believe I ever treated anyone bad, except maybe you, it's not in my nature, but *unreal* for sure, imagining my tall expensive wives were in love with me, certain it was never my fault if a picture died, I had a lucky streak that would always see me through, wasn't I the guy in charge and on top and calling the shots and a genius forever? and to prove it I made a huge down payment on a huge unnecessary mansion with a pool and poolroom and tennis court and projection theatre and gymnasium, black-tied butlers, a white grand piano, a diningroom with a table that seated twenty, a mirror on my bedroom ceiling just like Mae West, and can you believe it, *peacocks*, yes for a while I had live peacocks on the lawn, we summoned our guests when they spread their wings, that was my second wife Dawn's idea, Dawn who divorced me when she found out I was screwing Clara Bow, it cost me a fortune to keep it out of court, and although I felt like the hero of my dreams screwing the great Clara, remember I once told you what her dangerous curves did to me, I was no hero at all, it meant nothing to Clara who was sick and touched and hardly remembered whose bed she woke up in just then, and although she married her faithful cowboy star lover Rex Bell, and went to live on his ranch in Nevada, she sees a psychiatrist night and day, so I ask you what price screwing poor Clara, and a couple of other lunatic lovelies I might but won't mention, you must be getting the general picture now, I grow more irresistible but more unbearable every day, until my peacocks turn into turkeys, three in a row, an experience I believe you're familiar with, and I move toward the moment of truth, no longer believe everything I do is automatically great, and people ask what happened, how did you lose it, are you sure you're the real Jimmy Gabriel? you're beginning to look like a bad imitation, and finally the studio doesn't renew my contract, I'm not everybody's kid who made good and an all-American success anymore, I'm someone who makes pictures the public doesn't want to see, and I go on the lot for the last time to vacate my Irish cottage bungalow that used to belong to Janet Gaynor, and as I pack a suitcase there's a workman removing my nameplate outside the door, and as I leave I run into Ty Power, smile and joke and pretend there's plenty offers coming up elsewhere, and I drive home to an empty mortgaged mansion, sit up on top of a hill, call my agent, who says Jimmy right now it's cold everywhere, that's all I can tell you, so I sit at my piano and sing the blues, realize none of my tall expensive wives ever loved me, and not so many other people love me to judge from the way the phone doesn't ring, and finally I lie down on my big *round* sexy bed and stare at my reflection in the mirror on the ceiling, it doesn't look so good anymore, but I'm not the type who gives in or gives up, I start walking around, empty room after empty room, every corridor is Memory Lane, and I end up in the gymnasium where I decide to work out, body and soul, vowing to burn and rise from my own ashes like the phoenix, and that in a word is my story to date.''

I told Jimmy it was quite a story, and on the whole I certainly sympathized with it, but found something unfair in the way he expected his wives to love him while he screwed Clara Bow and others not mentioned. Jimmy called this a typically female red herring, because his wives were whores long before *he* started screwing around. "Stick to the point. I'm talking phoenix to phoenix and want to know how *you* felt when they let *you* go, and it was suddenly cold everywhere."

"I felt better than when it was warm everywhere. It was success, not failure, that really threw me."

"Your false modesty's showing. It always did, and I know where it comes from." Although he'd never met her, Jimmy went into a ruthless imitation of Mother. "Oh, I'm nothing really," he said in a demure refined voice. "They tell me I made Baby into the greatest little star the world's ever known, and built the biggest one-woman empire the world's ever known, and I keep so wonderfully young and glamorous — but I don't see it that way." He patted his hair. "No, I see it as nothing really. Fate has been *so* kind." Then he gave me an accusing look and said in his own voice, "When Mayer let you go, you sulked like a child. You got fat and ran off to Hawaii, which you only pretended to enjoy."

"I wanted to be anonymous. And did it so well, it got dreary. I mean, nobody ever noticed me."

Jimmy shuddered. "How could you even imagine living that way? But at least we're both older and wiser now. I'm free because I've finally got nothing to lose. I don't have to worry whether people will like me, because they don't. I just have to be unique, which I am."

With his new freedom and his last ready cash, Jimmy went on, he bought a unique script that had to be exactly what the two of us needed. Every producer in town passed it up because he found the leading characters so unlovable. It was the story of an American boy from an ordinary middle-class family who met an American girl from the same, which should have turned into a fine wholesome romance, but ordinary middle-class life happened to bore and disgust them. They saw through its hypocrisy and longed to challenge it. Deciding to challenge it together, they had an impulse to steal a car and drive to the next small town, where they held up a service station because they needed money for gas. One thing led to another, naturally, and in the next small town they robbed a bank and killed a man who gave them trouble. Soon they were outlaws, but laws unto themselves, driving happily around the USA on the Wanted List, like Clyde Barrow and Bonnie Parker in the good old days. In the end a posse of cops chased and cornered them, yet as it rained bullets they never really knew what hit them, they died cursing their bad luck and the world.

Jimmy saw *Two of a Kind* as a very big movie even though it would cost very little. "A documentary of our changing times as well as a sleeper," he said. I told him it sounded like an exciting story, but I had no idea the times were changing so much. "You were always too protected," he said, and reminded me of his warning, one Sunday afternoon at Mother's house, about violence in our time. That was ten years ago, and violence was still on the rise, especially out here, especially among young people bored with their ordinary lives. His old friend on the force, disillusioned because he saw so many families breeding punks instead of Andy Hardys, resigned last year, sat down and wrote a script from the horse's mouth. "When you read it, you'll see more than meets the eye. You'll see what's happened to the Dream." Staring at Jimmy, I saw a new side of his character, the sinner turned missionary. But the old showbiz side gave it strong competition when he outlined the deal with Republic, asked me to help him out and promised me equal billing, which in my present situation he considered I was very lucky to get.

Another martini and I felt extremely lucky in every way, eager to challenge hypocrisy in any form, small town or MGM, longed to burn my image alongside Jimmy's and rise with him to create the screen's most dangerous phoenix couple. "I'll see my lawyer and start losing weight tomorrow," I said. "And I'll take lessons in shooting up the world the day after. Last time I handled a gun was for laughs, when I played Calamity Jane at the age of nine." Jimmy almost cried because I was so understanding, then wanted to take me to his mortgaged mansion on the hill and screw me under his mirrored ceiling. He told me he was wildly moved and it had gone suddenly hard, urging him to recapture a past he should never have let go. "If you don't believe me, feel it," he said, and grabbed my hand. I felt it under the table and said, "I believe you, but it's a piece of the past I don't want to recapture. Let's keep things professional, warm and friendly but professional, and order a steak." He sighed. "Maybe you're right. I'm impulsive, remember, thank you for putting the brakes on. But as soon as I'm free, I think I'd like to marry you."

Later, as we walked to our cars with our arms around each other, I realized one of my ghosts had come back to life. Jimmy Gabriel no longer played piano in blackface in the MGM property department, he was solid and close. Looking at him, I saw no change in his face, no gray in his hair, and not because I'd taken off my glasses. I was hopelessly under the influence of memory, and still am.

Elva's Diary

December 15 • Three days ago Benjamin Siegel walked out of court a free man. Yesterday he walked into my house. At early evening I lounged in my bedroom, reading the financial page of the *Examiner* and wearing my Adrian housecoat of sheer organdie trimmed with moleskin. The doorbell rang, and since it was Hattie's day off, my new Filipino butler went to answer it. Jaime seems to be working out well, apart from the problem of making himself understood in English, so when he informed me a Mr. Siegel was waiting downstairs, I feared he mistook the name. There was no reason to expect Gentleman Ben, who never acknowledged my warm note of congratulation sent by Green Arrow Special after the verdict came over the radio. But in case Jaime got it right for once, I decided to remain in provocative trim.

Moving quietly down the staircase, I saw him standing in front of a mirror, combing his wavy black hair. He was too intent to notice me and I watched in secret, fascinated by the almost voluptuous care he brought to the job. As he finished I glided discreetly forward again, but only took one step before he wheeled around with an automatic in his hand, pointing straight at my decolletage! A second later he welcomed me with the smile and blue eyes I remembered so well.

"Just wanted you to know, nobody takes me by surprise, Elva." He raked me over frankly as he slipped the gun under his cashmere jacket. "That's some outfit you're not wearing. I really appreciated your note, and I've come to take you out to dinner. Let me hear you're free."

"Footloose," I said, and offered him a drink. He told me he was usually a very light drinker but felt like celebrating tonight, and asked for champagne. "I'll work it off tomorrow with twenty extra laps in the pool," he added, explaining he kept in shape with an exercise program, for he really believed in the old proverb: no healthy mind without a healthy body. When Jaime brought in the bubbly, Ben insisted on popping the cork himself, charmingly eager to show off his social accomplishments. We clinked glasses, he sat on the long white couch and I lounged on a white ottoman not far from his feet. "Some showplace you've got here, a real movie set," he remarked. "And how's Baby doing?"

It came to me in a flash, keep my enormous girl out of the picture until she slims down, at present she's fatal for my image as well as her own. And before they finally meet, I must warn her on no account to ask Ben how it feels when he presses the trigger. "We sat out her contract and now she's about to sign for an important new picture," I said, wishing again she was not about to play a killer, then changed the subject. "Where are you taking me to dinner? The Brown Derby, for old times sake?'' He raised his glass and said I could read his mind.

After that mildly suggestive entrance in organdie and moleskin, I inclined to a change of pace. I chose a severe, high-necked but form-hugging cocktail dress, over which I slipped an ermine pelisse against the chill of a winter's night. Much admired when I wore it recently to the preem of Mr. Disney's epoch-making *Fantasia*, it drew a low whistle from Ben and later a deep bow from the maître d' at the Brown Derby. At our secluded booth the talk flowed like the bubbly, we seemed to have known or been waiting to know each other for years. Ben plied me with questions about my empire, what real estate connections did I have when I started to build it, who passed on the knowhow, gave me hot tips, guided me to extend my grip to Motor Hotel Inns, furniture and sportswear corporations, the stock market, diamond mines, gold?

"It's nothing really," I said. "Even though I had no connections, never took a course, found myself in a man's world and had Baby's career on my hands as well, it's nothing really. I seem to have a knack for buying the right piece of land at the right time, and the rest just fell into my lap. Maybe I was born under a lucky star."

Ben said he would like to know the name of that star, also exactly how much fell into my lap and what I was worth today. With a different kind of man I might have felt wary, and suspected his motives, but Ben's boyish pride in my success was simple and touching. "This year's figures aren't all in yet," I murmured, "but you can value me, conservatively, at thirty-two mil." The words produced a long silence, then the tango signal of all time. His eyes if possible more magnetically blue than ever, Ben grasped my left thigh under the table. I looked away and speared a forkful of Waldorf salad.

"You're really shitting in high cotton, if you'll forgive the expression."

"No problem, Ben. The first time we met, I forgave you crapola."

He smiled. "Right. People with real class like to spread a little hot mustard on the language." He relaxed his grip but still kept his hand on my thigh. "Success *and* class. You've got it all, Elva."

"Don't make me blush. I've heard tell, anyway, you do pretty well yourself."

He shook his head and frowned. "I'm not in your class, and I mean class whichever way you look at it." The frown cleared, leaving a wistful expression on his face. "Okay, I don't always run straight, but what chance have I got? Every time I start moving ahead, something sets me back. That lousy trial set me back fifty grand, which may be peanuts to you but ain't to me."

"Ben," I said, "*one single grand* ain't and never has been peanuts to me. If your eye is on the jackpot, just one single lonely grand is pennies from heaven. Call that Elva's Law."

He smiled, then frowned again. "Dockweiler cleaned me out for thirty."

"Our new DA? How did he come in?"

"With a proposition. When shit-heel Fitts, our old DA, indicted me, elections was coming up. Dockweiler needed funds and my lawyer made a deal. If I reached in my pocket to help him win, he promised to throw the charges out of court."

"But you were innocent," I said. "You never harmed a hair of Big Greenie's head."

"I know it, and shit-heel Fitts knew it, but he counted on an indictment to bring in votes. Politics is the dirtiest business. Call that Ben's Law."

Having voted for Mr. Fitts, whose campaign against crime in our city struck me as sincere, I felt deeply shocked. "I suppose I'm naive. I always believed justice got done, and only the guilty had something to fear."

"Nice dream. Wish it was true."

Ben still looked so wistful, I decided to play it light. "But I've also heard tell you're a big spender. You like to ride high. When you ride high with a girl like Wendy Barrie, doesn't that set you back as well?"

"I never sink money in girls like that." He sounded truly indignant. "They're just Coca-Cola when there's no champagne around."

I felt another heavy tango signal. "So where does it go?" I asked, knowing some of it went on Ben's wife and family back East, knowing it would not be tactful to know.

"On Lady Luck," he said. "I lay out on the cards and the horses till it hurts. Don't you ever gamble?"

I shook my head. "Not in that way. Life's enough of a gamble for me."

"Life's enough of a gamble for me," Ben repeated. "I should have met you years ago."

Later he drove me up to the Clover Club, where doorman and barman greeted him warmly and my ermine pelisse drew more compliments. We had splits of champagne at the bar, listened to Ethel Waters sing a couple of moving spirituals, then Ben took my arm and led me upstairs to the gambling room. I had never seen it before, although I knew about it, how the owners paid for police protection and were never raided, yet the place turned me absurdly weak with fear. I almost asked Ben, as I asked Desmond Taylor twenty years ago, to take me out of it, but the sight of Mr. Selznick at a roulette table reassured me. Ben steered me to a window and we looked down at the lights of the city. Brushing my ear with his lips, he whispered that he planned to buy into the Club as soon as he got ahead. A big block of shares was coming on the market and he thought it would make an investment with class. "Maybe you don't like to gamble, Elva, but there's big money to be made out of people who do." He told me Mr. Selznick had been known to lose $20,000 in one night.

"Often, I hope? He passed up Baby to play Melanie in *Gone With the Wind*."

Ben laughed. "I just learned one of your secrets. You bear a mean healthy grudge."

"That's true. Never cross me."

"Likewise. It takes one to know one."

We were sparring like lovers in my favorite kind of sophisticated comedy, and when we got into his car again, Ben headed for Beverly Hills but drove straight past my street. I made no comment, then as we turned into a driveway and stopped outside his Bel Air mansion, I remarked on the new moon. He told me to make a secret wish, and did the same.

"So what do you think, Elva?" He pressed a button that switched on a row of chandeliers and a radio at the same time. The radio played Alice Faye singing "Wake Up and Live" in her inimitable cheery style. Glancing around the spacious livingroom, I noted a marble floor with Persian rugs, red lacquer cabinets and coffee tables, cane accent chairs with red velvet cushions, purple satin drapes. Dorothy's influence struck me as a mite too obvious, but Ben's look of innocent pleasure made it impossible not to praise everything. He pressed another button, and a silk-lined bookcase slid away to reveal a secret exit. "Takes you to a hidden garage at the back in thirty seconds," Ben said, and pressed another button. A gilt-framed mirror slid away to reveal a safe in the wall. He touched off the combination, a door swung open and I glimpsed piles of gold cufflinks, some plain, some studded with diamonds, emeralds and sapphires, a collection of small arms, and a gleaming gold object that puzzled me.

It was shaped like an enormous thumb, or maybe a spout. "A gift from the Countess," Ben said with a foxy smile, and placed it in my hands. Surprisingly heavy, it continued to puzzle until I read the inscription: *Dear Benjy's, Worth Its Weight in Gold*.

"You'd never see one like this at Fort Knox," I remarked coolly, and laid the heartfelt memento back in the safe.

Ben's last, or rather last-but-one specialty of the house, was the cellar. Cases of French perfume were stacked like wine. "It comes in on a run across the Mexican border. Only Chanel, only the best," he said, giving out trade secrets with a frankness that disarmed me. No doubt he was mildly euphoric on champagne. "I'll send you over a case in the morning," he went on, then looked anxious. "If you really like it, if you really think it's the best?" I assured him there was none better.

In the bedroom he opened a clothes closet full of cashmere suits and silk shirts, also a few brash plaid jackets I cared less about, although naturally I admired everything. There was a mirror inside the door, and he stood in front of it to comb his hair. "Does it look like I'm losing any, Elva?" I shook my head but he seemed unconvinced. "Three times a week it gets an alfalfa shampoo and a massage," he said, then asked about the men in my life.

"They'd hardly fill a book. I suppose I'm hard to please."

Ben nodded, took off his jacket and tie, slowly unbuttoned his shirt, and I saw his bare muscled chest. Like Clark Gable in *It Happened One Night*, he wore no singlet.

He walked toward me, his face unusually gentle, but reached out and grasped my wrist very hard. Then the night moved outside time, emptiness filled, there was submission without defeat, and as the only way to avoid an anti-climax, I felt ready to die! Finally I roused myself from a long silent trance and started to get out of bed. Ben's hand reached out and pulled me back. "Stay here, Elva, I'm ready for an encore." Tuned into that magical station of the air, I drifted afterwards into an even longer trance, roused myself at last and started to get out of bed again. "Champagne stays the night." He gripped me firmly. "I like to wake up with it in the morning."

Then he let me go, walked naked to the bathroom and rubbed cream from a jar over his face and neck. "Helena Rubinstein double-strength, anti-wrinkle night formula. It's the best." Slipping into my pelisse, I came over and took the jar. As I calmly rinsed my face, his look of disbelief was most enjoyable. I knew he never expected me to dissolve my makeup and show my extra years, under the x-ray of coldly lit mirrors, after a night of feverish love. But there was little makeup and not a single extra year to show. Ben slipped off my pelisse, audited my body and gave a low whistle. "Human velvet all the way," he said, hands passing from my shoulders to my wrists, then to my back. I silently blessed the Patter. "How do you keep yourself that way?"

"Living in Shangri-La!" I shot back with a smile.

A few minutes later he lay sleeping at my side. I listened to his breathing in the dark and pondered his mixture of wolf and lamb. But that's the male animal in a nutshell, I concluded drowsily, nature's most baffling creation, stranger even than bat or giraffe. Never expect too much of it, keep hoping as we may, and we are grateful for a few earth-shattering moments. The next thing I remember, a knock on the door woke me, and

I lay alone in the bed. A butler entered with a breakfast tray, respectfully informing me it was 10:00 and Mr. Siegel had to go out and take care of some business.

"Did he leave a message?"

"No message, Mrs. Kay."

Although miffed, I determined to behave like champagne and not Coca-Cola, stretched luxuriously, sat up and remarked how delicious the coffee smelt.

A husky bodyguard type, also most respectful, loaded a case of Chanel into the car before driving me home. I asked casually how long he'd worked for Mr. Siegel, and it turned out he was new on the job, having replaced an employee who met with an unfortunate accident two months ago. I recalled Dorothy's story about the bodyguard who promised to sing and fell out of a hotel window, and wondered if the unfortunate accident came out of Ben's expenses for leaving the court a free man. Then I noticed a single dark wavy hair on my ermine, picked it off and gazed at it in my hand. What the hell, Elva? I thought, Life is a One Way Passage, so enjoy the trip.

December 22 • On my way out of the house, I opened the front door and saw Gentleman Ben getting out of his car. "Glad you're all dressed up," he said. "I'm taking you out to lunch." I told him I had to pick up the Countess and take her to Romanoff's, where Elsa Maxwell was giving an intimate reception for Leopold Stokowski. He walked calmly into the hallway and dialed a number on the phone. "Make up an excuse," he said, and held out the receiver. "Tell Dorothy something's happened to change your plans."

"Is it always going to be like this with you?" I asked, and Ben nodded. Smiling, I took the phone and told Dorothy I just discovered I was running a fever. Meanwhile Ben stroked me here and there, and when I hung up, wanted to know if I missed him. "Such a busy week, I hardly had time," I answered quickly. "Except, of course, when I dabbed myself with Chanel." He liked the way I fell in with his rhythm, easy come and easy go, and I smiled again. The brute had no idea how hard I fought to stop his rhythm plunging me into the dismals.

As we drove off, Ben mentioned he'd had a busy week as well, most of it spent in New York, but gave no reason why he went there. Knowing better than to ask, I saw his eyes flicker uneasily and decided the visit was not successful. Most likely his wife pressed him to increase her allowance and set Ben back again. Then, at Café Lamaze, someone called out to him from the bar. He waved and continued steering me toward a booth. The

man hurried after us. "Ben, excuse me, I've got to talk to you very soon."
He was aging and paunchy, with small tired eyes. Ben introduced him as
Mr. Dragna and promised to drop by his house in the morning. "Mrs.
Kay, excuse me, I didn't mean to interrupt," Mr. Dragna said before go-
ing back to the bar.

"Is that Jack Dragna, the *capo*?" I asked. Ben grunted, and picked up a
toothpick from a bowl on the table. "I heard tell he had Thelma Todd
rubbed out," I went on, "after she got tired of her Roadside Rest being
used as a front."

Ben's face looked carved in ice. Even his eyes seemed to turn pale and
frosty. "You heard lies, Elva." I felt something jab my hand. "The only
thing to do with lies is forget you ever heard them, before they get you in
trouble."

The toothpick punctured my hand. I saw a drop of blood but felt more
shock than pain. Ben kept his eyes on my face, and they flickered uneasily
again. He gave my hand another jab with the toothpick, then the waiter
arrived with cocktails. "Compliments of Mr. Dragna," he said. Glancing
toward the bar, I caught the old man's eye. So did Ben. They smiled, and
so did I, but at the curious irony of it all, remembering I needed a connection a few years ago, considered Mr. Dragna and decided to stay clear.

Gentleman Ben looked down at my hand with a dazed expression, and
whipped the toothpick away. "Jesus, what did I do, where did my mind
go? Jesus, did I hurt you, why didn't you say anything?" He raised my
hand to his lips and kissed it. "Did I hurt you? I never want to do that,
believe me, Elva. Why didn't you say something — or take your hand
away?"

"I don't know," I said. And it was true. When I saw the drop of blood
on my hand, it was as if I'd landed in a movie, a Warner Brothers melo
about the Lady and the Mob. She got in too deep, soon they called her
Ex-Lady, then Marked Woman, finally they pulled a Thelma on her and
she breathed her last at the wheel of her Studebaker de Luxe, in a closed
garage at dawn. It was oddly exciting.

We spent a long, unforgettably romantic afternoon together, for Ben
insisted on taking a drive all over the city so I could point out every piece
of land I'd bought and sold, and the properties I still owned. "When I
really admire an operation," he said, "I like to check on it." It seemed
right to begin the tour by driving past my famous White House, a scaled-
down replica of the original, with its rose garden and West Terrace front-
ing Rodeo Drive. "Elva Kay Enterprises. EKE for short. Baby calls it the
Control Center," I laughed, then we rode on through Beverly Hills and
Westwood, passing various city blocks I acquired years ago and now

leased to banks, insurance companies, medical corporations, what have
you, and the lots I sold for markets, drugstores, motels, service stations, a
bungalow complex, various duplexes, plus undeveloped territories waiting for a bid to warm the heart.

Turning back, we purred toward Hollywood. "There's a lot more of the
same coming up, Ben, so if you're bored I can skip the more mundane
sights," but he told me to skip nothing, he wanted to get the big picture
piece by piece. I was able to break the monotony by pointing out land I'd
sold for different purposes, for movie theatres, Chinese and Italian restaurants, a beauty salon, a burial advisory service, a prosthetics center. At the
end of the Miracle Mile I told Ben to slow down. "We're approaching a
historic landmark," I said. "The first apartment house I ever built." Sniffing petroleum in the air, noting a multitude of pumps still at work on the
oilfield next to the Royal View Towers, I confessed to one of the few mistakes of my life. "Those were early days, Ben, and my capital was limited,
but I could still have grabbed the whole shebang by raising a bigger loan
on Baby."

He patted my hand. "You can't win 'em all."

"You can try," I said.

Soon Westlake Park came into view, subtropicals and real estate equally
in full bloom. Ben wondered why I never got in on the ground floor there.
"I just stayed away, don't ask me why," I said, remembering the night I
cast my secret on the waters, thinking the place was another historic landmark in its way. Then we reached downtown, where I showed Ben my
two blocks between Main and Fifth, one a department store and the other
an automobile center, my chain of parking lots, the armored car service,
and the mortuary on a hillside that fell into my lap for peanuts in 1927. As
we turned a corner, I realized One Big Look was only a stone's throw
away and asked Ben to stop off there, telling how Baby and I first happened on it a few weeks after we hit this town with stars in our eyes and
practically zero in our pockets. "We still haven't seen my subdivision
along the coast, next to Hermosa Beach," I added. "But it's a clear day
and I'll locate it for you from the observation tower."

Ten years ago, Baby and I stepped from the cable car to the platform and
heard birdsong all over the sky. Now the sky gave back only a tremendous hum of traffic. Yet the city had changed less than I expected. Like the
same person putting on weight with the years, it bulged in all directions
and all its parts overlapped. Pointing to a new oil refinery along the coast,
I told Ben my subdivision lay immediately beyond it. "All those gray
stucco bungalows are the Vista Pacifica housing development," I said. He
put his eye to the grimy telescope and called it a smart move. "Frankly I

wouldn't care to spend the night there," I said, "but people are still pouring into this town, and they'll live anywhere." Then I seemed to catch an echo of my voice, but it was another voice, very far away, with a prairie twang, and it belonged to Mr. Van Tassel, who said almost exactly the same thing twenty years ago, when Baby and I shared a taxi with him and saw people living in tents on a strip of scrub desert.

It was almost dusk, a tinge of purple and gold in the sky, lights starting to come on from the foothills to the ocean. "Some view, Elva." It was Ben's voice again. "That's some view of the good life out there, and you certainly helped yourself to a big slice of it." A neon sign began to flash SWELLDOM. He gazed at it. "Feels almost mystic," he said.

Another sign began to flash RICHFIELD, and for a moment just those two words winked across the city. Then DRUGS followed, and Ben turned suddenly away. "I'm going to level with you, Elva. I'm carrying a load on my back and it's too heavy."

I felt a quick shock in my hand, like the toothpick stab. "Dragna?"

He almost jumped. "You read my mind again." Now other signs were flashing, PARK, EATS, SPOTLITE, IT'S ALL YOURS. "I'm in business with that old shit-heel and I don't like it."

"What kind of business, Ben?"

"Very tacky." He sighed. "Dope and a call girl ring. Low class, high risk. I know a better way to get ahead, but they won't see it." Sighing again, he told me he went to New York to meet with some associates and ask for a loan to buy into the Clover Club. But they turned him down, thought he was doing just fine with Dragna, didn't care whether it was a class operation or not.

"You know something?" His eyes were bright yet sad. "Too many people worship the almighty dollar. They kiss its ass night and day. All I asked for was three hundred grand to get me ahead."

Ben's other side, as Dorothy called it, had never come out so appealingly. It stirred my protective depths. How well I knew that situation from the movies: reckless yet strangely naive kid from the New York streets falls for the lure of easy money, and gets in too deep with the wrong crowd. No wonder Ben's nerves were jangled at lunch, he felt the Invisible Stripes on his cashmere jacket, saw his Dangerous Paradise coming to a Dead End. The situation cried out for Sylvia Sidney, a woman born to stand by loyally and help. "You've got a right to a second chance," I said. "But I wonder if illegal gambling's the answer. Isn't it on the tacky side as well?"

He shook his head. "Illegal doesn't have to be tacky. Doesn't even have to be wrong if you've got a sense of values." And he looked very thoughtful. "When something's illegal in every state of the union, like peddling dope or flesh, then it's tacky, and maybe wrong, and touch and go for sure. But gambling's legal right next door in Nevada! It's big and swanky there, and that's the way it ought to be out here, Elva — if the Reno crowd wasn't paying off Mayor Bowron to kill the competition."

I remembered voting for Mayor Bowron because he seemed no less sincere than District Attorney Fitts in his campaign to rid our city of crime. "Oh Ben," I said, "politics is really the dirtiest business."

"What did I tell you? And what price illegal now? Will you back the Mayor who makes a deal to ban man's favorite sport, or the guy who wants to bring man his favorite sport in spite of the Mayor?" Ben put his arm around my waist. "The police department's standing in line to help me. All we got to do is pay them off."

"I do see your point, Ben. That way everyone gets a piece of the action, and no one's a loser."

A voice behind us called out, "One Big Look is closing now." We turned and saw the old attendant waiting by the cable car. On the way down Ben kept his arm around me and I kept silent, pondering his other side. Beneath the devil-may-care mask he had ideals of a kind, and made me feel warmly sympathetic when he talked about shaking off the past, yearning to start all over again and hit the jackpot. And as we drove off, further proof of his other side emerged. Switching on the car radio, I found it tuned to the classical music station. We listened to some inspirational Rachmaninoff for a while, then I said, "You'll get ahead, Ben. I'll stake you." He clasped my hand tightly. "But what about Dragna?" I went on. "What will you tell him?"

"The truth. I'm going out on my own."

"Won't there be trouble?"

Ben's hand almost crushed mine, then relaxed. "Jack's okay. He's tacky but he ain't in the killing business. I never ran with that crowd." We were passing the Coconut Grove. "Let's go dancing there soon. Nobody kills if you play it straight, Elva. And straight for Dragna means giving him a good deal."

"Don't let him buy you out too cheap."

Ben flashed me a look of surprise. "What are you talking about? *I'm* buying. Buying my way out."

"But you're selling your share of the business." He nodded. "And Dragna's getting it." He nodded again. "Why should you pay for something Dragna's buying?"

He didn't answer, but I solved the problem anyway. Shakedown, I thought. Payola's a real bog, it can sink you. "I'm an old hand at deals and I know how to beat people down," I said. "I'd be happy to help."

"You're helping enough. I don't want you involved, Elva. Apart from putting up the dough."

This sounded a bit ruthless, but Ben was under pressure and I shrugged it off as unintentional. We fell silent, caught up in the magic of Rachmaninoff again. An hour later we were caught up in an even more potent magic. I finally roused myself and started to get out of Ben's bed. "Don't leave, I'm ready for an encore." Two hours later I started to get out of bed and he reached for me again. "Don't leave, I've been thinking. Another hundred grand would buy us a controlling interest in the Clover Club. And I'd like to look into a couple of night spots along the coast." He stroked my face. "What do you say, Baby?"

I nodded, very happy if slightly confused to hear myself called, for the first time in my life, Baby!

Baby Looks Back

"Merry Xmas, you've got the wrong Baby," I told the Bug the first time I ever spoke to him, which was when I answered the phone and he thought he heard Mother. We were just sitting down to our dinner. Mother talked with him for awhile and came back disappointed. He couldn't drop by the house after all, because he had to spend the Day in a conference with Mr. Dragna, ironing out details of their deal.

"I thought only the movies believed The Show Must Go On when the rest of the world stops," she remarked. "But Ben's profession seems just as dedicated." Sipping champagne, she grew nostalgic. "Remember the time we went to Lon Chaney's funeral at Forest Lawn? He was hardly in his grave before Mr. Thalberg and two screenwriters hurried over to a limousine, which was waiting by God's Garden, and went on with their script conference."

Although Mother considered me just slim enough to meet Ben on Christmas Day, in my opinion there remained a few pounds to shed, so I took only a thin slice of turkey breast with my cottage cheese. She ate the works, treating herself to cranberry sauce, yams, creamed onions, mince pie, three splits of bubbly, and even had a Yuletide log blazing in the fireplace, although the temperature was above seventy. By tradition we kept Christmas dinner a family affair, the two of us snugly alone with our gifts to each other, diamonds, negotiable securities, a new automobile or whatever. I believe this was the year Mother gave me a small piece of Wilshire Boulevard.

Over mince pie she looked suddenly grave, and confessed that Ben's involvement with Dragna worried her. "How deep does it go? And how deep does Mr. Dragna's involvement go with Ben's business associates in New York?"

"You mean the Mob?"

"I'm afraid I do. I know beans when the bag is open. When Ben called to say he couldn't get away I heard a babble of crude excited voices in the background. Just like the soundtrack of a Warner Brothers gangster picture." She poured more champagne, then whispered, "*Each Dawn I Die.*"

Of course her secret affair quickly became an open secret. At Earl Gibson's open house, where Mother commented that the conversation pit alone must have held a hundred mil, Harry Chandler of the *Times* took her aside and said, "Elva, we voted you a Woman of the Year two years running, you're on a pedestal, don't fall off." It didn't faze her. She continued to give dinner parties for Ben at her house, intimate yet tremendously grand, caviar, truffled guinea hen, flaming crepes suzettes, champagne in silver goblets. Di Frasso was a fixture, playing godmother to the affair and wistfully congratulating Mother on steering Ben to a practical enterprise like the Clover Club, instead of hauling him off to search for buried treasure. Sessue Hayakawa, who once thrilled me in *The Tong Man*, brought his long-time housemate. They taught Mother and the Bug the ancient art of Japanese finger message. Miss Sophie, who sometimes brought Ramon Novarro, was no longer in fashion as hairdresser extraordinary, and no longer discreet as a saint about her fickle ex-clients. She dished out scandal as flaming as the dessert. Although WR remained very fond of Mother, he never saw his way to socializing with Ben, but Marion sneaked over when he was out of town. She put on a soft shoe or high kick show with the Mosconi Brothers, ex-vaudevillians who ran a dance school and gave me hoofing lessons in the early days. I usually brought Jimmy Gabriel, and sometimes Ben invited a sinister buddy who called himself a movie director. We never discovered what movie he made, but from their conversation it seemed they were planning to muscle in on a bookie service. After dinner we screened a picture, and in spite of my protests it was usually one of Baby Jewel's early triumphs.

Jimmy won Mother over with his imitations, especially his Carmen Miranda, although of course she never witnessed his Elva Kay. Unable to sabotage our picture, she became its greatest advance publicist and faithfully repeated Jimmy's slogans to the world. "Watch out for a sleeper. I read the script and it's a documentary of our changing times. Judge Hardy never had a case like this!" And one evening after everyone else had gone home, she stretched out on her white streamlined couch and kicked a silver ballet slipper into the air. "Isn't it strange, Baby, how the secret pattern in our lives threads on and on?" A smile. "We're both financing male animals." A raised eyebrow. "But is that one up to them, or to us?"

By this time Ben had apparently squared his accounts with Dragna, although Mother never learned the details, only what it cost. She signed the checks when he acquired two gambling spots near San Diego, but refused to go and visit them, clinging staunchly to her rule about staying inside the city limits. "What are you afraid of?" I asked. "Turning a hundred years old like Margo in *Lost Horizon*, when she ankled Shangri-La?" She gave a mysterious smile. "Make fun of me if you like. But the City of the Angels is my home, and I've always had a strong vibration I'll regret the day, or even the hour, I leave it."

Asking me for a signed photograph, sending over a case of bootleg French perfume, always standing up when I came into a room, Ben really worked hard on good manners and only scared me once. He listened to Mother extol the Violet Flame, grew fiercely excited at the idea of blasting enemies out of existence, and announced there were quite a few people he could use it on. I believed him. But he cooled off and almost sulked when Mother explained the technique was only for use against hostile entities, not personal foes. He promised her he was now free of everything tacky, but she never quite believed it, and neither did people like Mr. Selznick, for although they fraternized pleasantly at the Clover Club, Ben never got back on the top social circuit.

I told Mother I had the impression that he dreamed sincerely of class, but found it almost impossible to turn down a good racket. He moved away from Dragna because it felt too dangerous, but still went on smuggling Chanel and planning to acquire the racing wire service that tipped off bookies. But Jimmy, who had inside information from his friend the ex-cop and author of *Two of a Kind*, insisted that Ben did more than keep his secret ties with the Mob and pocket the money Mother gave him to pay off Dragna. He was a genuine authentic guaranteed killer who not only rubbed out Big Greenie, but in his New York days pumped "Mad Dog" Coll full of lead in a telephone booth.

"Please. Do not blow this story to Mother," I said, doubting it anyway. But for Jimmy it was more than truth, it was revelation. "Chew this over, Baby. An all-American grin like Gable, Come and Get It eyes like Flynn, a wardrobe even classier than Ronald Colman's — and the heart of Attila the Hun. The Bug is a very great actor." Studying the very great actor's habits and gestures, Jimmy was particularly struck by the way he kept combing his hair. "What a reflex for a killer, imagine shooting a guy dead and then primping in the mirror. I'll use it." Then the missionary in his nature stirred. "No. Tricky and shallow. I've got to reach further." He grew hushed, almost somber. "Behind that incredibly confident facade lies a mystery to freeze the heart. Blood-guilt. The dark night of the soul, when the Bug cries out in his sleep." Then he changed his mind and decided to use it after all, until our director said, "Watch out. When Bugsy sees it in the movie he'll put the finger on you."

Jimmy picked this director because he was an old hand who specialized in cutrate melodrama. Irish, fiftyish, weatherbeaten, with a rough no-nonsense front, Roy William Neill looked me over at our first meeting and gave a nod of approval. "You're real thin. That's good. Gives you an eager, hungry edge. Keep it that way." He sipped a dark beer, thick as mud. "Baby Jewel. They tell me you're sticking with that name, or stuck with it, and maybe it still sells a couple of tickets, but don't expect any star treatment around here. This is no MGM."

"I can see that," I said, looking around the basic dingy office. "In fact it reminds me of where I started out. Poverty Row. Working for a man called Sid Gordon. And you remind me of Sid, in a way."

He seemed pleased. "Mother of God. Whatever happened to Shylock Sid?"

"You knew him?"

"Sure. He never laughed. *I* started out at a studio in the next block, and once did Sid a favor. Took over some piece of junk for a week when his director took sick. Wonder what happened to old Shylock Sid." He opened another bottle of beer. "Now let me tell you something about myself. I'm not Fritz Lang. I'm not Hitchcock."

I gave him a deadpan look. "I guess you're not Lubitsch either."

"You bet." A thoughtful pause. "I'm not Jack Ford."

"And you're not Orson Welles."

"You like Welles?"

"He's got it," I said.

"He's got too much of it. You'll never catch me shooting through fireplaces. I just tell the story the best I know how."

"You're an honest-to-goodness pro," I suggested. "You're Howard Hawks on a budget."

He grinned. "Okay, that milks it." Another thoughtful pause. "But just telling the story is more than it sounds. I work to make things real."

"That's fine with me. I worked for years with directors who worked to make them unreal. No slur intended. On the whole they did a pretty damn good job of it."

Roy William Neill got up from behind his desk. "They're waiting for me to check a couple of locations," he said, started for the door, then turned back. "I'm going to like you. Frankly I wasn't sure. A star trying to make a comeback can be a big pain in the ass, especially when she's got money in the picture."

The first day on the set, Jimmy astonished me. I hadn't seen him over the weekend, and at 8:00 Monday morning he looked unbelievably intact, like a juvenile lead all excited over his first chance at a starring role. Yet physically all he'd done was to rinse the gray out of his hair. "When the inner man knows where he's going, Baby in Quotes, it shows. I've been working out body and soul." Then an assistant called us and we shot eight minutes of film before lunch. It felt like the Sid Gordon days all over again. Nervous as usual from lack of imagination, with no grip on my part as usual until I started working, I did what Neill, and occasionally Jimmy, said. Neill had a sharp, tough instinct. He wasn't Lang, he wasn't Hitchcock, maybe he disliked to expose his sensitive side and put out a cantankerous smokescreen, but he knew how a scene should be played. Jimmy often gave too much at first, and Neill jumped on him right away. "Silent movies went out more than ten years ago. I thought everyone knew that except Lionel Barrymore." I always gave too little at first, and he jumped on that as well. "Mother of God. Did you never meet a boy and feel an instant click? Or are you frigid? You deny it? Then give me some heat and we'll stay on schedule."

We stayed on schedule. One desert-cold night in the Valley, on location in some half-empty new suburb passing for Arizona, Mother came out to visit. She had trouble locating my trailer because the name Constance Moore was on the door. "Who is Constance Moore and why isn't *your* name up there?" she asked, furred and perfumed, unpacking a Waldorf salad, a cheesecake and a bottle of cognac from a picnic hamper. I explained the company switched to night shooting at short notice and had to grab any available equipment, including this trailer. "Constance is the resident Republic blonde," I added. "She just finished *La Conga Nights* and has forty-eight hours, which is all we need, before she goes into *Ma, He's Making Eyes at Me.*"

It didn't satisfy her. "They could at least send you fresh flowers. This picture only got off the ground with your money." She handed me a silver snifter of cognac. "And are they still barring you from watching dailies?"

"Jimmy thinks it would be bad for me, and I trust him."

"Why isn't it bad for Jimmy to watch dailies? Have a little Waldorf, Baby."

"I'm in his hands. He knows more than me. I trust him."

She shook her head. "I still think he owes you star treatment. I don't even see an icebox in Constance Moore's trailer. Talk about changing times, your situation here is a documentary in itself." A coyote howled long and distantly in the mountains. Mother shivered. "How I hate that sound. Coyotes feed on carrion, and there's no more disgusting animal habit in the world."

Then I was called to the set, to run down a dark street with Jimmy and fire a shot at the cop who chased us. When I got back to the trailer, Mother was standing proudly on the steps, and Constance Moore's nameplate was no longer on the door. "I borrowed a screwdriver, Baby. And you'll have flowers tomorrow night." She smiled, then shivered as the coyote howled again.

On the last day of shooting we drove out toward the desert to retake part of a scene. It was near the end of the picture, Jimmy and I holed up in a strange desolate building that had once been a motel. The crippled widow who used to run it still lived on the premises. She betrayed us to the cops and there was a gun battle as we made a getaway in our car. Neill thought the action came out too slow the first time, and had a touch he wanted to add. "A stray bullet's going to hit that widow in the face. It's a natural, I don't know why I never thought of it before."

We finished just before the light started to fade. While the crew loaded its equipment back on the trucks, Jimmy took my arm and walked me away. We were both covered with dust, caked with tomato ketchup from our wounds, and Jimmy had an artificial bruise on his cheek, which the widow struck with her crutch. He said he wanted to talk to me. I wanted to clean myself up and asked if it couldn't wait. He shook his head and led me around the side of the abandoned motel, to a veranda facing the desert.

"The greatest mistake of my life was leaving you and going back to Marie."

I felt irritated, wondering why Jimmy brought that up again at the end of a long day, when all I wanted was to wipe myself free of ketchup and dust.

"When you work with someone, you really learn about them," he said. "And when it's good, you feel so close. Every day I've felt closer to you, every day I couldn't imagine why I let you go and married three more wives." His arm was around me now. "I'll be free in a month. I want to marry you."

I was too unprepared to say anything at first. During the shooting I hardly saw Jimmy outside the studio, too tired to do anything on Sundays except get up late, lounge around the house, and have an early supper with Mother. One Sunday he wanted to go through a scene and kept things the way we agreed, warm and friendly but professional.

"Why?" I asked finally, and in the window of an empty room caught sight of our reflections, filthy and blotched, as Jimmy said how much he loved me with a love more than sex, a deep true romantic eleventh hour love. He said we were Two of a Kind. I opened the door to the empty room and walked inside. There was a musty smell in the air, a mixture of neglect and dogshit. Old newspapers lay around the floor, they crackled when I stepped on them, and the paint on the walls had faded to no color at all. As he followed me into the room, Jimmy said something about Mother, how I must loosen the tie or face loneliness at the end of the road. He respected the tie, of course, but it was no substitute for deep true romantic eleventh hour love. The newspapers crackled again as he stepped on them.

"I faced loneliness ten years ago," I said. "Thanks to you." Then I asked if he had a cigarette. He looked annoyed and reminded me he never smoked. "I'm sorry," I said, "but I left my cigarettes somewhere, and I need one desperately." Jimmy stood close to me and demanded an answer first. Outside, beyond the veranda, voices called our names, asking what had happened to Baby and Jimmy, everyone was waiting to go home. Jimmy backed me against a wall and kissed me on the mouth. He tasted of ketchup, and no doubt I did too.

"I can't imagine being married," I said.

"You always lacked imagination. But remember this." Jimmy sounded accusing. "Ten years ago you took off your clothes, lay on my bed and were so in love with me you even offered to pay for my divorce."

"I remember. I also remember you turned me down."

"I told you it was the greatest mistake of my life."

The voices called for us again more urgently. They asked what the hell was going on. "It's a good question," I said, stepped on a patty of shit, then my eyes released a few silent tears of exhaustion, confusion, surprise, anger, and worst of all a ghastly suspicion. Through a slight blurr, I looked at Jimmy. He was breathing fiercely, his eyes glared, dust caked on his forehead and chin, and he reminded me suddenly of the Phantom of the Opera.

"I only asked you to marry me. There's no reason to start weeping."

But there was. A moment later, confirming my suspicion that a fearsome thing was about to happen, I heard myself accept. My own eleventh hour feeling came out like a tooth that was hard to pull. "Look what you've done," I said. "You've twisted me around your little finger, unless

I'm twisted anyway, and if I am, it's your fault." Jimmy blinked with alarm. I must have looked and sounded very angry. "Goddammit, I'm going to be Bluebeard's Fifth Wife!" I shouted, ran out of the room and along the veranda, and found it was almost dark. Turning a corner I collided with Neill, who had come looking for us. I begged him for a cigarette, Jimmy appeared like a bat out of hell, and Neill said, "Mother of God, you're both mad."

Elva's Diary

May 27 • For an almost uninterrupted three hours I faced the cameras in the Oval Office of the executive suite at EKE this morning. *The March of Time* had honored me with a request to appear in their special feature on American career women, my co-stars including politician-playwright Clare Boothe Luce, novelist-missionary Pearl Buck, and all-around athlete Babe Didrikson. Wearing a brisk yet feminine two-piece based on a creation by the great Irene for Myrna Loy, which caught my eye in *I Love You Again,* I received many compliments on my informal charm and glowing energy. Also on the range of my professionalism, when I corrected the position of a key-light.

Around midmorning the director called a break and I arranged for the crew to sample my latest canned goods investment, EKE Coffee, which everyone agreed tasted incredibly fresh. (Earl Gibson of Ace Foods, watch out!) My secretary informed me that a Miss Hill was on the line, demanding to rent Falcon's Lair, so I took the call and heard a voice with a southern accent even more swampy than Mary Louise Cloud's. She sounded a most unlikely candidate for the great Valentino estate, and in need of a stringent checkup. Explaining I no longer handled such matters personally, except in special cases, I offered to switch her to Francine at my rental sector.

"I'm a special case, Mrs. Kay. Don't you dare switch me to anyone."

About to slay her with a comeback, I changed my mind. The arcs were suddenly brighter than silver again as *The March of Time* director began "sneaking" a shot of me in action. Framed in close-up for posterity, I summoned a gracious smile, told Miss Hill the cameras would be grinding away for hours yet, and suggested she come by after 3:00. But she came by much earlier and there was no way to avoid her. She stood right beside the camera and watched behind a pair of outsize dark glasses as I welcomed Baby, in a special guest appearance, to the Red Room, and asked her opinion of our projected takeover of the Wetherby-Keyser Shoe Company, Hollywood's most exclusive footwear store. Although deep in my role, I noticed Miss Hill wore an expensive white linen suit, carried a large morocco leather shoulder-bag, and had a mink coat draped over her shoulders. It was stylish, yet betrayed her lack of style. Furs always go into storage at the end of April out here.

The moment we got the last shot in the can, she walked over and demanded to talk business. I led her to the East Room, where she languidly tossed her coat on a chair. "Just got in from New York," she drawled, removing her dark glasses and looking like Joan Bennett since her wise decision to become a natural brunette. "I'm after the Lair because they tell me it's big and private. And that's the way I like things to be."

Two crackerjack diamond rings, a Cartier watch and the lavish mink inspired me to ask if she'd rather buy than rent. Her green eyes flashed me a suspicious look. "I heard the Lair's only for rent." I confirmed it, then explained there was another big and private mansion on my books, the famous adobe chateau of Jimmy Gabriel.

"No. I want the Lair. Everyone tells me it's my kind of place. A real party house." Miss Hill's voice was suddenly powerful enough to call the hogs home. "So don't try and pull any fast ones."

I raised a cool eyebrow.

"And come off that perch. You're aiming to do Jimmy Gabriel a favor because he just married your daughter."

First I wondered what kind of tough customer I was dealing with, then wished yet again I'd never agreed to handle the most notorious white elephant in Bel Air. "Baby and Jimmy are the romance of the year," I said calmly. "But there's no connection. His former residence merely happens to be one of the hottest properties in town. When would you like to see the Lair?"

"I don't have to see it. I just want to move in tonight."

"Snakes alive. Tomorrow might be possible, although it's unusually short notice. And I'll have to check your references first."

Miss Hill sighed. "I always forget the pace out here is real slow. How I do hate hotels, but I guess I can futz around for one night at the Beverly Hills." Opening her shoulder bag, she poured out roll after crispy roll of new greenbacks. "Here are my references, and don't tell me they ain't good enough." She pushed them across the desk. As far as I could tell, they were all $100 bills, and as far as I could see, she had plenty more left in the bag.

"I wasn't thinking of money."

"In a pig's eye." Miss Hill let another cascade fall from her bag.

"The Lair never rents for less than six months."

"No problem. If I get restless, I'll move out anyway and cut my losses." She began counting the loot. "But if I don't move in tomorrow, you can shove it. There's twenty grand and I'll swear it's a hell of a lot more than you usually get."

Bored, or impatient, or both, Miss Hill turned away suddenly and gazed out the window. I picked up a greenback and held it against the light, examining it the way Ben taught me. No doubt it was the genuine article.

Then I saw Miss Hill's green eyes watching me.

"Just checking your references," I said.

"You beat the band. Anything to drink around here?"

Opening the door that looked like a mirror on the wall, I revealed Ben's inspiration, a luxurious bar with a chandelier and a music box. Automatically, one lit up and the other played. "Name your poison, Miss Hill." She named a double bourbon on the rocks, and her hands trembled slightly when she took the glass.

"Shall we drink to the deal, Mrs. Kay?"

"I never drink in the afternoon. And there's no deal yet. I really have to know something about you."

Miss Hill drank too eagerly. "Twenty-four, twice married, twice divorced, the second time in Mexico last month, scads of other guys in my life, but I'm still waiting for the big wham bam." She gazed out the window again. "And the *Mirror* just wrote up one of my parties in New York. On the café society page."

"Did it mention you rob banks?" I asked, looking at the rolls of long green on my desk.

There was no smile on her face. "My daddy saved me from a life of crime," she said. "He left me a trust fund when he died." She finished her drink and picked up her fur. "Are you taking my money or leaving it, Mrs. Kay?"

I buzzed Francine and told her to get the Lair ready in twenty-four hours.

Miss Hill put on her dark glasses. "I love to gamble, even though I hate to lose," she said as she walked to the door. "Is the Clover Club the place to go?"

"It's the top." How nice for Ben, I thought, after his recent run of bad luck at the races, if Virginia Hill dropped half her trust fund there in a single night. From the window I watched her drive off in a new white Cadillac, and reflected there was more to my unusual client than met the eye. Even if almost too much met the eye.

May 28 • Resting after an encore last night, I described my unusual client while Ben stood naked in the bathroom trying out a new chinstrap. At first he made no comment, he was having problems with the buckle. Then he said, "So the Alabama heiress is back in town."

"You know the little lady?"

"Just saw her once in New York. I was meeting with my business associates and Virginia came by with a bag."

"Full of lettuce?"

Ben was still having problems with the chinstrap, so I got up and fixed the buckle.

"Around fifty grand," he said.

"From her daddy's little old trust fund?"

He smiled and ran a comb through his hair. "The Alabama heiress is the full crapola."

"You don't have to tell me."

"Virginia just carries the bag."

"Is that a profession? And is it as tacky as it sounds?"

Ben sprawled in a chair, sat me on his knees and asked me to massage his scalp. "Someone in New York wants to transfer funds to his business associates in Chicago, or vice versa," he explained. "It's got to be cash because these are not guys who pay income tax. So they need a person to carry the bag. It's a good steady job, pays nice expenses, and Virginia gets to ride first class on the Twentieth Century. Plus little Joey Adonis is nuts about her, and doesn't mind paying for it."

"I knew there was more to the little lady than meets the eye. And who's Mr. Adonis?"

"What can I tell you?" Ben sounded vague. "Wears lifts in his heels, built a bombproof house for his mother, crazy about opera."

"The Alabama heiress is crazy about gambling. She plans to pay a visit to the Club."

Ben frowned. "Her type I can live without. She's not the kind of client we need. And not the kind you should be doing business with. Move off now."

"The Lair's been empty for a while," I said, getting up and starting to put on my clothes. "And it was my easiest twenty grand in many a moon. I just couldn't resist it."

Ben grunted, stood in front of a mirror, slapped his cheeks a few times and then got into bed with his chinstrap. "Well, I guess I can't blame you for keeping your eye on the jackpot. Goodnight, Baby. See you around." As I reached the door, he called me back. "Loosen this buckle a notch, will you, or I'll never get to sleep."

June 3 • Dinner last night with di Frasso, the first in the new townhouse she decided to rent for the duration. (Yours truly masterminded the deal, of course.) An inner circle affair, just WR and Marion, Elsa Maxwell, Mary Pickford with her adoring Buddy Rogers. Mary wore six strands of pearls but looked out of sorts. Elsa whispered she still wakes up in the night and calls for her lost Doug, which can hardly make sweet music in adoring Buddy's ears. I wondered if the fatal click of the barber's scissors ever haunted her dreams.

When the others left, the Countess asked me to stay behind. "Let's make a night of it, Elva, and hit the Clover Club. I'm in the mood for action."

This was embarrassing. The last time Dorothy came to dinner, Ben asked me to do him a favor. "Phase the old broad out, Baby. She belongs on the shelf." When I protested, he stood firm. "Leftover wine, pour her away." But I could hardly refuse the friend who brought us together, and we drove to the Club in separate cars.

Al Jolson was just finishing his act in the downstairs room with "Swanee." "He's better looking in blackface," Dorothy said, and glanced around the bar. "Slim pickings. But it's an early town, and we're late."

Then I heard someone shout a raunchy oath in a southern accent, and Virginia Hill came down from the gambling room with Ben. She wore a long white dress and had a restless glitter in her eyes. One glance was enough to reveal that my unusual client had been losing and drinking heavily, and Ben seemed in a bad temper. "Didn't know you planned to drop by," he said in an unwelcoming voice, and muttered at the sight of Dorothy, "this is all I need tonight. Phase her *out*, Baby." Meanwhile Virginia disappeared to the ladies' room. "She'll throw the attendant twenty bucks," Ben said. "The dumb crocked broad has been throwing everybody twenty bucks since she got here. Even David Selznick. She took him for a dealer."

Virginia came back, reeking of bourbon and stale face powder. Some pig, I thought, and yet too much liquor gives her a curious sleazy glamor. I patted her arm and asked how she was enjoying the Lair. "It's a hell of a kick except for all those stopped-up johns," she said in her best hog-calling tone. "I'm planning a Fourth of July party, and you're invited, but get me a goddam plumber first. I need at least one straight flush." She started on another drink and it proved fatal almost at once. Her eyes glared, then closed. She went dead pale. "Okay, folks," she said. "Somebody drive Virginia home."

Ben whispered in my ear, "Sorry, Baby, I've got to do it." He gave her a disgusted look. "But if she ever comes back, we'll give her the bum's rush."

Our little party broke up not in the best of spirits.

June 5 • This morning Ben's butler called to say Mr. Siegel had gone to Mexico City on business, and would be away for a couple of weeks. This afternoon Baby phoned to cancel the screening of her picture. Seems the Hays Office hit the roof when they saw *Two of a Kind* yesterday, and demanded twenty-eight cuts to tone down the brutality. Five of them in the last scene, where Baby almost drowns in her own blood! Remembering the time Mr. Hays embraced her in front of the national press and declared her an example to the world, I wondered if he saw the picture himself. Baby said she hoped so.

June 7 • Francine from my rental sector called, asking what to do about those stopped-up johns at the Lair. Wanting to make sure someone would be home to let the plumber in, she'd phoned Virginia several times and got no answer. Finally, this morning, a maid picked up and said Miss Hill left June 5 on a business trip to Mexico City.

Faced with a coincidence too great to be a coincidence, I kept exquisitely calm. "Did she mention how long Miss Hill planned to be away?"

"A couple of weeks."

I slammed the receiver down and paced my bedroom, still exquisitely calm but unable to stop humming "South-of-the-border-down-Mexico-way." To get the wretched tune out of my head, I began talking nonchalantly with myself.

—You blind trusting fool, letting Ben two-time you with the Alabama heiress.

—I don't understand it. On our first date, I alluded slyly to Ben's reputation for boffing around, and he said there were times when he settled for Coca-Cola in the absence of champagne. But it was bubbly all the way with me.

—And still the brute slunk back to Coke.

—Swamp water's more like it. *Why?*

—Find the movie. There's no mystery of the human heart that a movie hasn't solved.

—So true. I need a movie where the male animal falls, and falls very low, on account of a ruthless worthless bitch. . . . And I think I've found a clear case *Of Human Bondage!*

—Go on. Remake it. Fade in.

—New York. Grand Central Station. Virginia steps off the Twentieth Century, carrying her bag. Takes a taxi to the bombproof residence of Mama Adonis. In the cellar, Mama serves drinks and her famed antipasto to the usual bunch of hoods. Virginia comes in to hand Joey the green stuff, and claps eyes on Ben Siegel for the first time.

—Bingo.

—It's *Riptide* and more.

—Go on.

—Los Angeles. Union Station. Virginia steps off the Super Chief. She's ditched Adonis to follow Ben out here. She gambles on enticing him to her Lair.

—Didn't take her long. And Ben certainly fooled you, saying Virginia was a type he could live without.

—No. He fooled himself. At first he really believed it. Then she began casting her spell, the strange feverish spell of an alley cat in heat.

—It's *Red Dust*. Harlow rutting for Gable.

—And more. Virginia's the type that never takes no for an answer.

—She even got *you* to hand over the Lair at twenty-four hours' notice.

—Alley cat cunning. She had *everything* worked out. Why didn't I realize it, the day she penetrated EKE?

—You were exhausted from facing the cameras.

—But it seems so obvious now. She *knew* too much.

—Yes. Knew the Lair was for rent and you handled it. Knew about you and Ben, and the Clover Club. A real thorough job of research.

—I wish to God I'd done the same job on *her*, instead of grabbing that twenty grand on the spot.

—You're not going to like this, but I just heard a voice from your past. Smooth. British. Mocking. It said: *"Gobble and shit, Elva. You always ask for more."*

I smashed a bathroom mirror by throwing my hairbrush at it, then lay on my bed, feeling exquisitely calm. Virginia had nothing but youth and crude determination on her side. The movies told me that a mature, wise, tastefully seductive woman always wins her man back in the end. Just let the end come soon, I prayed, with Baby in my life I'll never feel truly lonely, but I feel lonely enough right now without Ben.

An hour later I entered the gilded lobby of the Pantages Theatre and ascended one of the giant twin stairways leading to the mezzanine. Fifty-two is a vulnerable age for a woman to find herself temporarily alone, I thought, no matter how inviting she appears in the mirror. Then I glimpsed myself in a mirror. Let me record — maybe with a touch of vanity, but without a jot of exaggeration — that I *did* look inviting. And light years away from fifty-two. The front row mezzanine was empty. I chose a seat directly below the blue glass dome of the ceiling, and its lights dimmed for the matinee of *My Favorite Wife*. Opening my Tiffany's pillbox from time to time for a hearty sniff, I chuckled my way through this delicious marital mix-up with Cary and Irene, and by the end was laughing so much I had to wipe tears from my eyes.

Baby Looks Back

Dressed to kill, in a tight beaded gown, Mother drove to my house after the matinee, rang the doorbell frantically and slumped into my arms. I mixed a jug of martinis and heard her out.

"But didn't you tell me it was a law of nature?" I said. "They take what they want when they want it. And if it'll make you feel any better, Jimmy's been cheating as well."

She gave an astonished look. "So soon? Who's he boffing?"

"Some tall expensive girl."

"That's terrible. But it *does* make me feel better." Sipping her third martini, she remarked again how calm she felt, then clutched my arm desperately. "All the same, the situation couldn't be worse. I'm the older woman as well as the other woman. It's easy come and easy go. Sometimes I only learn where Ben's gone through his butler." A new thought seemed to disturb her. "There was a wretched butler once before in my life," she said.

"Before what?"

"It doesn't matter. Just a coincidence." She looked uncertain. "I hope."

This was yet another of Mother's remarks that took me thirty years to figure out. It only became clear when I read her diaries and knew she was referring to Desmond Taylor's butler, who used to call up and cancel their dates. At the time, I feared the movies were making serious inroads on Mother's mind. She talked of getting Ben back in the last reel, she dissolved to a hotel bedroom in Mexico City, she panned to two shadows locked in an embrace on the wall, she cast herself in the role of wronged but loyal helpmate and then slipped into the scheming other woman part.

It grew even more confusing when she remarked sadly, "Irene Dunne lost Charles Boyer in *Love Affair*."

"Norma Shearer got her husband back in *The Women*," I said, hoping to encourage her.

"I'm not talking of husbands, Baby. Anyway, they had a child, which gave Norma a top card to play." She brooded. "Margaret Sullavan lost Henry Fonda in *The Moon's Our Home*."

"No, she got him back," I said. "But lost him in real life."

"Are you sure it was only in real life?" When I nodded, Mother thanked me for setting the record straight, walked to a mirror and studied her reflection. "Would you say I look like $30,000,000 today?"

"I would."

"Then don't tell me youth can hold a gun at my head."

"I won't."

And a moment later it was over. Maybe she did a quick exercise and summoned the Violet Flame. Maybe she thought of another movie with the ending she wanted. In any case, when she turned back from the mirror, she was gleaming with that elegant, complete, uplifted sense of herself, and I wondered again how she found or stole or invented it.

"Ben's coming back, Baby. He knows where he belongs." A flashlight of a smile told me everything she believed in was totally real to her again. "What *really* worries me is you and Jimmy."

"I can handle it."

"That's my girl." She hugged me. "She can handle anything, no need to ask where she gets it from. I'm going home now, because I feel a little tired. Maybe overwork's catching up with me again, and I need two weeks of complete rest."

"Good timing if you do. And you always come back from that clinic looking like sunrise."

She hugged me again, walked out to her car and called back over her shoulder, "I'll show the bitch youth!"

This was not a remark it took me thirty years to figure out. At one of Mother's parties we screened *Girl on the Wing* after dinner because the Bug wanted to see it again, and Miss Sophie, who unloaded a cargo of secrets that night, whispered another to me as I died in the plane crash. "Ponce de Leon, move over," she said, and described how Mother found and peeled the Onion of Youth.

As Mother predicted, Ben came back and knew where he belonged, at least for part of the time. For the rest he belonged at Falcon's Lair, with furloughs that he spent at his own house, recharging the batteries. It was a threesome that would probably have ended in murder under the same roof, but with Mother and the Bug and Virginia installed in separate mansions, it had room to breathe. More than fifty rooms, if you added them up. Although the eternal triangle was a specialty of the movies, they never showed one anything like this, and it's amazing that I took it for granted. But I was brought up to take amazing situations (including my own) for granted, and this cruel voluptuous sexual contest struck me as just one more scene from the passing show. On your left, a gracious and ladylike plutocrat, the illegitimate child of a garment worker in Des Moines. On your right, a hard-drinking Syndicate moll posing as an heiress from the old South. Between them, their blue-eyed boy, the fashion-plate mobster, a slum kid from Brooklyn who made good. And looking on from above, maybe, the ghosts of slinky Louise Glaum and sultry Valentino.

I always knew when Mother got impatient with her role of patient help-mate and acted up as the other woman. For a few days afterwards, she had to wear dark glasses. "Seems the black eye is another secret pattern in my life, Baby. Getting one from Mr. Kay was a mundane thing, brutal but impotent, but in Ben's case it packs real libido."

At her Fourth of July party, Virginia wore dark glasses for the same reason. She and Mother acknowledged each other behind enormous shades, then turned their backs. On the wide sloping lawn behind the Lair, a tent with red, white and blue stripes flew the American flag, and a rented band played Sousa marches. Guests ate patriotic food in the tent, hamburgers, spare ribs, corn on the cob, sweet pickles, baked Alaska, or carried it out and picnicked on tables in the shade of eucalyptus trees. Waiters in Uncle Sam hats moved around with bowls of punch and pitchers of apple cider. Walking around arm in arm, Mother and I found most of the faces unfamiliar and overheard a lot of racetrack talk. "Virginia hasn't exactly rounded up the stars. See anyone at all, Baby, except George Raft?" I saw Harry Cohn helping himself to punch. "A bush-league player," Mother said. I pointed out that he put Columbia Studios on the map. "Not on *my* map, Baby. Take Mr. Capra away and it's still the same old peanut farm."

Later Hedda Hopper made an entrance in a Fourth of July hat, and I hid behind a tree. She stayed all of ten minutes and wrote up the party as a smash, tipping Virginia for stardom in the movies. Maybe she believed it or maybe no one told her that Harry Cohn gave Virginia a modest contract only as a favor to his friend George Raft, who asked it as a favor to his friend the Bug. In the end nothing came of it, because Virginia tired of voice lessons and took off for Mexico City again. Ben followed, but this time Mother said, "What the hell? It's important to grow from experience, and believe me I'm really growing, and can take anything now except the alley cat *becoming a movie star.*"

At the party I spoke no more than a hello to Virginia and never saw her again, but her image is still very clear. A series of images, really, like consecutive frames on a strip of film. Whenever she looked at Ben, which was often, her white dress gave off an aura of white heat. She seemed always to know where he was, a quick eager turn of the head and she

gazed right on target. Although I never saw her eyes behind the shades, I imagined them unblinkingly hungry. When Mother first outlined her scenario of the Virginia-Ben movie, it sounded like too many movies I'd seen, but when she passed on a confidence that Ben made in a burst of indecent pride, I changed my mind. "During their south-of-the-border idyll, Virginia fondly recalled how she turned up at Mama Adonis's house one day with her bag, stepped into a room full of paunchy or midget hoods, saw Ben standing by the pool table and ran a fever on the spot. After years of spreading her legs for the underworld and pretending she enjoyed it, you see, she was desperate for the real thing, the big wham bam, and just knew she'd found the dude to give it to her. *Hard all over.*"
So it seemed that some people led lives out of *Red Dust, Riptide* and Warner Brothers after all. And on that Fourth of July, Virginia certainly gave the impression of making up for lost time. At twilight the band switched from Sousa to Gershwin, lanterns were lit in the tent and braziers in the garden. Virginia took Ben off to her Lair, disappearing in a flash of hot white. Twenty minutes later she came out again, slightly disheveled, and seemed to be giving off smoke. Then I realized it came from a brazier on the terrace.

Nothing fazed Mother that day, experience made her grow by the minute. When she saw Ben and Virginia hotfoot it into the house, she sat down under a tree and timed the event on her watch. "The more they do it, the sooner they'll wear themselves out. Another law of nature, Baby. For *her,* of course, Ben is nothing but body, but for me he's body and soul." Ben's body was no small matter to Mother, and she used to complain that Virginia grabbed the lion's share, but she could always fall back on satisfactions of the soul, pride in embarking on her most romantic affair at an age when di Frasso and others got phased out, a tender belief in the Bug's *other side.* "Which Virginia never sees. And never forget I dared what no other woman dared. I stood by Ben all the way, and gave him his second chance."

Although Ben seemed to control the situation, maybe in the end it controlled *him.* Sometimes, I remarked to Mother, he looked at Virginia as if he hated her. "Only sometimes, Baby? I've never seen him look at her any other way — maybe it happens at moments when I would naturally not be present, but I wonder. She's white trash, and how can Ben ever forgive her for making him want her?" As we said goodbye, Ben looked at Mother as if he could never forgive her, either. He found his dream of success with class and found it not enough, he was grateful for his second chance and bitter about playing it false. He kissed us both, started to walk away across the lawn, then turned back to watch us leave. Lights blazed from the Lair, the band still played Gershwin, he stood near the tent with its lantern glow, and I saw a flash of gold on his wrist from the chain Mother gave him. Then Virginia in her garish white came up with a group of racetrack friends in tow. Just before they surrounded him, he looked our way once more and waved. Poor Ben, I thought, I can almost feel sorry for you for almost a minute, it must be terrible never to draw a simple ordinary loving breath.

Which brings me back to Jimmy, who drew so many. At his suggestion we got married in Reno, "where everyone goes for a quick divorce, so if you change your mind the morning after, you can stay on and file suit." At my suggestion he moved into my Mediterranean hideaway above the Strip, and turned his ghastly mansion over to EKE to rent or sell. "I won't really miss it," Jimmy said, "except for the mirrored bedroom." But I never shared his fascination with catching us in the act, in fact I tuned out when he admired our tangled reflections, as if checking to see how well the scene played. Once I accused him of shifting positions for an imaginary camera, so its angle favored him at the climax. And once, as we rested in each other's arms, dusk gathered and the room slipped gradually into darkness. "Don't move," Jimmy said, "lie very still and look at us up there on the ceiling. It's the most beautiful slow fadeout in the world." As the light dimmed, our reflections dimmed to black. "This is the only way to die." He held me tightly. "Making it, then watching ourselves disappear." After we disappeared completely, he said, "Feel my face." I felt tears.

A few weeks after we got married, *Two of a Kind* opened in various choice locations all over Los Angeles, downtown, Eagle Rock, Long Beach, Covina. Local reviewers found our effort distressingly sordid, and doubted that Jimmy Gabriel and Baby would recapture the hearts of the American public as a pair of delinquent killers. But *Time* magazine, the only national publication to give it a notice, called the picture an interesting primitive melodrama about youth running wild, and praised us for submerging ourselves so effectively in our characters. Maybe that explains the lack of comeback offers, we submerged ourselves too effectively, but I still like *Two of a Kind* better than any movie from my so-called golden age. For the first time I sat in the dark and really connected with my image on the screen. And I knew why when Mother said, "First time I saw you in a picture when you didn't *have* an image. I couldn't believe it was Baby up there!"

A few years ago I saw the movie again on TV around 4:00 in the morning, chopped here and there for commercials during which I switched to All-Nite Wrestling and Praise the Lord. I still connected. The violence that once stunned the Hays Office looked fairly routine, mayhem and blood count no higher than your average family hour show, but the mean, hard, funny excitement was still there. I remembered Neill saying he only told a story the best he knew how. His best could certainly hold its own against the best of all those B directors the movie buffs made a cult of later, and it struck me there ought to be room, in an unhealthy society, for a cult of Roy William Neill. I'm still waiting.

After *Two of a Kind* I waited for offers, but only one proposition came my way, from a German producer working on Poverty Row. Like many refugees at the time, he had a colorful story about escaping from the Nazis in Europe, something to do with reaching Lisbon in the back of a truck, disguised as a nun. He radiated class and sophistication in spite of the sleazy office, told me he saw my *Treasure Island* in Berlin with the great Pabst, and produced an early Dietrich movie in which she wore a monocle and looked weirdly like Conrad Veidt, and almost worked with Brecht. "But of course, that means nothing *here*," he said, and wanted me to star in a quickie about a blind girl detective. "Sorry, I don't see it," I said.

Jimmy was offered the part of Ali Baba in yet another low-grade Arabian Nights fantasy, and took it for the money, which he handed over to me as first repayment on the loan for his mortgage and divorce. "It's not necessary," I said, but he hated the idea of being in debt to his wife even more than he hated playing Ali Baba. At least our picture fulfilled his hope of turning out a sleeper, and netted us a profit of a hundred thousand. Nothing to boast about these days, in fact pretty shameful when you're supposed to make enough on your first movie to buy a studio or a Napa Valley vineyard or an island where you can retire for life, but it allowed Jimmy to clear the rest of his debt. "It's not necessary," I said again, and he told me I had some weird attitudes. "You don't seem to mind if a man lives off your money, for instance. I guess that comes from your Mother, but I'd like you to get a taste of the normal from *me*."

My first taste of the normal from Jimmy occurred when he told me about the girl in the chorus line of a Carmen Miranda musical. "I'm not the kind who cheats, Baby in Quotes, I never even think in terms of cheating, which is why I can look you in the eye and openly admit I screw this tall conniving broad. It's just a stupid physical thing and makes no difference to how *we* feel about each other."

"Are you sure about that?"

He put his arms around me. "We've reached a very special kind of understanding. No matter what happens, we *know* we're basically right for each other."

"How do we know?"

"It's obvious. I tell you about this girl and you don't throw a fit or walk out on me."

"Give me time. I could be working up to something."

Jimmy shook his head. "If I thought you'd be really hurt or jealous, I'd never have gotten involved with her." He gave me a solemn look. 'The One remains, the Many change and pass,' " he said. "Know who wrote that? Me neither, but it's some famous poet and it just came into my head, and it sums us up, so what have you got to worry about?"

"I'm not worried. Just impressed and aggravated by your incredible nerve."

When the Carmen Miranda musical opened, I asked Jimmy to take me to see it. "I'm crazy about her anyway," I said, "and I want you to point out the stupid physical thing." But he told me it wasn't necessary, they'd just broken up.

One Sunday morning, over a late breakfast, we heard a special bulletin on the radio. Jimmy sprang to his feet, caught sight of himself in a mirror and seemed disturbed by his own reflection. But he said nothing, and neither did I, listening to further details of the Japanese attack on Pearl Harbor, and having a memory flash of myself on the Royal Hawaiian beach at sunset. The rest of the day felt very long and silent. I read a couple of Erle Stanley Gardners. Next morning the radio brought us the voice of Roosevelt, saying America was officially at war.

Springing to his feet again, glimpsing himself in the mirror again, Jimmy seemed reassured by his reflection this time. He walked up close to it. "Here's one act I can't stay out of," he said. "Every bone in my body tells me to get into it. Otherwise I'll never be able to live with the guilt."

When the shock was over, I laughed. It was involuntary, like the dismal joke that followed. "You lived okay with the guilt of that stupid physical thing."

Jimmy called me a poisonous bitch, shuddered as if hurting all over, and backed away. I knew every bone in his body was really telling him he had to escape for a while, from a career that was still failing, probably even from our marriage. As he reached the door, I apologized and said, "I admire what you're going to do but it makes me very sad."

Tears came to his eyes. He walked up close to me, as if I were another mirror. "Remember you're only one of thousands of American wives, all facing the same situation at this very hour." I nodded. "This is unbelievable. But you know what happens when I'm wildly moved." He almost flung me on the couch. "It's gone hard."

Next day he volunteered for the air force. In due course it accepted him for navigational training, and in due course sent him to a base in Arizona.

Mother saw the whole thing as a movie, a replay of Tyrone Power in *A Yank in the RAF*. "Ty was so cocksure, so love-em-and-leave-em when he joined up, just like Jimmy, then he found military life more than he bargained for, stopped breaking Betty Grable's heart and began to *change*."

"Jimmy won't change," I said, but I found signs of change in him on the crisp, sunny winter's morning that I saw him off. Maybe he was only trying out a new part as he walked very stiffly to the bus with the other volunteers, and didn't even look back. As the bus drove off he leaned out the window and waved a last goodbye, brief, almost dutiful, like an afterthought. It seemed as if another world had taken him over, and I felt myself turning into a memory.

"Of course Ben feels very strongly about the war as well," Mother said. "He wants us to lick the hell out of every two-timing Jap." But in spite of his strong feelings he never volunteered, and apparently his police record kept him out of the draft. Instead he joined the black market and became its West Coast commander in chief, with the Clover Club as headquarters. The night after the great Los Angeles air raid scare, when sirens wailed and guns thundered at an empty sky, I went there with Mother and we sat at her special table downstairs. Ethel Waters, a regular favorite, sang "Stormy Weather" and some spirituals. Ben and his friend the phony movie director joined us, and after Ethel's first spiritual the friend said, "That lady really gets to me," then began discussing operational plans, how to corner the market in gasoline, liquor, silk stockings, draft deferments and other basic necessities likely to be in short supply.

Mother tuned out with an indulgent smile, and we talked of the previous night's false alarm, a mysterious attack of jitters that caused hundreds of people to imagine enemy planes swooping from the sky while Japanese gardeners signaled to them from the ground. "They say it's the end of *Mr. Moto*, Baby. Peter Lorre as a lovable Jap sleuth no longer fits the national mood. And you can be sure the government will go through with its plan to round up all our Japs now, and send them to camps out of state. Which means I'll lose Yoda and Fujita both."

When her Japanese gardeners were "relocated," in the official phrase, along with the rest, Mother cabled Roosevelt, offering to vouch for their loyalty and reminding him she'd once met Eleanor, who admired me so much. No answer came, and she denounced our president as a racist while denying that the Bug was a profiteer. "When there's goods to spare *and* money to spare, it's a simple case of supply and demand. What's so unpatriotic about recognizing a law of nature?" His clients at the Clover Club treated Ben like the man of the hour, and it made her proud. "The other night he suddenly thanked me all over again, and said he really feels like the man with the big cigar at last."

Mother awarded herself a big cigar when Virginia began drinking so heavily and swearing so vilely, because she lost at gambling, that Ben barred her from the Club. "It's the beginning of the end. She's losing her youth more quickly than I ever dared hope." Meanwhile, Mother's unique illusion of youth was kept up with booster peels, personal advice from Max Factor, daily isometric exercises followed by forty laps in the pool. And when Miss Sophie designed her new hairstyle, a modified Veronica Lake peekaboo, for the premiere of *Mrs. Miniver*, a columnist was inspired to nickname her She, after Rider Haggard's ageless princess. The label stuck, and it pleased her. "Not for nothing, Baby, was that immortal tale my favorite reading as a child."

Jimmy wrote short infrequent letters from Arizona, saying he missed me and loved me, but still felt good about getting into the act. He didn't want to spend his first leave in Hollywood, so I took a train to Phoenix, and found more signs of change when he walked into my hotel suite. The uniform was a shock, and the haircut that finally tamed his cowlick, but the biggest shock was his new habit of silence, which both of us found difficult to break. "There's something on your mind," I said. He shook his head. "Then why are you so silent?" He sighed. "Because there's nothing on my mind."

The day after I arrived, he taught me backgammon and the U.S. marines landed on Guadalcanal. The next day we went to see *Casablanca*, and Jimmy grunted with approval when Bogart told Ingrid Bergman that in times like these, personal problems amounted to less than a hill of beans. The next day we caught the bus to Albuquerque because Ginger Rogers was selling war bonds there, and we watched a local businessman pledge ten thousand dollars worth in exchange for a pair of her dancing shoes. On our last evening we admired yet another Technicolor sunset over the desert, then Jimmy told me what was on his mind. He had passed all his tests and would soon be sent to England, to go out on bombing missions. "So follow my example now, Baby in Quotes, and put yourself in limbo. When it's limbo time anyway, better move with it. Grow vegetables and make a victory garden, dance with lonely servicemen at the Hollywood Canteen, and if they offer you the trashiest movie, take it."

Next morning he left for the base and waved the same distant, dutiful goodbye. I went home and learned to jitterbug. One night, at the Canteen, Mickey Rooney joined the band and played drums. Some nights I took a lonely serviceman back to my lonely hideaway. I grew

corn, spinach and lettuce, hummed along with the Andrews Sisters singing "Praise the Lord and Pass the Ammunition" on the radio. And I
accepted the only movie offer to come my way, which came from Roy
William Neill, who signed on for the duration to make a new series of
Sherlock Holmes quickies with Basil Rathbone. As a joke and a good luck
gesture, he thought I might enjoy playing a murderee in each one, so in
Sherlock Holmes and the Voice of Terror, *Sherlock Holmes and the Secret Weapon*,
and so on, I acted a variety of the unbilled dead. Once, as a Japanese
agent, I was discovered lying on the floor in a kimono and rice-powder
makeup, with my throat cut.

Then two things happened almost at the same time. They had no apparent connection, yet I connect them now in my mind. One day the sky
turned a dirty drab yellow, the air smelt bitter and curdled, people complained of headaches, nausea, tearful eyes, and a scientist informed us on
the radio that all the booming wartime industries had created a new condition called smog. A few days later the phone rang and a man's voice
asked if I was willing for a limousine to pick me up at 1:30 a.m., and drive
me to a destination he was sorry he couldn't reveal. But he promised that
Mr. Howard Hughes, who was anxious to talk with me, would be waiting
there.

"Is this a practical joke?"

After a pause the man said quietly, "No."

By this time, of course, the gangling bewildered Howard who sat me on
his shoulders, and wanted to know if I liked flying, had become several
different Howards. He had flown his own planes to break the world
speed record and the around-the-world record. He had almost married
Katharine Hepburn. He had acquired TWA, and a reputation as a recluse
who liked to do business between midnight and dawn. He had given up
the picture business, then come back to it, discovering a foot doctor's
receptionist called Jane Russell and starring her in a movie called *The
Outlaw*. It had lain on the shelf for more than a year while he argued with
the Hays Office about all the shots of Jane's cleavage, which was supposed to hang over the movie like a thunderstorm over a summer's day.

Maybe, I thought, Howard has got plans now for some part for me.
"Okay, I'll see him," I said, and when a limousine took me way up in the
hills on that misty blacked-out night, it felt like the ultimate limbo time. In
a completely desolate area, with no glimmer of anything in view, the
driver pulled over to the side of the road. He opened the connecting window and held out a black velvet blindfold. "Mr. Hughes wants you to
wear this," he said. I felt stunned. "Any particular reason?" I asked, and
the driver, who was young and polite but never smiled, explained that

Mr. Hughes didn't want me to know where he lived. Fearing some joker or rapist had me almost in his clutches, I looked into the driver's eyes and searched them for crazy intentions. But they seemed rather bored, as if he'd been putting visitors through the same routine for months. So I let him blindfold me, and we drove on again. A coyote howled in the distance. I felt I was following Jimmy's instructions all the way, and moving with the time.

1951

Elva's Diary

March 15 • It was the first time I ever saw Virginia Hill not dressed in white. She entered the courtroom wearing somber black, had gained pounds as well as years, and looked more like a prosperous widow than a retired underworld queen. Remembering Eleanor Roosevelt's television debut on V-E Day, when she addressed the nation just a few weeks after Franklin died, I awarded Virginia equally low marks in the glamor department — but maybe, I thought, she's improved her chances in the dignity stakes. Then the cameras moved in too close for comfort. Sweat broke out on her forehead as she hollered at them to get away, and proved she could still call the hogs home any day of the week.

She settled herself at the witness table and fiddled with a bracelet as Senator Kefauver, a distinguished Walter Huston type, explained that his Committee was investigating organized crime in these United States. It wanted names and facts and figures, and had a few questions to ask Virginia about the racketeers she first took up with in the early Depression days. She looked up blankly. "I made it a point never to know anything about anybody," her voice twanged over the mike, and it seemed as if the louder she talked, the less she was going to tell. When the Senator warned Virginia that his Committee knew all about her frequent trips on the Twentieth Century, and the money that passed through her hands over the years, she gave him another blank look. "I liked to gamble and I was born lucky," she said, and it was impossible not to admire her nerve when I remembered Virginia at the Clover Club, cursing the wheel of chance like a drunken marine.

With a friendly smile, the Senator asked if Virginia could deny that she was once intimately friendly with Joey Adonis. With an unfriendly stare, Virginia admitted that she got to know him fairly well, but claimed he was introduced to her as Mr. Joseph Adams, and it took more than a year before she discovered his real name. "So what did you discover about him after that?" Kefauver asked. Fiddling with her bracelet again, Virginia allowed that Mr. Adonis had very nice manners, was devoted to his mother and the opera, but when the Senator pressed her for details of his business operations, she shook her head. "I never asked questions," she said. "You never answer them," the Senator complained wryly, getting a laugh from everyone except the witness. Virginia took a sip of water and reminded Kefauver that it all happened a long time ago, these days she was Mrs. Hans Hauser, wife of a skiing instructor and mother of a lovely baby boy.

The Senator stopped smiling and his voice sounded hard as he reminded Virginia that she only got married a year ago, so he refused to believe she could recall so few details of her life before that time. His Committee knew very well that Joey Adonis and other members of the Syndicate heaped a pile of money on Virginia, and would appreciate a serious effort on her part to come up with a few facts. She frowned, and seemed to make a serious effort. But she only said, "Some fellows gave me money and presents when I went out with them. What's so special about that?"

The Senator sighed, then smiled again as he addressed the court. "Those fellows were gangsters. I find that special." It got another laugh from everyone except Virginia, who sipped more water and said, "That's *your* story. I never asked what they did."

The Committee members whispered together, then one of them leaned forward, looking very stern and tough. "You moved to California and took up with another fellow out there. But if you never asked him any questions, it was because you didn't have to. Everyone knew about Bugsy Siegel."

I held my breath and watched Virginia hold hers as the cameras moved in close. Sweat glistened on her forehead, but her face was set like a mask. "Benjamin Siegel," she said. "His name was Mr. Benjamin Siegel and I can tell you all about *him*." An eager silence filled the room as she gripped the mike. "He was a fine man." Somebody laughed, and she glared. "A fine man," she repeated, with a twang like an angry guitar. "Promised to take me to Europe someday. Liked to travel and knew all the pretty places." Then she sat very still, her mouth clamped shut.

Senator Kefauver cleared his throat for another try. "You stayed in Las Vegas while Siegel was building his casino there." Virginia nodded. "Are you going to tell us you never met his partners?" She nodded again. "You must have heard Siegel talk about them," he went on, almost pleading. "You must have heard him mention names." She shook her head, and the more names Kefauver mentioned — Lansky, Costello, Buchalter, almost a Syndicate roll call — the more puzzled she looked. "Ben didn't want me to know anything," she said finally. "And I met nobody. Nobody at all."

The tough one leaned forward again. "So what did you *do* up there?"

"I stayed in my room," Virginia said calmly. "The sun was hell on my skin and the cactus gave me hay fever." She leaned back in her chair. "You can keep the desert. I cut out after a few weeks and took a house in Beverly Hills."

The Committee members huddled together and whispered again, then Kefauver dismissed her. Virginia walked out of the courtroom as cool as you please, until a camera moved closer than she wanted. She turned on it with a final holler that must have left ears ringing, and hoped the atom bomb fell on everybody.

It was a haunting exit line for a nifty characterization in the Claire Trevor mold, and as I switched off the set, I felt suddenly frustrated that the Committee never knew enough to subpoena *me*. As in the Desmond Taylor case, wisdom dictated that I remain on the sidelines, yet what a chance I missed to seize a truly classic star role! After reaching for a sniff I stared at the empty screen and daydreamed my entrance into the courtroom, elegant and mysterious as Rita Hayworth in *The Lady from Shanghai* and looking hardly a day older under the rude bright lights. Tension was high from the start, for I not only welcomed close-ups but told the truth, and responded to Kefauver's first question by dismissing Virginia as bush league stuff and identifying myself as the woman behind Ben Siegel. A row of stunned senatorial eyes fixed on me, and a great hush fell. Kefauver broke the silence by saying his records showed that I was no more than one of Ben's numerous acquaintances in the Hollywood beau monde. With a faint sigh I advised him to forget about his records, and began my story:

"Cast your mind back if you will, Senator, to October 1944, two years before Ben's casino opened in Vegas, and a few months before the end of World War Two. We both welcomed the prospect of victory and peace on earth, of course, even though we knew it meant the end of Ben's current era. Peace brings plenty, and as I'm sure you know, he'd been dealing in shortages. But with the future on his mind, he began to look way beyond the Clover Club — all the way across the Mohave desert, in fact, to Las Vegas, Nevada. Gambling's never been legal in California, and Ben always wanted to be legal. It was his secret dream.''

There was a brief, foolish outburst of laughter in the courtroom. I ignored it and continued calmly:

''For years Ben had a vision of building a really swank casino in Nevada. 'Baby,' he used to say, 'if I pull that off, I'll be running straight at last.' He picked Vegas because the Nevada mob was still busy sewing up Reno and hadn't moved in there yet. 'Okay,' I said, flashing my green light, 'I'm behind you on anything that doesn't start another war.'''

I had them now. An extraordinary silence gripped the courtroom, and the cameras moved in close as Kefauver asked how Ben financed the venture. ''Yours truly financed most of it,'' I said, ''after his associates in New York agreed to stake him for a mil.'' The Senators exchanged alert glances, then Kefauver asked me to identify the New York backers by name. I listened to the silence before answering. ''Unlike Miss Hill, when I say I don't know, I mean it. I never cared to meet any of them. But, unlike Miss Hill again, I asked a lot of questions and discovered the key man in the East was Meyer Lansky.''

For the first time, Kefauver gave me a sharply disapproving look. ''Is Meyer Lansky your idea of legal, Mrs. Kay?''

''Meyer Lansky is not my idea of anything,'' I replied with a Mona Lisa smile, ''even though rumor has it he was a founding member of Murder Inc. But gambling in Nevada is certainly my idea of legal, and I've always looked on money, wherever it comes from, as beyond the law. Has anyone ever tried to arrest a dollar bill?''

I not only had them, I had them on my side. A surprised murmur of understanding and approval rippled through the court. I seemed to have touched a vital nerve. Taking a sip of water, I resumed my saga at the Senator's request:

''When Ben Siegel asked me to go to Vegas with him and choose a site for his dream casino, I refused at first, for I always had this belief or superstition, call it what you will, that bad luck would follow if I ever traveled beyond the Los Angeles city limits. The pueblo had always been so good to me, taking both Baby and myself to its heart, and seemed to create a magic circle around the two of us. But Ben felt *I* created a magic circle around *him*, especially in business matters, especially after I bought him the Clover Club, and refused to go ahead without me. So I finally gave in, and found myself struggling with a vortex of emotion as the plane took off and Los Angeles vanished under my feet.''

The row of senatorial eyes looked sympathetic. I smiled discreetly at them, and went on:

"We rented a car at the Vegas airport and drove out on Highway 91. Did any of you know the place in those days? It had hardly begun. The downtown area was nothing but a few cheap slot-machine parlors and a few gaudy cathouses. They called it Glitter Gulch. Beyond it, the desert highway sported a couple of tacky casinos, and the rest was cactus and sagebrush all the way to Utah. As Ben and I headed toward the hot Mohave, we passed a driveway with a faded sign and it gave me a strong vibration. Turning in, we bumped along it and finally came to a motel that had gone out of business. But the owner still lived on the premises and was eager to sell the whole property, which amounted to some thirty acres. Under a little pressure from Ben, she agreed to a rock-bottom price. I produced an encouraging cash deposit, and floated a new company called Nevada Projects next day."

Although spellbound by my tale, Kefauver felt compelled to interrupt it. He asked how all my transactions of behalf of Ben, from the Clover Club to the Flamingo Casino, could so completely have escaped the Committee's notice.

I gave another Mona Lisa smile. "Frankly, Senator, the inner workings of my empire are *designed* to escape notice. EKE is a vast network with subsidiaries even harder to trace than the source of the Nile. Shall I go on?" He nodded eagerly. "An architect drew up plans and building started," I said, "just as the Japs surrendered. Progress was less easy than I hoped, and with so many wartime restrictions still in force, the bribes to get around them almost doubled our budget. And Ben almost doubled it again, for he was a perfectionist and refused to settle for anything but the best. Having traveled in Europe he knew the grandeur that was Rome, and wanted no tinsel shack on the edge of Glitter Gulch but a true palazzo with marble staircases, classical statues, gold satin drapes, even gold bathroom faucets. In his quest for perfection he even sold his own house, but still busted Nevada Projects in the process. When Mr. Lansky and friends declined to up their ante, I had to rescue the dream casino with a final $2,000,000."

The courtroom rippled with astonishment and one of the senators asked if I signed away a small fortune without trying to make Ben see reason.

"Of course not. I suggested axing the gold faucets, at least, but he drew a gun and fired several shots at my bedroom ceiling."

As the courtroom rippled again, the Senator supposed that I started to fear for my life.

I shook my head. "For *Ben*'s life. He was neglecting his health, you see, drinking too much, and it was most unlike him. Of course Miss Hill was to blame for this and a great deal more, for he was spending half his time in Vegas and she usually tagged along. Itching and sneezing on account of the cactus, swilling bourbon in her room, she hardly improved her disposition or her sense of reality. Such as they were."

Kefauver felt compelled to interrupt again, this time with a personal question. "You held the purse-strings, Mrs. Kay. Why did you tolerate a rival?"

"Early on in the game I made the mistake of trying to scuttle Virginia," I said, realizing a politician was out of his depth when it came to the passions. "It gained me nothing but black eyes, and even a punch in the stomach from the lady herself. You have to understand that Virginia was never a serious threat, not even a rival, just a sickness Ben could never quite rid himself of. It was better to ride the situation and stay in the wings while she grabbed the limelight as Ben's true love. And since I was playing *Back Street* with a touch of *Humoresque*, it even strengthened my role."

From the puzzled look on every senatorial face I realized politicians were also out of their depth when it came to the movies, most likely they only watched stuff like *Wilson* or *Mission to Moscow*. Filling them in on the *Back Street* situation, and Joan Crawford's great role as ministering angel to a handsome young musician in *Humoresque*, I noted how everyone in the courtroom listened and watched intently, imagined millions viewing my coast-to-coast image from their livingroom homes, felt the eternal magic of motion pictures reach out to the nation. "Ben and I may not have been everyone's idea of a perfect romance," I averred, "we may not have been June Allyson and Van Johnson, but few strike that lucky. I played the cards I was dealt. Shall I go on?" Every senatorial head nodded eagerly, and I continued:

"Ben excused me from attending opening night at the Flamingo when I begged him not to make me leave Los Angeles again, but I waited in fear and trembling for news of the event, because I knew that hardly any of the Hollywood luminaries he invited would show up. Maybe you remember how war veterans picketed the dream casino, claiming all the material poured into it could have built them hundreds of homes. Although, whoever heard of veterans' homes with marble staircases and gold satin drapes? Anyway, stars hate to appear unpatriotic and almost no one except fading vaudevillian George Jessel braved public opinion. I fear it was his greatest mistake since turning down the lead in *The Jazz Singer*. That opening night was a tragic bust, all the glittering taste in the world thrown away on the kind of crowd you'd expect to see at Miami Beach. Even more tragic was the way Ben refused to face facts, clinging to his dream against all the odds and finally bringing the temple down on his head. Although the Flamingo sank ever deeper into debt, he refused to lower his standards. And then, as you surely know, New York decided to take steps."

With a sigh I braced myself for Kefauver's next question. "Miss Hill knows more than I about the steps they took," I answered. "I played no part in the hideous events that followed." Then I guessed the next question correctly as well. "Of course I can prove it," I answered, and listened to the silence again. "The lady gave nothing away to this Committee, but she gave everything away to *me*. On the night of June 17, 1947, she honored me with a drunken phone call from her house in Beverly Hills. She said she was leaving for Europe because it was *time to cut out*, and wished me goodbye with every four-letter word in the book." I took another sip of water. "Two days later, Ben came into town on a business trip. He seemed to be at the end of his rope and I wanted to help. 'No, Baby, you've done enough,' he said, and I felt proud because he behaved like a real gentleman, yet sad because he spoke the truth. Then he said, 'Wait a minute, there's one thing you *can* do.' And his eyes looked so blue, I said, 'Anything.' And he gave me a strange smile. 'Never forget me,' he said. 'It's okay as long as we don't forget. But otherwise we're dead.' "

I sipped more water, overcome by the memory of that moment, which was our last moment together, then held my head high. "Virginia had left him the keys to her house in Beverly Hills. He went back there after a business meeting that night, sat on the living-room couch and began reading the paper. Seconds later, he was shot with seven deadly bullets by a person or persons unknown." The cameras moved in very close, and I looked them in the eye. "Don't tell me Miss Hill was surprised. Obviously New York warned her it planned to rub Ben out and take over the Flamingo — but instead of warning *him*, she loaned her house for the crime and *cut out*. When the police closed their books on the case, leaving our pueblo with yet another unsolved murder, she returned to these United States, bought herself a hunk of Teuton and now poses as a respectable wife and mother!"

Kefauver dismissed me with respectful thanks, and I left the courtroom to face a mob of excited reporters and reject an offer to serialize my life in *Woman's Day*.

In the here and now it began to rain fiercely. I stared at the blank television screen and felt sudden goose bumps as a ghost appeared on it. Like the man I loved before him, Ben sprawled dead on the livingroom floor, blood spilling over his face and his silk shirt. And the house felt suddenly dark and haunted, like my life.

Baby Looks Back

Although Mother's life was not as dark as she painted it, by now you know about her taste for high-voltage drama and the great trash movies that fed it, some of the lights went out after Ben Siegel died. Their last months together were spent mainly apart, her *Back Street* role seemed to go off the rails along with Ben's second chance, but she never doubted it was only temporary. "His new mistress is a dream casino, very beautiful and very jealous. But she won't hold him for long. Not to worry!" The day after Ben was murdered I went over to the house and found Mother sitting up in bed, staring at a photograph on page one of the *Times*. It showed a pair of bare feet sticking out from a drawer in the morgue, with a label attached to the Bug's right toe. *Homicide, Benjamin Seigel.* She complained the name was spelt wrong, then pressed the picture to her lips and kissed Ben's feet.

That night, insisting the show must go on, she took me to a Glamor Bazaar in aid of a children's hospital and bought a Waterford crystal chandelier donated by Anna May Wong. While we were there, the Mob sent a squad to Vegas and took control of the Flamingo. They called themselves stockholders, and with Ben still frozen in the morgue, held a meeting and voted to transfer all his assets to their own pockets. The moment she read about this in the papers, Mother held a meeting at EKE and informed her startled board of lawyers that it was *zero hour.* "Don't ask any questions, just let me brief you. There's one concealed asset at the Flamingo, three hundred grand in cash I gave Mr. Siegel as an emergency fund. I know where it's stashed and *I want it back.*" Then she laid out her plan for a rescue mission. "We'll move in right away with a task force wearing tuxedos, passing itself off as a group of wealthy gamblers. Don't tell me you can't organize that, I know your connections." The lawyers advised Mother to give the dust a little time to settle, they'd heard the cops were watching the situation up in Vegas, and any task force would have to get past them as well as the Mob right now. Fearful that Virginia somehow learned about the money and had left the country with it, Mother found the suspense hard to bear. But it didn't last long and the dust barely settled on Ben's monogrammed wardrobe trunk in the cellar. "Seems the brute they call Icepick Willie couldn't wait to ransack the place. He found the false bottom and shared out the boodle." She gave a violent exasperated sigh. "You heard me warn those deadhead lawyers the situation's like politics, always send in the marines *right away.* Now I'm truly up the creek. Any move I make will bring the cops on my tail, to say nothing of Icepick Willie. He's got a mean habit of poking an icepick in your ear, which makes it look as if you died from a brain hemorrhage."

She took to her bed and lay very still with the shades pulled down. "I've hit the dismals, Baby. Better leave me alone." It was too late to summon the Violet Flame, for the Master had died of cirrhosis a few years back, and although Little Dynamite claimed his spirit was still at work, the faithful lost heart. Going back to the temple once, Mother found them listening glumly to a phonograph record of his voice. "Doubt had set in and we blasted away in a vacuum. The Mighty I Am is no longer spiritual box office." Each time I looked into her bedroom, it was disturbing to see that famous energy running down in the dark. But I noticed the bed was strewn with copies of *Photoplay* and other movie magazines, and suspect that when Mother was alone she switched on a lamp and drew strength from the only world she never doubted.

For this is how she broke a long silence. "Did you ever hear, Baby, that the Japs admire Bette Davis more than any star in the world? They practically worship her as the goddess of self-sacrifice. It must be true, because when Yoda and Fujita came back from the camp where Mr. Roosevelt sent them, the first thing they asked was if I'd seen *The Corn Is Green* and *Mr. Skeffington.*" After I left she rose from her bed, pulled up the shades, got dressed, ordered her Thunderbird, told Hattie to invite me for cocktails later, and zoomed out of the driveway. Back from a matinee of a private eye melodrama called *Out of the Past,* she pronounced it even closer to everyday life than two recent favorites, *The Postman Always Rings Twice* and *The Strange Love of Martha Ivers.* Rattling the martini shaker: "You may smile, Baby, but I know a sign of the times when I see it. These movies create a new moral color, and it's neutral gray. Doesn't matter whose side anyone is on, because when the chips are down he's not on yours. And nobody loses because nobody wins. It's a booby-trapped world." She filled our glasses and recalled the emotional climax of her afternoon, gazing from the mezzanine at a close-up of ruggedly promising Kirk Douglas and imagining for a moment that she saw Ben. "The same equal parts of love and death in his eyes, and a dangerous smile that was truly Out of the Past!"

Over a second martini she suddenly decided that her white immaculate Moderne livingroom no longer expressed her mood, and resolved to sell the house. Love of splendor was always a big link in the chain with Ben, and I saw equal parts of love and death in Mother's eyes as she planned to create her own Flamingo in his memory. Next day she began shopping

around, briefly considered the old John Barrymore place and the former
Ann Harding estate, then astonished me by settling on Jimmy Gabriel's
mansion. She agreed it was almost as monstrous as the former Clara Bow
hacienda, but found it the only property on the market with *real scale*.
"Plus it's been on my books so long, no one else will buy it if I don't."
And unless a house was *historic*, which meant that a star had once lived
there, it was out of the question. Now she could inform her friends, and
the press, that she was moving from the former residence of slinky Louise
Glaum ("slinky Louise *who*?") to the former residence of versatile Jimmy
Gabriel.

She gave the house, like Ben, a second chance. She knocked out walls,
added windows, raised or lowered ceilings, replaced the gymnasium with
a tropical greenhouse-loggia, brought her famous Art Deco marble staircase with her, hung the Anna May Wong chandelier in the den,
goldleafed the projection theatre and loaded it with Moorish grillwork to
create a miniature Pantages, stripped the master bedroom of every mirror
and remodeled it on the lines of de Mille's *Cleopatra*, bed like a royal
barge, sunken bath, archways, gauze hangings, low couches. A tour of
the house was like a walk through a spectacular jumble of movie sets, and
Mother happily admitted she drew inspiration from other beloved costume romances, *Marie Antoinette, Camille, The Prisoner of Zenda, The Great
Ziegfeld* and *The Merry Widow*. "To judge from current product, of which I
fear *Forever Amber* is all too typical, they don't build them that way anymore. But at Villa Elva the Golden Age lives on."

The dinner parties started up again. "If only Ben had lived to see this!"
Mother used to sigh, reviewing her Arthurian round table with its parade
of monogrammed silverware, ormolu candlesticks, crystal decanters,
shining goblets and an outsized grail in which gardenias floated. But the
old trusted familiars lived to see it, although di Frasso was only an occasional guest. She spent most of her time since the war at her own villa in
Rome. On one return visit she described her great social triumph there,
throwing a dinner dance for the wedding of Ty Power and Linda
Christian, then annoyed Mother by predicting Rome would soon turn
into Hollywood-on-the-Tiber. "I've heard that before, Dorothy, and simply don't believe it. Wait till all our frozen dollars are spent, and we'll see
which is the real Eternal City." She sat up very straight, eyes even
brighter than her diamonds. *"Hollywood will last as long as the world."*

Now that Ben was out of the picture, WR sometimes came with Marion.
Gaunt and slowed down after a heart attack, convinced the Cold War
would soon warm up, he advised Mother to build air raid shelters in the
basement. Although he feared we were losing the battle against commu-

nism, he never seemed to notice Marion losing the battle against drink. When we screened one of her pictures after dinner she was still the star of *Page Miss Glory* in his adoring indulgent eyes, even if she'd gained more weight than WR lost and dozed off soon after the credits began, breathing heavily. In the same way, Mother found Ramon Novarro still blazing with retroactive glamor, although he was by now a paunchy character actor. "Contrary to appearances, Miss Sophie assures me, he's living more dangerously than ever."

I remember a couple of new faces at the round table. Ayn Rand found Mother a rare example of the pure capitalist spirit, even rarer and purer than WR, because even in her youth she never succumbed to illusions of altruism or the democratic process, but understood the wisdom of enlightened selfishness from the start. (Although she realized it was a compliment, Mother felt bound to protest. "Selfishness? It was all for Baby!" The author of *The Fountainhead* gave a smile that matched Mother's for Mona Lisa intent.) And Maria Rasputin, living in the Russian quarter near Silverlake after a successful career riding bareback at a circus in Paris, was pumped for anecdotes of her father. Primed with champagne, she poured out examples of the monk's occult and sexual powers, electrifying di Frasso with tales of his dick. She had seen it erect, and confirmed the rumor that it measured a jot over twelve inches. She had seen it after death and confirmed that it survived. Hacked off with a dagger by one of his assassins, it was somehow retrieved by an elderly female admirer, who smuggled the precious relic in her luggage and fled to Paris. Maria saw it there, in the bedroom of a modest refugee apartment. Amateurishly preserved in a velvet-lined box, darkened and mottled in places like an overripe banana, it was still recognizable. And brought back memories of happier times.

Although Mother found this story moving in its way, she was more deeply stirred by the monk's occult side, and held her breath when Maria told how her father was poisoned, stabbed, shot, put in a sack weighted with stones, thrown into an icy river and still managed to live for hours. "How I do wish I'd met the man. There's so much he could have taught me about mind over matter."

But not even Rasputin could have helped me endure life under Howard Hughes, in the end not much less of an ordeal than being stuffed in a sack and dumped in a river. On the night I foolishly agreed to meet him, I sat blindfolded in the back of the limousine until it stopped again, heard the driver get out and open the door, then felt his hand take mine. He guided me forward, rang a doorbell that someone answered, and led me inside a house. When he removed the blindfold I was standing in a room with

heavy drapes screening all the windows. The furniture was new, anonymous, motel-like. A corridor led to other invisible rooms, but I had the
impression the house was fairly small, maybe a bungalow. The driver left
without a word, I lit a cigarette, walked toward a window with the intention of peeking out, then heard someone coming and turned back.

Howard entered the room. He wore a suit and tie, looked neat and
relaxed, his face surprised me with its open and somehow innocent can-
dor. Then he frowned at my cigarette and I noticed his eyes were dark and
impenetrable, as if watching behind an invisible veil. "That's an unhealthy habit," he said.

"Well, maybe." I took another puff. "But I hope you didn't bring me
here, blindfolded, in the middle of the night, just to accuse me of an
unhealthy habit."

He seemed genuinely crestfallen and apologized. "I'm not accusing
you of anything, but I'm concerned for your health." And in his rather
monotonous Texan twang, gave me a lecture on germs. Both his parents
died while he was still in college, and he believed they might still be alive
today if they'd taken care to protect themselves from germs. "Germs are
everywhere," he warned me. "Most of all they're in dust. When you
blow out cigarette smoke, naturally you blow out germs, these germs mix
with the dust in the air and you get a double threat." His eyes went even
darker. "So it's more than just poetic to connect dust with death."

Then he began walking around me in a slow deliberate circle. "When I
saw *Two of a Kind* your clothes did nothing for you, I couldn't be sure what
kind of figure you had. Now I see it's pretty good."

"It wasn't a glamor part, I dressed ordinary." I sat down, putting an
end to the circular tour. "But I never felt my figure was my fortune, you
know. It's only average."

Howard shook his head gravely. "On the scale of one to ten, you rate
seven and a half. Maybe eight."

This man has dated some really well engineered girls, I thought, Gene
Tierney, Ginger Rogers, Olivia de Havilland, what's happened to his
sense of values? "From what I hear about Jane Russell," I said, "she rates
ten and a half. Maybe eleven."

He sat beside me and asked in a quiet, almost somber voice: "*How'd you
like to tussle with Russell?*" Naturally I looked blank, so he explained he
was quoting the ad-line for *The Outlaw.* "You'll see it on billboards everywhere when the picture opens," he said, and I promised to look out for it.
There was a long pause, during which he looked me over again. Then he
asked in the same muted voice, "Do you like flying?"

I smiled. "You asked me that before."

"I don't believe so." It startled him. "And my memory's pretty good."

"So's mine. Years ago, when I was a child star, we met at a party. You were with Billie Dove, another ten and a half. I told you I'd never been in a plane and you promised to take me up very soon."

Howard apologized again. "I remember you at the party, and of course I remember Billie. But I forget asking if you liked to fly."

"For a long time I hated it." As I told Howard about my first experience in the air with B.J. Langdon, and the phobia it gave me, almost as bad as my ocean phobia after I fell off a boat into the Pacific while filming an early *Kid Sherlock*, he began to look anxious. I reassured him. "Things are better now. I never go into the ocean but take to the air pretty well."

"There's no place on earth like it," Howard said. And as he talked aviation, a gleam appeared in the darkness of his eyes. He described a machine he'd designed for the Air Force, a huge flying boat made of wood, capable of transporting seven hundred troops and their equipment across the Atlantic. "Some people say it'll never take off, but some people used to say you'll never have lunch in Chicago and dinner in Los Angeles." He leaned close. "This is only a beginning. In a few years' time you'll look up at the sky and see planes big as ocean liners everywhere."

All this was quite interesting and friendly, but struck me as leading nowhere. But then the driver returned and asked if we were ready. Howard glanced at his watch and nodded. The driver took the blindfold out of his pocket.

"Just a minute," I said as he came toward me. "Where to?"

Howard picked up a cardboard box from a table. "I want to show you the most beautiful sunrise in the world."

And with his usual bored expression, the driver slipped the blindfold over my eyes.

This time Howard guided me out to the limousine, his hand pressing sharply on my arm, not letting up until we sat together in the back. Then he described another of his new planes, some kind of reconnaissance aircraft. I listened in the dark to details of flight tests, cruising speeds, whatever, until he removed the blindfold and asked how I was feeling.

"Pretty good," I said, and lit a cigarette. Looking out the window, I saw nothing but night and mist. "But won't you tell me where we're going?"

"I like to surprise."

"Of course. I should have guessed."

On the other side of a hill, the mist began to clear. I realized we were driving through the Cahuenga pass, heading for the Valley. In a few minutes we approached Burbank airport, which looked closed, not to say abandoned, but as we drove around to a side entrance, a guard saluted and waved us through. The limousine drove out to the airfield and stopped near a solitary private plane. Howard got out and hurried toward it. By the time the driver brought me over and I stepped inside, he was already at the controls wearing a flight helmet. As we got airborne I looked down, but because of the blackout saw only the vaguest occasional glimmer. Another view of limbo.

For a while Howard didn't speak, but from time to time offered me a cookie from the cardboard box. Finally he pointed for me to look out the window. It was still dark except for pale gray streaks low in the sky. He nodded encouragingly as we started to lose altitude. A tinge of yellow appeared in the gray streaks, then very gradually the darkness lifted. I took off my glasses and made out a wide empty stretch of land below, contours of mountains, then a hollow black area like an enormous pit. Howard turned and circled the plane, gained altitude, changed his mind, dropped down again, turned and circled some more. I was beginning to fear some kind of replay of the B.J. Langdon scene, telling myself all aviators were nuts, when he scribbled a note on the cover of the cookie box and handed it to me. It read: *The correct angle is very important.*

A gleam of light caught the wing of the plane. I looked down and saw the sun edge its way over the rim of the black pit, streaking it with sudden colors, green, bluish gray, reddish brown, exposing trees, rocks and a long deep valley crisscrossed with trails. Things opened up like flowers coming to life underwater in a bowl. As I realized we were flying maybe a thousand feet above the Grand Canyon, the plane veered away and flew almost directly into the sun. A yellow flare spilled across the cabin, then Howard made another turn and I looked down again to see the Colorado river like a flow of silver in the dawn.

We hovered for a long while. Howard seemed reluctant ever to land again, he wanted to stay up in the air. On the flight back he made a detour to the Painted Desert, circling it a few times, then went on to the Petrified Forest. I accepted more cookies and lit a cigarette after we encountered sudden turbulence. The driver was waiting on a corner of the field at Burbank airport, and as he sprang alertly from the limousine to open the door, I wondered how he managed to stay so brisk. He must have been on duty since midnight and my watch showed 8:30 in the morning. Actually it had stopped, since I forgot to wind it, and the time was past 10:00.

The blindfold came out again as we left the airport, and Howard asked for my impressions of the trip. Watching sunrise over the Grand Canyon, I told him, was like watching the creation of the world. And I heard him say, "That's almost exactly my feeling, except there's one thing different about it. Sitting up there in the sky, it feels like *I'm* creating the world."

The velvet darkness was a relief, I found myself not minding it at all. The limousine stopped, I felt Howard's hand like a claw on my arm as he guided me back into the house, and when he removed the blindfold I looked around the room with a sense of anti-climax. Lights burned and heavy drapes still screened the windows. He asked if I could eat some breakfast. I nodded, but wondered if he could produce a shot of brandy right away. After ordering brandy for one and breakfast for two, he stretched out on a couch. "I'm from Texas," he said. "In Texas we don't give up easy, we stand by what we believe in. For instance, I stood by *The Outlaw* for more than a year."

"You mean you refused to make those cuts the censor wanted?"

"That's right. I believe in every frame of that picture as it stands."

"But will we ever get to see every frame of Jane Russell?"

He folded his hands across his chest. "You will. Here's how I swung it. I showed the censors a copy of the Venus di Milo and asked them to prove it wasn't a work of art. They couldn't. Then I showed them all the frames of Jane they objected to, and asked them to prove she looked less artistic and more immoral than the Venus in any of them. They couldn't. So we finally get to open the picture in a month or two."

"With that fantastic ad-line you told me about."

"It can't miss. I'm really high on the movies these days and I've got a lot of plans." Sitting up, he gave me a somber, veiled look. "If you want, they include you."

"Well, that's the first offer I've had in two years. I'd like another brandy."

Howard ordered it and lay down again. He stared at the ceiling and said, "Reality's just a point of view. Some see it, some don't. *Your* reality is very clear to me."

Although exhausted, I felt suddenly alert. Somebody else's view of your reality, especially when you don't have one of your own, is always fascinating. Warren once told me he was the sum of his parts and I felt the same, except that my parts had no sum. There was Mother's view of the most natural innocent the world had ever known, Sid Gordon's view of the little trouper who was only herself in disguise, Mr. Mayer's view of the paper doll who grew up into one special yet typical American girl, and Jimmy's view of a wise sneaky Baby who knew the score.

"You've still got plenty to show the world," Howard said, then fell silent.

"I hope you're right."

He sat up and gave me another dark look. "You know it." And fell silent again, but keeping his strange eyes on me this time.

"You want *me* to tell *you* how I see myself now?" He nodded. "That's new," I said, and fell silent myself.

"I'm waiting."

The huge empty landscape at sunrise gave me a flash, and I thought of outer space. I took a sip of brandy and said, *"Thuvia, Maid of Mars."*

Howard's face went slightly dazed. I wondered if he'd heard properly, and repeated the title, but it turned out he simply hadn't heard of the Martian tales of Edgar Rice Burroughs. To put him in the picture I began by explaining their angle on Mars. "It's a planet divided into separate countries, just like the earth. And there are two major rival powers, Dusar and Ptarth, locked in deadly enmity and intrigue."

"Can Burroughs back this up?" Howard asked as breakfast arrived. "Does he have solid evidence?"

"No. Just imagination." Then I outlined the story, describing how Dusar agents kidnapped Princess Thuvia of Ptarth in a flying machine. Looking very sharp, a touch of excitement in his voice, Howard wanted to know the Burroughs angle on Martian aircraft. "You name it, they've built it," I said. "From everyday light transportation to giant passenger liners that land on special platforms high above the graceful minarets of the city."

He buttered his toast, then spread it thickly with jelly. "I like the way you're telling me this."

"Well, it's good stuff. Many adventures befall Thuvia before she's rescued by the intrepid Prince of Helium." I ran through the high points: Thuvia lost in a jungle of man-eating white apes and hairless fanged lions; Thuvia trapped in the valley of the Plant Men, ghoulish blue creatures with long tails, two mouths and one eye, then in the Hall of Doom that yawned beneath her feet as the royal couch dropped through a hole in the palace floor. Then I gave him the climax, on a landing platform high in the starry heavens, where the Prince fought off Thuvia's attackers while she climbed aboard an airship and navigated it to safety by the light of two glorious moons. "I always dreamed of playing Thuvia," I said. "I really feel for that girl and everything she went through."

He nodded. "What about sex?"

"You mean a love story?"

"I mean a sexy love story."

"The Prince is certainly wild about Thuvia. And at the end she accepts him as her royal mate."

He nodded again, then wanted to know what kind of costumes Thuvia wore.

"Jewelry is all. Martian Maids rope themselves with pearls."

This seemed to bother him. He hesitated, then asked in a flat clinical tone how Thuvia covered her vital parts. I told him Burroughs had no specific angle on the subject. "But I get the impression she handles herself like a stripper. There's something about a magnificently encrusted G-string."

Howard got up, asked me to remove my glasses and walked around me once more. This time he moved very close, and became a blur. Then he stood directly in front of me, very still, and I felt his eyes were meeting mine and searching for a response. Unfortunately my farsighted condition made it impossible to be sure, and I couldn't see him clearly enough to know what response he expected. In any case I preferred not to give him one, so I looked away.

He sighed. "Okay," he said. "You'll be hearing from me very soon. That's a Texan promise."

And as the driver came back, he blindfolded me fondly, holding my face in his hands for a moment. Then, on the way out, I heard his voice: "You think audiences will go for a picture like that?"

These days, of course, science fiction is the surest thing, but in the forties it was strictly for tacky serials like *Flash Gordon*. "They went for *King Kong*," I reminded him, uncertain where to address my remarks because of the blindfold, "and just recently for *The Thief of Bagdad*. So maybe they'll go for a combination of both. In space."

Madness is catching, I thought as I settled in the limousine, Howard Hughes flies me to the Grand Canyon at dawn, then gives me breakfast in a room that shuts out the daylight, and I try to sell him *Thuvia* before he sends me home in a blindfold. But it was a mistake, of course, to bring madness into it. Like reality according to Howard, madness is only a point of view.

When I called Mother, her point of view was to find me a very lucky girl and predict the beginning of a great new cycle in my life. "Don't forget, Howard Hughes is one of the living legends of our time." A pause. "What's he like?"

"A law unto himself," I said.

"Exactly what I imagined. I know we'll hit it off."

My attorney called to say a contract had arrived in the mail, and it seemed Howard was keeping his Texas promise. Mother set up a meeting to discuss it in the Oval Office at EKE. "Mr. Hughes has offered to sign you for three years, with an option to renew every year for five more," my attorney said. "*You* have no options of any kind. Mr. Hughes makes all the decisions, on material, scripts, casting, etc. Any publicity campaign you have to go along with. You're not allowed to work for anyone else or even leave the city without his permission."

"How much?" Mother asked.

"A thousand a week this year, with a 10 percent annual increment."

"Baby got more than that when she was twelve."

"When I was supposed to be twelve," I said.

"This deal could be improved," Mother said.

My attorney sighed. "Believe me, I tried. But Mr. Hughes makes only one kind of deal. Take it or leave it."

I looked at Mother. "Maybe I should write to Jimmy and ask his opinion first?"

Mother looked at the covering note attached to the contract. "The offer expires at midnight tomorrow, Baby." She handed me the papers. "At least he wants you. And it's important to be wanted."

HUGHES INKS BABY, the headline in *Variety* announced. Exclusive pact, it went on, and one project already in preparation, *Thuvia Maid of Mars*, tale of adventure and passion in space by the author of *Tarzan*. For the first time in years, Hedda and Louella called. "Where did you get to see Howard, is he in good shape, did he romance you?" they asked. "In his plane above the Grand Canyon, yes, no," I answered. The day their stories appeared, the phone rang. I recognized the voice, it belonged to the man who set up my 1:30 a.m. date with Howard. "Mr. Hughes requests you to report at Photo-Art Studios tonight, wearing no makeup of any kind," he said. "A car will pick you up at 1:00 a.m."

The studio was in an old building on a Hollywood side street, above a store that rented furs. A small egg-shaped man with red hair and matching goatee opened the door at the top of the stairs, gasped and kissed me. "Babushka! So beautiful to work with you again." Boris had been a still photographer at MGM during my golden age, and as I followed him into the studio he told me that Howard happened to see his pictures of Lana Turner in *Ziegfeld Girl*, went crazy over them and bought up his contract. "I'm on twenty-four hour call to photograph glamor pussies under consideration for the next Hughes movie," he said. "And I'm ready to drop."

"Are there so many?"

"You have no idea. And Howard has no idea for a movie."

In front of a photo mural of the Pyramids, a stranger stood drinking milk from a carton. He wore an exhausted sports jacket, rumpled pants, old sneakers, and had a growth of stubble on his face. "Good to see you again," he said, and with a shock I recognized the stranger as Howard. "I've been busy as hell lately," he went on, as if to excuse his appearance, then pointed to a battered suitcase on a chair. "There are some things for you to try on. I want to see how you look as a Maid of Mars."

"At 1:00 in the morning, not at my best."

He hesitated, then said in his flat clinical tone, "The way you described her. Roped with pearls. But no brassiere or panties."

Boris picked up the suitcase and led me to a cubicle. He whispered before drawing the curtain, "Babushka, you have no choice but to look like a million dollars. That's what you'll be wearing."

Opening the suitcase, I found Ali Baba's cave. Gold belts and girdles studded with rubies, pearl chokers, diamond and sapphire bracelets, tiaras, pendants, trinkets and rings flashing almost every known precious stone. Even a pair of emerald pasties which Howard must have included to take care of the brassiere problem. A cluster of pearls, held in place by a gold belt with a heavy clasp, solved the crotch problem. But it was hell to cover my ass reasonably. An elaborate jade chain seemed the best bet, only wouldn't stay in place, and I had to hold everything precariously together with my own chiffon scarf. After putting as many bracelets on my wrists and ankles as the traffic could bear, I went out to face Howard.

He sat in a director's canvas chair being shaved by a barber, who must have arrived while I made myself look like a million dollars. The barber held up a mirror when he finished, Howard nodded without looking into it, got up and came toward me.

"Glamor pussies don't wear glasses," Boris said, and took them off.

Howard began one of his circular tours. There was something eerie about him now, like a peeper watching a girl undress through a crack in the curtains. He paced for a while, then came close and made a minor adjustment to the jade chain covering my ass. "This is pretty much what I thought it would be," he said finally, and told Boris to take over. Boris giggled. "If Louis B. Mayer could see us now!" Then he set me in various poses, mysterious, frightened, virginal, seductive, trying to look like the Sphinx in front of the Pyramids mural, cowering against a wall, seated demurely on a stool, slinking along a fur rug. Occasionally Howard had an idea, always the kind we used to call "suggestive," but there was no apparent gloat in his manner, he pursued the suggestive with a firm, solemn detachment. I heard him breathing calmly as he peered up or down at all my parts, felt his cool hand on my ass as he rearranged the jade chain again to show more of it. Rummaging in the suitcase, he found a diamond necklace and clasped it around my thigh. When I posed on the rug, he told me to part my lips wider and strain my breasts harder. Groping under the emerald pasties for a brief professional check, he decided I was doing my best.

After a couple of hours, he turned to Boris. "That's good enough for me. What do you say?"

Boris giggled. "I say we covered the waterfront."

As I made for the cubicle, Howard called me back. "You forgot your glasses," he said. He stood very close but didn't give them to me. Instead he went through the old ritual of staring darkly into my eyes. Before I had time to look away he gave me a sharp, almost mean goose, and while I was still recovering from the shock, the phone rang.

He turned away to watch Boris answer it.

"For you, Howard."

Boris winked. I ran to the cubicle, stripped off my jewels and got dressed. When I stepped outside, Howard was no longer there. According to Boris he'd been called away on urgent business, but sent me a Texan promise to get in touch very soon. "You know this weirdy," I said. "What's your estimate of the situation?" Boris shook his head. "Nobody gets to know Howard Hughes. All I know is, he was planning to make a pass from the time he ordered a shave. It's always the sign." I thanked God the phone rang, but felt miffed that he put business first, however urgent. Boris shrugged. "He always will. Many times I see the man preparing to make a very great pass, then business calls him away."

"So what's your last word?"

"My last word, Babushka?" Boris picked up the suitcase and began switching off the lights. "The man likes a challenge, and this project would challenge anybody."

Two years went by with no further pass and no further word from Howard. It seemed the project was either not challenging enough, or so challenging that he needed even more time to lick it. When my attorney called Howard's attorney he always got the same answer: Mr. Hughes was very busy but hadn't forgotten me, would definitely be in touch next week. Meanwhile the salary checks arrived promptly and each Christmas I received a bouquet of roses almost as large as a float. I often wondered what kept Howard so busy. It wasn't making tests of more glamor pussies, I checked with Boris in case there was new competition and he told me Howard hadn't set foot in the studio for months. I read in the newspapers that he was in Washington, explaining to the Air Force why neither of his new planes had got off the ground. I read he was in New York, in Acapulco, in hiding. And I feared he was only a serious practical joker when Boris confided he knew where Howard always lived when he came to Los Angeles. At a rented bungalow in the grounds of the Beverly Hills Hotel.

"Are you sure? His driver took me way up in the Hollywood hills before blindfolding me," I said. "It was at least a half hour trip, and the Hotel's only five minutes from my house."

"I told you, nobody gets to know the man."

The Outlaw was premiered in San Francisco, got terrible notices and went on to make millions across the country. Mother and I saw it at a matinee, and when we came out of the theatre there were lines around the block for the next performance. "I agree it could easily be recut for comedy," she said, "but it's a hit and there has to be a reason." She gazed thoughtfully at the marquee display of Jane Russell chewing on a straw, in the Picture That Couldn't Be Stopped. "Nuns may be big at the box office these days, but they'll never be bigger than pin-up girls. Nobody boosts the morale of our boys overseas like a crackerjack pin-up." As we walked to her silver Cadillac executive sedan, Mother developed her theme. "Betty Grable lightened their dark days in the Pacific, Rita Hayworth was their mirage in the North African desert, and now Jane girds up their loins for the second front."

"But those are not our boys standing in line. Those are ordinary civilians like you and me."

"And they can't wait to case the latest pin-up above the bunk of every conquering hero, Baby. Whether or not his planes eventually fly, Mr. Hughes has made a historic contribution to the war effort with Jane."

Howard stepped up my own contribution, by remote control, when a call from headquarters ordered me out on a tour to sell war bonds. To reawaken his and the public's interest, Mother advised adding a touch of pin-up to my image, tight Grable skirt, Russell blouse with top buttons undone, ankle-strap Hayworth shoes. They earned me friendly whistles when I climbed aboard a platform to stand beside the Mayor of Tucson. He introduced me as a kiddie star who once made America's heart beat faster (shades of Baby Jewel Day when they opened *Treasure Island* there!), and had now grown into a fine young lady still out there pitching.

It wasn't always easy to keep pitching out there. At the Fort Worth baseball stadium the temperature in January was subzero and the town band's rendition of "In the Mood" blasted my eardrums. But my jokes got a laugh, my speech about the Four Freedoms got a cheer, I signed autographs and was begged by middle-aged couples to make heartwarming movies again. At the San Antonio rodeo center I chalked up the biggest sales of the tour, doing bumps and grinds and belting "That Old Black Magic" until it started to snow. Favorable reports reached as far as

Bob Hope, who invited me to join his next show for the troops in Europe, and I lived on a fantasy of surprising Jimmy at an airforce base until Howard, by remote control, killed it.

Then, while thousands boomed, I slumped. Los Angeles was still the great oasis in the desert, the war brought a new Gold Rush, people pouring in from all over the country to work in factories and aircraft plants. There was hope to spare, money to burn, and not enough places to sleep. Servicemen on leave even bunked down in movie theatre lobbies after the evening show. Dwayne from Colorado Springs, twenty-two and a ball of fire, was resigned to doing this until we met at the Hollywood Canteen. After a couple of dances we ducked out, and I took him to the Florentine Gardens. It was the raunchiest place to go, a big band playing while showgirls paraded half-naked and circus artists performed a trapeze act overhead. At closing time people streamed out to Hollywood Boulevard, mingling with the crowds just out of movie theatres. The sidewalks were jammed, nobody wanted to go home, everyone gave someone the eye. Dwayne from Colorado Springs could imagine no more exciting place in the world.

Prime cuts, gasoline and silk stockings were in short supply, but not movies. Life without celluloid was unthinkable and the theatres never ran short. The studios manufactured new stars as quickly as the factories turned out spare parts or canned food. Any chick bright enough to memorize a few simple lines of dialogue got her name above the title, for the duration at least. Would you believe or do you remember Lynn Bari? Arleen Whelan? Brenda Joyce? Only Baby Jewel, a prisoner of Howard Hughes, seemed to be missing out.

Maybe because Howard believed anything unpaid for was unserious, he made no objection when the Hollywood Democratic Committee asked me to join an all-star radio broadcast. It was designed to rally Californians behind Roosevelt when he stood for a fourth term, and I shared a spot with the glorious Carmen Miranda, who chick-a-chick-a-boomchicked while I sang a new version, with pro-FDR lyrics, of "A Good Man Is Hard to Find." Mother loved the whole show but still voted for Governor Dewey.

Next evening she gave a dinner party and Mr. Hearst kept frowning at me across the table. Later he took me aside, walked me out to the terrace and asked why I supported Roosevelt. When I gave the usual reasons he shook his head and warned that FDR was too soft on commies. They were infiltrating the movies, he continued, his hand tightening on my arm, and we had to combat their deadly influence. "Young lady, you must get in touch with the Motion Picture Alliance for the Preservation of American

Ideals." WR, who had put money and his newspapers behind the group, walked me further along the terrace as he confided that Coop and Walt Disney had already joined, Irene Dunne was on the verge, and his old friend King Vidor had pledged active support. "King's directing a picture at Metro right now, so you're bound to run into him. Ask him to tell you about our ideals." Although WR's hand still gripped my arm with surprising force, his memory had weakened. It was several years since Metro closed its doors to me. "I always thought of Mr. Vidor as a liberal type," I said. "People used to think of *me* as a liberal type," WR replied quietly. "But a man has to develop."

When the war ended I had a nostalgic urge to take one more One Big Look, and drove downtown. The platform and cable railway had been bulldozed to rubble, a solitary dwarf palm tree withered on the empty hillside. It struck me as an omen of loss, and sure enough two other landmarks disappeared a week later. At Mrs. Root's funeral, the undiscovered child stars who came to pay their last respects made a glum crowd, probably wondering where to take their somersaults and xylophones next. While a moppet sang "Abide With Me" more or less on key, I remembered the last time I saw my dear friend. Her English Tudor cottage had a neglected look, its windows smeared with dust and one pane broken. Still turbaned and braceleted, Mrs. Root was at her war work in the kitchen, baking cookies for the Hollywood Canteen. "Talent Hour grows more abject by the minute, my dear, not a budding Margaret O'Brien or Roddy McDowall in the wretched bunch." She rubbed an arthritic hand. "When peace comes, I'll lay down my arms and take a trip around the world. I've never seen it except in movies, where it's usually not in color."

I wept silently, not only because Mrs. Root was lost to me and never managed to see the world in color. The past we shared seemed on the verge of being forgotten. But when the second landmark disappeared, I wasn't sure what I felt. The *Times* carried a brief obituary of Ralph Haines, who succumbed at the Paradise Convalescent Center in West Covina. Highlights of his career, it noted, were *Lady of the Pavements* for D.W. Griffith and *Freckles* with Baby Jewel. His last role was in *Charlie Chan at the Wax Museum.* When I brought the item to Mother's attention, she nodded and said, "Deep down inside, I still wonder if he was really my father. But when the center called me last night, I ordered a wreath anyway. Anonymous of course. Two hundred mums in the shape of a cross."

I stared at her as she turned a page of *The Wall Street Journal.* "Why did the center call you? And how long have you known Ralph was there?"

"Since I put him there, Baby, almost three years ago." And she described how he collapsed in the street, alcoholic and broke. In the hope of saving him from public assistance, Ralph's doctor asked for the name of a relative who might help. At first Ralph insisted he had no relatives, then reluctantly breathed the name of Mrs. Elva Kay. "I agreed to help him on condition it remained top secret, and I never had to see him again."

"But why did you keep it a secret from me? I'd have gone to visit him."

"That's why." A spasm of alarm crossed Mother's face. "Suppose some news hound got hold of the story and unmasked me!"

Without understanding my impulse to call the Convalescent Center, I followed it. The voice on the phone told me the sanitarium was owned and run by the True Church of Paradise, and Ralph's funeral would take place next day at its chapel. Plain and bare, with frosted glass windows, and a nurse playing the harmonium as I walked in, it looked like a mission on the rocks. A dozen or so mourners, obviously from the center, sat wrapped in blankets. They dozed while a minister commended the soul of Ralph Haines to God. But one man stood by himself with an air of deliberate solitude. Tall and elderly, he wore a shabby raincoat, carried a dark felt hat, and his keen hooded eyes gazed at the only luxurious object in the chapel, Mother's jumbo crucifix of flowers. Once he glanced at me without a flicker of recognition.

Unlike Mother I've never been high on the occult, but it was hard not to believe my impulse to go to Ralph's funeral had something to do with the kismet plan. I walked close behind D.W. Griffith to the cemetery, and watched him scatter earth on the casket after it was lowered into the ground. His face looked as remote as Saturn. When the rites were over I walked close behind him again, followed him to the street and along the sidewalk. He stopped for a moment, looked at a passing car, and appeared confused. Then he walked on until he came to a bus stop, and sat on a bench.

"Excuse me," I said.

The face turned to look at me, showed no interest and turned away.

"We met a long time ago. In fact a quarter of a century ago. On the set of *Broken Blossoms*."

The face gave me another look, non-recognition added to lack of interest.

"I was with my Mother and danced the Dying Swan. After I died you told everyone, 'the kid's got it.' Which made a lasting impression, like you."

Mr. Griffith gave me a long stare now, but said nothing.

"A year later I became a child star. They called me Baby Jewel. They still do."

After a long pause Mr. Griffith said, "I usually knew talent when I saw it," in a voice exactly as I remembered it, although maybe even slower. Then he gazed up at the sky in a way I also remembered, and appeared to forget about me.

"If you don't have a car, I can drive you somewhere."

When he looked at me again, he seemed confused. "The friend who drove me here was supposed to come back and pick me up. Something must have occurred to change her plans. Or maybe I misunderstood." He looked away again, not up at the sky this time, but at a movie theatre across the street. Its marquee advertised Maria Montez in *Cobra Woman*. "I don't know what to do," he said.

I wondered if the friend might be Lillian Gish. People said she was almost his only friend these days. When I repeated my offer, since Mr. Griffith neither accepted nor rejected it, he frowned. "It probably wasn't your intention to create a problem for me, but that's what you've done."

"I'm sorry."

"Don't apologize. It's unnecessary. Your intentions were of the best." Then he stood up. "Did she change her plans? Or was it yet another misunderstanding? In any case, I'm living at present in a hotel on Hollywood Boulevard. Is that out of your way?"

"No problem."

It seemed strange that the Father and Master should not only have gone to the funeral of an obscure actor who played a small part in one of his pictures, but was prepared to return home by bus. As we drove off, he appeared to read my thoughts. "Poor Haines," he said with a last look at the Maria Montez marquee. "I had a fondness for Haines. Gave him a lot of walk-ons as well as the best role of his life. But what's your connection with the departed player?"

"He played my grandfather in *Freckles*."

Mr. Griffith gave no sign that he heard. "Perhaps you know I haven't been busy for a while." He sounded dry. "Unless you count my attendance at funerals. And on these sad yet necessary occasions I always find myself burdened with memories." He recited a long list of colleagues whose funerals he'd attended over the years, ending with Lupe Velez, star of *Lady of the Pavements*. "Poor Lupe. I had a fondness for Lupe. But although she died young, I fear the gods didn't love her. They must have abandoned her, if she took her own life." He closed his eyes. "They've abandoned *me*," he said, and I felt a solitude so complete that I decided not to invade it.

Finally I had to, because his eyes were still closed as we reached Hollywood, and I wanted to know the name of the hotel where he lived. The

Father came to and gazed out the window at another theatre marquee, Erich von Stroheim in *Storm Over Lisbon*. "Stroheim keeps busy, but the gods have abandoned him as well, you know. It's possible my friend will be waiting at the Hollywood Roosevelt. Maybe I misunderstood but let's go and see."

As we entered the bar I looked around for Lillian, but the Father didn't look around for anybody. His pace suddenly quickening, he signaled to the barman and strode to a table in the corner, where he sat down and seemed to forget about me again. He watched the barman pour a jigger of scotch into a highball glass and follow it with a splash of soda and a brace of ice cubes. When the drink arrived, he grasped it without a word and took a long deep sip.

So far Mr. Griffith had struck me by turns as vague and ornery, and during the drive I even wondered if he was growing senile behind a gallant front of pride. But now I knew him for a serious toper, mildly fuddled by years of knocking it back.

"You can't imagine," I said, "how long I've been waiting for our paths to cross."

Once more he gave no sign that he heard. "Forgive me. I should have offered you a drink. The sad but necessary occasion hasn't put me in a social mood." He looked thoughtful. "Of course, few occasions put me in a social mood anyway."

"I don't want a drink. And I don't want to think of this as a social occasion. It's very personal," I said, and described all the times I'd hoped to meet the Father in the past, when the first *Kid Sherlock* opened on the same bill as *Way Down East*, at my Baby of the Year party, on my visits to the abandoned set of Babylon. "If it sounds ridiculous now, remember I was only a kid. I wanted you to be proud of me. I wanted you to *know*."

He nodded understandingly. Then he said, "I'll tell you what I know. Motion pictures are not an art, they give us nothing to compare with the Greeks or Shakespeare. If you care about art, stick to the theatre. Lillian went back to it. I often regret I ever left it."

"Yes. But that's not what I was talking about."

He took another long sip of scotch. "Maybe I misunderstood. What *is* it you wanted me to know?"

"I was a kid seeking approval, longing to find out if you'd seen me in a picture and thought I was doing okay."

Mr. Griffith seemed to rack his memory. Finally he said, "Most likely. But next time you step in front of a camera, remember everything starts with the eyes."

"It may be a while before I step in front of a camera again."

"Don't wait too long or you'll get *unwound*."

When I explained the situation with Howard, the Father gave another understanding nod. "Sometimes, young lady, all we can do is wait. It's all I've done for fifteen years." He signaled to the barman for another scotch. "Now let's get back to what you wanted me to know. I used to call myself the Columbus of the movies. I made *Intolerance* and showed the history of the world in three hours. I taught people to see themselves in time as well as space, and they compared me to Homer." The drink arrived and he cradled the glass in his hands. "But those who came after," he said, "Chaplin, Stroheim, Lubitsch, Sternberg, young Mr. Welles, talented men, men of great talent, they make us *see*, but did anyone compare them to Homer? That's why I say now, motion pictures are not an art. And Mr. Welles takes too much from me, by the way, I built sets with ceilings twenty-five years ago, to say nothing of. . . ." His voice trailed off and he sipped his drink. "Now do you understand what I *know*?"

"I see it all."

He leaned forward to peer at my face. "What did you say they called you?"

"Baby Jewel."

It startled him. "Really? Did you make *The Bluebird*?"

"Yes. Did you see it?"

Mr. Griffith seemed to rack his memory again. "Most likely," he said. "And here's something else for you to remember. After the eyes, the hands. So many human expressions in the movement of a wing. Study our feathered friends and learn to flutter."

Then he noticed a woman standing in the doorway. She looked like a B girl, as we used to call hookers who worked the bars, black satin dress, too much eye shadow, dyed coppery hair. Suddenly anxious, the Father got to his feet and walked over. She scolded him loudly. "Old Daddy, you told me to go look for a bottle of scotch while you were at the funeral, and I couldn't find one in all of West Covina, but when I got back to the chapel you were gone already. Why didn't you wait?"

"Forgive me. I misunderstood." She took his arm and they left, the Father never glancing back in my direction. I waved to the empty doorway and got up as the barman came over. "Your friend forgot to take care of the check," he said.

"Can't you charge it to his room?"

The barman shook his head. "Mr. Griffith likes people to think he's got a suite at the Roosevelt, but he's living at a dumpy little place around the corner. Sad, isn't it? Still, you cheered him up."

"I wonder. He never smiled."

"It's all relative. I've seen him sit here for hours, really drooping, then *she* comes and takes him home."

I paid the check, and the barman called out as I reached the door, "I guess it was a thrill for you as well, talking about old times?"

Driving home, I tried to read between the lines. Was the Father's memory really slipping or did he find it convenient to forget? Did he truly fail to remember whether he'd seen *The Bluebird* or had he seen it and not been proud of me after all? "You'll never know," Mother said. "So stop worrying and get that old man out of your system. I warned you years ago he'd lost his touch."

"Yes. But I'm somehow afraid he saw *The Bluebird* and *hated* me."

"So strange of you to have a father complex. *I* never did, with just as much reason to." Then Mother confided she was about to take a one-day trip to Vegas with the Bug. "Ben believes it'll bring him bad luck if I don't go, *I* believe it'll bring one or both of us bad luck if I do, but how can I say no to the man I love?" When I smiled, she looked grave. "Make fun of me if you like, but things happen in this world way beyond the reach of your literal mind."

Years later, discovering the fear and excitement of that trip in her diary, I felt a chill. Mother stated all her beliefs, from the most sensible to the most absurd, with equal conviction. And yet, although her dread of leaving Los Angeles always struck me as absurd, memory tells she came up with another superstition that I fell for eagerly. "This can't be proved, Baby, but it's an unusually strong vibration. *Our government will never allow any movie star to be killed in action.* You can be sure it only sends them on riskproof missions, and I promise you that Gable, Ty Power, Bob Montgomery, Jimmy Stewart *and* Jimmy Gabriel will all come home without a scratch."

So they did. On my way to meet Jimmy after his discharge, I wondered who to expect. His letters never gave me a clue, like Mr. Griffith he left me reading between the lines and finding only empty spaces there. In the years he'd been away, I learned that he admired the British and despised their food, despised the French and admired their food, had dinner with Major Gable, reported the King in good shape. They agreed I was right to sign the contract with Howard, a hard man to get to know according to Gable, but never did anything without a reason. Also, Cagney as George M. Cohan in *Yankee Doodle Dandy* really knocked Jimmy out, moved him to tears every time he saw it, especially the last, which was the night Roosevelt died.

At first sight I thought Jimmy looked the same, only thinner. After we hugged and kissed, he said, "You look the same, only thinner." On the drive home it was difficult to pick up the threads, unlike the time we had dinner together after so many years apart, on my return from Hawaii. He refused to talk about the war. "Don't ask me if I was scared or thrilled or bored or disgusted, because I can't tell you. I was in limbo time all the time. And I'm not out of it yet."

We drove past a camouflaged movie studio. "What is this?" he asked, and I told Jimmy all the studios had been camouflaged after an intelligence tip-off that the Japanese planned to knock out MGM. When we got back to the house, he looked around and saw his photograph on the mantelpiece in the livingroom. "This is nice." I brought out a bottle of champagne and asked him to open it. "Where did you get it? I heard the supply dried up." Mother was kept in bubbly by the Bug, I explained, and sent over a case as a welcome home surprise.

It was a warm night, so we took bottles, glasses and a radio out to the pool, lay side by side on chaises longues listening to Dinah Shore. "This is nice," Jimmy said again, then asked how many times I'd been unfaithful while he was away.

"Not very often. An occasional stupid physical thing."

"Same with me. Was one of the physical things with Howard Hughes?"

"What a crazy question."

"I wouldn't have liked it if you'd gone to bed with Hughes."

"Me neither."

Jimmy opened another bottle of champagne and we chinked glasses. "It's not Hughes personally, just anyone famous I'd have minded you going to bed with."

"Nobody famous asked me, Jimmy."

After a pause he said, "You wrote me Howard fixed you up as a sexy Martian princess and had a lot of pictures taken. I want to see them."

"I don't have them."

He looked suspicious. "How is that?"

"Howard wouldn't let anyone see them. I never even saw them myself."

"I guess it figures." His face cleared. "But you certainly landed yourself in limbo time."

"And I'm not out of it yet. He's got me for another five years if he wants."

Jimmy opened another bottle of champagne and we chinked glasses. "Do you have any plans?" I asked.

He nodded. "I've eaten the bitter apple but I'm still planning to stick around the Garden of Eden. Just like you." He lay back and closed his

eyes. "But can Paradise Lost ever really turn into Paradise Regained?"
Shortly afterwards he fell asleep. It was 2:00 in the morning, very silent,
no wind, no movement of water in the pool, but a slight chill in the air. I
covered Jimmy's body with a blanket and went to bed.

Some time later I woke with a start and found him standing over me,
naked. "Sorry I was so down," he said. "It's been like coming around
after a long operation." He got into bed, made love and plans. He had a
great idea to play Al Jolson in the movies and create an even bigger sensation than Cagney as Cohan. He was determined to confront Howard and
make him shit or get off the pot. "Things are going to start happening, I
promise. Just give me time."

However, Howard disappeared again, even harder to find than to
know. And every producer that Jimmy tried to interest in the Jolson story
assured him Jolson was a back number. "Get into a Broadway musical,
that's the million dollar route these days," Jimmy's agent advised, so he
got into one, but it flopped. "Put a nightclub act together, you can't
miss," his agent advised, so Jimmy opened in Montreal, singing and
dancing, impersonating his favorites from Jolson to Carmen Miranda.
They loved him so much that his booking was extended, and the critics
compared him to a human tornado. I never saw the act, because Howard
refused to let me leave town, but the man turned up in Los Angeles again
while Jimmy was in Montreal, almost married Lana Turner, failed to return my calls, then went back into hiding.

Then Jimmy opened his act to great acclaim in Chicago, where the critics compared him to a human whirlwind. During the run a Hollywood
producer announced plans to make the Jolson story. As soon as he could,
Jimmy flew back to the coast and did an audition. The producer agreed he
could imitate Jolson's voice to a fare-thee-well. "But we're going to dub
Jolson's real voice for the songs, my friend, and we're after a taller romantic type to play him." Jimmy left town again and opened his act in Miami,
where the critics compared him to a human cyclone.

I was planning to fly out and see the act in spite of Howard, and
checked in at the airport desk. As I walked toward the departure lounge a
man came up and said he had an important message for me. He warned
that if I went to Miami against Howard's orders I was breaking the contract and must expect to be sued. I called my attorney from a pay phone.
"The man's got plainclothes detectives watching me now, this is really
getting out of hand, is there no way *we* can sue?" My attorney regretted
there was no way at all. "*Howard* has never broken the contract, you see. I
wanted a clause that he had to make a picture with you by a certain date,

it was one of many things I tried to improve, but he wouldn't agree. Better stay home."

A week later Howard turned up in Los Angeles again. He failed to return my calls but took to the air himself, in that reconnaissance aircraft promised but never delivered to the Air Force during the war. It had some kind of engine failure. Crash landing on a house in Beverly Hills, he fractured his skull, suffered multiple burns on his face and body, broke nine ribs and his nose. After a few days on the critical list, he began receiving visitors, and at the Good Samaritan Hospital I passed Ginger Rogers in the corridor, on her way out from his room.

Howard lay propped up in bed, motionless, encased in splints and bandages, his face invisible apart from the eyes and lower lip. In his flattest, most clinical tone he remarked that he was in great pain. "But yesterday I finally figured what went wrong with the XF-11. It had to be the right propeller." A somber gleam appeared in his eyes. "That helps me a lot in my mind."

I lit a cigarette. "You could help *me* a lot in my mind if you dropped my option next month."

A nurse came in with a glass of water and a pain-killing tablet. Howard examined the tablet carefully, frowned, blew an imaginary speck of dust away and washed it down. Then he said, "I thought you had more sense." He knew the gossip columnists had been sniping at him recently, with stories about the growing list of actresses he placed under contract and never allowed to work, but he couldn't believe I took them seriously. A man who ran several businesses at once had to sort out his priorities. "The only reason you're on the back burner is that I can't make you a top priority right now. Why are you looking at me that way? Don't you believe me?"

I shook my head.

Slowly, Howard reached out a bandaged hand to the bedside table, picked up a letter and told me to read it. A note from President Truman, wishing him a speedy recovery. "If the President believes in me," Howard said mildly, "that should be good enough for you."

After Miami, Jimmy took his nightclub act to New York. Near the end of the run he called with the news that he was going to London, where the Palladium had invited him to top the bill.

"I wish I could come. I've never seen Europe."

"Thanks to the man, you've never even seen my act."

"And hardly seen *you*. It's like the war."

"Try him again."

I called Howard at the hospital and he reproached me again for not believing in him. "Oh, I *do*, I really do," I said. "I just want a little time off to see my husband." But he refused. "Then here's the truth," I said. "You may be in pain, but any similarity between Howard Hughes and a human being is still coincidental."

"The pain's much better now." He sounded almost cheerful. "I'll be out of this place in a couple of days. And as soon as I've solved a couple of top priorities, we'll have dinner and plan your career."

I told Jimmy I'd go to Europe with him anyway, but the day before I was due to leave, the phone rang. A voice speaking on behalf of Howard Hughes ordered me to report for a week of photo sessions, starting that night. I called Jimmy again and said I'd still go to Europe with him, but he advised against it. "The man's got too much *power*. You're risking more than a lawsuit, you're giving him a *reason* to fuck you over long and good."

At 1:00 a.m., Boris waited for me alone at the Photo-Art Studio. "Isn't Howard coming?" I said, and he shook his head. "Howard's in Acapulco, seeing no one. He feels very tired. I'm sorry you suffer, Babushka, but I have to admit I feel a little happy. This is the first time in months Howard's given me any work to do." I posed in a swimsuit and asked, "What's your estimate of the situation now?" Boris reminded me to smile, then told the story of a starlet Howard brought over from Italy, confining her to a hotel room for several months, with guards outside her door around the clock. Occasionally he went to visit the girl. He took her downstairs to the empty hotel ballroom, where they danced cheek to cheek in the small hours to a rented orchestra, and she cried a little as he promised her a great future. Then he took her back to the room for a lay, and said au revoir.

"Boris. Why are you telling me this?"

He reminded me to smile again. "Things could be much worse and I wanted you to know. That's my estimate of the situation."

Elva's Diary

April 5 • For too much of her life Baby has been like a becalmed ship, always in need of some force to put wind in her sails. The male animal, of course, overdoes it and threatens to sink her, but the combination of yours truly and alcohol usually launches her nicely, so last night I took her to dinner at Romanoff's and got her well liquored up before starting to talk turkey.

"It's time you began to think about time," I suggested over our third martini.

Baby said she thought about it quite often but never knew what to think.

"Just remember it's always running out. When Mr. Hughes' last option expires next month, you'll be close to a secret forty. Of course I blame myself."

"You can't blame yourself because I'm getting older. It's a law of nature."

"I blame myself for not facing up to your situation sooner. But hope springs eternal and I simply couldn't believe the man would keep you in cold storage year after year after year." Even his flying boat finally got off the ground for five minutes, I pointed out, before Mr. Hughes shut it away in a hangar, and it seemed reasonable to expect a trial run for Baby one day. But that was the moment when I should have realized the secret pattern of his life. Keeping his most prized possessions, especially actresses, shut away in a hangar. Instead, when he bought the RKO studios, I assumed Mr. Hughes was becoming operative at last, and never dreamed the brute would merely close them down while he checked every employee's record to make sure there were no Commies on the payroll.

"Things could be much worse," Baby said, and I asked her in God's name to tell me how. "Suppose Howard had actually *made* a picture with me," she said. "When he opened the studio again, he threatened to star me in *I Married a Communist,* but decided I wasn't a natural anti-Red type and finished off Laraine Day instead." She gave a contented smile. "Things could be much worse. I'm in great demand to make recordings for the blind. They just asked me to wax the works of Erle Stanley Gardner."

"You always missed the point of charity work. Recordings for the blind will never get you in *the public eye.*"

"If it's Comeback Country you're after, forget it. I've been away too long, nobody knows who I am. Or was. There's nothing shorter in this town than people's memories, except maybe Alan Ladd."

"Must you wallow in the worst while your Mother as usual prepares for the best? I'm after more than a comeback, I'm shooting for Resurrection!"

Baby shook her head when I offered her another martini, claimed she was hungry and hid her face behind the menu as I outlined my plan. "There's a bandwagon around and I want you to hop on it. Right now I admit it's mundane, but that's only temporary. And as poor Ben used to remind me, when there's no champagne around we can't afford to turn down Coca-Cola.''

"I can afford to turn anything down." Baby spoke quietly from behind the menu. "I don't need to make any more money."

"Everyone needs to make more money, it's human nature. Besides, you're a natural fourteen-carat talent. The world's been telling you that since your moppet days. To thine own self be true, Baby, or risk spending the rest of thy life in a spiritual desert. Like the Divine One, lonely and adrift since she renounced the cameras."

Baby looked at me briefly over the top of the menu, but didn't answer.

"Here's how we walk off with the game one more time." After seeing my first nickelodeon drama about an alcoholic truckdriver who ran down his own daughter, I explained, it never occurred to me that the movies would develop into the eighth wonder of the world. In the same way, almost half a century later, most people believed TV would never offer anything more than roller derbies, strings of stupid puppets like Howdy Doody, and a talk show starring never-say-die Wendy Barrie.

Baby looked at me over the top of the menu again. "They're wrong. TV just offered Virginia Hill and Senator Kefauver."

"Smarty. The cathode ray tube is definitely on its way. And if Hopalong Cassidy can gallop off with millions every week, it's bound to start a trend. In fact the trend's already started. Superman and I Love Lucy will hit the home screens shortly, and I see *a very special future in filmed TV series.*"

Baby didn't look up.

"This is an A-1 vibration. I hear cash registers ringing, and they'll ring for Baby Jewel when she stars in her own series."

Baby put down the menu and lit a cigarette. "I'll have vichyssoise, then rack of lamb with a Caesar salad."

"Here's the clincher. I'll make you senior vice-president of EKE and we'll own the series together."

"But you know what they'll call that. Nepotism. Just like the time there were twenty-three Cohns working at Columbia."

"Don't let twenty-three Cohns stand in your way. What other girl in this town has the chance to star on the home screen every week *and* perform as top senior executive in a great financial empire?"

Although Baby said nothing she gave a little shiver, as if a faint wind was beginning to stir her sails at last. "It's another new image for you, and a blockbuster," I went on. "Besides, I really *need* you. In spite of appearances I'm not as young as I was, and just a little weary of being a one-woman show. Not ready to hand over the reins yet, but ready to share them. One way or another we've always been a two-woman show, so it's as natural as Fate. What do you say? If you say no, you'll be fighting the kismet plan."

After a while Baby said, "Honestly, you never cease to amaze me."

"I hope I never will."

After a while Baby said, "I'll have to think it over. In the meantime I'm changing my mind about that final martini. Make it a double."

April 12 • Since I offered her a new life last week, Baby has been walking around with a distracted expression on her face. "Just thinking it over," she tells me when I ask what's the matter. This evening I returned home from a Glamor Bazaar, where I bought an Edison Cylindrical Phonograph complete with original tinfoil record of Al Jolson singing "So Long Mother," and found Baby waiting in the livingroom, walking around with an expression more distracted than ever. "Haven't you thought it over yet?" I asked. "How much longer are you going to look a gift horse in the mouth?"

Tears suddenly streamed out of her eyes. I had a strong vibration that jolted my mind back to the night more than twenty years ago when Baby came home, and thrust a kiss-off letter from Jimmy Gabriel in my hands. And as I stared at her she began to sob loudly, then said, "People shouldn't ask for a divorce over the phone!"

I held out my arms, hugged her close, then led her to a divan and told her to lie down while I fixed a gin fizz. She agreed to lie down but protested she didn't want a gin fizz, she was trying to cut down on drinking. But I made it and she drank it, while I stroked her hair. "Jimmy Gabriel moves around so much," I said, "I'd sooner try and keep up with a bat out of hell. Where did he phone from?"

"Dallas. I thought he was still making a picture in Rome, but he just finished it, and flew to Dallas to open the first Jimmy Gabriel Academy of Acting." Baby stared at the ceiling. "It was love at first sight when Miss Bluebonnet of 1950 cut the tape. He wants to marry her."

"Any man who's planning to get married for the sixth time is obviously not the marrying kind." I got up to make another gin fizz. "Call me hard if you like, but it's the best thing that's happened to you in a long time. In this our life, Baby, we've got to fish or cut bait. And don't tell me you'll miss the brute. Since the war you've seen him about as often as you've seen Howard Hughes."

Baby sat up. "I suppose I just hated to read the signs. I read them once, and told Jimmy I got the impression he was avoiding me. But he denied it. He said everything would work out if we gave it time."

"There's no end to the tricks the male animal plays, and no end to the way we fall for them. Hateful to admit you've lost your man, Baby, but humiliating to try and hang on to him. I hope you agreed to a divorce on the spot."

Baby shook her head. "I asked for time to think it over."

"Thinking it over looks like becoming the story of your life."

She stood up and walked slowly toward the hallway. "Everything's so weird," she said. "This used to be his house."

"You'd never know it. I changed everything except the address."

Instead of answering she gazed at my marble staircase leading off the hallway. Then, in a shaky pathetic voice, she told me how Jimmy made love to her a few times in the master bedroom, and liked to watch their reflections in the mirrored ceiling. Once, as it turned to night outside, he held her very tightly, watched darkness blot their reflections out and said it was the only way to die.

"I find that remark almost as clear as mud. Now stop brooding on your past and concentrate on your future."

"Do I have one?"

"Until the day you croak. And — who knows — maybe even after that."

She walked slowly back toward me. "Jimmy's opening another Academy of Acting in Cleveland next week. There's going to be a chain. He took a leaf out of your book and formed JG Enterprises. He's getting into sportswear and toiletries for the modern man as well. The first Jimmy Gabriel sportswear and toiletries store opens in Vegas at the same time as his nightclub act." The tears started to flow again. "And he's putting Bluebonnet into the act. She's going to sing "It Had to Be You" while he does a softshoe shuffle in a spotlight."

I led her back to the divan and made her lie down again while I explained what I wanted her to do. "Fly up to Nevada and establish residence for a quickie divorce. You can sit it out in Reno, so you won't have to see Jimmy *or* Bluebonnet making her debut."

"Reno's where we got married." Another rush of tears. "I could never sit it out there."

"Kindly remember what I told you last week."

"Time is always running out?"

"Very good, but I was thinking of something else. You tend to wallow in the worst, Baby, like a pig in shit. Otherwise, of course, you're as close to human perfection as anyone can be."

"I'd wallow in the best if I could find it."

"It'll come your way if you take my advice. First you've got to sit it out in Reno." She started to protest but I laid a hand over her mouth. "Find a new hobby to take your mind off the worst. I understand there's no end of things to do up there, they call it the busiest little town in the world. Keep busy, then pick up your divorce and come home to a new life. Senior business executive and queen of video!"

I took my hand away from Baby's mouth. She lay very still and closed her eyes.

"When private love fails, there's always public adoration to fall back on," I said. "You've lost your man and you'd better find your audience."

Baby opened her eyes, sat up and glanced toward the hallway again. She sighed. "Jimmy once told me, it doesn't matter what happens to you. Only what you do when it happens."

"For once I agree with him. Get back to being *yourself*, with a little help from your Mother, and knock the world dead again."

Although the distracted expression left Baby's face, it was difficult to know what replaced it. She looked quite blank. "Don't run out of rainbows," I said. "I never do." Then I flung open a window with a grand gesture. "Just letting the Queen Bee in." I opened another window, then another. "And making sure the Queen Bee gets the message."

It was dark outside. A faint sweetness of jasmine drifted through the open windows and filled the room. I took Baby's arm and led her out to the terrace, where the sweetness was stronger. We might have been breathing honey. Baby inhaled deeply, then sighed again. She still looked blank and I had no idea what was on her mind. But then she began to smile.

"Well," she said finally. "Got to hand it to you. You certainly know how to make a deal."

Baby Looks Back

Mother failed to stage-manage only one thing that night. The moon. It should have come out from behind a cloud and turned us triumphantly silver. I remembered our first evening on the Boulevard, when we stood hand in hand outside the Hollywood Hotel and wondered whether we'd traveled a long way to the wrong place. We stood hand in hand again that night, but the moon kept its dark side to us, the sky and the planets were still just beyond Mother's control. But she made do by promising me a fresh image and a new world when all I had left was a discarded image and a dead world. Ex-star and almost ex-wife, I had nowhere to go except maybe to the ultimate Father and Master, no other deal to make except with the Catholic church. So chalk up another credit to Mother. She probably saved me from the long arm of the Pope.

For ten years I'd been trying to make a career as Jimmy's wife, and wanted to succeed not only because I loved him. If I lost him, it was a failure on the human *and* professional front. That night, knowing I'd lost him, I decided to stay with Mother and we went upstairs to her voluptuous barge of a bed. After she dropped off to sleep, I began to wonder if I genuinely loved Jimmy or was suffering because I'd lost my favorite role. It was a futile thing to do and I could only conclude that I always found Jimmy unbelievably interesting, vulnerable at his most egotistic, heroic at his most absurd. I remembered our first date, and the street light catching his face as he opened the door of his beat-up roadster. "Am I or am I not dreambait?" he asked. There's no accounting for tastes. He was. And then I remembered a day after the war when I sniffed the possibility, strong as jasmine in Mother's garden, of the dream fizzling out. "Now listen, we're together but apart, or apart but together, depending on the way you look at it," Jimmy said, and the way he looked at it was as a *born entertainer* who had to entertain wherever he could find a spot. Unfortunately the spot was never Hollywood, which his agent advised was still cold, but Montreal, Miami, London, Australia. After a while, when he came home and spent a night or two at the house, he no longer made love. But he had an explanation for that as well. "We've still got something deep and true and eleventh hour, even if it's not romantic any more. That's *my* fault, by the way. These days I'm too disillusioned ever to feel romantic again."

As I hear it now, there followed another of his long unbroken confessional sentences, at 3:00 in the morning after he'd flown in from Puerto Rico. "I know the times are always changing, but why are they always changing for the worse? with the big studios getting into big trouble, starting to lose out to TV after losing their theatre chains because some government law about monopolies took them away, can you imagine divorcing production and distribution, don't those idiots in Washington realize it *kills the flow?* and now there's a shake-up at Metro and they've forced the great Louis B. to resign, I never worked for Louis B., met him a couple of times and got the impression he didn't like me too well for some reason, but I always had this feeling, as long as the great Louis B. reigned at Metro there'd be more stars than there are in heaven and nothing seriously wrong with the world, now he's gone and I see the handwriting all over the wall, it's the *system breaking down,* no Louis B., no flow, no security, I guess all systems break down in the end, but *I* haven't broken down, my talent's still there (isn't it?), my energy, my enthusiasm, I still *love* this business even though terrible things are happening in it, Judy Garland starting her fifth nervous breakdown, Chaplin heckled and baited as a Red by all and sundry including Howard Hughes, that spook who's planning to open his latest turkey *Underwater* underwater, who has the nerve to invite *you* after all he's never done for you, knowing your phobia about the ocean he still expects you to watch Jane Russell with a mask over your face in an air tank under the coast of Florida, and don't forget the freezing out of Jimmy Gabriel, reduced to taking anything he can get, right now a so-called cameo in some mad Italian costume epic, twenty-five thousand dollars to play the Cyclops, one-eyed *and* dubbed.''

And so on until a car arrived to take him to the airport at dawn. ''Are you sure there's no one else around you're feeling romantic about?'' I asked as I rode with him. Jimmy denied it, insisted romance was a dead letter in his life, even boozy lust had subsided, and rumors never reached me, as they say, that he was telling anything except the truth. Apparently it took Miss Bluebonnet of 1950 to make Jimmy feel romantic again.

On the phone from Dallas: ''I don't know how to explain it. If life wasn't so crazy, I'd still be in love with *you*.''

''Can you explain why you're in love with Bluebonnet?''

''I detect a note of hostility in the way you keep calling her that. Her name's Coralyn.''

''How tall is she?''

''I still detect a note of hostility. Five eight.''

''Gorgeous? Expensive? Conniving?''

''Gorgeous, willowy and compassionate. And she can sing.''

''A star in the making.''

''Very likely. I'm putting her under contract to JG Enterprises. Now let's get back to the real subject.''

''I thought Bluebonnet *was* the real subject.''

''You want to give me a hard time, or bring suit and charge me with whatever you like?''

''I'll have to think it over.''

''Extreme cruelty is always a sure thing.''

''How about grievous mental suffering? Or killing me by inches?''

''Never known you so bitter before.''

''Never felt so bitter before.''

''I'm truly sorry.''

''What kind of stuff does Bluebonnet sing? 'Deep in the Heart of Texas'? 'The Trolley Song'? 'The Lord's Prayer'?''

''Make your lousy jokes if they give you a kick.''

"Can she twirl a baton?"

"It so happens she won a contest."

"I suspected it. Why not let Bluebonnet twirl a baton *and* sing 'The Lord's Prayer'? It's never been done before, even in Vegas."

Jimmy sighed. "How long do you need to think it over?"

"I don't know yet. But I promise you one thing," I said before hanging up. "Whatever happens, you can keep the Chrysler."

As soon as my contract with Howard expired I set out for Reno in the Buick and it felt like the day the world ended. Distant baby tornados were blowing up in the desert, the sky turned the color of dust. At Lou's Kitchen, a solitary shack on the highway, I stopped for a coke. In the diner, a man wearing faded jeans and check shirt stood with his back to me, gazing out the window. When he heard the door creak, he turned around. Whiskered and leathery, Lou looked like a retired gold prospector, but he gave me a quick excited look and said, "Holy Moses, here comes the first customer of the day and it's Baby Jewel as I live or die." Impossible, I thought, for an ex-Baby to walk into the middle of nowhere and get the fan's rush, then he told me he used to work as a movie extra, and the tornados on the horizon were stirring up memories like dust.

"I been looking out the window and remembering that fantastic tornado scene in a western I worked on back in twenty-eight, *The Winning of Barbara Worth*. Now what were *you* working on back in twenty-eight? *Treasure Island* if I'm not mistaken. Saw it twice. Did you ever see *Barbara Worth*? It had a fantastic flood as well as a tornado, and launched Gary Cooper." Lou smacked his lips. "Twenty-eight was quite a year. I did *Rainbow Trail* as well."

Lou called for his wife May and she came out from the kitchen, a trim pioneer type with sharp blue eyes and a weathered, pointed face. She wore an identical check shirt and pair of faded jeans, recognized me at once and said she used to work as a movie extra as well, she and Lou met on location for *The Covered Wagon*, courted on location for *The Iron Horse* and decided to tie the knot on location for *Barbara Worth*. "We made all those early westerns, honey. People thought us crazy, turning down cushy indoor ballroom and restaurant stuff to go out on *Cimarron*, but we liked the life. Pictures were really pictures in those days. No wonder you got out." She cut me a slice of fresh homemade pecan pie. "Eat up, honey. You're much too thin."

"Is that why you live here?" I asked. "For the same kind of life?"

They nodded. "How we love it still," May said, and Lou gazed out the window again at a swirling desert and a dirty sky. Then he wondered where I was going all by myself in the middle of Nevada.

"I'm driving to Reno to divorce my husband, but where I'm going after that is anybody's guess."

May clicked her teeth sympathetically and asked if I saw *Sunset Boulevard*. She was very shocked at Gloria Swanson lending herself to a picture like that. "How could she help them to knock down the old stars and the old movies that way? Know what Mae Murray said after she saw it?" Her eyes grew narrow and fierce. "She told everyone in the lobby as they came out, *'Now listen, not all us floozies were all that nuts.'* "

"I should say." Lou offered me another coke. I refused, and didn't tell them Mae was nuttier these days than Gloria as Norma Desmond, boarding a Greyhound bus to New York in her *Merry Widow* makeup under the delusion she had a new movie opening there. They wouldn't let me pay for the pie or the coke, waved as I left, then turned back to watch the dust storm through the window.

I drove on toward a blurred horizon, my own memories stirred up like dust. A cardboard pyramid appeared in the desert like a mirage and for a moment I became a moppet Cleopatra, rolled up in a carpet a few miles outside Palm Springs and gasping for air. Blinking her away, I let a very recent memory settle. I was lying on my livingroom couch the night before, waiting to catch an ex-Baby on a TV variety show. From time to time it was interesting to check up on the other kids, see what kind of shape they were in, and I wanted to take a look at Gloria Jean, who had her own radio program at five, entered movies as a rival to Deanna Durbin at ten, and went on the skids at twenty after a nervous breakdown on a singing tour. There she was again, with a determined smile, pudgy figure and perky soprano voice, warbling "Fools Rush In." Great to have you back, I thought, keep up the smile and the good work, but try and lose some weight. Leaning to switch off the set, I found myself face to face with another ex-Baby, cool and crisp in a polka-dot gown. Peggy Lynch, tipped as another Shirley Temple after she played an elf in *A Midsummer Night's Dream* but doing a commercial for dog food now. Then the front doorbell rang, I went to answer it and saw no one outside, but an old Chevrolet parked in the driveway.

As I wondered where it came from, a tall man appeared from behind a tree. Something ghostly and sneaky in the way he padded toward me. A familiar voice said, "When I saw your lights on I thought it would be okay to ring the bell. But you didn't answer at once, and I thought maybe you'd left the lights on but gone to sleep."

"Just watching a dog food commercial," I said and invited Howard inside. The last time I saw him was in hospital, his face almost completely masked with bandages, so I should have been prepared for a change, but the change stunned me even so. To hide the scars around his mouth he'd grown a mustache, but his eyes looked anxious and startled, his face almost twenty years older, his body shrunken and fragile. He wore a rumpled suit and a fedora. "You've got a dog?" He fiddled with a hearing aid. "What kind of a dog?"

"No, Howard, I never had a dog."

"I'm real sorry about everything that didn't happen." He frowned. "Although I move pretty fast when I make up my mind, sometimes it takes me a while to make up my mind." Then he reached into a pocket. "But I brought you a gift."

Inside a thin black box lay a diamond necklace. When I told Howard I didn't want it, he looked so puzzled and hurt that I changed my mind and let him put it around my neck. He apologized for fumbling with the clasp. "A couple of fingers don't work so good anymore. But I wanted you to know I'm real sorry." His hands brushed against my skin and felt clammy. "Maybe it's true I handle machines better than people."

He walked around me in a slow deliberate circle. "It looks fine. So do you." He started to sit down, then made for the door. "I guess that's all." But he stopped, turned back and walked around me again. "You look fine. If you still want to get back in the movies, it's not too late."

I said nothing, just wanting him to go away. Not because I felt angry. He seemed so sad and wasted. He made me think of a trick photographic effect, speeded-up motion that stripped away flesh to reveal the skeleton underneath. Death at work.

"Insist on color," he said, staring at me. "People should see you in color." Rambling on, he gave what he called pieces of valuable advice. "Keep out of war movies, nobody wants to see them. Watch out for the Reds. They're still around and Chaplin's the worst, don't let anyone fool you. If they offer you a picture in Italy, get the deal checked very carefully. They make a lot of false promises over there, and you could sit around for ever waiting for something to happen."

Then he shrugged. "But I'm losing interest in motion pictures."

"That's a shame, Howard. After all, you bought yourself a studio."

He told me he had no time to think about the studio anymore. No time even to play golf, for he spent almost every waking hour on his top priority, the Hughes Aircraft Company. It would soon become the biggest electronics center in the world. He was signing up scientists and engineers instead of stars now, and negotiating with the government for research contracts.

"You mean the government still speaks to you? Fantastic!"

The dark haunted eyes went suddenly blank. Then he shook his head, leaned close to me and spoke very quietly. "Nothing fantastic about it. As a newspaperman wrote the other day, you don't judge Howard Hughes on a few mistakes. *This is no ordinary guy.*"

He turned away, fiddling with the hearing aid, and was gone.

A few miles before Reno I swung off the highway and drove along a dirt road that climbed higher toward the Sierra Nevadas, until I reached the divorce ranch that Mother recommended after checking with friends who'd been through the quickie mill. "Lana Turner *always* goes there, Baby, and the cook is top-notch." I lay on the bed in my room, reading a Chamber of Commerce brochure and thinking over Mother's advice about finding a hobby, decided against skiing, bridge, boating, hunting game or rocks. A couple of days later I picked myself a hobby called Glen, the cowboy who looked after the ranch horses. He came up to me with a slow, confident lope and offered to give me riding lessons.

Nothing original about this. Several guests had picked themselves the same hobby. Cowboys, or rather ex-cowboys, were a dime a dozen around the place, they ran small businesses in Reno but still dressed the part, kept their boots and their drawls, rode over to the ranch every day with a spare horse in tow. Breakfasting on my terrace the first morning, I saw several ladies hefted into the saddle and trotting off eagerly to the pine forest. When we met, Glen had just said goodbye to an uppity Santa Barbara matron after she picked up her divorce from a citrus king. He complained of feeling lonesome. "Thought only the girls around here were supposed to feel lonesome," I said, and he shook his head sadly. "Everyone feels it. It's in the air."

Then he loped to the corral and chose me a horse called Star.

"All I ask is, you don't ride off into the sunset together," Mother said when I told her about my hobby on the phone. A week or so later I told her I'd decided to catch Jimmy's opening after all, and sneak a look at Bluebonnet in Vegas. "All I ask is, you make it happen like a movie," she said. "Go glamorously incognito and take your hobby along."

Because Jimmy was playing the Flamingo, we checked into the Frontier. I changed into a sleek New Look number, put on a long dark wig and kingsize dark glasses, and Glen dressed up in the tux I bought him, so we were both in disguise. Then we drove to the Bug's original dream casino. In the lobby I saw pieces of the original dream still lying around, marble columns, gold-leafed statuary, any number of elegant thugs who might have been Icepick Willie. And a piece of an earlier dream was playing a one-arm bandit. Dynamic as ever in spite of a collapsing figure, di Frasso hurried over and favored Glen with a long stare. Then she gave me a quick glance. "Baby, I'd know you anywhere. But who's your friend?" I begged her not to blow my cover, and at the bar she introduced me as her niece to a Beverly Hills decorator with a lifted face. It worked even though we'd met before, he designed Mother's greenhouse-loggia and found tapestries and a suit of medieval armor for her den. But like di Frasso he concentrated on Glen and hardly gave me a second look.

On the way to the nightclub di Frasso suddenly gasped for breath, sat down and brought out a pocket inhaler. When she recovered, she told us she suffered from asthma these days, and an attack could be brought on by strong emotions. Not Glen but the Flamingo brought them on, everywhere she looked she saw the shadow of the Bug. She even spoke to it. "Didn't you put Vegas on the map, Benjy? Didn't you found this place as sure as Brigham Young founded Salt Lake City? There ought to be a monument."

It was Vegas, so naturally Jimmy had a line of showgirls to back up his act. He clowned with them, joined them in drag, danced a shimmy shake with them during his salute-to-vaudeville routine, which brought down the house. As for Bluebonnet, she got to sing *two* numbers, "You Made Me Love You" as well as "It Had to Be You," in a loud clear voice with an echo of the Panhandle. With her pink strapless gown, ostrich plumes and hopeful capped smile, she looked gorgeous and willowy all right, although I couldn't judge if she was compassionate as well. At the end Jimmy led her onstage for a special bow and a truckload of bouquets, introduced her as his bride-to-be, and the audience cheered.

Glen wanted to gamble, so I gave him a couple of hundred dollars, stood behind him at the roulette table for good luck and watched him lose it all. Then Jimmy came in and sat down at a blackjack table. From the way the dealer greeted him and the frantic concentration he brought to the game, I guessed he had a mania for gambling now. I left Glen with another couple of hundred, went over to stand quietly behind Jimmy and waited until he'd lost a thousand.

"This is something new," I said.

Jimmy recognized my voice, turned around and failed at first to recognize my face. Then he said, "That's a hell of an act."

"Not as great as yours."

He took my arm and hustled me to the bar. "You really liked it?"

"Everyone in the world should take off his hat. Where's Bluebonnet, by the way?"

"Exhausted. Gone to bed."

"Well, two numbers in a single evening is pretty arduous."

"One more of your cracks about Coralyn and all communication between us is over."

"It's practically over anyway."

I lit a cigarette and he wondered why my hands were trembling.

"Dumb question. I'm nervous."

"Hard to tell *what* you are in that Cleopatra wig and those shades." Jimmy removed my dark glasses and inspected my face. "Your eyes are angry. They look ready to launch one of those death rays you used to talk about. Why are you taking the situation so hard?"

"Because it *is* hard, and there's no other way to take it."

Jimmy leaned back in the booth, stretched out his arms along the top of the seat. "Take it *philosophically.*"

"What is that?"

I saw his eyes crinkle with experience and his mouth pucker with knowledge as he prepared to play the wise old trouper. He leaned across the table and patted my hand. "Let's go beyond the moment. To the final truth. Which lies beyond love or lust or hope or fear." I noticed his cowlick standing up taller than ever. "You know what makes people different from the animals? *They change.* A dog loves you for life, but human feelings are more volatile. Sad but true. A law of nature."

"I've heard about laws of nature from Mother for years, and I hate them. They're never on my side."

Jimmy gazed into space. *"Change,"* he said. "Our feelings change like seasons, prices, automobiles, luck. . . ."

"Speaking of luck, I get the impression you're quite a gambler now."

His gaze returned from space. "Caught the fever a few years ago, Baby in Quotes. Guess I never told you."

"Do you ever win?"

"Not as much as I lose."

"So you have to work your ass off to pay your debts?"

He shook his head. "I'd work my ass off even if there were no debts to pay. I've always been impulsive, and an impulsive person is always a driven person. He lives right up to the edge of his instincts. All my instincts drive me to adventure, which makes gambling a completely logical part of my character."

"Assuming there's any logical part of your character." I laughed. "And assuming you've *got* a character."

I thought he was going to hit me, but he only stood up and called me a poisonous bitch. "As I-forget-who said when he walked out on a party, 'Don't think this hasn't been fun, because it hasn't.'"

He started to walk out on me as Glen appeared with a disgusted look on his face. "They fix the whole operation here, I just lost another two hundred," he said, then smiled at Jimmy. "Mr. Gabriel, you're the greatest. I'd like to shake you by the hand."

Jimmy smiled back, but not because Glen paid him a compliment. The smile was much too arctic for that. He let Glen shake his hand and went on smiling. Glen wondered if I had any more cash in my purse and I told him I was cleaned out. Still smiling, Jimmy took a wad of bills from his pocket and handed them to Glen. "How much have you got there?" I asked. "Let me write you a check." But Jimmy didn't want a check. All he wanted was for Glen to go back to the roulette table and enjoy himself.

Glen looked embarrassed. "I can't take this."

"Sure you can," Jimmy said. "I'm a student of human nature and I've been studying you. You're not the type to turn down any good offer."

Glen hit him on the jaw. As Jimmy fell over backwards, I screamed. Then I knelt down and asked if he was all right. His eyes rolled alarmingly but he muttered, "Never better." By this time people had gathered around and a photographer appeared out of nowhere. He took a flash picture as I said to Glen, "You dumb cowboy, why did you do it?" He took another as I said to Jimmy, "Shall I call a doctor?" There was a scuffle when Glen tried to break the photographer's camera. Two men pulled him away and he loped furiously out of the bar. Meanwhile Jimmy staggered to his feet. "No charge for this show, folks," he said, smiling at his audience, took my arm and sat me down in the booth. His audience continued to watch. "But there's a charge if you don't go away now," Jimmy said, and they did, and I ordered us both a drink.

"Who's Glen?" Jimmy asked, and gave me no time to answer. "Whoever he is, he's not good enough for you. You're a wonderful person and you shouldn't be fooling around with a gigolo who comes on like the Lone Ranger."

"No, I'm a poisonous bitch and he's better than I deserve."

"Don't weep. There's no reason to weep."

"You're weeping too." We both took out handkerchiefs at the same time and began mopping each other's eyes. "I know Coralyn's going to make you very happy," I said. "And you deserve it because *you* are the wonderful person."

Then I kissed him and ran out of the bar.

A while later there came a knock on the door of my bedroom at the Frontier. "Jimmy?" I said, and Glen came in. I told him to go away. He sat on the edge of the bed. I lit a cigarette and he wondered why my hands were trembling. When I didn't answer, he took the cigarette from my mouth, stubbed it out, and grabbed my wrists so tightly that the trembling stopped.

"If you ever call me a dumb cowboy again, it's over."

"I'm sorry. If you ever hit my husband again, it's over."

"He insulted me. And he's almost your ex-husband, anyway. You're weeping. Don't weep." Glen let go my wrists and began comforting me gently. "Jimmy Gabriel's no student of human nature," he said. I didn't answer. "Now look at me!" he commanded. "Look me straight in the eye and tell me Jimmy Gabriel's a student of human nature."

I looked Glen in the eye, but still said nothing.

"I'm waiting, Baby. Waiting to hear if you think I'm just along for the ride."

I burst out laughing. It took Glen awhile to understand the joke he didn't know he'd made, then he laughed too.

"Maybe *I* am," I said, and we laughed in each other's arms until he switched out the light. And later I said, "You're really better than I deserve."

He got dressed, kissed me goodnight, then frowned. "Is that Countess really your friend?"

"In a way."

"She and *her* friend both propositioned me during Jimmy Gabriel's act."

"Footsie-wootsie under the table?"

"It never stopped. I'm surprised you didn't notice."

"Guess I didn't notice anything except Jimmy."

The day after we got back to the ranch, Mother called. "Well, Baby. You certainly know how to put yourself on every front page in the West."

"I feel sick about it."

"I'm thrilled. Only sorry there was no time to take off your wig and your dark glasses for the pictures, and show everyone how terrific you still look."

"That's the only thing that didn't happen the way it happens in the movies."

"What a pity we can never retake life. But even though you looked like someone else in the pictures, you looked terrific anyway. And the press is behind you to a man." According to Mother, no one saw me as another Ingrid Bergman, deserting her family and these United States for a torrid runaway affair with an Italian director. On the contrary, everyone saw me as a perfectly respectable ex-Baby who brought her riding instructor to applaud her almost-ex-husband's Vegas debut. "And when the two men got into a fight, you were completely bewildered!"

"That part is true," I said. "But the *Reno Evening Gazette* is hedging its bets. It's sent a photographer to lurk around the ranch and sneak pictures of Glen and me."

Mother advised me not to let Glen try and smash the man's camera, the press might turn against us if it happened again. I said he was playing it very cool, just a few hours ago he took me out for a lesson and told the photographer what good progress I'd made.

"So you have, Baby. But watch your step now and don't get caught in a clinch."

Later I thought, something else failed to happen the way it happens in the movies. In the movies, after Glen hit him, Jimmy and I would have discovered we were still in love and canceled the divorce. As I went off for another riding lesson, I wondered whether it was a pity or a relief that we can never retake life.

The photographer gave up next day and Glen was disappointed. He felt the press wasn't paying him enough attention. Jimmy gave an interview in Vegas and gallantly explained that he was wound up after the show and the whole thing was a stupid misunderstanding. When Hedda called, I swore I wasn't carrying a torch for Jimmy *or* having a secret romance, and she announced in her column that she believed me. But nobody asked Glen anything and he complained of feeling left out, especially as the press soon forgot about all three of us and went back to the big stuff, which was poor Ingrid.

"I think I understand about human feelings changing now," I told Jimmy when I called to thank him for handling the situation so well in his interview. "But I'll always think of you as my dearest friend." Jimmy felt the same, then asked me to *say hello to Coralyn.* I took a deep breath and said, "Hello, Coralyn." After another deep breath I added, "I wish you every success and happiness." Coralyn sounded quite emotional, so maybe she was compassionate after all.

After picking up my divorce I went to say goodbye to Glen, wondering how to say it. I hoped he wouldn't really miss me, because I wouldn't really miss him. It had been only a six-week stand, or what dashing Warren William called an exchange of two momentary desires and a contact of two skins. And as it occurred to me, in a not totally pleasant way, that with the passing of time I found myself in Warren's shoes, Glen put his arms around me. "I'm really going to miss you."

"Really going to miss you too, Glen." The old sensation came back, of hearing myself speak and wondering who wrote my dialogue. "Maybe in a different kind of world we'd have more time for each other, but let's be grateful for the time we had."

He looked very sad. "I'll be lonesome. It's in the air."

I remarked there were other things in the air around this ranch besides lonesomeness, which made him grin, but then he looked even sadder. "Time for a change," he said. "I want to settle down." He put his arms around me again and kissed me on the mouth. "You're so special. Marry me. I want to take care of you, make you happy."

"But I wouldn't make *you* happy," I said, calling once more on my screenwriter in the sky. "I'm not ready to get married again."

"How do you know till you try it? We could have a great life here."

I stared at him. "You want me to marry you and live *here?*"

He nodded calmly, and licked my ear in between the murmuring of simple pleasures, going on a camping trip and waking up high in the mountains, seeing Black Rock desert by moonlight, sunbathing in a boat on Pyramid Lake. Then he started trying to take my clothes off and I had to push him away.

"Okay." He picked up his hat. "But you'll be lonesome too."

He was in the corral as I left, showing a horse to a new arrival who reminded me of di Frasso. No baby tornados in the desert as I drove home, just a flat empty stillness under a cloudy sky. Two cars were parked outside Lou's Kitchen, but I didn't stop.

Elva's Diary

May 22 • This morning my sinus problem was so painful that instead of calling Baby in Reno I phoned Miss Sophie to cancel our lunch date. "I can hardly breathe," I said.

There was a pause, then I heard an undertone in Miss Sophie's voice that puzzled me. "It's not the first time, is it? I've been watching you for quite a while and I'm amazed you've held out so long." The undertone began to sound menacing, and I protested that I had no idea what she was talking about.

"I think you do. I know *I* do. I also know the man to fix you up, because I ran into the same problem myself a few years ago."

"Good grief." I felt stunned. "How long have you been doing it, then?"

"Longer than you, probably."

"All these years we've been such close friends and it never came up."

"The closer your friend, the more you respect her privacy," Miss

Sophie said. "I only bring it up now because you seem to be in trouble. So get on the phone to Dr. Varconi, mention my name and he'll take care of you right away."

Miss Sophie may no longer be hairdresser extraordinary to the stars, but she remains extraordinary.

May 24 • The good Dr. Varconi, who reminds me somewhat of Bela Lugosi, examined my nose today and advised immediate relining. "You've hardly got a decent membrane to call your own," he said, and went on to describe his operation. "Ten thousand dollars may sound like a gouge, but my plastic membranes hold up better than anything God made. They'll mend you for keeps, Mrs. Kay. But shoot, don't sniff, for three months. You can't expect even plastic membranes to bear heavy traffic right away. Know how to shoot?"

I nodded, but explained I only shot occasionally, not wishing to brand my flesh with telltale marks of the needle. "Fine," Dr. Varconi said. "Ever take methanol?" I denied it. "Fine," he said again. "You should see what it's doing to Talmadge. Slow suicide. Promise me you'll never touch the stuff." He looked in his appointments calendar, booked me into his clinic for the day after tomorrow, and guaranteed to send me home sound as a bell in a week. I thanked him for fitting me in so promptly, knowing he must be unusually busy, for there were seven patients breathing heavily in his waiting room.

June 1 • Miss Sophie paid a welcome visit soon after Dr. Varconi finished his check-up this morning, pronounced me clear and signed my release papers for tomorrow. We settled down to a cozy chat about how we got on the stuff. I confided that William Desmond Taylor, a casual acquaintance, gave me my first sniff at a party way back in '19, and Miss Sophie confided that the Count, a casual acquaintance who supplied Mack Sennett's Bathing Beauties, shot her up on a double date way back in '15. "Did you ever consider cold turkey?" I asked, and her eyes grew bright with astonishment. "This bird doesn't foul her own nest," she said. "Some of my finest inspirations came after a fix. How else do you imagine I startled the world by turning Pola Negri blonde, giving Miriam Hopkins an Eton crop and sprinkling *real gold dust* on Marlene's hair? The studio made a test of that, by the way, declared it the most beautiful thing they ever saw, but too expensive in the long run."

"Isn't it the goddam truth?" I said. "*I* sniffed my way into disguising Baby as a boy and launched one sensational career. And just recently, wandering high as a kite in my garden, I laid plans for one sensational comeback." Naturally Miss Sophie wanted to hear about this, so I gave her a blueprint. "Elva," she said quietly, "I've known them all, Peg Talmadge, Charlotte Pickford, Lela Rogers, Gertrude Temple, Ethel Gumm Garland — and I want to tell you, no star owes more to her Mother than your Baby!"

Baby Looks Back

In top gear when I returned from Reno, Mother said a minor operation for clearing her sinus had given her new get-up-and-go. "Not that I've been lacking in that department, Baby. But as you know I've had a temporary sinus problem for at least fifteen years. My good doctor advised me to restore what he calls communication with the nostrils, and I must say it's been a real shot in the arm."

I wondered why she never called to let me know about the operation, and she seemed surprised. "It wasn't important. And you were obviously having such a good time up there. Now let's get down to serious business, the papers are ready for you to sign."

In the Oval Office I became VP of EKE at a ceremony attended by reporters and photographers from the Los Angeles papers, the fan magazines, *Fortune* and *The Wall Street Journal*. It started late because Mother took a long time deciding what to wear. Watching her shuttle between a copy of a Travis Banton for Claudette, an Adrian for Norma and an Edith Head for Kay, I realized that as a fashion plate she had begun to regress. Every outfit under consideration dated from the thirties or early forties. Yet when she finally appeared in one of the great Irene's creations for Hedy Lamarr, a mildly slinky jade-colored twopiece with matching turban, she seemed beyond time, or ahead of it and behind it at the same time, for she also pioneered the huge tinted glasses that Dior made popular in the seventies. (Pure decoration: her vision was always perfect.) And at sixty-two she looked maybe forty-six, so it was truly impossible to slot her into any epoch or style. She took the wheel of her marbled Thunderbird with its ELVA KAY license plate, a car she featured when anxious to stress her up-to-the-minute high-powered image, and as we entered the Oval Office she acknowledged the press and her corps of lawyers with a regal wave.

Sitting down at one end of the new black lucite conference table, she motioned me to a chair at her side. Photographers went to work as her lawyers handed me documents to sign, and I remember thinking about madness again and telling myself not to bring madness into it, for the press responded to Mother with its usual awe and I heard a *Screenland* columnist proclaim her the most glamorous tycoon in the free world.

When the signing was over, Mother stood up and offered champagne on the house. A reporter asked what my position at EKE would entail. She described it as more important than Alben W. Barkley's under Harry Truman and hinted at various *roving assignments* of which the first would be a TV commercial for our prize-winning instant coffee. This was news to me, but I smiled enigmatically like Mother as she told the press to expect further developments soon.

After the press conference Mother mixed a pitcher of stingers, buzzed a secretary and ordered her wire recorder brought in. She had recently stepped across the threshold of the electronic age by recording key business conversations in the Oval Office or on the phone, less for practical use than the pleasure of playing back her own performances. I listened to the phone conversation with General Sarnoff of NBC that occurred while I was still at the ranch, and although the sound was less clear than it later became on tape, technical shortcomings failed to blunt Mother's style. "Note my use of military lingo, I felt it appropriate to a two-star General." After advising Sarnoff that EKE planned to sponsor a TV series starring Baby Jewel, she offered the network the first crack at it. "And let me remind you, General, NBC's in need of reinforcement. CBS seems to be advancing on all fronts now with Lucille Ball, Jackie Gleason, Ed Sullivan and Arthur Godfrey, and you've had some serious defections in the field recently, Jack Benny, George Burns and Gracie Allen. Don't lose your shirt by withdrawing from the chance of a lifetime."

The General promised to call her back and did so a few days later, expressing the warmest interest in a deal and telling Mother to expect a call very soon from an NBC representative on the coast. That same afternoon, the secretary of a Mr. Gordon called and made an appointment for us to go see him. The name was ordinary enough to stir no memories, we even failed to read the nameplate on his office door at NBC as an early warning signal, and trembled as if seeing a ghost when old Sid got up from his desk. He gave us an impatient look and said, "Decided to surprise you. If you'd known it was me, you might have called off the deal."

"There's still time," Mother said.

Sid had a secretary now, a larger office, he drank coffee from a plastic instead of a tin mug, but seemed otherwise unchanged. It was even possible he hadn't changed his clothes since we saw him last, his suit was baggy and tarnished with age. "No wonder we thought you were out of the business or dead," Mother remarked after listening to a rundown of his life since 1925. "You've produced no movie we wouldn't cross the street not to see." The history of Sid's life since *Kid Sherlock* was the history of B movies. He turned out one of almost every kind: a Ken Maynard and a Cisco Kid western, a Torchy Blane and a Nancy Drew, a Blondie, a Boston Blackie, a Mexican Spitfire, a Mr. Wong and a Charlie Chan, a Crime Doctor and an Inner Sanctum. But only one of each. Always the victim of a power struggle, he was sold down the river, jockeyed or smoked out. He also paid a heavy fine for income tax evasion and lost his Poverty Row studio, renamed Midas-Art, in a fire. "Imagine," he said, "they arrested me and put me on trial for arson."

"I can imagine," Mother said.

Ignoring this, Sid turned to me. "The verdict was not guilty *and* I collected. I'm the kind that always bounces back." He described how he bounced back with a volcano movie, a Devil's Island movie, a zombie movie, a mad scientist movie, a talking chimp movie, a Red Menace movie and a dinosaur movie shot in the Philippines under very discouraging conditions, notably a kidnap attempt by Huk guerillas. "They thought I was some kind of capitalist pawn or spy. It really shook me up, but the President begged me to stay on, so I finished the picture under armed guard. Under budget too."

Mother had to admit she found this an extraordinary record in its way. "Still, I'm not sure it qualifies you as the man to make Baby queen of video."

It turned into a moment from the old days. Glaring with hate, Sid jumped up and swiped the desk. "You're still the Mrs. Rip Van Winkle of showbiz. Let me tell you what TV's about." He sat down again. "It's about B movies. That's why the network offered me this production job. It's costing one thousand dollars a minute to shoot a TV movie right now, so naturally Sarnoff turns to an old pro who knows how to cut corners and come in under schedule, even in the Philippines. So if you think I'm the wrong man for Baby, I've got no time to argue. I don't *need* her. I'm too busy lining up the Three Stooges and a lot of other stuff."

On an impulse I winked at Sid. He winked back. The wink told me several things, most of all that a part of me still belonged to him. Maybe the real father the cards dealt me was a prickly little oddball in a shabby striped suit. Sid never interfered with my life like Mr. Mayer, or with my dreams like Mr. Griffith. He just made me work my ass off until they loved me all over the world. On the surface he was all rage and panic, screeching to get one more chase or pratfall or homicide in the can every day, but underneath it he was all grit, a survivor who kept bouncing back. In my Babyhood I learned to trust his corny shrewdness, and I felt ready now to trust it again. Nobody else ever convinced me he could have Romeo without Juliet or Holmes without Watson, or for that matter Holmes without Holmes.

When Sid mentioned the Three Stooges, Mother shivered violently as if she'd just heard a coyote howling. She seemed to hear it howl again when he began throwing out ideas for my series, Charlotte Chan, The Woman in the Iron Mask, The Wolf Woman. "Disguise Baby as an oriental? Clap a mask over her face? Turn her into a wolf? This is even worse than the time you wanted to make her invisible!" Sid yelled at her for God's sake to stop interrupting the creative process. Anybody who knew anything about the creative process knew that you had to come up with a few wrong ideas, and discard them before you came up with the right idea, which he would reveal shortly. "Are you with me, Baby?" I nodded and he looked pleased. "*You* understand the process," he said.

I nodded again. "All the same, Sid, I'd like to interrupt it and hit you with something." He graciously agreed and I hit him with *Thuvia, Maid of Mars*.

"Fabulous. We're on the same wavelength, we're thinking B. I even thought of *Thuvia* myself, remembered you were going to do it for the man Hughes, it's a great story but I had to throw it out with the others. Too much science fiction on the home screen already, you can't compete with Superman and Captain Marvel. Even in a G-string, which we'd never get away with anyhow."

Some dreams die hard, as they say. I felt a twinge of loss as my last chance of being rescued by the Prince of Helium floated away, then Sid asked if I ever saw a silent movie serial called *The Perils of Pauline*.

"Baby wasn't even born when it came out!" Mother said indignantly. She still believed her lie about my age. In fact I was two years old at the time.

Sid ignored her again. "Pauline got rescued from danger in the nick of time every week of the year in 1914," he said. It struck me as an interesting coincidence that Sid had rescue for me on his mind, and I felt more ready than ever to trust his corny shrewdness. "We're on the same wavelength," I said. "But tell me this. What kind of girl gets herself into deep trouble every week of the year? Is she dumb or unlucky or secretly attracted to danger?"

Sid frowned. Then he said, "Who cares? Pauline was never any particular kind of girl."

"No particular kind of girl is not good enough for Baby," Mother said.

Sid glared at her. "It's perfect. She can make *anything she wants* out of the part." He turned to me. "I don't care what Pauline *feels*, as long as it *looks* natural. What I care about is the situation. A rich orphan with a Basil Rathbone-type guardian who's after her money and keeps trying to fake an accidental death for her. Every week we take you to the edge of the cliff.''

''Just like Kid Sherlock?''

''Just like every damn movie I ever made. Now you see how my mind works.'' He grew suddenly thoughtful. ''But I know why Pauline's so right for you. Some people want to be saved and others want to save. *You* want to be saved.''

I stared at him. ''What makes you say that?''

''Just a hunch. When you came into my office thirty years ago, you were cute but feisty. You started acting for me and it was like you could solve any problem in the world.'' The phone buzzed on his desk and he shrieked into it, ''No calls! I said, no calls!'' He took a gulp of coffee, stood up and walked toward me. ''When you came into my office today, you were the same but different. I don't know. You could be angry about something.'' He chuckled suddenly. ''Pauline tied to the railroad track just before the train's due to pass. I see you playing the hell out of a situation like that. Still cute and feisty, but really playing the hell out of it.''

I shocked Mother by jumping up and telling Sid he had a deal. Then Sid provoked her by saying he was glad Mrs. Rip Van Winkle's daughter knew the score. ''Why are you more insulting to me than ever?'' she asked.

''Because you always argue with me, Mrs. Rip.''

''I have to. I always disagree with everything you say.''

''Then keep away from me, it'll make all our lives easier.''

On the drive home, Mother gave a long sigh. ''*I'm* the kind that wants to save, Baby. I want to save you from Sid Gordon. TV may lack the magic of the movies, but it doesn't have to be *that* mundane.'' She nipped through a red light. ''And imagine a power struggle over something as picayune as *Mr. Wong*.''

Turning into her driveway, she sighed again. ''I want you to move forward now, but Sid Gordon wants to take you back where you started.''

''Maybe it's the same thing.''

''All this talk of *Mr. Wong* has put you in a fortune cookie mood. You don't *ask* enough of life. Almost as if you suspect you'll never get it. I can't understand an attitude like that.''

Rattling the martini shaker in her livingroom, she smiled. ''There's a clause, in those EKE papers you signed, giving me the right to veto any decision my senior VP makes.''

"Never read the papers, just signed them."

"Typical. But don't worry. I'm not planning to use my veto. Our new partnership mustn't begin with a power struggle."

"I agree. You'd obviously win it."

Mother shook her head. "My loss would be greater than my gain. I could never bear it if you bore me a grudge." A brave, sad, misty look came into her eyes, she was playing — no, *living* — one of the great Mother roles. Probably *Mildred Pierce*. "Everything I've done is for you. And I'll never stand in the way of anything you want to do. That's a secret clause in my heart."

I called Jimmy in Vegas to ask his opinion, as my dearest friend and the wisest old trouper in the world, on *The Perils of Pauline*. They'd paged him in the casino and I heard a croupier shout "Last bets!" before he answered.

"Dynamite."

"You're sure it won't expose me as a mental and emotional Baby? Peddling innocence on the verge of forty?"

Jimmy wondered whoever put an idea like that in my mind. I reminded him of our first date, when he warned me against refusing to grow up. He reminded me that feelings changed. "Now that I know you even better, I see a wonderful chance to show how innocent and childlike, after all these years, you still are."

I stared at myself in a mirror, saw an image there, wondered whether it was angry or innocent, asking to be saved or not asking enough for fear of asking too much. It looked weirdly deadpan. Like Buster Keaton, the more that happened the less it seemed to show. Maybe simple cunning Sid was right about something else as well: I was only myself in disguise and he saw through my face to my mask.

1968 – 1969

Elva's Diary

November 1 • It took more than one man to change my name to Shanghai Lily. Playback. Okay for sound. Elva Kay speaking. My hand grows tired of pushing a pen but my voice never seems to give out. Up slightly earlier than usual to catch the 5:00 a.m. movie on the tube, *Footlights*. Why the hell do they always air Baby's golden oldies around dawn? After viewing this ageless charmer across the gulf of time, I almost blew a fuse when I noted the ** (Flawed: Has Moments) rating in *TV Guide*, it's **** (A Classic) if I ever saw one, with Baby in full innocent bloom as a stage-struck hopeful, much cozier than Hepburn in *Morning Glory*.

Then came the news with its shocking headline story. My God. Years ago the late irreplaceable Mr. Mayer begged Ramon Novarro to stay out of trouble if he insisted on living dangerously, and Ramon managed this so well for so long, I assumed his luck would hold until he got too old to care. Seems we both reckoned without a pair of teenage hustlers. They choked him to death and plundered his hillside hideaway last night, a sadly unromantic fate for the Latin lover and hero of *Ben Hur* and partner of the Divine One in *Mata Hari*. But death is no respecter of persons, not even stars.

So many have followed the late irreplaceable Mr. Mayer to the Eternal Wheel, almost as if he started a trend. Ramon joins the host of all-time greats who are now but shadows on a cosmic screen, beloved Marion and reckless Clara, coolly seductive Kay Francis, mighty Clark and stalwart Spence, wayward Margaret Sullavan, witty Constance Bennett, flamboyant Flynn and straight-shooting Coop, eternally smiling Jeanette MacDonald, eternally sardonic Bogie, eternally boyish Ty Power. Not to

mention the cream of the new crop, mercurial Monty Clift and Marilyn
the troubled bombshell, enlisted all too soon in the ranks of the heavenly
choir.

Which reminds me of a last curtain call at the Ambassador Hotel. It left
me with mixed feelings, just as Robert Kennedy alive left me with mixed
feelings. The man who played fast and loose with poor Marilyn's affections, helped drive her to a fatal O.D., as President of these United
States? It didn't feel right from the start, and I pledged $1,000,000 to Mr.
Nixon's campaign if he won the nomination.

Difficult to get the grim reaper off my mind after the shocking headline
story this morning. I grieve not only for a world left with far fewer stars
than there are in heaven, but for Mr. Disney (who may yet return to produce his most sensational True Life Adventure, for rumor has it he's in
deep freeze), for Mr. Selznick (even though he never appreciated Baby)
and of course for the irreplaceable Louis the Great. *Life without Louis*, I
wrote, searching for words to express my loss, then gazed at tears falling
on a blank page. Closing the cover, I resolved to bury my past along with
the man who inspired the best of it, took the diary to the Tower Room and
stored it away with all the others. So Elva's story ground to a halt. Long
empty years. Finally Miss Sophie persuaded me to take it up again.
"You're short-changing posterity. *He* wouldn't want that." Bless her eternal heart, but my God, the memory of her open casket hurts like a salted
wound. First I touched her cold hand, its nails aflame with polish, then
her hair, sprinkled as she requested with genuine 14-carat gold dust. We
left the Chapel of the Psalms to the sound of an organist playing her
favorite song, "I'll Be Seeing You," and followed the bier in thick smog
past the spectacular Cecil B. De Mille mausoleum. Only one star besides
Baby watched Miss Sophie laid in the Sunken Garden, Miriam Hopkins
rushed over between takes of a TV film at nearby Columbia Studios,
made up and costumed as a whorehouse madam. At least my wreath
gave the occasion a lift, four hundred roses in the shape of Miss Sophie's
ornamental comb, famous trademark of her later years. Otherwise, a meager tribute to a crackerjack artist and human being. In the old days a
glittering crowd would have packed the cemetery.

But the old days are almost gone. How many moons since I saw a
Hollywood crowd, at cemetery or premiere, that really glittered? Although glamor is on the decline, I fly my own flag for it, and at seventy-
nine remain unfazed by other changes in our city, wild ragged hippies
roaming the Sunset Strip like coyotes, snipers working the freeways, rap-
ists working the hills. These are obviously high-risk times and you must
learn to live with them. Louis the Great once said I always looked as if I

was walking off into the sunset, like the stars at the end of his movies, and yours truly intends to go on looking that way. In spite of zero public support, I continue to campaign against the destruction and neglect of our historic local monuments, buying time on TV to proclaim the nitty-gritty — a bulldozed Hollywood Hotel is a more serious threat to society than Hell's Angels or Dr. Timothy Leary, and our Sistine Chapels, Grauman's Chinese and the Pantages, are now filthier spectacles than the bluest movies Santa Monica Boulevard has to offer. At Grauman's it's not the picture but the sticky blobs of gum that root you to the seat. At the Pantages the ceiling is more dust than gold, the mezzanine a jungle of slashed upholstery and broken springs, the toilet bowls in the ladies' room more polluted than the canals of Venice. And on the base of that glorious nude statue of Valentino in De Longpre Park, some twisted brute dared to scratch (but KTOL bleeped me out on this), Rudy Sucks.

When they demolished Marion's former beach house to make way for a parking lot, a small crowd and a TV crew gathered around my picket line of one with its simple accusing sign, Shame. Nobody joined it, I was obliged to retreat after causing the bulldozers a brief symbolic delay, but still walked off as if heading for the sunset and gave the five o'clock news a shot of glamor with my space-age Courreges suit, leotards and hooded cape. Glamor was again the watchword at my all-night wake for the Garden of Allah, razed to make way for a savings bank before I could put in a bid and save the place. Instead, for its last hours on earth, I took the Garden over and asked my guests to come as stars of the twenties, recapturing the spirit of the opening night party Nazimova threw when she acquired it. I not only played hostess but the late owner herself, wearing a gown modeled on one of her *Salome* outfits, and Baby came as immortal Valentino with a robe, headdress and whip inspired of course by *The Sheik*. To the music of mandolin players on a raft in the pool, we danced a passionate tango together. The real Francis X. Bushman, a guest at the opening as well as the closing party, called for an encore, and for a while it truly seemed as if the sands of time were not running out after all.

A few guests stayed until dawn, when the musicians left, and threw empty champagne bottles into the pool as a final salute to the madcap days. Seeing them bob on the water among the gardenias, I had a sudden twinge of grief, thinking that Mr. Mayer would never have allowed our monuments to be despoiled, and our movie palaces to go downhill like the movies themselves. But at least he departed before his stars began freaking out, which would have killed him anyway. Greer Garson fitted with buck teeth as Eleanor Roosevelt, Elizabeth Taylor rolling around as a blowzy boozy harpie, Joan Crawford served a dead rat for breakfast —

where has all the flair gone? Our epoch's gravest problem is the failure of the movies to comfort and inspire. Every teenager a candidate for Alcatraz, every U.S. President a Doctor Strangelove, every woman interested in sex beyond forty a nymphomaniac, nothing in our future except planet earth going up in smoke, the birds attacking us, devil worshipers or apes taking over. Without John Wayne I might lose confidence in the human race.

According to Baby, *her* confidence in the human race is growing shaky in spite of John Wayne. "Sometimes I look around and feel the apes might do better. Other times I can't honestly blame the birds. And other times the only majority I respect is the dead." Then she gives me race riots, assassinations, Vietnam, endangered species, fixed TV quiz shows, you name it. "All the more reason," I point out, "for the movies to help us *escape*. It's a law of nature for people to seek consoling dreams, and where are the dreams of yesteryear?" Baby shakes her head. "It'll take more than another Louis B. to bring back those dreams," she opines darkly, "and more than all the stars in heaven." But with the economy still booming, the GNP going up almost as fast as EKE's profits, and Vegas betting on Mr. Nixon for president, surely all our country needs is to rediscover the MGM spirit?

Seems my mind capers around like a grasshopper when I commit my life to tape instead of paper, but I always liked talking, and although my breakfast has just arrived (thank you Hattie, how are those noises in your head today?) I'm still sounding off. The silver tray with its familiar cargo of cooked Wheatena, desiccated liver powder in orange juice and Executive Vitamin Pack, brings on the usual shudder of gratitude. No one except Adelle Davis, nutritionist extraordinary, could have pulled me out of that slump triggered by the death of Louis the Great. More than that, her anti-stress formula attuned me to the possibilities of matter over mind. We are what we eat, but as Adelle points out, what we eat can also make us *much more than we are.* When I step up the B supplements as she advises in time of really acute stress, they boost me almost as high as a good old-fashioned snort. And no dismals later. Ramon's death certainly calls for a triple desiccated liver as well, but once it's under my belt I know I can put in a solid day's work.

Today's schedule looks like yet another backbreaker. To begin with, three giant steps in my crusade to keep the MGM spirit alive. Letter to the Postmaster General, urging him to commission a stamp with Mr. Mayer's head on it. Letter to the Mayor of Los Angeles, asking why he fails to acknowledge (and accept) my suggestion to rename Culver Boulevard after the great man himself. Letter to the Governor of California, hoping he will reconsider my proposal to declare Mayer's birthday a state holiday. At 9:30, off in my Phantom V to the Oval Office, to hear a financial report on my chain of suntan parlors. (Tanamatic profits apparently spiraling, but how to hide yet another windfall from Uncle Sam?) 10:30, show the former Jeanette MacDonald mansion to Baby's favorite rock group, The Doors. Home for a quick costume change, then zip over to Hollywood Boulevard at noon, where the Walk of Fame dedicates its latest sidewalk star — to Baby! Could wish for a better location, however. It's right at the end, in front of a porno bookstore. Then onward and upward with Louella Parsons to buffet luncheon followed by special screening of a new Lesbo drama, *The Killing of Sister George*.

Somehow, too, I must snatch a moment to dictate a blast to *TV Guide* for its infamous ** *Footlights* rating, coupled with another plea to reschedule Baby's old movies in prime time. I'll sign this one Alexandra Zuck, aged 12, Hidden Hills. . . .

(*Two minutes of silent tape, maybe Mother was eating her Wheatena and forgot to turn the machine off. Then an incoherent quarrel with Hattie.*)

Who was Alexandra Zuck? That secret, along with many others, goes into the time capsule. Elva Kay signing off for now.

Baby Looks Back

The day that Louis B. died, Mother warned it was the beginning of the end. She was talking about Hollywood, not herself, but I think she crossed an important line that day. Losing him disturbed her much more than losing the Bug, which was mystifying at first but simple when I realized the movies had taken her over completely and become much more real than life. She'd been working up to the situation over the years. Never a stranger to verbal inflation when she talked about the movies, she developed a new habit, around the time Mayer was retired from MGM, of reaching for the grandest historical parallels. She compared him to Napoleon in exile, and when Dore Schary took over the studio she was reminded of Benedict Arnold. After reading an interview with Schary and learning he had no use for the star system, which he considered out of date, she predicted that conditions in Culver City would grow worse than in Europe under the Black Death. "But *watch the numbers*, Baby. When the numbers are in, his head will roll as surely as Robespierre's." She watched the numbers in *Variety*, rejoiced to find how many of Schary's pictures fared poorly at the box office, and when he was fired she took me to dinner at Romanoff's, calling for caviar and champagne. A few weeks later, hearing that Louis B. hoped to persuade a group of stockholders at MGM to vote him back to power, she tried to buy her way in and swing the vote. "If I bring this off, it'll be the biggest thing since Theodore Roosevelt led the charge up Kettle Hill at San Juan, and we took over Puerto Rico."

Then the old man died. He had guided me to stardom, done the same for many of Mother's supreme idols, his studio had produced more stuff that dreams were made on than she cared to name, and his memory inspired her most dramatic and enormous floral tribute. A wreath with hundreds of hibiscus and camellias was shaped to form the letters LBMGM. "But without his guiding spirit the studio seems doomed to fall. And if Metro falls, can Hollywood be far behind?" She not only predicted the end of civilization as we know it but found a private, romantic cause for sorrow. "You once told me, Baby, that I inspired a secret passion in the great man, and I foolishly laughed the idea off. But now I remember so many things, the way his solemn eyes lit up when I entered a room, the vibrant clasp of his hand, the shy yet purposeful arm around my waist as he whispered I too could have been a star." Imagining herself as the final Mrs. Mayer, hostess and adviser to all-time greats, power behind the studio, she reached for another epic parallel. "I forget the woman's name, but she kept the Sun King on his throne. Loved by some and feared by others, she eventually retired to a convent. You may smile, Baby, but I missed a chance to rewrite motion picture history." She sat in her favorite thronelike Spanish chair with a lapsed, dreamy look on her face, and it reminded me of the way she used to listen to Valentino's record of "Pale Hands I Loved." "Think of luring the Divine One back to the lot, snapping up Burt Lancaster before Universal grabbed him, getting in first on hot properties like *Mildred Pierce* and *I Remember Mama*. And never letting *you* go, of course." She moaned faintly. "To weather the storm, all Louis needed was a few extra moneyspinners under his belt and a heap of controlling stock in my safe."

Getting up, she took her lost horizons to a darkened room, retired to exile in her royal barge of a bed. Instead of recovering quickly, as she'd done after Ben died, she ran a fever, complained of shooting pains, heart murmurs, skin rashes, ate practically nothing and refused to see a doctor. "This time I fear I've moved beyond the reach of human help." Tapes from her library of favorite movie music stood on the bedside table, and sometimes she played beloved themes from *Love Is a Many-Splendored Thing* and *Gone With the Wind* on her cassette recorder. One night it was *Kings Row* over and over again. "Always glorious, but it's acquired a special meaning now. Remember the scene when Ronald Reagan wakes up after they amputate his legs and asks, *"Where's the rest of me?"* With Louis gone and MGM going, that's how I feel."

She closed her eyes. Seriously alarmed, I decided to phone the talent scout of miracle workers, and Miss Sophie came around at once. As well as her eyes, Mother had closed the gauzy curtains around her bed, and lay with hands folded across her breast. She remained still and blurred while Miss Sophie spoke of a nutritionist extraordinary called Adelle Davis, whose diet programs cured depression, anxiety, forgetfulness, lowered libido. "She's found the answer for thousands of people, Elva, and I'm sure she'll find it for *you."*

Mother turned her face away. "There is no answer. Not with Louis gone and MGM going."

"It's so unlike you to take things lying down." Getting no response, Miss Sophie parted a gauzy curtain and said in a low urgent voice, "There are secrets of the human body you never dreamed of. What I'm suggesting is a step into the unknown, in its way."

Mother turned her face back very slowly. She didn't answer, but there was a gleam of interest in her eyes.

"You've been a pioneer in this field yourself," Miss Sophie went on. "You put Baby on yogurt and activated dry yeast, with fantastic results, as long ago as 1928."

Mother raised an eyebrow. Then she said, "1927."

"And only recently, medical bureaucracy defeated your Koumiz project. Mrs. Davis has had similar projects and similar experiences. She'll let you in on countless untold secrets."

Mother still didn't answer, but the gleam of interest brightened. Miss Sophie let go of the curtain, then signaled for us to leave the room.

"Our girl's rising to the bait."

"And I've just had a lesson on how to handle her."

"There's a child buried in every genius." Miss Sophie smiled. "I found it long ago in Elva."

Adelle Davis was not yet famous, although her *Let's Eat Right to Keep Fit* book had an underground reputation and people were starting to talk about her as the Ralph Nader of diet. She worked as consultant to a county health clinic way out in the suburbs, and Mother wore a kind of safari jacket with a dramatically high collar for the journey. It was copied, she told me, from the traveling outfit favored by Dietrich on her world nightclub tours. As I drove, she glanced through enormous tinted glasses at a landscape of arched freeway interchanges, grinning signs for Jack-in-the-Box drive-ins, pink suburban bungalows, bulldozed hillsides, automobile lots, stringy palm trees, oil refineries, storage depots, chamber of

commerce flowerbeds with massed azaleas in the shape of a heart, everything veiled in smog. We passed a new shopping center that looked like a
satellite space station, with a sign announcing Everything Slashed, and
Mother pulled up her collar even higher. "Talk about your step into the
unknown. This is it, and a hard act for Mrs. Davis to follow."

All the same, she was discreetly excited, hoping for a medical equivalent to the Violet Flame or the Veiled Mahatma. What she found, seated
behind a desk in a workaday office, was a plain-speaking strong-boned
woman with the outdoors look of someone brought up on a farm. After
Mother explained her symptoms, Adelle Davis commented cheerfully
that her engine had gone very sluggish and needed riboflavin for a start.
"Now let's take a look at those red splotches on your arm," she said, and
after Mother rolled up her sleeve with a wince, remarked that skin problems were always more than skin deep but often responded to niacin
amide.

We'd never heard of riboflavin or niacin amide and began to feel impressed. In a world of closed minds, Adelle said, drugs were common
knowledge but natural remedies almost unknown, and we'd be hearing
about a lot of things for the first time. Then she opened our minds to the
healing powers of vitamins, proteins and minerals, described water-
logged hearts repaired by B1, bacteria chased out of the tissues by C,
dying cells recharged by A, neuritis pains, heart palpitations and negative
thinking corrected by thiamin, insomnia relieved by calcium, porous
bones firmed up by fish-liver oil, lost energy recouped by stepping up all
the Bs, lackluster hair brightened by amino acids, sex drive revved up by
thyroxin. She spelled out the bracing interaction of trace minerals, zinc
and iodine, iron and copper, the dangers of inositol deficiency, she
warned against ingesting too much phytic acid from oatmeal and too
much high alkaline-ash from oranges, she frowned upon jello and dena-
tured white flour, applauded garlic and collard greens. Finally she drew
up a basic program, three meals a day plus supplements, midmorning
and midafternoon booster snacks, to saturate Mother with essential nutrients and restore her enjoyment of life's riches.

"There's nothing to worry about, Mrs. Kay, as long as you stop worrying. You've passed through the three major areas of *stress*—anxiety, resistance, exhaustion—and got trapped in the third, like the American people
as a whole."

"You hear that, Baby?" Mother was talking to me but gazing steadily at
Adelle Davis as if hypnotized.

"A doctor friend came back from Russia not long ago," Mrs. Davis said.
"They use hardly any refined foods, don't guzzle sugar or spray every

crop with insecticide. It's their health that scared him, not their missiles."

Mother nodded. "Are they going to come out on top?"

"Hm, nip and tuck," Mrs. Davis said. "There's still time for Americans to stop depending on empty calories, saturated animal fats, tranquilizers, the whole narcotic spectrum. Did you ever read the British historian Arnold Toynbee?"

"Make a note of that name, Baby." Mother's eyes were still fixed on her new guru. "I'll order his complete works."

"Toynbee believes that nations fall when they *decay from within*," Adelle Davis said. "And *I* believe the rot starts with poor nutrition. In 1937 an expert predicted France would soon collapse because it was hooked on white bread and wine, while Germany with its rye bread and fortifying beer would reach a new high." She gave a breezy smile. "So it went. If you want to reach a new high, Mrs. Kay, get healthy," she added, and lit a cigarette.

On the drive home Mother studied her diet sheets, marveled at a list of food values calculated in gammas, milligrams and international units, then we stopped at a health food store to buy a trunkload of special items. She observed the crowd and cocked an ear. "I hear cash registers ringing, but not for EKE. We really missed out on this one, Baby."

A step into the unknown worked its usual magic, but by the time Mother got home her flare of energy was dying down. She went to bed, took a long nap, then woke up and played several movie music themes on her cassette recorder, but not *Kings Row*, which I found encouraging. Later she ate a pep-up supper, liver for extra iron, oysters and collard greens for additional riboflavin, soybean salad to step up her thiamin, and drank a glass of skimmed milk to meet her calcium quota. "Not my usual gourmet fare, yet curiously stimulating." She swallowed a fistful of vitamin pills. "Do you realize it's more than a week since I saw a movie?" Another encouraging sign. She scanned the newspaper ads and almost wept to discover an old Kay Francis vehicle was closing at a revival theatre that night. "I never saw *British Agent* and always wanted to." She looked uncertain. "Wait a minute, am I confusing it with *Mandalay*?" Her face cleared. "Yes, I am. And is it B2 that jogs the memory? I'll boost my intake, no risk of an O.D., Adelle's diet sheet informs me all the Bs are water-soluble and you just piss the excess away." After a nightcap of blackstrap molasses spiked with vodka, she closed her eyes. Her face had the innocent euphoric look of someone confidently expecting a miracle, and I thought of Miss Sophie saying she'd found the child in Elva long ago.

A week later: "Physically I feel somewhat restored, yet still identify

with the great Swede at the end of *Queen Christina,* sailing alone to nowhere." Another week later: "How those vitamins pulse through the
bloodstream. I almost begin to believe in life after Louis." And finally: "I
believe in it." She drove off in her Rolls Phantom V to check out a new
MGM production of *The Brothers Karamazov* and returned in a state of
shock. "My God. What a vile slur on the studio's name. Tackiest sets you
ever saw and *no star chemistry.* Of course Louis would have known better
than to expect it from Yul Brynner and Maria Schell. He must be turning
in his grave." But anxiety over the future of the Culver City lot no longer
trapped Mother in the third stage of stress. Next afternoon she dived into
the pool, swam thirty laps, split a bottle of champagne with me, then
headed out to a birthday party for Clifton Webb.

Although essential nutrients restored her enjoyment of life's riches,
Mother was too addictive a personality to let a miracle alone. Megadoses
of thiamin soon made her thinking dangerously positive, a daily intake of
B complex 2000 percent above the normal requirement loaded her with
energy to misdirect. As she got over losing Louis, she enlarged her fantasies about him. One day she crossed a new line and actually believed she
was Mayer's widow. Dialing MGM, she asked the switchboard operator
to connect her with the head of production. "*Elva Kay Mayer* speaking."
The name created either a great impression or a great confusion, for she
got through. "Now listen to me. Just before the end, Louis opened his
eyes and made me promise to watch over the studio. So give me the
numbers on *Karamazov.*" Next time she only got through to a secretary.
"The boss just stepped into a meeting? If he knows what's good for him,
he'll step *out* of it and talk to me." A pause. "Very well. Then tell him if I
don't get those numbers on *Karamazov* pretty quick, he'll find himself on
the carpet. There's a heap of controlling stock in my safe." Next time the
MGM operators put Elva Kay Mayer on indefinite hold.

Slipping in and out of fantasy as quickly as she changed lanes on the
freeway, Mother complained of the way MGM treated her, then forgot
her mission to save the studio until something occurred to resurrect it.
Rumors of a stockholders' revolt or an executive shake-up, and it was
time to call in the marines. At first alarmed by Mother's instructions to
buy the studio outright, then weary of explaining it was not for sale, her
lawyers invited me to a behind-closed-doors meeting at the Control
Center. As senior VP I sat at the head of the black lucite table, listening to
grim talk of EKE's conglomerate responsibilities, the emotional strain they
imposed on Mother, a genius of course but pushing eighty. I sniffed
boardroom melodrama in the style of *Executive Suite,* which Mother saw
several times, and the types around the table must certainly have seen it

once, they gave performances as authentically scheming as Frederic March, Louis Calhern, Paul Douglas. With an unctuous paternal smile the Calhern type warned of so much power invested in one person, the March type twitched his eyebrows as he advised me to grant powers of attorney, and in a voice loaded with heartily false regrets the Douglas type feared that Mother was no longer responsible for all her actions.

I lit a cigarette. "Gentlemen," I said, "what can I tell you?" I blew a smoke ring across the table. "Let me report this conversation to the party in question and see how she reacts." I got up. "But since I can guess, let me also wish you goodbye and good luck." As I walked to the door they ran after me, the Calhern type actually blocking my exit, the March type claiming I misunderstood them, the Douglas type seizing my arm and insisting that all they wanted was to lay the MGM problem, frankly and openly, on the table. With the picture business in such an uncertain state, there was a terrible risk of Mother eventually finding one of her offers accepted. Genius as she was, as head of a major studio she might sink us all. "Gentlemen," I said, blowing another smoke ring, "I'm in complete agreement, why didn't you say so before? Let's leave it this way— anytime you're worried, just give me the nod and I'll be happy to talk things over with the Chief."

When I talked MGM over with Mother, reaching for the grandest historical parallels I could think of, she put up surprisingly little resistance. "If you really believe I'm heading for a personal *Titanic* or *Retreat from Moscow* or *Charge of the Light Brigade*, Baby, I won't attempt to intervene anymore. Besides, we must never engage in a power struggle." Then she confessed she'd just dropped plans to acquire a rock group. "Big money there, but after getting to know quite a few groups when I sold them houses, I fear any investment I make will freak out on me. They're all stoned out of their skulls and apparently incapable of metering the habit."

When she turned her mind to it, Mother continued to develop her flair for spotting business trends, made a killing in surfboards and bowling alleys, launched the first suntan parlors with her Tanamatic chain, and foresaw the rise of investment in art. A slew of Chagalls, Renoirs and Utrillos came her way before the market got super-bullish, and she sold them to collectors at a heartwarming profit. Because Adelle Davis scorned artificial preservatives in food, she disposed of her canned goods corporation to Earl Gibson, then invested the proceeds in condos, electronics and another pile of gold. Extending her sportswear interests, she cornered the market in printed T-shirts, a bittersweet winner in a way. Although she wore her L.B. Mayer T-shirt at a sales convention, dramatically parting an

Alaska sable coat to reveal the great man's name on her breast, it was the only one that never took off, trailing far behind Elvis, Lolita, Fabian, Big Brother, Ayn Rand, Dracula and Peace.

In the unclouded days before the death of Louis the Great, Mother and I had our only power struggle. A few weeks before my TV series was due to start, she reminded me of our press conference in the Oval Office and the announcement she made. "For our coffee commercial, Baby, I see you poolside in smart swimwear, pouring for a group of intimate friends." She claimed it was the kind of exposure I couldn't afford to turn down, before *Pauline* even hit the home screen my face would become a household word. "My face or your coffee?" I said. "Come off it. You'd really prostitute your own daughter in the cause of junk?" Mother grew very offended, but not at the thought of prostituting me, at the idea her coffee was junk. "No, advertising is junk," I said. "There's no product up there, just the hateful charm of whoever's pushing it. And I've got my pride. I'll never try to sell a new automobile by sitting next to the driver and hitching up my skirt, and I'll never play second fiddle to a cup of instant coffee." Mother felt betrayed, I felt bad, and for a couple of days we didn't speak. Then she called as if nothing had happened, deploring Irene Dunne's latest role as Queen Victoria in *The Mudlark*. "You can't *recognize* her. By the way, I'm shooting for Swanson to prostitute herself in the cause of our new improved mountain fresh, and if *she* turns me down I'll settle for Tallulah, who can't afford to turn anything down." She settled for Zasu Pitts.

When I walked on the set of *Pauline* to face a camera for the first time in over ten years, Sid Gordon gave me no time to feel nervous. "Just get in there. You'll be gagged and bound all day, nothing to it." There was certainly nothing to the set, either. I recognized Sid's unique touch of cut-rate sleaze from the *Kid Sherlock* days, but as Pauline was usually in peril out of doors, we moved all over the city and beyond. In spite of the changes, it was still a back lot where you could go back in time, literally turn a corner and meet the past. Sometimes there was a jagged hole in the past, and the Venetian Gardens dance hall, backdrop for my great women of history, scene of the marathon contest where I watched Jimmy watch his first wife without knowing it, had gone the way of the bulldozer. But around the next corner a derelict villa served as the studio of a portrait painter who drugged Pauline's cherry cola, put her in a sack and dumped her in a sewer leading to the Pacific. A Chinatown alley, as murky as the first time I saw it from the platform of One Big Look and mistook it for an open-air set, led to the opium den where Pauline was held prisoner. Mexican bandits captured me in a canyon near Malibu, and took me to a cave from which Kid Sherlock once rescued a deaf-mute millionairess. A corner of the old Santa Monica airfield, with its memories of B.J. Langdon, provided the secret landing strip from which I was hustled, bound and gagged, into a monoplane flying to white slavery. The Yucca Riviera apartment building, more Spanish than ever after serving a term as the Apache Arms, stood in for a Brazilian whorehouse. By the time I was thrown overboard from a launch and washed up in a cove beyond Malibu, supposedly an uninhabited island, the sense of déjà vu almost stunned me. Heat-stroke actually stunned me when I lay gagged and bound yet again on the railroad tracks at the 20th Century Fox ranch under a glaring sun. As a train chugged toward me and I heard Sid yell for it to pick up more speed, I tried to free my hands and remove the gag. "Baby Jewel! Sid Gordon! Thursday!" I wanted to cry out, even though Sid would be furious if I spoiled a take. Instead I lapsed into semiconsciousness and went on doing what everyone said, even though it was my forty-second birthday.

We still made the last shot of the day, someone pushing me down a well, after the actor who played my wicked guardian revived me with a shot of brandy from his pocket flask. This part had been turned down by Basil Rathbone and other character stars with a line in smooth menace, so Sid fell back on an obscure oldtimer, the villain of his Nancy Drew, Red Menace and zombie movies. At the end of each day's shooting, Craig Howland finished off his second flask of brandy, then went home to kill a third and fourth. Yet every morning he arrived on time and knew his lines. "Why do you live this way?" I asked. "Does nothing else interest you?" He gave me a stern look. "Nothing," he said. "And with a few drinks under my belt, I'm less afraid." When I asked what he was afraid of, he gave another stern look. "First of all my own mediocrity, which you might call a sober fact. Other sober facts I can drink my way out of are ambition, lust and the fear of death. So I'm uniquely contented, and how many other actors can say the same?" He patted my shoulder. "*Think it over,*" he said.

Mother and I watched the first episode together at her house, sitting on one of the red and gold banquettes in the den, under the glimmer of Anna May Wong's chandelier. She never took her eyes off the home screen, sighing faintly at the Zasu Pitts commercial, smiling at the EKE Hit Parade chorus singing the praises of her sportswear. At the end she poured more champagne, raised her glass and pronounced my new image a triumph. It confused me. How could she talk about a triumph when there was no audience, and how could anyone create a new image with a gag stuffed in her mouth most of the time? "What a strangely negative reaction, Baby.

There are millions of viewers across the country glued to their sets, exactly like us." I doubted there were any other viewers across the country remotely like us, then wondered how she knew the millions hadn't switched channels to Ed Sullivan. "You underrate public taste. Furthermore, your new image comes over very strongly because you *struggle* so well. You make a person feel what it's *like* to be trussed and gagged and helpless, which in my case is far from easy to imagine."

Later the phone calls began. "It's a knockout," Sid Gordon said, "and it's going to run for years. People love that kind of clean old-fashioned excitement. They root for you like they rooted for Mary Pickford in *Sparrows*, rescuing a bunch of orphans from that baby farmer and guiding them through an alligator swamp. Hey, why don't we steal that and throw you to the alligators sometime?" Miss Sophie was kept on the edge of her seat: "Not just by the suspense, but by how young you looked." Marion thought I was f-fabulous, a director from the old MGM days said, "A star is reborn," and after I got home and went to bed, Jimmy Gabriel woke me up by singing "Yes, Sir, That's My Baby" in perfect imitation of Eddie Cantor over the wire. Then he told me he was leaving town the next day to play Korea.

By the end of the show's first year I was getting fan mail of almost MGM dimensions, mainly from the middle-aged in small towns. But in spite of the cagiest handling, the white slavery episode provoked a few letters of protest and one crank threat: *Watch out, I'm coming to tie you up, and they'll never show what happens then on TV.* Autograph seekers stopped me on the street. The fan magazines described "Baby" Jewel Kay, Lucille Ball, Superman and Jimmy Olson as the first major stars created by the tube. Gossipwriters dug up my past, my marriage with Jimmy, profiled the legendary Elva and found my hillside hideaway surprisingly modest. "In fact, 'Baby' Jewel herself is surprisingly modest and you'd never guess she's one of the richest showbiz veterans in Tinsel Town, worth maybe twenty-five million and an active VP of her Mother's multi-faceted corporation. She wears hardly any makeup, no jewelry or designer-brand clothes, drives a 1950 Buick."

After this item appeared Mother gave me a Rolls-Royce, saying my new image demanded it. At first I doubted whether I could handle the huge silver thing, or even wanted to, then began driving it around and discovered a rare sense of security. A Rolls is a whole world in itself on wheels. Since that time I've never driven anything else, held meetings, given interviews, rehearsed scenes and watched my own show in it. Too tired to drive home after a long day on location, I've mixed myself a drink or two at the bar, eaten a dozen oysters and a take-out Brown Derby Cobb salad

kept in the fridge, then spent the night in the back seat. The only thing a
Rolls failed to do was upgrade my image, as a status symbol. It gave me
the wrong status, for after a fan magazine published a spread of my home
away from home, several hundred letters arrived asking why I gave up
my American car. TV stars were not supposed to act like movie stars, their
image had to be down to earth, ordinary and recognizable like favorite
brands of cereal or steak sauce.

Toward the end of the show's fifth year Jimmy woke me again around
one in the morning, but this time there was no performance over the wire.
A strange hoarse voice told me he was coming over right away and
blurted out something about a matter of life and death. He arrived looking
dazed and haggard, asked for a drink, gulped it down, began to sweat
and then to shiver. When I asked if he was sick, he shook his head, took
another drink and walked out to the pool. The night was chilly, unlike the
time he came home after the war, but he lay back on the same chaise
longue and stared at the misty sky. After a while he gave a racked, terrible
moan. I put my arms around him and said, "Now tell me about this
matter of life and death." He moaned again, stared at the sky again, and
grew calmer. "That was an exaggeration, Baby in Quotes. It's only a matter of death."

Earlier that night Jimmy returned to his house in Laurel Canyon, heard
the radio playing but got no answer when he called for Coralyn. He went
upstairs and found his sixth wife, the former Miss Bluebonnet, naked and
strangled in bed. "The cops told me they've had a couple of similar cases
in the area recently. Some traveling rapist. They were surprised we had
no alarm system." He gave me an anxious look. "Do *you* have one?" I
told him Mother insisted, she was very high on alarm systems. "That's
good," Jimmy said, turned away and retched. He lay on his back again,
heaving, and I thought guiltily of the cracks I made about Bluebonnet in
the past, remembered her singing "It Had To Be You" in a strapless gown
with ostrich plumes, remembered my clenched teeth as I wished her happiness and success. "The cops linked it to the others," Jimmy said, "because of the knife cuts." Then he felt cold and wanted to go to bed.

We lay with our arms around each other. He asked for music, I found
the all-night Mexican radio station and we listened to the usual Mañana-
Chiquita sobstuff for a while. "Are you surprised I came straight over to
see you? You shouldn't be surprised. In a way I've always felt closer to
you than anyone else in the world." Of course I'd heard this before, from
the time Jimmy stood me up and went back to his first wife, to the time he
told me over the phone that he wanted to marry Coralyn. He must have
realized it sounded familiar, because he added, "I mean it differently this

time." We'd both known the same kind of early success and later failure, he explained, over the years we'd comforted, encouraged and laughed at each other as friends, lovers, a married couple, enemies, then friends again. "That's pretty special. Nothing else in my life ever lasted as long as that."

"Wouldn't Coralyn have lasted as long?"

Jimmy gave an unamused laugh. "If she'd lasted much longer I might have killed her myself. Horrible, I know, but horribly true. Number six and I were on the ultimate rocks, even boozy lust had fled our house. We were living in a mortgaged graveyard. Wall to wall carpet and a sunset view." He held me more tightly. "We both knew she'd never make it as a star, we both knew I was having problems making it as an ex-star. Jimmy Gabriel Enterprises getting deeper in the red, Jimmy Gabriel himself wondering how he's going to pay those back taxes. But we both postponed the showdown because Coralyn had no better place to go, and if we divorced I stood to lose my only solid remaining asset, the loveless house with a sunset view. Get the picture?"

"It's clear," I said.

He gave the same laugh. "Hating to spend an evening alone with her dumb, greedy, disenchanted eyes, I run off for a stupid physical thing, a trip to Vegas, a booze night with friends. Tonight as usual I roll in late, and. . . ." He broke off, sobbing quietly, less for Coralyn than for the muddle of his life. "How can I have lived so long, seen so much and made so many mistakes? And why are the dice so cold?"

Then it was dawn and I had to drive out on location to the insane asylum where Pauline was held that week against her will.

Jimmy was still there when I got home. He lay on a couch, watching the story of Coralyn on the TV news. He didn't go out all day, he said, he wanted to avoid the press and friends calling up to commiserate. He made one call himself, to Coralyn's family in Dallas, and agreed they could ship her body back for burial in her home town. "Did you eat anything?" I asked, he shook his head and I ordered cold cuts and salad from a delicatessen down the hill. "I'm not hungry," Jimmy insisted, but when the food arrived he became suddenly ravenous. "You know," he said, spreading mustard on the pastrami, "if there's something tragic in a person's future, I always sense it. Even when I'm having a good time with the person, I get a kind of psychic chill. But not with Coralyn. I never felt anything like that with Coralyn."

"How about your own future? Did it ever give you a psychic chill?"

"Sure, but goose bumps as well. Always knew I was destined to run the gamut, Baby in Quotes, highs *and* lows beyond the usual range."

Then tears came to his eyes, he clutched me and wanted to go to bed. "If it's okay with you, if I'm not imposing?"

"It's okay."

"If you don't want me around anymore, I'll check into a hotel. But I can't go home."

"A hotel would be depressing."

I went to the bathroom, washed my face, brushed my teeth and changed into pajamas. Jimmy was waiting by the bed, stripped down to his jockey shorts. "If it's okay with you," I said, getting in and turning my back, "I'd like to get some sleep." There was no answer. My arms ached because Pauline had been wearing a straitjacket all day. I heard Jimmy go to the bathroom, come back, approach the bed, then walk toward the window. Without moving or speaking, I watched him. He scratched his head, walked back to the bed and sat on the edge, not looking at me.

"Can't you sleep? Want a pill?"

No answer, but he got into a crouching position, resting his chin on his hands, still looking away. Finally he said, "Do we like each other too much for romance ever to come back?"

"Definitely. We've arrived at our final solution, friends for life."

"There's only one final solution and I need hardly remind you what it is." Then he changed position, stretching his legs until he straddled me. "Romance is coming back after all. If you don't believe me, feel it."

"For God's sake. Just boozy lust."

"I didn't booze tonight. You look sad. What's the matter?"

"It's not fair. The way you always try to get me on the rebound."

He leaned close. "What rebound? You just split up with someone? Who?"

I began to see Jimmy through a slight blur, my eyes releasing the old silent tears of exhaustion, dread and relief. "It's not important. The basic rebound, even now, is still from *you*."

"Don't weep." He gripped my shoulders. "There's no reason to weep."

"I can't help it. I've caught a psychic chill."

After we made love, he held me so tightly that it was difficult to breathe. "I'll be damned," he said. "It feels like paradise regained. How about you?"

"I'll be damned. But give me some air."

Jimmy rolled over and lay on his back. Then he clenched his fists. "This is worse than crazy," he said. "This is shocking." He began pummeling the bed. "Do you realize what happened?"

"Romance came back."

"With Coralyn dead only twenty-four hours!" The pummeling stopped and he lay rigid as stone. "Monstrous," he said. "Unnatural." I reminded Jimmy he stopped loving Coralyn much longer than twenty-four hours ago.

He stared at me. "That's very true." And relaxed again. "I guess it's not shocking, just crazy, or not even crazy, just perfectly natural." He closed his eyes. "All the same, Coralyn's not in her grave yet. They bury her tomorrow. I'm too tired to sleep," he said and opened his eyes.

"So am I," I said.

"Then tell me about this other guy who's not important."

"I have to get up early."

"But you're too tired to sleep."

I sat up and lit a cigarette. Jimmy lay with his head in my lap. "Okay," I said, "bedtime story."

The Cartagena film festival doesn't invite you, it begs you to come, I went on, being one of those fringe affairs that takes any celebrity it can get. From Hollywood this year it got Sabu, one of the Gabor sisters and me. At the opening night party in a hotel by the beach, the air-conditioning broke down and a middle-aged Colombian put the make on me. He had an important somber charm, a powerful build and a terrific gleam, white teeth, almost black eyes, gold bracelets, manicured nails. It was too hot for an adventure and on the other hand too hot to say no. He hired a yacht to take me out to an island for lunch, drove me in a Mercedes for dinner at a castle transformed into a country club, flew me in a private plane to the orchid plantation of an important somber friend, then to a casino at another beach resort, where we stayed the night in a presidential suite. The windows were hung with velvet drapes and the velvet drapes were studded with bullet holes. Courtesy of *La Violencia*, he explained, then told me he was returning to Bogota next day to take up a government post. "You will miss me?" I nodded. "You will not miss me," he said, and before I could deny it, asked me to marry him. "Let me give you a new life. You need one." It had been a heady trip, culminating in a heady offer, and I knew he was into emeralds as well as power. But I couldn't see myself wearing a pair of shoes labeled Evita. "I'm afraid I'm going to miss you after all," I said, and for a moment he looked very sad. "What are you? Are you just another whore?" he asked, and before I could deny it, cracked me on the mouth with his fist. Then he walked out of the suite. I locked the door, but he didn't come back, and in the morning they told me he was gone. I caught a plane to Cartagena in time to attend the screening of *Moby Dick* with a mysteriously bruised lip.

"What happened to the man? Ever hear from him again?"

"*La Violencia,*" I said. "The guerrillas got him."

"That is some bedtime story. Imagine if you'd married him and the guerrillas got you as well."

"Imagine how close I came to letting it happen."

He stared at me. "*How* close?"

After a moment I said, "I really felt I could have used a new life."

There was no answer. He'd fallen asleep.

When he slept, Jimmy always had an amazingly young, contented, smoothed-out look on his face, the kind that makeup artists at funeral parlors try to give their clients. I got up at dawn and he still had it. I came home from a day of location shooting and he still had it, laid out on the couch in front of the TV. I sat and watched him sleeping off the past, then fell asleep myself and woke up to find Jimmy awake, watching me. We smiled vaguely at each other and for a long while neither of us said a word.

Romance was back to stay, but we had to keep its profile low. The TV networks, like the movies, had their Control Centers in New York that could blacklist you not only as a Red but for leading an un-American sex life. Jimmy sold his house and took an apartment where he officially lived alone, but one of Hedda Hopper's legmen must have spotted us together and identified the circumstances as romantic, because that was how Hedda identified them in her column. Glassy-eyed with fear, Sid Gordon told me the shit was hitting the fan in New York. "Our show's got *family appeal*, but you and your ex-husband carrying on again right after a sex criminal finished off his sixth wife, that appeals to no family General Sarnoff ever heard of." I insisted it was a wicked rumor and promised to make Hedda retract it. "Whatever it is, make her retract it," Sid begged me, "before the hate-mail starts pouring in."

With a crack of desperation in my voice I called Hedda to ask how she could believe such a wicked rumor, let alone print it. "You fooled me once, my girl," she answered, "over that filthy affair in Vegas, but you're not going to fool me again." Knowing she was vicious enough to be sentimental, or vice versa, I accused her of *adding to Jimmy's pain.* "We're friends for life and I'm helping him through a grievously traumatic period. What else are friends for? He turned to me like Clark turned to his old love Joan Crawford after Carole died in the plane crash."

Hedda only laughed. "*I* heard Clark was humping Joan again after that."

"Another wicked rumor."

"Want to bet?"

"No," I said. "You may be right. You usually are. But not this time, Hedda. This time Jimmy and I are turning to *you*. We need *your* help. And we appeal to your human understanding."

It worked. Two days later she firmly denied the wicked rumor, overlooking the fact she started it.

Mother suspected Jimmy of taking what he wanted when he wanted it again, but still relished the touch of *Back Street* in my life. "As you know, Baby, in my youth I lived through the sexual revolution of the twenties and it taught me a profound lesson. We only scale the heights of romance by casting off the shackles of convention. Maybe a secret affair with your ex-husband will succeed where marrying him failed." There was certainly one big change. Now that we were unmarried lovers, Jimmy turned faithful. He claimed to have lost his dangerous desire for beauty queens, models, chorus girls, he gave up gambling and pursued only the joy of domestic life. "Let's not go out tonight. We always have a better time at home." Illicitness made us respectable. Getting back after the day's work we swapped anecdotes over a drink, then sat down to supper in front of the tube and watched *Gunsmoke* or *Perry Mason* or my show or Jimmy's guest shot on *Dragnet* or *Alfred Hitchcock Presents* or a rigged quiz show or the Duchess of Windsor on *Person to Person* giving the lowdown on how to win at jacks.

Sick of hotels, casinos, audiences falling down drunk, and in a mood to stay home, Jimmy refused to travel around playing nightclubs anymore, even though he had enough offers to pay off his back taxes. But Mother solved that problem when she bought JG Enterprises and absorbed them into EKE. "You not only have a knockout figure and a deadpan technique I still envy," Jimmy said, "but you're without question the mad genius of all time. *I* come out rich by selling you a worthless washed-up corporation, and *you* come out even richer by writing off the deal as an *improvement*." Mother said it was nothing really, she'd turned greater liabilities into greater assets in her time, and always enjoyed a challenge.

In the black again, Jimmy made a few B movies, clawed to death in *Attack of the Killer Crabs*, doing a man-into-monster number in *The Incredible Doctor X*, then starred at a Hollywood theatre in a revival of *Charley's Aunt* which broke all records and ran six months. Near the end of the run, Sid Gordon came around to his dressingroom and said he was just closing a hot deal to produce *Mr. Wong* for the tube. "It's a series that'll sell like fortune cookies and put you right back where you belong." Jimmy had just taken off his matronly wig. He wore a black skull cap underneath it. Narrowing his eyes to slits, he bowed gravely and went into a Chinese detective number. Then he turned to me. "Jesus. If that's what it takes to put me back where I belong, I don't belong."

But Sid was jockeyed out of the rights, sold down the river again, and a serious ambitious young director, who'd done live TV in New York, came around to Jimmy's dressingroom with a script about a fading nightclub entertainer. "We'll make a low budget movie but quality for the price," he said. "And you can really *use yourself*." When Jimmy read the script, he agreed. "It also suits my mood. Ruthlessly downbeat." They wanted me to use myself and play Jimmy's neglected bitter wife, but there was no way to postpone shooting until I finished my *Pauline* episodes for the year. "Thank your lucky stars," Mother said. "Why does Jimmy Gabriel always want to *degrade* you on the screen?" For once Sid Gordon backed her up. "Preserve your image. That's basic."

A few days later I met Lucille Ball at a party, we got into the kind of overly friendly huddle that befitted rival stars of the tube, and she told me that *staying clear of the ugly* was basic as well. "Stick to that little something called entertainment," she advised. "Give the public the me it expects," and grew nostalgic over my MGM image and was glad to see I'd found it again, more or less. "The less we change, the longer we last. Especially when we're lovable."

Although Jimmy ended up despising his director, he got wonderful notices for the movie and felt back where he belonged. But his agent warned him *the jury was still out*. "This is a nice little prestige hit, not a blockbuster, and let's face it you are not easy to handle, people complain about your *star complex*, and although no one denies you were great, we need another great role to prove it wasn't just typecasting, a one-shot, you know how they think." And then, after nothing but junk offers came in: "If you want to stay on top, hit the nightclub circuit again."

"Now *there's* irony for you," Jimmy said.

The night before he left on another long tour, we sat home and watched *Pauline*. He yawned frequently, then remarked during the first commercial break, "No one can say you don't make the most of whatever they give you. No one knows better than you how to make an audience forget the dishes in the sink. But wouldn't you like to make it remember them? Don't you ever yearn and crave to connect with reality?"

"When I'm acting, I connect with the reality of acting," I said. "It feels like the most real thing in my life, even when I complain the part's unreal."

He stared at me. "So. Deep down, you've finally sold out."

"Is that what you call it? I thought I was just following your example."

And I recalled a Sunday afternoon when we were lovers but not yet married and Jimmy stripped naked, winding a shirt around his head like a turban and coming on as Valentino. "You told me then, all actors out here live in the movies and only find themselves when they try out a part. You told me then, they belong to their parts more than they belong to their lives." I went on to recall some other parts that Jimmy tried out and lived over the years, embracing the tinsel of stardom, rejecting it to challenge hypocrisy and middle-class values, turning gung ho at the beginning of the war, coming back from it too disillusioned to feel romantic, then casting himself as a romantic daredevil whose instincts led him to the edge of adventure every day.

"Then you think my whole life's just a case of *Three Faces of Eve?*"

I nodded. "Mine too. But you're more versatile, you've got nearer three hundred faces, which makes you harder to pin down. But one day, maybe, we'll catch up with each other."

"You're really laying it on me tonight," Jimmy said.

I watched Pauline being buried alive in a crypt. It seemed to interest Jimmy more than the rest of the show, and when it was over he smiled. "Kind of sexy, the way you lay there gasping for breath. Let's go to bed." Later he said: "We catch up with each other sometimes." And later: "If we're talking reality, you still look sharp as they come. But as an innocent helpless orphan, your days on the tube have got to be numbered."

"Advancing age is Pauline's greatest peril," I agreed. "We never expected the show to run so long, and I guess it's time to talk to the cameraman again."

Then Jimmy was off to Reno, Hawaii, the Virgin Islands, Jamaica, adding Elvis and the Singing Nun to his impersonations, while Pauline continued to battle her greatest peril and Sid Gordon developed an ulcer because our show was so successful. "In spite of the ratings I get this recurring nightmare. One morning I come on the set and Pauline's a little old lady." He sipped his milk and complained I made her too believable. "I believe everything about her, Baby, including the fact she's no spring chicken. You can keep on getting into the same kind of trouble just so long, then people think you're a mite retarded. Better start playing all the way for comedy. Laugh at yourself before they laugh at you." He nodded shrewdly. "Old showbiz tip."

"Sid, you ought to know my limits by now. The only way I get laughs is by playing it straight. These days I'm so straight, everyone calls us a *fun show*." I shuddered. "It's time we stopped playing for time."

He glared. "What else is there?"

"If you want Pauline to escape the Jerry Lewis syndrome, let her *grow*. Me too, by the way. Come to think of it, if she doesn't strike out as an independent woman on her own, I'll never get through the sixties."

As he sipped more milk, Sid gave a violent twitch, habitual disgust at not being allowed coffee. "So let's have your ideas on getting through the sixties."

"Anyone too old for the orphan act is too old have a guardian," I said. "The only solution is to *kill him off*. It may sound a terrible thing to do to your old friend Craig, but he's drinking so much he may not even notice."

After a moment, Sid thumped the desk. "Too bad if he does."

We blew up Craig in a tremendous explosion he intended for Pauline, but a few episodes later I realized the pattern hadn't changed, and the old retarded feeling came back. In charge of her own fortune, Pauline was endlessly duped by fortune hunters. When not falling in love and embarking on a perilous romance, she was taken for every conceivable kind of ride, unwittingly financed a spy ring and bought stolen jewelry, endured blackmail, kidnapping, frame-up. And when she picked a husband who looked even more perilous than Vincent Price, I told Sid it was time to commit her. "If she doesn't stop signaling patsy," I said, "there's no way I can get through the rest of the sixties." He thumped the desk. "Pauline is *trusting to a fault*. That's why we keep on having to rescue her." I almost wept. "But who's going to rescue *me*?"

Mother, of course. "Don't pass up the opportunity of a lifetime, Baby. Play what I believe they call the *subtext*. Like Crawford and Stanwyck in the movies of their classic mature phase, Pauline doesn't stand back and *talk* about the exploitation of women, she goes out on the barricades and fights for her life against the eternally unworthy male."

Elva's Diary

June 10 • She's as complex as a Bach fugue. Playback. Okay for sound. Elva Kay speaking. To bed slightly later than usual last night after catching Irene Dunne and Robert Taylor in *Magnificent Obsession* on the late late. Always one of the great emotional experiences of my life, but greater than ever after the shocking headline story on the 6:00 p.m. news. Beguiling Bob, like so many others, now but a shadow on the crowded cosmic screen.

The kind of American boy that gets under your heart and stays there, as irreplaceable Louis used to say. On the tube he got under my heart all over again, and surging with desperate hope I dialed a number on the phone. "Tell me it's not true," I said. "Tell me that report was a hideous mistake and Bob Taylor lives."

"You know they never make that kind of mistake." The Voice sounded tired but firm. "Yesterday at Cedars of Lebanon, aged fifty-six."

I first spoke to the Voice after hearing a midnight flash on the radio that Louis the Great was no more. Suspecting a malicious rumor, I called the *Times* and asked for the night desk. "Booked into the funeral parlor an hour ago, aged seventy-two. Are you kidding? Who is this, anyway?" On learning my identity, the Voice changed its tone, agreed on the loss to the world and seemed anxious to continue the conversation. In the emotion of the moment I poured out my heart to a stranger. By the time he hung up the Voice was no longer a stranger but an invisible friend, and although it's given me nothing but bad news over the years, never failing to confirm that another star just boarded the Eternal Wheel, we manage to say goodbye on an uplifting note.

The Voice particularly enjoys drawing me out on the subject of MGM, but also appreciates my nostalgic moods. Carried back to the golden years by *Magnificent Obsession* last night, I recalled seeing the movie for the first time with Baby in 1935, at the Pantages. Afterwards we walked around the corner for supper at Clara's It Café, dead and gone now like its dazzling owner. As the Little Princess of the Culver City lot, Baby was besieged by autograph hounds. She obliged one and all, then sat smiling prettily at one and all, sipping her gin and tonic disguised as soda pop.

"I just love it," the Voice said, and begged for more.

"So many memories, where to begin? In the golden age," I said, "every day was an event. Joan Crawford loyally christening a new battleship. Mae West launching the Goodyear blimp, packed with sightseers, on its first aerial tour of our city. Baby in Eskimo clothes opening a new ice-cream parlor in the shape of an igloo. The operators at Universal's switchboard refusing to take any calls because Lon Chaney lay near death and they were on their knees to a girl, praying."

"Can you paint a picture?" the Voice said. "And when are you going to let me come and see you?"

"If we met, we might lose the magic."

"Never think that. I've been going through the photos in your file here, and they look as fantastic as you sound. Promise you'll keep calling, anyway, and don't wait until somebody dies."

A goodbye, a click, and I'm alone again. In a way more alone than ever, with the Divine One's partner in *Camille* a confirmed shadow. But life has to go on, and after snatching an hour or two of sleep, I'm up for Baby in

Freckles on the early show. An actor playing the Mayor of Wabash looked uncannily familiar and I finally placed him as my alleged father, Haines. A more serious shock, though, was the picture's infamous one-star (Desperation Time) rating in *TV Guide*. I blew a triple fuse and fired off another blast to the editor, signing it Ella Geisman, aged nine, Lone Pine. So with another mystery name for the time capsule, it's over and out.

July 22 • Right after the news came through last night, there was a rumble of distant thunder and a flash of lightning in the sky. I called the Voice and said, "All nature seems to be protesting. Tell me it's a false alarm and John Boles lives."

"John who?"

I excused this on the grounds of youth, the star in question having been in semi-eclipse for thirty years. "But toastly and dependable in his prime. He partnered Irene Dunne in the first *Back Street*, a ticket to glory in itself, and Barbara Stanwyck in the second *Stella Dallas*. Then, unwise enough to play straight man to Shirley Temple, and you can guess the rest."

The Voice kindly offered to check the report, then brought its usual tidings. "Yesterday at his home, aged seventy-four."

I felt the usual pang of emptiness, but said lightly, "He'll be back. They all come back. Press a button, especially late at night, and there they are again."

"Old movies on almost every channel. Such a comfort."

"And with TV sets all over, the house really comes *alive* — Spence in the den, Lombard in the library, Bogie in the bedroom, Ronnie Colman in the poolhouse. The medium is the medium, tuning me into all my loved ones."

"Oh, I must remember that," the Voice said.

"Why do you suppose Baby claims I'm sinking deeper and deeper into false security?"

"You don't sound as if you're sinking into anything. But maybe it's a problem sometimes to know what's real and what's imaginary?"

I laughed. "What a strange idea. You forget I'm a child of the golden age — when everything we imagined *became* real before you could say MGM."

"Everything?" The Voice sounded amazed. "Really?"

"Everything," I assured it. "Whatever we wanted, we got — *up there*. Sometimes even before we knew we wanted it. Like a waking dream."

"I can't imagine that," the Voice said. "Take the other day, sitting in front of one of your TV sets and watching the first man set foot on the moon. Wasn't it an experience you could never have dreamed?"

"But I watched the same thing almost twenty years ago in *Destination Moon*, so much better done. The TV show was nothing in comparison, even though they shot it on the actual location."

"How about national disasters? Cameras on hand to record both Kennedy assassinations? You must admit. . . ."

I laughed again. "They just played the same scene over and over, with the same downbeat ending every time. No twist, no uplift, no *imagination*. A story has to *go* somewhere, *mean* something. . . ."

"I'm beginning to understand your point of view and it's another thing I could never have imagined," the Voice said. "But I've got a call on the other line. Take care now and keep in touch."

Now voyager, sail thou forth to seek and find. I'm tired of crooked streets and crooked people. Last night I dreamed I went to Manderley again. Was that cannon fire or is it my heart pounding? She's got a one-track mind, but what a track! "Come and see those dancin' fee-eet," *(singing)* "on the avenue I'm taking you to. . . ." Nobody really likes champagne, but it *looks* gay. When a girl goes wrong, a man goes right after her. Buenas noches from Elva Kay.

August 17 • Who was it said that true love is like seeing ghosts, we all talk about it although few of us have ever seen one? Whoever it was, his immortal words will haunt me forever. Last night, when I stepped outside to admire a brilliant moon, the air was warm and still, yet somehow charged. I had a vibration that I wasn't alone. No fear attached thanks to my infallible security system, with its network of alarms that scares the pants off all invaders. Humming under my breath, I walked boldly down my driveway, then stopped.

A trail of cigarette smoke drifted in the air. My eyes followed it, and I spotted Coop lazing under a palm tree in his Legionnaire uniform from *Morocco*. He stared, not at me but in direction of the summerhouse. I turned and saw Jeanette smiling and waving from the balcony in her merry widow's weeds by Adrian. And then, everywhere I looked, a pain and a consolation. The King in a provocative locker-room moment from *Boom Town*, wearing only a pair of midcalf long johns. Poolside, Clara bouncing with It in a swimsuit. On the lawn, a fantastic line-up of talent: Valentino and Ty Power each swirling a matador's cape in his own version of *Blood and Sand*, beloved Marion dancing up a storm as *Blondie of the Follies*, two great loners, Bogie and Alan Ladd, on the prowl in their homburgs and raincoats, and Ronnie Colman in costume for *A Tale of Two Cities*, unforgettably noble as he prepared for the guillotine. All this and Kay Francis too, in a long velvet gown, shoulders magnificently bare, clutching a small automatic. She was reliving *Jewel Robbery*, which I re-lived myself for a moment, then stepped back as Flynn galloped past leading *The Charge of the Light Brigade*. When the dust cleared, Jeanette was still smiling and waving from her balcony.

Always at home with the unknown, tremendously thrilled yet only mildly surprised, I strolled around with a casual air and pounding heart. So many ghosts, I thought, so many true loves. They smiled and waved and gazed only at each other, never at me, and although longing for a signal, I took care not to disturb them. Instinct told me they wished to be left alone, and *my* role was the fly on the wall at this unique class reunion. Time drifted by like the smoke trail of Coop's cigarette, which never burned out. But at the first faint glimmer of dawn everyone grew sud-denly still, then dissolved. Jeanette the last to leave, with a curious disap-pearing trick. Her body vanished piece by piece, until she became a face with a waving hand, then just a huge friendly smile in the air, then noth-ing at all, leaving only birdsong behind.

Exhausted but inspired by her all-night vigil, yours truly retired to bed and snatched an hour or two of sleep. You can imagine her dreams.

August 24 • No doubt about it, my loves are here to stay. More of a full house some nights than others this week, but always a solid turnout. Connie Bennett dripped with *Outcast Lady* furs while both Hunchbacks of Notre Dame, Mr. Chaney and Mr. Laughton, leered at her from the pool-house roof. Time and my heart stood still when the King arrived in his Fletcher Christian loincloth.

August 29 • That old putrid sound, a coyote howling in the hills, scared off my visitors last night. Feeling sadly alone, I dialed the Voice and whis-pered, "If I tell you a secret, will you promise not to laugh?"

"Have I ever laughed at you, Mrs. Kay?" the Voice answered smoothly.

"Some people refuse to take the occult seriously."

The Voice promised it took the occult very seriously indeed.

As I finished my story, I glanced out the window and saw there was now one visitor in the garden. Tireless Jeanette, waving and smiling in spite of that vile coyote's persistent howl.

"I love it," the Voice said. "Those wonderful old-timers picking on *you* because they know how much you always cared."

"Oh," I said, "you really understand."

"People forget so quickly. The old-timers could wander around for years getting nowhere if it wasn't for *you*. You're the greatest fan in the world." The Voice sighed. "But I wish you'd let *me* into your garden.

Inside your house, too. After all these years, I'm getting slightly desperate."

"Is it really so important to you?"

"You know it is. You know you're the most fascinating person I've never met. That's from the heart," the Voice said. "Remember, I'm always from the heart."

The coyote stopped howling and my garden became Eden again. Elva Kay signing off for now, not at all lonely and curiously at peace.

Baby Looks Back

If you suspected the Voice was a fantasy, like the stars coming home to roost, you were too clever by half. One Sunday afternoon I arrived at Mother's house to find her in the greenhouse-loggia, posed against her bright orchid jungle. The photographer was a blond, tanned faggot in a Nehru jacket. Dangerously smooth, but his eyes flickered with alarm when we were introduced.

I wanted to speak to Mother alone, but she wasn't in a mood to connect, hypnotized by the Polaroid and preparing another pose against her tropicals. "Don't let me interrupt," I said, wondering exactly what there was to interrupt.

Dressed like vintage Swanson in a long gold evening coat with a train, and draped sleeves that made her arms move like wings, Mother somehow still managed to look like tomorrow's fashion news. (On the Strip, as we got out of her Rolls, a group of hippies once surrounded her, stoned but deeply respectful. "Man," they said, and "Some trip," and "*Real unreal*.") Her secret lay in knowing where to draw the line after she'd gone too far. "If I adapted my style to the times, Baby, it would disappear. So I defy them, and it stands out. All the best surfaces are profound."

After the greenhouse, the mini-Pantages projection theatre. Posed against Moorish grillwork and twirling a rose, Mother recalled that Mr. Mayer often said she could have been a very great star herself. The Voice clicked his camera and smiled. I didn't like his smile, wondered again what I was interrupting, and watched Mother grow flirtatious. Lately she'd begun to hint at romantic secrets, mysterious admirers who sent flowers and champagne, followed her along Rodeo Drive, winked at her in movie theatre lobbies. "But maybe you knew that Mr. Mayer was hot for me?" She saw the look of astonishment on his face and added sternly, "Baby will confirm it. I was his ideal type and made him very hot. He was even ready to divorce his wife." She paused uncertainly, as if about to slip into her Elva Kay Mayer fantasy and claim they were secretly married. But then she shrugged. "I couldn't allow it. The greatest American of the age just never attracted me physically. The glorious primitive was *my* ideal type — but maybe you knew that Benjamin Siegel and I made beautiful music together?"

The Voice almost dropped his camera. "Bugsy? The gangster?"

"Never call him Bugsy *or* a gangster. Ben was a reckless animal from the New York streets who fell in with the wrong crowd. Until I rescued him." She pointed the rose accusingly. "You may smile, but I know what I'm talking about."

"I only smiled out of excitement. It's a habit of mine."

She lowered the rose and forgave him. "We mustn't get you *too* excited."

In the bedroom he photographed her on the steps of her sunken bath, then against the veiled barge, then lounging on a divan strewn with fur pillows and displaying her perfect legs.

"Fab," the Voice said. "I wish I didn't have to go now."

As they walked arm in arm to the front door, Mother invited him to come again. "And bring the pictures. I'll sign one for you."

"You are truly out of this world." The Voice kissed her hand. "That's from the heart. Remember, I'm always from the heart."

She gave him the rose, then waved as he drove off. "He'll never forget this day, Baby. It opened a door." She walked back across the hallway, raising her draped arms like wings, still posing. "Before you came he told me I gave an extra dimension to the word achiever."

I didn't answer. Mother posed at the foot of her marble staircase. "That's very flattering," I said. "But I'm not *just* an achiever, you know. Megabucks without romance would be dust and ashes." In the living-room she made her way past Empire sofas, glanced at her reflection in the mirror of her authentic Wild West bar, bought intact from a ghost saloon in Silver City, and stopped in front of an oriental swan-boat. Valentino had reclined there in *The Young Rajah*, naked except for a smattering of bangles, and a startlingly faithful mannequin of Valentino reclined there now, commissioned after Mother bought the prop at an auction. "Romance," she repeated, gazing mistily at his beaded crotch. "Anyone who comes to visit here had better forget about the Year of the Pig." It was obviously not one of her connecting days, no way to get through. Usually Mother's fantasies gave me almost as much pleasure as they gave her, but sometimes she went away when I longed for her to be near, and I felt waves of sadness and anxiety. I said nothing, deciding to go home, and she looked up suddenly. "You're running so silent and deep. What's the problem?" It was as if she'd never gone away at all. She walked over, sending out whiffs of starry tropical perfume, and took my face in her hands. "Let me check your eyes and see what message I get from your heart."

"I can't keep up with you today," I said. "You're really flying."

Her eyes were very close to mine. As they dilated with shock, and the weighted lashes fluttered, it was like the most exaggerated silent-movie acting. But hindsight tells me I gave Mother no mean shock, without intending to, because she *was* flying. Shot herself up, most likely, to get into top gear for the Voice.

After a moment, she grew calm again. "I know that look," she said. "It's all too familiar, like the eternally unworthy male."

She moved away, to a table with an arrangement of signed photographs in silver frames. Louis B., WR and Marion, the Bug, di Frasso, Miss Sophie, Max Factor, Adelle Davis, Mr. Nixon, crowned heads of a dozen corporations, Ramon Novarro, Sessue Hayakawa, Jimmy Gabriel and me. She ripped Jimmy's picture from the frame and threw it in a wastebasket.

"He only made it here on your account, anyway. He never truly belonged to the inner circle of my life."

"He did to mine," I said.

"More's the pity. But don't feel sorry. You're a fool if you feel sorry." She sat on a stool at her Wild West bar, pressed an intercom switch and ordered champagne. "It's the best thing that ever happened to you."

"Every time the same thing happens to me, you say the same thing."

"If you believed me the first time, it wouldn't keep happening. Now let's have the scenario, Baby."

"He called me from Nassau, a couple of hours ago. . . ."

"Typical. The typical Gabriel trick. Always a phone call or a letter when he runs out, only shows up in person when he wants to be taken back. Who's the new girl in his life?"

"Snappy young redhead he met in the casino."

"She sings, of course? He's going to put her in his act?"

"She dances. All the latest stuff, Watusi, Mashed Potato, Slop. . . ."

"Don't forget the Hustle. I'm sure she does that best of all."

The champagne arrived and Mother chinked her silver goblet against mine. "Here's looking at you, kid." She seemed elated. "And here's to your freedom. You *must* feel free!"

"If I drink to it, maybe I'll feel it. Oh, my great love," I said. "My great farce. All these years of my life. . . ."

"Concentrate on the farce and get that man *off your back*. How old are you now?"

"A secret fifty-eight. Thanks for reminding me."

She shook her head. "It can't be true. On the tube last night you looked not a day over thirty-five."

"We shot that episode ten years ago. It was a rerun."

Mother tut-tutted. "Sometimes the tube plays strange tricks. But don't worry. I was pushing fifty-two when Ben came along and felt me up at the Brown Derby, and as you know, I'm still getting more offers than I can handle. Rich and famous always makes out. Chin chin."

I burst out laughing. Mother saw nothing funny but felt relieved I wasn't crying, and so did I. In fact I vowed never to cry over Jimmy Gabriel again. "Maybe he grew from a feeling into a habit, and maybe habits are even harder to give up than feelings," I said. "But I'm in the mood for cold turkey."

"Good thinking, Baby. Don't lose your thread when the champagne wears off."

No danger of the champagne wearing off that night, we killed three bottles and chased them with brandy. Around midnight Mother dropped a fistful of Bs into our snifters, guaranteed they would ward off a hangover, and led me to a guestroom. I lay between John Gilbert's monogrammed satin sheets on Errol Flynn's bed from the Garden of Allah, more trophies picked up at an auction. "It's the best thing that ever happened to me," I muttered. Mother smiled triumphantly. "This is just like old times. You and I together again, ready to take on the world. Strange how the secret pattern of our lives winds on and on."

She left, but her perfume remained in the air. Dead drunk and yet painfully clear in my mind, like a drowning person the moment before going under, I replayed the phone conversation with Jimmy.

"How am I going to tell you this?"

The tone of voice, and the bromide, told me at least the half of it. "Where are you and who is she?" I said.

He gave me the picture. Then he added, "I've always had this unending drive for happiness."

"I know. I hope it doesn't make you too unhappy."

"Sometimes. But better to be swept along by dangerous dreams than stuck in noplaceville."

It sounded fairly insulting. But I agreed.

"And she makes me feel young."

Also fairly insulting. But no comment.

"There's really nothing else to say."

"You've forgotten the bit about hoping we're still friends for life."

I hung up, threw all Jimmy's belongings into suitcases and lugged them to the garage.

Just before dropping off to sleep, I heard a strange murmur of voices all over Mother's house, and realized she'd tuned her TV sets to different channels. Old movies were playing everywhere. When I got up in the early morning, very tired but with no hangover, voices still came from her bedroom. On my way downstairs I heard sweet music with more calories than chocolate spongecake, then a young girl's voice, almost as sweet and definitely familiar. The door to Mother's room stood half open. Glancing inside, at a mirror that covered most of one wall, I found I could see without being seen.

She lay on her barge with the curtains looped back. Her face was still sheathed in makeup and she wore a flowing embroidered caftan. The columnist who nicknamed her She, I thought, really hit the mark, then I saw her hands reach forward, cupped as if to warm themselves over the flame of eternal life. She was watching the early early show, Baby Jewel in *Footlights*, and I watched myself give dashing Warren William an innocent girlish smile as he casually slipped an arm around my waist. A close shot of our faces close together, and an undertone of warning in the music. Hard to say which of us looked more like a ghost on the black-and-white screen, even though Warren was actually dead, stricken with cancer years ago. Then, seeing Mother and myself years later in the mirror, I decided *we* were the real ghosts, even though alive and in color.

"Is someone there?" She sat up suddenly. "Is that you, Baby?"

"Yes. Part of me's here."

She looked at the screen again. "You brought every moment to life. And made the camera love you." Her voice seemed to come from far away. "How did you *know*?"

"Know what? I just did what they said."

"But it's so heartfelt. How are you feeling now, by the way?"

"Top of the world."

"*Top of the World*," she repeated. "That's one of your pictures they never show on the tube. I can't imagine why." Then she forgot I was there, except on the screen. As she watched, her voice went even further away. "You were nothing less than *immortal*," she said.

I drove out in my Rolls to the Pavilion on Balboa Island and got into tattered costume as Pauline. Abandoned to wild bears by her husband on a sightseeing trip in the jungle, she'd spent the previous week fleeing in terror through the tropics. This week, on the edge of collapse, she reached the ocean, spotted an empty canoe by the shore and somehow found the strength to paddle away toward the Pavilion. A relic of the oriental craze during the twenties, it looked like a pagoda over the water and was serving as our location for the house of a scalp-hungry tribal chief. Out of luck as usual, Pauline landed in a nest of headhunters.

She would escape, of course, but more trouble lay ahead. Trapped inside a nailed-down crate in the hold of a ship carrying smuggled cargo. Bound to a log destined for the chute and the buzz saw. Captured by a mad scientist bent on using her for a fiendish experiment. Strapped to a huge church bell about to be rung. Drugged and fired out of a cannon at the circus. Alone at the controls of a plane flying high above the Pacific at night.

But then we had to wind everything up, for our series was in its seventeenth and final year, run into the ground at last. A unique record, as the farewell tribute in *TV Guide* pointed out after our cancelation was made official, untopped even by *Perry Mason* or *Lassie*. (In the end, though, *Gunsmoke* topped it by a year.) And like it or not, *TV Guide* continued, Pauline had become "*part of the national consciousness. Throughout an unusually turbulent era of American history her ratings held firm, she straddled the armistice in Korea and the escalation in Vietnam, the rise of Castro and the assassination of President Kennedy, the civil rights and burn-your-draft-card movements, flower children, Black Power and a soaring crime rate. Sociologists have argued bitterly over the meaning of this, fans and detractors have called Pauline many different things, survivor and goon, Houdini in skirts and Miss Punishment Freak, but not even those who put her down as a compulsive loser could deny that she won an incredibly faithful audience.*" So why did her audience begin to fall away in the last two seasons, and her ratings slip from 12 to 31 to 49? *Batman* in the same time slot didn't help any, according to *TV Guide*, but it was only a symptom, not a cause. A long-running series had to attract young viewers as well as keep all the millions growing old along with the show, and when Pauline failed to do this it proved she'd lost her hold on youth.

The makeup man sprinkled dust on my face, the wardrobe lady ripped my skirt some more, and they called me for the first scene. It was no problem at all to look exhausted and totter pathetically on the sand. Then I spotted the empty canoe, got in, paddled a few strokes in the shallows and refused to go any further. While they switched to a double who didn't mind the deep, I tottered back to the Rolls and took a long nap. Jimmy kept his distance all day. Occasionally he turned up on the sidelines of my mind, like Warren, like a ghost, somebody with whom I made a black-and-white movie a long while ago. And for once Pauline didn't get on my nerves but suited my mood. When the headhunters chased and captured me later, it was a pleasure to act dumb and passive, too tired to struggle as they tied me up and carried me off in triumph.

With a heavy escape situation on the next day's schedule, I decided not to drive home and parked my world near the Fun Zone, which had closed for the night. Coastal mist was swirling across the empty, stationary merry-go-round and ferris wheel. I mixed a martini, then ate supper. While the radio played soft happy California rock, the Beach Boys, the Mamas and the Papas, I flicked through the *Hollywood Citizen-News*, which had pictures of noted psychic Peter Hurkos in the house on Cielo Drive, sniffing Sharon Tate's bloodstains for vibes. He claimed he got them and had told the police who the killers were. I drew the window blinds, locked all the doors, switched off the radio and pressed a button. My special convertible back seat became a bed. Jimmy still kept his distance and I felt sure of going to sleep at once, but ocean surf was breaking loudly and echoing all around. It made me nervous, just like Pauline when she heard tomtoms in the jungle. I switched on a light, tried the tube and got the last ten minutes of an early Jimmy Gabriel movie with a carnival background. He wore a cap and bow tie, looked exactly as he did on our first date, sang "Oh! You Beautiful Doll" to a midget carny dancer, and I didn't feel a thing. At the end I switched him off and wrapped myself in a fur rug.

Then I heard a car draw up outside, very close. There was the sound of a door opening, footsteps coming nearer. I let up a blind and looked straight through the mist into the eyes of a cop. He asked to see my driver's license, checked the name and photograph on it, then gave me a long accusing stare.

"I know I'm not wearing any makeup," I said. "But is it really that bad?"

He held the stare. Probably a cop mask, I thought, worn to cover up reaction and keep me guessing. Finally he jerked a thumb into the mist. "Didn't you see the sign? You're illegally parked."

"I didn't see any sign," I said, and explained my habit of spending the night in a world on wheels when I was working on location far from home. He looked inside the Rolls, noted the folding bed, TV and radio, bar and fridge. Caught by surprise, his mask relaxed slightly. "Quite a set up there. Don't you ever get lonely?"

"Not when I'm alone."

He thought this over, then asked what happened to Pauline in the episode I was shooting. I outlined the headhunter situation and he said, "A lot of us argue about this. Is your show for laughs or for real?"

I smiled. "Which side are you on?"

The mask relaxed a little more. "I like it anyway, you understand, but I get some big laughs out of it."

"That's fine. Only wish *I* did." Then I said, "I'm really sorry I didn't see the sign. But it's so late, maybe I can stay? No question of blocking the Fun Zone, I always move on at dawn."

The mask stiffened. "Tell you what." He held the stare again. "I'll leave a ticket on your windshield. You won't lose any sleep over ten bucks." He fingered his holster. "That way, everybody's happy."

Elva's Diary

September 19 • When you're slapped, you'll take it and like it. Playback. Okay for sound. Elva Kay speaking. Excuse me, Bogie, yours truly has taken it but my God she doesn't like it, and wants the world to know. Even though Baby tells me times have changed, the public doesn't shock so easy anymore, scandal sheets have lost their power to scandalize. "And now Hedda's dead, the stars actually seem to miss her. They feel *neglected*. That's why they write their *own* kiss-and-tell life stories, and let it all hang out on talk shows."

"Maybe so, but this is a case of wicked humiliating lies about your own Mother, and she feels *betrayed*."

"I warned you the Voice was a two-timing faggot. Did you take your extra Bs for stress?"

"The situation calls for more than extra Bs. You don't seem to realize I've been given the finger, *all the way up*, and it's made me fighting mad. My God. Just a moment."

I went to the bathroom for happy dust, ignored Baby's advice to cool it when I came back, and called Mr. Chandler at the *Times*.

Courteous as ever, he asked what he could do for me.

"Don't tell me you haven't read the latest *Enquirer*?"

"I never read it."

"Well, I'm *in* it, and the whole town's buzzing. People I haven't heard from in years, like Lillian Coogan, calling up to find out if I'm all right. Thanks to a two-timing faggot on *your* night desk, who gained my confidence over the phone, came to the house, took pictures and made a secret tape of my voice. Now, on checkstands at supermarkets all over the country, there's a screaming banner headline, THE TWILIGHT OF ELVA KAY."

"What can they be thinking of?" Mr. Chandler said. "Everyone knows you're at eternal high noon."

"That's some haha." I laughed bitterly. " 'Once acclaimed the most glamorous tycoon in the free world, noted figure on the Los Angeles scene for years,' " I quoted, " 'the Mother of Baby Jewel Kay is now a sex-crazed octogenarian. Friends are embarrassed by the fantasies she pours out to anyone who will listen. Louis B. Mayer wanted desperately to marry her, but she turned him down because she was having the affair of her life with notorious gangster Bugsy Siegel. The ghosts of Hollywood stars visit her garden at night, and as she crows over Clark Gable and Errol Flynn in beefcake poses, she works herself up to a pitch of excitement really shocking for her age. . . .' "

"The lowest thing I ever heard," Mr. Chandler said.

"Rock bottom's to come. 'Another fantasy is very embarrassing for her daughter. Elva repeatedly insists that Baby Jewel began drinking heavily at the age of ten. . . .' "

"No one will believe a word."

"Lillian Coogan believed *every* word, until she called me. And as for my photograph, it's a deliberate travesty, a hoax and a fake. You won't recognize me."

"These people always pick an unflattering shot," Mr. Chandler said.

"You don't understand. They've picked an impostor. The picture is *not me*. My God, I'm a three-time Woman of the Year, and Dorothy Chandler's Music Center acknowledged my extremely generous donation with a special plaque, and I want that skunk on your payroll bounced all the way to. . . ."

"Just a minute, Elva, and I'll see to it right now. Let me put you on hold."

Unable to keep a note of admiration out of her voice, even though she felt I was over-reacting, Baby remarked that I certainly knew how to raise the roof. I told her to order champagne on the intercom, the two-timing faggot was getting his. Then Mr. Chandler came back on the line with unwelcome news. Seems the Voice resigned his job at the *Times* a week ago.

"Has he made enough money, moonlighting as a secret agent over the years, to start a filthy rag of his own?"

"He's going to work as a legman for Walter Winchell."

"That's another haha." I laughed bitterly again. "And what a vile combination. We're in for a reign of terror."

"Elva, try playing this whole deal down instead of up. You're a woman of unique reputation, dignity and wealth. *Too big* to be hurt by cheap gossip."

"Thank you for those words, Chandler, but in a personal sense I *am* hurt. And I hate to see someone *getting away with murder*."

I hung up and was drawn against my will to gaze at that awful picture. Knowing it was a travesty didn't ease the pain. "There's nothing to celebrate," I said. "Cancel the bubbly." And felt suddenly cold.

Baby gave me an anxious look. "Are you all right?"

"Everyone asks me that." I laughed bitterly again. "Now I'm beginning to ask myself." That absurd cruel photograph still drew my unwilling gaze, still wounded me even more than the article itself. "It's someone else," I said.

"Yes, it's unrecognizable," Baby said.

"But it's got my name on it. And it's winking. All because that weasel kissed my ass and I fell for it. Maybe twilight's coming on after all."

Baby was riffling through *TV Guide*. "Jennifer Jones in *Song of Bernadette* on Channel 5," she said. I shook my head. "Then how about Channel 9? Edward G. and Jean Arthur in *The Whole Town's Talking*."

"An unfortunate title at this moment, Baby." I shook my head again. "As we speak, millions are talking about your Mother. Sex-crazed octogenarian clinging to the illusion of youth! Dressed for the party that was over long ago! Fading away to a world of tinsel Hollywood dreams! Almost as much a ghost as the ghosts she claims to. . . ."

(Mother breaks off, begins to sob quietly, and after a minute or so the tape runs out.)

Baby Looks Back

"Maybe twilight's coming on after all," Mother said again. "Yes, better face it. No point in reloading the camera. Kill the lights. It's a wrap. Everyone go home."

"I can't believe what I'm hearing."

She gazed at her picture in the *Enquirer*. "I can't believe what I'm seeing, Baby. And yet I'm seeing it."

There were several Venetian mirrors in the livingroom. Mother walked over to each one in turn, studying her reflection for a moment. She stopped in front of the last one, standing very close to it, her face almost touching the glass. "This could be the last reel starting. I often wondered how it would feel, and now I know. It's Bette Davis at the end of *Mr. Skeffington*. Remember what happened after she caught diphtheria? She looked at herself in the mirror and found she was no longer the great desirable beauty." Mother looked at herself in the mirror. "It felt like the end of the world and she couldn't admit it at first. It's not easy to admit you're *unrecognizable*."

I went over and tried to pull her away. "Will you come back from there?"

She went on gazing at herself. "But I'm not so lucky as Bette. Her husband was blind and never found out. Everything's always better in the movies."

"Wherever you are, will you please come back?"

But she didn't seem to hear me. "My image trampled in the dust. For all the world to see. So wicked and unfeeling. I suppose they don't understand romance anymore." Turning away from the mirror, she moved right past me as if I wasn't there. "It's a bright, guilty world." A pious hush came over her voice, as it always did when she quoted sacred lines of movie dialogue. "Trust no man further than you can kick a lemon pie." She drifted into the hallway and paused at the foot of her marble staircase, clutching the handrail. "But what's going to happen when someone unties the knot that holds you together?"

Talk about the power of the press. Convinced the *Enquirer* had toppled her image, Mother set about rescuing it and making it over. Like her famous instant coffee, it came out new and improved. And inspired her last great role, which she played for the rest of her life. "Apart from the fact that I was quoted *out of context*, time will show what is fantasy and what is truth. In the meantime, yours truly will show that twilight can be the most beautiful hour of the day!" Socially speaking, she took the veil and became a fascinating recluse. But although mysteriously unavailable to the common world, she wanted the world to know it, and "granted" the society correspondent of the *Times* an exclusive interview over the phone. "I've lived a long time, but I'm not *old*. Just rich in experience. And rich period. I don't need the madding crowd any more, I've had my fill of *external stimuli* and like the Hindus feel detachment coming on." In fact she grew more dependent on external stimuli than ever, not only media-conscious but media-dominated. In this last phase she had no direct contact with the present, knew it only through newspapers, magazines, TV, and she relived the past through old movies, her scrapbooks, her beloved ghosts. No use trying to persuade her it wasn't necessary to run for cover, or that she took the *Enquirer* story far more seriously than anyone else. She fell back on two contradictory lines of defense, either denying that she gave the article a moment's thought or hinting at a deep wound. "Tell Mrs. Rip she's a fool to hide," Sid Gordon said. "If you've got what people want, in her case a hundred million smackers give or take a few, you can get away with anything. Tell her that's *the bottom line.''* I told her, but she didn't like it. "I have nothing to *get away with*, Baby. I'm just retiring to inner space."

The photograph, not the article, was the real bottom line. Any reference to it dealt Mother's new air of Hindu detachment a knockout blow. "I see now it was not, in the strictest sense, a fake. But what happens to the Mona Lisa when you repaint her with a mustache?" She trembled slightly. "The Voice kept clicking and clicking until he finally got *one* unflattering shot, which he retouched to make me look older than history." Did she really believe this? I can only tell you she had become afraid to show herself in public.

On the rare occasions that she ventured out, Mother came as near as she could get to a low profile. The classic Phantom V and marbled Thunderbird had been placed on blocks in the garage, she merged with crowd by driving a white Porsche, with specially tinted glass, at breakneck speed. Her face almost invisible behind dark glasses and the sweeping brim of a hat, she sidled into a movie theatre as the lights went down and arranged private visits to her cemetery lot at Forest Lawn. Laying flowers on her future grave, she viewed it with peculiar satisfaction. "Let the world say what it likes about me, I shall spend eternity only a stone's throw from Carole Lombard."

Her sole companion, apart from me, was Hattie. Well into her eighties, very stout and testy, physically slowed down but still quick to predict Armageddon around the corner, she encouraged Mother's isolation. "Come to her senses at last! Didn't I always tell her to lock her doors against Satan?" Sometimes they struck me as a kind of Laurel and Hardy, Mother so slim and remote, Hattie so large and smoldering. They seemed locked into each other, especially when they had loud violent quarrels, accusing each other of the vices of old age, forgetfulness, muddle, impatience, incompetence, not paying attention, but they also succeeded in running the enormous house together, kept it immaculate and gleaming and brimming with flowers. Of course they had what Mother called a skeleton staff, nine servants plus gardeners, to help. And on occasional restless nights, when coyotes or a thunderstorm scared the ghosts away, or there was no old movie worth watching on the tube, or she felt a vague nameless anxiety in the air, Mother herself became a compulsive housecleaner, waxing a floor, polishing mirrors, vacuuming chandeliers, scrubbing her sunken bath, spraying everything against imaginary ants. Otherwise she lived in a planned dream. Her day began with the 5:00 a.m. movie, followed by breakfast according to Adelle Davis, followed by an hour or two at her desk with its In and Out trays, followed by a swim in the pool, a sampling of midday movies on the tube, a couple of martinis and lunch. A nap, a session in her private Tanamatic parlor, a visit from her hairdresser, cosmetician or manicurist, and it was time to prepare herself for the afternoon tour bus. Villa Elva was on the itinerary of movie star homes, and although not strictly speaking a movie star, Mother had acquired the status of one and was considered historically significant. Out-of-town visitors peered through the heavily locked wrought-iron gates to the driveway, noted the Protected by Silent Security System signs, and hoped for a glimpse of the legendary owner. Mother usually supplied it, stationing herself at a distance like the ghost of Jeanette MacDonald, smiling and waving in an Adrian gown. Then she returned to the past, settling herself in the mini-Pantages theatre. Jaime, her faithful Filipino butler, had been trained as a projectionist, and she screened a favorite from her private collection, a Baby Jewel or a Marion, a bootleg Garbo or *Back Street* or *Red Dust* or *A Free Soul*. After the cocktail hour, a pitcher of martinis at her side as she browsed through newspapers and magazines, glancing up occasionally at the news on TV, she dined alone at her round table stacked with crystal and silver, ringed with empty chairs. Then she took a long stroll through the garden to check out her ghosts, retired to bed for the late and late late shows, and finally snatched a few hours of sleep.

At least three times a week she sneaked out to current movies, but I only heard her express real enthusiasm for bike pictures. "Call me a devotee. So pretty and exciting to look at. They plug me into *American youth*, speeding through the West on its Harleys. I know its motives are less pure than the good old U.S. cavalry, those boys have got rape and destruction rather than rescue on their minds, yet my heart goes out to them. There's a true spirit of romance in the way they'd rather die than conform."

In keeping with her role of recluse, she decided to step down from EKE. "No room at the top for a sex-crazed octogenarian," she said grimly, then glanced in a mirror and firmed her chin. "I'm giving you full power of attorney and making you chief operating officer, Baby, so you can keep a sharp eye on the boardroom junta. As you know, I feel pleasantly detached from high finance these days, but from time to time I *may* ask you to push a special project through." And late one afternoon she asked me to come over to the house right away, saying she'd had an A-1 vibration. I found her lounging on a banquette in the den, the Anna May Wong chandelier lit, copies of *Fortune* and *The Wall Street Journal* scattered everywhere. "Help yourself to a martini, Baby, I just made a fresh batch. The best financial brains in America agree that the biggest commodity of the future is oil. I missed getting my hands on the stuff out here and I'd like to take a crack at the Middle East."

Around the black lucite table at the Control Center, the junta discussed Mother's memorandum, Black Gold Is Where You Find It. They seemed impressed but uncertain how to proceed.

"As I read her," the Calhern type said, "Mrs. Kay wants us to buy crude at the lowest going rate, then refine it and sell it at the highest going rate."

"But where do we go to buy crude?" the Fredric March type said. "And is she expecting us to get into the refinery business as well?"

They all looked at me. I blew a smoke ring and suggested calling the Chief.

"My God." She sounded fairly impatient over the phone. "After all these years do I still have to spell everything out?"

"Looks like it. They want to know if we should buy a refinery," I said, "or go into partnership with an existing company."

"At this stage of the game I don't go into partnership with anybody."

"Check. I guess they can find a refinery to take over, but they don't have any idea where to buy crude. On the spot market?"

"Where it gushes, Baby. It's cheaper. One of those shysters has got to haul ass to the Middle East, put his ear to the sand, make contacts and start dealing. This operation's like real estate in California in the old days, a scramble, a scrimmage, you get down on your knees if necessary." Then she chuckled. "By the way, I just went through an old scrapbook and found a darling picture of you and B. J. Langdon after he took you up in his plane. Publicity-wise, we really beat the shit out of Jackie Coogan that day."

The Calhern type suffered from high blood pressure, the March type had a locked knee, so it was decided to put the Paul Douglas type on a plane to Saudi Arabia. I thought, anyway, that his line in false geniality was most likely to succeed, imagined him slapping shoulders and picking brains in hotel lobbies out there, and in fact encouraging messages soon arrived on the telex.

"Big deal," Mother said impatiently. "He doesn't have to tell *me* the market's wide open and a smart independent operator should be able to grab a piece of it. Why does he think I sent him there?" But when EKE added a petroleum company to its empire a few months later, she was grudgingly pleased. "So now I'm an oil sheik. Not bad for an old lady who's supposed to be fading away into a world of tinsel dreams." She didn't want to hear facts and figures. The object of the operation was to settle her score, yet again, with the *Enquirer*.

And then a great fire broke out in a canyon beyond Bel Air. It frightened the ghosts from her garden, she stood on the empty terrace, saw the sky turn red and felt a piece of ash fall on her cheek. "Drop everything and come on over, Baby." Her voice sounded oddly frail and desperate on the phone. "I want us to face the end together." Watching the progress of the fire on TV, I knew she was in no danger and told her the wind wasn't blowing her way. "To hell with the wind," Mother said. "The movies predicted this years ago. Don't you know what's happening? Did you never see *When Worlds Collide?*"

At first she refused to believe that flames in the sky, and falling ash, and helicopters buzzing overhead, could mean anything except cosmic disaster. She'd seen that movie and she knew the signs. "Last night they showed *The Thing* on TV," she added. "Remember the warning at the end? *Watch the skies!*"

"If you watch the skies on TV now," I said, "you'll see it's just another brushfire."

It was strange. When Mother saw an actual fire, she began living in a disaster movie. She only got herself out of it when she saw the same fire on the tube. Images on a screen led her away from reality and brought her back to it, as if she could only recognize something by its shadow.

It made me start to miss her. Even though I saw her as often as before, we were no longer "we," traveling companions always looking out from the same window. And when we looked back, I began to miss her in the past as well. She brought out an old photograph of Marion's famous fancy dress ball at the Ambassador Hotel, our hostess in costume as a southern belle, Chaplin as Napoleon, John Barrymore as a tramp, Mother and me as Dearest and Little Lord Fauntleroy. Mother saw a living image of reality there, it conjured up memories of a golden age that she polished to an unearthly glitter. I saw a faded picture of visitors from outer space, and the most unlikely member of the group was a midget in a velvet suit and ruffled shirt. She had a practised knowing smile, but her eyes betrayed it. They were too intensely anxious to please.

"We've hardly changed, you know!" As Mother looked around the glorious junkyard of her livingroom, I caught another unexpected glimpse of us in a mirror. Almost fifty years later, she at least was still in a fancy dress situation, in a set as splashy and more fantastic than that Hawaiian ballroom planted with coconut palms, jacarandas and Birds of Paradise. As for the midget, she had a practised knowing smile, but this time her eyes didn't betray it. They were just as knowing, although maybe a little tired. Fifty years, she was thinking, is too long at the goddam Fair.

The same thought was in Jimmy Gabriel's mind when he called me a few weeks before Christmas. I hadn't heard from him since the summer, when he kissed me off from Nassau. This time it was early evening, cool and cloudy, with a wind getting up. His voice sounded slurred, and then there was a heavy clatter, as if he'd dropped the phone.

"Are you drunk?"

"No."

"Alone?"

"Completely. Taking, uh, the sleep cure."

"Where?"

"I forget." He seemed to go away. Then he said, "The Tumble Inn, Ventura."

"Am I getting this right? You checked into some motel up the coast and swallowed some sleeping pills?"

"Felt so tired. Been around so long and wanted to rest. It's my third day on the barbiturate diet and I may stay on it awhile longer." He laughed. "Jimmy Gabriel is on vacation in limbo."

"You could take one pill too many and join the majority."

"Always believed in keeping my options open."

I asked about the dancing redhead and Jimmy said it didn't work out. He said *nothing* worked out anymore. Nothing he *wanted*, anyway. His time had come and gone. Maybe he should quit.

"The business? Or life?"

He laughed again. "You sound fine. That's all I really wanted to know. 'Toot, Toot, Tootsie, Goodbye,'" he sang off-key, and hung up.

What kind of crap is this? I wondered, and it began to rain. As I got in the Rolls, there was nothing so boring as the return of romance on my mind, but I knew a cry for help when I heard it. And there was something in his laugh that jarred on my ears, like the tearing of silk.

It began to rain harder, which as usual made the night seem darker, and as usual the drivers on the freeway went crazy. When conditions were risky, they always took more risks, as if they felt electricity in the air. I passed several cars that had skidded into each other, and one that had hit a central divider, before I turned off on the coast highway. The Tumble Inn was an old stucco building in bungalow court style with neon signs that advertised TV in Every Room and Special Monthly Rates. The reception lobby had cigarette, junk food and soft drink machines, a WELCOME mat, a vase of plastic flowers on the desk. Behind it sat a hefty shoulder-length blond with an APATHY button on his T-shirt. Student earning himself some pocket money, I thought, asked for Mr. Gabriel's room, and he said "111," jerking a bored thumb toward the patio.

Business at the Tumble Inn did not seem to be terrific, a dull yellowish light came from only two other rooms. I stepped around pools of water,

knocked at the door of 111, got no answer, found it was unlocked and
went inside. The air felt stale, as if the room had been closed up for a long
time. The TV was switched on with the sound turned down, a pile of
sandwiches wrapped in plastic on the top, and Jimmy lay asleep on a
large rumpled bed. For the first time he didn't look young or contented in
sleep. His face was haggard, seedy, terrible. On the bedside table stood
several bottles of pills and a quart of scotch.

I shook him violently. His eyes opened, gave a blank stare and closed
again. I picked up the pills and the scotch and told him I was going to
flush them down the toilet. His eyes jerked open and his hands clutched
at me, struggling to get hold of the bottles. I jabbed him with my elbows
and he fell back, hitting his head against the wall. I heard him moan while
I carried out my promise in the bathroom, but came back to find him
sitting up in bed, wrapped in a sheet, glaring at me. "I can always get
more," he said. "Give me a cigarette."

"You don't smoke."

"You took my pills and my booze. I need some kind of crutch."

I threw a plastic-wrapped sandwich at him.

"You seem to be in one hell of a rage," Jimmy said, unwrapped the
plastic and began to eat.

"What kind of crap is this? *Valley of the Dolls?*"

"Wish I had some potato chips." He threw the sandwich away. "Something else is missing around here as well." The same dry, grating laugh.
"I've lost the rest of my life." And he began to weep. "What is *wrong*
with me?"

"I'll tell you later. Get dressed now."

Jimmy shook his head. "You're not going to rescue me, Baby in Quotes.
No one can do that. It's too late."

"Then what kind of cheap trick was it to call me, and make me drive up
here in the rain? Oh, I'm truly disgusted," I said, and made for the door.

He threw off the bedsheet and got up, naked. He swayed on his feet,
seemed about to faint, and I ran forward to catch him. But he shook his
head again. "I'll make it." He steadied himself, holding on to the back of
a chair. "I'll make it if you stay. But if you leave, it's the end of Jimmy
Gabriel. And what an end. Alone, forgotten, unwanted, in a cheap motel
room."

"You look awful. I can't believe that belly."

"Just give me a cigarette."

I lit one and gave it to him. The first drag almost knocked him out. He
began to lurch, and I ran forward again to catch him. This time he fell

against me. I led him back to the bed, where he sat huddled and trembling, his face very gray.

"I wish you'd get dressed."

"No way. I'm going out as I came in."

"Okay," I said. "Before you go, here's what's wrong with you. It's not the way you keep chasing after those long-legged numbers who keep taking you for all they can — although, at your age, the situation can only get worse. It's not even the way you kid yourself it's true love, and want to marry them. It's the way you kid yourself they have *talent*, and put them in your act."

Jimmy stopped trembling and began to straighten up.

"Your *act*," I said. "Anyone with any sense should stay out of it. There's no room. You're a one-man show, always were, and you need a supporting cast, maybe, but not a partner. If one of those girls began showing signs of real talent, you'd have fired her."

"I need a glass of water."

I fetched him one, he drank it and asked for another. I fetched him another, he drank it and asked for another sandwich. I gave him another sandwich, he unwrapped the plastic and began to eat. "Hard words," he said between mouthfuls. "But I probably deserve them. Why did you never tell me this before?"

"I was in love with you. Didn't want to face facts, or hurt your feelings."

"And now you want to hurt me."

"A little. Your whole act's making me so angry."

He nodded and got up again. More or less steady on his feet now, he walked to the window, drew up the blind and stared out at the dark rainy patio. "What is acting? Can you tell me what acting's really about? Is it a way of looking at yourself, checking your development as a private *and* a public person?"

"You're feeling better. Yes, I guess acting is something like that. Or ought to be."

"Ah! *Ought*. One of the saddest words in the language. When acting's not what it ought to be, it's a way of *indulging* yourself, *failing* to develop as a —"

"You're right. But goddamit, will you please get dressed? It's time to make tracks."

He sighed. "Where? Where do I go now? How do I find myself?"

"In front of an audience."

Jimmy turned around suddenly. "So many smart answers tonight. But how come *you* never found yourself? Never truly developed?" Scowling at me, he came over and stood very close. "How come you let your Mother run your life? She could die tomorrow but it's too late. I see nothing ahead for you, Baby in Quotes, but enormous loneliness. At your age you'll never find true love. Or develop into a real actress. You settled for the personality thing too long ago. After all these years, all you've come out with is a slick bright mask — plus millions in the bank, of course. But that's *dead money*, and it's taking you with it."

Then he hit me in the face. I hit him back and we had a fierce ludicrous struggle, aiming kicks and blows, Jimmy twisting my ear hard and holding on to it until I managed to bring down my heel on his bare foot, when he yelped with pain and let me go.

"So we finally spoke true," I said. "You were always a crazy hopeless egotist and I was always a piece of dust in the world's eye. And we've been longing to hit each other for years."

Jimmy laughed. "I only hit you to make an impression. You stood there looking as if you didn't believe me. Almost *cheerful*," he said accusingly, "when I wanted you to cry. I still do. I want to stand and watch while you shed a tear. Go on. Cry your heart out."

"Later. I want to go home now."

"*Home*? No place like it, if you can find it." He shrugged and started to put on his clothes. I looked out the window and heard him say after a while, "Don't seem to have any money. No credit cards either. What happened? Where was I?" The lights in the two rooms across the patio had gone out. "Now I remember," I heard him say. "Came here from Vegas, that's why I don't have any money. But it doesn't explain the credit cards." The rain was tapering off. "Wait a minute. Someone drove me here from Vegas and I took my first sleeping pills on the ride. . . ."

I went to settle his bill. The blond student stretched out on a chair behind the desk and a girl wearing a Navajo headband knelt at his feet. She was painting a psychedelic heart on his sneakers. The student looked up as Jimmy came into the lobby and said, "Hope you enjoyed your stay."

When we walked out to the street, Jimmy saw my Rolls and gave a low whistle. "Don't tell me you drove up here in that thing."

"That thing is my friend. We go everywhere together."

"Where shall I sit?"

"In the back if you want to stretch out and watch TV. Up front if you're in the mood for interesting conversation."

He sat in the back. On the drive home it started to rain again, but there was little traffic on the freeway. Long, slicked, mainly empty lanes stretched ahead. After a while Jimmy contacted me on the intercom and told me to pull over, he wanted to move up front. "Let's sing," he said, "I feel like singing," and launched into "Singing in the Rain." We duetted, then he opened the window, stretched out his hand, cupped it to catch a few raindrops, and began crooning "Pennies from Heaven." I harmonized, then we segued into "Thanks for the Memory" and "Happy Days Are Here Again." "Enough of the old stuff, let's get with it," I said, and led us into "This Is the Dawning of the Age of Aquarius." We followed it with "Homeward Bound" and "Feelin' Groovy."

"I just had a fantastic idea," Jimmy said. "Why don't we do a Broadway musical together?"

"I'd rather cut my throat."

He nodded, closed his eyes and went to sleep. From time to time I glanced at his face and saw it gradually smoothing out. By the time we reached Hollywood it looked almost uncannily young.

"Wake up now." I stopped outside his apartment. "This is it."

He sat up with a start. "Where are we?"

"Tinsel Town. I've brought you back where you belong."

He stared at the apartment building. "But it's years since I lived here." Then he turned out his pockets. "And I don't have the key."

"The man on the night desk can let you in."

"There'll be such an empty feeling." He held my hand. "Can I face another empty room?"

"You'll find all your clothes and stuff there. I sent them over after you called me from Nassau."

He held my hand more tightly. "So when will I see you again?"

"By chance, maybe. But not by appointment."

"That sounded pretty chilling. And final."

"It wasn't meant to sound chilling. Just final."

"I don't understand how you can rescue a person and then leave him in the lurch."

"Whatever I did was for auld lang syne. For the good old days long past. And you're okay now, more or less."

"May I kiss you?"

"On the cheek. Like a brother. You once told me you always wanted a kid sister."

He kissed me on the cheek but still held on to my hand.

"You've got to let me go," I said. "Let me go home, drop my slick bright mask and cry my heart out."

But I started to cry then and there, on the spot. I couldn't control it. Jimmy put his arms around me and finally I stopped. "Let me go," I said. "I'm okay now, more or less."

He kissed me on the cheek again, got out and went into the apartment building. I waited until I saw a light come on in his window. Then the drapes closed.

On Christmas Day, Mother and I ate our dinner together as usual. When I arrived, she was sitting on the floor in her Courreges leotards, with a note pad on her knees. Flashing with tinsel and winking with colored lights, the tree above her was almost as tall as an Arizona pine. She went on writing for a while and then said, "The tube finally aired *Top of the World* this morning and I was up at 5:00 to catch it. Imagine how many fuses I blew when I found your dream sequence had been cut."

"Are you sure the picture *had* a dream sequence?"

"My God. I can't believe it's slipped your mind. You were climbing a flagpole that grew taller and taller, and took you all the way to the gates of heaven."

"What a memory. Sometimes it's even better than mine. Are you firing off another blast to *TV Guide*?"

She nodded. I knelt down to see how she signed the letter.

"Tula Ellice Finklea, aged 11, Calabasas," I said. "Your names are up there with the best of W.C. Fields. If you ever run out of inspiration, by the way, remember Oliotha Shugg. It was always my favorite."

"Oliotha Shugg doesn't sound quite real to me."

I glanced through the letter with its carefully faked childish penmanship and deliberate spelling mistakes. "I'm afraid you blew it," I said. "How could Tula Ellice Finklea aged 11 know about that sequence? The picture came out almost forty years ago."

Mother looked confused. Finally she said, "Sometimes your literal mind pays off. I'll redraft the letter, make Tula one of your oldtime fans instead of another kid who just discovered your early genius on the early show. You may smile, Baby, but I shan't rest until I've whipped up enough national interest to create a *Baby Jewel revival*. I want you recognized and hailed as a classic. Now open your present."

She pointed to a package under the tree. It was the size of a large attaché case. "I hope you like it. Quite a change of pace from the condominium I gave you last year."

"The year before. Last year you gave me a parking lot chain." The package was too heavy to lift. "Oh," I said after opening it. "You really shouldn't. It's too much."

"No such thing as too much gold." As Mother patted the gleaming ingot, the phone rang. She jumped smartly to her feet. "I've got a strong vibration who's calling," she said and went to answer it. "Elva Kay speaking." She gave me a nod to confirm that her vibration had paid off.

"And a very merry to *you*, sir," she went on. And then: "No, just Baby and me at home. I never go out anymore, you know, I'm sick of being hounded by the press." And then: "I thought you'd understand. Please give my warmest greetings to your lovely wife."

When she hung up, there was an almost trance-like look on her face. "Such an honor. Although I was sure Mr. Nixon wouldn't forget. You don't forget the kind of donation I made to his campaign." She glanced at the ingot, then sat in her favorite throne-like chair. "I'll be happy to reach in my pocket the next time around, by the way. When we met at that fund-raising dinner last year, I felt such an affinity with the man. Nothing physical, of course. But *he plays to win*."

"And he understands your feelings about the press."

"Completely. Distrusts them as much as I do. Knows how they can hurt. We agreed we're both fundamentally introverts." She sighed, then gazed at the tree. "Remember our first Christmas in this town? You'd just made your first Kid Sherlock, it hadn't come out yet, and we were renting a place that was hardly more than a hillside cabin. We ate our modest fare, then took a stroll along the Boulevard, which was so empty and closed-up and silent, we thought everyone had died."

"That's right. Then we went over to Mrs. Root's for eggnog."

"That's right. And look at us now. All this," Mother said, her gaze traveling from the ingot to Valentino's swan-boat, from the Wild West bar to the table of signed photographs, "and a phone call from the President too. We've come a long way, Baby!"

1980 - 1982

Elva's Diary

October 3 • Maybe I'm just a dame and didn't know it. Playback. Okay
for sound. Elva Kay speaking. To bed slightly later than usual last night
after catching Bette Davis in *Dark Victory* on the late late. Timeless as ever,
of course. Is there any subject more vital than Death? And Bette's death
scene hit the spot even more than the Divine One's departure in *Camille*
or Merle's exit in *Wuthering Heights*. For Bette had no lover at her bedside,
no arms to pick her up and carry her to the window for a last glimpse of
this temporary world. She made it the way yours truly intends to, on her
own. Stricken with an incurable disease, knowing her time had come, she
lay down on her kingsized bed and *waited*. THE END. My God.

That's the ticket, I thought, switched out the light and lay down feeling
brave and calm. THE END. A few hours later I woke and rang for breakfast. Another false alarm, but you can't be too careful. Death is no moment to be caught napping, and ninety-three a vulnerable age for a
woman living alone. My heart and guts may be sound, my memory still
good and my figure classic as ever, but I never ignore a strong vibration.
Many times over the last few weeks, even as I swallowed my Executive
Vitamin Pack, this one has warned me to *get set*. "Mission accomplished,"
it whispers firmly. The mad race is run, *and* won! And who am I to quarrel
with such a verdict? What more can I ask, now that a wonderful new era
has opened up for Baby?

Like any thinking moviegoer I've always known this life is a One Way
Passage and every damn one of us lives On Borrowed Time. No Sad
Songs for Me, then. Going it alone holds no terrors, for when the count-
down reaches zero we're alone anyway. Even the separation of body and

[369]

soul, the spirit kissing off the clay, is just a law of nature to me. *Nothing to it.* As she felt the big sleep coming on, poor dear old Hattie reached for my hand. Her lips formed silent words, then I heard "*closer*" and leaned close, expecting a last warning to keep Satan at bay. An hour earlier she'd been very doubtful I could manage that on my own. But she only said, "You old rattlebrain, try and remember to switch on your security system at night," and a moment later it was over. Time passed before I thought to disengage my hand from her dead one, partly because its grip was so fierce, partly because the TV was on with the sound turned down, and I got caught up trying to guess the title of the Constance Bennett picture on the screen. Then Connie appeared in an aviatrix outfit, climbed into the cockpit of a plane and made a smart take-off. With Hattie's dead hand still gripping mine, I exclaimed "*Tail Spin!*" Strange how the mind wanders unexpectedly.

The sun's going down. I look out the window and see the light fading, shadows growing longer. When I stop talking for a moment, the house is very silent. The vibration strikes again, telling me to say whatever is left to say, get those famous last words together, then go upstairs, lie down and *wait.* Will I wake up again after a few hours, ring for dinner or give myself a toot? Or will I . . . ? The house is very still. The light is fading, no color anywhere. As if I'm slipping into an old black-and-white movie.

I look back on my life and feel, as Mr. Sinatra sings, that I always did it "My Way." Nothing to regret except my failure to rescue MGM. But then I look forward and can hardly wait to meet Louis again. We'll talk it over and he'll explain where I went wrong. Timing is all, of course. There's a time to strike and a time to prepare to strike, and with MGM, it seems I missed both. But with the boardroom junta and even Baby against me, maybe the odds were too great. Or maybe I went wrong much earlier, pretending not to notice Louis's amorous eyes and his busy hands and his — "Are you packin' a rod or are you just pleased to see me?" as the one and only Mae used to ask, and Louis wasn't packin' a rod, no sirree, Louis wasn't packin' a rod. When we meet next time around he'll make it pretty clear where I went wrong, we'll have a few laughs and shed a few tears over it. One tango signal from Elva Kay and the great man would never have divorced his wife to marry a jumped-up cooch-dancer. One tango signal and I'd have hooked the mogul myself, then kept him on his throne until he died and it was mine. All the same. Mr. Lubitsch's pictures taught us that history is made in the bedroom, and history for yours truly was made in the bedroom of Mr. Benjamin Siegel. I chose romance and am proud of it. But wasn't there *some way* to grab the Culver City lot as well?

The sun's going down. Don't torture yourself. Check the machine again instead. Give my love to the sunrise. Playback. Okay for sound. Elva Kay taping her last. Where was I? The one that got away. If we're talking dollars and cents, mark MGM in the black, but if we're talking *dreams*, mark it deep in the red. The new boss may have taken over a studio, but his heart's in Vegas. And his Grand Hotel should be a hobby, not a hang-up. Louis ran his racing stables with one itchy finger of his left hand. I know the name of the game these days is diversification, all the studios are into ski resorts, the record business, pharmaceuticals, whatever, and I understand their thinking, always pick up the bucks where they fall. My God, I was diversifying forty years ago, before the word was invented, but it never stopped me *looking beyond the deal*. Then as now, the romantic spirit was my inspiration. And why? *What I was born into, I had to escape*. Yearning from my earliest days to breathe free. So it was for Louis, mogul extraordinary. He and his cohorts never forgot their humble beginnings, never lost touch with your tired, your poor, even as they thanked God for making them rich. "America, land of opportunity," Louis used to say. "It set me up in this great business of flowers for the living," simple words that brought tears to his eyes and mine. Even little Mr. Zukor, who was foolish enough to reject my terms for signing Baby — the memory of swatting him over the head with my purse still raises a chuckle — once spoke very wisely. "Imagine a boy like me becoming part of a great institution like this," he said. At least I think that's what he said. Wise or foolish, old Creepy always spoke thicker than goulash.

The new types running the studios came up *the easy way*, Baby tells me. No ghettos or back streets in their past, nothing to escape. They know every business aspect of the business, they're eager for the good life, jacuzzis, BMWs, wine, but never had a vision. Glorious shadows used to change the world, and this year's fantasy used to be next year's reality. Movies led. Now they follow. No trail blazing, just trailing.

"It takes all the romance out of crime," I said to Baby after *The Godfather*. "The Mafia took it out first," Baby said. "They turned their people into organization men working 9:00 to 5:00 outside the law. Just like the dreary crowd in the movie. The underworld's really gone downhill since Ben's day."

"Outer space has really gone downhill since Flash Gordon's day," I said to Baby after *Star Wars*. "Didn't he fix that evil planet for good and all? How could the new lot allow it to start acting up again?" Baby shrugged. "The new lot are not as bright as Flash. Chalk it up to the decline of education, which has even hit outer space and set it back God knows how many years."

"It takes all the romance out of monsters," I said to Baby after *Jaws*. "Two hours with a mundane killer shark leaves a person feeling distinctly snappish. Remember when monsters used to be *real characters*, scaring themselves as well as us? Kong made you sorry for every dim lovesick gargantuan brute in the world. Likewise another great symbol of the male animal, Dr. Frankenstein's husky childlike robot vainly searching for his soul. Where have depth and compassion gone?" Out to lunch, according to Baby, who tells me the world's gotten shallower and most people only pity themselves. "But if we're talking *dreams*," I began, and she cut me off with a laugh. "The shrinks are killing them. They treat dreams like early warning signals for cancer. So if you *must* have them," Baby said, "make sure they're healthy. Go to U.C.L.A. and take the Positive Dreaming course."

Everything very still now. The light's almost gone and the house feels so silent. Not a single familiar voice. My God, how could I *forget*?

(The tape goes silent. Mother must have gone from room to room switching on TV sets and tuning into old movies. When she speaks again there's a buzz of dialogue in the background, occasional bursts of music, gunfire, bells.)

Better recheck this machine, here comes the big vibration again telling me to go on record while I still can. Give me a whisky with a ginger ale on the side and don't be stingy, baby. Playback. Okay, where am I? This afternoon I took a nap and dreamed the land God made, and made on purpose, had reverted to type. If you don't keep watering the desert, it goes back to rock and sand and wrinkled joshua trees, which is how I saw the City of the Angels in my dream. A wind moaned through the dunes of Beverly Hills and Death Valley reached all the way to Universal. In Hollywood the land began to crack and explode with drought, buildings toppled crazily as another volcanic age began. Soon only saber-toothed cats prowled the ruins of the Pantages Theatre, and out Culver City way the most famous studio in the world was a nest of mammoth snakes.

My God. What a warning of the end of an era. *Apocalypse Now* and how to avoid it. The decline of Mr. Brando — no, the problem's even vaster than that. The problem is that sixty years ago we had no past here, if we're talking style, if we're talking aspiration, and then the movies turned a creative desert into a new Athens or Rome. But now, with the old spirit drying up, we could return even more quickly to desert again. And as the City of the Angels goes, they say, so goes America. Unless. . . .

Another classic voice speaking in the dark. Mr. de Mille once reminded us that the Divine Projectionist always makes the reels nearest THE END move faster. A cosmic hint, he used to say, that there's no time left for anything but our best work. So before it's too late, let's buckle down to the remake of *Mr. Smith Goes to Washington*! Turn Mr. Capra's finest fantasy to reality, get America back on the track with an alumnus of Hollywood's golden age in the White House! This has got to be the blockbuster package of the century: Washington provides Mr. Reagan with the big chance and the big picture Warner Brothers always denied him, and Mr. Reagan provides the nation with the image it's been waiting for. With a head full of folk wisdom and a heart as great as the world, small-town American boy walks off with the game. An image to rank alongside Garbo's for romance and Baby's for eternal childhood. An image to erase the shameful memory of the Carter family turning the White House into *Tobacco Road*. Ignore the nitpickers objecting that Mr. Reagan never made the Top Ten. No man who played a scene with Bette Davis or a whole picture with Barbara Stanwyck is likely to forget what we stand for. Bred in our unique tradition, he'll move heaven and earth to restore it. As Mr. Nixon said when I called him recluse to recluse at San Clemente, "Once you're in the stream of history you never get out."

Just hope I live to see this one. At least I've lived to see the greatest casting coup since Mr. Selznick found his Scarlett O'Hara. And when the time comes to audition some other important roles, I'm sure Mr. Reagan will remember that movie stars have always been our best ambassadors. But why do I feel a sudden headache coming on? And why is everything so dark? I can hardly—my God, would you believe it, they forgot to switch on the floodlights in my garden—what the hell are my visitors going to think? (*on the intercom*) LIGHTS!

(*Mother goes out to the terrace*)

No moon tonight. But why ask for the moon when we have the stars? Coop.

Bogie. Here's looking at you, kid.

Marilyn. Too shy to show her face for many years, very late when she finally turned up around 4:00 a.m. last spring, now obviously having a ball. God bless her.

But Pickford couldn't wait to get back where she wanted to be. Little Mary time all the time. A white bow peeping out of those famous ringlets, grown again in all their glory. God bless her.

Strange how Doug avoids her. And gives her dark looks, as if he expects her to turn into an *Omen*. Or a case for *The Exorcist*. Does he know something we never . . . ?

Such a different story when the King first saw Joan again. Before you could say *Possessed* they started reliving it. Me too. One of the great emotional experiences. It launched Joan's *haunted glamor* cycle, the world at her feet, yet secretly lonely and afraid, some dark mysterious force always driving her on and on to — *who knows?*

Duke.

Beloved Marion.

Flynn. Did he and Truman Capote *really* have a one-night stand?

La Grable, in showbiz for two very good reasons and standing on both of them. God bless her.

Spence.

"More stars than there are in heaven, Elva." Louis's voice in the night, very close. "And Baby among them."

I see Jeanette waving.

My kind never runs out of rainbows.

Baby Looks Back

That evening I was taping the Merv Griffin show and when I got home the phone was ringing. One of Mother's servants told me to come over quickly. The wrought iron gates to the driveway stood wide open and the grounds were dazzlingly floodlit. The front door and the french windows at the far end of the livingroom stood open as well. Nobody had thought to turn off all the TV sets, a shot rang out and for a moment I was in a Raymond Chandler novel, summoned to the vast hidden estate with its lawns, fountains, cypresses, roses, its grand Mediterranean villa, anxious squad of servants and body on the terrace.

Mother lay crouched on her side, unconscious but disturbed, her face violently flushed, her breathing and pulse very rapid. Only her eyes were calm, but seemed locked open. I picked up the battery recorder she must have dropped before blanking out and played back the last moments of the tape. "I see Jeanette waving. My kind never runs out of rainbows." The servants told me how they found her by accident. Everything was as usual that evening, except they forgot to switch on the garden lights and Mother shouted for them over the intercom. A few minutes later they heard a crash and felt the house shake. In the den, the Anna May Wong chandelier had mysteriously fallen from the ceiling. They stared at the glittering wreckage, then the housekeeper noticed Mother beyond the window, lying on the terrace in a glare of floodlights.

I sat with her in the ambulance, holding her hand. It was very warm, but limp. She still breathed furiously. At the hospital they wheeled her into a lab for emergency tests. I waited in the corridor outside, frowned at for smoking by an intern and a nurse as they passed. Then a young doctor came out. "Imagine the human equivalent of an earthquake around 9, or even 9.5, on the Richter scale," he said. "That was the kind of massive cerebral hemorrhage your Mother suffered." He described her heart as the strongest he'd ever heard, even though she was blind, paralyzed on one side and in a deep coma.

"Super-survivor type, she might even come out of it," the doctor said. "But I don't think you'd want her to. Unless you believe in survival at any price."

"I believe Mother will name her own price. She always did."

A few minutes later I watched her die. Her breathing turned to a dry rattle, slowed down, quieted down and stopped. Her eyes remained stubbornly open. They checked her heart and pulse, pulled a sheet over her body and I felt hideously relieved. Mother had such romantic hopes for her death scene, at least she never woke to see them defeated. The smell of vomit was ghastly. But as they started to wheel her out, I felt hideously cheated. Not only by the fact of her death but the way it arrived without warning, denying us a last moment together. How could you leave without saying goodbye? I thought, drew back the sheet and kissed her face. It was still purplish, shocked and angry. I followed the stretcher down a corridor and remembered the last time we talked. Two days earlier she was lounging on a canopied swingseat by the pool, wearing huge tinted glasses and sipping champagne. I looked over her shoulder and saw us both projected on a large screen in the poolhouse. She'd recently installed a TV camera that scanned her estate night and day, and the videocast appeared instantly in her new poolhouse media room as well as her private theatre. "Call me hypertensive but I've got another crackerjack project for the boardroom junta." Usually, she explained, she never encouraged EKE to compete in an overcrowded field, but the video-stereo home entertainment center was a development we'd be fools to ignore. "Even though I disapprove of the whole trend in a way, think how our movie palaces will sink into even deeper neglect. But people *are* staying home nights because of violence in the streets, so let's pick up those bucks where they fall. Like land in the old days, the rights to a slew of old movies are still up for grabs. And did you know that cassettes of *Psycho* were selling like hotcakes, coast to coast, as a Mother's Day gift last year?"

When I got back to Villa Elva the servants were waiting up. I told them to switch off all the TV sets, it was over. A great silence filled the house. After the garden floodlights were switched off as well, the cypresses stood out darker than everything else, and very still. Then I had what Mother would have called a vibration. Appearances were so important to her, I thought, and they would still matter when she was dead. Mortuary cosmeticians usually botched the job. I remembered Miss Sophie in her casket, looking as if she'd had a cheap face-lift.

The tropical perfume still lingered in Mother's bathroom. She'd forgotten to close the safe and the door hung slightly open, like a sign. I stepped inside, to a small room with soft concealed lighting and shelves built into the walls. Producing a weird yet familiar thrill of terror, the door began to swing back behind me. I was on the Kid Sherlock set, Mother and Will Hays watching as I broke into a safe and got trapped inside, then heard Hays whinny like a horse with laughter. In fact there was no reason to panic this time, the door was off the latch.

Mother kept her cosmetics and rejuvenation formulas in the safe, and its shelves were stacked with bottles, jars, brushes, pads, vibrators. Starting to pick out a few things, I noticed one shelf with a display like a head shop. Disposable hypodermics in plastic wrappers, Tiffany snuff boxes, gold sniffing spoons, rolled hundred dollar bills with fake art nouveau wrappers marked COCA, and a collection of mirrored silver cigarette boxes, all except one full to the brim with sparkling white nose candy.

I took a sniff which gave me a quick but not sensational boost, nothing to compare with stumbling upon Mother's secret. Or rather, the first of her secrets. This one, when I look back, seemed to explain more than the rest, the energy hardly slowed down by time, the shifting moods, over-aroused and remote, pitiless and soft-hearted, competitive and cool, the eternal slimness, the "temporary" sinus problem. But it also set me the biggest puzzle. How did Mother's vital functions hold up so well? Although she kept to her Adelle Davis health program, she only started it in middle age, continued to drink me under the table, and was still sniffing and even shooting at ninety-three. Then I remembered why she considered rock groups a risky investment. "Stoned out of their skulls, Baby, and apparently incapable of metering the habit." Once again, I supposed, she knew where to draw the line after going too far.

It was late. I lay down in a guestroom right below the Tower Room added when Mother remodeled the house. "A touch of old Spain, I got the idea from *Adventures of Don Juan* and the spiral staircase from an auction," but she only used it to store junk. Faint scurrying sounds came from the Tower Room but I paid no attention. I was exhausted and finally alone, as they say, with my grief. It was a far cry from the grief I used to play in movies, when directors warned me against making it *ugly,* and reminded me that my sad situation was taken care of later in the story. If my grief had been on camera that night, the director would have ordered a retake, cooled off and played down.

It was later, but I couldn't sleep. I turned from one side to the other and was always facing the past. A year ago, coming into the house and hearing Mother on the phone. The famous Hollywood sign in the hills had fallen apart, the chamber of commerce had formed a committee to restore it and was soliciting contributions. *"If you can't save the sign, you can't save Hollywood,"* Mother said. "Yes sirree, that's one hell of a slogan." Then she promised twenty-five thousand dollars to save the second O, but refused to have the letter dedicated to her. "Helping to preserve one of the great symbols of civilization is enough. I prefer to remain anonymous."

"For years you were a crazy publicity hound, now you prefer to remain anonymous," I said. "Is it still just because of the *Enquirer?*"

"That wound will never quite heal. But something else hit me later." She lay back on an Empire sofa. "The more important you really are, the less you give people to talk about."

"What a complex character. So vulnerable and so tough."

"Any woman born into a man's world is vulnerable, Baby. Any woman who survives it has got to be tough."

"Such a romantic, yet such a realist."

"Why settle for one or the other? It only creates problems." She smiled. "Given my unusual circumstances, I'm the simplest woman who ever lived. *You're* the complex character."

It was later still, and a caravan of one. I thought of all the passengers who boarded our caravan for a while along the way. Compared with Mother even the brightest, even Jimmy Gabriel, seemed to have come and gone like shadows. "Everything I've done is because of you," she used to say, but wasn't it also true that everything I'd done was because of her? "Strange how the secret pattern of our lives threads on and on," she used to say, making it sound like chance, but wasn't it part of the kismet plan? Before I was born she carried me around like her future, and after she died I was carrying her around like my past. We blended into each other.

"Hold it, I'll be right over," I said when the cosmetician from Forest Lawn called to ask about Mother's chief personality traits, so he could recreate her image. He'd read the obituaries and the tributes from the executive world, knew he was getting a Very Big Picture but needed human detail. Half an hour later I turned my Rolls into the mortuary driveway and the past. "Among the stars and under the stars," she murmured approvingly, checking famous markers the day we went out there to choose our graves. After touring the Columbarium we followed a guide through the Mystery of Life garden and faint Wurlitzer music was piped in from behind hibiscus bushes. Now she lay on a work table in a white hospital gown, her face drained of color, worn, shattered. The room was chilled and full of sweet beauty parlor smells. The cosmetician was washing his hands at a sink. "This is where I take over," I said, and he said, "*What?*" I opened Mother's makeup case, and his face went almost as pale as hers. "You can't do that, it's unheard of." I began laying out pots and brushes. "One of your slogans here is Comfort to the Bereaved," I said. "If you don't live up to it, I'll take Mother somewhere else. And no one has to know. I don't want a credit, officially you did another great job."

He backed away, as if expecting me to pull a gun from the case, then watched silently as I set to work. It wasn't difficult. I had seen Mother set to work so often, knew how to apply the special Pan-Cake mixture that glazed her skin, knew how she stretched it and smoothed out facial lines with gauze tape stuck under her hair, knew the correct amounts of green eyeliner and silvery coral lip gloss. Finally we slipped her into an Adrian creation I'd brought along, a blue and gold cocktail number with Egyptian motifs and a headdress. "The image is She," I explained. And there was a touch of Tutankhamen as well.

It had taken maybe half an hour, which passed like a minute. "That was a true labor of love," I said to the cosmetician, lighting a cigarette. "Please go away now, I'd like to be alone with her." He closed the door. I stared at Mother and remembered her saying there was no movie in which she would rather die than *Lost Horizon*. Serene and beautified, she was now the pride of Shangri-La. Nowhere a trace of the cruel actual movie of her death. I shivered a little on account of the artificial chill, and felt we had our last moment together after all.

But when the funeral service ended and her body whizzed discreetly down a chute, I felt cheated again. Why should that last loving tribute to Mother's image be burned to a crisp? "Because that's the way I want it, Baby. Promise you'll never let me rot six feet under until I look like something out of a horror cheapie."

After the funeral I followed the junta's limousine to the Control Center, where Mother's will was to be read. We began at 2:30, broke for cocktails at 6:00, resumed half an hour later and called a wrap around 8:00. The reason it became such a marathon affair was that Mother left instructions a mile long for the dismantling of EKE. "It was never really Baby's baby and I feel sure she'll be happy to get the great pyramid off her back. *But let's see to it Uncle Sam's pickings are as slim as possible."* Her plans for mergers, reshuffles and cross-collateralizations were too technical for me, but held the board spellbound. The Calhern type even hummed Hail to the Chief under his breath.

The disposal of Mother's fortune began with legacies to household servants, bequests to charities and "small but I consider *perfectly adequate* tokens of esteem for my Cabinet." The junta grimaced a little at being found worth only five thousand dollars apiece in government bonds, less than the servants. Mother left the remainder to "my daughter Baby, alpha and omega of my life," and proceeded to list her earthly goods, all sums raised after EKE went on the block, her real estate holdings, her cash in hand banked in Switzerland, Luxembourg and the Bahamas as well as Los Angeles, her gold reserve, her diamond mine shares, her house and its entire contents. I lit a cigarette and a long silence fell while the Calhern type scribbled calculations on a sheet of paper. Finally he said. "An amount in the area of two hundred fifty million dollars will be coming your way."

"Before or after taxes?" I asked.

"After."

Another long silence fell, then a final surprise item was read out. Mother also left me a package she called Special Project Tomorrow. It was a survival hideout, secretly built to order and paid for out of yet another private account, afterwards closed, in Singapore. In her grandest real estate brochure style, she described an underground fortress set deep in the heart of a Colorado pine forest. This unique property was equipped with bullet-proof, radar-protected entrance, generator, air-conditioning plant, subterranean reservoir. It was comprised of livingroom, dining area, master and guest bedroom suites with bath, all-electric kitchen, cellarage stacked with enough canned and freeze-dried food, bottled spring water *and* champagne to last a decade, small arms and machine gun depot, special safe for the storage of gold and jewelry, guaranteed to fool any metal detector. "Yours truly has never been a pessimist, but wishes to rest assured that in the event of world catastrophe, Baby will emerge a winner."

After the others left I stayed behind in the Oval Office. A portrait of Mother, commissioned from the artist who did Gene Tierney's portrait for *Laura*, hung on the wall. Our eyes met, and the concentrated weight of her love seemed even more overwhelming now that she was dead. I thought of Jimmy saying, "You let her take you over," and wondered how anyone could have rejected or curbed or escaped such generous, ravenous, fixated love. I mixed another martini and raised my glass to the portrait. If Mother was resting now, she was resting assured. Her love continued to operate and rule. Two hundred fifty million dollars after taxes on its way to the alpha and omega of her life, and in the event of world catastrophe I'd be safely sipping champagne in my underground stronghold, beside a safe full of undetectable gold. No one could emerge more of a winner than that.

The weight of her love struck me again when I found her diaries in the Tower Room. There were scuffling sounds as I climbed the spiral staircase, and as I opened the door, mice scattered in every direction. Moths flew out of a trunk of discarded finery, and right outside the window, which was open a few inches, rats nesting in a palm tree watched with small wary eyes. It was like the scene in *Freckles* when I wandered into an old shack on the edge of the Limberlost at twilight, and met a company of bats. They squeaked and fluttered as if I was disturbing secrets. This time I was rescuing them, diaries, scrapbooks, letters and photographs gnawed and mildewed over the years, often smeared with mouse droppings as well.

There was a smell of time, old and greasy and nauseating, like standing water. "I felt *historic*," I read as a page fell open. "My life was going to be one of a kind and future generations will want to know!" But a sign of the spaced out times was that Mother failed to notice how her history lay moldering. A few pages later she was firing her gun at William Desmond Taylor's heart. "There's more in my Pandora's Box than you ever guessed." How *much* more? I wondered as a wild idea occurred. Maybe, on other pages too ruined to decipher, Mother fired again? Then a later entry made me sad. "With Baby in my life I'll never feel truly lonely, but I feel lonely enough without Ben." She certainly paid enough for those nights outside time. Elsewhere in her life she seemed starved for human intimacy, except with me.

"What I was born into, I had to escape." In her elaborate showcase of a livingroom I listened to her voice on the cassettes. It spoke on and on, funny, angry, nostalgic, planning, fantasizing, but always alone. "A goodbye, a click and I'm alone again, in a way more alone than ever." Filling the house, her voice and aloneness began to spook me. In her will Mother asked me to consider preserving it as a national monument, but I looked around and knew the place had died with her. All those earthly goods needed her presence, walking down the marble staircase in some brilliant theatrical creation, watching TV from her *Cleopatra* bed, mixing drinks at the Wild West bar, playing the songs from *Top Hat* in her greenhouse-loggia. Or the two of us eating Christmas dinner like royalty in exile, too many servants waiting at the round table with eighteen empty chairs. "Glorious shadows used to change the world." The house had become almost as cozy as a tomb. Better to let it go, like her tricked-out body, down the chute.

For several days quiet expressionless men in dark suits moved around the house, checking the inventory. With a mortuary air they reckoned up movie star furs and gowns in a series of closets, diamond jewelry in a series of cases. They counted silverware and crystal, Venetian mirrors, Empire sofas, oriental rugs, they evaluated all the marble and gold fittings, and the movie mementos from the candlesticks used in *Queen Christina* to the record of Valentino singing. "This kind of thing has extraordinary market value now," one of them told me after asking permission to play "Pale Hands I Loved" and making sure it was still in good condition. "I recommend upping it to two thousand five hundred dollars." He also recommended upping the John Gilbert monogrammed sheets. "Miss Dietrich owns the only other certified pair."

I felt sure he'd have priced the stash of coke with the same professional solemnity. It had taken me awhile to decide what to do with all that happy dust. I wasn't about to become a user in my late sixties and flushing it down toilets seemed a boring waste. Two or three sharp young studio exectives I'd met struck me as likely customers, but why risk a social error? In the end I poured the stuff into sandwich baggies with twist ties and dropped them stealthily in the ladies' rooms at top restaurants like Ma Maison and the Bistro, in a corridor in the Thalberg building at MGM, underneath the newsstand counter at Schwab's, behind racks at expensive Beverly Hills stores, Neiman Marcus and St. Laurent. No news story ever broke about plastic bags of C turning up mysteriously all over town. I guess they were found and carried off in nothing flat.

A long procession of trucks hauled everything off to antique stores and auction company warehouses. I watched it move slowly down the driveway, then turned back into the empty house. The air was hazy with dust. It gradually settled in Mother's former bedroom, which for the first time in a long time I remembered was Jimmy's former bedroom as well.

When a petro-rich Kuwaiti bought the house he remodeled it once more, in early Maria Montez. And after bulldozers leveled the White House, a black plexiglass high-rise took the place of EKE. All the same, I felt Mother continued to rest assured. When I visited her grave with a concealed loudspeaker not far away, Wurlitzer music drifting softly, eternally across banks of eternally bright flowers and the weather-resistant gold plaque with her name traced inside a star, it was impossible not to believe she'd walked off into the sunset.

Professionally speaking, so had I. For a while after my series folded I was offered cameo roles in TV movies, but it's amazing how much you find in a part when you're under contract or need the money, how little when you're footloose and taken care of. No way I would get up at 5:00 a.m. to play your warmhearted widow or coldhearted spinster, or even your mythical lady gunfighter. "We're shooting for legend on this one, but tongue in cheek, the relevant image is Kate Hepburn in *African Queen* set down in the mythical man's world of the old West," the producer explained. "Dig," I said, aware there was a very sharp new executive type sitting behind the desk, but turned him down and decided to get through the seventies recording Edgar Rice Burroughs sci-fi for the blind.

Then, a year or so before Mother died, I received a letter from a Mr. Leonard E. Guidoboni, who described himself as a great fan and movie buff. He begged for an interview in connection with his forthcoming book, *The Films of Baby Jewel*. "You may smile, but I always knew you'd be hailed as a classic," Mother said. "Starved for romance, wit and beauty, thousands have turned back to our golden past." A copy of *The Films of Basil Rathbone* lay on her lap. She set it down on a coffee table beside *The Irene Dunne Story.* "Movie buffs are opening the eyes of the world, Baby." All kinds of movie books were certainly pouring off the presses, there seemed to be a demand for them, and for revivals of old movies as well. Even in Starlight City, where most people only cared about the latest anything, a salute to Busby Berkeley or a tribute to MGM drew packed houses. But as far as I knew, only Mr. Guidoboni's eyes were opening to Baby Jewel. When I scanned the flier for the MGM series, it reminded me of the time I used to report for no work at the studio and check the billboards advertising current productions. Every name on the star roster was there except mine.

Mr. Guidoboni was younger than I expected, in his early twenties, lean and small, wearing old faded denims. He had a white goatish face with an indoor, almost cave-dweller pallor, as if he lived in movie theatres, which he confessed that he did, except when he sat home watching old movies on the tube. *Footlights* on the dawn show, it turned out, introduced him to my unique talent. He was already researching a study of early screen vamps, *The Rhinestone Years*, but dropped everything. "*Words cannot describe*," was how he described his first exposure to Baby Jewel, but I begged him to try. After a while he said, "I hope this doesn't sound inadequate. Ten minutes into your pciture, I knew I was watching the greatest child star of them all."

"Mr. Guidoboni, I would like to offer you a drink."

He asked for a Tab and went on, "I only got up to watch your picture because of a letter in *TV Guide* that week, singing your praises and demanding to see more of your old films. It roused my interest even though I knew the letter was some kind of weird hoax."

"No hoax, it was Mother and she meant every word. She's been singing my praises to *TV Guide* for years, hoping to start what she calls a Baby Jewel Revival."

"But the letter was signed Rauff de Ryther."

"She likes to invent slightly offbeat names."

Mr. Guidoboni shook his head. "This name was not invented. It's the real name of David Manners, remember *him*? Hepburn's leading man in her first movie, *Bill of Divorcement*, and he claimed he was descended from William the Conqueror. It made quite an impression at the time. More than his performance did, frankly."

I remembered thinking as a child that Mother, like God, moved in mysterious ways. I also remembered, a few years back, suggesting the name Oliotha Shugg to her, which she turned down because it didn't sound real. "Let me lay a few more names on you," I said. "Alexandra Zuck, Tula Ellice Finklea, Ella Geisman, Ann La Hiff."

"Sandra Dee, Cyd Charisse, June Allyson, Nancy Carroll." He didn't hesitate. "Carroll was another actress of strangely luminous talent. She died in mysterious circumstances, on her knees in front of a TV set."

"You're so young and so full of unusual information."

"I believe in information." Mr. Guidoboni sipped his Tab. "You have to *know*. It's the only way to become an expert." A sudden gleam appeared in his rather dull brown eyes as he opened a notebook. "For instance, here's an interesting point I'd like to clear up. Was your original story for *Top of the World* influenced by Capra's *Lady for a Day*?"

Mr. Guidoboni seemed disappointed when I told him it was influenced by watching Shipwreck Kelly climb a flagpole. But for almost two hours he tried to clear up other interesting points, until I said, "We've only talked about my early serials and my films for MGM. Why don't you ask me about the one movie I really like?"

His eyes were dull again, almost murky. "But we've covered them all except *Two of a Kind*."

"That's the one. And I'd like to put in a word for Roy William Neill as a great unsung craftsman of Poverty Row."

He seemed disappointed again. "Of course I admire your work in that picture, but it comes across less *personal* than your MGM triumphs. Even though," he admitted, "you're right in a way about Neill. *Sherlock Holmes and the Spider Woman* was full of brio as well. But when you view him in perspective, from the early *Black Room* to his swan song *Black Angel*, which had a real gem of a performance by Dan Duryea, something's missing. You ask yourself finally, who *was* Roy William Neill?''

"Did you never ask yourself finally, who *was* Baby Jewel?"

Mr. Guidoboni smiled. "You've got to be joking. Ten minutes into *Footlights* I felt I'd known you all my life. And certainly wished I had. You were one of the great *role models* of your time." It was the time of Mary Pickford, he reminded me, and later of Shirley Temple, the time of the easy road to moppet popularity, Cinderella types rescued from garbage cans, smuggling favorite ponies into their orphanage beds and, excuse him, shit like that. Scorning this approach, Baby Jewel was a loner and rebel from the start. Her career opened like a pistol shot. Who else would have dared to disguise herself as an adult male detective, the only Sherlock Holmes secure enough to dispense with Watson? And who else could have topped this by going on to play colorful dominating woman of history, giving us an incredible gallery of powerful queens, cunning whores and spies, even a saint in armor? Then MGM signed her and she still refused to be tamed. Unlike Andy Hardy she broke away from her family to become a famous novelist or actress, and when she agreed to stay home, as in *Top of the World*, it was to set her family back on its feet. Like her older contemporary Garbo, she walked alone and extended the female horizon.

I listened and was amazed. Long after I'd given up acting, the image factory continued to work for me; long after Baby Jewel was forgotten it invented a new one. "Now listen, you can't ignore Sid Gordon, Mr. Mayer, Mr. Thalberg, all those writers and directors," I said. "I was just a creation of other people. And when they ran out of ideas, I ceased to exist."

Emotion seemed to make Mr. Guidoboni's face grow even paler. "So who *inspired* all those people? Forty years later, who inspired *me*? When I see you on the screen, I understand why audiences loved and envied you, like they love and envy all great stars. Your kind of childhood, your kind of springtime, they'd have given anything for. I know *I* would," he said more quietly, and looked away.

When I asked Mr. Guidoboni about his own childhood and springtime, he continued to look away and didn't answer at first. Then he said, "*Words cannot describe*," and asked for another Tab. His face was almost ashen.

A few moments from the life of Baby Jewel came back to me. Orphans in an institution who stared at me in a longing silence I feared would never break. A shipload of gifts from people all over the world, filling half a stage on my official eleventh birthday. The woman who rushed up to Mother and said she'd kill to have a daughter like me. Mr. Griffith stroking my curls and saying, "The kid's got it," and Mrs. Root saying, "Everything up there is because of *you*," and Howard Hughes saying as he stretched out on a couch in a room that shut out the daylight, *"Your* reality is very clear to me." Then I suddenly laughed and asked Mr. Guidoboni if he ever saw my TV series. "Nobody could have been inspired by Pauline," I said. "Or envied her, or for God's sake taken her as a role model. What a dope. But the same person you felt you'd known all your life. Or was my Babyhood just a flash in the pan? Did I burn out?"

He only shrugged. "Frankly I see *Pauline* as a kind of footnote to your career."

"Seventeen years is a hell of a long footnote."

"Every great star," Mr. Guidoboni informed me, "even Crawford, even Davis, even you, is *diminished* by the tube. There seems to be a sinister process at work. When I think of your series, I think of *The Incredible Shrinking Woman*. It was like you were too big for the medium, and it cut you down to size by passing you through a deadly invisible cloud of pollution."

"I really like that idea," I said. "But then I'm a sci-fi addict. Always was. At the age of eight or whatever, I imagined some kind of invisible ray turned me into a movie star, and I was changed without knowing it."

He nodded. "May I quote you?" he asked. "And don't tell me, incidentally, that the tube ever felt like *home*. The way a movie studio did."

"You're right. It felt like a motel. People in the next room always checking out in the middle of the night, because the ratings were no good."

"I believe we've taken care of the *Pauline* question," Mr. Guidoboni said. "We could sum it up by saying you were *not really yourself* in that series. Could I impose on you for a last Tab? I'm always thirsty."

Between sips he told me that he worked for a couple of theatres specializing in old movies, wrote program notes and thought up new ideas for tributes. "To coincide with publication of my book, I'm planning a Baby Jewel Season at the Hollywood-Sunset. Will you consent to take a bow opening night?"

"Baby Take a Bow," I said. "Remember Shirley Temple singing that?"

"In *Stand Up and Cheer*, 1934, directed by Hamilton McFadden if I'm not mistaken." He frowned. "It's a mystery how McFadden got the assignment, considering he'd done little except Charlie Chan features before. And afterwards it was back to the Bs again."

"I'll be around if there's anyone left to stand up and cheer at the end of the program."

When Mr. Guidoboni finished his Tab, I showed him out and saw only my Rolls parked in the driveway. He moved toward a pedal bicycle propped against the wall, movie books almost spilling out of the carrier basket. I imagined him pedaling devotedly, come rain or shine, to all the revival theatres scattered across the city. Out of doors he looked even more abnormally pale. And strict, like a monk.

"Was it a long ride over here? This is a pretty steep hill, anyway."

"I'm used to that." He seemed unconcerned. "And I'm centrally located."

"Hollywood?"

He nodded. "The Alhambra Lodge. It's one of the oldest apartment buildings in town, used to be the Apache Arms, and opened in 1913 as the Yucca Riviera. You can go anywhere from there."

"I guess you can. Wait a minute." I went back to the house, wrote a check, and came out again. "Please accept this. You need proper wheels."

He looked ready to faint. "You mustn't do this."

"Please take it. I've always heard writers are underpaid in this town anyway."

"It's too much." He was staring at the check. "You wrote one zero too many."

I shook my head. "What can you get for five hundred dollars these days?"

He smiled suddenly and said, "This is like the movies."

"Like they used to be."

Mr. Guidoboni folded the check carefully, put it away, got on his bicycle and raced downhill. He waved before disappearing around a corner. I felt puzzled and touched and somehow doubtful whether *The Films of Baby Jewel* would see the light of day. But an advance copy arrived in the mail, on the cover a photograph of someone who looked the way I felt in my golden age. The face was hopeful and suspicious at the same time. It had a stubborn energy and a touch of jailbait. I tried to react to it as a stranger, someone who never saw me in my distant prime. Would the face stir imagination or desire? Would a stranger open the book and marvel at the Many Faces of Baby Jewel, as Kid Sherlock with a magnifying glass held up to one eye and magnifying it, eating an ice cream cone on top of a flagpole, roaming the Limberlost with a butterfly net? Would he glance through the text, light on Leonard E. Guidoboni's passage about my instinct for truth, and decide to risk $6.95?

"Never doubt it. Greatness shines out from these pages." I put it down to coincidence that Mother happened to be looking at a page with a pho-

tograph of herself. Super-glamorous, waving, wrapped in her ermine pelisse at the premiere of *Fantasia*. "A volume to treasure, to come back to
again and again," she went on, lapsing into publishers' hype. Then she
added, "I only wish they'd left out the picture of you and Jimmy Gabriel
in a pool of blood. Somehow it breaks the spell."

For a moment she resolved to come out of seclusion and accompany me
to the opening night of my Revival. "Don't we owe the world one last
triumphant entrance together, Baby?" Then a look of veiled fear crossed
her face and she clutched my hand. "Maybe so, but it's *your* night and I
don't want to take anything away from you."

I told Mr. Guidoboni not to expect me until the program ended, sitting
through my old movies was out of the question. "All that part of my life is
in flashback now," I explained. "It's memory, and we get along with each
other best that way. I don't want the past suddenly leaping out at me like
a mugger on a dark night." And it was certainly a dark night, no moon,
thin high clouds, a dimly lit boulevard halfway between Hollywood and
downtown. The Hollywood-Sunset theatre was an Aztec-style relic from
the twenties standing in a typical nowhere area, scrawny palm trees,
liquor and delicatessen store, TV and stereo center, dry cleaner's, Credit
Dentist and a bar called The Lasso. To judge from the pickup trucks
parked outside and the western types going in and out, it catered to the
gay urban cowboy trade.

The area was typically nowhere but had once been somewhere, for the
theatre stood almost opposite the site of Mr. Griffith's studio. Every trace
of him had vanished, of course, and Babylon was a subdivision of family
homes. I tried to remember how everything looked sixty years earlier and
felt pretty sure there was only the studio, a view of Babylon and poppy
fields. Like so much of the city, it was just beginning. Now it was ending,
or getting ready to begin again. Next to the theatre was a bulldozed lot,
the fence around it covered with posters for rock concerts. And a billboard
announced, Watch This Space.

There was no parking space within two blocks of the Hollywood-
Sunset, so I left my world on wheels in the red zone right outside the
entrance. Maybe the theatre was full, but its lack of glamour would have
appalled Mother. "Remember our premieres in the old days, Baby?
Searchlights sweeping the sky, crowds straining against the police cordon, and the almost savage cry that went up as yet another star alighted
from her limousine?" In the empty lobby the popcorn-soft drinks counter
was closed. A few unsold copies of *The Films of Baby Jewel* had been locked
away in the display section, beside the peanut brittle. Posters for my movies decorated the walls and there was a display of stills, but the budget

could never have run to all those flower arrangements. Dahlias, roses, birds of paradise everywhere. I knew Mother must have ordered them, and Mr. Guidoboni told me later that she even sent workmen to set up hanging baskets from the ceiling.

I sneaked a glance into the auditorium. *The Bluebird* had almost ended, and Mytil was leaving the Land of Memory as I waited to enter it. A title appeared, something about the secret of happiness, tinted blue. Then the lights went up to decent applause.

As Mr. Guidoboni led me to the stage, banked with more flowers, the applause grew louder. I noted some middle-aged couples, and a handful of the very old, but on the whole the audience was young. It didn't conform to any popular image. This was obviously not the beach crowd, or the student crowd that packed Westwood on a weekend night, not the health-food store or singles or Legalize Marijuana crowd. In fact it was *not a crowd*. It was the silent minority, and very silent at first when Mr. Guidoboni invited questions from the floor. Finally a woman weighing maybe two hundred fifty pounds, with long red hair, doll-like painted face and a sundress, told me she used to sing on the radio at the age of five and was known as the San Antonio Baby. She wanted to know why child stars went out of fashion. It was like a timer's gun fired in my ear. "Anyone in the house tonight who'll admit to being a child?" I asked. A few youngsters gazed furtively at me, but not one of them volunteered. "There's your answer," I said, off and running. "If children are out, naturally child stars are out. Teenagers have been in for years, of course, but that's a different kettle of fish. Look at the way they wiggle their sharp little asses as they plug brand-name jeans on TV." I told how an editorial in the *Times* once begged me never to grow up, a weird and shameful idea today, but very big at the time. I recalled waiting in Sid Gordon's office to be auditioned for *Kid Sherlock*, surrounded by Mothers who had heard about the high value placed on eternal childhood and brought their eternal children all the way from Oklahoma.

"*Do you have any regrets?*" a voice called, and the gun went off again. "Just a couple. I regret never being directed by Mr. Griffith and I regret signing a contract with Mr. Howard Hughes." I told how Mother gate-crashed the *Broken Blossoms* set while Gish screamed in a closet, and how the great man bestowed his seal of approval when I danced and improvised for him later. I described being driven to meet Howard in a blindfold, flown over the Grand Canyon at dawn, photographed wearing only a few sparklers, then locked in the stable for ten years.

"What was Louis B. Mayer *really like*?" Plenty to draw out from the memory bank there. "Did you ever meet Garbo?" Another withdrawal slip, and out came the story of Mother meeting the false Garbo. "Did you ever feel *cut off from normal life*?" Almost drew a blank there. "Not that I can recall. My life seemed incredibly ordinary at the time. Except for one thing. I missed out on a regular education." Someone said, "Lucky you," then Mr. Guidoboni announced it was almost midnight and he had a few points to make before we closed this memorable occasion.

"It was hard to grow up in the sixties. There was this terrible backlash against movie stars. All the kids I knew were saying, gods and goddesses are out of date, this is democracy, give us *ourselves* on the screen, people in tune with *now*. And a monster was created." Mr. Guidoboni was deathly white. "The *anti-star*," he said. "Claiming to reject the old ways, thinking it smart to live anywhere but here, taking *political stands*, carrying on about personal freedom. Meanwhile society almost disintegrated for lack of true gods and real stars. The Moonies were taking over, and Hare Krishna, and LSD. Return to the dark ages. People lost their way in the dark. Now they're beginning to see the light again and realize what they lost." Scattered applause. "Tonight we saw a real star in a classic Hollywood picture and it was an amazingly profound experience. She led us on a personal quest for happiness through time and space. She brought us face to face with death and rebirth. *Words cannot describe*," Mr. Guidoboni said, looking at me with his strange dull eyes. "But let me try. When you made *The Bluebird*, you pre-empted *2001*."

In the lobby I signed autographs. A neat old lady in a fading silk coat told me she worked as a secretary at MGM while I was there. "In the transport department," she said sadly. "We never met, although I met Mr. Gable once. I always loved all your pictures. It *was* the best time, wasn't it?" Meanwhile a young man was giving me sad looks. He turned away and I overheard him remark, "Doesn't she *know* she's a freak?" And then someone unshaven was holding a card in front of my face. "I am deaf and dumb but wrote the bluebird for you." I thanked him, saying it was one of my favorite scripts, and he smiled happily as someone led him away.

After saying goodnight to Mr. Guidoboni and thanking him too, I walked to my Rolls. Waiting beside it was a tall, deeply tanned, silver-haired man in a safari suit. "I don't suppose you remember me, but I played your little brother."

"I'm sorry. There were so many little brothers." Then I looked him over carefully. "The Dressler picture," I said. "You were going blind."

He shook his head. "In the movie tonight."

The scene-stealing moppet bastard I hated so much. "But why didn't you introduce yourself before?" I asked, and flung my arms around him.

"It was your night, Baby. Guidoboni's a nut but he's right about one thing. You are more than terrific, especially in person."

"Well, thank you. I did feel a click, as if the performance was suddenly coming together."

"What performance?" It seemed to puzzle him. "That was you."

"Still in the business?" I asked.

"I gave up acting at sixteen. Went to U.C.L.A., took a degree in psychology. . . ."

"So you got out."

"Wait a minute. For a while I taught and lectured. Then I wrote a paper on the psychology of market research for radio, which landed me a job in the promotion department at NBC. Later of course I moved into TV. Ever watch the Mike Douglas show?"

"Now and then. We all get strange moods."

"Mike will love you. The past is *in* again and nobody talks old Hollywood the way you do. Crazy, wonderful, authentic."

What can I tell you? Mike loved me. My friend had primed him to love me, of course, and by the time we met the *Times* and the *Examiner* had done stories on my Revival, finding my vehicles on the flimsy side but my talent unique. Anyway, Mike loved me. After the first show viewers called in to say they loved me too, and he asked me back. Same thing happened with Dinah Shore. Then came the big time, out of the memory bank on the Merv Griffin show spilled glamor and tinsel, heartbreak and farce. What can I tell you? "The way you talk it is the way people want to hear it," said my friend in market research. "You know how to *put it across*. You always did. Born with the secret, I guess."

Mother lived long enough to catch my first shows, and approved everything except my story about the day Mr. Mayer compared me to the paper doll in his hand, crumpled it and threw both of us away. "*Maybe* it happened, though it sounds out of character to me. Easy on the bitters, Baby. Otherwise you were totally heartwarming. So *real*."

I reminded her that people used the same word to describe my movie performances.

"There's no other. And it proves you haven't changed."

"Who are we talking about? *Myself* now, but still giving a performance," I said. "A talk show situation is an interview situation, which is a performing art, which turns you into somebody else. You're pretending the camera isn't there, but playing up to it. Just like the movies."

Mother nodded approvingly. "And because of your training, you come across more real than ever. *No problem*, Baby."

In New York they revived *Top of the World* at the film festival, and I went on the Dick Cavett show. (What can I tell you?) Next day Mr. Warhol and company interviewed me for their magazine *Interview*, and I said, "Here it comes again, another interview situation, I love this restaurant and you're all making me feel so relaxed, but do you mind if I turn into somebody else? I'd like you to know who you're not talking to." Mr. Warhol said, "That's okay. It'll be like watching a movie of your life and knowing they hadn't found the right person to play you. More interesting, in a way, than if they *had*."

I always admired the way Mr. Warhol carried a non-attitude so far that it became a new attitude, and throughout that lunch he never let me down. In his view I was everything and nothing, no more and no less than what an audience saw in me. If you made a career out of appearing in movies and on TV, who could you be except who you appeared to be? "Which is great," he said. "Everything comes across much better on the screen than it does in real life. The screen makes a person into a personality. And if there's any secret bit of you left over somewhere, don't worry. It's off the record." Then he checked his recorder to make sure the tape was still running.

I flew home to play myself again on another Merv Griffin show, where Mr. Welles was also playing himself again. A great role, yesterday's rebel genius still flashing behind today's mellowed out sage, and he played it superbly. I told him about Mr. Warhol's idea of the movie camera as a machine that made us more real, and asked if he agreed. "And if you do," I said, "do you think there are any private parts of you left over from all your public moments?"

Raising an eyebrow, Mr. Welles wondered what I meant by private parts. When Merv stopped laughing, he grew solemn and opined the situation might be even more serious. "The Medusa's eye," he said as a camera held him in close-up. "Know what I mean? Whatever I look upon finally dies under my gaze." The camera went on looking at him. "Somebody once told me about that," Mr. Welles said, as if he'd suddenly remembered it. But he was creating a public moment that fooled me completely, because he went on to explain he was quoting dialogue from one of the movies he never finished. "The money ran out," he added, then slipped back into the character of his imaginary film director. "*The eye behind the camera.* Maybe it's an evil eye. There were some Berbers up in the Atlas mountains that wouldn't let me even *point* a camera at them. They think it dries up something in the soul. . . ."

Merv interrupted with the news it was time for a commercial break. I asked Mr. Welles if he truly believed the eye behind the camera could do such an evil thing. He shrugged. "Who knows? Maybe it can." But I wasn't about to be fooled twice. "Is that a personal opinion or are you still quoting?" He smiled. "Both," he said. Then Merv announced we were due back on camera, and although the subject was fascinating he wanted to change it.

Next day a stranger stopped me in the street and said, "Loved you as Baby Jewel last night." A new move in an identity game that began years ago, with the first stranger who ever stopped me in the street. He looked at me and saw, fresh from *The Secret Garden*, the original eternal child. A generation later, with the eternal child a back number but my TV series a success, a stranger stopped me because he saw Pauline. Almost another generation later, with Pauline a back number but the eternal child back in circulation, a stranger stopped me because he saw—"Who exactly did you see last night?" I asked, wondering if he meant the Baby in a clip from one of my old movies or the old lady on the tube. "The one you always were and always will be," he said. "You start talking about her and you *become* her, all over again."

Dissolve to a few weeks after my seventieth birthday, and the president of the Academy of Motion Picture Arts and Sciences is on the phone. "For the unforgettable way you imprinted the romance of childhood and youth on the screen, we want to honor you with a special award at our next annual ceremony," he tells me and hopes I will accept it in person. I thank him, promise to come and feel it has to be the final move in the game. There's an old-fashioned phrase, a woman with a past, and old-fashioned people used to say a woman could never escape it, the past always catches up with her in the end. The running time of my old movies was never more than ninety minutes and yet half a century later the movies are still running, still catching up with me, and I can never escape them. If Mr. Welles is right, I'm freeze-framed in a rearview mirror. Everything about me except the movie image has died under the gaze of the Medusa's eye.

However. Late that night the phone rings again and an unknown, unfriendly voice asks, "*Who do you think you are?*" No time to answer. "I never heard of you," he goes on, "until you started turning up on talk shows, yackety-yackety-*yack*. Never saw your movies, but those clips they keep running are a real turn-off. Those clips are garbage. But *in person*, which is what I'm calling about, you make me shit in my pants. How can anyone so disgusting appear in public?" Heavy, angry breathing. "I hear you're filthy rich, and I guess that's why the media goes on kissing your ass. What a racket, this old hen sitting on all that money, letting them kiss her lousy ass, lending herself to media hype when there's zero minus one to hype. You are disgusting. You are the lowest. Get my point?"

Several times I thought of hanging up, but it was too horrible to walk out on, like *Alien*. Several times I tried to interrupt, but he gave me no chance. Finally he paused and I said, "About the money. It's not the reason I get on TV and it's not filthy. I honestly earned or inherited it, and I'm leaving most of it to charity."

"That's your story."

"And about my movies. I don't really care if they're great or terrible. But they happened and I'm stuck with them, like a piece of baggage with a label. It says I was *there*. And people want to know about *there*, so I tell them."

"You jerk off in public." He made a gross puking sound. "And you live in the past."

"There are worse places. Don't you ever feel that living in the present is like sitting on a chair with broken springs? Or slipping on a banana peel every day?"

"Spare me the philosophical crap."

"Then about me personally," I said. "You can't take the hype out of the media. All the same, when I talk about the past, something clicks. I feel a click, as if I'm sorting out my life."

"*What's left of it.*"

"Okay, I'm seventy, but I've always been healthy."

"You don't understand," he said. "You don't understand *anything*. I've had enough. Enough of you and the whole fucking culture of narcissism you stand for. A line has to be drawn and I've decided where to draw it. Get my point?"

"I'm not sure." But I was feeling suddenly sure, and feeling a chill.

"Then let me spell it out. Obviously you're the type that needs everything spelled out." He sounded weary. "The only way to stop you is to kill you."

After a moment I pretended to laugh. "That won't stop me," I said. "My movies will live on."

"Once you die, *they* die. Without the hype, there's nothing. Zilch. That's my real point and I'm going to prove it. Soon," he added. "Very soon. When I come to a decision, I like to act quickly."

I hung up. The phone rang again almost at once. I didn't answer. It stopped, then rang again. I thought of leaving it off the hook, but was scared that he knew my address as well as my phone number, and might come over in a rage to prove his point right away. "You dumb bitch," he said when I answered. "You'll be sorry you hung up on me." He gave a low whistle. "Now I'll hurt you when I kill you. Are you listening?"

"Yes."

"You can hang up now but first I want you to say, 'Goodbye and thank you for calling.' "

"Goodbye and thank you for calling."

I was led down an empty corridor, with doors open to empty rooms, to a room at the end. A lieutenant-detective sat at a desk, tapping his teeth with a ballpoint pen. It was one in the morning. Tired but friendly, he said he enjoyed me on a show the other night, settled me in a chair, offered me a cup of coffee, lit my cigarette and told me to relax. People who were serious about killing celebrities, he explained, hardly ever warned them in advance. "This sounds like your typical threat-freak, fixing on someone to scare. Who do you know who hates you?"

"I could be living in a fool's paradise, but I can only think of a couple of actors from the old days. Both dead."

"You described the voice as very young, so it's unlikely to be anyone from the old days. Did you meet anyone very young recently?"

"Not in a while, not to get to know," I said. "The last one was a movie buff. But he loves me. And it wasn't his voice. This man was a stranger."

The detective nodded. "It usually is. There's a lot of anonymous hate going around."

"So I hear, though I never met it before. And it comes as a shock. I was brought up on a lot of anonymous love."

He gazed out the window. "Where's it all gone?" he asked, suddenly gloomy.

"The worst that ever happened to me was at a premiere years ago," I went on. "Some rowdy called me Baby Pig Meat and opened his fly. But you could take that as a compliment, in a way."

"Every week now it's Hate a Celebrity Week." The detective sighed. "You don't know how many cases we get. She's young and beautiful, they're going to throw acid in her face. She's got a kid, they're going to kidnap him. They're going to rape the guy's wife. Or his mother." He tapped his teeth with the pen. "Celebrities bring us a lot of problems."

"We never used to." He was making me feel apologetic. "Is it our fault?"

He shook his head. "*Shifting sands,*" he said. "The sands are shifting. They used to look up to you. Now they feel cheated and envious. They've grown hostile. But look on the bright side. They make all these threats but seldom carry them out." He offered me more coffee, then some advice. "Change your phone number right away. If it'll make you feel better, go to Mace class. Only takes an hour, then you're allowed to carry a can in your purse. A lot of you are doing that, by the way. And keep the profile low for a few days, don't provoke him by going on another talk show."

"In three weeks' time they're giving me a special Oscar," I said. "Think I should stay home?"

The detective looked shocked. "You can't let him take that away from you." He congratulated me, then added, "Besides, he should have cooled off by then."

"Maybe it's my show business training, but I feel there has to be a third act."

He smiled. "Not in this line of business. Not with your threat-freak. I told you, he's not the type who follows through." He shook my hand warmly. "I'll be watching you Oscar night. A real pleasure to meet you."

It occurred to me as I drove home that neither Mr. Warhol nor Mr. Welles had the answer after all. To at least one person I was *not* who I appeared to be. He saw through my movie image all the way to my soul, and it drove him up the wall with disgust. Freaks and drugheads had their crazy moments of truth, so it wasn't enough to write him off that way. By the time I reached home, he'd raised the ghost of an old fear. I poured a shot of brandy and remembered Mr. Mayer threatening his Little Princess with a terrible public backlash if she ever put a foot wrong. Mr. Mayer swore that public love could turn to public hate overnight, he saw millions of fists raised in the air and heard millions of voices shouting Down With Her!

"Only one person so far, but he could be the tip of the iceberg. Where did I put a foot wrong?" I asked Sid Gordon, who always boasted that what he didn't know about the public could be written on the end of a pin. Sid was in forced retirement now, finally out of the business after he survived a heart attack alone in a screening room. It happened during the first reel of an old B movie and the projectionist only discovered him slumped on the floor eighty minutes later. Now he sat for hours every day on the terrace of his high-rise apartment, eyes bright and angry with boredom, dead cigar in his mouth.

He shook his head impatiently, assured me I came across as *one of the greatest*, and talked about fame. "This kind of thing goes with the territory. Big money's always a target as well. So don't take it personal just because some junkie threatens and insults you on the phone. You're in danger anyway, Baby. We all are. Nobody's safe in this town anymore."

The view from Sid's terrace reminded me of One Big Look. It faced west to the sunset, to an endless geometry of streets and low buildings. A few high-rises broke up the flatness, but a long shot couldn't take in the city anymore. It had grown too vast, without enough points of focus. To make personal sense out of it, you had to move in close, as Sid began to do now. "Westwood okay except for those underground parking lots. Watch those parking lots, and the stairs leading up from them, when no one *seems* to be around. Plenty of bad news waiting in the shadows. Hollywood at night is asking for trouble, all those sex shops and porno theatres and greasy spoon restaurants draw a horrible crowd. Junkies, hustlers, freaks, muggers, even drag queens pull knives on you. Venice any time of the day or night is *out*. You'll get caught in crossfire from a gang war or stabbed in the back by some druggy Latino or dinge. The Strip is mucho weirdo early morning and after sunset. Downtown is nightmare alley like it always was, only worse. And if you're driving anywhere, even Beverly Hills, late at night, and you come to an empty intersection, *never wait for the stop light to change*. You're a sitting target, so jump it."

I thanked Sid for the rundown. "We're lucky to be old," he said. "We had the best of this place," and sat glaring at the view. "All the same," I said, "that stranger was so personal, it's hard not to take him personally. Everyone from Swanson to Shelley Winters has written an autobiography and plugged it on talk shows, but do *they* get hate threats? Are *they* accused of being too disgusting to live?"

"Why don't you ask them?" Then he thumped the arm of his chair. "But why waste your time? You're over-reacting because you grew up too protected. And we know who's responsible. Mrs. Rip," he said, "the most impossible woman who ever lived, may she rest in peace. She stuffed your head with all her grand half-assed ideas. Made you believe Baby Jewel Week was going to last for ever. Let you grow up convinced the world was your oyster." He closed his eyes suddenly. "The world is nobody's oyster. I learned that at the age of seven. Now go away. I love you but I'm tired, sick and tired, a very old man."

He closed his eyes, the smog-ridden city stretching away below, and I went home to call Shelley Winters. We'd met on a talk show and she was friendly. "No," she said. "No, dear, I never had a hate call. Just a lot of sex calls and some of them pretty exciting."

"Aren't you the lucky one. But tell me this. Am I over-reacting?"

She laughed. "I wouldn't know. I've been over-reacting all my life."

I still waited for the third act. It changed the way I looked at strangers but didn't change the way they looked at me. No enemy glances from passers-by in the street, from kids in a car in the next lane as we waited for a stop light to change. The store assistant, the gas station attendant, the boy who delivered groceries, they all still smiled and said, "Have a nice day." But as long as the third act didn't happen, it could always happen.

"*Only in your mind*. Only if you send out bad thoughts," Jimmy Gabriel said. I was still nervous when the phone rang, almost didn't pick up when it rang after midnight, almost wept with relief at the sound of Jimmy's voice and told him why. "You're the least disgusting and most lovable person I ever knew, unless I never knew you," he said. "So what lingering far-off chord of fear has been struck in your mind?"

"Far-off? It's damn close. He threatened to kill me."

"Just another fan," Jimmy said. "Fans have all kinds of fantasies about us. Believe it or not, a woman once asked for a snip of my pubic hair. But whether they go the fetish route, or copy the way we look, or want to make it with us or kill us, it's the *desire for communication*. Think positive, will you. Any gut reaction, even if it's on the twisted side, means you've got *impact*. Now I just came in from New York and I'm bushed. Let's have breakfast tomorrow at the Beverly Wilshire. If you get there after ten, I'll be soaking up the sun at the pool. God is love."

The reference to God didn't come as a surprise. From reading *People* magazine I already knew that Jimmy had been Born Again. "Like finding the Right Person at last," he described it. "The Person who was there, waiting patiently, all the time." From reading the Milestones column in *Time* magazine I also knew that he found another right person soon afterwards. *MARRIED. Jimmy Gabriel, 69, actor, nightclub entertainer, currently trying out a new Broadway-bound musical; and Cheri Fox, 29, singer-dancer; he for the ninth time, she for the first; in Toronto, Canada.* Here are a few other facts I knew about Jimmy from reading the magazines. His musical was an enormous hit on its tryout engagement, everyone predicted a long run and a personal success in New York. He had given Cheri a special number in the show. He was coming to Los Angeles to attend the Academy Awards ceremony, nominated for his supporting role of a satanist in *The Seventh Victim*, remake of an old devil-cult movie.

Although it was only 9:30, Jimmy was already out by the pool at the Beverly Wilshire Hotel, and already eating breakfast. There was no one else around. He looked trim and healthy, wearing flowered Hawaiian trunks and a quartz watch. Obstinate as ever, the cowlick stood up from his thick gray hair. "I got hungry," he said after flinging his arms around me and kissing me on the mouth. "Can I order you something?"

"Just coffee. I had breakfast. There's no reason anymore, but I still wake up very early."

He looked me over. "You sounded shaky on the phone last night, but the appearance is sharp."

"Yours too."

"Gave up the booze. It helps, you know."

One side of the table was in shade. I sat opposite Jimmy, on that side. "Where's the new wife?" I asked.

"Out shopping. It's her first time on the coast and she couldn't wait to go out shopping. Cheri's a lovely girl. She's longing to meet you, saw you on a show and thinks you're fantastic."

"Did *you* ever see me?"

"Never got a chance. The timing was wrong every time. But it's a shame and a loss that you gave up *the real thing*."

"Once you reach a place called Over the Hill," I said, "which lies way on the other side of Comeback Country, the pickings get very slim."

"It doesn't make sense. They're giving you a special award."

"Flowers on my grave. An old story, let's not make too much of it."

"Or too little." Jimmy reached across the table and took my hands. "It's a shame and a loss, Baby in Quotes, because you had a great talent. Don't make a face. I've got a nose for talent. You're making another face, will you stop it? All the years I've known you, I never heard you accept a compliment as if you believed you deserved it. Remember what you used to say when someone liked you in a picture?"

" 'I just did what everyone said,' " I said. "That's how it used to feel."

"Always so damn suggestible. A fine quality sometimes, but *needs watching*. Look what happens when some creep calls you a load of disgusting media hype. You practically *agree* with him."

"Maybe you just stumbled on the story of my life," I said. "My first day on a movie set, everyone was amazed how well I took direction. As if I was born to it." I looked at Jimmy's hands covering mine. "But maybe I'm just taking direction from *you* now," I said.

"I could still be right."

"Yes. It's confusing."

He shook his head. "It's perfectly clear. When it comes to your talent, you pass the buck. Why can't you acknowledge it as *yours*? Must you always act as if you owed it to someone else? That's a sin, you know, and makes you a kind of sinner, because your talent was given you *on trust*. Don't make a face."

"My name on a poster, or in big letters outside a theatre," I said. "It always seemed to belong to someone else. And those crowds cheering me at a premiere. Did *I* have the power to make them cheer like that? I just couldn't believe it."

"Most of us react that way at first. Even I did," Jimmy said. "Then I made the connection you never made. And once I felt *integrated*, I never looked back."

Remembering the last time I saw Jimmy, gray and lost and bloated in a bedroom at the Tumble Inn, Ventura, I supposed he'd forgotten it.

"Never?"

"Never," he said firmly, then looked at me with sudden curiosity. "Now you've got nothing to do, what do you do all day?"

"Still recording for the blind. Still reading a lot. I go for long walks, see a few friends and a few movies, take trips to New York to catch up on theatre. . . ."

"Will you come to my opening?" He smiled. "It's a one-man show, I have to tell you I get to do everything, but they seem to love it."

I nodded, and slipped my hands from under Jimmy's to open my purse and take out a pack of cigarettes.

"*What is that?*" He was looking into my purse. "What are you carrying?"

"Mace." I held it up. "The police advised it."

"No and no and *no*," Jimmy said urgently. "You took really bad direction there. Let me tell you, if you go around with that stuff in your purse, you are *lost*. I'm not talking about physical survival, although in a life or death situation you'd be dead before you could use that stuff. If this guy really means to kill you, if it's the only way he can communicate, *forgive him*."

"With my dying breath?"

Jimmy sighed. "Now. This minute. Understand his lonely pathetic spaced-out anger and forgive."

"You mean he'll get the message? And settle for a snip of my pubic hair?"

Jimmy sighed again. "Don't fight me so hard. Since I found God," he spoke very quietly and simply, "anybody vicious or destructive I come across, I forgive. In my heart. And since I started forgiving, you'd be amazed how little of the bad stuff I come across. You can't scare it away, but you can love and understand it away."

Remembering the Tumble Inn again, I saw the rage in Jimmy's face before he slapped me, even felt the shock of it.

"Climate of reconciliation," he said. "We all need that now." His eyes were fiercely blue. "Give me your Mace, hand it over and let me throw it away." Then he leaned forward and ran his forefinger across my cheek. "Oh, a tear. It feels like I touched a part of your soul."

"You touched a drop of perspiration."

"Don't fight me so hard. I understand your fear. I was the same way at first. Living alone, like you. In a kind of prison. And unable to see the way out when. . . ."

"Goddammit," I said, and handed over the Mace. "It's all yours. But I'm not fighting anything, not in any kind of prison. Just taking direction again."

Jimmy was no longer looking at me. He jumped to his feet as a willowy girl with long streaked hair came toward the table, wearing something long and white and semi-transparent. He kissed her on the mouth and said, "This is Cheri, my wife."

"Great to meet you." Cheri flashed me a smile, then turned back to Jimmy. "Forgive me, sweetness, but I almost bought out Holly Harp's boutique."

"Who is Holly Harp?"

Cheri turned back to me. "Honestly. He lives in a world of his own."

"Do *you* know who Holly Harp is?" Jimmy asked me.

"I never went to her store, I'm a little old for it. But I've heard she keeps a harp there. To make a statement."

"You're not too old for Holly, she could do terrific things for you," Cheri said. Then she told Jimmy, "Her statement is the floaty moody look. She makes it for Barbra, Jane, Raquel, I mean *everybody*. And for special occasions she makes a fun glitz statement too. Please order me a Bloody Mary."

Jimmy frowned. "Sweetness, it's kind of early for a drink."

"How do you know? You don't drink." She flashed another smile. "Order it please."

"I'll join you," I said.

Jimmy went over to the house phone and Cheri sat beside me in the shade. She shook out her hair and said, "Of course, my life didn't really begin until I met him."

"Were you Born Again too, Cheri?"

"I'm not quite ready. You can't force a thing like that, it has to happen naturally. If it's not natural, it's not good. Where do you go for shoes here?"

Jimmy came back. "This is so great, you girls having a instant lovefest. Cheri was a bit scared to meet you, Baby in Quotes, even though she found you so fantastic on the show. I told her you'd been very bitchy about my wives and girlfriends in the past."

"Only when I was married to you or living with you," I said.

"I understand that and I'd feel the same." Cheri shook out her hair again. "Take it as a warning, sweetness." Then she laid a hand on my arm. "But the moment I saw you, everything felt relaxed and warm. It's your loving aura, I'm very sensitive to auras."

She kissed me, then Jimmy kissed me, then the Bloody Marys arrived and she said, "Boy, did I need this."

Jimmy looked up at the sky for a moment. "This sun feels so great. Cheri, remember what I told you on the plane coming out?"

"You told me Baby was the only person out here you truly wanted to see, and you hoped I'd understand why. I sure do." Cheri held my hand. "Do you mind? I'm a very touching person. I like to reach out."

"Climate of reconciliation," Jimmy said, looking benignly at both of us, and the world.

The climate was beginning to overpower me, and Jimmy's latest role was not my favorite, but I tried not to knock the situation, even to myself. He'd found an unbeatable combination, God and Cheri, and seemed so happy. I freed my hand on the pretense of wanting another cigarette, and Cheri decided to change into a swimsuit. She blew kisses as she left, and Jimmy's eyes continued to bless the world.

"What a lovely girl," I said.

"Paradise Regained. And wait till you see her in a swimsuit."

Cheri came back wearing a white bikini, and looking as if she could sell anything on TV. "Isn't it fantastic," she said, "how this guy almost seventy years young keeps hanging right in there? Doesn't he have the most *ongoing* aura?" Jimmy kissed her hand. "The aura is *you*, sweetness." She flashed her smile and said, "I'm certainly hanging in there, right beside you, for life. But so is God."

They lay in the sun together. From the shade, I almost broke my vow and cried over Jimmy Gabriel once more, suddenly envious of the happiness he sprayed around like room-freshener. I wanted to be hanging in there myself, right beside him, while he loved and understood all the bad stuff away. Then an image came back from the past, from a night half a century ago, after Jimmy left me for the first time. I went to the apartment where I thought he was still living and a bleary stranger opened the door. When I looked over his shoulder into the livingroom, it had changed so much there was nothing to recognize and nothing to miss.

"Sure you don't want to join us?" Cheri called. "You could borrow one of my swimsuits. Your figure's so great I know it would fit."

I told her I had to be going. They got up to kiss me goodbye and Jimmy said he'd see me tomorrow night in my hour of triumph. "Yours too, I hope," I said, then went home and put another can of Mace in my purse.

Sid Gordon was waiting impatiently outside the apartment building next evening. He wore a sky-blue tux and a silver bow tie, and carried a small leather case. "Oxygen," he said as he climbed into the Rolls. "I could go out like a light any moment."

"You started the whole damn thing, so you've got to live long enough to see me accept my award."

"Don't count on it."

"You look great. That's a very fancy tux."

"Eighty-nine dollars for the night. Highway robbery." He glared. "But they had me over a barrel."

We followed a red carpet past a spotlit fountain to the lobby of the Dorothy Chandler Pavilion, where Sid Gordon blinked at the chandeliers, the floaty and glitzy statements, the ruffled dress shirts and the Cartier identity bracelets. "I am dying," he said, "but not before I finally get in on a class act." Everybody's mood was resolutely upbeat and the smiles reminded me of dress extras ordered to whoop it up for a party scene. A tanned, skinny, overwrought girl in moody chiffon came over to tell me how much she enjoyed *Footlights* at a recent Academy screening. She looked as if she might have been in *Dallas*, but then she was not the only one. "Goddammit," Sid said, clutching my arm, "there's Mrs. Rip's name on the wall." For we were standing close by a row of plaques acknowledging the generous donors who made it possible to build the Music Center. He gave Mrs. Elva Kay a wary nod and said, "Be seeing you soon, I'm afraid."

The theatre was lit for TV, too hot and too bright. Just before the show started, Jimmy appeared with a super-glitzy Cheri in harem pants and beaded blouse. They had seats across the aisle from us. Jimmy waited almost two hours not to win the award for best supporting actor, but when I glanced at him there was no sign of disappointment on his face. He jumped to his feet and applauded the winner more loudly than anyone else. Then the TV lights dimmed while home viewers got another commercial and the theatre audience got a dance number in space suits on the stage. Wondering where to look, I felt a tap on my shoulder and Jimmy beckoned me to follow him. We slipped through a door backstage. "Most closely guarded secret of the year," he said. "Guess who's going to present your award?"

And then the number was over, and the orchestra began to play Pretty Baby. The stage darkened, empty except for a blank screen. As I stood in the wings, Baby Jewel as Kid Sherlock appeared on the screen. It was followed by a montage of my eternal childhood and youth, and in the closing shot I was upside down on a flagpole on top of the world, standing on my head and blowing bubbles.

The stage was bright again as the president of the Academy announced my special award, then introduced Jimmy Gabriel to present it. "I've known this wonderful actress and person for fifty years," Jimmy said. "She's still my favorite ex-wife." He got his laugh and turned solemn before speaking the official tribute. A moment later I was standing with him out there, receiving my Oscar, and another moment later I was alone on the stage.

"Will Mr. Sidney Gordon, who started the whole damn thing, please take a bow?" Sid took a quick unsmiling one, clutching the oxygen case to his heart. "There's a lot of other people to thank," I went on, "but that's a long route to go, and I'm afraid in most cases it leads to the cemetery. So I'll just thank all of *you* out there, the living people who've always been closest to me, the audience."

Another performance, of course, and what can I tell you? I bowed. The living people stood up and cheered. I took off my glasses to see them more clearly, and they were all my audiences, the thousands of strangers who made me feel like someone else. But not this time. This time I seemed to vanish into all those images on the screen. I was the sum of my parts at last, and finally caught in the act, and I knew how it felt to walk on air.

Jimmy was waiting offstage. He took me to the pressroom, where all the winners were describing their emotions for TV. A TV person came up and asked me to describe mine.

"Well now," I said. "You are looking at an old lady clutching her award for the wonder and promise of childhood and youth. Which is something I always felt I missed out on at the time. And was dumb enough to let it bother me. Why didn't I realize the life I never led was my best life? Other people did. Millions of them. They envied me in the dark and wrote to me like lovers. And tonight I believe I've finally joined the club. I envy like hell that million-dollar moppet who made the hearts of the world beat faster. Really wish I'd been in her shoes."

Then I went off in search of Sid, and found him waiting in the lobby. "You should never have dragged me here," he said and stared with a kind of reluctant fascination at the plaque that acknowledged Mrs. Elva Kay. "Go on to the party without me. I'm sick and tired and I'll call a cab."

I shook my head. "I'm tooling on quietly home myself. I'll drop you off."

We joined the tide of glitz following the red carpet on its way out. Jimmy and Cheri were standing by the spotlit fountain. "We'll see you at the Beverly Hilton," Jimmy said, and I shook my head again. "In that case," he said, "God bless you and bless you forever. I'll send you tickets for my opening."

Sid napped for most of the drive home. As I turned off the freeway at the Hollywood exit, there was a police helicopter with a searchlight in the sky ahead. It had to mean trouble on the Boulevard again, teenage gangs battling it out on the Walk of Fame with its names of stars engraved inside stars. My own star lay at a safe distance from the action, in the quiet nowhere block east of Vine, by the entrance to a store that used to sell sex books and recently switched to punk clothes. But some of my peers would have to be cleaned up in the morning, and it was strange to remember the old days when people danced under famous names instead of dripping blood on them. I thought of Mother describing those golden stars on the ceiling of the Hollywood Hotel ballroom as we stood together our first night on the Boulevard and she recited the names like a prayer. Of the moon coming out from behind a cloud, and the vista of silent empty streets as we walked back to the Yucca Riviera. You can go anywhere from there, as Mr. Guidoboni said, and we went to a yard with a caged monkey and an acid smell in the air.

Sid Gordon woke up with a start and clutched his oxygen case.

"You look hardly a day older," I said, "than the day we first met."

"That's because I always looked old. You haven't changed much either, even though you're history now."

"You and I both, Sid."

"I'm just a footnote. In very small print." Police sirens wailed. "Or your shadow. And whatever I am, I'm fading into the past."

He took a dead cigar from his pocket and stuck it in his mouth. Then he leaned back in his seat and stared ahead as if sitting on his little terrace above the city. And I had a quick shocked vision of myself a few years from now, sitting by my pool, eyes bright and angry with boredom as I gazed at a row of empty chaises-longues.

"Not me," I said. "I've got my eye on the future."

The cigar trembled. "There's no future for an old-timer in this town."

"Who said there was?" I heard my screenwriter in the sky speaking. "That's why I've just decided to take a trip around the world."

Sid went rigid with alarm. "You'll be hijacked or kidnapped or caught in a revolution. And the airlines will lose all your luggage."

"All the same, I'm getting this terrific urge to travel before it's too late."

"It *is* too late. Save your illusions and your money."

"I can afford to lose a little money, Sid, and I've got illusions to spare. I know it's too late to run into Marlene on the *Shanghai Express* or Gable and Harlow on the *China Seas* or Kay Francis in *Mandalay* or Jeanette MacDonald in *Cairo* or Bogie and Ingrid in *Casablanca* or Fred and Ginger *Flying Down to Rio* or Irene Dunne standing on *The White Cliffs of Dover. . . ."*

He gave a violent, grim nod. "You can say that again. These days it's a whole different ballgame out there."

"Then I won't feel played out."

I pulled up outside the entrance to his apartment building. Sid clambered out of the Rolls, looked up toward his tenth-floor balcony. "Me," he said, "I'd rather fade." Then he turned around and thumped the car door. "Smallpox, malaria, typhoid, yellow fever. Don't forget to take your goddam shots." He put the dead cigar back in his pocket. "Goodnight and thanks. Give me a ring tomorrow. If I don't answer, you'll know why. But no flowers."

I drove all the way to the top of Laurel Canyon, got out and stood facing the glittering city below. In the years I'd seen it grow from hopeful hick town to anxious metropolis, it couldn't have changed more than the world. The moon came out from behind a cloud, a police siren screamed in the distance, then there was perfect silent stillness. After one last One Big Look, I turned the Rolls into a dark winding dead end lane and parked in front of a vacant lot. No lights came from the only nearby house with its rows of black plastic garbage bags at the entrance to the driveway. I drew the window blinds, pressed the button that turned the back seat into a bed, wrapped myself in the fur rug and felt the third act starting to happen. Not the one I'd been waiting for, the one waiting for me.

Recharging the batteries in my isolation tank, I heard Mother's voice. "So you're taking a step into the Unknown? As an expert on that area, let me give you a word of advice. Always trust your vibrations and always travel first class. (I still do.) Then I promise you'll be your own Baby, and *definitely* on your way." Outside, trees stirred faintly in the midnight breeze. Before dropping off to sleep I closed my eyes to everything except what I remembered, and felt enormously glad to reach the end of somewhere and be moving on at last. *Music. Fade Out.* But as the curtains closed I heard a stranger's voice. "Just a moment," it said. It had a warning note, like someone questioning a story point at the end of the picture. "You really expect everyone to go home now, envying you in the dark, wishing they'd led your life? There's such a terrible empty gap in that life. You missed out on one of the basic human experiences. You never had a child!"

Just a moment. Good as I was at taking direction, not even Mr. Griffith could have helped me turn that role into a basic human experience.

They'd have said, "She's faking it." They'd have said, "She's out of her depth, Baby really blew this one." For I cannot remember a time when I liked children, which maybe explains why I became, for a while at least, such a great little actress. Even when I was too small to play a midget, children made me ill at ease. I never trusted or understood them. In fact, they scared me. As if they knew something I would never know.

Also by Gavin Lambert and published by Serpent's Tail

The Goodbye People

"Decades before it was fashionable, Gavin Lambert expertly wove characters of every sexual stripe into his lustrous tapestries of Southern Californian life . . . His elegant stripped-down prose caught the last gasp of Old Hollywood in a way that has yet to be rivalled" Armistead Maupin

"*The Goodbye People* is (Lambert's) dark glory, melancholic, becalmed and effortlessly resonant . . . Lambert's studies of lost lives are more accurate today than ever before" *Independent on Sunday*

"Lambert has such a controlled, poetic, imagistic writing style . . . What a beautiful novel" *Uncut*

Long before the term Generation X was coined, Gavin Lambert captured the seedy landscape of Los Angeles in absolute moral and physical decay. *The Goodbye People* is a *danse macabre*, with a group of ill-assorted people who are "always changing their addresses and phone numbers as well as their lives". In an atmosphere of self-indulgence, blight and emptiness, they revolve around one another weaving together their dreams and nightmares to create a complex pattern of despair. The beautiful people who populate Lambert's novel are both the very rich and the very poor: what intrinsically links them is an all-pervading sense of aimlessness.

First published in 1971, *The Goodbye People* is an enduring classic, and one of the most incisive takes on Hollywood ever written. With *The Slide Area*, *Inside Daisy Clover* and *Running Time*, *The Goodbye People* forms a revelatory "Hollywood Quartet" of lives in one of the most extraordinary cities in the world.

The Slide Area

"A brilliant piece of work, terse, compassionate, and beautifully made. It earns a place on anyone's shelves along with Scott Fitzgerald's *The Last Tycoon* and Nathanael West's *The Day of the Locust*" *Times Literary Supplement*

"Most of all there is enormous skill: the author has the playwright's flair for taut, meaningful dialogue; the novelist's feeling for mood; the short-story writer's love of plot; and the good movie writer's capacity for deft characterization that is visual as well as psychological" *New York Times*

"These are the most truthful stories about the film world and its suburbia I have ever read" Christopher Isherwood

"A moody and visual novel which mercilessly conveys the last days of old Hollywood and its desperate insiders" *Big Issue*

"An insightful, dream-like novel" *Neon*

The land along Pacific Palisades is apt to slip away without warning, hence the road-side signs — SLIDE AREA. Narrated by a script-writer, Lambert's widely-acclaimed 1959 Hollywood classic of lonely souls marooned on a glittering wasteland is a perceptive and sensitive study of human emotion.

Inside Daisy Clover

"Resembling Armistead Maupin on Benzedrine, it's hard to believe this was first published in 1963" *GQ*

"A classic . . . ****" *New Woman*

A precocious teenager chronicles her own rise from trailer-camp squalor to singing stardom by way of a supermarket talent contest. In her journals, Daisy Clover tells the story of how she is discovered by a Hollywood movie producer at 14 and proceeds through large doses of work, sex, and Benzedrine to a 24-hour marriage, a nervous breakdown, retirement, and finally obscurity in New York. A has-been before her late teens, she makes a vaudeville comeback in Atlantic City at the age of 24. A very campy, very funny look at the frenzy of late '50s Hollywood. The film version is frequently on cable *very* late at night.